HORIZONS

THE FOG CHRONICLES
Horizons I-III

HORIZONS
Trilogy

VIRGINIE BONFILS-BEDOS

INTRODUCTION

KEY CHARACTERS & LOCATIONS FROM 'GATEKEEPERS'

THE FOG & THE FOGGIES
(aka the Gatekeepers)

The mysterious thick Fog makes its appearance every 231 years, roughly in the same locations, give or take seven miles, and roughly on the same dates, give or take seven days. The Fog has some healing faculties for those who cross it. They can break a leg, hurt themselves, and the Fog won't help, but it will get rid of viruses, microbes or infections. It is as if the Fog cleans you when you go through it, preparing you to be relocated without transferring diseases and viruses, too.

For each Fog, there are seven Switchers, seven Crossers and seven Facilitators.
Switchers = Fog creator. Need help to access our world (with Facilitator) and new world (with Crosser). Otherwise Fog-bound.
Crossers = need help to access our world (with Facilitator) or direct access alone to the new world.
Facilitators = assist Switchers and Crossers to come to our world.

The Foggies have a unique bond between themselves and with the Fog. If they don't cross it at least once in seven weeks, they start to develop terrible migraines that worsen until the sufferer is completely incapacitated; A kind of Fog-withdrawal syndrome.

Aside from the Foggies, some people cross the Fog and are unaffected – nothing happens aside from a body-healing – and some are completely affected. Referred to as Relocated, one in seven of the people crossing the Fog are sent to the Other World and can't come back.

LONDON (U.K)

The four housemates with whom the whole story started:

Yoko Salelles (**SWITCHER**) – the narrator: Mediterranean-looking with French, Italian and Japanese origins, she is an energetic 30-something with a positive attitude and a stubborn personality. She moved to London for her studies and saw many of her dreams crash before meeting the housemates who turned into her adopted family in the UK.

Zenone 'Zeno' Grande (**CROSSER**) – Caucasian-Italian in his early 30s, he is an entrepreneur and Jack-of-all-trades, with a curiosity only deterred by wolves.

Enrico 'Rico' Scelti (**FACILITATOR**) – Italian of African origin in his early 30s, he is an artist, fitness addict and irrepressible flirt, hiding his oversensitivity behind a macho façade.

Harry Braxton (**FACILITATOR**) – Early-40s, Caucasian Englishman and University Lecturer in his early 40s, he embodies the quintessence of Britishness, sarcasm included.

Simba – Yoko's adopted wolf from WII, born in the Fog and able to cross and facilitate to both worlds at will.

ESSEX HOUSE (U.K.)

The Foggies who were originally based in Rome left the Italian capital for England, as they lacked a Facilitator and did not want to be stuck in WII.

Jack (SWITCHER) – A young gay Caucasian American who discovered he was a Switcher while studying fashion in Rome, Italy. A sweet guy whose main flaw is his depressive streak and being the unlucky one, always.

Dante Bopani (CROSSER) – A Roman architect and Leo's best friend. Mediterranean- looking man in his early 30s, he is focused, serious, and one wonders where his chilled Italian-side is.

Leo Lumbrosi (CROSSER) – In his early 30s, he is a real charmer who seduced Yoko online and got caught at his own game, falling in love with her. He gives up everything to embrace the life of the Gatekeepers, but struggle to cope with the independent tendency of Yoko. She just won't let him look after her!

ALASKA (US)

Rosario (SWITCHER) – Mid-20s, blonde American. She returned to Alaska to look after her mother after her studies at Berkeley University and set up an event and travel agency there. She is engaged to Tony, and nothing will get in the way of her bliss with him. She marries Tony in GATEKEEPERS.

Mitch (CROSSER) – Rosario's older brother, in his late 20s: a loner who loves the countryside and spends most of his time in it. He organises expeditions in the Alaskan mountains as a passion, so he is unfazed to do the same in the Other World.

Tony (FACILITATOR) – Early 30s, New-Yorker and insurance specialist. He met Rosario on a flight to Vancouver. Dropped everything for her and never looked back: he is ready to take on the Fog challenge for her and feels useful for once in this wilderness

NEVADA (US)

Adam Koplat **(SWITCHER)** – Jewish financial lawyer with a positive spirit and a sharp mind, struggling to cope with the constant bickering between his second wife Sophia and his daughter Michelle.

Sophia Koplat **(CROSSER)** – Second wife of Adam Koplat and stepmother to high school teenager Michelle. A socialite, she likes being the centre of attention, and can't stand Michelle's rebellious streak.

Michelle Koplat **(FACILITATOR)** – 17-year-old yearning for her independence. Though loving her father and supporting him, she would do anything to irk her step-mother. She is the daughter of Adam Koplat from his previous marriage to Penny Thompson, a journalist.

KENYA

Clare **(SWITCHER)** – Advisor on Human Rights to the Kenyan Government, in her 60s. Ecologist, independent and disillusioned with society. The Other World is the answer to her prayer of going back to humanity's roots.

Mary **(CROSSER)** – Clare's daughter, in her late 30s; psychiatrist and headstrong. Like her mother, she believes WII is better than her original world and has no wish to live anywhere else. She falls in love with a bushman from WII and they get married.

Putu **(FACILITATOR)** – a young doctor in her late 20s, dedicated to tending to the poor and the young in need of medical treatment, she is unimpressed to have to deal with Clare and Mary.

MOROCCO

Christophe de Rocque (**SWITCHER**) – Classic French arrogant flirt, a banker living in Paris with a summer residence in Morocco. He gets stuck there with his mistress Louise and his pregnant wife Isabelle (relocated in the desert). Annoying, useless at relationships, but not a bad guy once he faces his responsibilities.

Louise (**CROSSER**) – Christophe's French mistress, based in Morocco. Young, wild, emotional and deeply in love, she is heartbroken and terrified at the messy situation.

Helo (**FACILITATOR**) – Young Indonesian boy separated from his family when they get lost in WII Indonesia and the Fog disappears. The poor child is passive for now, having to on strangers for his survival. He is now in Morocco to be raised within a family of fellow Foggies and to help as a Facilitator.

OUR WORLD (aka WI)

Leila Al Bassa (**The Society**) – Main liaison agent of the Society with the Foggies, she is American with Middle East origins. Her warm and open attitude never wholly compensate for her mysterious story. She is dedicated to the Society and the cause it defends: the protection of the people and nature in both worlds. But is it always in the interest of the Gatekeepers?

Phil (**The Society**) – Yoko's devoted bodyguard, budding friend and silent witness of her relationship problems.

Ingis Chen (**Chen & Co**) – Charming Chinese businessman brought up in the United States, for whom the end justifies the means. He believes in making everyone on the planet cross the Fog for the survival of humankind by stopping overpopulation, while getting rich in the process. He has an ambivalent relationship with the Foggies, first aggressive, then he revises his approach by highlighting he wishes to help them - or use them, depending on the point of view.

Ushi Tsou (**Chen & Co**) – Mercenary from Chen's Corporation. She is relocated during a confrontation between the Society and Chen's Corporation. Tough, unemotional, dangerous and impossible to read, she is both hot and scary.

Sam Riverson (**British Secret Service**) – Believed at first to be an introvert photographer intrigued by the Fog, he turned out to be a secret agent from British Intelligence whose instinct was (rightly) telling him there was more to the Fog than met the eye. When he discovers the truth, he interrogates the London Foggies. The authorities enter the scene, and then GATEKEEPERS ends HORIZONS begins.

THE OTHER WORLD (aka WII)

THE RELOCATED

Jazz (**WII London - 'Woodfellas'**) – Yoko's best friend, she is a 20-something of Asian origins, and with a posh attitude which is both funny and endearing. A strong woman with a mouth where her heart is. After a period of adaptation and feeling low, she perks up when she decides to create a lounge between two worlds; *The Jazzin*.

Big Tom (**WII London - 'Woodfellas'**) – Big Englishman with a bald head and tattoos, a builder by profession and with dodgy connections in East London. He is relocated when curiosity gets the better of him while on a construction job, next door to the fogged house.

Nick Baker (**WII London - 'Woodfellas'**) – Mercenary from the Society, in his 20s. He was a professional boxer before enrolling in the army. He leaves out of disappointment for what he considers a lack of humanity. He is approached by the Society for his values and experience, and he immediately becomes an asset to them.

James Fisher & his children, Maisie & Owen (**WII London - 'Woodfellas'**) – Civil servant performing his round for a survey. He gets relocated when he puts duties before apprehension and crosses the Fog to interview the housemates. When he and his wife learn about the healing qualities of the Fog, they decide to make their daughter, Maisie, cross to save her life from incurable hepatitis. Her brother Owen accompanies her, and both are relocated. Only the wife comes back to her normal world and now faces

Edward and Kimberley Epcott (**Essex House**) – Edward Epcott is a policeman who crossed the Fog at the Essex house. He was on duty when the alarm was raised following the sound of gunshots during the raid by the Society against the Chen Corporation. His sister Kimberley manages to get hold of him and is relocated, too, when she visits him.

She is the one who got in touch with an acquaintance of hers, Sam Riverson, sensing he was more than a simple photographer.

***Isabelle de Rocque* (Morocco)** – Christophe de Rocque's wife. She comes down from Paris at his request and ends up relocated in the desert of WII. She is heavily pregnant and not impressed by being relocated in a desert, and even less to have to share the house and her husband with his mistress, Louise.

***Julia & Eudes* (France)** – Yoko's obnoxious sister and her toddler son: and a source of anxiety, sadness, and guilt for Yoko. She blames herself for their relocation as she brought the Fog to her parents home in the South of France, then having to deal with her sister jealousy and wrath.

WII COMMUNITIES

The last Fog Gate opened in 1782 and lasted for about 40 years. By now, the total population known in WII South East England is around 22,000. The two main towns are Lil'London and Newtonsee, the former being the closest to the Fog Gate, the latter being by the sea. The third largest community is Yerushaleim, home to the Jews of WII. The WII English are a very strict community putting an emphasis on having as many children as possible for the survival of their race. To that end, the wealthier a man, the more wives he will have. The women's roles are to have children, raise children, and look after their husband and the household, the old-fashioned way.

In their appearance and everyday life, they remind the onlookers of the Amishes.

***Augustus Hoare* (Lil'London)** – Member of the Council and Sheriff. Stern and inflexible on the traditions to maintain, he reveals himself to be a good man at heart with a curious mind for technology. He becomes friends with the relocated Nick and Big Tom through their shared passion for boxing.

***Clémence Hoare* (Lil'London)** – young wife of Augustus Hoare. She is fascinated by Maud Poff's liberal and free spirit and is in awe of Barbara Snayth.

Edmund Poff (**Lil'London**) – Member of the Town Council and Church Leader. Introverted and shy at first, he reveals himself to be the intellectual of the town and their most open-minded man. His family has kept a library and a diary through the years, and this has enabled his wife, Maud, to gain a knowledge and understanding that there is more to both worlds than the little town they live in. He is madly in love with his wife and does not want any other.

Maud Poff (**Lil'London**) – Wife of Edmund Poff. Avid reader and liberal, from an early childhood she has gone against the grain of the Lil'London's social diktat. She dreams of changing the norms to a more egalitarian society between genders. Yoko and she immediately strike a friendship.

Benjamin Snayth (**Lil'London**) – Member of the Town Council and Mayor. He is the biggest landowner and businessman of the small town. A politician, he is charming at first though soon proves a manipulator with only his own interests in mind.

Barbara Snayth (**Lil'London**) – First wife of Benjamin Snayth. Cold and rigid, she considers herself the guardian of the values and old ways of Lil'London and is especially keen to protect the privileges of the few ruling families.

Hugh Ashby (**Newtonsee**) – Member of the Council and Sheriff. Tall and lanky, in his early 30s.

John Chester (**Newtonsee**) – Member of the Council and Mayor. He is a lookalike and character-like of Winston Churchill.

Walter Makepiece (**Newtonsee**) – Member of the Council and Church Leader. He is always trying to keep everyone at peace, even when no one is arguing.

Ariel Ben-Chaim (**Yerushaleim**) – Physician, apothecary and mediator for Yerushaleim, the Jewish village and only Jewish community known to WII. He looks like Santa Claus with very soft and intelligent eyes, and always seems to know more about someone than they know themselves.

PROLOGUE

The Fog Chronicles is my story. This is how it all started: what I have observed, heard and learned, in my own clumsy words.

My name is Yoko. I am a thirty-something half-French, half Japanese-Italian woman, and one morning many years ago, my life turned upside down. Much has been written and said about what happened and much has been distorted. So, I wrote GATEKEEPERS, a first-hand account of the seven weeks following the apparition of a mysterious thick white Fog shrouding my home. HORIZONS will complete the extraordinary adventure that is my life, which is also a constant source of stress, conundrum and anxiety. It is not easy being a Foggy…

When it all started, I lived with my three housemates in a charming, bohemian house in central London: Zeno and Rico, from Italy, and Harry, a British university lecturer. A couple of years back, I had lost the man I loved and was going to marry, taken away from me by an illness. Slowly, I was rebuilding my shattered life and they helped me greatly. My housemates were a colourful bunch and we had a lively and warm household. Life threw us together and that was a good move, but was it a coincidence?

After yet another cold winter night, we woke up one Sunday to find our house enveloped in an unusual Fog. As Zeno and I ventured through it and exited our front patio, we suddenly emerged in the clearing of a wild forest. The mystery deepened when Rico and Harry walked out with us and we all came out in our good old London. After a few trials, we understood that depending with whom we stepped out, we would reach either London or the mysterious forest. It was even worse in my case as, on my own, I could never get out of the Fog in which I would start suffocating the further I went through it. However, the house itself remained the same even though linked to both worlds, so we benefited from the Internet, electricity and phones, as usual. It was also accessible to people from both worlds but we did not know that yet, nor were we aware of the rules attached to the Fog. Oblivious to my bond to the Fog and its secret workings, I visited my parents in France and spread the Fog to their home, sending my obnoxious sister, Julia, and toddler nephew, Eudes, on a one-way trip to the unknown new world. The situation could not be any worse, or so I thought! We had created a bridge to another reality, one with which we had special links.

The online discovery of someone like me, in Morocco, prompted a mysterious person called Leila to contact us, with claims that she could shed some light on the strange Fog phenomenon. We were desperate to understand what was going on, but what she told us was mind-blowing. When I finally met her, I learnt that the Fog opens a passage every 231 year to a parallel earth. Leila also revealed the complex hierarchy of permissions for the Foggies – so called because of our bond to the extraordinary Fog – to travel into that other world, nicknamed World II (or WII). I was one of seven Switchers, individuals switching a place into a gate to WII on Saturday nights. A Switcher cannot escape the Fog alone or go to either world: to do so, I need one of the seven Crossers (who can go into the new world on their own) or one of the seven Facilitators (who enable Switchers and Crossers alike to come back to the original world). This clarified that Zeno is a Crosser, Harry and Rico are Facilitators. It also indicated that there should be 17 other Foggies spread across the planet. In addition, the Fog also has a healing power for anyone who crosses it: it cleanses the body of harmful viruses and bacteria. This may turn the Fog into a gift, or a curse, depending on what the day brought and if you have had enough coffee to face it.

When I enquired how Leila knew all of this, she revealed the existence of the Society; an old association created during the last Gate opening, for which she has been working all her life. Back in the late 18th century, a group of people affected directly and indirectly by the Fog realised that lack of preparation, injustice and rivalries caused havocs and dangers. This would only get worse with the advance in weaponry and technology. '*When so few people have the control to create and access this Other World, it gives them power*,' Leila told me, '*Where you have powers, they risk being overused and abused either by the owner or others. There is a whole world to discover and to protect, along with those who are living in it*'. This alternative world offers all the richness of ours, untouched and easily accessible. Should the almighty States and large corporations of our world decide to exploit WII, the local communities would have little power to stop them. The Society wants to study and protect this Other World. They have a purpose, an ideal, and have built up the means, knowledge and people to support those over the past two hundred years.

Local communities … We did not know who we were to meet, or how welcome we would be. Leila also insisted that the Society wished to help the Foggies in dealing with and learning from the indigenous people of World II. But that was not all! Indeed, most people in our world are unaffected by the Fog and will cross it without any apparent consequences, but one in seven of them are relocated to WII and can never go back to their original world. I had had the unfortunate experience with my sister and more followed, like my best friend Jazz.

The only link these Relocated have with their original World is the Fogged Gate, acting like a bridge between both worlds. So, when the Gate closed in the early 19th century, the Relocated grew into relatively small local communities developing differently from the modern societies of our world (WI). The first encounter of our household with the representatives of Lil'London confirmed Leila's accounts. Lil'London, the closest town to us in WII, had priorities and ways of life still very close to those of English society in the 1800s. For both sides, the encounter and discovery of the other's customs was a shock, to say the least.

The question of whether or not to inform the British Government of the existence of another earth, of the Gate to access it, and of the Fog healing attribute, was heavy on our minds. Our household feared the Foggies would be overwhelmed if the authorities knew and WII became an official matter.

The military would, doubtless, get involved. We would lose our freedom and turn into pawns torn between two worlds as well as be subjected to countless experiments, to understand the Fog and our connection to it. Under constant watch and analysis, we would lose our individuality as human beings, transformed into assets and tools with regards to the Fog and WII. The Foggies and I were also concerned by the general tendency of human nature to seek domination – as history had proved so many times - in this case, by the attempt to colonise this new world and its inhabitants. We understood, too, that the healing attribute of the Fog needed careful managing and preparation before being disclosed. Finally, we had concerns that WII communities were not ready to welcome a large-scale relocation of people.

Therefore, involving the authorities was dismissed quite early on. We decided instead to put our faith in the Society, as long as it kept its role as advisor and respected us as individuals in our own rights. We set up to work together.

What started with an eerie discovery by four friends soon turned into the creation and management of the 'Inter-Worlds Relations' between local communities, the Relocated and the Foggies. I had to quickly learn the intricacies and subtleties of being an Ambassador. The natives of WII, including the friendlier ones, struggled with the newcomers and the changes we brought, even though they expected the Fog to return and the Gate to open. The wide gap in technology, the clash in cultures and ways of life, and the risk to their balance of power generated fear and bitterness at best, violence at worst. Buried dissents resurfaced. The Relocated would pay the price if the Foggies' diplomacy did not manage to establish good relations between the people of both worlds. Within weeks, I faced a failed abduction and two attempts against my life in WII. The last one almost killed Nick, a relocated ex-mercenary from the Society turned bodyguard.

Things were far from simple in WI either. The Society was well organised and efficient, but the ripple effects of the Fog could not be controlled, despite a couple of hundred years of preparation. For example, they could not prevent

UPRISING

WEEK I

Day 1 (Sunday)

It was still strange to wake up in my former home, yet not in my old room. It was now my best friend's house, and on Saturday nights, I occupied the new guest room. The smell of coffee shook off my nostalgia and soon I made my way downstairs. Coffee was paramount! Sleep had evaded me for days. There was too much on my mind.

Jazz was at one of the bar tables on the ground floor, pouring coffee from a large pot into her favourite cup. She had organised breakfast already, with toast, butter, jam and honey. It was not for her: Jazz was content with only caffeine until lunch.

I loved what Jazz had done with the place; it looked amazing. She had successfully transformed the living-dining room into the warm and modern lounge she dreamt of. The large room had comfortable armchairs and 2-people sofas at the front and small tables at the back, with a small kitchen and bar in the far right corner. Her little business was the latest attraction in both worlds. Well, from London the visitors were limited to the family of the Relocated in-the-know and us Foggies, but it was still a good start. I sat down heavily and she poured me a full cup, without a word. She knew better than to engage in a conversation before it was empty and one toast was gone.

The British Secret Service were one of the reasons for my sleep deprivation. In the three months since they got involved in our life, because of the Fog, they had slowly but surely pushed the limits of our initial agreements. At first, we had managed to win all our demands in exchange for working in partnership with them: no surveillance inside our protected terraced houses area, freedom of movement in and between worlds, contracts for trading and information signed with the Foggies' company, Gatekeepers Associates.

We even imposed Ingis Chen – our former nemesis and now, reluctantly, business partner - as intermediary in business deals. We had also managed not to disclose information on the Society and any of the Foggies. All we had to do was to be cooperative in our everyday life. We shared a general understanding of the Fog and its workings; we agreed to maintain the Essex house fogged for the use of the British Government, with Jack, Dante and Leo based over there. Kim and Ed Epcott also had to compromise and stay in that house, working for the authorities.

The most unpleasant were the tests: they were incessant. Within and outside the Fog, in this World and the other, day and night, Foggies and Relocated gave samples of blood, hair, skin and urine etc. We even convinced the WII locals to undergo some of these tests, as well. We had our daily routine, habits and food scrutinised and altered for the sake of additional analysis. Throughout the first month, wires and tubes covered our entire bodies.

The British Authority now aimed to develop its own diplomatic strategy on the inter-world relations and asked us not to interfere with its policies. The Foggies, via Gatekeepers Associates, already presented themselves as a neutral private entity. In practice, non-interference was difficult to achieve, as we were de facto at the core of every encounter between the WII Town Councils and the representatives of the British Government. Soon, as I was still the Foggies' ambassador, I became the mediator, the ombudsman, or the pacifier. It was challenging, my being inexperienced in the world of diplomacy, though I found it thrilling and personally rewarding. I loved it.

It was an elusive equilibrium. It could not last.

During the past few weeks, the British authorities had grown increasingly demanding towards Gatekeepers Associates and I didn't like what they had in mind. Not one bit. The deployment of drones over WII England did not satisfy them any more: they wanted real presence on land. They wanted to attempt mass relocation for their men. The WII Town Councils relented on this, fearing the sudden wave of professionally trained military men, armed and independent from their control.

That was just one of their new demands. Sam Riverson's visit the previous day was the last blow: they wanted to fly Zeno, Rico and me to the Middle East as a team of Switcher, Crosser and Facilitator. We were to 'fog' the small caretaker house at one of their Embassies, travel for Zeno and I through WII Middle East, and create a gate between the two worlds in a specific location the following switching night. The aim was to plant a bomb in the middle of a terrorist camp's weaponry and blow it up, relying on the vintage Italian military training Zeno had received long ago, and a quick brush-up. If the plan worked, the bomb would explode and destroy the whole camp along with the key leaders of the terrorist movement. They assumed the Fog would be reduced to a blanket on the ground with no passage possible between worlds. We were then to make our way back safely across WII to the Embassy.

I could see many flaws to their plan. First and foremost, it was based on too many assumptions to be solid. What the hell were they thinking?! No one knew the effects and consequences of an explosion within the Fog. What if it spread the Fog to a larger surface? What if it opened the door to yet a third world? This was irresponsible. The second flaw was the lack of knowledge of WII Middle East. Did I want to end up in a Bedouin harem in WII: no thank you! Third, I was clumsy, Zeno was forgetful, and relying on us to carry around and activate a bomb sounded like a bad - very bad - idea. Last, the Foggies' code of conduct specified that we would not create bridges without the Foggies Board's general support: each gate needed maintenance and control, maintenance by a Switcher, control from abuse in use. We were cautious about opening a portal that any government would be free to use as they wished, as we felt responsible. Authorities have a tendency towards exploitation of new opportunities and land. In just three months, the Society, the Foggies and even Ingis Chen had already noted the tendency towards control, invasion and maybe even colonialism by the British. Maybe, once a great Empire, they consciously or unconsciously worked their way towards a new one.

Besides, of all the Foggies in London, only one was British: Harry. Zeno, Rico, Leo and Dante were Italians, I was a mix between French, Italian and

Japanese, and Jack was American. We had no patriotic allegiance to the Queen and the British Government. Of course, if we didn't do what the Government wanted from us, they could kick us out of the country. It was the last thing they wanted.

One thing I had learned, in my months as an Inter-Worlds diplomat, was not to express my position on the spur of the moment and instead, give the impression the proposal was under consideration. Even when I already knew the answer.

Sam expected to hear our decision today. His new partner, McRae, would join him. Sam had mentioned, the previous week, that his boss wanted him to have a partner to cover for him, in case he was indisposed or otherwise unavailable. Sam had lobbied to get the Scottish man assigned to work with him. He trusted the man. We all hoped we would, too.

Rico was fuming and ranting against 'the nerves of those Brits' to involve us in their war against terrorism. Harry had reminded him that, for the government, we were not *private citizens* any more, even if we were still civilians. Nick, my WII bodyguard, had also been indignant afterwards. He had now completely recovered from his knife injury incurred saving my life and was more dedicated to my safety than ever. He would not abide me being put at risk.

'And who would protect you in WII during that mission? No one!' he raged. 'This is exactly why I left the army and joined the Society. Lots of good guys in the system, but within their priorities they are forgetting the individuals.'

'No, they don't', Rico started. 'They know exactly what they are doing. They just don't give a damn about the little people like us.'

'Rico, you and your conspiracy theories…' I interrupted him. 'They hardly consider us as 'little' individuals. Really, it surprises me they would put us at risk.'

'They must be desperate', commented Harry, frowning.

'Which is not reassuring at all on the status of the war against terrorism', Zeno said.

'Or they never intended to send you to this Embassy. In reality, it is a trap to kidnap you three and to have their own Switcher, Crosser and Facilitator a dramatic slaughter in a Fogged resort of Mexico at the hand of WII Mayan, angry that their civilisation was destroyed in our world. Moreover, the Society faced competition in working with us Foggies. Another party knew about the Fog: a large corporation with very specific interests in the Other World, economic and opportunistic ones. This competition stopped at nothing to gain direct access to the WII and its unlimited potential, from threats and bullying to kidnapping. When the antagonistic approach failed, the man behind the corporation decided to change tactics to entice the Foggies away from the Society. Ingis Chen, a Chinese-American at the head of a complex and wealthy international company, came in person to seduce us Foggies into trusting him. A capitalist, focused on the economic advantage and profit that a monopoly trade with WII would give him, Chen also had an idealistic goal: that was what he tried to sell the London Foggies. For him, the source of all plagues in our world is overpopulation and, by transferring one seventh of mankind to the other planet, he believed we could save the humans on this earth. We did not deny there could be some truth in his reasoning, yet we disagreed with his methods to achieve his objective. For Chen, the means justify the end, but not for my friends and me. However, Chen's Corporation had a lot to offer which was tempting for some Foggies among us: money, luxurious homes, recognition and prestige…

But there is always a dark side to the glitz. If the Foggies do not work as a team, our future is gloomy. We can only make it work in the long term if we stick together. Any Foggy who decided to follow him, abiding by his decisions, would be cut off from the other Foggies. They would be stranded and that is a daunting prospect. Relations between Foggies were neither simple nor easy within each location and internationally. Personalities, interests and ambitions differed strongly and the temptation to side with Ingis Chen's substantial rewards for 'Foggies Services' was mounting for some, until we decided to work hard together to set up a structure with rules and a deontological charter everyone can agree on, including serious consequences if broken.

On a personal level, I faced an emotional dilemma, too: seduced by the Italian Crosser, Leo, increasingly attracted to my Society bodyguard, Nick, and struggling to balance my private life and new role as a mediator within the Foggies and with the WII communities, my mind was in a constant battle to remain level headed. Honestly, most often I felt I was walking blind. Additionally, the fate of my sister and her nephew was in my hands and I was at a loss to know what to do next. I also had a secret of my own, kept with housemates only: the ability of my wolf cub, Simba, to both cross and 'facilitate' between the two worlds. It was unheard of that any being from WII could pass to WI. It made Simba unique and I knew I must protect this secret tightly.

The Fog is a huge challenge to face, for the Foggies and me; a challenge that cannot be eradicated but one that brought opportunities and hope for the future, alongside fears and dangers on an individual and global level. We all have the power to fight for what we believe in: it does not mean the fight is easy. As Leila wrote to me: '*Life is meant to be unpredictable for us. Your life, as you know it, will never be the same… you will open new avenues in the lives of many. You have started something amazing*'. Honestly, I often doubt there is anything amazing about having this 'power'. Extraordinary, yes, but amazing? One thing is certain, it has turned my life into one hell of an adventure!

When, at last, we Foggies reached a balance amongst us and created Gatekeepers Associates, and when an agreement was reached with Ingis Chen, I started to believe we would be able to face the complicated future ahead of us. But the reality of our world caught up with us and the British Government entered the game, opening new horizons.

Yoko.

DEDICATION

To Antoine, a better brother than I could ever have hoped for.

~

to use as they please,' Rico intervened, back on his pet beef of scheming governments. It triggered a general eye-roll from everyone.

It had become a little tradition for the previous housemates and Jazz to meet on Sunday mornings at 10am, when possible. Harry, Rico, Zeno, Jazz and I cherished this quality time together. Today, Rico arrived in a particularly good mood. It surprised us all and added to Harry's stoicism and Zeno's big hug; our breakfast reunion started well. Rico even arrived with a gift for Sam to let him know his anger was not personal but towards the outrageous requests from his department. Sam was not a bad guy. In fact, we were pretty lucky to have him in charge on the Intelligence Service side.

Sam Riverson arrived at 11am. Sam's face was set and tense. He was under no illusion the Middle East proposal was not our cup of tea. Instead of joining us at a table for discussion, he asked if we could move to ours. His new partner, McRae, wished to attend the meeting but not to cross the Fog.

*

We settled around the table in our big house, Harry, Zeno and I. Rico had disappeared into the kitchen the second we entered the house. I observed McRae. He was a big tall guy with a good head of ginger hair and a round cherub face that made him look early twenties instead of his probable thirties. Despite his serious and observing attitude, there was a mischievous glint in his eyes.

Rico soon brought fresh coffee from the kitchen. He also brought a delicious-looking cake for our visitors. It looked homemade and I eyed it suspiciously.

'Rico, where did you get that cake?' I asked.

'I made it especially for Sam and Mr McRae to apologise for my outburst yesterday,' Rico replied with a smile I knew all too well. There was something fishy going on. Then I remembered the last time Rico had baked a cake. It was to soothe Nick's pain after his knife injury. He had prepared another space cake! Sam and McRae thanked Rico and took the large slices he served them. Harry held out his plate as well and after a little hesitation, Rico cut the smallest piece possible for him. Harry frowned at the portion but said nothing. It confirmed the last of my doubts. Rico smiled wickedly and Zeno stifled a little laugh, so he knew. Rico did not offer any to me, which suited me fine. The last thing I needed was to get stoned. It was important to keep my head clear.

'So, we have some serious matters to discuss,' said Harry, helping himself to another larger piece of cake, as the first one had disappeared in one mouthful. I threw a glance at Rico who winced as he watched Harry eat. We had to stop him. He never took pot: who knew how it would affect him!

'Ahem… Harry, you seem hungry this morning. Do you want some toast?' I attempted a subtle approach.

'No, I am ok with cake, thanks,' he replied, surprised. 'Oh! Sorry, is it just for the guests? Apologies, Rico,' Harry looked genuinely sorry.

'No worries, mate. Have some. There is plenty for everyone,' Sam said. He and McRae cut two big chunks of cake as their second helpings.

'Great. Thanks,' Harry replied, finishing his second slice.

'Want some more?' Rico suggested, mischievous.

'No!' It had escaped me, and now Harry and everyone were looking at me with concern, except Rico. Rico had his hand hiding the bottom half of his face in an attempt to hide his laughter. Zeno was struggling as well.

'Yoko. What's up?!' Harry asked.

'Well. Rico made the cake. You know Rico. Do I need say more?'

'Bugger!' Harry blurted. 'Rico, you are unbelievable! You…' he stopped himself mid-sentence, turning towards Sam and McRae. Sam was looking suspiciously at Harry and Rico. McRae was scowling at the cake.

'What did he do?' Sam asked me with intensity. Silence settled.

McRae grinned and told his colleague: 'He made us a space cake.'

'What?!' Sam shouted.

'You got the best of the crop, too. You wouldn't find better marijuana anywhere in London,' Rico added, looking pretty proud. Sam's mouth hung open in disbelief. It closed slowly and his eyes became a mere slit. His jaw clenched, he was making a supreme effort to contain his anger.

'Must be a strong one. You made it extra sweet to hide the taste, right?' McRae asked Rico.

'Yep. I see you are a connoisseur,' Rico nodded, looking at McRae with newly-earned respect.

'Well. One happened to have a life before entering the Services of her Majesty...' McRae replied non-committedly.

'At some point, maybe you could tell us a bit more about you? We could start with your full name maybe? All we know is 'McRae', I suggested.

McRae gave me a long look with a crooked smile, then took a sip of coffee without answering. Sam smiled. There was a complicity between them that revealed a real friendship. He answered the question for him.

'The name is Thomas Lochlan Alasdair of the great McRae clan,' Sam teased.

'Just call me McRae,' Thomas Lochlan Alasdair McRae said, simply.

'Yes, everyone calls him McRae. Or Lochy for the ladies,' Sam noted.

'Lochy? Why not Thomas, or Tom?' Harry broke in, not lifting his eyes from his FTab.

'It seems the ladies find 'Lochy' more exotic,' McRae replied.

I leaned over to see what Harry was up to. He was searching online on how to annihilate the effect of the drug and keep a clear head to face the day ahead. Good luck with that, I thought. It read that it could take a good hour before the effects of the cannabis begun. Harry would be out for the count later. For now, we had to deal with the current issue and fast. Sam had the same thought.

'Right. You and I will have a talk later, Rico,' Sam said, through clenched teeth. 'We have little time now to go through the Middle East crisis. So, with no further ado, it is your duty to say yes.'

'Our duty towards whom?' Zeno asked. Rico was about to say something, but a look from Harry stopped him. Rico leaned back in his chair, crossed his arms and remained silent with a surly face for the rest of the meeting.

'I understand it can't be to the British Government, so it will have to be your duty to the international fight against terrorism,' Sam replied, severe and sincere.

'Let's not be over-dramatic here,' I told him, 'and let's review why we are inclined to refuse your proposal. First - ' My sentence was interrupted by Zeno.

'First your plan sucks! It's irresponsible. A bomb in the Fog, what a joke!

Risking Yoko's life, especially with no back up, is completely mad. Nope. Ain't going to happen!'

McRae gave a nod, which seemed an approbation of Zeno's comments. Sam scowled at him and McRae hunched his shoulders and opened his hands in a way that indicated he thought Zeno had a point. So much for Sam's supporting act.

'Plus, we had an agreement; we were to help you liaise with World II and act as neutral intermediary. We do not want the Fog used as a military weapon, or kind of,' I added.

McRae nodded again approvingly and Sam snapped at him.

'McRae, you are getting on my nerves.' Sam was always perfectly in control, but his tone betrayed he was bound and determined.

'Mate, we pass on the message; we don't have to agree with it,' McRae replied to Sam. 'No camera here, so I will say it: personally, I think only professionals should come near those terrorist camps, whatever road you take to go there.'

'This is not the…' Sam started, passing a hand through his hair.

'And I know you agree with me anyway. It is a great risk of rare assets,' McRae turned to look round at us and added, 'No offence. That's what you are to the authorities, singular assets. As well as a source of puzzlement and disbelief, still. It is impressive the controversy and problems you have created internally, not least to protect your existence from leaking to other governments, mainly the US!'

McRae had certainly a more chilled attitude about his job and in expressing his opinions than Sam, who closed his eyes and clenched his jaws anew.

'Right,' Sam concluded, 'so this is a 'no' to the Middle East. Well, that will displease a few. You are the only one for it, Yoko. Considering Jack's deepening depression, we can't rely on him for such a mission. You know guys, you will have to give in at some point and open more portals for us.'

'We made it clear from the start we don't want this. We agreed,' I said, slowly.

'I know, but it was a first agreement. You must have known that our superiors were never going to settle for it in the long term, that it would be… renegotiated.'

'It is not manageable for us to create many portals. Plus, the people of WII are fearful of a large arrival of armed professionals. Who could blame them?' I replied.

'We need to get ready,' Sam replied.

'Ready for what?' I persisted.

'For what comes next.' Sam was laconic as usual.

'What are you talking about?' Zeno asked, before anyone else had a chance.

'That's the point. We don't know. That is exactly why we need to make the odds in our favour,' Sam finished. His comment unsettled us a little.

'Don't forget that aside from being messengers and keeping an eye on you,' McRae commented, 'our principal role is to protect you and the secret of your existence.' He eyed the cake and added, to Rico, 'Do you do doggy bags?'

*

It was quite the anti-climax, this lack of fuss or argument with our refusal of the Middle East mission. Whether McRae's relaxed attitude of the cannabis cake helped smooth the encounter, or Sam already knew our position prior to coming and was prepared for it, all that mattered was that we had avoided that ordeal. For now. It still left a sour taste in my mouth. Sam was right: soon the Government would push for more. It would be difficult not to concede something, but what?

*

I left the boys to return to Jazz's house with Simba, my adopted wolf. She had grown so much in only a few months, that she needed a lot of time outside to get rid of her enormous energy. Nick also wanted to see me for a review of the situation in WII. I had taken this opportunity to organise a meeting with Maud Poff in the afternoon. She was a great source of information on Lil'London's life outside the official line of the town's Council. I wish I had someone similar in the other town, Newtonsee.

I spent some time with Jazz, sharing my concerns with her about the British authorities, until Big Tom, the ex-builder now Relocated, arrived at midday. After a quick hello, he headed to the kitchen and bar corner. His apron on, he began preparing the selection of simple dishes on the menu of my friend's café and lounge business, suitably called *The Jazzin*. Big Tom had proved a keen cook, and he and Jazz made a good team. His mother was a regular visitor in the afternoons: he had finally told her the truth and she had taken the news of his extraordinary situation very well. She laughed that she spent more quality time with him now than before. She was also glad that he had distanced himself from the thugs that were his friends.

*

Nick entered the house shortly after and greeted me warmly, with kisses on both cheeks. Gone was any decorum between us. He looked worried though and wasted no time in dragging me outside in WII. The clearing of the forest had changed. A small development of a few simple houses formed the hamlet of Woodfellas, home of the Relocated. I only had a chance to wave at James Fisher and his children, Owen and Maisie, as Nick continued to lead me at a fast pace on one of the paths in the forest.

'We need to talk. Now!' he said in an urgent whisper. The ground was uneven and I struggled to keep my balance. Simba was with us of course, following without problem. When I winced at Nick's strong grip – he had trained as a boxer and often forgot his own strength – she growled at him. Nick had competition as my best bodyguard.

'Nick, what is it?' I asked him, massaging my free wrist.

'Not here. I want to make sure no one can hear us. No one.'

'You are alarming me!'

'Nutty, you should be alarmed.'

Only Leo and him called me Nutty. No matter how much I protested, they continued. Nutella, my original nickname, was so much better.

Once we were further into the forest, he stopped and scanned the surroundings.

'I think Clémence Hoare is the one attempting to kill you,' he said when he was satisfied no one was around.

'What?! Clémence Hoare? That young, fragile little thing? Nonsense!'

*

Clémence and I were not close. Clémence, the youngest wife of the stern and rigid sheriff of Lil'London, Augustus Hoare, sometimes accompanied Maud Poff when we met. She never spoke much and always seemed unsure of herself. She was both fascinated by and longing for the attention of the non-conformist Maud. Clémence was also in awe of the haughty and ultra-conservator Barbara Snayth, wife of the town mayor. Why would this poor creature want to kill me? The teenager who had tried to kill me a little more than three months ago had been seduced and indoctrinated over months. She didn't fit the profile. Surely Nick's obsession in finding who was behind the failed assassination attempt had made him lose sight of reality.

'Nick, come on. Clémence Hoare is too insecure to even talk to a teenager, let alone seduce him into committing murder. She is a sweet woman who just needs to find her voice.'

'Your '*sweet woman*' is not that innocent. There is one thing she doesn't know: we can track someone from their hair, thanks to our DNA technology. I found a few strands of hair in the teenager's hidden cabin, where he met his mentor. It took me long enough to gather samples to match the hair with someone, but I did.'

'Are you certain of the match? How did you get a sample of Clémence's DNA?' I asked, unconvinced. I had great respect for Nick, but his claims of Clémence were far-fetched.

'Hoare and I meet weekly for boxing and we often go to his for dinner afterwards. It enables us to have an informal discussion on their frustratingly slow investigation. Last time I decided to check his household, too. You won't believe the clumsy reputation I have in WII, bumping into people at all times to get samples? Anyway, this time round was easier: to thank my hostess for her repeated hospitality, I brought her a gift: a modern boar brush. I even kindly gave her one stroke with it to demonstrate how it massaged the scalp. Hoare frowned; she was ill at ease, but I got my strand of hair. There is no doubt, it is a match!'

'The hair strand you found could have fallen from Hoare when he was gathering evidence.'

'Yoko, what do you take me for? An amateur? Do you really think I would not dig further?'

'I am sorry. I don't mean to insult you or anything. It just doesn't make any sense.'

'Like you, I needed to be sure so I followed her. Your 'little one' is more active than meets the eye! She is very regularly travelling to Newtonsee on the pretense of running errands. Well, she never buys anything. Whatever she brings back to Lil'London is brought to her by one of her followers at the meetings she organises.'

'What meetings? You have lost me.'

'Your sweet Clémence Hoare organises religious meetings several times a week in Newtonsee. Their official purpose is to teach the ways of a good woman and exchange ideas and crafts between the towns. In reality, she has created a cult around her and promotes the rise of women in WII.

'Excuse me?!'

'She wants the women to rise against the men who control them. And her movement isn't a pacifist one, either.'

'What the …?! No! No way!' I was incredulous. It was too unbelievable to be true. 'Come on, Nick… You are pulling my leg, aren't you?'

'No. I am not. I managed to use a bug and record one meeting. You should listen to some of it.'

I nodded, in shock. Nick took out his tablet and selected a recording. He then placed an ear bud in my ear and pressed play. Clémence's voice came out clear, but it was confusing. It was Clémence yet it wasn't. Her voice was deeper, graver and more confident than the one I knew. Each word came out both honeyed and powerful. They conveyed the strength, power and conviction of a person with great oratory art. I was captivated, first by the voice, then by the message it carried.

'(…) oppression for centuries is not acceptable anymore. We are no better than slaves at the mercy of the ruling men, despite being the most valuable individuals of this land. They ought to treat us with respect. They ought to give us pleasure. They even ought to be at our service, grateful that we ensure the survival of our kind. Instead, they order, impose and condemn the barren and dissident to their repugnant brothels that they use at their leisure, dismissing their duty towards their wives for their own pleasure. We women should not have to share our husbands with other wives. We should be the ones to choose the men we want as fathers for our children. Men, not man. Our bodies do the hard work; they

should have the privilege of having pleasure, too.'

'The reverend read…', came a hesitant voice, rising from the audience.

'Do not let yourself be influenced by the words of men! They are teaching you their faith to better control you. They impose their Bible, written by men for the power of men over women. God is merciful and just. He would not abide women, who give birth to his children, to be treated in such an unjust fashion. The men of Lil'London created the Bible we read in church. They twisted its meaning in such a way to dominate this world. We have known this for years. Today we have the proof. The Gate has shown us the truth: a woman has been chosen to open the bridge between our world and the one of our ancestors. Miss Yoko Salelles, and I insist on the Miss, is showing us the way. She obeys no one, belongs to no one. She…'

Nick cut the recording and I took the ear bud out. I was both enraptured and shaken. Clémence's speech was gripping. No wonder Nick talked of cult and followers. I would follow her!

'But, Nick, that doesn't explain why she would want to kill me? On the contrary. You interrupted, but she was talking about me as…'

'As a role model? Yes. She does. Constantly. She always uses you as an inspiration, as a model, as a tool to assert her convictions and gather her audience more strongly around her. One of the sentences she often uses to finish her meetings is *'No one will ever grant us power. We have to take it!'* Then all the women shout *'Yes! We take it! Yes! We will have power!'* As a man, I find it scary.

'So why would she want me dead?'

'That I haven't been able to understand yet.'

'So maybe it isn't her?'

'And you find it just a coincidence; her double nature and rebellious scheme along with her hair linked to your aggressor? You have just heard how she can seduce a crowd, how she extols that women should be free to choose their men. She would have no difficulty in seducing a teenager and making him do what she wants.'

'Except that the teenager was against the Foggies and wanted the door closed. That would not help her cause.'

'The ways of a cunning woman's mind are mysterious,' Nick commented.

'Maybe you are right... Hell, I don't know what to think! I grant you, Clémence is not the innocent flower I thought she was. But a murderer? I need to talk to her.'

'No!' Nick yelled. Afterwards, he looked around the woods suspiciously for anyone eaves-dropping.

'You will do no such thing,' he continued in a low voice. 'Knowing you are aware of her true nature would only make her more dangerous. You might trigger her to launch her *Battle of the Sexes*.'

'She is going to do it anyway, by the sound of it,' I commented, sarcastically.

'Yes, but now we can prepare for it.'

First the meeting with the Secret Services: now that. A headache was building up slowly. An urge for chocolate chip cookies was building up, too: a clear sign from my gut that tough times were coming my way.

'Okayyy... And how do you intend to prepare for this *Battle of the Sexes*?'

'No idea.'

'Well, that's helpful.'

'We need to keep it quiet though. If any men, especially Hoare, hear about it, they will take action against the women involved and that wouldn't be pretty.'

'They are their wives and daughters. They wouldn't really harm them, would they?'

'Don't put it past the men to destroy the threat to their rule, mentally if not physically. It could even make them relent to the British Government's wish for more military relocation to help repress Mrs Hoare's rebellion.'

'This is so messed up!'

'One last thing. You remember when Ushi Tsou kidnapped you in the forest of WII?'

'How could I forget this charming escapade in the woods with a ruthless and upset relocated mercenary?' I hadn't nicknamed the dangerous woman 'Tsou Bitch' for no reason.

'Well, if you recall, she had a secret meeting with someone you couldn't distinguish, between your exhaustion and the drugs she gave you. It must have been Clémence Hoare.'

My headache had hit home.

*

Talks about Ushi Tsou brought back to mind another sore point. Neither she, nor my sister and nephew, had returned from flying by helicopter from my parents in the South of France through World II. I blamed myself for this. This mission to rescue a stranded Relocated had been much too early, and with a loose cannon for a pilot, as well. To satisfy my difficult sister's demands, I threw caution to the winds. What was I thinking?! For weeks I had woken up hoping it would be the day they would show up. Every evening, my parents called and I had to crush their own hopes. They did not blame me, but I shared their pain. I had very little hope now. At first, their disappearance could have been due to a technical fault or bad weather and they had to stop on their way. Now... Now we feared the worst.

Nick read my mind and put a friendly hand on my shoulder, telling me that it was not my fault. That I could not have predicted what happened. Everyone was repeating this to me constantly. It didn't help. I felt guilty about their disappearance – I still refused to use the word *loss*. Sensing his gesture was not enough, Nick came closer and hugged me. It was comforting and warm. It was a beautiful summer's day: nevertheless, I felt cold inside and Nick's sincere kindness touched me. When I separated, he took my face in his hands and kissed my forehead, then looked into my eyes.

'In these moments, I wish I could kiss you.'

'Nick, you know I like you, but...'

'You fancy me,' he said, with a cheeky smile.

'Nick, we talked about this, I don't want any relationship right now. There is too much...'

'Yoko, you are a strong woman. It doesn't stop you being scared of getting hurt. Sometimes you may want to keep it light. I like you. You like me. I am a man. You are a woman. No big deal, just a bit of fun.'

'Nick, please. I am not in the mood.'

'I know. This is not about me and it won't happen. It is about you loosening up the serious and intense. I do respect you. You are a good person.'

'Thank you, Nick.'

'And what about Leo?'

'What about him?'

'You broke his heart.'

'No, I didn't. We hadn't had the time to fall in love.'

'Yes, you had.'

'No.'

'Yes. Time does not matter, you know that.'

Leo, the charming Italian Crosser from Rome. What had started as a flirtation through messages turned real when he came to settle in London. We kept it quiet for a time, and then it became official. That is when I backed out. If my feelings had not been so ambivalent about being involved with a fellow Crosser, or even anyone linked to the Fog, maybe I would not have. However, the prospect of a relationship going wrong with someone bound to be around me for life because of the Fog stopped me. The chances of future dramas were too high. This was my official line, only partially true. It didn't fool the ones who knew me, including Nick. Long conversations ensued with my parents, Jazz and even Maud about my needing to let someone into my life, about learning to be vulnerable, about letting down the walls of my inner core. They raised a strong case, but at the end of the day I wasn't going to force myself into a relationship if I didn't believe in it. If I wasn't ready, I wasn't ready, and that was that.

The last thing I wanted was to extend this type of conversation with Nick. So I thanked him for his wise words and turned to go back towards *The Jazzin* for my meeting with Maud. During the walk back, I reassured him that my lips were sealed on his revelations about Clémence Hoare, then briefed him on the morning encounter with Sam Riverson and McRae. I suggested that he joined next time to give us his professional opinion on the newcomer. Nick reminded me it implied McRae crossing the Fog and risking relocation. Would McRae be prepared to do it as part of his job? He seemed pretty laid back, but being relocated was no trivial matter. Crossing the Fog or not was a life changing decision: a 1-in-7 chance to be a one-way ticket. Aside from his personal decision of course, did we, the Foggies, want to allow a British spy to go through? I brushed that matter aside as non-priority for now. No one had requested it so far, so it was irrelevant.

*

Maud Poff was waiting for me when we got back to the clearing. She had brought a basket full of Lil'London pastries to share with the Fishers children. Our little Woodfellas community liked her good nature and kind attentions. She even brought a bone for Simba. Putting aside in my mind, as much as possible, the troubling news about Clémence Hoare, we discussed the differences between our Worlds and talked at length about the *Lil'London Tales*, a collection of historical notes the Poff family had gathered over centuries. It had been my bedtime reading for the past few months. After a difficult start getting used to its style, the stories and main actors were now beginning to make sense for me. There were gaps and a lack of detail sometimes and Maud was helping me fill in the blanks. In truth, these were not the most exhilarating tales, with little action and suspense. However, the stories were a captivating analysis on a sociological and social level. Slowly, it revealed how the indigenous communities had evolved towards polygamy, the breeder role of women or the simple but rigid structure of the town councils. I still had a long way to go before reaching the part when Edmund Poff had taken over from his forefathers and had written the contemporary history of their known part of WII.

I also had a gift for Maud: a brand new pair of rollerblades. She looked at them in awe as they looked so different to hers. Next, she smiled and claimed she would teach me how to rollerblade better on the roads and streets of her little town. And to think I would finally improve my wheelie skills, taught by someone from another world!

Day 2 (Monday)

Jack tried to kill himself. Last night, he tried to kill himself.

The American ex-fashion student never completely adjusted to being a Switcher and how it changed his life. He was subject to depression and was always struggling to sleep. He used this to convince the doctors to give him sleeping pills. Leo, Dante and Jack lived in a small house built in the back garden of the fogged Essex house, so that during the week they would not need a Facilitator to wander around in England. It was the middle of the night when Jack tried and failed to swallow enough pills in one go. He decided the only way was to mix them with some food. However, as he was in a daze, Jack somehow managed to blow up the kitchen – matches, gas and microwave is never a good combination - and got himself projected out into the garden and against a tree. Rico immediately went to the Essex house to help boost Jack's morale, as Jack had a crush on him. He and Leo were still by Jack's side at the hospital.

My chest was tight as I gripped my coffee cup in bed, absently stroking Simba, the sun barely up, digesting the news after Rico's call. How did it come to this? Should we be more worried for his mental health or for the physical damage after the explosion? All things considered, Jack had had the worst deal among us. Stranded abroad with strangers, twice kidnapped, depression… Nothing was spared to the poor young man. When the UK government got involved, Jack felt left out. He had come to England with the hope that the situation would somehow be lighter than in Rome. Everyone spoke English, the group of Foggies were larger, and Rico was kind to him even if Jack's attraction for the Italian was not reciprocated. Sadly, it was not enough. His mood did not improve. Slowly, he retreated more and more within himself, hardly ever leaving his room and dozing most of the time. The Society had discreetly organised a therapist to come and see Jack weekly. Evidently, that was not sufficient.

*

I was still lost in sombre thoughts when Rico called again around 6 am.

'Jack is gone!'

'What! You told me he was comatose and under perfusions, incapable of leaving his bed?'

'His bed is gone too! They took him! Yoko, they stole Jack.'

'Hang on, calm down. Who is 'they'?'

'If I knew, I would go there and give them a piece of my mind! Bastards! I bet it's the British Government. You can't trust these people. I keep telling you, Yoko: you can't trust these people!'

'Wait. Let's not make assumptions here. First tell me exactly what happened.'

'Right. Thirty minutes ago Jack was here, now he isn't. That's it. His bed is gone, the perfusions and machines and stuff are gone. The Government guy by his door is gone. Simple.'

'Shit. And you say the Security from the Government is gone too.'

'Yep.'

'…'

'I think it is pretty telling. It is them.'

'I am calling Sam.'

Sam picked up my call, grumpily, after four rings.

'Jack,' I said, between clenched jaws.

'What about him?' he said, in a rocky voice.

'An accident happened last night. Jack ended up in hospital.'

'What?! Is he ok?'

The tone of his voice was of real surprise. He really sounded shaken out of his sleep. Moreover, if he didn't know Jack had had an accident, he couldn't know about his disappearance either.

'He was doing fine. Although comatose, there wasn't anything serious. The real issue is that he has disappeared, along with his bed and the medical equipment attached to him.'

'WHAT! I'm on my way. I'll call you back in five!'

Our next conversation did not last long. Sam was driving to his office to clarify, first and foremost, if his Secret Services department was involved. He would contact me afterwards. In the meantime, I showered, ate a little, and of course contacted Leila to find out if she knew any more. She didn't. Jack had evaporated without leaving a trace: it was the work of professionals. All the cameras had been disabled. The Society's men on site could not check the ambulances coming and leaving the hospital as they had no authority, so Jack could have been in any of them in the minutes preceding the alarm being raised. Now every room, every floor, every corner of the hospital was being checked. I couldn't shake my fear that Jack was already far away in a place inaccessible to us.

The young American was, again, the victim of kidnapping. I shook my head: some people really have bad luck.

*

I had to inform the other Foggies in Kenya, Morocco, Nevada and Alaska. Our relations were amicable and efficient now. Mainly because all of us had adjusted our lives to the existence of the Other World and kept each other in the loop with our different connections to that World. In the past three months, we had settled into a routine of two video conference calls for the Foggies Board Meeting, every Monday and Friday at 6pm GMT. I prepared an email for them all, hoping there would be better news in the evening.

In Kenya, the love story between Mary and her WII Maasai hunter was still strong, even though her mother, Clare, was finding it difficult to cope with. She was worried for Mary's future life in this community. Putu, their Facilitator, was coping with her Fog requirement more easily now that Mary was not constantly demanding her help to return to Nairobi.

In Nevada, Adam Koplat had developed good relations with the Native Americans, with whom he loved spending time and exploring the culture. He had started a business of selling their fur blankets and carpets, which gave Sophie, his wife, something to do with her days other than argue with her stepdaughter Michelle. Michelle… It was a sore subject for the Koplats. She was headstrong and against any of her father's decisions. Her constantly challenging attitude was taking its toll on the nuclear family's morale.

In Alaska, everything was well. It seemed nothing could disturb the blissful mood of the newlyweds, Tony and Rosario, or the content life of her reclusive brother, Mitch.

In Morocco, the situation was, of course, more complex. How could it not be, with a very pregnant betrayed wife, an over-sensitive mistress, an orphaned foreign child and an unfaithful husband-lover all stuck with each other? The original arrangement for Helo failed: he was supposed stay with Christophe de Rocque who, every other day, would stay with either Isabelle-the-wife or Louise-the-lover. Unfortunately, within a week, Christophe escaped from Morocco and headed for Paris. He had been in touch with the cleaning lady there to send his passport by mail to Louise, as Isabelle had destroyed the identity papers, purposely, to stop him leaving her. He stayed there for five days to reorganise his business and run errands before returning on the Saturday, just in time for the 'switching night'. Louise and Isabelle were furious! Christophe argued that Louise could travel as she wished – she had come to visit us in London a few weeks prior - so why couldn't he? Louise had replied she was not sneaking away from a pregnant wife and his responsibilities. Louise and Isabelle still hated each other: however, instead of screaming at each other or ignoring the other's presence, now they managed to keep their relations cordial. The Society had acquired a remote villa in the Atlas Mountains for them, protected from view both from the ground and the air, thanks to mountains and trees. The security was high, aided by the latest technology, including a medical room for the baby delivery and future health support for parents and baby. When the house was ready, Christophe switched it into a WII portal. Isabelle and Christophe moved there, travelling through World II. Louise remained in the Marrakech house even though it was not a portal anymore, and visited the wife and unfaithful husband only occasionally when she needed access to the Fog. Christophe would go and see her much more often. Helo was now staying with Christophe and Isabelle full time.

*

Sam and McRae arrived shortly before lunch. Harry, Zeno and I were ready for them, waiting in our living room. Sam looked really upset and agitated. McRae looked serious, though relaxed. Sam immediately told us that the UK Government had taken Jack.

'This is unacceptable!' Harry banged his fist on the table. It took us all by surprise. He isn't known for his display of anger or lack of emotional control. Zeno and I promptly agreed with him and soon the room was filled with demands for explanation, in loud and rude terms.

'I am really sorry. I have nothing to do with it. I... I do not approve it. However, there is nothing I can do...' Sam tried to explain.

'This is not good enough!' I shouted. 'You have to release Jack to us immediately! What do you think you are doing? Why...'

'Because they want more than what you are giving,' McRae interrupted. 'As you refused, they decided to take.'

'May I point out that you belong to the 'they' you refer to?' Harry snapped, back in control with a dangerously calm tone. There was a tempest underneath.

'They are not 'us'. The department is split in sections of operations. It is the military branch that wanted to send you to the Embassy. And who took Jack,' McRae explained. 'They saw what looked like an opportunity and grabbed it. Him.'

'They claim Jack is too precious or dangerous to be left in a civilian hospital,' Sam continued, 'so they brought him to a more 'secure' location while he recovers from his trauma, both mental and physical.'

'Which means they intend to keep him for a long time,' I replied. 'His depression is never going to be cured if he is locked up all day long! What about Saturday night; 'switching' night?'

'They have been after access to the Fog without limits for months, to send people of their own across for relocation,' Zeno said to me, while looking at Sam and McRae. 'They want their own exploration team on site. Maybe even their own army.'

Sam and McRae kept silent.

'Re-lease-him,' Harry enunciated each syllable, slowly.

'It isn't possible. I would if I could, but this is not in my power,' Sam replied.

'He shouldn't be in a normal hospital anyway. A military one is much more suitable considering the circumstances,' McRae added.

'And on Saturday night, what will happen?' My voice was high-pitched in frustration by then. I was squeaking like an angry little bird. 'You must release him!'

'Well, obviously the arrangement hasn't worked out so well for him so far, as he tried to kill himself. So maybe he needs something else,' McRae argued.

'Bullshit!' Zeno exploded.

Our only leverage was to refuse to cooperate, by withdrawing ourselves from further tests, or not reporting World II. It was better for them if we willingly worked in partnership to get the full benefits and access to WII, but if we didn't, they could use us by force. It would still give them a minimal contact with the Other World. The balance of power leaned towards them. It did not matter. We would not give Jack up. Harry, Zeno and I warned the British authorities, via Sam and McRae, that there would be repercussions for their kidnapping. Sam protested that kidnapping was a grand word when really they were looking after him, but even he was not convinced by his statement.

When talking with Sam and McRae, my Ftab rang several times. Without picking up the call, I checked the caller ID. Ingis Chen. I returned his call as soon as the British agents left. After a brief exchange with one of his assistants, I was put through to him.

'Dear Yoko, thank you for returning my call so fast.'

'You are welcome, Mr Chen.'

'Please call me Ingis,' he said as usual. 'Yoko, we have noted a sudden rise of activity around you and the Essex portals. May I enquire if everything is ok?'

*

His enquiry did not come as a surprise. For the British Government, Ingis Chen was our private and official security back up. Our real support, the Society, was kept secret from the authorities. Ingis knew about their existence without having any details about our mysterious protector. His security was just a screen, but he used it to keep an eye on us, as well.

The Society was proving invaluable in blocking the Secret Service's repeated attempts to listen to us with remote devices, to access our data, or to track our private communications. They also enabled us to hide the existence – albeit one the Secret Services suspected –of the other Foggies. So far, the Society had been true to its word: it has respected our independence, never imposed its suggestions, and we worked in a good partnership. Their objectives had proved true: to gain knowledge of the ecology, history, climates and people of the WII, as well as protect the doors from abuse. I had come to assimilate them in my mind to a non-governmental organisation. For example, the description of the UNESCO (United Nations Educational, Scientific and Cultural Organisation) fitted the Society like a glove:

'The "intellectual" agency of the United Nations... created in order to respond to the firm belief... that political and economic agreements are not enough to build a lasting peace. Peace must be established on the basis of humanity's moral and intellectual solidarity. UNESCO strives to build networks among nations that enable this kind of solidarity, by mobilising for education..., building intercultural understanding..., pursuing scientific cooperation..., protecting freedom of expression.... Its message advocates the creation of holistic policies that are capable of addressing the social, environmental and economic dimensions of sustainable development.'

It was reassuring that such organisations existed. It restored faith in humanity. It was also comforting that we might not be complete fools to believe that the Society, as an organisation with positive goals, really did exist.

I briefed Ingis Chen on Jack's accident, omitting the suicidal part, and his current disappearance.

'So Jack is in the hand of the British Government?'

'Yes. You are our business representative with them. Anything we can do to make them understand it is unacceptable?'

'I will look into it right now,' he replied promptly, adding, 'They intend to have their own portal, it is clear. From a business point of view, this is not good for me. I lose my monopoly.'

'And I presume, as a second thought, you are also upset for Jack.'

'Of course.'

Our conversation was short. Ingis Chen and I never had long chats and they were always over-polite. I had an uncomfortable feeling hanging up. Ingis Chen was first and foremost a businessman attracted by power. The British government had done what he would love to do himself. In fact, he had tried and failed, and somehow managed to find a compromise with us. He was no State though. The fragile equilibrium between the British authorities, the Foggies and Chen had just been shaken. Should we lose our freedom and the government take over, he risked being dismissed. He had reacted too calmly on the phone. The steel in his voice concerned me.

*

I called Leila to get an update on the situation.

'Any news on Jack's location?' This had a taste of *dejà-vu*.

'Not yet. We are working on it.'

'Ingis Chen called. He knew something was up. His team followed the ambulance to the hospital. I asked him if they had seen anything that could lead us to Jack but he replied negatively. I am not sure he would have told me, anyway.'

'We will monitor him as well.'

'We must find Jack.'

'We are doing our very best,' Leila said, in an exhausted and frustrated voice. 'The Secret Services have done a good job at erasing their tracks. We will keep an eye on Chen in case he has a lead. If... No - WHEN we do, Jack will have strong protection around him. We won't be able to just go in and get him.'

'This is never simple, is it?'

'The Fog is not a straightforward phenomenon.'

'It's a pain in the backside.'

'Ah, but...'

'No Leila, don't even start. I know what you are going to say: we have had this conversation often enough. *'It is an amazing event, a great learning opportunity about our planet, a sociological wonder,* blah-blah-blah. *The Foggies are unique, entrusted by Nature or whatever with a special gift and again,* blah-blah-blah'. It is still a huge pain in the backside! All I wish is to sit comfortably on my little – or not so little – bottom, once in a while!'

Simba needed a walk afterwards. When we returned, I went straight to the kitchen and helped myself to a pack of chocolate chip cookies. It had been a long time since I'd had such a strong urge. I had only recently managed to zip up my favourite jeans again, and now... I sighed, prepared a cup of tea and dipped the first of many cookies into it. My excuse was that I'd had no time to prepare lunch and it was already mid-afternoon. After a couple of cookies, I dialled Jazz. She didn't know yet about Jack.

*

I was right to worry about Ingis Chen.

If I thought my life was complicated then, it was nothing in comparison to what was coming. Still, to give him credit, he gave us more leverage and more power than we had ever imagined.

Day 3 (Tuesday)

Last night, the Foggies bi-weekly video conference call was the most unusual we'd ever had. The original agenda was Jack's kidnapping and the threats posed by the British Government. Instead, we anxiously followed a live birth.

It was beautifully bloody, eerily captivating and nervously exhausting. Isabelle gave birth to Chloé at 12.43am. The new-born baby had all her fingers, all her toes, was of average height and weight, and screamed out all the air in her lungs seconds after arriving into the fogged house in the Moroccan mountains. She was born in the middle of two worlds. So it was to everybody's relief that she was alive and well, that the mother was fine and that the birth had no complications. Christophe de Rocque showed a new side of him: he dealt with the situation like a professional. He explained afterwards that he had watched videos on how to support a birth and practised daily with the nurse who looked after Isabelle. He demonstrated more care, attention and patience than I would have thought him capable of. That night, I glanced at the man both Louise and Isabelle loved, and I could understand why they did.

The birth was fast. Isabelle lost her waters at the start of the video conference. When we suggested we should leave them for this private event, Isabelle refused. She said she was always alone and had nobody but us. If something happened to her, we would all have to look after the baby, not just Christophe. 'Even you,' she added, for the attention of Louise. She said to the other woman that she would always hate her for stealing a part of Christopher's heart, but also knew she would never abandon her baby if something happened to her. Louise nodded, tears building up in her eyes. Christophe placed the Ftab on one of the tables along the wall, at the level of Isabelle's head. The best angle in my opinion: there are body parts during the birth I didn't think necessary for me to witness.

*

A call woke me up late the next morning. I was still in a state of wonder and bliss at the marvel of birth. I eagerly took Leila's call, expecting some news of Jack or Chloé. Had they found Jack? Was the baby girl Relocated? Was she the missing Facilitator? Was she like Simba, also born in the Fog and able to cross at will between the two worlds?

'Leila! How are you? Any news on…'

'We have a new problem.'

I immediately tensed and sat up in my bed. What was wrong with the baby?!

'Go on.'

'The Internet is flooded with news of the Fog and the parallel World.'

My head went numb and my breathing stopped. Everything froze in and around me. I frowned, repeating her words in my head and trying to make sense of them. The panic was not linked to the words, but their implications. Internet, Fog, the Other World. Everyone. Billions of people. No!

I wanted to scream, yet my voice was only a whisper. 'How is it possible? How could it be on the Internet? You… You monitor… What does it say? I don't… What happened?'

'You remember Michelle's mother? Not Sophie, who is the step-mother, but the real mother, the journalist.'

'Well, I know of her.'

'Michelle talked to her mother.'

'Ah…' Focusing was still a real effort. My head was buzzing. Internet! The urge to go on Google was growing fast.

'Michelle's mother went to see from afar the fogged house in Nevada. She observed the new business of the Koplats with Indian products. She made a parallel with the mediatised events in Mexico and in Jakarta involving Fog. Even though the Fog has now disappeared in both locations, she travelled to the sites and asked a few questions. We did our best to contain her. We thought we had. It had been two months already and she seemed to work on other things now.'

'So, why now?' I asked.

'Because we were not the only ones aware of her enquiries and interest.'

'Who? No… No! Ingis Chen!'

'Yes, the one and only.'

'How did he do it?'

'Well, we are partially at fault. For months, both his team and ours were blocking and controlling Michelle's mother. When we saw he had already placed strong blocks, we only added minor ones. It made the checks simpler. We didn't imagine he would just lift them all of a sudden and launch an information campaign on the net.'

'And the journalist, does he know her links with Michelle and the Nevada Foggies?'

'Hard to tell but it is possible he doesn't. There hasn't been an increase of activity around them. We think the journalist kept that quiet to protect her daughter.'

'But now… What is going to happen now? Can you do anything? Can you stop it somehow? What damage control could be done?'

'At this point, none. All we can do is follow-up where it's going and increase security around you guys.'

'What the heck was Ingis Chen thinking? Has he lost the plot? I am calling this bastard right now!'

*

I was walking in circles in my room, Simba, on the bed, was looking at me, confused. I wanted to shout my anger and frustration at someone. Zeno knocked on my door and called out: 'Yoko?'

'Not now!' I replied. I felt a burst of adrenaline and energy and wanted to use it.

I dialled Chen's number and after one ring his assistant picked up.

'Anna. Hi. I need to speak with Chen,' I blurted, as best as possible with clenched jaws. She didn't even reply and transferred me immediately.

'Hello, Yoko. I was expecting your call.'

'You were, were you?!' My jaws, too tightly clenched, prevented me from exploding just yet.

'Of course I was. I know you are quite the Google fan.'

'Chen, you bastard!' I couldn't hold it any longer: I exploded. The door of my room opened and Zeno, Harry and Rico entered, worried and with inquisitive looks on their faces.

'How could you do that to us?' I continued. 'The Internet?! You leaked us to the Internet: you disgust me! You... You... Mean nauseating vermin! Scum of the earth!'

Zeno, Harry and Rico's faces went pale and their jaws dropped. Rico went for my Ftab but I didn't let him catch it. I jumped on my bed, still insulting Chen profusely. Zeno demanded angrily that I give him the phone. Rico swore he was going to kill the 'Fucking mother-fucker bastard c***' (Only quoting - Sorry). Both Italians were trying to get on the bed where I was unleashing my anger, insulting Chen. The latter remained silent on the other end of the line. It was even more annoying. Simba was at my feet, protecting me by scratching and biting any of the boys attempting to reach me to get the Ftab. Only Harry had not moved. From ashen- faced, he had turned lobster red in rage. I ignored them all, lashing out verbally over the phone. When at last I had to take a breath, Chen said:

'If I may say, I did you a service.'

'What? How dare you!'

'Now that your existence is known, the Government will have to be open about their connection with you. They won't be able to do as they please. You will be the centre of worldwide interest. Now you have all the leverage you need, my dear, to make any demand you want.'

This made me freeze on the spot. As a ripple effect, Zeno and Rico stopped as well, wondering what had just been said.

'Mr Chen...' I tried to speak as calmly as possible.

'Please call me Ingis,' he smoothly interrupted, his voice the epitome of control. That was so irritating!

'What about asking us FIRST? Do you think we want to be displayed on every screen on the planet? NO! WE DON'T! Now every government on the planet will want its own portal, not just the British! The French, the Italians, the...'

'Exactly. So the British Government will have to be very nice with you

Foggies to keep you here. And I, as your business interest representative, will make sure you have the best deals.'

'For which you will take a good cut.'

'Fairly so.'

'Mr Chen,' I tried to regain control of myself and not let emotions cloud my judgement. 'You went behind our back. You put your best interest before ours.'

'No I didn't. Your best interest IS mine. If I had told you what I was about to do, you would never have agreed or taken too long to do so. It would have been a loss of precious time. At some point, your existence would have been revealed anyway. It is better to have it done in a controlled fashion and Jack's situation made it urgent.'

'Oh! You think leaking the information to the press and Internet is controlled… Next, will you control the reactions of the public? You do not act on our own initiatives when it comes to us. Never. As to you representing us to the big world out there, after today, forget it!' I hung up.

*

The room was silent. Still standing on my bed, Simba continued growling at the boys. I was fuming. Harry spoke first, slowly, as if unclenching his teeth was an arduous task. He suggested going downstairs and organising an emergency meeting to brief everyone. We also needed to go online and check what had been leaked and the first reactions to it. We had a big crisis on our hands. I thought of Isabelle and how this could affect her baby. Chloé was barely a few hours old.

*

Online, we found reference to the Fog immediately. The consequences of Ingis Chen's decisions were already unfolding for the worst. We clicked on a video news report and watched in silence:

'Riots have erupted in Kenya following the controversial information released, by the renowned journalist Penny Thompson, concerning the extraordinary apparition of localised 'Fogs'. Thompson makes a parallel between events in Mexico and Indonesia four months ago. There, mysterious Fogs created chaos

with the horrible deaths of more than thirty people in a Mexican resort and the disappearance of a family in a slum in Jakarta. Her claims are that this Fog phenomenon opens a bridge to another planet, one identical to ours, but preserved from the havoc caused by mankind. According to Thompson, the Fog has healing powers as well as a mind of its own, selecting about one in seven who cross it to access this other earth. Without possible return. Her fantastical claims, although lacking proof and out of character with the reputation of the journalist, went viral at surprising speed. The Fog scam, as some people already referred to, turned out more real than expected on the East coast of Africa, in Kenya. Indeed, a few Nairobi inhabitants claimed they had seen such a Fog some months ago around a property in the wealthy quarter. The villa was later boarded up and hidden from view. Galvanised by various reports supporting Thompson's strange theories - reports whose sources remain undetermined - and by the sheer magnitude of her claims online, those inhabitants went to that villa. To every sceptic's surprise, the house was indeed covered by a very thick fog. A few of those who crossed it were unable to come back into town. They were adamant they had emerged in the wild instead of Nairobi, the capital. It didn't take long before the house became flooded with people trying to access this Other World. Some who had been unwell failed to reach the wilderness, but they did not display any of their previous symptoms. The rumour that the fog had healed them spread like fire. The police were prompt to intervene at the first sign of riots, people demanding access to the Fog. The whole area is now blocked. If Thompson's sources are correct, there are more of these Fog-bridges in the world. It is unclear at present what causes it, if the Fog's healing powers are real or if this is all a grand hoax to shake the regime in power in Kenya. Without doubt, the local government will investigate. Will such a fog-hunt develop in other countries? As to the implausible theory of doors opening to another planet, it sounds more relevant in a movie studio than in a news channel studio. We live in strange times.'

Clare! Mary! Putu! Had anything happened to them?! Were they safe? Harry had attempted to call them but no one could get through. It was now 9.30am in London, so 11.30am in Kenya. How could so much unfold in such a short time?

In Morocco, Christophe and Isabelle were safe in their remote house in the mountain, but Louise was unreachable in Marrakech, where she had returned after the birth to give the new parents some privacy. As her Ftab was gone too, we hoped she would be in touch soon.

In Nevada, the Society had already contacted them and warned they should be moved to another location for their safety. They were packing a few essentials and would get back to us as soon as they were on secure ground. Leo and Dante were already on their way here.

We couldn't get through to Leila. It was so rare, we felt lost in the dark.

We couldn't stop browsing the web. The first articles were all based on Penny Thompson's 'theory', with similar information about the Fog. Soon, other articles and comments criticised and laughed at her claims. However, the more we read, the more articles appeared supporting the journalist's position, especially from Africa. Twitter crashed in Kenya. Instagram crashed in Nairobi. Soon witnesses began to come forth claiming the Fog had been seen in Marrakech months ago. A crowd was gathering around the house where it had once been. At home, we were glued to our devices' screens, helpless and with rising panic. Where was Louise? Why had she not contacted us yet? Where was Leila?

*

Our search was interrupted by Sam and McRae arriving about 30 minutes later. As we let them in, they headed directly towards the living room.

'It is clear from your faces that you know,' McRae commented, adding, 'we will all need a lot of coffee. Mind if I…?'

'You think I'll let you go to the kitchen alone and make bad coffee? I'll prepare coffee. You stay here.' Rico went next door, leaving the door open to listen in on the conversation.

'We would have come as soon as we were told, but we had to go for a briefing first,' Sam began, in an apologetic tone. 'So, what do you know about Penny Thompson and where did she get her information from?'

As usual, we had to practise the art of answering without divulging anything about the other Foggies and the Society.

'We have never met this Penny Thompson,' I replied. 'She is a journalist.

Evidently, she found a trail and linked the fog in Mexico and the ones in Jakarta.'

'Did you know about those two locations?' Sam asked.

'Of course we knew!' Rico shouted from the kitchen. 'It was in the news. Doh! We are not brainless, we made the connections!'

Sam did an eye-roll and McRae took over: 'Did you have any contact with those two locations?'

'No,' we replied in unison. It was the truth: we had had no contact with anyone in Mexico, and although we had connected with Helo, it was only later when he came from Indonesia.

'Are there any more locations we should know about?' McRae continued.

'Well, I think you might have read about Morocco?' Harry mentioned.

'OK. So anything you could tell us about Morocco and Kenya?' McRae asked, taking one of the biscuits Rico had brought over from the kitchen. He sniffed it and peered at Rico. The biscuits were safe so I grabbed one and took a bite. McRae copied me. Munching slowly to gain time before answering, the boys and I avoided looking at each other. We always attempted not to lie in case it would turn against us in the future.

'We can't tell you anything about Morocco,' Harry told the two secret agents. 'We have no idea what is happening there right now and we really wish we knew.'

'Do you know them? Were you in contact with them before?'

'Honestly man, what is it with all these questions? Don't you think we should talk about what is going to happen to us instead?' Rico arrived bringing a new pot of steaming coffee.

'Rico is right.' Harry leaned back in his chair. 'What happened in Kenya is terrible and it could happen here. Too many people observed the Fog when it first started, before we enclosed it, away from the prying eyes. Neighbours, firemen, postmen, policemen, friends... Same in Essex. I think by the end of today we...'

'The street is being blocked as we speak,' Sam jumped in. 'We have special services on standby to upgrade the security and install a barricade. Now we need to talk about you all.'

'I am not moving,' I declared, pre-empting his request. Maybe the others disagreed and wanted to go into hiding, but I couldn't. Here were Jazz and the other Relocated, and my sister and nephew knew only this place to go to. I felt it my duty to stay around this house. I was not good at being told what to do. Plus, my rebel streak had resurfaced.

'This is not a safe place. We will protect you better in a remote location with military structure. Somewhere where people would not know your Fog-linked abilities.'

'Somewhere with Jack, I presume?' Harry intervened.

It hit me. News of the Fog was spreading, but the Foggies were not mentioned anywhere. Switchers, Crossers and Facilitators did not exist for the public yet. If the Government took us now, we would be under their control. If we stood strong and faced the public, if our presence was known, then we couldn't just disappear anymore. Ingis Chen had a point.

I turned to McRae and Sam. 'You came to get us, didn't you? It is not a suggestion.'

'Indeed,' McRae answered. Sam was looking uncomfortable.

'Sooner or later, the roles of the Foggies will be known, and then, people will look for us. They will demand to know where we are, and the Government will have to answer to that,' I continued.

'We are only obeying orders. They are to take you in,' Sam retorted, shaking his head. 'It's not our call.'

'I must admit, I am not keen on having a crowd of journalists and people gawping at me when heading out to work at the university,' Harry announced. 'I think it would be wise to take refuge elsewhere for the time being.'

'It doesn't have to be under the British Government surveillance though!' Rico exclaimed. I was about to agree with Rico when McRae's mobile rang. He picked it up without looking at the caller's ID, answered 'yes', and spent the next minute listening. All the while, Sam looked apologetic and unhappy with his messenger role.

'A press van has been stopped at the top of the road by our people,' McRae told us, hanging up the phone, 'The London Fog is about to make the news.'

'We must go now.' Sam stood up and indicated for us to follow him.

'Fine. Can I gather a few clothes and personal items first?' I asked. After a brief hesitation, Sam gave in. The boys and I ran to our respective rooms. I threw together a few essentials in a large weekend bag, as well as some comfortable and practical outdoor clothes. Then I sent a message to the boys, letting them know my intention was to escape to WII, and asked Zeno if he wished to come with me. He was keen, too. Without Zeno and me, the British Government would have less control over the Fog. As we met downstairs ten minutes later, Rico was missing. Sam went to get him and came back down shaking his head, incredulous. Rico was in the bathroom, retouching his hair and refusing to go until it was perfect. He had been in there all that time.

*

Once outside, I checked the Secret Services' security. As usual, they were at the main entrance to the gated houses. No one was checking the inside of the ground. I held Simba close on her leash and announced: 'Simba needs a quick walk. Give me a minute.'

I leaned towards her to undo her lead and muttered in her ear 'Jazz. To Jazz.'

Slowly at first, then speeding up, she made her way towards the walled area behind which the Fog and Jazz's houses were hidden from view. Zeno was speaking quietly, though at high speed in Italian, to Rico next to him, who was nodding approvingly while glancing at me. I acted as if I wasn't paying attention and slowly peeled from the group. Simba was almost by the Fog's wooden wall. It was time for me to go and join her.

'Hey, Little One, you must be done by now.' I started walking towards her as nonchalantly as possible. When reaching the wall, I picked up Simba and made a show of struggling with carrying both bag and wolf cub. It was not difficult, as Simba was growing up fast and was almost too large and heavy for me to carry. Dropping his bag, Zeno started to walk towards me, saying: 'Hang on. I'll take your bag so you can carry Simba.'

I waited for him by the door of the wall leading to the Fog. From afar, I saw McRae frown and say something to Sam, but the latter was talking on his mobile.

'Hey! Stay where you are!' McRae shouted to Zeno, adding 'You too!' for my attention. He began walking towards us.

'Run, Zeno!' Harry shouted and Rico jumped on McRae's back to stop his advance. Zeno broke into a sprint. Harry blocked Sam, who had started to sprint towards Zeno. McRae had got rid of Rico and was catching up with Zeno surprisingly fast. I opened the door to the Fog and got in. I waited for Zeno mid-way in the Fog, putting Simba down. When Zeno rushed in, I caught him and we quickly moved to the gate again. We exited the Fog into the forest clearing, thanks to his Crosser's abilities.

'Wow! That was close. The Scot is a runner! He grabbed me by the jacket just as I was coming in. I left my bag behind, though. You have yours?'

'Yes. With Ftab inside. We'll need it! We must contact Leila now and let her know what's up.'

'Poor Rico and Harry, we abandoned them...' Zeno looked genuinely concerned.

'Zeno, they backed us up: they approved our move, no? In any case, we are going back.'

'What!' Zeno blurted.

'What was important here was to prove a point, which was that aside from locking us in the fogged portal, we always have an alternate world to escape to. They have no control in WII. And really, what is the point of locking us in if they want to interact with that other world.'

'They could just invade it with the relocated soldiers. They will make the whole army go through the portals if necessary, but their intent is to get a position of power in the Other World. We are not going back. Especially not you: You are the one creating the portals. I am actually less important here.'

'The Society gave me a special pair of earrings with a tracking device a few months back, and I constantly wear them. It could be a way to find Jack.'

'The Secret Services didn't spot them?'

'No, they look like old family jewellery. I only took them off when they were dangerous for medical tests, like scans or MRI, and even then they're on the nearest chair.'

'They spotted my watch. The Society was looking for an alternative.'

'And Jack's stayed with his clothes at the hospital.'

'Damn!'

'So we have to go back. It might be the only way to find him.'

My Ftab rung. I checked the caller ID with thumb authentication. It was Sam.

'Hello Sam,' I replied.

'Yoko. What do you think you are doing?' He sounded weary.

'Reminding you all that there is and always will be another world where you have no power over us.'

'We know that! For God's sake, why do you always act as if we are your enemy?'

'Because you are not acting as true friends?'

'The world is not black or white, don't you get it yet?'

'Listen, we will come back and go into hiding with you, but only if we are going somewhere neutral and if Jack joins us. No military camp, no demonstration of power, no attempt to take this as an opportunity to use us.'

'This. Is. Not. In. Our. Power.'

'Then make it! Call me back when the deal is confirmed, and when you have Jack with you. Throw in Leo and Dante as well while you're at it.'

I hung up. Zeno was looking at me, shaking his head.

'So we're not going back yet, I presume?' he said.

'Well… What do you think? Do you agree?'

'You know what will happen next, Nutella? They will bring Jack just for the show. We have no guarantee, once we get in any of their vehicles, that they will keep their word.'

That thought had crossed my mind. So I had a solution. I really needed to speak to Leila urgently.

*

Nick joined us within seconds. With all the security system he had set up around the house, he could not have missed our presence. He and Zeno listened to the call with Leila and nodded their approval. Jazz arrived before we got a chance to fill Nick in on all the details of the situation.

'Yoko! Zeno! I didn't see you come through the house? Why didn't you stop to say hello?'

'Because we didn't come through the house,' Zeno replied. He explained that if we had done so, Sam would have just come in to take us.

'But why do they want to take you?' Jazz's voice was full of sudden anxiety. Zeno and I turned to look at Nick, who evidently had been kept up-to-date by the Society about Ingis Chen's leak. I took a deep breath and answered her.

'News of the Fog has spread around the world.'

'WHAT!' She shouted and put her hands on her mouth. 'But how? What does that mean for us? Are you safe? Are you - will you leave London?'

Jazz was panicking. She stretched out an arm and leaned on Nick's chest for support. She looked as if she was struggling to breathe. I quickly went and grabbed her in my arms.

'We are not leaving Jazz. We will not abandon any of you! Never!' As I was hugging her, Nick's eyes met mine and he mouthed 'thank you'. He was another one of the people we would not abandon.

*

Twenty minutes later, Jazz, Zeno, Nick and I were still talking on the grass by the edge of the forest. We had borrowed some chairs from the Relocated cabins – an upgrade from their first mobile homes. Jazz was reluctant to go back into the house in case they kept her captive inside as a way to get back at me. My Ftab rang. Sam.

'Sam. So how's it going?'

'Bad.'

'Do you have Jack?'

'No.'

'Leo and Dante?'

'We told them to hide in the Fog.'

'Excuse me?' The call was on speakers and we all looked at each other in surprise. What he had said did not make sense. Why would he tell them to hide?

'Yoko, my side of the department does not approve of the military side. I got to know you all in the past three months. You are stubborn pains in the ass sometimes, but you are all decent people. They don't handle you the right way.'

'Wait!' Nick broke in. 'You decided to tell the Essex-based Italian Foggies to hide so that you wouldn't have to give them up to the people you disagree with?'

'Well… Let's just say we don't deal with pressure very well,' Sam replied.

'Are you acting on your own here?' Nick persisted.

'… Let's just say that it is not our official assignment. That none of you can quote me on my recommendations,' Sam answered.

'What does it imply for us?' Zeno asked.

'It implies we - my department - wants to work with you. We want to negotiate.'

'Negotiate what?! All we want is the respect of the original agreement with Gatekeepers Associates. And Jack. Until Jack is free, there is nothing to negotiate.'

'Yoko, if you stay there, they will try to send people through the Fog for relocation, and those people's mission will be to get you out. If you totally refuse to cooperate, we will not be able to help.'

'How do you propose to help?' Nick asked in a steely voice.

I was biting the inside of my cheeks, a clear sign of stress. I was unsure what to do next. We had agreed with Leila on a plan of action, and this would work even better with Sam's help. After a quick exchange with Zeno and Nick, we decided to take the risk and tell him.

'Sam, this is where we stand,' I began. 'We need to find a way to cope with the press and public knowing about us. It will be overwhelming. So we are willing to negotiate new ways to work with the British Government.' As I spoke, images of the crowd forcing their way into the fogged house in Kenya filled my head. There was no way round it: we needed the government's support.

'Glad to hear it, Yoko,' Sam said.

'Waiting for the 'but',' McRae commented.

'We will not come with you to negotiate. You are coming with us,' I continued.

My last sentence was followed by a silence until Sam replied: 'The Other World is not accessible to me, Yoko.'

'I don't know if it is to me and I am disinclined to check,' McRae added.

'In ten minutes, be by the wooden wall of the Fog.'

'Wait!' Nick intervened. 'One of you needs to get to the Essex house and check on Leo and Dante, making sure things are fine there. It will have to be you, Sam, as you can cross the Fog unaffected.'

'No way! I want to participate in the negotiations!'

'The fellows of the military department are not stupid. They know that if they try to relocate some of their military staff in the London fogged house, they'd have to deal with many more people than in Essex. Me, Relocated people and all the inhabitants of Lil'London, Newtonsee and Yerushaleim. That is why they haven't done it so far. In Essex, no one would stop them trying to go through to retrieve Leo and Dante. They even have some people there in WII already.'

'Let me remind you: we do not like their methods or their way of imposing a pro-military and defence approach, but they are not the enemies here,' Sam retorted.

'So what are they?' Zeno asked.

'Bullies,' Nick replied. 'In any case, you have to go there and prevent them taking over that house. McRae, be by the Fog with Harry and Rico in 5 minutes. Tell them to take their bags and Ftabs with them. And Sam, don't worry. You will be able to join the negotiation table. Leo and Dante have their tablets, too.'

Nick hung up the call and returned the Ftab to me.

'Sorry I took over, Nutty,' he told me.

'No problem. You knew what you were doing. Sam was less keen.'

'I know. I am right though and he knows it.'

*

Zeno and I were waiting in the Fog, ready to exit via the front gate when Harry or Rico stepped in to get us. We heard the helicopter above our head and Simba howled.

'I guess the plan is for us all to escape by helicopter. The Society?' Harry said, when he appeared with Rico.

'Yes.'

'Well, I want to make a slight amendment.'

'Harry, we need to be quick here. We need to go!' Harry did not let me continue.

'Zeno and you are staying here in WII. It is safer. Like Leo and Dante, you'll negotiate via Ftab.' He shoved Zeno's bag in its owner's arms and ran back out, leaving us behind in the Fog. Seconds later, we heard the helicopter leave. The noise was loud and Simba resumed her howling. Zeno and I quickly returned to the clearing and explained to Nick and Jazz what had just happened. Harry called us soon after.

'Sorry, guys. We couldn't let you take the risk. The helicopter might get intercepted or something like that. For your peace of mind, McRae has confirmed Sam is on his way to the Essex house.'

'Where are we going?' McRae asked, in the background.

'Tell him. He'll like the destination,' I told Harry.

They had a long trip ahead of them. First the helicopter ride, then travel by car with regular change of vehicles and to finish, an air trip to reach their destination: a remote corner of the Scottish Highlands .

*

We stayed in touch the whole afternoon with the Essex house and travelling Foggies, via our tablets. Our tension was palpable. We all worried about Jack, the involvement of the authorities, and of course about the consequences of the Fog leaks.

The reactions in the British Isles were mixed. The press was sceptical about the allegations that the Fog was a gate to another world, especially as so many people in Kenya came back disappointed after having crossed it. However, the claims of miracle healing and the few disappearances of Relocated were puzzling. Most presented the whole thing as a large-scale sham and wondered about its purpose. A few commentators expected that someone would soon come out, claiming to be the new Messiah. Others speculated that this was the prelude of a political coup in Africa, or a new cult in the making. Regarding the London Fog, journalists interviewed several of our former and current neighbours. The Society was efficient: the lack of available information was a big impediment for the press. The neighbours knew only our first name, too. Still, there was little hope of remaining anonymous for long.

Because the Fog had gone from the Marrakech house, there had not been any riots there, unlike in Kenya. Many, who were curious, had tried to break in and the press was camping in front of it. Images showed policemen in heated discussion with the Society security guards. It was clear that such security, in addition to the claims of the previous cleaner and workers, was raising suspicions. It was not good; not good at all. The Society also had search teams around the Moroccan town in the hope of finding Louise, with no luck so far.

With the status of the Foggies abroad, the situation in Kenya and Marrakech was alarming. The Koplats in Nevada had not been in touch either but we knew they were on their way to Alaska, a safe place to stay at present. The Alaskan Foggies were stunned by the images from Kenya and Morocco. News that the Fog might have reached central London also concerned them.

*

Leila wrote, late afternoon, with a proper update…

'*Dear Yoko,*
Sorry it took me so long to contact you again. We are juggling with quite a lot here! We had planned ahead for when this day would come, yet this is a mess. There is only so much one can predict about people's reactions: Kenya took us by surprise! If only Ingis Chen had consulted with you first, even if only to give us a mere couple of days warning.

Kenya is bad news. Putu, whose friendship and visits to Clare and Mary were known, is hiding with us. She is considering whether or not to turn to the Australian Embassy for protection. Mary and Clare have gone into the bushes of WII, hopefully hiding with the tribe of Mary's beloved. So far we haven't heard anything from them. Mary should still have her Ftab but Clare hasn't. One of the rioters took it, in the house. We tracked its movement across Nairobi and blocked it from use. We finally retrieved it in a slum, buying it for a pittance.

Morocco is also a big worry. We are in constant contact with Christophe, Isabelle and Helo. Mother and baby are doing fine. Obviously, the major problem is Louise's silence. Christophe is preparing to camp in the WII Atlas Mountains if necessary. We are providing them with food and everything to survive several weeks. They will be also given the materials to try and head west towards the coast, should they be stuck longer than we hope and need to move to survive.

In Nevada, the Koplats departed just in time. The US Government reacted fast in tracking down any sign of Fog. We could not stop their satellite search: we can mask and tamper when they are not looking for something specific; we cannot when their focus is on it. They are currently at the property doing all sorts of analysis. They also contacted the British Government about the London Fog. We are not privy to the information they are exchanging, or not, but there is a lot of activity going on there. Please watch out!

So far, the Alaskans are safe. There is no local abnormality around them. The Fog around their house is held within the forest and not visible from the ground or the sky. They should be fine, but we are keeping a good watch. The Koplats should reach their destination in the early hours of tomorrow, at best. We are not taking any risks: they are taking the long journey to get there.

Last but not least, the situation in the United Kingdom. We monitor you all with hawk eyes. Harry and Rico are off radar. They should reach their destination within the next 45 minutes. As for Leo and Dante, whatever Sam Riverson told his superior - it worked. There were military vehicles heading for the house, but within twenty minutes of Agent Riverson's arrival, the vehicles turned round. Security was reinforced on your street and the whole area around, but there was no attempt to break into the Essex Fog complex. We were not expecting them to be so reasonable…

To finish, I wanted to inform you that we did as thorough a check as possible on Agent McRae. The available data is limited of course, his belonging to the British Secret Service. So far, he came out as a good agent, though, with the reputation of a loose cannon, not afraid to speak his mind to his superior. He has had quite a few warnings on record! In turn, McRae has been digging on Nick Baker, your known bodyguard in WII. He even went to the trouble of visiting, in person, some of Nick's friends from the army and his old boxing club, as well as a few family members. We are not sure why he has such a high level of interest in Nick, but this cannot be good. McRae is smart.

Please let me know if you need anything, and we will try to provide it despite the blockade. I have never been so stressed in my whole life!

X Leila '

Zeno and I were bound to the Other World for an indefinite time. I had never spent a night in this world, nor had I felt blocked in it, except that one night, months ago, when kidnapped by Ushi Tsou. Now, even *The Jazzin* was out of bounds as the British authorities could be waiting for us there. Frustration and homesickness kicked in within a few hours. I empathised with the Relocated even more now.

*

Rico and Harry called at dinnertime to let us know they had arrived in the North of Scotland. They were staying in one of the Western Islands to McRae's joy: he kept muttering 'Home Sweet Home'. The Scotsman came on the phone.

'Yoko, when should we start?'

'Everyone is exhausted tonight. Shall we say 8.00, tomorrow morning?'

'Fine by me.'

'Have you been in touch with Sam and your boss?'

'Yes.'

'Anything we should know?'

'No.'

It had been a pathetic and tired attempt on my part to pry for information on the US-UK communication regarding the Fog.

'Sam and I have convinced our boss to deploy more of our men around your Fog complex,' MacRae continued. 'We have also posted two agents inside. I know you want it to remain private. We believe the additional security might be necessary, but if you want them out, we will have them removed.'

Zeno and I hesitated. Nick mouthed 'stay' to us.

'They can stay for the night. We will review tomorrow,' I replied to McRae.

'I noticed something,' McRae said, changing subject. 'You left with your young Malamute dog in your arms. As you and the Relocated are in WII, shall we ask one of the guys to walk and look after her in London for you?'

'Argh!' I thought. He had it all wrong. First, Simba was a wolf. Second, she was not from 'our world': she was from the Other World. Last, and certainly not least, she could go in any world she wanted if she put her mind to it. Literally. We assumed her ability was linked to her birth on the first night of the Fog. Over the past 5 months, her training to lead me to 'London', 'Forest', or 'Fog' had produced excellent results. This was one of the reasons we didn't want any British services representatives on the ground of our complex. It was sometimes complicated to do her training without attracting attention. But now, what was I to tell McRae?! As I looked around, trying to think of a reply, the Relocated cabins gave me an idea.

'Actually, this reminds me of a point we need to sort out. The Relocated have two regular visitors, Big Tom's mother and Maisie and Owen's mother – Ann Fisher. We must ensure they can still come through to visit their families. When they do, they will look after Simba. She is a puppy so she can be a bit scared by strangers. She knows them.'

'Simba is quite an impressive dog.'

'She is, isn't she?'

'Where did you find her? She is still young: did you get her before or after the Fog first occurred?'

'You sound like Sam! Aside from the Fog, his first questions were about my little Simba. What is it with you spies? You all have an obsession with dogs?'

'Sam is right: you are not answering the questions. He mentioned you do that when you are uncomfortable with them or wish to hide something. I am now even more curious about Simba.'

'I think you are reading too much into it. I am protecting my private life, that's all!' As the most convincing tone in my repertoire did not sound convincing enough to me, I feared the professional on the other end of the line would hear right through it.

'There is another subject I would love to explore. Nick Baker, your protector in WII. His role in all of this and how he came to be a Relocated is shady. His link to Ingis Chen is too unlikely. I would like to have a little chat with him.' McRae continued.

I winced. Nick frowned. Zeno almost spilled his drinks. McRae had a knack for asking the questions we wanted to avoid.

'McRae, why don't you make a list of all those random points? They are not the current priority. Or were you taking the opportunity of Sam not being with you to ask them?' I counter-asked.

'I will prepare a list,' McRae retorted. 'Sam's presence is no bother. We think alike. Why do you think he asked me into the team? Those are queries he wanted to look into but his increased duties with the Fog and Foggies took too much of his time. He was overwhelmed and needed someone he trusted 100%. We go way back: he knew I would pick up just where he left things and would be as intrigued as he was. Aye, let's speak tomorrow then. Good bye.' He hung up. He was strange, that one. I kind of liked him. Sam choosing him was to his credit. Mysterious Sam was not always fun but he was a decent and a reliable person. It was also true that Sam was inquisitive. The Society often told us that he was doing checks behind our back when our answers were unsatisfactory. Now McRae was taking over. These enquiries were dangerous. As happened so often when the Fog was involved, we were walking on eggs.

McRae's reference to Ingis Chen made me think of the man. I was still angry. His keeping his cool at all times, even when he was pushing the limits, was so irritating it made me lose my cool and risk losing the argument, like that morning. In a battle of words, self-control is everything, whatever the strength of your point. We would have to deal with him in the morning too, once all the Foggies had agreed on our position towards him.

*

'So. How are we going to handle the mess this time?' Harry asked on the video-conference between Foggies. It was the evening. He was seated next to Rico in what looked an old-fashioned and rather run-down cottage room.

'Why Scotland?' Rico asked, surly, looking out at the window. 'It's cold and raining. Could you not pick somewhere warmer? Gibraltar is British, that would do!'

'Because you think that Gibraltar is big enough to hide you?' Harry replied.

'Have you been?' Rico asked.

'No,' Harry responded.

'So how do you know?' Rico persisted.

'I know my geography,' Harry said, in a cynical tone.

'You two, drop it. This really is not the time,' Zeno interrupted.

'You are right, Zeno,' Harry said after a pause. 'How will we regain control of the situation here?'

'Which situation? The public discovery of the Fog, Ingis Chen back-

46

stabbing, the missing Foggies? Maybe the struggle of power with the British Secret Service? Or just how to get Jack back to us?' I snapped. That day had been a long one. I was not in the best mood.

'Yoko, eat a cookie...' Zeno handed me a pack of biscuits, as well as a cup of tea, all brought over by Nick, the latter then retreating back into the motorhome parked by his cabin. It was still the main security control centre around the forest clearing where the Fog and Woodfellas were located.

'Everything is linked,' Leo jumped into the conversation. 'It all started with Jack and the Government seeing an opportunity to have their own Switcher. Then Ingis Chen – this bastard - disclosed and promoted the information about the Fog to the public, his reasoning being that if the public knows, the government can't act in total impunity with us. Everything else is just consequences.'

'Fine. So how are we to handle these consequences?' Rico asked.

'Yes, we have to get some kind of control,' I intervened. 'Annoyingly, I think Ingis Chen may have had a point.'

'Yoko, you cannot be serious. This...' Leo began. I didn't let him finish.

'Ingis Chen will always act in his best interest, long or short term. I am furious with his unilateral decision, and he will pay for this. His decision to inform the rest of the world of our existence, behind our back, is outrageous, but we could benefit from it. If handled right, that is.'

'And how would you suggest we proceed, Yoko?' Harry asked, before Leo or any of the others had a chance.

'I think we should come clean,' I replied.

Zeno broke the silence.

'What do you mean, exactly?' he asked, with a suspicious look.

'I think that we should let the public know of our existence and roles, working as a team. We ought to confirm that the Fog is real and explain its abilities, as well as its limits. We should warn about the possible Relocation. This might prevent misinformation or exaggeration being spread. It might also help Clare and Mary in Kenya. Maybe Louise, too.'

'Do you realise what you are saying?!' Rico exclaimed.

'I agree with Rico,' Harry said. 'So far, the Fog is not being taken seriously by the western media and in most parts of the planet. At best, it's a curiosity or bafflement. In Kenya, the riots are mainly due to a culture being open to the paranormal and surreal, combined with a rather precarious life for most. No wonder they want to believe in the Fog: it gives them hope for another chance, for an alternative to their tough life, or for better health. Once the local government gets involved and stops the access to the Fog, the buzz will die out.'

'If it does, then the Kenyan Government will also control the Fog. The local authorities are bound to discover the local Foggies. Who will protect them?' I replied.

'Us! We know about them. The Society knows about them. Ingis Chen knows about them,' Dante and Leo replied.

'But what can we do to protect them? I mean, what weight do we have? With global information, mass media and public pressure behind us, we would have more strength and power. We would have a voice. We could not just disappear or be taken for granted. Besides, it would also be good to defend the neutrality of the Fog.'

'Wow! Yoko!' Rico exclaimed.

'How long have you been harbouring these radical thoughts?' Harry asked.

'I don't know. I'm not sure.' I pondered the question for a couple of seconds and continued, 'I think when Ingis Chen mentioned it this morning; it kind of hit a nerve. The Foggies are a team and we are doing, overall, relatively well. We are working beyond nationalities and countries. The Society was right; there is an idealistic side of us that makes the whole thing possible. Which leads to another one of my arguments: the Society could continue to support us behind the scenes, like a private Secret Services.'

'What about Ingis Chen? Do you see him as our public relation? Because I...' Leo stopped himself talking any further, not trusting his words when it came to Ingis Chen. He always had a strong antipathy for the man; an almost irrational one.

'No, I am not inclined to,' I told him. 'I might credit him with having made a clever move: I do not trust him.'

'I say we ditch him!' Rico exclaimed.

'He is already tricky as an ally. I am not sure I want him as an enemy,' Zeno pondered. He would know: he was the one dealing with him on Inter-Worlds trading.

'Then how about a middle ground?' I suggested. 'We deny him representing us on the political and public scene, as he has always wished. However, we let him continue to be our business representative because of his undisputed skills in the domain.'

'Still too close,' Leo grunted.

There was another heavy silence. I was about to suggest we all sleep on it when Harry spoke.

'Yoko might have a point,' he commented. 'We need to have a proper public status. When I said earlier we needed to gain control of the situation, I wasn't sure how. The whole leak this morning took us by surprise. I don't want this to happen again. So let us be in charge of announcing our presence to the world. It will happen eventually.'

'What about the other Foggies? Shouldn't they have a say?' Dante asked.

'Of course they should! We are a democratic group!' I exclaimed. 'We should have a unanimous vote on this. What? Did you think I was going to act like Ingis Chen and just put them in front of the fait accompli? Come on!'

'Good. Because I see your point but I am not convinced yet,' Leo said.

'Neither am I,' Rico added. 'Everyone knowing about the Foggies... Cazzo, I hate the name...'

'It's just the rough outline of an idea for the moment,' I protested. 'Let's call Leila and ask her opinion if breaking the news ourselves would be manageable. By the way, Rico, I am surprised you're not a determined advocate for being one of the rare Foggies around. Imagine how attractive you'll be to girls.'

Rico's head perked up and sparkles lit up his eyes. It was a cheap win; almost too easy.

'I'm in, as well. Not because I like the idea of being exposed to the general public, but because I don't see what else to do,' Dante pointed out.

Everyone nodded at that.

'What about the Secret Services? What are we to tell them tomorrow?'

'Nothing,' Harry said. 'We need to contact as many Foggies as possible in the meantime, prepare an action plan with Leila, discuss if there are alternatives. Then vote. So we say nothing and gain time if they ask about our strategy.'

'Let's ask THEM a few questions,' I added. 'Like how they intend to proceed with their internal divisions.'

'Now that, I totally approve!' Leo exclaimed. 'Although let's not forget: we need it all sorted by Saturday and to get Jack back before Switch night. We also need to make sure they don't suspect what we are up to behind the scenes.'

'It won't be easy. If we don't make any demands, they'll be suspicious. I would be!' Rico pointed out. I rolled my eyes; he was always suspicious, anyway.

'We could tell them we are working on some kind of deal to get Jack back, and it would help if we knew where they stood,' I suggested.

'It's worth a try,' Harry said.

'Right. Shall we call Leila?' I proposed.

'One more thing,' Leo interrupted. 'Are you going to tell Ingis Chen afterwards about your idea to limit him to business partner only?'

'This affects all the Foggies, so we must first all agree on this.'

'Fine by me. Thank you, Nutty,' Leo leaned back in his chair and added, 'I like the way you think, even if I don't always agree with you, either on Foggy or personal matters.'

I ignored the reference to the 'personal matters' and we contacted Leila, for her to join the video conference call.

*

Our first concern was about the other Foggies. Sadly, there was no news on Jack, from Clare and Mary. Putu was still hiding with the Society. The Koplats had reached Alaska safely. In Morocco, the Society was monitoring all the official lines to discover if the local authorities had taken her, yet so far they had come up with nothing. The police were not even aware that Louise lived in that house as it was under the name of Christophe de Rocque. Leila now focused on the unofficial channels.

The conversation with Leila was brief. She had a lot on her hands with the turmoil created by the Fog on the African continent. When we explained we wanted her opinion and suggestion on the Foggies coming into the open, she listened without comment, taking notes with an exhausted look. Then she confirmed she would get back to us in the morning.

Afterwards we dropped a note to all the other Foggies, hoping that those we had no news from would soon reconnect. Our message summarised our discussion about taking control of the information released to the public from now, before leaks or misinformation occurred. We included our split opinion and doubts on this. We also explained that Leila would get back to us on what was feasible. To finish, we proposed to vote on the matter the next morning - Wednesday. The matter was too urgent to wait for the evening.

Despite my original plans, I was too tired afterwards to contact Ingis Chen. Instead, I dropped him a note mentioning my feelings about his actions, that though I understand his reasons, his methods were unacceptable.

One thing was certain: should the Foggies vote for full disclosure, we were not going to warn him.

Day 4 (Wednesday)

The day had started fast and well. As agreed between us the previous evening, we only asked Sam and McRae to state their department position and what they wanted. It was apparent they were surprised by our proposition. They were expecting a more determined approach from us and to react to it, not the reverse. They were on the defensive, rather than the offensive. They had no clear position to share with us on behalf of the British authorities. Their pronounced goal was a peaceful partnership with us. Contrary to their military division's strategy, theirs was not to antagonise us. This aside, McRae requested a private conversation with Nick later that day. Nick agreed to it. To my relief, he didn't enquire again about Simba.

All the available Foggies voted pro disclosure of the Foggies' existence and roles to the public, providing we agreed on the information to reveal. Fear was omnipresent in the communication between us. None of us really loved the idea of disclosure and the exposure to unknown dangers and threats that came with it. However, the fear of how things could evolve if we did not regain control was greater. We even felt lucky that, right now, one side of the

United Kingdom officials wanted to play nice with us.

As promised, Leila sent a breakdown of the Society's suggestions on how to go viral with the information. It was very simple yet it required a good control of social media, blogs and all online news broadcasts. Her suggestions included the need, in the long term, to introduce at least one Switcher, one Crosser and one Facilitator to the world. I felt my heart stop. The logical choice, and one all the Foggies agreed on, was for Harry, Zeno and me to represent the 'Gatekeepers'. We already had links with our Government and we were the ones who needed protection from that Government, too. Leo had given in on releasing information, but protested vehemently at my being put in the spotlight.

'You already have enough on your plate as Foggies' ambassador to Lil'London and Newtonsee!'

'We all have plenty on our plates,' I countered.

'I could take your place.'

'You are not a Switcher.'

'Being in the open puts you in too much danger! I can't abide that.'

'Leo, if not me, someone else would be in that dangerous situation. It is logical that it is me as I'm already known as a Switcher outside our group! Then I can't just be made to disappear without the public asking questions. That is the whole idea!'

'Why not lie and say I am a Switcher?'

I let out a sigh. He was very sweet; his worry and care were real. My heart felt a twinge. I still cared for him, too. Moreover, I still found him so attractive. We faced each other, via our tablets, in a silence betraying what we meant to each other. Silently, too, I scolded myself for the hundredth time for being so protective about my feelings. One day, would I let my heart rule, instead of my head?

Immediately after the vote and review of Leila's information, Harry, Zeno and I messaged her to say she could proceed with the global disclosure scheme. Then I headed to the kitchen and took out some dough from the freezer. Time for a special batch of chocolate cookies. Large size.

*

Mid-morning, I was sitting on a chair in the clearing with a cup of tea, lost in those gloomy thoughts, when Nick came, bringing his own chair to join me.

'Things will be shaken soon, won't they?'

'Yes. They will.'

'How are you doing?'

'I'm not sure. I will cope. I don't have any other choice.'

'You are allowed to let your hair down from time to time, you know. You are human. Why aren't you kinder to yourself?'

'I will keep this luxury for when I have the time.'

'Are you scared?'

'Terrified.'

'Can I indulge you? Take your mind and body to another place for a while?'

I looked at him suspiciously and he laughed.

'Not like that Yoko! I would have said 'blow your mind and body away!' No, come with me: we are going to practice self-defence.'

'The Secret Services already gave me some training for that.'

'Trust me: it's not the same when you do it with someone who cares for your safety as much as I do.'

*

As I lay on the grass, Nick blocking me underneath him and totally in his power, I could only agree: his self-defence practice was very different to those Sam had organised for me. For one thing, the teachers from the Secret Services did not linger on top of me, arranging my hair and whispering in my ear that we ought to practice more positions like this one. Nick had certainly succeeded in taking my mind off any worry about any looming dangers except the present one. His desire was obvious and very much felt, and my libido had hit the roof. When his lips brushed mine, my body responded in a millisecond. His kiss was soft for the first second and passionate the following three. My mind went numb while my body took over, giving him its assent.

The beep of my 2-way radio stopped him in the heat of the moment, just when he was about to pull my top off. I was mentally grateful to the caller, though my body was not. A relation with Leo was not a good idea in my opinion and neither was one with Nick. 'Yoko! Get a grip!' I told myself, as I nervously brushed a leaf and gave a slightly awkward look at Nick. I picked up my radio.

'Yoko speaking.'

'Yoko, this is Maud. Please forgive my unscheduled call. I hope I am not interrupting you during an important task?'

'Well…' I thought. 'Not at all,' I replied.

'I am with Clémence Hoare. We are quite upset about a position taken by the Council of Lil'London. Would it be possible to see you today?'

'Certainly.' I was immediately alert. Clémence? The Council?

'Would you be free in an hour for lunch? We would love to have your advice. Your help even.'

'Lunch? Yes, that would work. Would you like me to come to yours? I could be there in no time with my vehicle.'

'No, no, no,' Maud protested. 'We would rather come to yours and find a place where we could talk undisturbed.'

I frowned. Maud had never felt it necessary to hide her visits or mention a need for privacy from Woodfellas's inhabitants. I glanced at Nick and all his cheekiness had gone. He had his professional poker face on. Clémence Hoare's surprisingly strong and revolutionary voice on his recordings resonated in my mind. Had she enrolled Maud into it as well? What was she up to?

'Mine it is. I'm sure we will be able to find a place to talk. I will see you both in an hour.'

'Thank you, Yoko. We shall bring a picnic with us, so as not to inconvenience you in any way.'

'Really you shouldn't! I…'

'I must insist. We would not want to put you to any trouble.'

The call finished, Nick didn't say a word but put one hand on my back, indicating the way to the clearing with the other. His hand lingered a little before he let go.

'You taste sweet…' he said, a little later.

'It was a thing of a moment.'

'I will just have to recreate a moment then.'

I smiled. I was still turned on, but my mind was back in control. Officially, I had other priorities than any kind of relationship in a time of crisis. Unofficially, I just had relationship issues. To add to them, I had felt I was betraying Leo when Nick kissed me. I sighed, inwardly.

*

Maud Poff and Clémence Hoare arrived exactly an hour later in a small coach pulled by a single horse. Instead of both stepping down, only Maud came towards me to ask if I would care to join them. They had spotted a perfect plot of grass for a picnic on the way. Nick stepped in.

'I am afraid I will have to join in, as well. Due to recent threats against Yoko, I am not to leave her side.' He came right by my shoulder as he said this and looked determined to be like glue on me.

'Maybe you could make a concession to not leave her out of your sight instead of your side?' Clémence intervened, having heard Nick from the coach. 'The matter we wish to discuss is quite a delicate subject, relative to women.'

'I do not make any concession when it comes to Yoko's protection,' Nick said in a firm tone.

Maud and Clémence looked at me. Nick would stick by me whatever I said so there was no point arguing. It was not my intention, anyway. In reply to my silence, Maud just nodded and Clémence became stern. I wondered if the mask was falling off her face. I had never seen her show any sign of determination before. Now, even in her sentence to Nick, she had betrayed a new confidence.

Maud got back on the coach with Clémence. Nick and I followed them on the quad for 15 minutes. We couldn't hear them, but Clémence was talking vehemently to Maud who kept shaking her head. From time to time, Clémence glanced at us and it was not full of love. I still couldn't believe she had organised the attack against me: however, Nick had planted a seed of doubt.

*

The tension was palpable as Maud and Clémence laid out the food on a large blanket. Maud set aside a small basket and gave it to me, saying it was a little gift with a few treats her twin children had prepared for me. So we left it on the quad.

'Now that we are here and you can see there are no threats, maybe you could give us a bit of privacy?' Maud tried again with Nick.

'Sorry. You never know where the danger could come from,' Nick replied.

'Very well, then. In any case, you know quite a lot already, don't you?!' Clémence exclaimed. This surprised both Maud and me but Nick just stared at her, deadpan.

'You really think you, a Relocated and Yoko's bodyguard, could walk around unnoticed in Newtonsee?' she asked, rhetorically. 'I know you are aware of the little gatherings I organise there. Obviously you know I am not the poor frightened little lamb I have let people think, in my hometown. Yoko, I take it he informed you?'

'Yes, he did,' I replied.

The one who didn't seem to understand was Maud. She kept looking at the three of us with incomprehension all over her face.

'Please! Someone explain what is going on,' she finally pleaded. 'Clémence, what is happening?'

'Maud, my dear Maud: you are so sweet,' Clémence began. 'I used to admire you so much for your independence and your equal relationship with Edmund. Then I came to realise you were just lucky to have met the right man. Otherwise, you would have ended up either tamed or alone. You have your heart and mind in the right place, but you are too soft to change how things work in this world.'

'What?!' Maud was shocked by what she was hearing. She had always been the advocate of women's rights, and always been frowned upon for her bold ideas.

'Why are you surprised?' Clémence continued. 'What have you achieved so far? Nothing. You have changed nothing. Your ideas are right and I embrace them, but I go further. You have too slow and soft an approach, just loudly speaking your beliefs that the roles of women in our Society are unacceptable. Words are not sufficient, we need action!' As she spoke, Clémence took an apple and crunched into it. She was calm and self-possessed. Strong, confident and sure of her power. She had an aura about her that inspired respect; it was not difficult to imagine her gathering a crowd of women followers around her.

'Clémence,' Maud was breathing slowly, working at regaining her composure, 'I don't recognise you. Where does this come from? How long have you… What are those 'gatherings'?'

'It is about a Revolution! You see, I followed your example long ago: I taught myself to read and write. And I read a lot. I have gone through all that I could find on the French Revolution and any other people uprisings. It is time for a role reversal here, too. We women are the most important humans in this world, and we should be treated as such!'

'A Revolution? Women in power? What are you on about? Have you lost your mind?!' Maud was beginning to get heated. Instinctively, Nick and I leaned backwards away from the two women, to put some distance between us and danger.

'I have always told you,' Maud continued, 'that men and women should be equal. We should have the right to read and learn as thoroughly as men. We should be able to have our own shops like they do. We should be able to choose our husbands like they choose their wives. We should have representation at the Council. But I am talking of equality! Not taking over!'

'You live in a dream. There is never equality! The balance of power is never perfect. Never! You are in a privileged situation with Edmund. It's all talk: you do nothing. The only woman you are really convincing of your equality dream is your daughter, but all she will face is a rough world when she grows up, because unles she meets a man as understanding as Edmund, she will fall hard. Your words would never make a difference. Me, I will change things. Wait and see!'

'May I ask,' Maud's voice was full of anger, 'what you intend to do to the men of Lil'London and Newtonsee when they disagree to your intended changes?'

'They won't have a choice.'

'Really. They will just sit there and accept you kicking them out of their seats, will they?'

'What can they do when the women suddenly refuse to bend to their will? When we refuse them the bed. When we refuse to look after the house. When we educate the children against them. We will break into the Council, the prison, and more. So what can they do? They cannot kill us: they need us! They need us to breed!'

'So do we! We cannot breed alone?!'

'They need many of us to have many children. We need just one of them.'

Maud looked at Clémence, bewildered.

'You are mad,' she said, slowly.

Clémence burst out laughing: 'No, dear Maud. I am the realist. You are the idealist.'

I decided to intervene: 'Clémence, why now? Why have you suddenly...?'

'Golly! Surely you don't think I have started this just now? I started years ago. Little by little, I began to target the wronged women, the unhappy, used and abused ones. And the ones who saw clearly the unbalanced system we were in and fumed about it. I told you, Maud: you inspired me at first, and I wanted to gather a group of followers around your idea. Then slowly I saw your flaws. I saw the limits of your ideas. I saw the lack of actions. I came to understand I was stronger and more determined than you. I was the one who was to lead the Revolution towards a new order, the order of the Women!'

'Clémence Stalin Hoare,' Nick whispered to himself.

'I knew long ago the best moment would be just after the opening of the portal,' Clémence was on a roll. 'If we wanted to change things, we had to use a special turning point in our lives. Annoyingly, it was still proving difficult to launch the change, but the men helped! They provoked it! On this we agreed, Maud: they went too far with banning the new classes to women.'

'What do you mean?' I asked. I wasn't aware of any banning for women.

'This is what we came to see you about.' Maud turned to me, adding, 'or at least I did. I cannot talk for Clémence anymore. The councils of Newtonsee and Lil'London have voted, in a majority, to block women from attending the 'online' classes you wish to organise for us with... How do you call it?'

'Open University or distance learning,' I replied.

'Yes, this is it, Open University. Well, the men decided that they ought to try it first to confirm the content would not be detrimental to a woman's mind. They believe it is dangerous to provide too much education to women, anyway, as '*it makes them waver from what should be their main focus and activity, making and looking after children and the household'.* Edmund, of course, was against the ban, but the majority won.'

'My followers and I are not going to let them cut any more avenues from us. The time has come to react. The time has come for us to reign.'

Maud turned her head and fixed Clémence for several seconds before bursting into a loud laugh.

'Listen to yourself! *'The time has come for us to reign'.* You have lost your mind: we are not a Kingdom!'

'No. We are not a Kingdom. Just wait and see, we might be a Queendom,' Clémence said, with a cold smile that made me shiver.

Maud stopped laughing. A heavy silence settled as we all stared at Clémence. She leaned over and cut herself a piece of cheese and bread while we remained silent. She ate it slowly, and still no one could speak. She couldn't possibly intend to create a monarchy?

'You should try this cheese, it is delicious,' she suggested. 'And please, stop staring at me so seriously. I was just playing with words. It annoys me that everything has to be male by default, even in language. After all, Yoko, you have a Queen in your England, so why should it not be referred to as a Queendom and not a Kingdom. Anyway, I think I will try one of those ham sandwiches next. They look irresistible.'

Maud had clearly lost her appetite. So had I. Nick had not, or played the cool card. He had moved to sit closer to me, between Maud and me. He helped himself to a small ham sandwich and asked Clémence:

'There is another point I was hoping you could clarify.'

'And what may that be?' Clémence asked.

'The assassination attempt against Yoko three months ago... Were you the person behind the perpetrator? The woman who indoctrinated him?'

Clémence did not reply at first. She took another bite of cheese and chewed slowly, her gaze passing from Nick to me, from me to Maud and back to Nick.

'Of course not. What a ludicrous idea,' she finally said, in a sardonic tone. At that moment, I understood she might have. Her smile felt more like a maybe than a no. I finally accepted Nick's theory. But why? Surely she had more to lose than gain.

'Clémence, why did you want to see me today?' I asked her. If she had come here for my support, I was still of value to her.

'To establish what you know. Then, depending on what you know, to establish what side you are on.'

'What side? I am not taking sides. I am not from your world.'

'You belong to both worlds. You are here, aren't you? You have a say and an influence in both. You can't remain non-engaged.'

Story of my life! I already had divided allegiances since birth due to my parents being from different cultures. I never knew who to support at the Olympics or football matches.

'I see your point. However, my role is an ambassador on behalf of the Foggies. I do not take sides in the political views and dissensions inherent in both worlds.'

'Ohhhhhh… So you mean you are above the little problems of the people in both worlds because of your privileged status, a status that protects you in either. How convenient!'

Clémence smirked with a belligerent stare. How I suddenly missed the weaker, even if fake, Clémence!

'OK. Let me make one thing pretty clear for both of you, Maud and Yoko,' she continued. 'As far as I am concerned, if you are not with me, you are against me. Against all of us: the women. I suggest you have a good think about it.'

She stood up, went to the coach and grabbed a bag behind the seats. Nick placed himself in front of me and put his hand on his back, ready to pull out his gun. Clémence pulled a pair of their local roller-blades out of the bag.

'I have to say,' Clémence commented, 'since you came and the roads were improved for your vehicles, rolling around has become an even more enjoyable experience. I will be home in no time!'

She was about to go when Nick asked one more question.

'What about your husband? How is he taking your ideas?'

'Augustus? He is not a bad man; he does not treat me so badly,' she laughed as she continued. 'He is blind to my true ideas and activities. My husband is convinced I am a fragile little one who needs to be looked after. Poor him,

I think he will be in for a shock! Ah well, you can't change things without sacrificing a few of good ones. He is still a man after all, and because of him I had to bend to the will of the dreadful Barbara for years. If only I had been a first wife… Farewell! Choose your side with care.'

*

Nick and I went back home shortly after that. Maud was dazed from her encounter with the real Clémence. She was eager to return home to Edmund for him to expose Clémence to the Council as soon as possible.

'Would they believe him? Could anyone believe her transformation without witnessing it? Even you are still struggling with it,' I pointed out.

'We must warn them that… Gosh! You are right; they already think I have dangerous ideas. They could turn against me, instead. Maybe… Maybe we should let her reveal herself. This Revolution of hers… It will never work. Never! But it could shake things a bit. Maybe if she tries and fails, they will realise they have to make life better for us. Treat us more as equal. Oh I don't know! What to do? What to say? I need to go back home! Yoko, please forgive me. I must go.'

On the way back, hungry despite the stress of the situation (or maybe because of it), I checked the contents of the basket prepared for me by Maud's twins. She had left a note in it. It was mainly on the Open University issue and her fury. There was also mention of her worrying about Clémence, who seemed to have a lot of anger and feistiness these days, and that she hoped the pressure at home was not taking its toll. Without comprehending them, she had seen the signs of the pending disaster.

*

So on the menu for the days ahead we had a looming revolution in one world, a global public disclosure in another, a rescue mission for Jack and a search for missing Louise. I wanted to crawl into a cave and hide.

A little later, while Nick was on the phone with McRae, I was on the phone with Ingis Chen. He was playing it cool, telling me the revelation of the Fog didn't go down so badly. I was still angry towards him when I told him that he had backstabbed us. He retorted that the end goals justified any means to achieve them.

'What about ethics?' I asked.

'It only gets in the way of efficiency,' he replied. 'Especially if the high end has a strong ethical side. It balances, don't you think?'

'No.'

'So are you always fully good? You never lie or hide anything, even if only to protect someone's feelings? You never put your own interest first? You never go against your own ethic, or give it a little flexibility?'

Damn him! No one is such a saint. I knew I was not… I swiftly moved on to telling him that I saw his actions as an abuse of his position with us, and intended to do a review of our agreements as a partnership. Then I hung up.

Nick wouldn't tell me about his discussion with McRae, but it left him preoccupied. What was up?

*

The rest of the afternoon was spent discussing the details of our existence going public with Leila and the Foggies. Aside from initial scepticism, the reactions to the news were unpredictable. Ideally we would have liked to be filmed live from a location in WII, easily recognisable despite a missing human footprint, like a landmark building. It was not such an easy find around London. Moreover, with special effects and technological advances nowadays, it would still be debated whether we were where we said we were. The best would have been the Mount Rushmore National Memorial in the USA, where in WII there would be no sculptures of the four American presidents in the mount's granite. Unfortunately, that was too impractical to organise at this short notice.

The Relocated were also concerned with the revelation of our existence. On the positive side, they would not have to hide the truth behind their disappearance from family and friends any more. How long it would take for the information to settle and be accepted was anyone's guess. On the negative side, the unknown reactions of the public may affect them, too. Kenya's uncontrolled mass reactions, leading to death and riots, had initiated fears in all of us. We still all agreed it was better to take the lead and pave the way, rather than be pushed, pulled or bullied later into dealing with the public.

*

Taking advantage of a nice summer evening, Jazz joined Nick and me for dinner outside in the clearing. We reviewed and remarked again and again on the events of the day, without being any wiser about the future.

'Only three nights before Saturday and we haven't moved an inch towards finding Jack,' Jazz said.

'I think you'll find we have,' Nick commented.

'Have we?' I perked up. Could it be what McRae and he had talked about?

'In a way, yes. I will tell you more tomorrow.'

'You can't do that!' 'Come on!' Jazz and I exclaimed.

'Sorry. Nothing is confirmed yet. Tomorrow I will be able to explain further. You will not like it though,' he replied putting his hand on my back in an appeasing gesture. It felt so nice that I immediately mistrusted myself and moved a bit further away. Jazz noticed and she looked at me with a knowing smile. I shook my head slightly and she sighed, hunching her shoulders. She would like me to have a bit more of a life. Looking up at the stars, I wanted to focus on the present. It was such a lovely night to spend with friends. The blissful 'carpe diem' saying was easier said than done: I could not put my worries aside. Instead, I went to bed early inside the mobile home and wrote down a summary of the day, the door safely shut to the other occupant of the vehicle for the night; Nick.

Day 5 (Thursday)

The revelation of the Foggies was not going to be direct from Gatekeepers Associates. We were to 'leak' it to the press by an anonymous source inside the British Government, which did not exist and thus would never be found. Once the Foggies were known, my name along with Harry and Zeno's would surface, and we would 'reluctantly' be put in front of the media to admit our links to the Fog. The more unwilling we were to come forward, the more people might be inclined to believe us. It would not look like either self-promotion or like a scam.

During the night, the Society had pre-released the information on the Foggies to the American, French and Italian Embassy. In giving them advance notice on the press, the Society could then create more 'leaks' from the Embassies for the media.

The Embassies' reactions started early. At 6 a.m., the Ftab rang. The caller had hidden his ID. A female voice introduced herself as working for the French Embassy. When I confirmed my name, she transferred me directly to another interlocutor who did not give his name, and who insisted that my presence was requested at the French Embassy today. They wished to discuss the claims relevant to my links with the so-called 'Fog'.

My reply to the Embassy was ready: it would be difficult for me to come to any appointment. I was currently homebound by the British Government and incurred the risk of being taken to a remote and unknown location should I try to leave. The Embassy immediately asked how long the British Government had been holding me against my will. After a (fake) hesitation, I told them the British authorities had started to show concern and be controlling after the revelation of the Fog's existence earlier in the week. I weighed every word I said: it was important to avoid creating a diplomatic incident between the two countries. My hesitant tone also aimed to give the impression that I was reluctant to talk about the Fog. The Embassy informed me they would send a car with someone to pick me up. I refused, adding that I had little trust in anyone these days anyway, including the French authorities. Then I hung up.

*

Divide and conquer. The game had started. The French, and most probably the Italians too, were going to be on the British case to have access to us. We knew the Americans were already in touch with the British Government. Did they also know about the Foggies? Leila had passed on the information to them as well, in case they did not. She left out the existence of Jack, though. I smiled, thinking of the mess we had created. It was a little petty, but I enjoyed this small revenge on the mighty powers. I stopped smiling when I realised how good an actress I had become in a few months. Before, my lying about the slightest matter would have been obvious to a toddler. Now I could confidently lie to my own Embassy with the intent of making them play the cards my way. My ego was proud; my conscience was less.

I did not have the time to dwell on this thought. Within minutes, I received a call from Sam.

'Hello, Yoko. You're up to no good, aren't you?'

'Me? I don't know what you mean…' I replied, innocently.

'Oh please! The timing of it all is way too convenient, and those 'leaks' to the Embassies. I presume the press is next?'

'Sam, it's too early. I haven't even had coffee. So either you tell me why you're calling before 7am, or call back after breakfast,' I replied.

'Fine. I will tell you straight: some very relevant specific Embassies have received overnight information on the Fog and have immediately contacted the British government with your names on top of a list of questions and demands. Moreover, we are monitoring key people in the press and media and they have just 'leaked' that the Fog has 'Gatekeepers'. So many coincidences and perfect timing. Strange, isn't it?!'

'It sounds like you have a leak,' I commented.

'We have no leak!'

'Whatever you say, but it sounds like it.'

'Yoko. We have no leak and you know it. I could bet you my car the same people who disclosed the information about the Fog last Tuesday are behind this.'

I remained silent, even though I could have got a new car.

'And I think you are all in cahoots on it!' he continued. 'Look! You don't even seem surprised by what I am telling you.'

'That's because the French Embassy called me just before you did. They want me to go and see them. I told them I couldn't. I wouldn't risk it. The house was under the British authority control…'

'Ah! This is why they are making such noise all of a sudden! It had been busy but quiet until now. I've been up all night!'

'You probably need coffee even more than I do.'

'No, I've had too much. It's as close to intravenous as it could be. Now, Yoko, don't quote me on this: do not go to the house and do not try to leave.'

'I am afraid to ask …'

'We can't let you go to your Embassy. On this, the whole Agency agrees. And they will use any legal or less legal way to stop you. They might even use blackmail with Jack, or say that you are a terrorist they must contain.'

'You've got to be kidding! The terrorist card?!'

'I know. I also know that you don't wish to be under the thumb of the French government, any more than under the British one. Anyway, you have been warned. Please keep in mind I never made this call.'

'Thank you, nonetheless.'

'Also, McRae is speaking to Nick about something and there is hope there.'

'Hope for what? Is it Jack related? Is your department preparing action?' I enquired.

'That depends.'

'That depends on what?'

'On McRae. He can be a bit negligent on following the department lines of action sometimes and go above and beyond… So he might use the department's instructions more as a suggestion and inspiration. I have to go now. We're in a kind of diplomatic communication crisis here because of you. Take care of yourself, okay?'

'You too.'

*

I left my bed and the small room, immediately stepping into Nick's minute kitchen. Nick was already up, reading the paper, with a cup of tea at the nearby small table. He was wearing a tight T-shirt and boxer shorts and it was a good look on him. He eyed me up and down. I was in boxer shorts, too, with a long out-of-shape T-shirt that had seen better days. It was too early for me to care about my appearance. I needed coffee. He turned back to the papers with a smile.

'Good-morning. Love the messy hair. Real sexy,' he said without another look at me, sipping some tea. I ignored him, put the kettle on and took a cup out of the cupboard. Only when the coffee was ready did I reply with a simple 'Good morning. Coffee?'

Nick laid the newspaper down on the table as I sat down with two cups of coffee, one for him and one for me. He pointed to the headlines, which read 'Foggy Business'. The one-liner underneath went further: 'First we had the Fog, now we have the Fog-people'.

The article went on, introducing the Gatekeepers with the three categories that characterise us: Switcher, Crosser and Facilitator. It explained that anyone else crossing the Fog is either unable to access the Other World, or relocated there without the option of coming back. The journalist insisted the only common ground for anyone going through the Fog was to benefit from the Fog's healing ability. The tone was very sarcastic yet the writer was clearly intrigued by the existence of the Fog and the mysteries around it.

Nick and I switched on our FTabs. On one, we selected a live news channel and on the other, we browsed the Internet, various social media and the press. When Nick heard that the identity of the so-called Foggies remained unknown at this point, he commented out loud:

'Don't worry, mate, you'll receive the information later on tonight.'

'I am not looking forward to having my name on tomorrow's headlines!' I said, in a grump.

'In a way, I am. That means you may want to spend more time in this world where it is my job to look after you. And I will only ever give you my very best,' Nick commented, his eyes on my legs.

*

We spent several hours reading and watching the news. From time to time I exchanged messages with my peers in Scotland or in Essex and with Leila to share our views and get an update on the situation. Ingis Chen sent me a laconic 'Smart move' text message, about which I had mixed feelings. Mid-morning, Sam and McRae called.

'We need to talk,' Sam began.

'Nick included,' McRae added.

'We are both here,' I replied.

'Good. So here is the situation: McRae is not officially working with us.'

'He resigned as a British Secret Agent?' I asked, surprised.

'No, but officially, he is not working on the Fog case anymore.'

'Go on,' Nick said.

'On paper, McRae has been on a break, recuperating after a mission in the Middle East,' Sam continued.

'Let's be clear, I am never on a break. I don't do breaks,' McRae corrected. 'I have been made inactive because some of my actions were slightly outside the outlines of my mission, which was nonetheless a big success.'

'What did you do? Did you kill a few people too many?' I enquired, only half-joking.

'Nope. I applied my conscience to the statistics on which the mission was based. Anyway, back to the point, I have never met you and you don't know I exist,' McRae replied.

'Ah… Ok… And you are telling me that now because…?' I asked.

'Because you must not talk about him to anyone other than me,' Sam replied, 'and because only my boss and I know he is involved.'

'So why is he involved?' Nick asked.

'For emergency situations. Like now,' Sam answered. 'Jack is 'retained' by the most militarised departments of the Agency: you cannot leave the house because they, the Embassies, or even unknown members of the public, could put you in danger. The information to the public has gone out of control. So it is crucial that we have a good working relationship and right now, officially, we are stuck. We need to unlock this.'

'Sam and I have worked together in critical situations in the past. We know we can rely on each other without doubts,' McRae took over. 'Sam cannot act freely on this one. He needs to report his actions and interactions with any of you. I don't. He brought me in exactly for the type of intervention now required.'

'Removing the leverage your colleagues have on Yoko and the other Foggies by getting Jack back,' Nick stated.

'Exactly. And Nick will provide essential support and back-up for this,' McRae added. 'I checked your background at length. We talked yesterday so I confirm my opinion about you. My conclusions are that there is no way you would offer your services as a mercenary for someone like Ingis Chen. You left the military because of your ideals and values. Working with Ingis Chen would be like selling your soul to capitalism. It is the reverse of who you are. You are not working for Ingis Chen.'

'No,' Sam took over. 'You are working for someone else. Someone or an entity behind the Foggies that gives them the real back-up; someone we suspect to be creating the chaos within the diplomatic world between your homelands' Embassies and the United Kingdom. Divide and Rule.'

'Interesting theory,' Nick replied.

'We are going to put the theory to the test. Tomorrow, I plan to go on a rescue mission to get Jack without the Agency back-up. I will need help and I'm hoping you'll provide it.'

'That's what I gathered from our little conversation yesterday. You know I won't confirm your theory in any way,' Nick said.

'We do,' Sam and McRae both replied.

'I will neither provide information on any help you might receive for your venture, nor how or why,' Nick continued

'Yes,' Sam replied.

'Pretty clear,' McRae added.

'You are not to ask any question whatsoever.'

'Fine by me,' McRae replied. 'As long as you provide the support, the rest is not my concern; at least not on this mission.'

'Good,' Nick replied. 'Now, we will need Zeno to determine Jack's location.'

'I don't see how Zeno...' I did not finish my question when I realised I knew the answer. Sam confirmed it.

'We need a bait to lead the way to Jack.' Sam said.

'No!' I exclaimed. 'What if something goes wrong and then they have both Jack and Zeno? No way!'

'Yoko, sometimes you have to take risks to move forward,' Nick said.

'No, no, no! It's too big a risk,' I protested. The men didn't seem to care.

'This is not your call. It is Zeno's,' Nick persisted.

'It's not fair! You will present it in such a way he won't be able to refuse. You know it's true!' I was enraged. Zeno was like a brother to me: I couldn't let him take the risk.

'Yoko, stop!' Sam's voice was controlled and icy. 'First of all, you are not his mother. He can make his own decisions. Second, do you have another solution? No, you don't. Now, where can I find Zeno?'

Despite knowing he was right, I was sulking and refused to answer. Nick did: 'He is at Ariel Ben-Chaim's, the rabbi and physician of the Jewish community, here in WII.'

'At Yerushaleim? He picked this time to go to a village with neither mobile reception nor radio signal? It's the worst timing ever!' Sam exclaimed exasperated.

'He needed a break. He went last night and said he would be back before lunch.'

'You lot really need to get your priorities right sometimes,' Sam said, shaking his head. 'Please let us know the minute he's back. We need to get this thing going.'

'First, if he agrees, I will set a plan of action and organise it with him. Then we will be in touch,' Nick corrected Sam.

'And what if he refuses?' I asked.

'We will have to ask one of the Foggies in Essex.'

So it would put Leo in danger, too. My heart felt a pinch.

'What about me? Not that I want to do it, but you've eliminated me from the start. You don't think I could do it, is that it?' In my frustration and anger, I was picking for a fight. Neither Sam nor McRae fell for it. They just ignored me.

'You are the only Switcher here,' Nick replied. 'The three Crossers and Two Facilitators will always have to jump in before you do in risky situations, Nutty. Also, you are under my protection. I would never let you take such a risk.'

Annoyingly, I knew Nick was right. I stopped arguing but sulked some more out of principle.

Afterwards, Nick disappeared to plot the rescue mission with Leila. So when Zeno arrived, I was first to grab him and provide an update on the situation. I did my best to put aside my personal feelings about the risks involved in order to discuss the pros and cons of the mission with him. The result was the one I expected: he wanted to go ahead with the rescue mission.

*

When Zeno went to Nick, my Ftab finally got my attention. It had rung incessantly since the morning until I switched it to silent, for some peace. Most of the calls showed no number and several messages were from the French Embassy. They were probably the ones behind the unidentified calls. I called a number they indicated in their messages. In the politest tone, they informed me they were sending someone to pick me up in an hour, and asked if I would be so kind as to be ready, maybe even pack a bag, just in case. In the same tone of too-excessive-to-be-sincere politeness, I declined their invitation due to a prior engagement in the Other World. Obviously, this remark caused a brief silence, soon followed by enquiries about the Other World and my activities there. I laconically replied that it was private. In conclusion, the call was very frustrating for my interlocutor, though very amusing for me. It cheered me up to refuse to abide by their rules.

*

Nick and Zeno were out of sight until the evening, working on the big plan for the next day. I spent my time glued to the Ftab, exchanging messages with the Foggies and watching the news. In Alaska, the Koplats family had arrived safely. In the Moroccan Atlas Mountains, Christophe and Isabelle both worried about Louise. Isabelle was feeling guilty about her old nemesis's disappearance, saying she should have insisted that Louise stayed after Chloé's birth. She would be safe now if she had. The new mother kept crying: her lack of sleep due to night breastfeeding heightening her sensitivity. In Kenya, Putu remained in hiding, hoping for news from Clare and Mary. She would be needed as a Facilitator to bring them back to our original world. Unfortunately, Clare and Mary had no means to communicate and it was clearly not safe for them to go back to their house at the time. We had little hope of hearing from them any time soon.

The Fog was proving a very popular phenomenon in Kenya. Despite its government's best efforts to block access to the house and control the press, rumours of the Fog's healing powers had spread fast, thanks to the large number of people who had already crossed it and returned home. In addition, it was impossible to control the Internet: Leila informed us that 28 people had placed calls or broadcasted videos from WII via their mobile phones. Those were 28 newly Relocated. There could be more that the Kenyan Government had not disclosed. According to Leila, the Americans, the British and the French had sent special 'advisors' to help the local authorities deal with the situation. Russia and China wanted in, as well. It was a logistic and political nightmare and we were only at the beginning. My main preoccupation was with Mary, Clare, Louise and Jack. They desperately needed help that we could not provide.

*

Towards the end of the afternoon, Leila called with bad news. Someone was tampering with Louise's Ftab. Worse, they were dealing with competent computer experts who had managed to blur the tracking device. The Society's only resort was to remotely fry the device, rendering it useless to anyone. Louise's fate worried us even more: who were these people? Were they the Moroccan Government? The CIA? They could be Mossad, Russian mafia or Chinese Triad for all we knew. The Society was hitting a wall. That was a very, very, very bad sign.

*

A call from Edmund Poff, via the two-way radio, interrupted my conversation with Leila. The Council of Lil'London had held an emergency meeting following the disappearance of Clémence Hoare the previous night, along with the vanishing of an alarmingly large amount of married and unmarried women from Lil'London and Newtonsee. They decided to contact me to enquire if I would have any information on the missing women. Edmund Poff had volunteered to do so, as our mutual appreciation was now renowned.

'I am very concerned. What is going on?'

'Edmund, I do not know where the women are.' As the Foggies' representative and WII Ambassador, I was not supposed to get involved in local politics. And yet...

'I asked Maud if she knew anything,' Edmund's voice was anxious. 'She was very flustered. She is not herself. She can't look me in the eye and seems uncomfortable around me. This is unlike her. She knows something. Why isn't she telling me? Yoko, please, if you know something, you must tell me.'

'Edmund, are you alone right now?'

'Yes, I am.'

'Good. I am in a very delicate situation here. This is not my place to get involved in the politics of your world,' I answered.

After a few seconds of silence, Edmund replied.

'What do you mean by 'our politics'?'

I smiled. He got the hint.

'Well, do you think Maud could be ill-at-ease because she is unsure of how to react to the current event?'

'Yoko, you do not make sense!'

'Edmund, I will tell you as a friend what I think is troubling your wife, but I cannot give you the details: she is possibly split in her allegiances.'

'I still don't understand.'

I sighed heavily and tried again. It can be difficult to reveal something without saying it.

'Edmund, what has Maud been advocating all her life?'

'That women should have a better place in our Society?'

'Exactly.'

'What is the link with the missing women?'

'Are you sure they are missing?'

'Very much so!'

'That is your choice of words. One can say they are missing, or one could say they are gone.'

'Are you saying Maud knows the women have gone willingly? You are saying it has a political cause, a link with their place in our society?'

'I am not saying anything: only suggesting you may want to see the current situation in another light. After all, the opening of the portal between our Worlds may have changed the mentalities more than you have realised. Maybe...'

'Oh Lord! You mean the women are... Have... Left us? And Maud is not sure if she should stay or go?'

'Edmund, Maud loves you! She has no reason to leave you. This is exactly why I don't want to meddle with your ways and politics. Just talk to Maud privately and remind her she can be open with you about everything, as she always could. Please do not share what I told you with anyone, as they could easily get the wrong interpretation. Please talk to your wife. If you wish, you could both call me again afterwards: we may discuss the matter in hand as friends.' What we could discuss, I was not sure. I had no clue how to handle the situation, really.

*

My name was everywhere. Leila had warned me, before pressing the button that revealed my existence to the world. Harry, Zeno and I were making the headlines within one hour. The press had got hold of some photos from my former job and a few more online, generously provided by the Society for them. Leila's team also leaked a telephone number they would manage for me and transfer calls to me only when appropriate. In the meantime, they acted as an in-between, making sure that any caller was aware that I was upset by the disclosure of my identity and not willing to talk. The French Embassy called again. I told them I was in shock and hoped they could respect my need for privacy until further notice. They disagreed but I hung up.

Everything was going according to the Society's plan. As we did not deny the leaked information, combined with my reluctance to talk, the media took this as an admission we had links to the Fog. The concept of Switcher, Crosser and Facilitator was quite fascinating for them, whether or not they believed it. Their investigation of our former neighbours, employers and backgrounds revealed a sudden recent change in an otherwise normal life, which further fuelled their interest. During that Thursday evening, my ex-boss and some former colleagues were interviewed on the news. They confirmed my becoming more distant before resigning three months ago, at a time coinciding with neighbours, police and fire fighters noticing the Fog on our house.

*

Back then, Rico was never officially living in the house. He paid Harry in cash and used his art studio as a mailing address. Only his close friends knew he lived there. We hoped they were true good friends and would not publicly reveal that he might be involved. Zeno was ignoring all his calls, especially as most of them came from his ex-girlfriend, Cris. She was the last person he wished to speak to. Harry had lost his usual poise. The revelation would put an end to his career at Imperial College. Even if he had known this when he agreed to the revelation, it was still a blow. He attempted to cheer himself up in our presence by saying that they would have so much to deal with in the days and weeks and months to come, there would be no time for looking back at the interrupted career.

The three of us, Harry, Zeno and I, worried mostly about the repercussions of the news on our family. Both Zeno and Harry had kept the Fog secret from theirs until now. It had been easy for Harry: he had very few close relatives who were not that close anyway. It was more complex for Zeno: he was on the phone with his mother and sister daily. Harry and Zeno had contacted their relatives prior to the news being leaked to the public. It took so much toll on Zeno that it triggered his departure to Yerushaleim for a change of scenery. The old rabbi and physician had an appeasing presence, and Zeno loved spending time in his apothecary, learning about plants and natural balms.

*

Maud called me by radio after her chat with Edmund. It surprised me, as after dinner was an unusually late time for them to contact me.

'Edmund is furious with me for not telling him about Clémence's abrupt change. He says I should have gone to him immediately after the picnic. He is very upset, Yoko… I fear he thinks I betrayed him.'

'What do you think?'

'I think I may have betrayed his trust a little.'

'Did you tell him why you didn't speak?'

'I tried, but I find it hard to explain, even to myself.'

'May I talk to him?'

'Yes. Of course. I'll go and give him the radio.'

A minute later, Edmund was on the radio.

'Good evening,' he spoke in an icy tone, full of anger. It did not match the voice of the Edmund I knew.

'Good evening, Edmund. Please accept my apologies for this intrusion into a private matter. I just hope I might clarify the situation.'

'Very well,' Edmund coldly replied.

'Maud has said that she mentioned the events of last Wednesday's picnic to you. Has she told you about the personal attack Clémence made on Maud?'

'It seems Clémence talked a lot of balderdash. Which attack are you referring to?'

'That Maud is all talk, no action.'

Edmund remained silent.

'Maud has always advocated the case of women being as intelligent as men, that they should be recognised as such. Her status as your wife and your understanding protects her when she speaks up. However, it also puts her in a rather comfortable situation: she expresses her opinions, lives the life according to her beliefs, yet she hasn't actively changed the status of women. When Clémence pointed it out to her and affirmed she would do what Maud has never achieved, Maud got into an awkward situation. If she blocks Clémence because of her extremism, she might prevent the possible change within your society that she has always dreamt of. If she goes along with Clémence, she rebels against a system she only wanted to amend, not overthrow. Talking to you, to a man and to member of the Lil'London Council, is already taking a side. By neither talking, nor siding with Clémence, she was trying to remain neutral. In a way, it is not dissimilar to my approach.'

'I see,' Edmund replied after a short silence.

'She is your wife. She loves you. Yet she is also a woman with strong opinions about her gender being enslaved. The same way you are her husband and her best friend, you are also a man and a member of the Council.'

'I understand.'

'If I may add one last thing: she was distraught at the picnic. Her immediate reaction was to think of how to talk to you. She needs you more than ever now. On that last note, I shall leave you two to deal with it. I have pushed the limit of our friendship enough already.'

'Yoko,' Edmund replied, in a softened voice, 'I am pleased you did. Thank you.'

Day 6 (Friday)

Zeno left early in the morning. He crossed the Fog of *The Jazzin* equipped with three tracking devices implanted on him: one under the hair at the nape of his neck, one in a copper bracelet and one under a fake nail.

McRae had wondered how Zeno would be able to cross back to London without a Facilitator. As Harry and Rico were known Facilitators and thus at risk, we had to use a third. Helo was the fastest option. Sam had applied pressure so that relatives should still be allowed to visit the Relocated at *The Jazzin*, and we briefed Big Tom's mother to come with Helo as a distant nephew. The boy flew overnight from Morocco, and Big Tom's mother came with him to visit her son for breakfast. Zeno was waiting for him on the way out, hidden in the Fog, and joined them walking out to London. As he stepped out, he kneeled to lace his shoe, making sure that the boy and the elderly lady left swiftly. The boy attracted attention by acting being in tears and running forward. He was a surprisingly good actor, that one! Evidently, the presence of the additional man raised attention and Zeno was soon apprehended. We had bet on a delay before the agents made the connection between Zeno's presence and Helo, and we won. By the time they realised Zeno could not have crossed back to London alone, and that the old woman was not a Facilitator, the boy was gone. The man from the Society had promptly driven him away.

Big Tom's mother had her story prepared. She claimed that the boy had come to her begging for help, as he was sick. She could not bear refusing a simple crossing to him. She knew nothing about his origins or whereabouts. Obviously, Zeno told them nothing about Helo, either. Instead, he declared he wanted to go to the Italian Embassy. He wanted to go back to his home country, firm in the belief that they would treat him better. The British authorities' immediate reaction was to put him in a car going to a destination that was, unsurprisingly, not the Italian Embassy. Behind them, McRae was following the signal emitting from Zeno's multiple trackers in a standard, black Mini Cooper. He had travelled overnight from the Highlands.

*

I woke up at 8.30am to the beep of the 2-way radio. Benjamin Snayth sounded angry.

'Miss Salelles, we must see you. We have organised an emergency meeting with all the members of the councils of Newtonsee and Lil'London for today at 10am, and would really appreciate your attendance.'

'Good morning, Mr Snayth. I hope you are well?'

'Yes - good morning. Will you come?'

'May I ask what it is regarding?'

'Women! It is about women! They are making ridiculous demands. We need to address the issue and stop this nonsense at once. The stability of this world is our common interest, as I am sure you will agree.'

'I am not certain this is my place…'

'Miss Salelles, the Relocated will be affected by this, and in any case you are already involved. It would never have happened without the opening of the gate between our worlds. We are counting on you at 10am. Please do not disappoint us. Goodbye, Miss Salelles.'

He hung up.

It was the first time Benjamin Snayth had used his authoritarian nature towards me. Attending this meeting was not something I was keen to do, though if backing out, I risked antagonising both towns' leaders. People really had to stop contacting me first thing in the morning before coffee, let alone breakfast!

When I stepped out of the very small room to enter the mobile home's kitchen, Nick was already there, reading the news on his tablet.

'So, what did Snayth want? Was it worth making you grumpy for the rest of the morning?' he asked.

'How do you know it was Snayth?'

'I am the one who supervises the 2-way radio system, remember? They are now all linked to my Ftab.'

'Ah…' I replied, preparing a very strong coffee.

'So, what did he want?'

'He wants me to attend an emergency meeting of the councils this morning at 10am. It's about Clémence and the missing women.'

Nick frowned. He was not aware of Clémence and the women missing. He grew more and more tense as I filled him in.

'First, I will come with you. I will be one step behind you at all time. Second, you will carry a gun.'

'If you are coming with me, why should I carry a gun?'

'One can never be safe enough.'

'You saw me at shooting practice, I am pathetic!' I exclaimed.

'They don't know that. You can still scare people. When you look angry, it is terrifying,' he added, with a smirk.

'I don't look that bad!'

'I will pass on commenting. So, are we going or not? I need to organise someone to liaise with McRae in the meantime. And don't you use this as an excuse to tell me to stay! It will not work.'

'Fine. We are going.'

*

When we arrived in Lil'London, the main square was full of men. Disparate small groups of agitated women were gathered on the side, keeping out of the way. The men looked both serious and confused. They stared gravely at me as Nick and I made our way through to the Town Hall. I sensed anger and blame towards me. For the first time since the gate opened, I felt unwelcome in this town.

Edmund Poff greeted us at the door of the Town Hall. The other members of the Lil'London and Newtonsee Councils were already in the main room. He warned me that the atmosphere was tense and antagonistic towards me, as I was now as a negative role model to the WII women. In Edmund's opinion, it was not fair as any bad influence on the women from me was unintentional.

After some dull and half-hearted greetings, Hoare cut directly to the chase and asked me if I knew anything about Clémence's whereabouts. Edmund Poff had informed him of her revolutionary ideas and attitude at the picnic. Maud had refused to talk to them and remained at home, supposedly in shock. She might be; it was still a clever move to avoid having the men's wrath fall onto her. Hoare disbelieved her report, deeming it too implausible, too unlike Clémence. She was his wife, he knew better. Someone must be using her and her name. As a direct witness, I confirmed what Edmund had already told them. The six men around the table listened without a word. Jack Chester, mayor of Newtonsee, Churchill-like in physique and demeanour (not less in his whisky consumption), broke the heavy silence:

'Were you aware of Clémence's hidden side before Wednesday?'

Admitting that I had been was not an option. It would open a brand new can of worms, revealing that Nick had been following an investigation of his own accord without informing them. In addition, I did not want to dissect

Clémence's possible antics with them! It was possible that she had planned my death, mentored and used a man to attack me, and maybe used sex to achieve her control over him.

'Clémence always presented as such a reserved and shy woman: my last encounter with her was a real shock. I never expected this,' I replied, as diplomatically as possible.

'This is unacceptable!' The other mayor in the room, Benjamin Snayth, exploded. 'This sly and contemptuous woman needs to be stopped! Hoare, you are the sheriff of this town, and you had the worst snake of this land under your own roof. We will have to discuss this.'

'Pointing fingers is not going to help here, Benjamin,' Jack Chester interrupted. He turned towards me. 'We understand that you might have had some reasons to suspect her of not being all that she seemed?'

Of course, Maud must have told them about Nick's suspicions. I hesitated. Nick intervened.

'I did. Being in charge of Yoko's security, I took it on myself to further investigate the assassination attempt on her person. It took some time before discovering Clémence's link to the women's meetings in Newtonsee, as well as their real purpose. I have some suspicions, yet no concrete proof, that she was linked to Yoko's attacker. Without presenting proof, I was reluctant to disclose my conclusions.'

'This is preposterous!' Hoare protested. 'Clémence would never harm anyone! She...'

'Hoare, I wouldn't say another word if I were you. Obviously you do not know your wife that well,' Jack Chester interrupted. He asked me: 'Are you aware of the demands made by that silly woman?'

'Well, aside from what she said on Wednesday, no.' I answered.

'She wants us to abdicate from power, give up the councils to women elected among their group, and fill our shoes,' Jack Chester said. 'She wants the women to take control of all official positions in town, and for us to be at their service. She even wants our men of religion to be under their supervision until the women-folk have revised the Book in a female-oriented light. Then I presume the ministers will only be women. She is a lunatic. This could never work.'

The mayor of Newtonsee leaned back in his chair and took a large sip of whisky. I was impressed by his self-control. Snayth less so.

'She IS a lunatic! She is dangerous! She MUST be stopped!' Benjamin Snayth banged his fist on the table. Edmund jumped, as did everyone else except Jack Chester.

'She demands that the women have priority access to your education system. PRIORITY! And the closure of the Women's Punishment System too!' Snayth continued.

'You mean your official brothel-like prison?' I did not resist. I hated their way of punishing the women by making use of their bodies. It was revolting! Snayth shot me a distasteful look.

'It all started when you arrived. You and your over-liberal way of life,' he said, between clenched teeth. 'Can you confirm that you did not voluntarily contribute or participate, in any way, to Clémence's sudden twist towards the so-called women's rights?'

'Without hesitation, I confirm! I did not approach Clémence with suggestions to make the women rise against the men, let alone a 'Women's Revolution'. I told you before, Clémence took me by surprise earlier this week.'

'Very well. So you will not mind announcing publicly that you do not approve of her ways and claims,' Jack Chester added.

'I beg your pardon? I will do no such thing,' I remained composed and firm. 'I will not take sides in your community. I will not get involved in your politics and disputes. I am here as a Foggy representative and my home-world ambassador, not to support one faction or another.'

'You are already involved by your own presence here. Your independence and free spirit are at the source of the problem,' Snayth snapped.

'No. They aren't! Clémence has led her double-life and organised her women's freedom meetings - or whatever she calls them - for a long time before the portal opened.'

'You do agree with her, don't you?!' Snayth banged his fists on the table again. I focused on my breathing before replying.

'I sympathise with a system giving equal chances to all. Yours does not, but neither does hers. I do not agree to a role reversal that would then discriminate against men. Also I have doubts about her methods.'

'Would you say this in public? That would still be useful,' Jack Chester suggested.

'No, I will not. As I said, I should not make any public appearance of any kind towards either side.'

'You are impossible!' Benjamin Snayth banged his fists one more time. Didn't it get painful?

'Yoko, will you not help us?' Edmund Poff spoke for the first time since we sat down.

'Dear Edmund, I cannot. I have to remain neutral.'

'It is not in your interest that our community be in turmoil,' Jack Chester leaned on the table. His calmness, this time, did not hide how seriously he was taking the situation. He should. One never knows how a social uprising might unfold.

*

On the way back, Nick and I stopped to see how Maud was faring. Edmund was not with us: he had remained with the other members of the Councils to work on a response to Clémence and her followers' demands. As I had refused to partake in their plan, I was not privy to it. Maud's housekeeper told us her mistress was not available to see anyone, even us. She gave me a letter from her 'to read at home'.

'*Dear Yoko,*
It was so sweet of you to call on me and enquire of my health. Please accept my apologies for not seeing you. I am a bit poorly and find it difficult to recover from the discovery of Clémence's true nature, severe positions and extreme actions. My mind is confused and torn between my inclination to support social progress and her excessive demands. They are too radical. I wished to thank you for your kind words to Edmund yesterday. I needed his support so desperately, and you helped him understand my distress. I felt so lost.
My state of confusion has worsened this morning, as while you were at the Lil'London Town Hall, Clémence came to visit. She reiterated her wish, or

rather command if one considers her tone and demeanour, that I join her group of women. She alarmed me by informing me her last count is of 160 women, and that their ranks are growing fast! How could there be so many disquieted women without any of us realising it. Oh Yoko! What are we to do? I long for Edmund to return and to discuss this with him. Clémence will certainly try to contact you again. I do not recognise my friend and am frightened by her. She seems so strong, so fearless, so adamant. I am anxious she will never compromise on anything, and compromise is necessary in the democratic rule of a society.

Please be assured, I intend to be back to myself promptly, and I will then come and see you as soon as possible.

Yours sincerely,

Maud.'

This was not boding well. Maud was right to be worried. Fearless people always push the limits of the reasonable and Clémence was already going too far. '*I am anxious she will never compromise on anything*'. This could not end well, especially for Clémence.

*

The matter of the women's uprising was set aside when Nick came back to the mobile home with a lunch prepared by Jazz. He was bringing news on Zeno and McRae's mission.

Prior to being driven to an undisclosed destination, Zeno had been subjected to a quick search. It was a rudimental one, the agents not expecting anyone in Woodfellas to equip the Crosser with tracking technology. They found none of the trackers. McRae had followed them at a safe distance until they reached a destination in the middle of England. Zeno's trackers stopped moving, and McRae went to investigate. He soon reached high walls topped with electric wires and hidden security cameras. McRae withdrew and called the number provided by Nick to report the situation. Shortly before lunch, McRae met with two men from the Society in the pub of a nearby village. They provided him with satellite photos of the location behind the walls, photos they should not have had. It showed one large old-fashioned building at the centre of the land, surrounded by more recent and smaller structures covered with satellite dishes and antennae on their roofs. The pictures also showed civilians and men in military uniforms. McRae and the two men were now working on finding a way to break in and take Zeno and, hopefully, Jack out.

As Nick updated me on the McRae-Zeno-Jack situation, my spirits spiralled down. This felt like a 'Mission Impossible' scenario, except that McRae was not in a movie. How on earth were we to rescue the two Foggies from such a well-protected location? Nick was more optimistic. He said there are always options if you have the means and the guts. Here though, time was of the essence. We had 36 hours before Jack switched this new property into a portal to the Other World.

Jazz joined us with dessert.

'*The Jazzin* is temporary closed. No visitors are allowed from London, and here people are under the shock of what is like a Women's Liberation Movement. For the first time in my life, I actually want to scream *Vive La Revolution!*' Jazz said, as we helped ourselves to cheesecake.

'Oh, come on!' I objected. 'Agreed, things do need to change for women here, but it was bound to happen anyway with our arrival. Clémence is an extremist, and any extremist, of any faith or ideology, is dangerous. I do wish for a major social change for women down here, but I have a bad feeling about this Revolution talk.'

'Well, it is not just talk, from what I have heard,' Jazz replied. 'The gossips have reached us here in Woodfellas: in town, men are worried and women are confused. No one knows how to react. This may play well for the Clémence bunch. She surprised me, that one!'

'She surprised everyone,' I replied.

'She is more dangerous than you think,' Nick said. He explained to Jazz his belief that she was behind the assassination attempt against me, a few months back. He also made her listen to the recordings. Jazz's jaw clenched and remained so for the whole time Nick spoke.

'OK. I get it. She is on the right path in her fight for women, but she might be a Stalin in the making,' Jazz commented, with a worried look.

While Nick was busy working on the rescue mission, Jazz and I went for a walk. The minute we had stepped out of the mobile home, Nick leaned out of the open door and called for Big Tom to watch us. Big Tom appeared out of nowhere, a gun in one hand, another tucked in the back of his trousers. Jazz whispered to me that he was always watching over her these days. Big Tom treated Jazz like a fragile little doll who needed protection. He was very fond of her and Jazz had grown to appreciate the big bear of a man who helped her run *The Jazzin* kitchen and bar. They made quite a funny pair; she the little sophisticated woman, he the tall rough thuggish man.

'Do you think I should tell my family I have been Relocated?' Jazz asked me, when we reached the forest.

'It's really up to you. You know best,' I replied.

'Now that the Fog has been revealed and now that your name is all over the net, I can. I have avoided talking to them all morning, but they keep calling. They were bound to add two and two; the timings of my sudden 'move' to a far-away land and the apparition of the Fog at yours, along with our friendship... Yes, they must know already,' Jazz was talking to herself more than to me.

'Problem sorted then,' I put my arm around her shoulder. 'How do you feel about it?'

'I'm not sure yet. Happy to be able to talk to them openly. I just... I don't want them to take the risk to come and visit. Also... Also I had just started to get used to the idea of my new life. It is just all... Confusing. Stressful.'

'I am sorry...' I began.

'It's not your fault. Anyway, the house is off-limits to anyone right now, so I still have some time to think about it.'

'It must be because of Helo's help in getting Zeno out.' I winced. Everything we did with the Fog had wide ripple effects.

'It affects Big Tom the most. His mother is distraught not to be able to visit but glad to have helped. He is furious. He is not blaming any of you though... What about you? How are you coping with your name plastered in the headlines?' Jazz asked.

'I haven't had the time to think about it, really.'

'When did you check the news last?'

'Briefly, this morning…'

'Ah! You missed a lot. Your ex-boss was on an interview. He spoke highly of you and how lenient they were in letting you go. He said he felt you had a lot of personal problems to deal with…' Jazz started.

'What?! The man shouted and insulted me!' I exclaimed.

'I know.'

'What an arse!'

'Some old dates also talked about how you broke their hearts.'

'No comment.'

'Wait, I kept the worst for the end… Your brother-in-law who left Julia for his gay mechanic: he is having fits!'

'Yes, I know. He has raised hell over the past few months with the courts in France to find his wife's whereabouts and have shared custody of his son.'

'Well, now he claims that the disappearance of his son, Eudes, matches the Fog's appearance and that you probably made his soon-to-be-ex-wife and Eudes cross the Fog to hide them from him. He demands to see his son. He wants full custody.'

'Noooooo! No, no, no, no, NO!' As Jazz mentioned Eudes and my sister Julia, a flood of emotions hit me. Sadness, guilt and fear. A little bit of hope still crept in afterwards as I tried to convince myself that no news was good news. They may still be alive. I had to keep believing.

'Oh, Jazz. The last thing I want now is to have to deal with Julia's husband. What would I say to him? That his son has disappeared in the WII three months ago? I can't… I can't…' Tears welled up in my eyes.

'He has a right to know, Yoko. I understand you couldn't talk before, because of the Fog. But now…' Jazz started.

'As far as we know, no one is aware that my parents' house was fogged back then. Couldn't we stick with the story that they went on a trip to escape him?'

'I know you. The lie would not rest well on your mind.' Jazz said.

'To keep the old lies going for the sake of simplicity and consistency would be much easier,' I replied, knowing full well Jazz was right about me.

'My turn to say it is your call. You know best on that one,' Jazz winked at me.

We walked a little bit more in silence, Big Tom following a few steps behind. We reached a small river and the sounds of the forest were soothing, the flowing water mixing with the birds singing.

'Anyway, you should really check what the media are saying about you and the Fog. They are starting to take the story seriously, despite a general scepticism. The involvement of the police and authorities in the matter intrigues them. Oh! And of course, the involvement of the Secret Services, embassies etc. has been leaked to the press, as well.' Jazz had efficiently changed subject from the disappearance of my sibling and nephew.

I was about to reply when Big Tom jumped towards us and pushed us behind him, raising his gun with his right arm and grabbing the second one from his back. We were blocked between him and the river, his sudden move taking us by surprise. Jazz and I had not paid attention to our surroundings while talking and failed to notice the appearance of a group of 10 women, merely 10 metres away. They wore trousers with heavy boots and light blouses, their hair attached in low ponytails. Some vintage-looking guns or shotguns hung on their belts or on their shoulders. They all carried bulky satchels across their backs: from their shape, they contained their local type of roller-blades, among other things.

Clémence, followed by two women holding their guns down by their sides, walked calmly towards us. We looked at each other in silence. Big Tom kept his guns up. Clémence asked Jazz and me if she could have a friendly word without Big Tom in the middle. Big Tom immediately said no. I leaned and switched on Big Tom's 2-way radio, attached to his belt. The instant Nick picked up, I said, 'Trouble. Need back-up'.

Clémence smiled.

'We mean no harm,' she said.

'You have guns. I ain't going to take no chances,' Big Tom replied.

'Our guns are to protect me; not to attack you,' she retorted, the smile fading. 'I have no doubts that some of the men out there would not treat me kindly if they were to lay their hands on me.'

'Whatever. I don't care. You have guns. No one will harm the girls under my watch,' Big Tom replied.

Clémence looked at him for a while and made a face of approval.

'I actually appreciate that. At least you have respect for womenfolk and look after them. I will speak in your presence then. Yoko, Jazz - I wish to discuss your position regarding the Women's Revolution. You met with both Lil'London and Newtonsee Councils this morning. You know our demands.'

'You are well informed. I take it that you kept some of your followers in town as spies,' I replied. She smiled.

'Wouldn't you?' she replied. 'It was good of you not to make a public appearance supporting the councils. Now I would like to invite you to join our fight. This will be my final offer.'

'I appreciate your offer. You have good reasons to want to change the status of the women in your communities. Some of your laws or practices are, in my view, archaic and unacceptable. However, my neutrality is crucial for the Inter-world relations. I cannot get involved in your politics. If I were to do so, the role and respect for the Foggies on both sides of the portal could be affected in the long term, and in ways we don't know.'

'I hoped you had changed your mind when I heard about your refusal to speak for the councils this morning. I am disappointed in you,' Clémence replied and turned towards Jazz. 'Jazz, you do not have the same ambassador role as Yoko. You would benefit greatly from the changes we - up-to-now repressed - women intend to make. Join us.'

'Thank you, but no thank you. I am all for the changes: indeed, you got that right. However, I don't support violence or extremes. Moreover, I am for equality. You don't seek equality: you seek total control and revenge. This I cannot condone.'

Clémence's face grew dark. She spat her reply.

'I do not understand how two strong, free women, like you both, could watch us be treated so badly and not react. This is wrong! Because you have a privileged status, because you already have the freedom that we seek, you will let fellow women deal with their own fate without taking part. What for? Being able to be an 'ambassador' for both worlds? You should refuse to deal with men who abuse their powers and treat your peers like slaves. You should not accept their representations. Your role is to help repair what the centuries without the portal have done. You are no better than the men, thinking of your own interest first. Both of you. If you are not our friend, then you are our enemy. So be it.'

*

With those words, Clémence turned around and returned to her group, the two protecting women watching her back. We remained still until their group disappeared from view. Within minutes Nick was by our sides. He had arrived when Clémence was beginning her last tirade, unable to hear her, but reading her facial expression showing how displeased she was with us. He decided to remain hidden and ready to shoot, if needed. We returned to Woodfellas, Nick walking in front and Big Tom walking behind.

Once back at the settlement, I called my parents for an update on the situation with my brother-in-law Charles-Antoine. I also wanted to check how they were dealing with my name being spread all over the press. Thank goodness their property was surrounded by walls and located in a friendly small village! The villagers did not welcome the press with open arms. On the contrary, they were doing their best to protect their neighbours and friends. The Society had also placed a protection around my parents. However, the French 'special police' had summoned them to their office in Marseille, the main city in the vicinity, that same afternoon. I had called just before their departure to the police headquarters. For safety, the Society had provided them with tracking devices and would keep a close eye on them. On the matter of Eudes' father, they had told him an abbreviated truth; that they did not know where Julia and his son were and that they were worried. Charles-Antoine was to visit them the following week.

*

I spent the rest of the afternoon in the mobile home, reading what the press had written about me. I ignored many calls from friends, distant family members, ex-colleagues and of course, members of the press and the French Embassy. I also had voicemails from the Japanese and Italian Embassies. They had never bothered being in touch before as I didn't even hold their nationalities, even though I could claim them via my mother.

The media had dug up stories about me that were impressively detailed and accurate. Little was said about my background growing up in France or on my studies; mostly the press focused on my time in London, my failed attempt to run a bakery and my former job. To my distress, they developed at length the most painful period of my life: the death of my fiancé and the depression I suffered afterwards. This was not something I wished to be broadcast all around the globe in strangers' voices. They even found photos of Michael and me and posted a clipping of his obituary. This was sickening and infuriating. It had nothing to do with the Fog!

The day, with its emotional baggage, had drained me. I longed for an early night but first, we had a video conference call with the Foggies in Morocco and Alaska. They thanked me for agreeing to go public, along with Zeno and Harry, even though the other two were not on the call. The Foggies had grown close to each other, even if we had our own little spats from time to time. We were all anxious for the rescue mission and frustrated not to be able to participate. It could have been any of us in need of help; if not this time, next time. We also worried about Louise, Mary and Clare. We hoped that the latter two had found refuge with Mary's boyfriend in WII, at least. Louise's silence was more worrying. The complete absence of means to track her, missing minutes on the street security cameras, the Ftab professional tampering; everything indicated that Louise might be in the hands of an unknown party. The situation reminded me of when Ingis Chen had abducted Jack months ago, on the day the Foggies first arrived to England from Italy. I hoped Chen was not involved this time. He was trouble as a foe.

Day 7 (Saturday)

The Society provided McRae with the support of twelve mercenaries for Jack's rescue mission (and Zeno's). They had obtained the map and structure of the land and building, then devised a plan to drop McRae and six mercenaries from a stealth glider onto the roof of each building. Each man was equipped with modern bat wings to direct their landing in silence. Their goal was not to invade the premises, but to access the air-conditioning systems and administer a strong soporific drug to pervade the building. Within fifteen minutes, everyone in the premises was sound asleep. In the meantime, the rest of the mercenaries had neutralised the soldiers outside, using special guns shooting mini-syringes with a somniferous liquid, like those used to restrain dangerous animals without killing them. The mercenaries and McRae had to act fast to locate Jack and Zeno and bring them out. The abnormal silence on site and lack of communication would raise the alarm.. The whole rescue took less than thirty minutes before McRae, the mercenaries, Jack and Zeno were out, the last two in deep sleep. The rescue team split. McRae left with Jack and Zeno by car, heading towards Scotland with regular changes of vehicle on the way. The mercenaries simply disappeared.

*

Waking up to the smell of brewing coffee, I had stepped out of my room to the sight of a breakfast table fully set and ready for a feast. Nick had pulled my chair out with a 'Good morning, Sunshine!', then had given me a ten-second shoulder massage before putting a mug of coffee in front of me. Only then did he join me at the table and said, in a happy tone, that the mission had been successful. Zeno and Jack were still asleep, so my longing to speak with them had to wait. As I sat in the mobile home and listened, captivated, to Nick as he related the previous night's events, all the tension of the past weeks alleviated. Elated by the successful rescue, I had not felt so light and comfortable in a long time. What happened next was the result of this sudden feeling of bliss.

The synergy between Nick and me was palpable. It would have been similar to my friendship with my housemates but for the strong sexual vibes between us. Weeks ago, I had made the decision that my life was too complicated to get into any intimate relationship. It had not been an easy decision to make: I was really fond of Leo, his company, his spirit, his sense of humour, his body. Ours had been an instant attraction and connection. I was already getting attached. This was why I had to cut that relationship short. It would have rapidly developed into a serious one.

Now, overjoyed, in the cramped space of the mobile home with a hot hunk who looked at me as if I was candy, it was not the prospect of a relationship that crossed my mind: it was wild sex. The animal attraction between us eclipsed anything else. My eyes glazed and my mind went back to that kiss in the woods a few days prior: passionate, intense.

'You are thinking about sex', Nick said, bringing me back to the present.

'Me? Not at all.' I lied.

'Yoko, Yoko, Yoko… Do you think you can fool me? And you looked so cute thinking about it, with your messy hair and frumpy t-shirt. And those shorts….'

He leaned over and wiped a spot of honey on the corner of my mouth with his finger. He took me by surprise, and before I realised what was happening, he leaned further and kissed me. My mind went blank. My impulses had taken over with hunger for his lips, for his body, and for much more. The kiss went deeper: the fragile table saved me. It couldn't handle his weight and collapsed, along with what was on it. Broken glass spread everywhere. In silence, we cleaned the mess. My libido calmed down. Afterwards, I hastily announced I would go and shower, then would check with Sam on the British government's reaction to losing both Jack and Zeno. There must be quite a panic there! I swiftly disappeared before Nick could grab me and I lost my self-control again. Under the shower though, it was Leo I had on my mind. We were not together and still it felt like a betrayal, somehow, to feel attraction for someone else.

*

Mid-morning, in the clearing under the sun, Jazz came to sit next to me. I shared the good news with her regarding Zeno and Jack.

'Oh Yoko! This is fantastic! I am so relieved! So all the Foggies are safe now,' she exclaimed.

'Well, it's not looking that good in Africa: Louise is still missing in Morocco. We hope Mary or Clare are safe somewhere in WII.'

'And Helo, is he going to stay here now? Or are they going to send the poor child back to Morocco?'

'He has to go back. If Helo remains in England, no one can facilitate Christophe,' I reminded her.

'He must be disappointed his daughter didn't turn out to be a Facilitator, isn't he?' she asked.

'Christophe is completely smitten with his daughter. He wouldn't be upset,' I replied. 'However, it's too early to tell the effect of the Fog on Chloé, as it's impossible to make her cross the Fog. Any time they try to get Chloé outside with anybody other than Isabelle, the baby cries as if in pain. No one has the courage to pursue the experience for now. Christopher mostly worries for her future. He wants to find a way to have mother and daughter leave the WII Morocco for either the U.K or U.S. Both are long and possibly dangerous trips through WII for a young child and Isabelle,' I said, thinking out loud.

'Maybe by helicopter or plane trip in WII?' Jazz suggested.

'The Switchers would have to fog houses along the route for the necessary fuel stops. And it's unpredictable. Dangerous…'

Julia and Eudes were on my mind, of course. How could they not be? Nick, arriving discreetly behind me, put a hand on my shoulder and told me not to think about it. Jazz nodded. They both knew why my mood had suddenly turned dark.

The British Secret Service were panicking. They had no clue as to who had organised the abduction of Jack and Zeno, and to what end. The bug they had implanted in Jack and Zeno had been crushed. Now the military branch of Sam's department was frantically trying to track any vehicles spotted in the vicinity of the property the previous night and early morning. They were also trying to determine how many people broke into their site and what drug had been used. Sam's boss was playing along, blaming the military branch for their negligence and for taking the wrong initiative in the first place.

Only McRae joined the conversation with Sam. He had arrived in the Highlands with Jack and Zeno, but the Foggies were still under the effects of the drug and were in bed and asleep. He gave us a few more details on the events of the previous night, commenting on how impressed he was with the service of the mercenaries. They were efficient with extensive access to technology, weapons and data. All he asked was for Nick to confirm they were not from a foreign government. Once Nick appeased his fears, McRae declared he needed a quick nap.

*

Afterwards, when we were alone, Jazz raised an eyebrow and asked,

'This is all very good but I have one more question: what is happening with Nick?'

Sometimes it was annoying to have people knowing you so well.

'Nick made some moves on me. Even though neither my head nor my heart are inclined to anything more than friendship with him, my body seems to differ.'

'Woohoo! Any juicy details?'

'No. Only snogging a couple of times. It is really purely physical and there is nothing behind it. I need to get a grip: it's pointless.'

'Girl, let go and have some fun!'

'No. I will talk to him. We need this to stop. I want to keep my head clear.'

'What about Leo?'

'What about him?'

'Are you still thinking about him?'

'No,' I said. 'Yes,' I thought.

Jazz just looked at me silently. She didn't believe me, rightly so. She switched to another subject. 'Jack and Zeno are safe in the Highlands with Harry, Rico and this new McRae guy. Leo and Dante are blocked, yet safe, in the Essex house, and you are with me. So what's next?'

'Soon I will have to speak to the press. Leila is organising a live interview for me, in which I will appear unenthusiastic and cautious about disclosing information on the Fog and us 'Gatekeepers'. We will use that term instead of Foggies. It may help us being taken more seriously.'

'How will you do the interview? Via the web? You'll never manage to get out of this house without interception from the British Intelligence Services.'

'No, it has to be in person to be taken seriously. It's important I send the right image. We still need to work out how to get me out for it.'

'Wouldn't it be easier if they didn't take you seriously and we could go back to our lives?'

I sighed. I had just started to rebuild a close-to-normal social life in London in the past few months and reconnect with friends, whilst living in an unfogged house. Jazz and I had even organised dinner together with friends. Thanks to technology, once every other week, I placed a screen at the end of the table, in lieu of her plate, and invited a few friends in common. Jazz joined via our online video system. She was able to see everyone and participate in the conversation. The friends thought she was in a remote exotic location and found the whole experience fun.

'Some of our friends have called,' I told her. 'I didn't pick up. Returning their call is another item on my long 'to-do' list.'

'Like reading the *Lil'London Tales*... I struggle with it, too. I can't get used to the style. If it wasn't for you telling me about the last opening in 1782 and how this girl switched both a mansion and a house in a Jewish community, I would know nothing.'

Recalling the opening of 1782, a light bulb flashed in my head. It could be the solution to the problem! It was almost too perfect to work! I stood up abruptly and rushed to pick up Nick's copy of the Lil'London history book, still unopened by its owner. Leafing through the book, I found the part explaining how the Jewish community of WII saw their Fog destroyed.

In 1782, after unknowingly and unwillingly creating a gate to the Other World, the Switcher managed to flee her controlling family and found refuge in a Jewish community. Weeks later, having turned her rescuer's home into a portal as well, her family caught up with her and burnt the Jewish fogged house to the ground. It had cut the access between both worlds. I punched the air in victory. We needed a temporary door to London, and now I knew how to do it! Nick looked at me - not for the first time since we first met - as if I had lost the plot. It didn't bother me. I picked up my tablet and dialled Leila's number. I signalled to Nick to listen in: the task ahead was a team job.

*

Later that day, map and high-tech compass in hand, Nick drove the quad on the wild hills on WII in the direction of a northern forest. This forest still existed in our England, so it was perfect. On that Saturday night, I slept in a small basic cabin, quickly built for the occasion. I would switch it into a Fog gate overnight and, thanks to Simba, would exit in the morning into the English forest. Then I would be free and the world was my oyster.

WEEK II

Day 1 (Sunday)

For once, when opening my eyes in the morning, my first thought was not coffee and breakfast, it was to check if this tiny cabin had been successfully switched into a portal. Upon stepping out and facing the familiar wall of white fog, I heaved a sigh of relief. I stepped back inside and proceeded to dress up. Simba would not let me put on my jeans, pulling the trouser legs to play. I called Nick from the Ftab.

'It worked!' I exclaimed on the phone, happy.

'I can see that. Shall I come in with coffee before you head off to your London trip?'

'I'm coming out. It's too small for the three of us in here.'

Nick was waiting for me by his tent, preparing breakfast with a camping gaz kit. Coffee was nearly ready. He had laid out a picnic blanket on the ground and set up some bread, butter and jam for breakfast.

'Eat. You'll need it. Without knowing the details of your diary, I am sure you'll require a lot of energy for the day ahead.'

'Very thoughtful of you. Thank you.'

'You're welcome. One must look after valuables.'

His comments dampened my spirits a little. Our little flirtation and borderline relationship had to be stopped.

'Nick...' I began.

'No need. Your immediate serious face says it all. As you wish, I'll keep my hands off, but ... Yoko... You are always so kind to everybody: when will you be kind to yourself as well and be open to your emotions?'

'Thank you for understanding,' I said, a little sheepishly and quickly

96

changed the subject. 'Now, once I am back in England, this gate needs to be destroyed promptly. Leila is on the other side and will dismantle the house and set fire to the planks afterwards. Might you stay until it is all done and confirm the portal is gone here, as well?'

'You needn't ask,' Nick said, in a business-like tone.

'Thank you.'

We had breakfast in silence. I was anxious the door could be destroyed and munched my food at the speed of light.

*

I had not seen Leila for at least a week; not since this whole mess with the media started, and could not wait to hug her. She was now a real friend, aside from her support through the Society. I missed her. Back inside the cabin, I took a deep breath and said to Simba, 'London, Simba. London.'

Leila was on us for a big hug as soon as Simba and I reached England. We were delighted. The plan was working so far. I was back in my home world, a few kilometres from London and free from the Secret Services' control. The next step was to dispose of the newly created door to WII. Some men from the Society, known to be unaffected by the Fog, soon started to dismantle the cabin. They were efficient, finishing the task within an hour. It was a strange sight: the planks were put in a pile forming a Fog-covered mound. After spilling petrol over it, they set it on fire; extinguishers in hand to keep it under control. The fire was going to last for some time. Leila suggested we made a move towards London with some of the men as protection, leaving a couple of them on site to ensure the fire burned everything to the ground, erasing any trace of what had happened. Staying would not change the outcome and we had plenty to accomplish ahead, so soon we were on our way.

Leila and I were on the terrace of a coffee shop in Soho, munching a salad for lunch. Simba was on a lead at my feet. Simba's hair was all black; dyed to be less distinguishable: she was still an impressive sight, although closer in looks to a young Newfoundland dog than a wolf or Malamute. My hair was black, too; a waist-long black wig with thick bangs now hiding half my face. Contact lenses changed my eye colour to black to complete the goth look. When Leila and I looked around at the other tables, my picture was on the cover of all newspapers. I put on my oversized sunglasses to hide even more of my face. Most titles were either ruthless or sarcastic. Or both.

'Fog-gate, a global information Watergate?'

'To Fog, or not to Fog, that is the question.'

'Bored of this world? Yoko Salelles, Gatekeeper, at your service.'

'The Pharmaceutical Industry against the Fog: 'The claims of Yoko Salelles & Co are preposterous."

'The Fog conspiracy: hoax, or latest secret files' leaks?'

'Are Yoko Salelles and the Gatekeepers real people or computer fakes?'

'The Fog phenomenon, a marketing campaign for the launch of a Hollywood blockbuster gone out-of-control?'

*

The 6pm interview was to be a live broadcast with a team from the BBC. They did not have the exclusive rights and the interview would then be passed on to all the major channels around the world and online. As it was live, despite the Society's efforts, it was impossible to stop them asking unscripted questions. It was up to me to deal with them as best as I could and in preparation, Leila and I spent the afternoon reviewing potential aggressive and intrusive questions. It was not going to be a walk in the park; we expected that much. We were about to go to a hotel room to do one more mock interview when her mobile phone rang.

'Yes?' Her line was protected, the calls screened, but as a double-security she never stated her name in case the caller was not supposed to know it. While she listened to the caller in silence, the frown on her face grew deeper and deeper, anger and anxiety more and more obvious. When she hung up, she hailed a waiter and asked for the dessert menu. Her reaction surprised me, but I went along with it. We both chose the carrot cakes.

'What is up?' I asked her when the waiter left.

'I will tell you in a minute, when the cakes arrive,' Leila said, turning to look at the door of the coffee shop, eagerly waiting for the desserts. Within seconds, they were on the table.

'Louise has returned,' she began. 'She walked for days and got lost in the rocks and emptiness of the Moroccan countryside before finding the Fog house in the Atlas Mountain.'

'What? Why did she go on the journey alone?' I was relieved to hear Louise was now safe. I knew from Leila's look that it was not all good news. So why had Louise faced the desert alone?

'Ingis Chen,' Leila said, matter-of-factly and pinched her lips. I picked up my fork and dug into the carrot cake. Now I needed it, too.

'Go on,' I said, as I munched.

'So Louise was at home in Marrakech. She woke up early and put the radio on. When she heard about the Fog revelation to the public and the riots in Kenya, she instantly realised she should vacate the house. Too many people in town had seen the Fog, like in Kenya. Louise quickly packed a few key essentials, deciding to contact us and the Foggies when she was at a safer location, a public café or something, where we could come and get her. She put everything, including her Ftab, in a large holdall. Louise had only made a few steps into the street when a man stopped her. He introduced himself as a member of the Chen team. Ingis Chen was never told about the Marrakech Foggies, so his team should not have been there. She glanced around for her Society's bodyguard. She spotted one coming towards her, on the other side of the street, but a truck arrived and blocked the way by stopping in the middle of the road. It created confusion in the traffic. Another of Chen's man appeared next to her and grabbed her bag. She tried to stop him but the first man held her still, telling her not to worry; they would take care of her. They dragged her behind the truck where another vehicle was waiting for them. The back passenger door opened. She looked behind her to see if she could spot the Society's man, but he was not in view. Trying to put the basic self-defence methods taught to all Foggies to good use, she struggled to free herself from the first man's grip. Failing, she went back to the good old tactic of kneeing him in the groin and running for her life. Soon Louise was in the middle of the local souk market. The shopkeepers knew her. She asked one of them if she could sneak out from the back door, saying she was trying to avoid a stalker. She did that several times in different shops to be sure to lose whoever was behind her. In a rush to free herself, she did not think that her actions would also make her lose her bodyguard from the Society. And, in a rush to leave the house, she had forgotten to put on her earrings with the hidden tracking device.

Louise had no paper and no money, so she decided there was only one thing for her to do: walk to the Atlas Mountain. As she had explored the bare and wild countryside in WII around the mountains, she believed she could find the house. She also knew the direction from Marrakech and ever positive, she thought it feasible for her to reach it within a day. The shopkeepers kindly gave her some essentials; one a bag with a bottle of water; another a pack of biscuits and more water, and a third one, a bag of Medjool dates. She had water, food, youth and was determined not to be caught by Ingis Chen or anyone else. Fear gave her wings and determination. The dates, a staple diet of the Middle East for millennia, gave her the sugar boost needed and she set on her way. Unfortunately, her sense of direction was not as accurate as she thought. In fact, she completely lacked an inner GPS: it took her from Tuesday to Sunday to make it to the mountain. She arrived severely dehydrated, ravenous and exhausted. Louise quickly told her story and collapsed. She was burnt out.

'What on earth was Ingis Chen doing in Marrakech? Had he tried to kidnap Louise, or was he trying to protect her?' I thought. I was relieved that Louise was back and safe, yet anger was bubbling in me against Chen. Again. What was he up to?! Leila had been right to order the carrot cake; it soothed my nerves and kept me calm.

'I need to call Chen,' I told her.

'Yes. And you can ask him to give us the Ftab back. We had to fry its system, but we still want the hardware. We would rather not have too many of those out there.'

'Still no news from Mary and Clare?'

'None.'

There was a pause before I broached another subject.

'Leila, will you look after Simba during the interview? I don't want her to be in the picture. Too many people already know I have a dog, or what they think is a dog. Let's not make this public, shall we?'

'Of course: no problem. Shall we go to the hotel and practice for the interview now? Have you had your fill of freedom in London for the day?'

'Yes. That was considerate of you: I appreciate it. I don't know when I'll be able to do that next.'

'Tomorrow, if all goes well.'

'If nobody recognises me.'

'Trust me, with this wig you are a different person! We might have to start building a collection of styles of you. Also, in London, no one is surprised to see a woman walk around in a burka.'

'A burka? Isn't it the attire that some Muslim women wear and that covers all the body and face?' Never in my life did I conceive that wearing this, one day, might be a welcome option to protect myself.

'Yes, we got you one. I know it isn't the most exciting, but we have prepared several bags for emergencies with different types of outfits, wigs, niqbab or burka, sunglasses etc. to hide your identity as you wander around. It also includes several DIY pet hair dyes for Simba. Similar bags are ready for each Switcher, Crosser and Facilitator. They also include a locator and an emergency number to call. You should learn it by heart. Will you?' she asked, with a smile.

'After what happened to Louise, I want to learn every key telephone number and address by heart!' I exclaimed.

*

We made our way to the hotel nearby, arranged by the Society. Leila told me to make sure to take my time when answering, and not to let anyone pressure me into talking. It was important to emphasise that I was a normal person, unprepared for what was happening to me. We decided that I would not call Ingis Chen and demand an explanation for his men's action towards Louise until after the interview. Talking to him would wind me up; I needed to keep my cool prior to meeting the press.

We were in an empty office on the top floor of a high building in the City, in the centre of the financial district. The large windows gave us an aerial view of the main London landmarks. A van organised by the Society had picked up a team from the BBC, a journalist with a cameraman and a sound technician in tow, and drove them to us after many detours to lose whoever could be following them. The Society had used several tools to ensure no devices could trace them to where we were. As the television team set up their cameras, microphone and other technology for the interview to start in ten minutes, I stood by the windows admiring the view. London was my home and I was very fond of it. The path of the Thames in the middle of the beautiful city was familiar to me, yet it still touched me. That was one of the beauties of this town, always ready to surprise and enchant. Now, as only minutes separated me from the global broadcast, a strange peace took hold of me. The quiet view in front of me made me feel all was what it was meant to be, despite the millions of people buzzing around like ants in the web of streets, houses, offices and shops underneath us. I couldn't define why or how, but it filled me with confidence that I could handle it all.

'Miss Salelles, good evening,' the interviewer began.

'Good evening,' I replied.

'First of all, thank you for agreeing to speak with us tonight.'

'You are welcome.'

'We must inform our viewers that this interview is live from an undisclosed location in London,' the journalist said to the camera. 'Nothing in this interview has been prepared or pre-recorded.'

The journalist then turned towards me.

'Miss Salelles - your name, unknown until a couple of days, is now on everyone's lips on the planet. The same goes for this curious Fog phenomenon occurring in various locations. Thankfully, the chaos and riots it caused are now under the control of the local governments. So my first question is: are you indeed linked to this Fog?'

And so it began. I sat straight in my chair, trying to keep my face and demeanour friendly, yet displaying unease about the position I was in. I had to appear like a regular person forced into a situation over which she had no control, and one she would rather keep secret. After a few seconds, just long enough to take a discreet deep breath, I answered.

'Yes, I am.'

'In what way?'

'I seem to create it.'

'Really?' The journalist's comment sounded sarcastic. I dismissed his tone and made a show to play nervously with a ring worn especially for that purpose. Later, fidgeting alternatively with my pendant and bracelet would also convey I was nervous about the interview.

'As far-fetched and unbelievable as it sounds, I do,' I continued, a little hesitant. 'The whole thing is not... Easy to explain. And it is not something I can control.'

'So it just happens and you don't know why or how?'

'Yes.'

'And what is this Fog?'

'I don't really know. I mean, its functioning, its components - all of this I don't know. What I can talk about is what it does. There has been lots of rubbish about it in the media, which is understandable as it is unknown. In a nutshell, the Fog is a passageway to another world; an alternate earth.'

'Could you be more specific?' The interviewer was doing his best to be professional, and only a limited scepticism showed on his face

'I will try.' I paused to compose myself and gather my thoughts. 'So, when you cross the Fog, approximately one in seven people come out, not on this earth but on the other one mentioned earlier. There is no way of knowing who will be selected to relocate to that Other World. It seems totally random. The others are just crossing the Fog none the wiser that this can be a gate. On that alternate earth, it is pretty much like ours, just more raw, without the tell-tales and amendments to nature linked to human presence. A preserved earth, if you will.'

'A Greenpeace's dream come true.'

'Something like that.'

'When did you realise this Fog was, well - magical?'

'Magical? I prefer the word extraordinary.'

'Fine - 'extraordinary'. Transcendental. Supernatural.'

'I knew something was amiss when I first stepped into a wild forest instead of my street in London.'

'It must have been rather terrifying.'

'I was too baffled to be terrified at first.'

'And afterwards?'

'Honestly, it is all a bit of a blur. Things happened so fast; it was one discovery after the other. But the local inhabitants really helped.'

'Excuse me?!' The journalist looked shocked. I had innocently dropped a bomb. No one knew yet that WII was inhabited.

'Yes, there are small communities on that planet, as well. They are the descendants of the previous Fog openings, when some people were relocated without being able to come back.'

'I am starting to find it difficult to follow...' the journalist frowned.

'Right. Let me summarise. Please don't ask me why this happens because I do not have a clue, ok? It is just what it is. The Fog is recurrent, every 231 years. When it happens, a small group of people become bonded to it: the Switcher, who creates and maintains the Fog on a weekly basis; the Crosser, who can cross to the Other World and the Facilitator, whose presence by their sides enables the Switcher and Crosser to return. Aside from these three people - let's call them the Gatekeepers - anyone else crossing the Fog will either be unaffected and unable to access that Other World, or 100% affected and transferred to that other world. So those last ones, the Relocated, have formed communities since the previous Fog happened. They knew the doors would open again and were waiting for us.'

The journalist was gobsmacked and could not say a word. Finally, he whispered: 'This is unbelievable...'

'I know. Why do you think we didn't want the Fog to be known? We knew nobody would believe us! Or if they did, the reactions would be unpredictable and uncontrollable. The events in Kenya proved us right.'

'What proof do we have that...' the journalist began.

'Honestly, it doesn't matter to me whether you believe me or not,' I interrupted. 'It is the least of my problems. I am here with you because of the media's harassment for confirmation and answers, because the French Embassy is on my back, because the British Government is trying to control my life, and because people relayed so much rubbish on what was happening, it was getting dangerous. I just want to set the facts right, get rid of all this pressure and try to reorganise my life back to normal, or foggy normal.'

'I see… Hypothetically, let's say your story is true: how could you possibly lead a normal life being the guardian of the door to an entire new planet?'

'There! Now you understand my real problem!' I exclaimed.

What I really wanted to say was: 'When circumstances are not in your control, whatever happens gets integrated into your life, and that becomes your normal life. We all go through difficult times, and everyone – EVERYONE – wonders, during a crisis, how they will go through this. When you come out of it, you have gained strength. You get resilient with time. That's what we do: we adjust to a given situation the best we can, to make this life our own.'

The journalist shook his head with dubiety. He looked down at his notes to regain countenance.

'There were also claims of the Fog having a healing effect?'

'Indeed. It has.'

'Is it like one of these holistic modern age healings?'

With a sigh, I prepared myself for confirming a fact about the Fog that would trigger considerable interest.

'Again, I can't tell you how it works or if there is anything holistic in it. What I understand is that crossing the Fog eliminates viruses from the human body. It won't repair a broken bone or a genetic flaw; it won't cure cancer - it is a malfunction of some of our cells. Just things like flu, hepatitis etc. - the Fog clears it.'

'Wow.'

'Indeed.'

'Do you realise the implications this healing effect would have, should it be real?'

'It is real. And yes, I do realise. Anyone with an ailment linked to a virus will want to cross the Fog. Of course, let's not forget they would incur the risk of being relocated to the Other World and unable to come back.'

'Would it be so bad, if you have your health back? People move around all the time.'

I raised my eyebrows. Did he think that being a Relocated was like being an Expat?

'I think you are not seeing the whole picture here,' I chose my words carefully, struggling to avoid being either sarcastic or patronising. 'The Relocated do not move to another country. They move to another PLANET. For example, in what would be South East England, they are barely twenty-five thousand people. Maybe that's the total population for their Europe: we have no idea. Also, their technologies date from the early 19th century, when the last door closed. The Relocateds' link to this world for trade, communications, family and friends, or anything really, is through the Fog Gate only. Forget Internet, central heating, electricity and television. No modern hospitals, no cars, no...'

'It is like a blank canvas?'

'Not exactly, but close to it.'

'That also means that the possibilities are endless. People could get a brand new chance in life, the same way emigrants went to America or Australia to begin anew and left their past behind?'

'In a way... There are also pitfalls to avoid: uncontrolled numbers crossing, protection of that other earth's nature and inhabitants from potential abuse from us. The list is long.'

'Incredible! This is really an extraordinary story. Would you say you have a gift?'

'A gift?' I didn't know how to answer. Was it a gift? Did it feel like a blessing?

As I was pondering on the last question, Phil interrupted the interview. He came by me and leaned forward, saying we had to go. Then he proceeded to unhook the microphone from my clothes. Another member of the Society's team joined us with my bag and jacket. In no time, we were on the roof of the building to escape by helicopter. As I got in, Leila was inside the aircraft already. She signalled the sound was too loud to speak and she would explain later.

*

Eventually, the views from the building windows would reveal the interview's location: we knew this. As soon as the Society identified there was a danger, they alerted Leila and Phil. They were right. As the helicopter flew away, the building below us was swiftly surrounded by cars and all the skyscraper's exits were blocked. Minutes later, the helicopter landed illegally in the middle of a park in East London, where a car was waiting for us. The helicopter was not discreet enough for a safe escape. In the car, nobody spoke: the atmosphere heavy and tense. I only broke the silence to enquire about Simba. Leila replied she was waiting for us at one of the next car changes. Thirty minutes later, Simba greeted me with an effusion of yelps and licks, her excited tail slapping Leila's face as she got inside our new ride behind the wolf.

'Where are we going?' I asked Leila.

'Up to you. The Highlands? Unless you wish to sort a few things here, first.'

I thought of my pending tasks and all I had to deal with: the Embassy, my ex-brother-in-law harassing my parents for answers, the unopened emails and calls to return…

'No. Happy to go. I have heard the Highlands are breath-taking.'

'Typical,' Phil grumbled, in the front passenger seat. 'We couldn't just go where it's sunny and warm, could we? Seriously, I hate haggis.'

Day 2 (Monday)

After changing vehicles several times during the trip, we finally made it to remote Scotland in the early hours of the morning. Supposedly, the countryside was stunning. I would not know: the Highlands' roads were not lit and it was raining too heavily to see anything. Upon our arrival, everyone was asleep in their rooms, except for Rico who was in the living room where he had fallen asleep on the sofa waiting for us. Rico was tenderly hugging a cushion, a wool tartan throw spread over him. He looked adorable. The television was on, the video-on-demand indicating Dirty Dancing as the last seen movie. After giving Rico a good night kiss on the forehead, I collapsed into bed.

*

The next morning, when I opened my eyes, a bright light filled my room. A glance at the window showed that the sun was shining. Soft-looking white clouds floated in a deep blue sky. Simba was reluctantly waking up next to me. The night had been too short for both of us. I surveyed the bedroom. It was small but cosy. The walls and ceiling were whitewashed, with wooden beams that gave a unique charm to the space. The bed was set against the wall, facing the window, and took most of the room. Only a small antique wardrobe, an old-fashioned armchair and a small side table could fit in as well. A tiny door, not even my size, was on the right; a larger, more regular one was on the left. Wrapping myself in the blanket, I opened the tiny door and entered the smallest and cutest bathroom. The bath was barely more than a shower with high edges; the toilet more adapted for a 10-year-old child and the sink the size of a dessert plate. The dolls' house style of this room was endearing, at least for a short stay. I ran a bath that took under 3 minutes to fill, during which I gazed dreamily at the bathroom's window. The views were magnificent. The house was nestled in a narrow valley surrounded by mountains: an eerie festival of colours on display. Trees, bushes, flowers... Each was violently affirming its rights on the land by a vivid colour contest. It was a painting with rough brush strokes of greens, reds and pinks. An array of brown and rust shades broke in whenever they had a chance. The intermittent cloud's shadows on the slopes added to the enchanting effect of the land. Leaning out of the window, a small yet defiant waterfall grasped my attention. Its path was uneven, wiggling and crashing against rocks before falling into a low river paved with pebbles, reflecting here the blue sky, here the clouds.

Even though the bath tub was minuscule, I stayed in there for a long time looking through the window, marvelling at the sight of goats climbing the high slopes, or the birds of prey in the sky. The peaceful silence, aside from the wind and the birds, was striking. It reminded me of my first Fog crossing and discovery of the WII forest. The serenity of nature and the feeling of magnitude, of something bigger than ourselves, appeased me. I was gripped by pure beauty. There were many places around the world upon which I had marvelled, yet nothing had compared to the Other World, unique in its purity and absence of human presence. That day, I was taken by the rawness of the Highlands. There was a strength and a fight in this nature to exist, to survive, despite the elements. Something indefinite and infinite touched me, deep into my core. It was unexpected.

I went down for breakfast feeling high and serene. Not even getting lost in the corridors of what looked to be a rehabilitated old inn could dampen my spirit. I located the kitchen from the smell of coffee and bacon before hearing Zeno's unmistakable laugh. As I entered with a smile on my face, my old housemates stood up and rushed to greet me, followed by Leila. She was now officially with us as part of Gatekeepers' Associates. For McRae's sake and to protect the secrecy of the Society, we had agreed on a story about her during the journey here: she was an old friend of mine and I had turned to her when in need of help. We messaged all the boys and from Leila's relaxed demeanour, the story had been adopted.

'Breakfast?' asked McRae.

'Say no!' Rico exclaimed.

'Me?! Saying 'no' to breakfast? Have you lost your mind?!' I teased him.

'He will serve you haggis! I am not kidding you! I checked: this thing is made with sheep's offal mixed with oatmeal, suet and stuff like that, all boiled in the animal's stomach!' Rico continued with a disgusted look.

I looked at McRae, inquisitively.

'You are in Scotland,' he replied. 'The English have their English breakfast. The Scottish have a similar one with haggis as an additional treat. Some do it for the show: I do it because I like it. So, a portion for you?'

English breakfast had never won me over. I liked my morning meal the continental way, preferably with lots of honey. So a Scottish breakfast was not tempting me at all. Plus the prospect of haggis with my beloved coffee did not seem a match made in heaven.

'Maybe I could keep the haggis for lunch?' I suggested.

'Come on. Where is your adventurous spirit?' said McRae, putting a plate full to the edge in front of me. There was much more than haggis on it. It could feed me for a day or two. 'Full Scottish breakfast for the lassie: haggis, scrambled eggs, bacon, black pudding, grilled tomatoes, fried mushrooms, baked beans and tattie scones. Toast is in the breadbasket. Kippers did not fit in. Enjoy!'

He sat back down at the table with a mischievous grin.

'They told you about the importance of breakfast for me, didn't they?' I asked him, looking suspiciously at my friends. They either avoided my eyes or displayed a similar grin to McRae's.

'I am not big on breakfast,' Leila said, pulling a face as she looked at my plate. 'A cup of tea usually suffices for me. I am so grateful for that today.'

McRae shot her a glance and commented: 'Not a brave one, lass?'

Leila did not seem to care not to be a brave one. She sat down at the table and along with the others, waited for me to dig in. So I complied, starting with the scrambled eggs and making my way round each element in my plate. I could never finish it all but tasted a little of each. It helped that I was unsurprisingly ravenous, as usual for me in the morning. The food went down well, until saturation hit, halfway through my plate. All of a sudden, my stomach felt heavy and full and I knew it would take hours for me to digest it all. It would provide me enough calories and energy for a trek in the country, I thought with eagerness.

'So, what's the plan for today?' Rico asked me. 'Why are you here?'

'What about a bit of fresh air? It looks unbelievable outside,' I replied.

'I think Yoko needs a mini-break,' Leila explained.

'Wait! We are in the middle of a crisis. As an active agent of British Intelligence, let me remind you that we don't have the time for a mini-break,' McRae said, raising an eyebrow.

'Oh! McRae, don't be a killjoy!' Leila told him, flirtatiously. That was a first: never had she used her charm to get what she wanted before.

'Lassies call me 'Lochy'. Lads call me 'McRae',' McRae said, flashing her a flirty smile in return to hers. He then turned to me and added: 'This applies to you both.'

'Lovely. So, Lochy, just for one day, let's chill a little, shall we? What can you show us about Scotland that will enrapture us?' Leila pursued.

'You promise that we will return to London tomorrow and finally sorts things out?' McRae asked, looking around. He frowned. 'Where is Jack?'

'In his room,' Rico answered. 'The 'lad', as you say, is not an early riser.'

'So, can we go for a walk in the countryside? Do you know your way around here?' I asked.

McRae hesitated. He was heavily outnumbered, but duty was playing on his mind.

'Come on Lochy. Pleeeeease!' Leila bent her head sideways and gave him a soft smile.

'All right then,' McRae relented. 'I'll show you around. But tomorrow, back to being serious before the situation worsens in London and elsewhere. There is only so long you can disappear before the military side decides to launch a takeover of the two Fog gates in Britain.'

'We promise - tomorrow morning, back to business. Now let's get ready! Do we have a map?' I was getting excited about wandering into wild Scotland.

'No need of a map. I know this country like the back of my hand. I grew up on a property only a few miles from here. This is where generations of McRaes have come from; the land of my clan.'

'Really? Wow! What a coincidence!' Zeno exclaimed.

'Is it? I wouldn't be so sure,' McRae looked at me, suspiciously.

'I had no idea where you came from. Nor do I know anything about your clan.'

'Obviously, I am from the McRae clan. And it is not difficult to know where I am from, as I am the next chieftain and heir,' McRae commented.

'Well, all this is new to me,' I said, dismissively. It was true. Leila must have known, though. She had run enough checks on Thomas Lochlan Alasdair McRae to be privy to any details of his Scottish roots. Had she picked this place on purpose to get him on our side?

'It would not surprise me that your mysterious protector – who I don't believe to be Ingis Chen - knew this when choosing this place. I would be curious to know why.'

I gave a little laugh that was highly unconvincing of my innocence and stood up. The weight of breakfast in my stomach immediately made me feel like a stuffed goose. I longed to walk it off.

'I will check the news and check on everyone for you today, including the Relocated. Everything is an emergency these days, but anything of extreme urgency, I'll let you know,' Leila told me, having accompanied me to my room.

'Thank you. By the way, you are good at flirting!' I teased her.

'Of course! I know how to flirt! You may think the Society is just a bunch of historian geek adventurers: we do have a private life, I'll let you know. I even have dates. Sometimes.'

'Are you interested in McRae?' That would be interesting to watch, a Society member dating a British Secret Agent.

'Certainly not! The man is a player.'

'He is rather charming and good-looking. I agree that McRae has a fun and mischievous streak, but he doesn't strike me as such a player.'

'Don't be fooled by his cherubic look: the man knows how to use his charms. Streaming through his file, he has impressive success with women. Most of them even forgive him his flirts and flings with others because he is so endearing.'

'You are describing James Bond, not McRae.'

'He is even more dangerous. In James Bond, the playboy is obvious: with McRae, it takes you by surprise. The man is smooth.'

I laughed. She genuinely sounded as if every woman was in danger in his presence.

'Seriously, you saw how the seducer came out when I started to flirt with him,' she insisted.

'From the little time spent with him, what I know is that I appreciate him and his intelligence. He is good company, can think for himself and is very helpful.' McRae had been on our side so far, even though working for the Government.

'Yes, McRae is an asset for us, I agree. He also seems to be the right kind of friend: Sam Riverson pointedly chose him for discreet support to his team. Still, when it comes to women, we should protect our hearts against his charm.'

She eyed me suspiciously. 'You're not falling for him, are you?'

'Well, if there had been any chance before your speech, you annihilated it!' I replied with more laughs.

'Good. Not that your private life is my problem, but as your friend, I don't want you hurt. I had to warn you.'

'Leila, I don't think you should be worried. The man shows no interest in me.'

'Let me quote an acquaintance of his: "McRae simply cannot be 'just friends' with pretty women". So the man is interested,' Leila concluded.

*

It was a glorious and warm day. The Highlands had conquered my heart. It was a hard and raw country on the surface yet underneath the rough beauty, the land had a true softness. The sensitivity and purity in the air captivated me. Simba shared my positive feelings about the place. She ran through the land as if rediscovering an old friend. Phil and Jack joined us too. Only Leila had remained inside to liaise with the Society and stay on top of the news. We walked along in silence, followed at a distance by Society mercenary bodyguards.

We returned from the mountains mid-afternoon, exhausted but filled with positive feelings. McRae announced that he had organised a special plan for us for the evening to further complete the Scottish experience. We were going to a pub he knew that offered a local beer and traditional dancing. He turned to Leila.

'You're coming too, lass. You won't get away with working tonight.' He had a glint in his eye.

'Thank you but no thank you. I don't drink much,' Leila blankly refused.

'Lass, that was nae a question,' McRae retorted.

'If you start speaking with Scottish idioms, we won't understand a word from you before long,' I told him.

'I'll keep it to a tiny wee bit then,' he winked at me. I was beginning to see why the man could have a string of women around his finger. Leo came back rushing in my mind. With him, the seduction was not a game.

'I have quite a lot to do and...' Leila began.

'Leila, just one night off,' he interrupted. 'If Yoko can do it, as well as Jack, Harry, Rico and Zeno, or me, so can you. Your job can't possibly be as stressful as their situation right now.'

We all agreed with McRae, and Leila could not fight long against her united friends. She arranged for Phil to cover for her with the Society. He would also look after Simba.

McRae had enrolled us not just to watch but to participate in Scottish reel dancing. For a couple of hours, McRae made us learn the steps and figures of the dances. I never thought I would love Scottish folk dancing so much! We were still painfully bad and unprepared at the pub, but the locals welcomed us with warmth, laughter and many pints. I had not felt so free in my being and my mind for a long time. For one day and one evening, every worry disappeared. Back in my tiny room, lying in my bed, I was breathing anew.

Day 3 (Tuesday)

Upon waking, the first thing I thought of was not 'coffee', it was 'window'. I jumped out of bed, to Simba's surprise, and opened the window wide, taking in the fresh air. Gosh! It was so beautiful!

After soaking for a while in my doll-like bathtub, I popped outside before breakfast, as Simba had her urgent needs. Zeno arrived behind me.

'I enjoyed last night… I don't usually like dancing.'

'A good thing you liked it. It is good practice for when Lil'London and Newtonsee invite us for their dances.'

'They are not Scottish.'

'No, but their traditional dances must have some similarities.'

We stepped back inside. Now I longed for my coffee. Arriving at the kitchen door, we heard Leila laughing at something McRae had just said. Inside, Harry was reading the paper, ignoring them. Rico looked at us and shook his head.

'I don't get it,' he said in his strong Italian accent. 'It wasn't that funny.'

'It's not your fault, Rico. Not everyone has the privilege to understand refined British humour,' Harry commented without lifting his eyes from the paper.

'Sarcasm is not humour,' Zeno replied in defence of his compatriot, Rico.

'Boys, boys, boys, please. Don't throw your toys out of the pram because only one of you managed to make the girl laugh,' I intervened.

'As McRae didn't come back with us last night, I would say the British win with more than one girl,' Harry continued, ignoring my comment. 'Which one did you pick, McRae; the bubbly ginger head, the sultry brunette or the doe-eyed blonde?' Harry asked.

'I must admit, I'm impressed,' Rico approved. It was a big compliment: the self-declared Italian Master did not rate other men's seductive skills lightly.

'I can't smell coffee? How come I can't smell coffee? Rico?!' I noted.

'We have run out...' Rico answered.

I looked at him in awe. How could we run out of coffee!?

'Yoko,' McRae turned to me, changing to what he considered a more serious subject. 'Sam and I - and the boss - won't manage to prevent a military action much longer. Gatekeepers Associates needs to work with the Government in London. You must find a compromise...'

'I don't see how I could deal with this without coffee,' I whispered to myself. 'Is there tea at least?' I asked no one in particular.

'Tea coming up,' Rico answered, already grabbing a mug for me.

'Please make it strong, black, no sugar. Thank you, Rico!'

Jack arrived, bleary-eyed and puffy-faced from sleep.

'Coffee,' Jack just managed to emit, before slumping down in a chair.

'Out of coffee, mate,' Rico told him.

Jack slowly turned his head towards Rico with an effort that was painful to watch. He grunted 'noooooo' in such a broken voice that we all felt sorry for him. He folded his arms on the table and let his head fall down on top. Jack was an even worse morning person than me.

'I'll never make it through today,' he groaned.

'You've all had a day off from the media bombarding you with news. A full day without your impenetrable Ftab. Let me brief you on the updates from... Our side.' McRae glanced at Leila, then me.

'Leila is our friend. She can be privy to this discussion,' I told him.

'From your side, maybe. However, she is not privy to whatever I have to say on behalf of who I work for,' McRae replied.

'I already know you work for the British Secret Service. You are a spy,' Leila said, looking rather innocent.

'Well, you shouldn't. It was not for you to know,' he glanced at me again, disapprovingly, and shook his head. 'Ah well, we all know that girls talk. Still, it would be better if you would leave now.'

'As you wish, Lochy,' Leila gave in without a fight and smiled. As she turned her back to him and faced us, she winked. She was playing with him.

'Leila, wait,' I stopped her as she passed by me. 'If you don't mind, Lochy, I would rather YOU leave us while WE catch up first on what we have missed and share our opinions and positions, prior to listening to yours.' As I spoke, I switched on my Ftab to browse the web and check the news.

'No offence, but we may like to check first-hand what is happening in the world out there,' I added for McRae's attention as the others also activated their tablets, except Leila who didn't want him to know she had a similar gadget provided by the Society.

'Fair enough,' the ever-chilled McRae replied. 'I'll be outside having a smoke and a chat with Sam on the phone. How long do you think you will be?'

'Can you give us an hour?' I asked, checking with a look that the boys and Leila agreed it would be enough. When they did, I turned to McRae who nodded and exited the room. Soon we heard the front door close and saw him appear on the other side of the window, lighting a cigarette and pacing the grass.

'I could do with a few more days...' I said with a sigh. 'One day of holiday; it really isn't enough.'

'Si, though I'll be glad to go back to normal meals, proper coffee and somewhere with a gym,' Rico commented.

'Rico, this is better than the gym. Running up and down the hills in the country and swimming in the lochs. You could train outside and fill your lungs with pure air!'

'I prefer the gym. Especially my new home gym. I can put the TV on when exercising. It's much better.'

By now, even Leila was rolling her eyes and head-shaking in consternation at Rico's latest complaint.

'Right, going back to the big issue here,' Harry said, speaking over Rico's grumbling. 'On leaving, where to?'

The past 24 hours had given me some time to breathe, away from the complexity of the last events and actions. It had also been beneficiary towards new ideas.

'How about we continue with what we have started? We have informed the public first of the Fog, then of us. Most still don't believe us and who would blame them? We should give them proof,' I said.

'Don't they have proof enough in Kenya?' Zeno said, firmly. 'We still have no news of Mary and Clare. Or… Do we, Leila?'

'No, we don't,' Leila's face was instantly business-like. She was also worried; she cared for us all.

'Yoko has a point,' Harry intervened. 'From what I read, the Kenyan government is now trying to control information and belittle the claims that the Fog can heal, as well as the existence of the Other World. This is hardly surprising: dismissing the Fog's attributes is their best way to stop the flow of the curious and the desperate people running to the gate.'

'If I may say something,' Leila interrupted. 'Governmental intervention will be extremely important to control the population. You will need their support to make sure order is kept when everyone knows about you. Many, many, MANY people will be willing to take the risk to cross, for whatever reasons: health, adventure, escape, hiding, business opportunities. The Fog is a chance of a new beginning, of a clean slate. There is a limit to what private security can do; ours or… Chen's.'

'Do not pronounce the name of *Il Bastardo* in this haven of peace!' Rico exclaimed.

'I thought you didn't like this place?' Zeno picked on him.

'You know what I mean!' Rico snapped.

'Boys, boys…' I attempted to appease them before it escalated into an argument. They were both tense and ready for one. 'Rico, let's chill here: Zeno is only teasing. Zeno, you know the man hasn't had coffee!'

'Leila is right,' Harry put us back on track. 'And so are you, Yoko. So what would you suggest?'

'Something like an organised crossing, by way of a lottery for a small number of people, involving the British Government and the press,' I said. 'It should provide proof to our fellow citizens of the world that we are telling the truth.'

My suggestion brought silence. I continued, 'Of course, we need to work on the details. In a nutshell, the idea is to announce a draw 24 hours before it happens, limit the applicants to a manageable number, and have several independent experts supervise the application process. Or something like that.'

As usual, the Society's support would be key. The Government was bound to try and choose who will cross. We needed them to stop this from happening.

'British Intelligence is going to be thrilled!' Harry burst out laughing.

'Do we care?' Rico looked around, challengingly.

'Wait, does this mean you agree with my idea? If so, we need to run it through the other Foggies as soon as possible.' I looked around, inquisitively.

'Yoko, we will have to do something like that at some point,' Leila commented, 'so it might as well be now.'

'Let's drop a line to the Foggies after the chat with McRae,' Harry continued.

*

Leila had a pocket notebook opened in front of her with a few notes scribbled as a memento. She proceeded to go through her list, ticking the items off, once talked about, for a full debrief on the Fog and Foggies' situation.

'First, the Foggies. As I have already mentioned to you, we are still in the dark about Mary and Clare. We don't know what is happening in WII Kenya. As Harry guessed, the local authorities are frantically trying to control both riots and information on the Fog. They are keeping a tight control on the house. They even attempted to block Yoko's interview about the Fog to broadcast in their country. It was bound to fail; the interview is all over the Internet. Putu is getting edgy. She worries not just for her friends, the children she was looking after - even though we provided a replacement for her – but that her Embassy is demanding to see her. She has agreed to meet them today, in a neutral place.

In Morocco, Louise remains in the Atlas Mountains Fog location with Christophe, Isabelle and Baby Chloé. The young Helo is with them too. They are safe and well protected, enjoying access in both worlds with no immediate danger that we know of. The Moroccan Government is doing a series of tests on the ex-fogged house in Marrakech, with the presence of British advisors. Oh! I forgot to mention this: the Kenyan authorities also have such advisors in tow. And tests are being made on Leo's old B&B in Rome, too. As to your parents' house, Yoko, there has never been any suspicion that it was fogged, even if a few people wonder why it was out of bounds for any of your parents' friends for the 7-week duration of the Fog. However, your ex-brother-in-law is insistent now that your sister and you are in cahoots and have abducted his son. You may want to contact your parents soon about that...

On the American Foggies: they are all in Alaska, and like the ones in Morocco, all are safe. Well, maybe not from each other. Michelle and Sophia are still snapping at each other every chance they get.

In Essex and London, nothing has changed: Sam has managed to maintain the fragile equilibrium since last Sunday. Leo and Dante are well, although if Dante is busy with his architectural plans, Leo is bored. He turns round and round, like a lion in a cage. He is very worried about the consequences of the interview for your security and life. He cares, Yoko, he really cares...

In Nevada, the American army took over the house. Special Forces have set up a base around it. Elsie is wonderful, though: she is not letting anyone through without disarming them immediately. You all remember Elsie? I told you about her weeks ago. We are so lucky that she was Relocated. She works for the Society, and although she doesn't have Nick's mercenary training or background, or my historian family tradition, her competence as a psychologist is proving invaluable. Elsie was great with Michelle: we knew she would be and that is why we sent her, but she is even more useful now. Her charm, open-mind and thirst for life have won over the WII Native Americans: they trust her to have their best interests at heart. So now when she tells them that anyone crossing the Fog must be stopped, disarmed and their technology removed, they comply! She is keeping us in the loop daily via her Ftab. The Americans have cut the former Internet signal, so instead we are using theirs without their knowledge.

Next, and this one is going to irritate you all: Ingis Chen.

The man did not waste time when the opportunity presented itself to him to go on the front line and introduce himself as your official spokesman. He affirms to the world that you chose him to protect you and your affairs, as well as act as your official public relation spokesperson. Chen emphasised that the revelations regarding the Fog and your existence, followed by the live interview, were a traumatic experience for the Gatekeepers and that you wish to limit your public appearances to the minimum from now on.'

*

McRae knocked at the window and tapped on his watch. Harry signalled that we needed five more minutes. The Scotsman lit another cigarette.

'So, Ingis Chen.' Leila frowned and checked her notebook. 'He is proving excellent as a public figure already when speaking to the press on your behalf. Of course, he has no idea where you are, though it doesn't stop him being very active. I have to give him credit: he is doing a fantastic job. His business approach, his explanation of what happened in Mexico with the indigenous WII killing everyone, and his mention of the Indian and Chinese legends on the Fog, they all help in making people on the planet take you more seriously. He has also contacted your respective embassies and is directly liaising with the Home Office and Defence Department in London. The details of what he negotiates, you should ask him. There is a lot to say against this manipulator; a dangerous, devious, duplicitous, amoral man. I do not like him, yet he is brilliant right now! You could not have dreamt of a better spokesman, advocate and business manager. Except us, of course, we are not media material.'

'What do you think of the public's reactions to the interview?' I asked her.

'It is a difficult one. A minority believes you, a minority is hard against you and the concept of another world and … the majority is waiting.'

'Waiting for what?' Zeno asked.

'Waiting for confirmation. People are going back to their old ways: they are waiting for a person or an institution of recognised authority to give credit to your claim.'

There was a knock at the door and McRae walked in.

'So, when and where are we off? London?'

*

Leila and I sat next to each other in a train from Edinburgh to London. Phil was in front of me, McRae in front of Leila. Harry and Zeno were flying back to London by helicopter, Jack and Rico by plane with British Airways. Each group had incognito Society bodyguards protecting them. The set-up of our return to London made McRae grumpy. As we separated, two thirds of the Foggies were not under his watchful eyes anymore and he did not like that, even if we had efficient backup with us. This splitting was the last drop of a bad morning for the British Intelligence Services, aside from the good news of us returning to London.

First, Phil, Zeno and Rico destroyed the wooden cabin that Jack had fogged the previous Saturday night. They had also implemented my solution for a temporary Fog in Scotland; to make Jack sleep in a separate dismountable structure they could burn afterwards. Zeno, Jack and I had a glimpse of what the Highlands in WII were like: we could not see any distinguishable difference to ours. Nonetheless, the purebred Scot in McRae was curious. Very curious. We saw him, more than once, wander around the small fogged structure. Rico and Zeno placed a bet on him finally stepping inside or not. Zeno bet on McRae's adventurous streak and lost. Now, even though he didn't take this opportunity, McRae deplored losing the gate to the Other Highlands.

The second cause of McRae's low spirit was the Gatekeepers' decision to give the public proof of the Fog's benefits to health. He surprised us, not for the first time, by agreeing that the option was good for us. What he jibbed against was having to break the news to Sam and his boss. He didn't rejoice, either, in the practical implications of our decision. It involved not only British intelligence, but more generally the police. So far, working with the police force had been easy, as they couldn't ask questions. From then on, there would be more internal politics within and between each organisation, more paperwork and more delays.

Last, McRae wanted to travel by air. The agent, who appeared so chilled and unfussed, liked the luxury of the first-class lounge and had a thing for earning air miles. Leila might have been able to cheer up the Scot with her mild flirting but she was focused on her laptop for the whole journey back, organising the strategy to prove the Fog's healing properties.

The long train journey was a good opportunity to read online the reviews on the interview, and to contact fellow Foggies and Relocated. Even though we were now officially labelled as 'Gatekeepers', between us we still referred to our group as the Foggies, despite our original misgivings about the word. The nickname had stuck.

As soon as I logged in, my profile showed I was online and Jazz sent me an instant message. She always kept her tablet with her to stay in touch with her old and modern life. She longed to have news from me. Her first question concerned my whereabouts and expected return. I answered I was on my way back with Leila, officially an old best friend of mine, as well as Phil and McRae.

'Yoko, I hate to be the bearer of bad news, but we are wading in a deep mess here,' Jazz turned serious.

'What's the matter?' I asked, fearing whatever news she was about to give.

'Clémence Hoare, who else?! The woman broke into Newtonsee women's prison, aka the legalised-brothel-rape-institution, and freed all the women. Unsurprisingly, they all joined her growing rank of supporters.'

'How are the councils of Newtonsee and Lil'London taking this?'

'They are furious! They've put a reward on Clémence Hoare's head! They condemn her in everything she says or does. And... I can't.'

'Me neither. I don't like her ways and her extremism, but...'

'But this women's prison is an abomination! I hate it! This is unacceptable! I don't understand how a whole community could do such a thing.' I could visualise Jazz fuming and waving her hands in anger, and shared her rage.

'Sadly, there is still the Lil'London one,' I said.

'Yes, and a big part of me is hoping Clémence Hoare will do something about it and raid it, as well.'

'I doubt Augustus Hoare would let this happen. The security around it will be reinforced. Not only does he have his reputation as Sheriff to uphold, he wouldn't want his personal humiliation to grow any further.'

'If only they could learn from this and change their ways!' Jazz exclaimed.

'That swiftly? Has the ruling power ever changed its way of thinking overnight in the history of mankind?'

'There must be a case... Even if nothing comes to mind,' Jazz wrote.

'Nothing here, either,' I replied.

'Ok… Changing subject, or I'm going to scream with frustration. How does it feel to be a celebrity?'

'It would feel better if it was for my skills, talents and/or intelligence. Not my phantasmagorical imagination, or my con-like qualities.'

'Well, not everything is negative or doubtful. Some people think you are the latest catch: gorgeous, single and guardian of a brand new world full of opportunities.'

'So thrilled. I cannot wait to have all these non-calculating gentlemen queuing at my door.'

'Oh, it's not that bad. Sure, you are the talk of the news and most of them don't take you seriously. It's still an improvement from when none of them did.'

'You sound like me when I try to cheer you up! It's scary!' I wrote, giving a little laugh that made both Phil and McRae turn and look at me, quizzically. Leila was too deep into her work to take notice. Earlier, I had spotted that McRae was giving her the once-over and showed a little smile of approbation, before taking a sip of tea. Leila was right: he was a hunter. She had started a flirt game with him; I hoped she knew what she was doing.

*

After my exchange with Jazz, I checked on the other Foggies around the world. Leo and Dante were grateful to Sam, though utterly bored with being blocked in the Essex house. Sam had turned out to be a great ally in protecting the London Foggies from intrusion by the more aggressive branches of British Intelligence or, more generally, from anyone. They discovered a new side to him too, when one evening he came along bringing his guitar. Kimberley Epcott, his friend who first informed him of the Fog's existence, was also at the house with her brother Ed. Together, they participated to this impromptu jam session. It was thanks to evenings such as these, and other little pleasures of life, that all of us Foggies still had a semblance of a normal life. It was more difficult to adjust for the Koplats in Alaska. Their cover was to be Tony's distant family coming to visit. They still had to keep a low profile, especially as Adam was anxious to protect his daughter from being associated with the Fog. He hoped that no pressure would be put on his ex-wife and journalist,

Penny Thompson, to disclose her sources. Sophia was finding Alaska's social life lacking and not to her standards. On the contrary, Michelle loved it: the ratio of men to women was highly in her favour and she enjoyed the attention she received. It seemed she was not missing her boyfriend much.

*

Even though there were no Foggies in Nevada any more, I was surprised to receive a message from there. Elsie Wood, the psychologist sent by the Society who Leila had referred to in the morning, had written to me to express her support to us in dealing with the public. Her situation was not a simple one. She was relocated in an alien world with a community of Native American descendants for new friends, unable to access the house and the benefits of our world; in her case, for trading. However, she had two major assets: her access to the Internet via her tablet, chargeable via solar energy, and her positive thinking. She had managed, so far, to control the two Relocated from the American Army. The man and woman no longer had any contact with WI, no weapon, and were learning the ways of the locals. Elsie was not sure how long she would be able to keep this going. The Army was bound to try and send more people across and with the numbers growing, they would be more difficult to control. She asked if I would keep her in the loop of any information, should I hear of anything from my British spy friends about the next American moves. It was unlikely I would know anything more than Leila, but I replied in the affirmative. In return, she would write about her learning on Indian traditions, including shamanism. The Native Americans' spirituality and medicinal knowledge had always intrigued me. I also wanted to make a parallel with the apothecary and physician, Ariel Ben-Chaim, in Yerushaleim. Both cultures were very different in origins and religion, yet they both shared a faith that was part of the healing process itself, along with respect for nature and its use to cure ailments.

*

Time dragged on the journey home. Finally, in the early evening, we were reunited with the old gang in our shared large house – Harry, Zeno, Rico, and me – as well as Leila, Sam and McRae. I had happily got rid of the wig and contact lenses, feeling much lighter. We sat around the dinner table with a bottle of red wine (or two) to review the situation. Leila had emailed us Foggies the Society's plans for the 'Fog Health Test' and it looked perfect. We introduced it to the two agents.

'So, will your bosses back us up with this?' I asked Sam. McRae had delegated the negotiations on the matter to Sam, under the excuse that his own role was not official.

'We don't really have the choice. One: people will ask questions and demand answers. Two: you made it clear that either we work in partnership with you and it all happens in a controlled way with government supervision, or you will do it behind our back.'

'I also believe that if we are seen working in partnership, it would strengthen the British government's position as advisor on Fog matters to other states around the world, like in Kenya, in Marrakech, and the US,' I added.

'Personally, it reminds me of something you said to us once, Sam,' Harry jumped in. '*It is too big a discovery, too big an opportunity*: how could you even think of not sharing it with everyone?'

Sam didn't reply. He leaned over and took one of the chunky double chocolate cookies on the table. McRae smiled and poured himself another glass of wine. Maybe the rule of not drinking while on duty did not apply to secret agents. Or to Scots.

'So, how do you suggest we proceed with your 'Fog Health Test'?' Sam asked.

'Well, we propose that tomorrow, mid-morning, we contact 10 of the main London hospitals and announce that 10 of their patients suffering deadly viruses will have the opportunity to participate in a 'health lottery'. Application will be open for 6 hours, at the end of which we will draw 10 names out of the 100 provided. That is, if 100 people are brave enough, considering the risk of relocation and its implications. Then, the following day in the morning, they will come here and cross the Fog. A hospital appointment will be planned afterwards for each of them to demonstrate they have been cured.'

'Health lottery... You are aware how much controversy this will cause?' Sam commented.

'Do you have a better idea?' Leila asked. She had been silent until then; intent on protecting the active role she had taken in the planning, or in her link with the Foggies in general.

'No. I was just asking,' Sam replied. His eyes narrowed on Leila. 'I am surprised you are privy to so much information. The Foggies are not often that open about themselves, even to Yoko's good friend.'

'Like with so many things, she can be very protective over our friendship,' Leila replied.

'Don't worry, Sam. I've got it covered. I intend to do a thorough check on Leila,' McRae jumped in, a wide grin over his face.

*

Back in my room, I wrote to the other Foggies to confirm we were going ahead with the Fog Health Test. We also had to agree on our position towards Ingis Chen. It was not acceptable that he acted first and justified himself afterwards. If his reasoning may have some grounds on occasion, it always left us all uncomfortable. It was part of the foundations of Gatekeepers Associates to be unanimous in our decision to cut our direct link with him, even if he did a good job defending us. He was just too much of a loose cannon. It was not a light decision: he knew about the Society's existence – even if only vaguely - so it would put the Society's position in jeopardy. He could let the government and anyone know about our mysterious backer.

As often happened of late, when switching the light off, I wondered what new problem would arise on the morrow.

Day 4 (Wednesday)

Some mornings, leaving the comfort of your own bed is just so hard! There is this tiny unrealistic hope that by staying in bed longer, the day would somehow clear itself of any of its daunting chores. There was one I couldn't postpone though; Simba needed to go out. So I dragged myself from under the duvet, put on my slippers and went down to the back garden. The proper walk would wait until after breakfast. I had taken the Ftab with me and quickly checked my messages. Each Foggy had replied in agreement that Ingis Chen had gone too far. However, Sophia, Adam and Christophe were the most moderate. They were the ones who promoted working with him in the first place, with some good arguments in favour of a partnership. Now, even though Ingis Chen had broken our trust, they still pointed out he had been useful and represented us well. They recommended we told him that our decision was temporary, to be reviewed at a later date depending how things evolved and how he acted. This would help in not alienating him and keeping the decision purely professional, as the partnership was with Gatekeepers Associates, not with the Foggies as individuals. The thread of emails between Foggies confirmed that Koplat's position was accepted unanimously. We were still severing the link with him, but doing so diplomatically and leaving room for a change of mind. I decided to call him immediately so that the prospect of this conversation did not ruin my breakfast, a key pleasure of my day.

*

Chen's personal assistant transferred me to him within two seconds.

'Good morning, Yoko. I was hoping for your call. We have much to discuss,' Ingis Chen began.

'Good morning, Mr Chen.'

'Please, will you call me Ingis? I believe we have known each other long enough now.'

'Everything is relative. Anyway, I wanted to discuss with you a few facts that we, at Gatekeepers Associates, have had the displeasure of noticing on your services.'

'This sounds terribly auspicious. What a pity: I was looking forward to a nice chat with you.'

'I don't believe we ever had *a nice chat*.'

'I have always enjoyed talking with you.'

'Thank you,' I replied, without much enthusiasm. By then I was immune to Chen's flattery. 'Going back to the reasons for my call, I am sorry to inform you that in view of your involvement in recent events, specifically leaking information about the Fog's existence and characteristics to the world, and your attempt to kidnap Louise...'

'Kidnapping Louise? Certainly not! I just wanted to help bring her to safety,' Ingis Chen protested.

'Let's not get into the details, shall we? There are many ways to help, and yours were not adequate. Anyway, in the list of your annoying practices, we don't appreciate your repeatedly taking discretionary decisions regarding the Fog and the Gatekeepers without consulting us first. Whether or not you are doing a good job at it, you should not have introduced yourself to governments and the media as our spokesman. We had told you ours was a business partnership only. You are neither our representative, nor our lawyer.'

'Nor your protector?' Ingis Chen snapped. Now the battle had started, I thought.

'This you had agreed to appear to be, as part of our deal to be our business partner. Appear only.'

'Well, if our agreement is now cancelled, this is a pretence I will not maintain.'

'Our agreement is cancelled for the time being until we sort our situation and until you learn your lesson, which is that you need us more than we need you.'

'So you mean that if I am a good boy and keep a low profile for some time, you might reconsider a partnership with me.'

'Indeed.'

'But there is no certainty that would be the case. I don't find this a very attractive proposal.'

'This is not a proposal; this is the situation. You don't know, and we don't know, what the future will bring. Tomorrow – today even - is unpredictable, and this is mostly your doing.'

'Very well. You make no promises. I shall make none. I hope you will not come to regret your decision.' Ingis Chen's deep and beautiful voice was hard as steel.

'I do not wish to make an enemy of you. Sadly in life, whatever you do or do not do, you will always end up having some. I hope you will not decide to be one of them.'

'Good bye, Yoko, and good luck. Until we speak again.'

'Good bye, Mr Chen,' I hung up.

I needed coffee. And breakfast!

After a big breakfast and a long shower, it was time to go out into London for a walk with Simba. I made it to the top of the road until I reached the blockade. There, Phil, always nearby for my safety, told me that it was not a good idea for me to go roaming in the park. He also remarked I shouldn't let the dog off the lead: she was still young and could be snatched away. The thought made me shiver. Simba was too important to me, both emotionally and practically. I would mourn her loss terribly! Phil suggested that he walk Simba instead. I relented and accepted the offer. I knew the man and trusted he would look after my beloved wolf.

Later, I sat at my desk; Simba at my feet, gnawing at a bone. It was time to sort another matter I had been postponing for too long: dealing with the French, Italian, Japanese and even American Embassies. They were attempting to contact me non-stop. I would have to meet them eventually. Once the existence of WII and the healing effect of the Fog were proven, they were bound to request the creation of a Fog door on their soil, and aside from the Americans who would certainly offer the most money, the others would play the emotional card of allegiance to my country or roots. Blah, blah, blah. At present, the only thing I was ready to provide was information and proofs. I contacted Harry and Zeno with the suggestion that we deal with embassies together, being the known Gatekeepers. They were in the same situation as me. We discussed how to proceed and agreed easily, then called Sam to organise the details. The latter grunted that we really made his life more complicated every single day.

The 'Fog health test' was launched afterwards. The hospitals were informed of the opportunity to apply for Fog crossing under specific criteria for a limited number of patients. The plan was that Harry, Zeno and I would go in the afternoon to one of the hospitals, where all the names would have been gathered, and pick the ten 'winners'. The Society was doing a thorough check on each of the 100 people pre-selected. If no one chickened out, they would come to *The Jazzin* tomorrow morning for the crossing. I called Jazz to let her know she should expect visitors tomorrow, and to inform all the Relocated as well.

*

'Yoko! I was about to call you! You have to come!' Jazz answered my call, sounding in the grip of panic.

'What? What's happening?' I asked, anxiety bubbling inside me.

'Clémence! It's Clémence, of course! She took Maisie and Owen!'

'What!' I was shocked.

'She demands weapons in exchange for their return! Oh Yoko, what are we going to do?!' Jazz's voice was cracking. She was holding back tears.

I swore between clenched teeth.

'I am coming now! Where is Nick?'

'I called him on the radio but he hasn't answered yet. It's his morning for boxing practice with Augustus Hoare and Big Tom. This woman is clever, Yoko! She picked her time right. She knew the big guys would be away just now. Poor children! And their father, James - he is devastated. As if the situation was not difficult enough for the family. I hate her, Yoko, I hate her!'

'I am on my way! Stay inside and lock the doors.'

'Already done.'

Running out to inform Phil that I was going to WII, I also called Leila to give her a brief update. I then messaged Zeno and Harry, asking them to pass the news to everyone. Zeno announced he would join me shortly. I thought of Leo, wishing he were by my side. I missed him… I quickly brushed away that thought and contacted Sam to let him know I was going to WII to deal with a problem there. I wasn't sure how the British Government would react to the demand for weapons, so deferred from telling him the details of the issue. Simba sensed my sudden stress and was nervous. Harry was not around, so she would come with me to help my return to London. Sam and McRae were already suspicious something was up with her: I would have to be careful coming back thanks to her gift. All these thoughts zoomed through my mind but none kept my attention for long. Worry for Maisie and Owen, as well as for Jazz's safety, had taken over. As I placed the key in the door of *The Jazzin* and unlocked it, Jazz was immediately on me, pulling me in with Simba, then closing and locking the door again behind me.

'What about James? We can't leave him outside alone,' I said.

'I'm here,' James Fisher said, from the living room. He soon appeared, his face livid. 'My children... I haven't had the courage to call my wife to let her know. I don't know what to do... We must get them back!'

I gave him a hug. He was a good man.

'We will work out something.'

'She wants weapons,' James Fisher said.

'We will think of something. We will. Now, tell me in detail what happened,' I asked them.

'All I know is that Maisie and Owen went in the forest this morning to shoot at birds. They are learning to hunt, as a means to defend themselves as well as gather their own food if necessary. They had guns! Why didn't they use them to defend themselves - you know, against Clémence Hoare and her women?!' The father started to cry.

'They are young. Even I cannot be certain I would be able to shoot someone. Anyway, we don't know what happened there. How do you know Clémence Hoare is behind their disappearance?' I continued.

'A woman left a flower basket for my attention with one of the watchmen from Lil'London,' Jazz answered. 'Inside was a note with Clémence Hoare's demands. Included in the envelope was Maisie's necklace and Owen's diamond earring.'

'Can I see the note?' I asked. I was trying to appear calm and in control to reassure them. In reality, I was working very hard to think what to do next. I had no clue. Jazz went to get the envelope from the table and handed it to me. I opened it and read.

'*Dear Jazz, dear Yoko,*
Your stubbornness and obtuse vision of the situation leaves me no choice but to use drastic methods to get what I need. We have thus taken young Maisie and Owen Fisher hostage. We will only deliver them back to you in exchange for the below. We urgently need them to pursue our fight and win the Women's Revolution. You have it in your power to obtain these for us, I am sure, even though you might have to bend your misplaced principles to achieve this. Maybe, in doing so, you will realise which side you belong to and join the rank of your gender in what is now your world.

You have until Saturday this week to provide us with the following items:

500 rifles, each complete with 500 ammunitions

500 of your two-way radios

500 of your torch lights with what you call batteries.

500 of your military 'rucksacks' equipped with the flasks, knives etc that we saw the Relocated from the British army carry.

2000 of your 'tinned cans' that have high longevity.

Should you not comply with our demands, you will leave us no choice but to punish the two innocent children as an incentive for you to understand we are serious. This brings me no pleasure; this is the price of war. They will bear the price of your inaction and you will have proof of this until you agree to our demands. I deeply regret it has to come to this. However, the goal is too important to let anything stop us.

I trust you will not disappoint.

Clémence H.'

I read the letter several times, and each time, breathing was increasingly difficult. So it was real: Clémence was on the war path. I thought back through history and images of the revolutions and guerrillas mixed with tales of the Amazons.

'Is Clémence Hoare a terrorist?' I thought. Most governments' policy, when dealing with terrorists, is to never negotiate with them or bend to their demands.

The three of us in the house glared at the letter in silence. We were out of our depth on how to deal with terrorists, and aware of it.

'At what time will Nick be back?' I asked Jazz.

'Big Tom told me he would be back around noon. Nick should be with him.'

'They will be on the road at 11.30am, latest. We should be able to contact them by radio in about an hour,' James Fisher added.

'Not that it will change anything. They won't make it any quicker,' I said.

'Maybe, but they won't waste time,' James Fisher said.

'They wouldn't,' Jazz snapped. 'If Big Tom says he will be here at noon, he will be here at noon. He is reliable.' Her protective reaction towards Big

Tom surprised me. She did not need to be.

*

Leila was sombre when she heard the news and the content of the letter. She had no solution to offer us: our means to find and retrieve the two children were limited in WII. She also warned us that the Society would not provide us with any of Clémence's demands. It was against their ethics to provide her with weapons. Tears ran down silently down the father's cheeks, until he could hold it no more and collapsed on one of the sofas, sobbing, head in his hands. My heart ached for him. At 11.30am, we contacted Nick and Big Tom on the radio. First, we asked them not to talk to Augustus Hoare about the situation and the letter, not until we clarified our position. Clemence might consider involving the councils of Lil'London and Newtonsee as an alliance with them. So far, our adopted line of conduct was neutrality: was it time to break it? Then, there was the British Government and the few relocated soldiers in Essex. They trained for various types of mission: maybe they could help? Then again, it would feed the British Government's argument for more involvement from the army if we started to require their help. Maisie and Owen were worth any concessions with our 'allies', though… The only thing not to do was grant Clémence Hoare's wishes, but it twisted my stomach: if all else failed, could we let her harm these children?

*

A knock at the door. It was too early for Nick and Big Tom to be there. I went to the door and, on hearing Leo's voice, I released a big sigh. I had been holding my breath in fear. Leo gave me a warm hug that immediately made me feel better and safer. After a quick hello to Jazz, he went to James, kneeling in front of the man and giving him words of comfort. Afterwards, he pulled me with him to the kitchen to prepare coffee and a large pot of tea for the afflicted father.

'How bad is it?' he asked me, in a low voice.

'Very, very, very bad. We are deadlocked and I can't see any good way to get out of it. Even if we enrol the relocated British soldiers and everyone from Lil'London, Newtonsee and Yerushaleim, there is no certainty that we can find the children and get them back safe. This is a nightmare!'

'Don't they have trackers? I thought everyone wore trackers as a security?' Leo asked.

It had slipped my mind! There was a ray of hope! If we could locate Maisie and Owen, we had a chance to solve the situation. I attracted Jazz's attention for her to join us in the hallway.

'Jazz, has Nick given trackers to everyone here?' I asked her.

'Well, yes. I have this ear clip. But I forget… I keep forgetting to put it on. No one does it.' She looked ready to explode into tears.

'What about Owen? What type of tracker does he have? A watch?' Leo asked, having joined us.

'I don't know,' Jazz answered, distressed at her lack of knowledge.

'Well, as soon as Nick is here, which is soon, he'll check the trackers and we'll have answers. Let's not mention it to James to avoid giving him false hopes that could be crushed too soon.'

Leo finished preparing tea and coffee and we brought the tray to James. I sat next to James, putting my arms around his shoulders. The other two joined me and we waited in silence for Nick and Big Tom to arrive. The air was heavy, the tea tasteless and the coffee bitter.

*

'Owen isn't wearing his tracking ear piercing,' Nick said, in front of the locator. 'The icon shows him in the clearing outside.'

'We have it, the diamond earring,' James said, in a weak voice.

Everyone's jaw was clenched, hoping for better news as Nick switched the tracker to Maisie's.

'Yes! Yes!' He turned to James and pointed at a dot on the top left of the screen. 'She's miles away, but still on the screen. We will find them!'

A surge of relief filled the room.

'Can we track down where she is?' her father asked, adding anxiously, 'When can we go and get them? Now?'

Nick turned to look at him and didn't reply immediately. His eyes narrowed as he assessed the situation and reviewed the options.

'No. We can't,' he replied. 'They already outnumber us and have basic weapons. We need to enlist more people, pinpoint the exact location, and plan a rescue operation properly. We want to minimise the risk of casualties, especially with Owen and Maisie on site.'

'That means we have to involve the councils. Dammit!' Leo reacted.

What was Clémence thinking? Didn't she understand she would push us towards the men she loathed! And how could she threaten the lives of innocent children!?

'It doesn't make sense,' I murmured to myself. 'Clémence is extreme and ready to do anything to reach her goals, but this is not a good move. It is unlike her. Moreover, I don't believe she would harm those children, or that the women in her group would accept it. Children are too precious in their world.'

'Her message is very clear, though,' Big Tom snapped. I whispered louder than I thought.

'There is one thing missing though,' I replied.

'What?' Big Tom and Nick replied in one voice.

'How to contact her,' Jazz replied for me.

'She made it pretty clear she would be in touch by next Saturday latest,' Big Tom retorted, unconvinced.

'I need to see Maud.' I grabbed my 2-way radio to contact her. She replied immediately.

'Maud, I am sorry to ask you this at the last minute, but can you come to *The Jazzin*? Now, if you can? This is urgent.'

'What? Well, I… I… Yes, of course. I will be on my way shortly,' Maud hesitated only briefly.

'Maud, please make sure that you don't travel alone. The journey is not safe any more,' Nick suggested.

'What?'

'Clémence,' I explained.

'Oh! Yes…' Maud murmured, sadly.

*

An hour later, Maud knocked at the door. She was sombre, expecting the worst. Almost immediately, we presented her with Clémence Hoare's letter. Maud read it with a frown, her mouth quivering in anger as she reached the end of the letter. She shook her head.

'This is wrong!' she said, in barely contained anger.

'We couldn't agree more,' Leo retorted.

'Everything about this letter is unacceptable and wrong. Clémence would never have done this! This is ridiculous!'

'Obviously she did!' Nick snapped.

'No, she didn't. She didn't write this letter,' Maud snapped back.

'You have the proof in your hands, Maud,' Leo told her, in a soft yet stern tone.

'It's not her handwriting, is it?' I asked Maud, and turned to my friends. 'Actually, this is why I wanted Maud to come, to authenticate the letter.'

'True. I know her handwriting very well, and it isn't hers. Someone tried to copy Clémence's and made a bad job of it.'

There was silence around the room. What did that mean? Were the Fisher children with Clémence or not? Who wrote this letter? The situation was getting more frustrating by the minute.

'This is giving me a headache! And I can't think with an empty stomach. We should eat something.' Jazz suggested. 'Maybe we could open a bottle too, just to get rid of the stress?'

'Yes to the food. No to the drink. None of us. We need complete focus,' Nick replied immediately, as Big Tom was already on his way to the bar. Big Tom's shoulders fell and he changed direction slightly towards the kitchen instead.

*

'We need to talk to Clémence to know if she has the children or not. And if her demands are real,' I said, over a plate of mashed potato and cold cuts of beef.

'This is ridiculous. How are we supposed to do that? Smoke signals? We are not in Nevada here, playing cowboys and Indians!' Zeno planted his fork in the mash with anger.

'Why don't you call her by radio?' Maud asked, looking round at us with surprise.

'Because we never gave her a radio,' Nick said.

'But, I thought you knew, she took Hoare's when she left,' Maud replied.

We stopped eating and stared at her. So all this time we could just pick the radio up and call?

'No, obviously we didn't know,' Nick stood up and went to fetch his radio, handing it to me. The plates were left untouched from then on.

'Why didn't he tell us?' Big Tom fumed. 'For fuck's sake! We were with him all morning, boxing. You would think he....'

'It's hardly surprising that the council doesn't want us to be in touch with Clémence. That is hardly in their interest.' Zeno commented.

'They are control-freaks!' James exploded. 'It is my children we're talking about!'

'Well, they don't know that...' I stopped in my tracks. Maybe they did know. This was really a big mess.

*

'Clémence, this is Yoko,' I said.

'Yoko. Good afternoon. I was waiting for your call,' Clémence's voice was slightly muffled, but otherwise clear.

'Well, it took us some time to work out how to contact you,' I replied.

'I don't understand. It was in my letter.' This confirmed we did not have her real letter.

'The letter we received was not yours.'

'You are not making much sense.'

'Let me enlighten you.' I proceeded by reading to her the letter we had received. She listened without interrupting.

'No, I never wrote this. The first paragraph is mine. However, I never listed these demands, and would certainly not, not even hint, at harming the Fisher children. Sacrifices need to be made to win the revolution, but not against children. Never. Especially Relocated ones. That would be stupid. Why would I provide you with reasons to officially ally with our worst enemies? You claim to be neutral, which for me is already being against me, but at least you are not with them. I have no wish to turn you officially into a foe.'

'What about the children? Do you have them?' James shouted over my shoulder to the radio.

'Yes, I do, but…' Clémence began.

'You bitch! You whore! Give me my children back!' James immediately reacted with fury.

'I will never harm them. In my letter, I mentioned that I only want to teach every child, yours included, about the purpose of the Revolution and why they should care and be involved. This is only until next Saturday.'

'No! I want…,' James begun.

'So now you know the feeling of being helpless and angry,' Clémence interrupted him, 'at having your life stolen from you. Because your children are your life! Now you realise how unfair it is to be forced into a situation without any control.'

Several of us begun to speak in outrage, but Clémence continued to speak regardless.

'In my letter, I had mentioned weapons; though not as a demand, as an object of negotiation in exchange for anything we could provide you. The towns will continue to receive the trade, technology and weapons from you that they might need, whereas we will not. If, indeed, you claim to be neutral, the least you could do is be fair and trade with us as well. We are the ones who need it most.' Clémence's voice was slightly shaking.

'What you did remains outrageous. Taking the children against their will and the will of their father is unacceptable!' Leo retorted, having been the most composed amongst us.

'Really … And letting you believe that I would harm them, is it better? Trying to manipulate you into a war against me, is that acceptable? Hiding that you could contact me and get some news on Maisie and Owen directly, is this fine? REALLY?'

'Bring my son and my daughter back! Otherwise…' James jumped in.

'Otherwise?' Clémence snapped. 'Please think carefully before you side with the snakes that were ready to have you attack us, and by doing so endanger your children. Maisie and Owen will stay with us until Saturday. They are safe and well and do not mind being with us. Owen, Maisie, please come here.'

We heard muffled sounds. Everyone in the house held their breath, waiting expectantly: then we heard both Owen and Maisie call their father. He burst out crying as he grabbed and cradled the radio in his hand.

'My darlings! Are you ok? Are you hurt?'

'Dad, we are fine. They are treating us very well, aside from not letting us out of their sight,' Owen replied.

'They are teaching me how to cook and sew, and we are talking a lot about what I think the role of women should be, and why I should fight to be respected,' Maisie continued.

'It is like the most boring school trip ever,' Owen took over. 'I don't have any problem valuing women. I think women are awesome. Mum and Maisie are top women. I don't need to be here to learn this. Though it is a bit much to say that women are superior beings…'

'You may go now, Owen and Maisie. Thank you.' Clémence said. 'So, Mr Fisher - satisfied? Your children are absolutely fine and just consider themselves on a 'school trip'. They will be back with you on Saturday. By then, I am certain they will have grasped the importance of women in our society and the changes that must be made. In the meantime, I hope you will agree that we deserve as much help as any other community in this land. I look forward to working out some arrangement when we meet on Saturday. Now I must go. Feel free to contact me when you wish.'

As an afterthought, Clémence added: 'Oh! Please mention to Benjamin Snayth to stop harassing me on this radio. I have no wish to hear his constant rambling and recriminations. I despise the man. Good day.'

'Wait! Clémence - why didn't you call by radio in the first place? Why send a letter?' I asked.

'Writing is better. Each word is weighted and picked with care. Words should always be chosen with care. Spoken words fly away: written ones remain.'

And she cut off the call.

*

After Clémence hung up, we contacted Benjamin Snayth. We told him that we had managed to make contact with Clémence, hoping to get a reaction from him about the children. We needed to know if he knew. All he did was grumble that he hoped we tried to reason with her in being less obtuse. Big Tom tried another approach and went to town for a word with Hoare, regarding his silence about the radio. He explained later that the Council had thought it best not to mention the loss of the radio. It would have further weakened Hoare's position. Also, as we had refused to get involved in their favour, they did not feel they had to keep us abreast with details of their handling of the rebellious women.

'Rubbish!' I thought. 'You intercepted her letter and tried to use us to get to her, to force us into requesting your help. Between Ingis Chen and you, we are surrounded by manipulators!'

I felt anger and frustration, but I had no proof. In the end, we decided not to ask anyone's help. As no harm was done to the children, we had more time to review the situation and try to free them ourselves. If it proved impossible and we had to leave them there for a week, we would make sure we talked to them daily. This was not ideal and it pained James. Yet we all agreed it was better than the risks of an armed action when children were involved, and not just Owen and Maisie.

*

It had been a busy day in London as well, with polemics on the health lottery for crossing the Fog. It had been expected. Whatever people thought of the Fog, the health project and the Gatekeepers, right now, I could not care less. They would discover soon enough that it was all real. Thinking of the future, knots gripped my stomach and throat. I could see only more problems ahead. It was late afternoon; I was on the sofa at *The Jazzin* with a cup of tea, staring through the window at the Fog. My eyes began to tinkle with tears. Leo and Jazz were in front of me and he immediately noticed – had he been looking at me all that time? He came to sit next to me, hugging me tight. Jazz chose this moment to go and disappear somewhere in the house. It felt amazingly comforting. Leo and I talked. We talked a lot, of everything and nothing, and he even managed to make me laugh. I had forgotten how good it was to be with him. Leo took the plunge and invited me out for dinner the next day. I said yes.

The range of feelings and emotions that can be packed into a single day never ceased to surprise me. Anguish and anger in the morning, fear and astonishment at lunch, relief and anger - again - in the afternoon, and tenderness in the evening. Maybe even love.

Day 5 (Thursday)

The day was lined up with meetings. I was looking forward only to the last one: the dinner with Leo. I knew he had wanted to kiss me the night before. He did not because he was unsure if I would welcome it. In truth, I did not even know myself, even if I couldn't leave his side.

*

First, Zeno, Harry and I were to meet with representatives of our respective embassies at 9am. The meeting was in the Society's office, part of the terraced houses, instead of our own home. We had opted for this venue so we could show them the Fog afterwards, if they wished. No crossing it, just showing. So, minutes before the meeting, we were bracing ourselves for the most international official encounter to date; a selection of coffee, tea, orange juice and biscuits on a side table of the meeting room. We had no idea what the outcome of today could be. Leila would 'act' as our Personal Assistant to help us. To the outsiders, it would make sense that we turned to a trusted friend to help us deal with the additional strains and demands, now that we had ditched Ingis Chen. For the Foggies, it would simplify our life not to have to de-brief the Society on everything after each meeting, from now on. They would have the information first-hand when we wished to involve them. It also enabled them to provide faster support.

The meeting table was full. We were already four from our side. Sam and McRae showed up after everyone had arrived and imposed themselves as observers: we let them stay to avoid a scene. The invitation was for two people, maximum, for each government, so we expected eight people with the British, French, Italian and Japanese representatives. At the last minute, we were informed that two members of the Kenyan embassy would join us, as well. Considering they were in the middle of a local crisis due to the Fog, it was difficult to close our door to them. I was surprised the Americans had not sneaked in, too. McRae explained, afterwards, that they had placed a request and applied pressure but the French were adamant they had no reasons to be there unless they had Fog on their territory, like the Kenyans. The Americans relented: they were not keen on revealing this piece of information just yet.

To keep the story of a boring encounter brief, all of the officials, except the Kenyans, were after the same thing: having a Fog Gate on their own territory. The Kenyan Embassy wanted to learn more about its origin, and if there was really no way to learn how to unblock the passage both ways. When we refused the requests of Fog creation, the Japanese protested, in Japanese, that it was my duty to my ancestors (I got the translation later). I replied in English that I did not speak Japanese. I guess that alone had already angered my Nippon Ancestors. The Italians told both Zeno and me that the country faced hard economic times and needed this to boost the morale of our compatriots. The French immediately intervened to say that it was also true for them, and that I should not forget how – should I wish to create a Fog near my hometown – it would benefit all the people I cared about there; specifically my parents. It was basic emotional blackmail. None of the British - Secret Services and Harry included - said a single word. They were in a privileged situation. They should not take us for granted and so I addressed all the people gathered.

'In view of our personal links with the countries represented around this table, we will consider giving you priority on business dealings with Gatekeepers Associates. Also, should our excellent relations with the British authorities deteriorate and should we need to establish ourselves somewhere else, please be certain you would be the first ones that come to mind.'

This was not welcomed with applause by any party. However, none had a chance to react as Leila handed me a note saying we had to end the meeting urgently. I stood up and indicated the meeting was over. Everyone left while Harry, Zeno, Leila and I stayed in the room with Sam and McRae. Within minutes, Rico joined in.

'Frecking terrible! Have you heard?' he exclaimed, coming in. He took one glance at the side table and picked a plate.

'This stresses me out. I need this.'

He then proceeded to pile a selection of biscuits onto it.

'No, they haven't heard yet,' Leila answered. Seeing that Rico already had his mouth full, she continued with a sombre ashen face. 'The Kenyan Fog is gone.'

Rico put down his plate, full of biscuits, in front of me and I automatically took one. I was in shock; it was a reflex.

'Clare,' I mumbled. 'The Fog gone. Oh no... No... And Mary! What about Mary?!'

The table was silent. Rico was in full stress-eating mode. He was stuffing one biscuit after another in his mouth, washing it all down with coffee. I felt faint. I turned to look at Leila and saw tears falling silently down her cheeks. McRae stood up and put one hand on her shoulder, handing her a napkin with the other. Without looking at him, she took it and murmured a thank you. He tightened his grip for a while. I wished Leo was by me. I wanted to snuggle my head on his shoulder and cry. Then, out of nowhere, two arms circled me and my head fell back against a torso. I recognised Zeno's aftershave, and my whole body gave up. I burst into violent tears. Sam came and presented me with a handkerchief. He gave one to Rico and Zeno as well. They were sobbing. Leila broke the silence and, sniffing, told us she had already requested further information and enquiries from her team, but right now we had to get ready to welcome the winners of the Fog health lottery. The ten 'lucky' ones would be here, shortly, to cross the Fog. The second important meeting of the day could not be postponed.

*

After Leila and I quickly went back to mine, to freshen up our faces and use make-up to mask our puffy eyes as best as we could, we met the others outside on the old parking area. A mismatched bunch of ten people was led through, shortly after. A quick look showed them to be between their 20s and 50s; six women and four men of all sizes, weight and skin colours. They shared the same nervousness and - yes, fear. They had been informed of the risk of relocation incurred by crossing the Fog. That they were ready to cross, nonetheless, to save their lives did not mean they were not scared or wanted to be relocated.

I took out my mobile and called Jazz. She was expecting us. She had tea, coffee and stiff drinks waiting. It was time. We led the people to the wooden partition that hid away the Fog and opened the double door. Behind me, I heard their intake of breath at the sight of the wall of Fog. I asked them to make a line and to follow me. Harry and Zeno would come last.

*

Once inside, Jazz greeted us eagerly.

'Hello. Please come in. Please take a seat somewhere, anywhere. Tea? Coffee? Would anyone want something to eat? My name is Jazz. I live here. You will see, whatever virus you suffer from, you will feel better soon!'

'Jazz, I don't think they are here to consume anything, you know,' Harry told her.

'But I'm just trying to be nice! And it is on the house!' she replied, exasperated.

'And that is very sweet of you,' I intervened, as she and Harry started to glare at each other. 'Just, this is no social visit. If I were them, I wouldn't want to linger but check right away whether I am relocated, and if not, go back to the hospital to test my health status.'

'I know, I know,' Jazz nervously brushed a strand of hair from her face. 'This is so rare for me to have new people around. Normal people: not agents, or police, or Society members. Like, people next door. I was looking forward to it so much.'

'Don't worry, there should be new people soon enough,' Harry retorted, rolling his eyes. Those two had little patience for each other these days, even though they both knew they could count on each other if they ever needed help. They had spent too much time in a closeted situation and in the end, their personalities clashed.

*

We began to make each 'winner' cross back through the Fog. Zeno was going with each of them so that they would not be alone if they came out in WII. Also, if one was the missing Facilitator, it would be revealed immediately when he and Zeno exited in London. None were. Most returned to London with relief: they would undergo a thorough medical check-up in the afternoon. However, one person walked along with Zeno to the forest clearing: a dark blonde and petite woman in her mid-20s, jittery and animated. She was wearing a vintage dress from the 80s, conservative aside from her generous cleavage. This woman had two amazing assets and knew how to display them without being provocative, thanks to her otherwise conventional outfit. Rico was going to love her. When Zeno tried to reassure her everything was fine, his eyes found it difficult to leave her décolleté and look at her face. She was too agitated to notice.

'Hi, my name is Jazz,' Jazz jumped in. They were about the same height.

'Hi... Sorry... I am Molly. ... So sorry... I'm a bit lost.'

'Don't worry: it's normal. I was, too, at first. We'll take care of you. So, why don't you take a seat. What would you like to drink? Champagne? Or Wine? Beer? Maybe whisky?'

'I don't really drink... Sorry. Would you have a diet coke?'

Jazz batted her eyes in surprise. I could see her thinking that, in a moment like this, no one should want a diet coke.

'Sure, we do. You are sure you don't want anything stronger?'

'Well... The only drink I like otherwise is coffee martini.'

'I can do that! Wait a minute!' Jazz almost sprinted to the bar and started to prepare the cocktail, leaving Molly even more scared than before.

'So, are you ok? Your life has now irrevocably changed: you are aware of that?' I said to Molly, sitting next to her.

'Yes... But my old life was going to be short anyway if the Fog couldn't cure me. Now I will live. It is true, isn't it? I am healed, aren't I? Sorry, sorry - I know you said it before.' Molly looked really sweet.

'Yes, you are fine now. Whatever it is you were suffering from is gone; at least, if it was a virus. What was it?'

'HIV,' she whispered, without further comment.

'Well. It is gone now.'

Jazz returned with a perfect-looking cocktail glass, along with the sugar coated edges and the coffee bean on the light mousse of the coffee martini. She had taken lessons, one could tell. Molly took a sip and hummed with pleasure. She gave a strained smile to Jazz.

'Delicious. Thank you.'

'There is more where it comes from. I have prepared plenty to be sure you can forget all your apprehensions.'

'Thank you. You are very kind. I don't... It is not... Oh! I'm not making much sense. I...' Molly looked like a fish taken out of its tank, now confused in a large pond.

'Just drink,' Jazz suggested, in a firm tone.

'So, why don't you tell us a bit more about you?' I asked.

'I am a teacher. I teach children aged 8 to 11.'

'Wow! That's great! We could do with a teacher here. They have a lot to learn about us, about our history,' I exclaimed.

'That's what I thought when I heard about this Other World. I said to myself that if I were relocated, my skills as a teacher would be valuable here. And to cheer me up, I thought of the flexibility I would have without the big State administration and guidelines constantly on my back. Hooray for creativity!' Molly said, not looking particularly cheery.

'Can I tell you though, about the HIV?' she added cautiously and tense. 'I don't sleep around, you know. This is not how it happened. My boyfriend, he was not the man I thought he was. He fooled around and caught it, then gave it to me. And the unfairness of it all: it didn't degenerate with him. With me it did, and the treatment doesn't have a strong effect on me.'

'Molly, don't worry about it any more. It's over. You are fine now,' I said to her.

'You are so sure...' Molly sipped her coffee-martini. It was starting to have an effect; she was relaxing.

Harry kindly went to get Simba, stuck at home since the morning and in need of a proper walk. If I wanted to do it myself, I could only take her to the forest. In London, it was not safe for us to appear together alone. I left Molly and Jazz getting slowly drunk in the lounge, where the newly Relocated listened to Jazz' biased information on the communities of WII. Outside, Nick, James and Zeno accompanied me. James looked wan. He had large blue shadows under puffy eyes and might have lost several kilos in a single night. He told us he would rather wait for the return of the children on Saturday than risk them being hurt. He trusted his son and daughter to be strong enough to come out mentally undamaged. As long as he could talk to them every day, he could cope with it.

'I am pleased you reached this conclusion, James,' Nick told him. 'This is what I would have recommended. Although…'

'Although? You think there is a problem with it? Do you think we…' Anguish filled James' face.

'No, there is not. Although I was hoping that Maisie could help us,' Nick said, in a calming voice.

'How could she? She's thirteen! Please don't make her do anything dangerous. I refuse!' James was panicking already.

'James, please. I would not do anything that could endanger Maisie. I would not!' Nick reassured him. 'Only if she could find a way to get her locator to Clémence on Saturday, it would be useful.'

'We could keep an eye on Clémence at all times…' I said, thoughtful. It was a good idea. 'But how could we say this to Maisie without raising Clémence's suspicions?'

'I don't know. I haven't worked it out yet. Until we think of something, we're not going to proceed with the idea. I don't want any harm to come to our wonderful Maisie.'

'It would have to be a very, very safe way of telling her!' James was adamant.

'I think I have an idea,' I said. 'When are you supposed to call them next?'

'Whenever I want!' James replied. 'What is your idea?'

It was simple and it took no time for me to explain. They both agreed it could work. It was dependent on his son or daughter to get the hint, of course. It was worth a try.

*

When we returned to the clearing, Jazz and a jolly Molly were giggling outside the house setting up a table for lunch. Big Tom was looking at them and shaking his head, a big smile on his face. They were struggling at the simple task. He looked at Jazz with a lot of affection, and it struck me he had a crush on her. We told them we had to do something first and would join them for lunch afterwards. Jazz looked happy: I did not want to kill that moment. I also thought of Clare. I had not yet told Jazz about the Fog disappearance that left no doubt of her passing. It would wait until later.

'Maisie, Owen - hello my darlings,' James said to his children. He sounded emotional, even though he was trying to be cool. I wondered if he would have the courage to tell them what we had agreed. He chatted a little more with them and then said to his daughter,

'Darling, my love. I am so sorry; I think I have lost one of your earrings. The one dear Nicky gave you. I have only one.'

'What? No, Dad. You're mistaken. I...' Maisie started to say.

'Don't worry Dad. Maisie has the other one.' Owen jumped into the conversation.

'Ah! Make sure she doesn't lose it, then. She is so forgetful always!'

'What? But no. Of course I won't! Dad!'

'You always lose everything,' her brother interrupted Maisie again. 'Even I would be upset if you misplaced Auntie Nicky's earrings.'

'I...' While Maisie sounded confused, Owen's reaction assured me that he understood we wished the reverse of what James had said, that Maisie would loose her earring and ideally in a 'safe' place among Clémence's belongings.

'Gosh, I am sorry my darling,' James had decided it was enough. 'I am sorry. It doesn't matter. They are just earrings. I love you, my darling. The most important thing is for you to keep safe. I love you, I love you both so much!' He couldn't bear to hear his daughter getting distraught that her father was upset with her, especially in those circumstances.

*

We were about to go back outside for lunch when Leila came in and indicated my presence was needed. With the help of Simba, I returned to London with her. She explained she needed an hour or so to discuss a few things in private and we could do it over lunch. She looked absolutely drained of all energy.

'Yoko, I can't think anymore. I don't know what to do or what to suggest. I feel lost,' she started.

We were sitting outside in the sun, having a simple lunch of salad and sandwiches at a restaurant by the Serpentine lake in Hyde Park. To avoid attracting attention, a cropped dark red wig with a large fringe and large sunglasses covered and changed most of my features. My own mother would not have recognised me.

'I can't believe it, either. Clare gone. And still no news from Mary...' I replied. I had a knot in my voice. I thought of my sister and nephew, too.

'Yes... What to do next? Shall we re-create a Fog portal there and send a search party for Mary? Is she still alive? What about Putu? I'm out of my depth. We all are at the Society. We are your advisors, though we don't know what advice to give you. The safest option is clearly for you not to get involved and not to go to Kenya to create a Fog. Who knows what happened? Whatever it is, it could happen to you! Maybe she was killed by people now waiting to do the same to any of you. Also, if the Kenyan Government knows any of you are there, they would stop you leaving their soil. Same for the Relocated there and their families over there. On the other hand, not reopening the doors would mean leaving Mary – if she is alive - stranded in WII without any means to contact us or return. Plus, there is the Fog withdrawal effect: it could render her mad! We don't know if this is still applicable in this case of Fog disappearance. There again, she might be dead, too, and there is no point opening a Fog Gate... I just don't know...'

'There is no perfect solution. The Foggies will have to come to a tough decision on that one.'

'Whatever you decide, we will try and help as much as we can.'

'Thank you, Leila. And as usual, your support is and will be invaluable.'

'Now, your new Relocated,' Leila opened a file on her tablet to debrief me on Molly. 'She is a teacher, living alone in London. The rest of her family is spread around England. She is part of the peerage of England, has good character reports from her employers, parents and friends. A thorough analysis of her communications reveal her as a kind and dedicated person. Another analysis of her health report confirms the story of her being HIV positive and not responding to treatment. She is both a sensitive character, easily affected by her environment, and a strong personality. Her profiler report indicates she will cope well with the change in the long term.'

'Well, profiling her is very nice, but I don't think anyone could predict depression and breakdown. You can't predict her reactions to fears, to the unknown future, and to the encounter with another planet culture and habits.'

Leila remained silent for a couple of seconds before replying.

'I know. It is still better than having the profile of a sociopath.'

We munched our meals in silence. I did not finish mine - my appetite was limited that day. With Leila's help, I summarised the situation afterwards in an email to the Foggies and the conundrum about Kenya, and asked them their thoughts on how to proceed next. The situation reminded me of the military's motto: 'never leave one of us behind'.

*

'McRae keeps digging for information,' Leila broached a new subject.

'It's his job, isn't it?' I replied, wondering if a BLT sandwich was a good thing to feed a wolf, as I couldn't finish it.

'Yes, but I would rather he didn't dig every sensitive spot.' I looked at her inquisitively and she continued.

'Sam and McRae are smart. They are checking each tiniest detail that does not match in your everyday life. Simba, your links with me, Nick… Their whole department is still attempting to break into the Ftab and the communications between Foggies. They are also still on Helo's case, the boy who facilitated you out of the Fog. They are hunting for him and who he could be. Thankfully, he is out of reach.'

'I am not really worried about the communication investigations. I know you can easily interfere with it,' I winked at her and smiled. 'However, I am more concerned with Sam and McRae's private ones. Those two have good instincts. They seem to scent when something is just worth looking into and they don't give up.'

'I totally agree with you. This is also my main preoccupation,' Leila shook her head, 'which is why I need to update you on our friendship.'

'This is an interesting turn of phrase. Go on.'

'So, my dear friend, we met long ago when I visited your tea shop.'

'That's impossible to check: perfect! I presume you always paid cash?' I asked, with a smile.

'Absolutely! You get my drift. Whenever I came to London, I visited and even worked from your café. We joked that we should have an old-fashioned friendship. We decided that we would be pen pals. We wrote to each other, never emailed.'

'Brilliant! I like that.'

'Exactly. So what do you think? That's a cool friendship we've had!'

'I actually wish we had it for real. It would totally have worked between us. A very private friendship, it explains why nobody else was aware of it. You are a genius.'

Leila parodied a courtesan bow as a thank you, and we laughed. It was a short laugh, the thought of Clare and the tasks ahead cutting it short.

*

Sam called on our walk back to the house. He wanted to check that we knew about the disappearance of the Kenyan Fog. He was aware it meant the person who created the Fog must have died, and that he or she might be a friend of ours. He presented his condolences and added that Kenya was too unstable and unsafe for us to go out there. I believed there was real worry for us in there, not just that the British Government could not afford to lose us on African soil. How I wished I could be an ostrich and just hide my head in the ground for some time!

I couldn't escape it any longer and went to see Jazz, to inform her of what had happened. She would be sorry for Clare and Mary, of course, but mainly she would think of how the same could happen to me, how she could lose me.

'How could it happen? The Society is so efficient usually; they can sort any problem. How about the tracking device - don't they have one, too?'

'We assume that they had to leave the house in a hurry and hide in WII, that they didn't get a chance to take any of the devices,' I told her.

'But… How? What happened? Do you think someone killed Clare?'

'We know nothing, Jazz. Anything is possible. It happened in WII, so it could be a wild animal, a rival bush tribe, an angry Relocated, a snake!'

'And the only way of knowing is to - no! You are not going there! You are not going to reopen a Fog gate there! You can't! This is too dangerous! I… I… I forbid you!' There was no anger in her voice but an incredibly high anguish.

'Jazz, I don't know yet what the Foggies are going to do. We are exchanging emails and ideas on it right now. But you have to understand, we have Mary to think of.'

'She has her bush man! He and his tribe will look after her!'

'We don't know that.'

'This is ridiculous. She could also be dead. They could all be dead! No. You can't go. You are too valuable. If you guys decide that a door must be open, let someone else do it.'

Except promising that I would not go, nothing would reassure her, and this was a promise impossible to make just then. I stayed with her until the last minute when I had to go home for my dinner with Leo. We went for a walk in the woods, staying close to the clearing, under Nick and Big Tom's watchful eyes. She was shaken. I suggested I could stay with her, but she would have none of it as she had high hopes for me and my date. I knew Jazz would cry when I left.

*

Leo came to pick me up for dinner at 8pm. We changed car several times, always under Phil's supervision. In the last one, my chosen wig for the night was black with curls all the way down to my waist. Black contact lenses and vintage glasses with a red rim on top of my nose, I completed the look with a red top and black jeans, red lipstick, and red ballerina pumps. Leo had chosen a restaurant in Ealing, on the edge of London. A large Indian community had established itself there and unsurprisingly, curries were all over the menu. Once the order was placed, Leo took my hand in his across the table.

'I worry about you. Constantly! You are all over the news.'

'I have stopped following the news. I don't have the time or the inclination to care about what people say about me or the Fog,' I announced to him, gravely.

'But… It's important to keep informed!' Leo was taken aback by how resolute I sounded.

'Why? What would it change that I read my critics or praise? It would incur the risk of affecting my capacity to think clearly. Plus, I told you, I don't have the time.'

There was something eerie about knowing that the world was talking, writing and just bitching about you in wonder or in awe, in laughter or criticism, and me not caring. I was surprised by how detached I felt and how much I enjoyed it. I preferred being unconcerned and my spirit not being dampened by the media.

'What about the rest of the news you are missing, that is not about the Fog?' Leo persisted.

'Not enough time in the day for them, either,' I replied, dismissively. 'And you know what? Life has been lighter since I made this choice. It got rid of so much negativity: now I can focus better on the positive in my life. When I can find it.' At least that was my goal. I was still in training.

This made Leo smile and he tightened his grip on my hand.

'Well, I am pleased you are looking after yourself, one way or another. Now, I wanted to tell you something important.'

'Yes?'

'You are not going to Kenya.'

'What? Jeez… I already went through that with Jazz.'

'Maybe, but she did not speak on behalf of Gatekeepers Associates.' That statement surprised me.

'And you are?' I asked, even though I already knew the answer.

'Yes. We had a conference call this afternoon. I organised it last minute. I will be honest with you: I was told you were not available and it suited me. For once, you would not be able to put yourself on the frontline of danger. I told the Foggies that you were already acting as the spokeswoman and front figure for the Foggies and that was enough. It would be impossible for you to make the trip to Kenya incognito and safe. So someone else had to take care of it.'

'Thank you. Even if you should not have kept me out of the call.' The warm wave of relief going through me made me forgive him when I would normally be furious. It lasted only a second, before I worried again. 'Someone else? Who?'

'We are still working it out: the options are limited for a Switcher. Christophe is a new Dad and should be kept out of it. So the choice is between Jack, Rosario and Adam. Rosario and Adam both have specific roles within the company, unlike Jack. He is also the one without dependents…'

'He is also the weakest, psychologically!'

'I know. This is why we are very hesitant. Except him.'

'You must be joking. He wants to go?'

'Yes. He says that he has nothing to lose and that, maybe, it would help him find a purpose.'

'But... Jack?!'

'I know.'

'Jack!'

'I know.'

The first dishes arrived and that gave me a couple of minutes of respite to assimilate the news. When the waiter left, I went on. 'Right. So let's say that Jack is going to Kenya to create a Gate. It is useless without a Crosser and a Facilitator with him. I am afraid to ask...'

'That was actually easier. Tony volunteered to be the Facilitator. Mitch and Zeno went there already, so they were ideal choices as Crossers. Mitch will go, but Zeno can't. He is the Crosser known by the public and it would be too dangerous for him.'

'So Crosser and Facilitator are sorted.' I had a sense of foreboding: it was too easy.

'No, not really. We believe it would be too dangerous for Mitch and Jack to wander in the wild, just the two of them. So I will go with Mitch,' Leo said.

'No!' I exclaimed aloud. Everyone stopped to look at me. Phil frowned and Leo discreetly shook his head, indicating to him we were fine.

'No! No, no, no, no, no!' I repeated in a lower voice.

'Lovely Nutty, think about it: it makes sense. We all agree we must check on Mary. We cannot leave her there alone, without knowing whether she is alive and safe. This is why Gatekeepers Associates exists: to watch each other's back. A team must go. And two people are not enough. Really, there should be several of us there, but we cannot afford the risk of losing more than two Crossers.'

'We cannot afford to lose ANY Crossers! This is beyond ludicrous! Mary needs us, we must go, but you, no!'

'Yoko...'

'Please, don't go. Please... Please...' I was pleading now.

'Yoko, I am sorry. I must.'

He couldn't go. He couldn't. I knew in that moment that I could not bear to lose him. Despite how hard I had tried to bury my feelings deep down, I loved him. I did not want to and was scared of feeling attached right now, but it was too late. Maybe Leo read this in my eyes, or maybe he had known all along, he leaned forward and kissed me. I kissed him back, hungrily.

Day 6 (Friday)

I woke up at the sound of Simba howling and scratching at my door. Being outside my room was meant as a punishment for last night. I had come back with Leo, and as he joined me in my room, Simba had followed. She had not taken his intentions very well and had been determined to protect me against his passionate Italian assaults. For Leo's sake, I had to put her in my home office, next door, which did not go down well with her. She howled to the moon. I went to calm her down before she woke the whole neighbourhood. When I came back to the room, the moment was gone. Leo took me in his arms, kissing me goodbye, saying he must go and get some sleep as he was leaving early the next day for Kenya. Leo whispered in my ear that he would continue where we left off, upon his return, making sure this time to charm not one but two females, Simba and me. After he was gone and although it wasn't fair on Simba, I was upset at her for ruining the night with Leo and so decided to leave her outside.

Now, thinking of Leo leaving towards unknown dangers in two different worlds, my heart felt sick. My Ftab rang and I answered it, walking downstairs with Simba.

'Hello, Leila,' I greeted my friend.

'Yoko. I'm sorry I did not tell you about Leo. He asked me to keep it quiet.'

'I know. When is the flight?'

'Later this morning, but they are already on their way to the airport. Tony and Mitch are unknown to the authorities and the public as Foggies, it is easy for them to travel. For Jack and Leo, it is more complex. The British government knows them. So first, we must ensure to lose their tails, and then they will travel in disguise with false IDs and special make-up that will fatten and age them. Not simple, but we are almost there. The Foggies will reunite in the plane from London to Nairobi.'

'OK.'

'Once there, we will create a temporary Gate, like you did, by switching a small cabin that can easily be dismantled and destroyed. Our local team has already rented a villa with a park for this purpose. We…'

'Leila, will they be safe?' I interrupted her.

'You know that I can't give you the answer you want. I can't give you full guarantees,' Leila replied with sadness.

*

I took a couple of minutes to prepare a cup of coffee on my way out, which I drank in the back garden as Simba was doing her most urgent needs. 'Meditation, that's what I need. Yes, I should start meditating,' I thought. I tried to empty my mind and think as little as possible. I focused on how the hot bitter liquid slowly woke my body up, and on the beautiful day to come. The peace and quiet did not last more than a few seconds.

So I called Jazz to reassure her that I would not go to Kenya. She wanted to know about my date with Leo, but I brushed the subject away. It would lead to talking about his departure, and I was not ready for that yet, not before a sturdy breakfast. I would visit her later and would tell her everything. She chatted away. It was nice to listen to her, coffee in hand, in the peace of the morning.

With Molly as a new recruit, Jazz and Maud had decided to get more involved in the current events of Lil'London and Newtonsee. Jazz, after researches online and long talks with Maud, had decided to offer a different approach to Clémence's Revolution in favour of women's rights, using political pressure and diplomacy. In brief, they planned to create a political movement as an alternative to the frustrated women, enabling the Council to make concessions without appearing to bend to the Revolution's demands. Jazz and Maud presented themselves as a positive counter-offer to women's freedom. Maud was taking risks. Her position as the wife of a member of Lil'London Council could jeopardise both her credibility and his. Also, this would stir Clémence's ire. They had to tread carefully. The whole situation reminded me of Sinn Féin, the Irish political party extolling separation of Northern Ireland from the British Isles. The party was often portrayed as the political branch of Irish terrorism against England… Definitely, Maud, Jazz and now Molly's endeavour could appear as such for the Women's Revolution. They were treading on dangerous territories. As I listened and despite foreseeing new problems ahead, their energy made me smile. I approved their position, appreciated their strengthening bond and liked how they united with a purpose. Jazz had been careful to avoid asking me to get involved. It was getting boring, this constant diplomatically correct attitude. Thinking back on history, I was inclined to adopt what many diplomats had done before me: maintain a neutral façade and less than neutral practices behind closed doors… The thought brought up a smile. Cronyism was a given between Jazz and me; of course she would have my support. We just both knew it was unofficial.

*

Laughter filled the house back inside. I followed the origins of Zeno's unmistakable guffaws to the dining area and noted Harry, Zeno, and Rico around the table watching the screen of one of their tablets.

'Yoko! Have you seen this?' Rico exclaimed, leaving some room for me to watch the screen.

'No, I don't watch the news any more.'

'Come! Come! Sit!' Zeno pulled a chair. 'You are going to love it.'

'Wait,' Harry stopped the video and eyed me up. 'Have you had breakfast?'

'Just coffee,' I answered.

'Not sufficient,' Harry stated and stood up.

'Yeah. She might not think it's funny if she's hungry,' Rico agreed. 'You want some tuna omelette?'

I pulled a face. His famous protein-boost-tuna-omelette breakfast 'treat' smelt and looked disgusting. I could never get used to the sight of it. I was not going to put this thing near my mouth. Not for my sacrosanct breakfast.

'Rico!' Harry shouted from the open kitchen. 'You are making it worse. We want her to eat, not throw up.'

Rico's face fell and he mumbled something about the English or

Scottish experience being no better. Then his eyes fell on the screen again and he giggled.

Half an hour later I was crying out with laughter, watching a spoof news report from the Other World. Without proper information of what WII was like, they had envisioned the population of a Palaeolithic village. Each villager was in awe at our arrival and treated us like God after we used a lighter to start a camp fire. Yet behind the fake huts, aliens were controlling the Paleo human - in reality robots - and having a blast on how they were fooling Harry, Zeno and me. The spoof show was excellent and so well done! We browsed for more like this, and sure enough, several mockumentaries were already online for our entertainment. We watched many. We had not laughed like that in the house for a very long time. Sadly, it stopped when we came across one that, contrary to the others, had a sour taste. People with all kinds of physical malformations were made to cross the Fog and would emerge on the other side looking like fashion models. This was a dangerous concept in a vain world and certainly not one that we wanted affiliated with the Fog. It was important we were not considered as a miracle solution to cure everyone and everything! The Fog was limited to viruses and eliminated only harmful external elements to the body. Images of wealthy millionaires' wives after the perfect skin and perfect body, trying to bribe a crossing, went through my head. Harry closed his Ftab, saying he was beginning to see my point about spending too much time online.

'Ridiculous. These people are stupid!' Rico said, waving his hands vehemently. 'Don't they know they are making things worse with this type of show!'

'Rico, we did laugh earlier,' Harry told him. 'Probably everyone aside from us is laughing at this.'

'Only we realise, or care, what consequences the last video might have,' I added. 'They are just making fun.'

'Bastardi! Well, I am going to prepare more coffee!' Rico stood up and left the room, annoyed.

*

The doorbell rung and Rico changed trajectory to open it. We were not expecting visitors and it was either someone from the Society or from the British Intelligence. McRae and Sam both came in and joined us in the dining area. McRae took one look at the table and disappeared into the kitchen, coming back with two cups and two plates. He put a paper bag full of pastries on the table and was about to pour coffee for Sam and himself but the jug was empty. With one glance towards the kitchen where Rico was busy, he knew a fresh brew was coming and sat down. Sam, in the meantime, had opened his laptop. His seriousness was not a good sign.

'Penny Thompson. Do you know her?' Sam asked.

'The name is familiar,' Harry replied, looking pensive. Of course we knew who Penny Thompson was! She was the journalist who, informed by Ingis Chen, had spread the news of the Fog's existence to the world. She was also Michelle's mother.

'The journalist?' I replied, after Harry.

'Yes, the journalist. Well, she claims her daughter has disappeared,' Sam continued.

'Shouldn't we wait for Rico?' McRae asked. 'What about Leila, isn't she here? I thought she was helping you as your assistant now?'

'If you had informed us earlier of your visit, she would be here.' As I said this, the doorbell rang. McRae stood up to greet Leila with a charming smile and kissed her on both cheeks before going to the kitchen to get her a cup and a plate. Leila shook her head with a smirk to indicate there was nothing between them but she enjoyed the flirting. Once everyone, including Rico, was at the table and drinking fresh coffee, Sam spoke again.

'So, as I was saying, the journalist claims that her daughter's disappearance would not be our problem if she were not claiming, as well, that her daughter Michelle is a Facilitator abducted by the US Government, along with her ex-husband and his new wife. The US Government denies the claim but the army refused her access to her ex-husband's home, alleging that the area is closed off for military operations. She also asserts that she had to go into hiding for her own protection.'

'Interesting,' Harry commented. 'May I have an almond croissant?' Rico handed him a croissant with pride at his friend's nonchalance.

'You are not going to do your act again, are you?' Sam looked round at each of us. 'Haven't we proven, McRae and I, that we are your allies?!'

'What is it that you want from us? You haven't asked us anything,' I retorted.

'Is it true?' McRae asked. 'Is Michelle Koplat-Thompson a Facilitator?'

'What did the US Government say?' Rico asked.

'Nothing. They give us no information, even though they ask us to part with ours.'

Harry, Rico and I looked at each other: it was our call. Each of us nodded slightly in favour of talking.

'Penny Thompson is correct. The Koplats house is a Fog Gate, and the US government has indeed taken it over,' I told the spies.

'And Michelle?' Sam asked.

'The US Government is not being a fair partner to you guys!' Rico blurted, his mouth full of carrot cake. He washed it down with coffee before continuing. 'They don't want to admit it, but they have their own Fog and they are trying to get as many Relocated soldiers as possible there. I bet they think it is a race to who will have a better knowledge and control of the Fog first! Typical...' he took another mouthful of cake and had to focus on chewing. McRae took this opportunity to speak.

'And are they working with Foggies, as well?' he asked, not mentioning Michelle this time. He knew we are not prone to give information on other Foggies.

'Not as far as we are aware. That is a point they will certainly not want to let you know. You are ahead of them on this.'

'Cool,' McRae said, while staring at Leila who ruthlessly ignored him.

'So the Americans are following their own agenda...' Sam said.

'Don't they always?' Rico cut in.

'Interesting...' Sam finished.

'See - you and I agree,' Harry told him.

'That still leaves blank the roles of Penny Thompson and her daughter in all of this,' McRae intervened, moving his eyes off Leila for a brief instant.

'You know there are other Foggies around the world, and you know that we watch each other's back. We will not give you details on them if we can avoid it. I am sure you understand this, Lochy,' I told McRae. Calling him Lochy immediately made him turn and give me his dangerously charming smile. Leila could not possibly be immune to it.

'Let me make a guess: Penny Thompson must be a Facilitator or a Crosser. She travels all the time, so she can't be a Switcher. She was travelling when the Americans went to the house and that is how she escaped,' Sam stated. 'Now the next question is, are they all safe? Her daughter, ex-husband and the new wife?'

We didn't answer his question immediately, as we all shared the same thought: Sophia was the Crosser, not Penny. Be that as it may, we had a Facilitator unaccounted for and it could be Penny! It would make sense. So far, the Foggies of each original Fog were connected in some way, by genes or deep friendship. Should we try to check Penny Thompson as a Facilitator? I made a mental note to discuss it with the boys and Leila afterwards. Harry was the first to emerge from his thoughts.

'They are safe, both from the authorities and anyone else. Don't worry about it.'

'Good to know,' Sam replied. There was a moment of silence.

'Well, I guess we can leave the American deal with Penny Thompson to sort the situation themselves. What do you think, Leila?'

'McRae, I know the girl is pretty but will you please stop flirting?' Sam snapped at McRae.

'What? I am just asking?' McRae replied with a not-so-innocent pout.

'Lochy, thank you for valuing my opinion,' Leila replied. 'Yes, you should let the Americans deal with that one. Still, the attention is bound to turn to London and eventually, she will contact the Foggies here. She is a mother who wants answers. She will open as many doors as possible to find her daughter. I would.'

'I think we should meet with this Penny Thompson,' Harry broke in and caused a new silence. My previous thoughts and his matched.

'That is logical and should be easy to organise. She broke the news about the Fog,' I supported him. 'She is on the front row when it comes to the Fog story in the media. Whether or not we approve of her doing so, she deserves our attention. Let's organise an interview,'

'What!' Rico exclaimed. His Ftab beeped. Reluctantly, he checked his message and gave a quick look at Leila. He took a few seconds to read it and then sat back in his chair, calmer.

'As I was saying, let's organise an interview,' I continued. 'That will confirm her statements on the Fog and show that we care about her distress regarding her daughter. Plus, we will then have a better idea of what she knows and what she wants.'

'I like the idea,' Rico said, in a high-pitched unconvincing tone. Whatever Leila had sent him had worked.

'Yoko, shall we look into it later?' Leila asked. 'Do you know how to contact this woman?'

'Not yet,' I smiled at her. The Society and she would work their magic in no time.

'Good. So that is one subject closed. Now, Kenya.' Sam closed one folder on his screen and opened a new one. 'The Kenyans have asked our Prime Minister for support in their situation of crisis, and for you to go to Kenya and reopen the Fog Gate.'

'No,' I replied without beat.

'They insist that would be a good way to prove that you can indeed create the Fog and the gates to that Other World,' Sam added without enthusiasm or conviction, only reading his instructions.

'We already proved the health benefits of the Fog yesterday...' Harry began.

'About that...' McRae interrupted.

'And I think it will be enough for now,' Harry continued, ignoring McRae. 'The rest will come in its own time. Yoko has enough to deal with right now, without having to fly to Kenya in an insecure environment. Even if she wanted to, we would not let her. We don't know what caused the death of the local Switcher. I – we!- will not put Yoko in a situation where she could face the same fate. No.'

'You did not let me finish. I was informing you of what the Kenyan

Government requested. Our Government relayed it, but did not approve of it,' Sam said.

'I am relieved,' McRae interrupted again. 'I did not want Yoko on a plane to Africa. Not a place for such a valuable –and gorgeous - lady. Pleased that you will not go of your own accord on the side, either.'

'Thank you, Lochy,' I gave him a grateful look.

'You see me glad too,' Sam smiled at me, a true smile. 'I would not have cared for the position of our Government on that one. Stay put, right here in London.'

Not for the first time, I felt a wave of warmth, Whatever the odd and stressful events in my life over the past six months, I was lucky to have around me people who cared. I believed Sam Riverson and Lochy McRae to be trustworthy, even if I was still cautious about them. They had been invaluable of late.

'Going back to the Health Lottery of yesterday: the results are amazing!' McRae went back to an earlier point. 'Every single test result came back clear. They are all healed.'

'Well, that was expected,' Harry replied. He was rather snappy with Sam and McRae of late.

'By you, yes. By the 'winners' of the lottery, it was more hope than expectations,' McRae corrected Harry. 'The rest of the world was failing in giving you the benefit of the doubt.'

'Have the results been announced to the press yet?' I asked McRae.

'We stood no chance of hiding the information from the general public for long.' Sam replied. 'What has happened to Ingis Chen, by the way? He would have made a press conference on the results.'

'Aye, Ingis Chen's silence is not to my liking,' McRae commented.

*

It turned out that the media had jumped on the information like children in a puddle. There were still sceptics who claimed this was all a hoax, although the purpose of such artifice was unclear, even to them. The rest of the morning we went through each result and analysed the comments and responses from the press on the healing powers of the Fog. The existence of another World beyond the Fog had been relegated to secondary information. For now. It was less easy to prove and so far, Molly had kept a low profile. She was the only one who had not appeared in the press, nor made a public declaration on her healing. Already, several lobbying groups demanded access to the Fog, either for further analysis or for urgent medical cases.

It was past lunchtime when we separated. Tony, Mitch and Leo were already in a plane flying across land and sea towards Nairobi, Kenya. In an attempt to escape and empty my mind, I decided to go for a walk in the woods of WII. Nick insisted on coming with me but I told him I needed to be on my own for a while. He puffed and grunted and finally seemed to give in, only to announce he would follow at a distance and that I would be none the wiser. When telling Jazz my wish to go for a walk, it was like pressing the replay button. A simple walk to clear my head, that's all I wanted!

Simba understood from my choice of shoes that we were headed to WII and she led me there without my asking. We were twenty or thirty minutes into the walk and my overall tension was beginning to recede, when the howl of a wolf nearby made both Simba and me stop. There had not been any wolves heard around Woodfellas in months, not since Lil'London had organised watches day and night to protect us. It took Simba by surprise, too. Another howl sounded, closer, after which Simba replied by a long deep howl of her own. I was unsure how to react. Were we safe? Was Simba threatened in any way? Was I? Seconds later, Nick was by my side with his shotgun raised and ready to shoot at any wild animal coming our way. No one spoke: we were intent on listening for any noise revealing signs of danger. Another howl. Again, Simba responded. Then she made a few hesitant steps forward. Nick and I remained motionless, observing her. I longed to understand what was said between her and the howler. Simba turned and looked at me, straight in the eyes, and my blood turned to ice. She was asking me to let her go. I didn't know how I understood the plea in her eyes, but I did. Simba wanted to go, she needed it, and I didn't have the right to stop her. She was a wolf, she was my companion, but I didn't own her. I nodded to her and smiled, mouthing a soft 'go'. She looked at me for several seconds, then turned towards the forest, remaining still. Time seemed to have come to a standstill. Abruptly, she ran away. Soon I lost sight of her. I had lost Simba. She was gone. Nick remained silent by my side and I felt incapable of moving. My eyes kept searching the depth of the forest for her, hoping she would come back. More howls broke the peace of the forest, and I recognised Simba's. They all came from the same area. My hands were frozen and I shivered, despite the summer warmth. Nick put his hand on my back to nudge me into motion. I told him I wanted to go home. He nodded, and we returned to Woodfellas in silence.

*

Once in the clearing, he invited me to his cabin for a cup of tea. I didn't want to talk about what had happened, not even to Jazz, so I accepted. Nick knew how to be a silent friend. I was heartbroken. The tea he offered me was very milky and over-sweet, a bit sickening, the way the English prepare it for someone in deep sorrow. It worked though and I sipped it slowly. Simba had grown to be a part of my new life, a part of me. It was rare for us to be separated. She would know when I was tense or sad, and she would come to play, console and change my moods for the better. She was a *confidente*, a companion, a friend, loving me whatever I did and only asking me to love her too. Simba reminded me to live in the present and enjoy the simple pleasure of life. She reminded me to care about something else than just the problems I faced. It was not her invaluable capacity to make me cross to both worlds that was on my mind as I cradled my cup of tea in my hands: it was my bond to her as a friend. Little by little, the worry crept in, taking over the feeling of loss. Would she be ok? Would the other wolves welcome her amicably? How would she survive in the wild? She was not prepared. She had never fought or hunted for food in her life. Gosh! Why did she have to go?

The image of Leo popped into my mind. This was a lot in one day: Simba gone, and Leo, on his way to the most dangerous place for a Foggy currently known. I had wasted so much time with him. More exactly not being with him. Why? I could be so stupid! I was shaken out of my dark thoughts by Nick as he came to sit by me and put his arms around my shoulders. My body tensed. Nick felt his contact was not welcome and he retrieved his arm. Poor him, I thought: he did not deserve that.

'Nick, I am sorry...' I began.

'Don't mention it,' he replied, sipping some tea.

'Simba. She is more than a pet to me, and...'

'I know. I am sorry.'

'I must tell you. Leo...' I took an intake of breath. 'He left today for Kenya. With Tony and Mitch. They must try to find Mary and understand what happened to Clare.'

'I see. And you are worried about him, too.'

'Yes.'

'That made you realise you are more attached to the man than you wanted to admit to yourself.'

'Yes.' How come any friend seemed to read me like a book and I was the only dumb one who couldn't accept the obvious?

'You took your time.' There was kindness behind his words.

'I can be a bit slow sometimes...' I tried to smile. It was a pathetic attempt of a smile.

'Well, I'll have to get used to women being slow into action. The women of Lil'London or Newtonsee will not be any faster, especially with what is going on around here right now. Let's not even mention the women of Yerushaleim.' Nick sighed. If he was trying to cheer me up, it worked. I imagined him trying to woo one of the local women. He was a very eligible bachelor in this world, but the prospect of an either over-submissive or revolutionary wife would scare any man.'

'What about Kim? She is attractive. And Molly? Cute, no? There is Jazz, too!'

'We'll see. Anyway, they are not the one I fancied the most,' he winked at me. 'And Jazz is already engaged elsewhere.'

'Excuse me? Jazz?'

'Come on, haven't you noticed? There is definitely something going on between Big Tom and her.'

The match between the strong, bald, tattooed and pierced builder from East London with dodgy connections and the posh sophisticated fashion conscious half-Asian, half-Caucasian woman was not an obvious one. There again, Big Tom had proved a valuable addition to Woodfellas, a good chef, a protector and a good companion for Jazz. And she was showing more flexibility and adaptability to her new life than I expected. The two of them shared a lot of time together, and they had a simple complicity and understanding that make a good base for a deep and lasting relationship.

'Do you know if they are already more than friends?' I asked Nick. I was berating myself to even have to ask. Jazz was my best friend. I should have been more observant. Had I been that bad a friend lately? Why had Jazz not told me?

'I don't think so. In my opinion, they are growing fond of each other but haven't realised the implications of their bond yet. More tea?'

'Sure.'

'Cookies?'

'Need you ask?' I answered, with a grin.

A wolf howled again in the background and my heart felt a pinch. Maybe Simba would be back soon? Maybe she just wanted to say hi to her family and she would join me tonight?

*

Following that last idea, I decided to stay at Jazz's for the night and organised for Harry to come to get me first thing in the morning. Jazz was thrilled. We both wanted to spend some time together. As Molly was keen to get to know me a little better, the three of us would have a drink together before dinner, and then Jazz and I would retire. Molly was good-natured and readily agreed. She aimed to work on reorganising her old life as a Relocated as soon as possible and had her hands full for the evening. It was no small task. She was under pressure from journalists around the world to disclose information on her whereabouts, regained health and plans for the future. It was the same for the members of her family. Nonetheless, she did not want to satisfy them with any information until she had clarified to herself where she stood in her unknown future and daunting external pressure. Neither Jazz nor I could blame her: we knew the feeling…

Jazz noticed that Simba was missing from my side and that my spirits were down, drowned even, but acted as if all was normal in Molly's presence. It did not take her five seconds, after she closed the door behind Molly, to ask me what was up and where was Simba. I burst into tears and told her everything I had on my mind and heart. I told her about Simba, about Leo and about Nick. I went on about my fears about Kenya, about the dangerous silence of Ingis Chen, about the looming issue of the demands of health crossing by sick people. I was mentally drained. I was so exhausted I couldn't even sleep any more.

'You keep trying to think and do for the best of everyone around you. You forget that you are a human and that you ought to think of yourself as well, otherwise you won't be able to hold on for long. Be careful, Yoko. You will not be able to help anyone if you don't look after yourself.'

'There is no holiday from being a Switcher.'

'I know, but you are still a normal person aside. You risk a burn-out.'

'I do have to have mini-breaks! Look, I went for a walk today for that purpose! Or now, spending the evening with you. Or the day in Scotland. It's not as if there aren't plenty of other things I should work on.'

'Yes, but do you feel bad about it? Because if you do, it spoils the breaks.'

I thought a little about that one and concluded,

'No… I don't feel bad about it. I am no Super-hero and glad to be able to say '*Time for me-time*'. It's the worry that is the worst to bear.'

Jazz couldn't think of any comforting words, so she poured more bubbly in my champagne flute.

'Now, enough about me. Tell me more about YOU,' I asked her.

'Well, Big Tom and I are getting ready for when *The Jazzin* will be the trendiest place on both planets! I think the waiting list is going to be long… We'll have to find a way to prioritise. We still have a problem with both councils, as they are strongly monitoring visitors. They are really doing their best to dissuade women and children to even come close to the woods. Only the men with an interest in trade are coming, and hesitantly at that. More often than not, as Zeno is wandering the lands, they don't have to. Whatever! Time will come for *The Jazzin* to be full and the beat will groove this land! '

'I think you might have to expand a little,' I laughed, and added, as a nudge for her to talk, 'Big Tom and you seem to make a good team.'

'Yep,' Jazz nodded, avoiding my eyes.

'Anything you want to tell me?' I tried.

'Nope. Not really. Not sure yet,' she replied with an uncertain note in her voice. I waited. She soon continued. 'The more time he spends here, the more I get used to having him around. I miss him when he leaves. I know what you are going to say… It is true: I like him. He is really sweet and helpful. He looks after me without ever trying to control or dominate me. This is so respectful. Not once has he tried to take over *The Jazzin*, or been upset if I didn't follow one of his suggestions!'

'It sounds like he has a great nature.'

'Yes. But…' She bit her lips, hesitating. I waited. 'He isn't really my type.'

'Physically?'

'Yes. He is almost twice my size. It's ridiculous! And he is bald. And yes, he is strong, but he also has a beer belly. Oh! Let's not forget the tattoos. I hate tattoos. They are just so vulgar.'

'Tattoos are also called body art. It depends how you see it. You can work on that.'

'Also, we don't really have the same education, you know…'

'You mean you don't belong to the same world. Except that now you do.'

'Ha-ha. Very funny.'

I smiled. It was an involuntary pun. She knew it was the truth.

'I know what you are thinking, Yoko, and I agree. It's the personality and the person that count most of all.'

'Well, yes. Still, physically, it would help if you were attracted to him…'

Jazz smiled back at me with a mischievous smile. Now that was good news!

Day 7 (Saturday)

Jack, Mitch and Leo had arrived in Kenya. From tonight, they would be off the grid for a week. Anxiety about it woke me up in the early hours of the day. I opened my eyes, gasping for breath, my heart and lungs constricted by a seemingly heavy burden weighing on my chest. The situation was ridiculous. Just a few months back, Jack was a young fashion student, Mitch a mountain guide and Leo a web master and B&B manager: they did not belong to the wild bush of Africa, let alone the Africa of another earth. And yet part of me wished I could have gone with them to Nairobi: the new portal was a tree house! How brilliant! Even though it was basic enough to be destroyed easily when the time came, it still had a proper kitchenette and a shower, with a little living area and a bedroom with two twin beds. Leo had given me a Skype tour the previous night. The Society had outdone itself again, and we were suitably impressed. It was risky, as we had no way of knowing if that tree also existed in the WII. The alternative of a grounded Gate could also be amidst a family of lions, so I much rather a risky tree.

Waking up without Simba by my side did not help lift my spirits either. The bed felt empty and cold. A double espresso was in order. In fact, desperate times called for desperate measures: I would make a full pot of strong coffee just for me. I walked down to the kitchen in my shorts and frumpy T-shirt and prepared a large mocha pot in the old-fashion Italian style coffee maker. Just as I was pouring my first cup, my Ftab beeped a message from Leila who wanted to know if I was awake, and if yes, could she pop by for a chat. Leila was now one of my favourite people: my answer was an immediate yes. I took out another coffee cup for her and put the kettle on to prepare tea in case she wished for some. She was at the door just as I was slicing a baguette for breakfast. The smell of coffee made her smile, or maybe it was the sight of me with my frumpy outfit and messy hair.

'How long do they last?' she asked, pointing at the hotel slippers I was wearing.

'One week, if lucky.'

'Do I need to restock you?'

'We still have 8 or 9 pairs since your last supply, so it's fine for now.' I should explain that Simba had a slipper addiction. She couldn't see any without gnawing at them. Gone were my beloved fluffy blue-starred slippers, and gone were many pairs after them. Leila had taken it upon herself to supply us with a bunch of disposable hotel pairs. Simba had gone through slippers from Shangai, Cape Town, Berlin, Dublin, Vancouver and more. She was well travelled.

*

Leila needed to see me about Penny Thompson. The journalist had jumped on the offer to meet with us and ask about her daughter, in addition to getting our side of the Fog story. She was already on her way to London. Leila suggested the earlier we met the better, so the interview was set for mid-afternoon. Penny Thompson had also eagerly agreed to come to ours and cross the Fog. I wondered why she was taking the risk. Maybe she was unwell or simply, should she be relocated, she hoped to reunite with her daughter. Not for the first time, I wondered if I would take the risk to cross in other circumstances.

'Nick told me about Simba. I am sorry...' Leila broke my reveries.

'I don't really want to talk about it.... The call of the wild... I had no right to stop her,' Against my own will, my eyes began to water. I told myself to get a grip, but only another knock at the door helped me hold my tears. McRae stood with a large bag full of pastries in one hand, and a box with eight large Starbucks cups of coffee in another. He looked me up and down, his eyes twinkled and his mouth broke into a large grin. I let him in without a word, my eyes fixed on the coffee he was carrying. He went directly to the dining room and put the box and bags down on one of the tables. He then went to the kitchen to grab plates, filling one with fresh pains au chocolat, croissants and raisin pastries. He then kissed Leila on both cheeks, did the same to me, put a Starbucks cup each in front of Leila and me and sat down, a pain au chocolat already in his hand. Leila looked at him enquiringly, while I focused on savouring my gift cappuccino. I couldn't make up my mind what I would have next: a croissant or a pain au chocolat.

'I was told you came for a visit and thought it would be nice to pop in and say hi,' McRae said to Leila.

'What if it was a girlie catch-up?' Leila asked.

'I took my chances. I just pre-empted the arrival of one of the Foggies,' McRae replied. 'Always such a privilege to have a moment with two beautiful ladies on my own.'

'Lochy, you are such a Casanova,' Leila told him with a smile.

'Absolutely not. I am just an amateur of the beauties Mother Nature provides us.' Leila and I rolled our eyes in unison.

'Spill the beans, Lochy. You didn't come here just to see me or sneak a view at Yoko in the morning, even though she is pretty damn cute,' Leila said.

'I have to agree she is. The bird's nest hair is a winner. And the shorts are delightfully short,' McRae bent over to check out my legs under the table.

'Lochy, what do you want?' Leila said. I was munching and sipping, nonplussed by all his smooth talking. Breakfast was my priority. I did not care about his flirting; I knew that he really had eyes for Leila only.

'Sam and I were wondering about Jack and Leo. We haven't seen them since yesterday. They have suddenly disappeared from our radars,' Lochy conceded.

I indicated to Leila, with a gesture of the hand, that I would take care of that one.

'They have gone on a little trip. Foggies' business. Don't worry about it,' I told him with a sweet smile.

'Foggies' business?' McRae repeated my words.

'Yes,' I took a bite into my second croissant.

'Is this a safe business trip? Something that doesn't involve the African continent?' McRae asked, casually. The three of us knew it was a pretence: there was nothing casual on that subject.

'I am afraid there is no such thing as a 'safe trip' in our life anymore,' I replied.

'Then maybe we should have been informed to help increase the safety for whatever business you are referring to,' McRae commented, his hand over the pastries plate, hesitating on which to pick. He still had an unfinished pain au chocolat in the other hand.

'We have taken the best possible measures to protect ourselves.'

McRae was looking at the ground around the table. I understood why he had not finished his pain au chocolat. He had saved it for Simba. He raised his eyebrows to me.

'She has gone to the country for some time,' I answered the implied question.

'A dog's holiday?' McRae asked.

'Something like that,' I replied.

'When looking for Leo, I checked the video surveillance footage. She hasn't left the ground of the Fog in the past 24 hours,' McRae stated.

Both Leila and I immediately became alert. McRae had an annoyingly good intuition. We refrained from commenting, as a way to dismiss the question. After eating the treat he had saved for Simba, McRae continued.

'Something was off about your dog since the start. Sam sensed it, I sensed it and now I think I get it. She is from WII, isn't she? And somehow she manages to follow you around, and if I am correct, that is a big, BIG thing. I don't even think she is a dog. You say she's a malamute because it is the closest breed looking like a wolf, but I think she IS a wolf.'

I didn't know how to reply to that. For some time I wondered whether the secret would hold against the inquisition of Sam and McRae. They had suspicions about Simba, and so they were bound to keep their eyes on her and discover the truth, sooner or later.

'What I don't understand is that only objects from WII are supposed to be able to cross, not live beings, so how would it be possible? And if she can, what other animals, or beings, could? Yoko, do we have a problem here?' McRae's eyes were fixed on me with a seriousness and intensity I had hardly seen with him before. 'Could we face an invasion from the Other World?'

*

Realising the dangers of McRae's train of thought, I decided to put my trust in him and hoped to be a good judge of character. I revealed the details of Simba's special birth: a couple of weeks after the first Switch, the guards from Lil'London had found the young wolf cub by the house, alone, yelping from hunger, or thirst, or fear, or all three. They had rescued her and, as a thank you to us for our previous gifts, they offered her to me. Simba had adopted me as her mother in no time and followed me around everywhere in the house. She was scared to cross the Fog alone at first, but one day, to our surprise, she showed up by my side on the parking lot in London. Our theory was that she was born in the Fog during the original switch night and it gave her the ability to cross to both worlds, at will. As her mother, she did not wish to be parted from me and unconsciously followed me around to whichever world I entered.

McRae understood how sensitive this information was and why the household had decided not to impart this to anyone else so far. Should it fall into the wrong hands - the likes of Ingis Chen – they would attempt to force births on switching nights to recreate multi-crossers like Simba. This was dangerous for the babies – we had no idea of the consequences this could have on them – and it was not ethical. This opened the door to designer babies, who would be under the control of who created them for their whole life.

McRae listened to me without interrupting. When I finished my long tirade, silence settled. I was so nervous about his reaction I forgot to eat.

'This is an important piece of information,' McRae said. 'Very important. It means the Fog has even more possibilities than we think.'

'It is dangerous...' Leila started.

'I agree,' McRae interrupted her. He looked at both of us, in turn. 'Which is why I will keep it to myself. For now. I need to think it through. So where is Simba now?'

'She is in WII. Somewhere in the forest. Maybe forever. I think her pack called her back to them.'

'You must miss her.' McRae was looking at me softly, revealing his kind heart, once again.

'Terribly. So much so I'd rather not talk about it,' I replied. I looked down at the untouched Starbucks cups, in which the coffee was getting cold, with the fleeting thought of microwaving them. Rico, the coffee-lover and purist, considered it a crime. It was so practical, though.

'As we are talking with an open-heart and have established I would keep the information to myself, may I ask more questions?' McRae was all seductive and charming again. That made me suspicious about what was coming next.

'You can always ask,' I replied. 'It doesn't mean you will get the answers you are seeking.'

'I'll try,' he continued. 'Let's assume Jack and Leo are in Kenya: are you helping the Kenyan Government or attempting to rescue the Gatekeepers there?'

'Why would we help the Kenyan Government? Why would we risk our lives for them? Come on, Lochy!'

'Thank you,' McRae replied, with a smile. We had implicitly confirmed that Leo and Jack were on a rescue mission. He didn't know about Mitch and the Society, although he was aware of the existence of the latter, even if unsure about its structure and nature. So it made sense that his next question was about our mysterious backers.

'Very well then: you will not tell me more, I know. However, whatever trip they went on, they had help from your secret supporters. So, who are they? Another government? Should we worry about them? Or, on the contrary, should we try to work with them? And you, Leila: are you linked to them, too?'

'Lochy, Lochy, Lochy… Why are you always implying I am not just a friend of Yoko? This is getting silly,' Leila batted her eyes to him.

'Your story of pen pals becoming close friends, beautiful as it is in this modern age, is just too conveniently untraceable and timely. My intuition is telling me there is more to it, and my intuition has saved my life many times. I trust it.'

McRae and Leila shared a smile. There was definitely a strong connection between the two, an attraction even. The front door opened and Zeno entered the room in a good mood.

'Any coffee left?' he asked, eyeing the display on the table.

'You have the choice: cold Starbucks cappuccino, cold espresso pot or cold tea,' I replied.

'And this?' He pointed at the plate of pastries.

'Pains au chocolat, croissant and raisin buns. And there is a baguette in the kitchen.'

'I'll prepare some fresh coffee and I'll join you.'

'And I have to go. I need to repeat to Sam the news about Jack and Leo being on a 'business' trip and that there are no details on anything else. Yoko, Leila: as usual, it was a delight to spend some time in your company.' McRae stood up and bowed his head to Leila and me. 'I already look forward to our next encounter, which I hope will be as relaxed and intimate.'

It was already mid-morning by the time McRae left us. Time had passed rapidly, and there was still much to discuss with Leila and the boys. Soon, Rico and Harry joined us downstairs. Harry put his cappuccino in the microwave to heat it up, to the horror of the Italians. The British man did not pay attention to the pained expression on their faces for the coffee sacrilege, and sipped his hot drink with unmistakable pleasure.

*

First, we went through the latest group message sent by the Koplats. The tension between step-daughter and step-mother had resurfaced. Adam and Sophia were bored. In Nevada, Adam had continued working as a lawyer and Sophia was occupied with their business of Native American artefacts (from WII, but people did not know). Now in Alaska, they had nothing to do all day long. Contacting their friends or relatives was also out of question as it may open a door for the American Government to track their location. Penny Thompson's latest declarations had made things worse, as Michelle was torn whether or not to contact her. What stopped her was a feeling of treason regarding her mother's revealing of the Fog and the Gatekeepers' existence. As a result of their boredom, Adam and Sophia considered a move to England would be good for them. It was where the action was and where the Government was mostly respectful towards the Foggies. They wanted to come to Essex, which was not as much in the limelight as London. Michelle refused to move. To everyone's surprise, she loved being in Alaska. She and Rosario got on like two peas in a pod, having started working with her host, in her event business, to fill her free time. Sophia also hinted that Michelle's crush on Mitch was the real reason for her refusal to leave Alaska. In her eyes, it was a ridiculous infatuation: the age difference was too large for anything to happen between them. As Adam would not leave without his daughter and could not force her onto a plane, Sophia was fuming. Adam was trying to be a pacifier, but Michelle was delighted that her wish to stay opposed Sophia.

We informed them that Penny Thompson would be in London today to interview us in the afternoon. Additionally, she was ready to cross the Fog. We asked the Koplats, especially Adam and Michelle, if they wanted us to provide the journalist with reassurances about their safety. It would reveal we were in contact, but she was a mother, desperate to hear from her daughter.

Michelle replied that she would like that. However, she also had a message for Penny Thompson, which was: *I am shocked that you put my life in jeopardy by breaking your promise. I talked to you in confidence, from daughter to mother and not to the journalist. I could never trust you again, even though I still love you.* Adam backed his daughter's decision and words.

*

Information from the Foggies in Morocco was sparse. Following Louise's disappearance, they were all living in a relative truce under the same roof, hidden in their modern fortress in the Atlas Mountain. We all hoped it would last for as long as possible, but a truce is just that: a truce. It is not peace. They could not escape from each other, and this was not by choice: the cheating husband, the wife, the mistress, and the new baby, all under one roof. It was not an ideal situation, even with Helo being there to help facilitate Louise or Christophe.

In Kenya, the Foggies had arrived in the house, one by one, discreetly and at different times to avoid attracting attention. Leo and I wrote to each other that morning, just the way we used to a few months ago when we had not even met. I was falling for him all over again. It was typical of me to let go of my self-control, to be open to love and be loved, just when the object of my affection might disappear and die in another land.

Finally, we dealt with the most urgent: the upcoming interview with Penny Thompson. The journalist was a professional, as well as a personally involved mother. Which side was to take over? Would she keep it professional, or would she make it a personal crusade to have access to her daughter?

Before we realised, it was time to meet her. Leila received a message informing us that Penny Thompson would be with us in 30 minutes. When the journalist arrived, we received her in the Gatekeepers' formal office, formerly and still unofficially the Society's. She would cross the Fog after the interview. It gave her a chance to change her mind once her questions were answered. She might not be so keen any more. Penny Thompson was a good-looking brunette in her early-forties; an age betrayed by the experience detected in her eyes only, not the wrinkles on her face. The years had been kind to her and she could have passed for 8 to 10 years younger. She was wearing a formal trouser suit, a white shirt perfectly ironed, her long and lank hair straight on her back and no make-up. Every vibe about her sent the message she did not arrive in an amenable mood. Her stare was stern without an ounce of charm and her handshake firm. She meant business. We sat down, around the table and without a word, she opened her notebook and looked round at the people in attendance: Harry, Zeno, Leila and me.

'Thank you for suggesting this interview. I was hoping to liaise directly with you sooner, but you proved difficult to get in touch with. You are well guarded.' This was true both in contacting us and getting to us. The police had set up several checkpoints to go through before arriving at the house. It was more difficult to come to us than visit one of the Royal Palaces nearby.

'You are welcome. It was overdue,' I replied.

She took a voice recorder out and put it on the table, pressing the record button. She indicated the date, time, and location and checked her notes.

'Mr Grande, Mr Baxton and Miss Salelles.' She turned to Leila who sat at the end of the table, her tablet raised in front of her. From it, Michelle was watching the live interview. Leila was also taking notes behind it.

'Leila, Personal Assistant to the Gatekeepers. Please don't mind me,' Leila answered the silent question.

Penny Thompson gave a preliminary summary of the revelation on the Fog and our special links to it. She then explained her theory - based on an analysis of the facts and her secret sources - that the Government had been covertly backing us from the start. To support her claims, she referred to the advanced technology behind our private communication system, the secure accommodation from which we benefitted and the financial means we received to help the Relocated. She pointed out that the Government never denied our existence when the news first broke out. So, as usual, they had hidden major information from the public. She was turning the whole situation into a Governmental conspiracy. It sounded as if she was using this interview to further build a case against the US Government. Some of her information was not public knowledge and well detailed: either Michelle had talked to her at length - and too much - or Penny Thompson had an excellent source in the person of Ingis Chen. My suspicion was that he was involved and his silence for the past few days was not a good sign!

At last, Penny Thompson stopped her monologue and asked me a direct question.

'Miss Salelles, are you, or are you not working for the Government?'

'I am not.'

'Is your assistant Leila working for the Government?'

'She is not.'

'Are any of the Gatekeepers working for any governmental organisation?'

'Not that I know of. You surprise me, Ms Thompson. We offer you an opportunity to meet us; we are willing to answer questions relative to the Fog and the Gatekeepers and these are your first preoccupations, heavy with accusation? If I assure you that Gatekeepers is an independent company acting freely, will you start asking valuable questions about the situation?' I asked.

'My questions are beneficial to understanding what is really going on with the Fog. This discovery is a scientific, political, economic and historical phenomenon of the utmost importance. We have the right to know who are your backers.'

'No, you don't. We are normal people who are protecting our private lives and Gatekeepers is a private company. The Fog is a truly outlandish discovery, but we are a private venture, we are under no obligation towards anyone. Our wish to be more open and to help is a choice, not a chore.'

Penny Thomson did not flick a muscle. Her face was a painting of austerity. She leaned forward and stopped the recording.

'Listen, my daughter is a Facilitator. I am sure you know that. She has disappeared. What was their house is now a Gate and is not accessible to me. The US Government is controlling it. I want my daughter back! I will write and do whatever is necessary to get the truth out and get her back. I will stir whatever shit is necessary!' Her words came out through gritted teeth, her voice controlled. The contained anger was irradiating through all her pores. Forget the professional journalist; we had the furious and determined mother instead. It was much more dangerous.

'My mother was Dutch and blunt. We don't beat around the bush. So let me tell you: I will be relentless. I can write articles that will destroy your image. I can and I will, if I don't hear from my daughter. It is nothing personal against you; I must simply use whatever leverage I have at my disposal.' Again, her voice remained quiet but contained a hiss that made me shiver. Her eyes were mere slits. Her jaw was so tense and stiff it was a wonder she could articulate at all. I shot a glance at Leila typing on the tablet; she noticed and winked at me, turning her Ftab around. I let out a long sigh of relief. Michelle wished to speak to her mother.

'Ms Thompson, again - I repeat - we are not working FOR the Government. We have to work WITH them in certain circumstances, but they do not control us or our finances. We are sorry you have been through this worry with Michelle. She is fine and she will tell you so herself.' I indicated Leila's Ftab with a gesture of my arm and Penny immediately turned her head and fixed on the screen.

'Mummy? Can you hear me?' Michelle asked. It was early morning for her, but she had made sure she looked awake and dressed, and that nothing could indicate her whereabouts or the time of the day.

'Michelle! Oh my God, Michelle!' Penny leaned forward towards the Ftab, suppressing an automatic gesture to take it.

'I'm ok, Mummy. I heard what you said: you don't have to worry. We escaped before the military arrived at the house,' Michelle said, in a sweet tone but with a stern face. There was an undeniable family trait in this look.

'Why didn't you contact me? I was worried sick! I…' Michelle interrupted her mother.

'The risk of someone listening and trying to track me down was too great. Anyway, you can only blame yourself: you started this by feeding us to the media, remember? You are ripping the fruits of seeds you planted. I love you but I can't forgive you. You betrayed me. You betrayed us.' Michelle was clearly hurt as well as blunt, like her mother.

'That wasn't my intention. I only wanted to protect you. As your mother, sometimes I have to make hard choices to protect you against yourself or what you think is best.'

'And now, do you still think you're right?'

'Yes. Without my disclosure of the Fog to the world, in a controlled way, who knows how it would have been! I will fear for you all my life. I already sacrificed having you by my side because my globe-trotting wasn't an adequate life for you, and this even though I miss you every minute of every day. I…'

'Disclosure in a controlled way? Really?! You mean like in Kenya? A woman, a Switcher, is now dead. You call that controlled?' Michelle interrupted, raising her voice for the first time.

'Michelle, darling, you don't und…'

'Oh fuck! Don't give me this bullshit, Mum. The *'you don't understand'* speech!' Michelle was now letting go, dropping all civilised pretence. 'You are not in my shoes, Mum. You are not a Foggy! YOU can't understand what it feels like, what it means, how it blows your mind. I will never have a normal life, Mum. NEVER EVER. And you know who gets it? Dad! And the other Foggies or whatever you call us! I know you love me, Mum. I know you do, but you fucked up! You fucked up big time! Get a grip Mum! YOU BETRAYED YOUR OWN DAUGTHER. Do you get it?' Michelle was crying by then. Penny Thompson could hardly breathe, expending all her effort into not crying, in turn.

'Fuck Mum; sometimes you should learn to lose it. You know what I think: you haven't sacrificed anything for me. Nothing. If you had really decided to sacrifice something for your daughter, it would have been your career. You could have chosen to be a journalist in the country, in another branch, and stay with me. Now THAT would have been a sacrifice. But no, you preferred to continue having the job of your life and seeing your daughter at your convenience. You sacrificed being a mother, not being a journalist. I am not stupid, Mum. I am your daughter, after all,'

'Cupcake, this is not…' Penny Thompson didn't have a chance to finish. Michelle would not let her.

'No, that's it. I am done. I just wanted you to know that I'm fine. I am even quite happy. Yoko, Zeno and Harry are my friends. I didn't want to talk to you today but you went too far. I don't want you to bug my friends. But now I've had enough. Goodbye, Mum.' Michelle hung up. Leila turned the Ftab screen back towards her. Maybe Michelle would continue to follow the meeting virtually. Penny Thompson was thinking along those lines too, as she glanced repeatedly to the Ftab in the minutes that followed. She apologised for her lack of professionalism and for us witnessing a family scene, but coldly. The journalist did not switch the voice recorder back on. Instead, after an awkward silence, she asked if crossing the Fog was still on offer. I dropped a quick line to Jazz telling her we would be on our way shortly.

Penny Thompson did not hesitate when she came face to face with the Fog. She stepped right in and we followed. Jazz had organised a piano music background. She had also prepared a pot of coffee and some muffins, giving a delicious welcoming smell to the lounge. As soon as she stepped inside the house, the journalist turned on her heels to cross back and check if the Fog had had any effect on her. It turned out Penny Thompson was neither Relocated, nor a Facilitator. She did not linger after crossing the Fog. She was gone within five minutes.

*

As it was already dusk, I stayed at *The Jazzin* and settled for the night. Big Tom told me the wolves were still around. He had asked the watchmen not to kill any of them, as Simba was 'visiting' her family. They thought he was mad but they had agreed. Afterwards, Jazz and I went to the room where a home cinema was installed. We watched one of the latest Hollywood romantic comedies. It was good to have a laugh together and think of nothing.

In the middle of the night, the nearby howling of wolves woke me up. I struggled to go back to sleep, thinking of Simba. I looked around and there were earplugs in a drawer of the bedside table. The howling still resonated in my head until the early hours of the morning.

~

CHAOS

DEDICATION

To my nephew Mathieu and my goddaughters Heloisa, Chloé and Louise.
May you always pursue your dreams and believe in life.

~

WEEK III

Day 1 (Sunday)

James Fisher's eyes did not leave the monitor as they followed the movements of Maisie's earring tracking device. Maisie and Owen were next to him, their father's arms around their shoulders. Nick was sitting in front of the controls, everyone in the house standing behind him. The Fisher children had returned the previous afternoon and spent the rest of their day with their father and Nick, the latter intent on learning as much as he could about their misadventure and about Clémence. Afterwards, they had retired for some valuable family time in their cabin, their mother joining them via a video call.

Now, after breakfast together, we focused on the screen, as Clémence was on the move. Nick believed it was to ensure Maisie and Owen could not lead anyone back to their camp, despite her efforts to keep her location secret.

'I kind of sympathise with their views,' Owen said, tentatively. 'The way they treat women in this land is just... just... unacceptable! If anyone ever looked at Maisie that way, I would ...'

'I would kick them in the nuts!' Maisie exclaimed. 'Then I would sucker-punch them!'

I looked at the frail young teenager in disbelief. So did her father.

'Maisie!' James reprimanded his daughter. 'I agree this is the appropriate defence, but please speak correctly. You can't have learned these terms with Clémence Hoare.' The father eyed his son with suspicion.

'Owen, Maisie, we all agree they need to amend their attitude towards women here,' I told them. 'However, I am more inclined towards the Gandhi, Martin Luther King or Nelson Mandela approach of peaceful activism towards civil rights.'

'You are referring to the ones who succeeded in their fight. Sadly the majority of the others failed disastrously,' Nick said, playing the devil's advocate.

'Well, have no fear, you people! Maud and I are on the case: we will be the Gandhis of this world,' Jazz jumped into the conversation. 'And now Molly is joining our ranks, too. Clémence has her Amazon Warriors' Rebellion: we have our Ladies' Equality Movement.'

'Where did you leave the earring?' James asked his daughter.

'I attached it to my scarf, which I left behind. I made it look as if the earring got hooked onto it by accident. I didn't want to put the earring somewhere it could fall and be left behind.'

'Hopefully they will spot the scarf and Clémence will keep it, with the intention of giving it back to you later.'

'Is she really that dangerous? She was nice to us,' Maisie said to her father.

'I am sure she can be nice in private, and you were her guests. Forced guests, but guests nonetheless,' her father replied, weighing his words. 'Still, her methods and ultimate goals are extreme and dangerous. Maybe Hitler also had friends who thought he was nice.'

'Dad! She is no Hitler!' Owen said.

'You never know, son: you never know. She did ask for weapons.'

'She asked for equal treatment between Lil'London, Newtonsee and her group, and that whatever we supplied to one, we supply to her as well,' Jazz corrected.

'Are you defending her?' James Fisher's eyes narrowed on Jazz.

'Certainly not. I'm not defending her, I am just amending your statement to clarify the situation so that all parties are treated fairly, and that your children have the facts, not biased opinions. You'd want them to make up their own minds with all the information, wouldn't you?'

James Fisher grunted and tightened his arms around his children's shoulders. The little family left soon after.

*

'Do you think the children have been indoctrinated?' Rico asked, in an overly dramatic tone.

'No, I don't think you should start worrying,' I answered him. 'However, I think she did manage to make them empathise with her cause.'

'I must talk to them!' Rico exclaimed, agitated.

Jazz and I gave a sigh. Nick and Big Tom rolled their eyes.

'You will leave these children alone,' I told him. 'We don't need you to indoctrinate them with your conspiracy theories. Plus, I'm not sure YOUR way of treating women is any better that the WII men.'

'I don't understand what you mean. I absolutely adore women!'

'As individuals or in your bed?' I said.

'That is not true. You are like a sister to me: I don't want you in my bed. Neither do I want Jazz, because you would kill me for it.'

'I would first! How about Leila?' Jazz asked.

'I wouldn't say no...' Rico replied, pensive.

'Interesting. I've never seen you flirt with her. Are you intimidated?' I teased him.

'Me? Never! It is just that the Fog business got in the way at the start, and now McRae has taken the lead in the race. I am like the hidden leopard, observing the scene, waiting for the right moment.'

Jazz and I sighed once more. Big Tom and Nick rolled their eyes again.

'What?!' Rico asked, looking around as if his comment were a matter of fact.

We all ignored him and instead, Jazz turned to me to ask if I would have time today to meet with Maud, Molly and her for a discussion on their political movement. They were quite keen on my unofficial input. I could hardly refuse anything to Jazz, not just as a friend, but also because she would be on my back until I gave in. It was easier to say yes, straightaway. We agreed on a lunch meeting, then I left for London, with Rico.

*

McRae had asked to see me. As I came out of the Fog boarded area, he was on the old parking ground, smoking and drinking coffee out of a paper cup. His mobile rang. He ignored it, smiled at me and threw his cigarette in the paper cup. He looked exhausted and pale, with large bags under his eyes. At first, I thought the Scot was under the weather or suffering from the strain of his job's demands. When we reached the gate of the houses' secure area and one of the agents gave him another coffee, it hit me: the man was suffering with a tough hangover. And yet he was impeccably dressed, holding himself tall and straight. Aside from his haggard look, unshaven face and his messy hair, it could have been a normal day in the office.

'Tough morning? Getting too old to handle a night of drinking with your mates?' I teased him.

'My dear Yoko, the drinking will never be a problem. It is the lack of sleep because of it that I suffer from,' he replied.

'Sounds like you really had a late one with the guys.'

'It is not the guys who kept me up.' The glint in his eyes and his mischievous smile brought his Casanova reputation back to mind.

'Are we leaving the secure grounds of the house?' I asked, as he took out a set of keys. 'If so, I need to retrieve a wig. I'd rather not go out in the open as Yoko.'

I left him by the door, sipping his coffee, and went back inside to change and disguise myself. For once, I remembered to put in the earbud linked to my Ftab. Back outside, McRae had finished his coffee and cigarette. He handed me a helmet. We were off for a bike ride.

'You warned your security that we are going and where, did you?' He put the helmet on my head, himself.

'Yep,' I replied.

'Tell them we are heading to Hampstead Park,' McRae said.

'OK.' I made a sign to Phil and provided him with our destination.

The motorbike was a black Ducati with sleek lines, shiny leather seats and the ability to make anyone on it look very cool. McRae indicated for me to sit behind him. Speed and its adrenaline rush was a big winner for me. I was looking forward to the trip.

*

We were on a bench on top of a hill, overlooking London. The view was striking. The city stretched in front of us, overtaking the whole horizon: a sea of old and new buildings, roofs, monuments and landmarks, seemingly so close to each other.

'I thought it was about time we had a one-on-one chat,' McRae said, as he sipped a cappuccino he had bought on the walk to the hill.

'Please don't tell me this is a date.' I was nursing a cappuccino,.

'Sam has forbidden me to even contemplate the idea. I had to swear on my Clan's honour before he let me in on this mission. I'll get my revenge on him for that later.'

'Good to know I am safe from you. He forgot to mention Leila, though. What about Jazz?'

'He didn't mention anyone else but you,' McRae smiled to himself. 'I can't wait to meet Jazz. She seems quite a character.'

'To think you seemed such a gentleman on our first encounter...'

'I am. I treat women with a lot of respect.'

'I am curious as to their point of view on that matter. Anyway, you haven't told me why you brought me here.'

McRae took out a cigarette and lit it. He took a couple of puffs before speaking again.

'I want in.'

'What do you mean you want in?' I turned to him, with a frown.

'Your private security: I want in. I like their methods. Your bodyguards, the likes of Phil and Nick, they all check out when it comes to character and profiles: good people. Ingis Chen is simply NOT their employer. Not a match. Now, as Sam told you, you can't just rely on your private security. You need to work with the British Government in addition. That's where I would come in, as the intermediary between both.'

'Are you suggesting being a double agent? If so, who would have the upper hand, your country, or the Foggies? I have doubts it would work,' I replied without much hesitation, even though his suggestion had surprised me. I was immediately on guard.

'Yoko, a double agent is not normally known as a double agent. I do not intend to betray my country and reveal anything crucial to you or the people backing you up. I just want to be able to fulfil the goal of my mission, to protect you and the other Gatekeepers properly. For this, it seems obvious I need to work with your private security.'

'Well, aren't you already doing that?'

'Only ad-hoc. We need something more constant; more viable in the long term, more efficient.'

'I'll pass on the message. Is that it?'

'Mainly.'

'Mainly, not yes. So what else is on your mind?'

'Where are Leo and Jack?'

'I don't want to talk about it.'

'Why?'

'Because you wouldn't like the answer.'

'They ARE in Kenya, then.' He stood up and threw his cigarette butt in the empty cappuccino cup, and lit another one. McRae was annoyed.

'There are plenty of other possibilities you wouldn't like and plenty you can't even conceive, so don't jump to conclusions,' I continued.

'I don't get it. You obviously trust me, otherwise you wouldn't be here with me now, so why not tell me?'

'I trust you don't intend me any harm and I trust you want to help the Foggies. However, we might differ in opinion on what our best interest is.'

My earbud beeped and I discreetly brought a hand to my ear to take the call. Mitch announced himself.

'Yes, Mitch?' I answered.

McRae took a couple of seconds to understand I was addressing someone else, guessing I had an invisible device in my ear.

'Ingis Chen is on his way to you. Do we stop him?' Mitch said.

'Not if we have enough security around,' I replied.

'We're good.'

'Then I'll meet him, but him alone,' I said.

'What about McRae?'

'I'll handle it if necessary.' My confident and professional attitude was all bravado and improvisation. I turned and spotted the distinct and unique figure of Ingis Chen walking elegantly towards us. He was alone.

'Lochy, we have a visitor,' I said to McRae. He turned and squinted in the direction of my gaze. I turned back to face the view, bracing myself for the encounter.

'Good or bad surprise?' he asked.

'If only I could be certain of the answer,' I replied.

'My dear Yoko, it is always such a pleasure to see you. Why is it so rare?' Ingis Chen said when he reached us moments later.

'Maybe because the pleasure is not mutual?' McRae answered before I had a chance. Ingis Chen gave McRae the once-over. He failed to show any sign of approval at what he saw.

'Your new boyfriend?' he asked me.

'Just a friend,' I replied.

'He is not the type to be content with a simple friendship where a pretty woman is concerned,' Ingis Chen replied, ignoring McRae. They had just met and already, there was no love lost between them.

'May I ask the object of your visit, Mr Chen?' I enquired. The sooner we skipped his little games and addressed the reason for his presence, the faster he would leave.

'Please, call me Ingis,' he said, paused, and continued, 'I have tried to reach you but you have lacked time for me of late.'

'I am busier than usual since my existence as a Gatekeeper became public knowledge, as you should have expected.'

'I would be delighted to help relieve the pressure your recent celebrity status is causing by taking some of the burden from your shoulders.'

'Thank you, we will manage for now,' I retorted, rather sharply.

'Oh dear, you are not still bearing a grudge, are you?' Ingis Chen put his hand in his inside breast pocket. McRae jumped in front of me, pulling out his gun and aiming between Ingis Chen's eyes.

'Take your hand out. Slowwwwly!' McRae said, in a whisper.

Ingis Chen slowly pulled his hand out, holding a USB memory stick.

'In proof of my good faith, I wanted to give you this. This is my sister's complete work on the Native Americans of North America. This is the study during which she encountered the old Indian man who mentioned the Fog to her. Thanks to her work, I found out about your existence. Even if she did not believe in the folk tale herself,' he said, with a broad smile.

'It may be useful for your people on the ground in the US. You never know, there could be something of interest for them,' he added. 'There is no mention of the Fog, aside from that old man's comments, but it reveals a lot on their culture and practices.'

'What makes you think there are Gatekeepers in the States?' McRae hissed.

'Penny Thompson says so. And Penny Thompson seems to have excellent sources of information, wouldn't you agree?' Ingis Chen replied, always poised. 'Why are your boyfriends always so abrupt with me? This, I wonder. Sadly, they have no reason to be jealous.'

Ingis Chen took my hand and bowed to kiss it, taking his leave. I frowned as I watched him make his way back to the gate of the park. I opened my hand and the USB memory stick was inside my palm. He was too kind and nice. No argument, contest or request. I had a bad feeling about this.

Ingis Chen had killed the mood: we did not linger in Hampstead Park for long.

*

Back in WII, Jazz, Maud and I were lunching in the clearing.

'You'll be pleased to know that Barbara Snayth has put a veto on her husband's suggestion that taking you for his wife would be excellent for Inter-world relations,' Maud said to me, as we dug our forks in the tomato and ham tart that Big Tom had prepared for us.

'Very pleased! Did he really believe that was even an option?!' The thought of joining the Snayth household was as appealing to me as eating raw snails.

'Benjamin thinks he is rather irresistible...' Maud smiled. 'However, you still have a chance of being a Snayth. They have a couple of teenage sons at the marrying age ...'

I could not work out whether she was joking. It was spoiling my appetite.

'Snayth AND teenagers? The thought is a nightmare,' I told Maud.

'I agree! Let's change the subject before you mention their plans for me!' Jazz cut in. 'Let's discuss political strategy. Girls, what is our next move to establish our Women's Equality Political Movement?'

'Well, it seems every political party has a programme with key elements they promote, no? So maybe we should have some?' Molly suggested.

'Good idea!' Jazz exclaimed.

'That is easy. I have a list of ideas that I have been promoting for years. They are within our reach should the men give in a little,' Maud said.

'And the women, too. It seems to me that some of the women of Lil'London and Newtonsee are very content with their sorry fate...' I added.

'That is due to ignorance,' Molly intervened. 'All they need is education.'

'I have been thinking about that,' I said, 'and I have discussed the matter with our associates. (We had still not given the full details of the Society to Molly, mostly referring to them as our 'associates'.) They will create access for us to the various online education programmes. However, we will edit out the most sensitive information to avoid shocking the locals.'

'What do you mean, *shocking the locals*?' Maud interrupted me. Her presence was so familiar by now that I had forgotten she was one of the mentioned locals.

'Maud, you have an open mind and, because of your avid reading of your family's broad library, you were fast to adjust to our world. Most are not like you here. On the contrary. It is true that some elements in our history are not casting a good light on humanity... We don't want our world to be judged only on the negative side of our recent history! We would rather prepare your people first,' I explained.

'Control of information is wrong, for whatever reason. This is the problem with this land and should not be repeated by you! It could also diminish our trust in you. What would you want to hide and why? Would you always choose what you reveal to us? It sets a bad precedent. No, I say you must be open and give us access to the bad and the good.'

She had put me back in my place, rightfully so. Who were we to think we had any right to sugar coat anything?

'I am with you,' Jazz replied, before I did. 'You should have access to all aspects of information, though you should have a look first before we open it up to everyone.'

'I concur with Jazz,' I said. 'Maud, we are not trying to control you, only to protect you. There are things that may disturb your peers, the same way you do not tell everything or show everything to children until they are ready. However, you are adult and we need to trust you the same way you trust us. To start with, maybe we could give you, and maybe Edmund and Ariel Ben-Chaim - the ones I would call the intellectuals of WII - full access to the Internet and the Open University. From your reactions thereafter, we could then expand the access to more?' I suggested.

Jazz shook her head.

'Poor them,' she said to herself. 'They could spend their lives in front of the screen and only dip a toe into the sea of knowledge and information available. And a toe is being a generous assumption. Worse, the waves that crash on their shores might not be the most relevant or interesting for them,' Jazz continued.

'So let's try differently, then,' I suggested. 'Let's start from the educational point of view. Maud, with the online Open University, you can browse the wide variety of courses and subjects. There must be thousands. It is also a good way to start learning without getting lost in the web. It is a good path for the WII inhabitants to widen their horizons and understand our world, as well as raising awareness that women deserve a better place in your society.'

'People will have a choice of classes,' Molly jumped in, excitedly. 'I can organise that and offer student support. This is my area. Brilliant! Just arrived in this world and already I get the best job ever! I am going to get this world the gift of L.E.A.R.N.I.N.G. That's totally brilliant!'

'Education of the masses. No less. Now that's a good start for a political party. What's next?!' Maud exclaimed.

Molly was already scribbling frenetically in her notebook.

*

Over lunch, we reviewed many ideas we could put on the table as a counter-approach to Clémence's movement. We needed to make most of them attractive to Lil'London and Newtonsee councils and to the Yerushaleim community. This would not be easy for some, like the right of women to divorce, the right over their bodies - forbidding rape in any shape and form (including in the brothel or from the husband) - or against the practice of husbands physically punishing their wives. Just talking about those practices made me shiver in disgust and anger. Subjects like abortion were not yet discussed. Jazz, Molly and I each saw, from Maud's reaction, that it was a subject best not broached at this point. At the mere mention of the word, Maud was distraught. This illustrated my beliefs that the inhabitants of WII were not prepared, at this time, to face everything available on the Internet. In her world, human beings were rare and their survival necessary to maintain a steady flow of births to ensure their population's growth. Their whole society was based on having babies for the perpetuation of mankind.

Health was an additional raised matter. Like a growing number of people in WI, the indigenous inhabitants of WII were keen to have access to the Fog in order to fight against their various viruses. *The Jazzin* now had regular visitors passing through, just long enough to clear their bodies of illness and satisfy their curiosity. Numbers were manageable just then. However, we believed the locals should be educated on the basics of medicine, like disinfection, cleaning with soap etc. Their doctors could do with stopping their antique methods to heal ailments. Maisie and Owen had in mind dedicating themselves to medicine and adapting it to WII, working alongside Ariel Ben-Chaim. They aimed to use the best of ancient practices and combine it with modern medicine.

*

Their approach reminded me of Elsie: the ex-Society psychiatrist-turned-Relocated was fast becoming a specialist on Amerindian culture and traditions. She had started writing about shamanic practices and it was fascinating. Although her focus was on the Shaman traditions on the American continent, her research led her to scrutinise every continent, from the steppes of Siberia to the Amazonian forests, from the jungles of Africa to the depths of Thailand, with a detour on the aboriginal practices in Australia, Hawaii, or the druids, gypsies and ancient cults of Europe. All of them displayed uncanny similarities. These cultures embraced the shaman at the same time as the priest and doctor, counsellor and teacher, as intermediaries or messengers between the human world and the spirit worlds. I also learned that most shamanic traditions, whatever the culture or terms used to define them, had been practically erased from our planet, either because the organised religions hunted them down as heretic practices, or because western invaders considered the tribes who practiced shamanism as retarded.

It suffered condemnations as witchcraft, as danger against communist beliefs, as malevolence etc. With the rising New Age movement in the 60s or 70s and ever since, the Western world had tried to revive shamanism, which was now becoming fashionable along with many other spiritual or even esoteric practices. However, so many of the traditions were lost. Elsie was now in the unique situation of being able to learn directly how it was all practiced more than 200 years ago, in Nevada. It was a dream for an anthropologist, historian, spiritualist, or merely a curious mind. Elsie was slowly growing from a practical and sceptical scientific mindset towards becoming a rational and spiritual believer. I could glimpse the pleasure of such discovery for myself during my regular visits to Ariel Ben-Chaim's apothecary in Yerushaleim. The traditional remedies, the concoctions, the old ways of healing both body and mind as one - and how efficient it was - still surprised me. It was my wish to introduce him to acupuncture and the energy-flow medicine of Reiki and Tai Chi, and to observe if and how he could combine it with his Jewish Doctor ways inherited from his Middle East origins.

It was in these moments, during these discoveries, that I was reminded of how lucky I was to live such an adventure, to experience such an incredible time of exchange between two worlds, between old and new. With the everyday struggles and the pressure from the communities of both sides, I too often forgot the extraordinary and the wonder of my situation.

*

It was late afternoon. The four of us were done with political talks and enjoying iced tea in the sun, when the howling of wolves rose in the forest in front of us. A shiver went up my spine. Jazz, Maud and Molly tensed next to me. Big Tom came out of the house in a hurry, carrying a shotgun. I glanced at the shotgun and looked at him with panic in my eyes, thinking of Simba.

'Don't worry, Yoko. Nick gave me this. It is one of those shotguns with special tranquiliser bullets. No risk for Simba.'

My shoulders immediately relaxed and I looked towards the forest, wondering if my beloved young wolf was with the howling wolf pack or if she was already long gone, forever lost to me. I picked a biscuit and nibbled at it.

'Yoko,' I heard Big Tom whisper. 'Look behind you, by the house. A wolf. Is it…'

I quickly turned around. Yes, it was Simba! I stood up and walked slowly towards the wolf. She didn't make a move. Had she forgotten me already? Mid-way, I stopped and kneeled on the ground, extending my arms and calling her softly.

'Simba? Simba, come. Come, darling. Come, Simba.'

My heart was beating fast. I longed for her to come to me! Suddenly, she jumped towards me and ran into my arms, pushing me onto the ground and licking my face as if it was ice-cream. I laughed and cried. She was still my beloved Simba. And she loved me, she loved me! We played in the grass for some time, and she yelped out of joy. Maisie and Owen heard her and immediately came running to see her. She yelped, licked and gnawed everyone's shoes. Big Tom ran inside and got some bacon and milk for her. She ate it ravenously. Nick came out, a shotgun ready in the arm.

'You can put that away. It's just Simba.'

'Her pack is still around and we don't know what they are going to do next.'

'How do you know the pack is still around?'

'From the feeds of the cameras I placed in the forest. The wolves are circling the clearing.'

That calmed us all down. Were they planning an attack? Was Simba only saying goodbye? Nick took out his tablet and checked the camera feeds on his screen.

'Still there?' I asked.

'I can't see them anywhere,' he said, swiping his screen to change angles. 'But that doesn't mean they are not there, only that I can't see them. I am going back inside to check the motion detectors.'

He left and I returned my attention to Simba. I could not believe she would let any danger come my way, even from her peers. My Ftab beeped. It was an instant message from Nick indicating that the wolves were gone from the Woodfellas neighbourhood.

*

'Next, we need to check if Simba will stay with you or return to her pack,' Jazz said.

So I stood up and went to the house, making a point of not calling her. It had to be her choice. I crossed the Fog and got inside *The Jazzin* without looking back, leaving the door open behind me for her to follow, should she wish. I sat on the staircase by the front door and waited. Within 30 seconds, Simba had crossed the threshold and came to put her muzzle on my lap. Her eyes seemed to say to me 'Of course I am here. What did you think? You and I forever!' I took her in my arms and hugged her for a long time. Then I stood up and called Jazz on her Ftab to let her know I needed to check if Simba could still make me cross to London. If yes, I would not return immediately, so if she could pass my goodbyes to Maud and Molly... I then stood by the door facing the Fog, Simba by my side, saying 'London' twice for her attention. We stepped forward together, crossed the Fog, and came out on the old lot of the London terraced houses. I sighed from pleasure and relief. It was a good day! I headed home, where Simba was greeted by a very excited Zeno. He didn't hesitate to take his socks off, roll them in a ball and throw them around for Simba to catch. Rico soon went to the kitchen to prepare her a special 'welcome back' dinner, and Harry stared at her for ages with a broad grin on his face. Simba was part of the family. She was back home.

*

'Are you cooking for us or for Simba? I am confused now,' I said to Rico, when I joined him a little later in the kitchen.

'Both. I am preparing a selection of ribs. I couldn't make up my mind what to choose, between pork, beef or lamb, so I am preparing them all. Simba will have a selection of bones to gnaw at for days.'

'You will spoil her.'

'Babe, she's part of the family. We are now complete in the household.' Rico began chopping vegetables to roast, as accompaniment to the meat.

'You haven't had a chance to check the latest craziness from this world, I presume?' he said to me, wiping the tears caused by a particularly strong smelling onion he was cutting. I picked up a knife and started slicing the courgettes.

'I am afraid to ask,' I said.

'I could lie and say it is not about the Fog, if you wish?' Rico replied. The return of Simba had placed me in such a good mood, it felt that nothing could shatter my good spirits, so I told him to go on.

The Americans had conceded to the British Government that they had a Fog gate on their soil, but that the Gatekeepers there had fled before their arrival. They also revealed that they had issues with the WII locals – some Indian tribes who blocked any attempt of communication. They asked the UK Government to assist by sending some of 'their' Gatekeepers to help. Incidentally, they also enquired if we had any information on the Koplats' whereabouts and would we provide details of our interview with Penny Thompson. The journalist was wanted for questioning, back in the US, but so far she had been unresponsive to their demand.

'So, do you fancy a trip to the US?' Rico asked me.

'No.'

'Me neither.'

'And Harry or Zeno?' I asked.

'Nope. They don't find the package deal attractive enough,' Rico said, popping a cherry tomato in his mouth.

'What about the position of the UK Government? What did Sam or McRae say?'

'Officially, the UK Government is willing to help, although they pointed out to the Americans that it is our call. Unofficially, they welcome the fact that none of us is keen to go.'

'I wonder if the Americans know about Elsie…' I spoke my thoughts aloud.

'Well, we couldn't really ask Sam about that, as I expect he doesn't know about Elsie. I doubt the Americans would have told them if they know about her, either,' Rico said.

Later, exchanging messages with Leila, I asked her the same question. So far, Elsie's presence remained undiscovered and her communications with the Society safe. The US military had not yet picked up that someone was hacking their communication system to liaise from WII to WI.

The US Government was not going to take no for an answer that easily. My pleasure in having Simba back in my life, even though I had to relinquish most of the bed to her, was clouded by a call from Sam. It was Sunday evening,

10pm. 'Why couldn't it wait until Monday morning?' I fumed as I picked up the call.

'I bet you're not calling to wish me goodnight, are you?' I answered.

'I promise to give you a warm goodnight at the end of the call,' Sam replied. I grunted, and he continued. 'The Americans asked for a meeting with you lot in London. The ones they know of, obviously; so Zeno, Harry and you.'

'The diary is full. We're very busy.'

'We'll have them on our back until you accept.'

'And?'

'And they are a pain.'

I very much wanted to tell him it was not my problem. It was their back, not mine. I was just grumpy and knew it.

'I'll talk to the boys in the morning. There, happy now?' I replied.

'Well, at least it is not an immediate no,' Sam replied. I grunted once more.

'Good night, Nutty!' Sam said jokingly. I could hear the smile in his voice. It brought out a smile on my side too.

I hang up the phone and Simba moved closer to me, putting her head on my shoulder. I fell asleep with a grin on my face.

Day 2 (Monday)

At breakfast, Harry and Zeno agreed to meet with the Americans. We were about to call Sam to inform him when Simba suddenly ran to the front door. Half a minute later, the doorbell rang and Harry went to open the door. Sam and McRae came in, the first holding a cardboard tray with cups of coffee, the second carrying a large paper bag with croissants from the bakery. McRae was already munching one. We all sat around the table and helped ourselves from the bag.

'So we have agreed to meet with the representatives of the US, although it has to be here in London,' I told Sam and McRae.

'May we be present?' Sam asked.

'Are you concerned they'll make us an offer we can't refuse?' Harry retorted.

'Among other things,' McRae replied.

'I don't think your presence is necessary...' I said, checking the reactions of the boys for their approval or not. The household seemed to agree so I continued. 'You are welcome to stay nearby, and we will call you in if required.'

Sam and McRae did not react to this. They both put their cups to their lips and sipped more coffee, giving them further time to think. Simba jumped to her feet and ran to the door with a joyful yelp. Leila walked in and greeted me with a hug, then went directly to the dining table and sat down. McRae presented her with a coffee cup.

'Arriving late for work already?' he said, the corners of his mouth lifting.

'I've been working for hours already,' she replied. She was agitated and unhappy. Whatever she was bringing up on her Ftab for us to see was not good news.

'Ingis Chen struck back,' she said. Leila turned the Ftab on and we all stared at the screen. Ingis Chen was behind a podium on stage, talking into a microphone. The tension around the table went up a notch. Penny Thompson was behind him. Leila pressed play and we concentrated on his speech for the following couple of hours.

*

Ingis Chen had indeed struck again. He had come back on the media scene in full force with a press release. He stated that, sadly, the intervention of the British and American Governments in the management of the Fog had forced him to quit his position as the Gatekeepers' Public Relations Manager. The pressure from both States was unbearable and against his principles. He regretted that, due to our circumstances, we didn't have the option to quit from them as well. Ingis Chen was a talented orator and he easily won over the crowd of journalists filling the audience. His strategy soon became clear: Ingis Chen was presenting himself as a Fog specialist and the defender of the people's rights to have access to the Fog. He advocated that the United Nations Organisation should meet with representatives of every country on this planet to discuss and agree on how the Fog should be managed not by one State, but all States. Chen continued that it should establish rules concerning where, when, why and under what circumstances the Fog should be created, as well as its access. In a sentence winning a round of applause, he emphasised that, from now on, the Gatekeepers should not be considered in terms of nationalities, but recognised as 'Citizens of the World' and should be given free access and equal advantages wherever they went. This point was important to him, as it led to another crucial matter: the access to the Fog. Ingis Chen insisted several times that everyone – i.e. not just sick people - should be given the opportunity to cross the Fog. This left the boys, Leila and me feeling dubious regarding his charitable motivations. Not that long ago, in a conversation with us, Ingis Chen was blunt in exposing that his final goal was an obligation that every individual could cross the Fog. An obligation; not just an opportunity. His philosophy was that all the problems of the world – ecological, economic, religious, to name only three – were due to over-population. The Fog was the solution to get rid of one person out of seven from our planet. Even if there might be some truth in the over-population issue, his approach was dictatorial and thus unacceptable for us. Chen also aimed to profit from his charitable intervention to save the people and the planet, and we had doubts that should he have to choose between profits and people, the right one would win. To gain further sympathy for his cause, Ingis Chen said to the press that we, the Gatekeepers, were good people and he felt very lucky to have worked with us and met us. He praised us highly, blaming the Governments for the lack of openness and thorough information on the Fog. He also revealed that, during his time with us, he had struggled with an undisclosed and mysterious support watching our back, which added to his suspicions that, in the shadows, some Government military branch or secret services were controlling us. He concluded by playing the card of governmental conspiracy and the military 'controlling everything'.

*

After the questions and answers period, which never seemed to finish, Leila put down her tablet. McRae's jaws were set and his coffee cup was crushed in one hand; the other a clenched fist on the table. Sam was already up and pacing in the living area, on the phone with their boss.

'Clever move,' Harry whispered to himself, with both admiration and venom.

'Ma perché? What does he have to gain in doing this?' Rico asked. 'He is not trading with WII, he is not working with us, and he sets the

Government against him!'

'Yes, but he becomes the voice of the people. Yes… He is back in the game,' I replied.

'Can't we refute what he just said? Can't we tell that WE are the ones who didn't want to work with him because he's dodgy?' Zeno jumped into the conversation.

'What about our mysterious support? Or any of the information he has not revealed yet? Plus, he is right you know, all things are relative: for the rest of the world, he is a Fog specialist,' I said, standing up and getting the USB memory stick he had given me the day before. I handed it to Leila.

'He appeared out of the blue yesterday when I was in Hampstead Park. This supposedly contains his sister's research on the Indian culture in the US. It may have malicious software included. Do you think you might pass it on to the tech team to double-check it?' Leila took the memory stick and nodded.

'We could do that, too,' Sam replied. 'We might be better equipped.'

'That's ok: we have it covered,' I told him with a smile.

'Or your mysterious support has, as Chen put it,' McRae said.

'What were you doing in Hampstead Park?' Rico asked.

'Lochy took me for a ride and a private chat,' I replied. Rico's attention was immediately on McRae, his eyes narrowed on us, as he looked back and forth between the agent and me, before turning to observe Leila's reaction. She was focused on her tablet with a confused face.

'Have I missed something here?' Rico finally asked. 'I thought if whatever was going on it was between Leila and the Scot?'

'There is nothing between Lochy and me,' I snapped. 'Lochy has a motorbike. I needed a break and it was a perfect way to empty my head.' I played a little with the truth there, as I hadn't had had a chance to discuss with Leila yet McRae's proposal to work in partnership with the Society. Also, it wasn't clear if Sam knew about it or not.

'There is nothing going on between Lochy and me either,' Leila added to my comment.

'Well… Not yet,' McRae added, without a look at Leila and giving a pat to Simba, instead.

'Not ever. I have no wish to be just another box for you to tick before you move on to the next girl. No, thank you,' Leila said and stood up. 'I could do with some time with the Foggies alone, if you don't mind?'

*

Once Sam and McRae were gone, silence settled around the table.

'Look at that; it's almost lunch time already,' Rico said, after a glance at his watch.

'It is only 11am and we have been eating non-stop since waking up,' I told him.

'Pastries do not make a proper meal. In a couple of hours, you will be hungry,' Rico shook his head and spoke thoughtfully. 'I think I will prepare pasta for lunch, and then I will go and train, and then I will work in my studio,'

'I thought only the French talked about food all the time?' I asked Zeno and Rico. 'Don't you think we have other pressing matters right now?'

'Yes! And that is why food is important. It gives us energy. Additionally, cooking is therapeutic,' Zeno said. 'I think we should all prepare a lunch.'

I looked at the plate, empty of pastries, and at my own empty plate. Then I checked the belt of my jeans. There was still room: I could handle pasta.

*

We spent the rest of the morning discussing Ingis Chen's new and old antics. We decided the best approach was to ignore him for now until we had a clear strategy. He had not done any obvious harm to us so far. It might even be in our favour to have a counterweight to the Government. This was the single argument that had made sense when Ingis Chen was on the receiving end of my wrath for disclosing the existence of the Fog to the public, and it still applied. However, the boys and I were not keen on potentially having everyone and anyone claiming access to the Fog: it was unmanageable for us and would overwhelm the WII communities. Did we have the right to either allow or block this, though? In doubt, we decided to see how things would evolve in the next few days or weeks before making a decision.

Regarding McRae; Harry, Zeno, Rico and I had no objections to his working alongside the Society as long as the Foggies' privacy, identity and any key details remained secret. There was already a partnership de facto. Leila would talk to the Society's headquarters in New York and get back to us with their opinion.

I reflected on the antagonism between Freedom and Authority. Real freedom could not exist without some authority or chaos would soon rise. On the other hand, authority without freedom would be tyranny. There were many demands of freedom these days - freedom for us Foggies, freedom for all to access the Fog, freedom, freedom, freedom… Where would the authority come from, to balance and manage such freedoms?

*

Leila accompanied me on a short walk with Simba while the Italians prepared lunch, arguing about which sauce to make for the pasta today.

'If the Society agrees to use Lochy as a direct link between the British Secret Service and them, does that mean your true role will be revealed to him?'

'Probably.'

'You will have to spend much more time with him…' I smiled at her.

'Please stop it. The man is trouble! He can't help himself. I was wondering how long it would take for him to try his moves on you… And then he makes flirty comments to me, like *not yet*. The nerve!'

'He didn't try anything on me. I told you, he just needed to see me alone to discuss his proposal.'

'Of course, and the only way to do this was to take you on an impromptu bike trip to one of the most striking views of London. There are empty rooms in the office, just next door to yours.'

'Hang on a second: are you jealous?' I was only half-joking with her.

'Nonsense,' she replied. I smiled to myself. Leila was already a little hooked on the charming Scotsman.

'Indeed. There is nothing to be jealous about so you can put your mind at rest.'

Leila frowned and looked at me annoyed, then her face lit up and she exploded in laughter.

'Well, I won't let anything happen to me with this man.' she said, and I let her remark pass. McRae certainly had a way with women, but this time his special skills reputation, in this domain, was his worst enemy.

After lunch, sitting with Zeno in the back garden at home, I broke my recent resolution to limit my news intake to the minimum and browsed the web on the reactions to Ingis Chen's press conference. They were unsurprisingly mixed. What struck me the most was how fast people got used to the idea of the Fog. Statistics indicated that 50% of the British population now believed the Fog existed and had healing powers, though they were more hesitant when it came to the existence of a parallel world. The consensus within the public was for access to the Fog to anyone who needed it, and that it should be a priority and a duty for the Government to organise. Aside from the sick, an increasing number agreed with Ingis Chen that everyone should have a chance. Debates on the matter were even turning aggressive. Additionally, I noted with both regret and alarm that a few fanatics were already depicting the Fog as a biblical sign of some form. These types did believe, without a doubt, that WII was a reality: unfortunately, they then made up what this reality was.

'Yoko! Look at this one!' Zeno exclaimed, pointing a finger on the screen of his Ftab.

'What's this article about?' I asked, putting my Ftab down on my lap and focusing on his.

'A complete nutter. Read: you'll see!' Zeno was serious.

The article depicted a self-proclaimed preacher who exhorted to his audience that the Fog was the first step of the Apocalypse, that our planet was doomed and on the verge of disappearing. The Fog was the gift from God to ensure the survival of the Chosen Ones, limited to one in seven of us. We, the Gatekeepers, were the representatives of God on earth, some kind of semi-deities to be worshiped. The whole article displeased and unsettled me. It sounded like a cult venerating my name and those of my friends. My frustration with the journalists, commentators, bloggers and whomever kept making up these ridiculous statements kept growing. They made me want to stand up and scream all the air out of my lungs in frustration. Every second of every day, I relied mostly on common sense and my *vibes* for what to do next. It was the same for all the Foggies: we had no clue what we were supposed to do; even less if there was a grand plan behind the apparition of the Fog.

'Some nutters can be dangerous,' I said to Zeno.

*

As the household was sitting for dinner, just when I thought we had gone through a day without major crisis, multiple beeps were heard around the dining table from the various Ftab of those present. My Ftab's ringtone blasted and someone insistently rang the bell. Harry, Zeno, Rico and I looked at each other. What now?

Leila stormed into the room, followed by Harry who had gone to open the door for her.

'Morocco is under siege!' she announced and collapsed in a chair. 'If I were drinking alcohol, this is when I would ask for the whisky bottle.'

'Leila, what do you mean *Morocco is under siege*?' Harry asked her.

'The Foggies. In the Atlas mountain. Under siege. We don't know how and when, but someone must have found them, and ...' Leila began.

'I bet this is that Chen - that bastard - again!' Rico burst out.

'No, it isn't. It would have been better!' she snapped, harshly. 'We are dealing with extremists. Muslim extremists. They want access to the Fog.'

'Oh my God...' I was in shock. So were the boys.

'The security in place spotted them just in time and we have managed to hold the fort so far. We're sending more people over, but we have lost two men already, and another one is... Dying. He is dying.'

'Oh Leila, I am so sorry...' I told her.

'And... Isabelle and the baby? And Christophe and Louise and Helo?' Zeno asked.

'They are fine. Shaken but fine. Isabelle, Christophe and baby Chloé have taken refuge in WII. Louise stayed in the Fog house with Helo.'

'But why? Why do those terrorists want to take the house? Have they made any claim?' Rico asked, shaking his head.

'No, they haven't,' Leila replied.

'How do you know they are Muslim terrorists?' Harry asked.

'We intercepted their communications. And when you have a look at them, there is little doubt…' Leila replied. 'Rico, would you mind - I could do with one of your strong coffees?'

'Coming right up!' Rico was already heading towards the kitchen. 'I still don't understand what they have to gain?!'

'Maybe it's not the house that they want, but the Foggies,' Harry replied. 'Imagine if they got hold of one and they could create Fog Gates anywhere in the world and access places they would never be able to, otherwise. They could create chaos.'

'Jeez…' I whispered to myself.

'Leila, is the Society equipped to fight them?' Harry continued.

'Our people are the best of the best, but we are not an army. Members of the team from here and from Kenya are already on their way to strengthen our position.'

'What about the Moroccan authorities? Could they help?'

Leila hesitated before saying, 'They are our last resort. We would rather not involve them. The consequences of their participation and reactions are too uncertain. Anyway, I hope you don't mind, but I have called our international man of mystery, Lochy McRae. He should be here shortly. He wanted a partnership; he could hereby have it, with immediate effect.'

'So New York has given the green light?' I asked her.

'Yes, on condition that he doesn't ask too many questions. Well, no questions really. We will give him the briefest description of who we are and our charitable goals, and only one point of contact: me.'

'And what do you expect from him in Morocco?'

'To set up an unofficial rescue mission with the British Secret Service. He says that he can be an open double agent but that's unlikely to work in practice. Instead, he will be the direct point of contact with them and me. Both of us will have to provide the least information possible on our respective sides. That is the basic principle. We need to talk about the details and how – or if – this could work.'

Rico came back with a large coffee pot and enough cups for everyone, including McRae's impending arrival.

'So, the beautiful Leila urged me to your humble abode at an unlikely late hour. Judging by your stern faces, the emergency is serious.' McRae said soon after.

'Yes, it is,' I replied. 'You made a suggestion yesterday morning that you wished to get closer to our protectors. Well, they are interested.'

'Brilliant! So who are they?'

'As you will continue to work for the British Secret Service, and they will not require you to betray your country, they will only disclose the minimum. You will act as a liaison agent rather than a double agent. You remember when you helped us rescue Jack? Well, the rule was *no questions asked*. This rule will extend to the whole partnership. At least to start with, then let's see how things evolve afterwards. We will expect mutual respect and mutual support when needed.'

'I was expecting a bit more information than this,' McRae commented.

'It might come later,' Leila intervened.

'What about communication?' McRae asked.

'If there is anything to communicate, you will be talking to me,' Leila replied.

McRae looked at the boys and me with a frown, meaning *'Shouldn't it be them?'*

'We still hope you'll stop by regularly with coffee and pastries for breakfast,' I said.

'But otherwise you will discuss matters directly with me,' Leila repeated.

McRae's mouth lifted into a smile as he understood the meaning of Leila's words.

'So my gut feeling was right: your mysterious friendship with Yoko was all made up.'

'We are friends now,' I replied on the defensive.

'So who do you work for?' McRae asked.

'The Society,' Leila answered.

'The Society? What Society? Care to tell me more?' McRae asked.

'They are a bunch of geek-historian-adventurers in the lineage of Indiana Jones,' Rico replied.

Leila rolled her eyes. McRae lifted an eyebrow.

*

Leila succinctly described the Society's purposes. McRae listened without interrupting.

'So you are pretty much modern good Samaritans,' McRae commented, when Leila finished.

'I like to think that we are,' Leila smiled.

'However, we only have your word for it,' McRae added.

'We have been working with the Foggies for months now and haven't disappointed them. Or so I hope?' She turned to look at us.

'You haven't. It took us some time to give you our full trust, but now we are fully enjoying both your help and your friendship,' I replied.

Leila beamed and turned back to look at McRae with a triumphant smile. It didn't last when McRae brought her back to the problem of the day.

'You didn't make me come here to tell me only this. This could have waited for tomorrow. What's up?'

'We have a problem in one of the Fog locations,' Harry said.

'Kenya?' McRae asked.

'No. Morocco,' Leila told him.

'It was my understanding the Fog there was long gone.'

'The one in Marrakech is. However, the situation is a bit more complex. The wife of the local Switcher was relocated and pregnant. We couldn't just close the Gate and leave her behind in WII. So the husband opened a new Gate in a remote location in the Atlas mountain, where the wife gave birth recently,' Leila explained.

'What a way to start a family,' McRae commented.

'You have no idea. The Crosser is the husband's mistress.' Rico told him.

'You are joking?!' McRae exclaimed.

'No. They are French,' Harry said.

'Ah! That explains it,' McRae said, looking at me with a mischievous smile.

'Don't you start! This is so clichéd. Not all the French have lovers...' I snapped.

Leila jumped in before McRae wound me up any further. She briefed him on the terrorist situation and the help required. When she finished, McRae immediately asked which room he could do some work in and pulled out his mobile to call his key people. Two hours later, he was on a private plane to Marrakech.

Day 3 (Tuesday)

I dreaded opening the Ftab to read my emails and see there would still be none from Leo. No news since Sunday. I also feared the updates coming from Morocco. I postponed checking for as long as possible. Mid-morning, I could not play the ostrich any longer: there was work to do.

A quick browse made me sigh, as indeed there was no email from Leo. A message from Sam confirmed a meeting with the Americans today at 4pm. Next, I opened an email from Christophe, from the Atlas Mountain.

'*Dear Yoko,*

That is it! That is the last straw. We have endured enough here. So far, the Society seems to be in control of the situation: I think those morons outside the house are fucked. They will never get to us! They will have their asses kicked in a matter of hours when the back-up arrives.

But we are done here. Isabelle and I have decided we can't live like that, and we can't have Chloé growing up in this shithole. It's time for a trip to England. After what happened to your sister, Isabelle refused to travel anywhere except on the ground, so we will make the journey by car. The Society will provide us with the latest vehicle for a rough trip with no road at our disposal. Now, it would really help if you could do a couple of things for us. Obviously we will need to refuel regularly, which will prove a problem in WII without Fog Gates. Next Saturday, I will switch a temporary cabin in a pre-agreed location in Spain so that fuel will be ready for us. Could you switch one further up on our way as well? We will transport tanks with us, but we can't last all the way up to England with them. Without highways, the journey is bound to take more time. When we arrive, we wish to be in the Essex house, not London, so we can stay clear of all the attention. We want to protect Chloé for as long as possible from the media and authorities. There are a few Relocated there already - right? - so Isabelle wouldn't be lonely.

What do you think? Would you do that for us?

Best,

Christophe.

P.S.: Fucking terrorists. I hope the Brits are going to kill them all!'

As usual when annoyed, Christophe's language was colourful. However, his confidence about his family's safety, despite their assailants, was reassuring. He gave me a new worry though, with their upcoming trip through the WII equivalent for Spain and France. Those lands were, as far as we knew, just wilderness. The family would be unreachable most of the time and left to their own devices with a baby. This was crazy. I could understand their decision, but wouldn't it be safer to wait until the baby was a little bit older than a couple of weeks?

*

My parents wrote too. Naively, I had hoped they would not suffer too much from the revelations that their daughter was a Gatekeeper. As I said, I was naïve. The security from the Society had to be increased. My parents were harassed for information about me by the media and the French Government. They had received threats and been offered bribes to have access to me. My mother could hardly see her friends any more and longed to escape the house for errands. They asked if they could come and see me in London. They needed a break. I loved the idea: I had not had a chance to see them in three months.

Jazz interrupted my nostalgia as I daydreamed of the childhood house in France, where I had little hope to go in the near future.

'Yoko, do you have a minute?' Jazz asked.

'Sure. What's up?'

'We have a problem here,' she said, whispering.

'Why are you whispering?'

'I don't want the council members to hear.'

'Why would ...' I began.

'They are in the lounge downstairs. I am in the office,' Jazz interrupted to explain.

'Ok. Which council? Every one of them?' I asked.

'Yes. Can you come? It's about the women…' Jazz explained.

'I expected that much. What has Clémence done?'

'It's not just about Clémence. It is also about Maud, Molly and me.'

'Oh no! What have YOU done?'

'Nothing! You are not taking their side, are you?!' Jazz was on the defensive.

'Of course not. I am on my way,' I replied with a sigh. I grabbed a few essentials, including the Ftab, and packed all in the large pockets of a light summer jacket. I quickly walked the few steps to *The Jazzin* with Simba by my side.

*

'Thank you for coming,' Jazz said with obvious relief as I walked in. In the lounge area, Edmund Poff, Benjamin Snayth and Augustus Hoare were waiting for me, sitting on one side of a table, Maud and Molly opposite them. They all stood up to greet me. Hoare had lost some of his confidence since Clémence had come out of her shell and revealed herself a feisty warrior princess. He had mellowed somewhat and his shoulders were a little slouched. Snayth had changed too: he had gained a constant look of bitterness in his face and hissed more than spoke when referring to Clémence and the women's issues. As for Edmund, he looked at his wife not only with love and admiration as before, but also with worry.

'Miss Salelles, let me raise our concerns straight away,' Snayth hissed. Clearly, he was about to talk about the women. 'We are very disappointed in your decision to support a self-proclaimed political movement promoting a so-called equality of the women in our society. You assured us of your neutrality in the affairs of Lil'London and Newtonsee. Such support goes against your words. We are hoping this is a misunderstanding and you do not intend to meddle in our politics?'

'Dear Mr Snayth, I am sorry to hear of your concern.' I needed time to think, not knowing what Maud and Jazz, or even Molly, had said that triggered such a reaction. 'May I ask what exactly troubles you?'

'What troubles me? Your involvement in our politics!' Snayth was struggling to contain his anger.

'I am confused, Mr Snayth. I am not involved in your politics: I am neither a member of this party, nor participating in their promotional campaign. Nor do I walk by their side as they approach the women of your towns. However, if as an Inter-world Ambassador I cannot officially promote them within your community, I approve of their cause which benefits our Relocated women. It preserves the rights, culture and ways of life they had grown accustomed to in their original world. So we cannot dismiss this new party and I personally sympathise with their purpose.' I told him, with a bright honeyed smile.

'Rhetoric!' Benjamin Snayth stood up, clenching his fists on the table. 'You know very well that your expression of sympathy is a strong support for their political aspirations and preposterous claims.'

'May I point out that I have never expressed my sympathies in public?' I retorted. Maud was proudly holding her head high. Jazz had her hand over her mouth in a pensive pose that badly hid a smug smile.

'They are known, nonetheless!' Benjamin Snayth was fuming.

'Well, it must be by hearsay and word of mouth, then. Nothing that is in my control,' I opened my arms in a helpless gesture. Augustus Hoare put a hand on Benjamin Snayth's arm to restrain him and spoke to me.

'Miss Salelles, I am sure you understand the importance of the situation. We are already fighting against Clémence's appalling demands and actions and ...'

'Exactly. Which is why I am surprised by your reactions to the Women's Equality Movement that Maud, Jazz and Molly are launching,' I looked at the men with what I hoped could pass for genuine surprise.

'What do you mean?' Hoare asked, while Snayth narrowed his eyes in suspicion.

'Well, have you not considered that many women follow Clémence because they are unhappy with their fate and she provides the only option of escape? Granted, a core of her followers have a thirst for a revolutionary change, and even for revenge against what they consider male oppression. However, Clémence's extremism and aggressive approach must render others, if not most, uncomfortable. Yet they don't have the choice if they want to improve their life or that of their daughters. Thanks to the Women's Equality Movement, those women will have an alternative. Thanks to the pacific political movement, they can have a voice without breaking from their families. It may also prevent the women who hesitated to join their ranks in doing so. Should you make a little bit of an effort and accept cooperating with the Women's Party, Clémence's radical strategy will be less appealing. You would gain credit by appearing more reasonable and in tune with modern times, instead of obtuse, stubborn, retrograde men who can't understand that women are a force to be reckoned with.'

My little speech left Snayth aghast, Hoare thoughtful, and Edmund relieved. Poor Edmund was split in his allegiances and beliefs… For a minute or so, no one spoke, and then Snayth hissed anew.

'They support *education for all*!'

'As I said, 'in tune with modern times'. With our Internet, a new wide pool of information is accessible at the touch of a finger. However, as global information could also be too much information, I recommend we stick to university programmes to start with.'

'We must approve the programmes first,' Benjamin Snayth said.

'It would take a lifetime to review them all. In addition, one of the problems you have with the women is that you have kept your people on a tight leash. Too tight. With our arrival, the situation has changed. You need to adjust.'

Leila rang on my Ftab. I wrote to her that I would return her call shortly. Augustus Hoare had taken in my hesitation and understood some business waited for me elsewhere.

'Miss Salelles, thank you for joining us at such late notice. We have noted your suggestions and will consider them. We will be in touch shortly.'

Snayth grunted a goodbye that was far less appreciative. Edmund whispered thank you in my ear, keeping a low profile.

Once they were gone, Maud threw herself at me and hugged me tight.

'You were fantastic! Thank you, Yoko!'

'I only said the truth, at least as I see it. I do wish for the women of WII to be treated with more respect and consideration than they currently are, but -

and please don't be offended - my priority is, of course, the Relocated. There is no way they would accept being treated the same way as you. Most of them would turn rebellious and could be more dangerous than Clémence!'

'About Clémence,' Jazz cut in, 'She's at it again.'

'What now?' I turned to look at Jazz.

'She has attacked the Lil'London primary school and taken the children in attendance. They range from 5 to 11. Boys and girls. Some of them had their mothers in the ranks of the Women's Revolution already.'

'Oh no! How many children?' I asked.

'One hundred and seventeen,' Maud replied.

'One hundred and seventeen! That many?!' I blurted, stunned. 'We do not have that many schools...'

'Why didn't the Council mention it earlier during the meeting?'

'As they are not happy with your 'involvement' as they put it, it's not that surprising...' Jazz remarked. She was right.

Leila messaged me again.

'I have to go,' I told Jazz.

'Is something up? Leila seems real eager to get in touch with you.'

'Well, we have our own issue with extremists. In Morocco...' I replied.

'What? Extremists? You mean, religious extremists?' Jazz exclaimed. I updated her briefly and she shook her head in disbelief.

'I hate those guys. It is terrible!' she said, in shock.

'Yes, it is. Thankfully, the Society and McRae are on the case. The worry is mainly for Louise, Helo and the mercenaries of the Society. Christophe, Isabelle and Chloé are hidden in WII. When it is all over, they have decided to make the trip to the UK and move here. You will have more company soon.'

Jazz didn't hide her lack of enthusiasm at the idea of Christophe moving into her vicinity. She abhorred any sign of French arrogance.

*

I crossed the Fog thanks to Simba and contacted Leila. She was anxious to give me updates: the Marrakech situation was not as easy to get out of as they had hoped. McRae had to set up a team via the British Embassy - not a simple task - on a no-questions-asked basis. In the end, he had recruited only a few trustworthy ex-colleagues and approached a section of the French Foreign Legion to complete his team. He remained vague on their involvement, saying only they had a favour to return to him. In the meantime, the terrorists had assaulted the Fog house several times, coming close to succeeding on the last one. The Gatekeepers' advantage was that the terrorists wanted them alive and so did not want to blow up the Fog house. The mercenaries had no such limits and were shooting on sight. McRae planned to launch an offensive at dusk.

On Kenya, sadly, Leila still had no news. I was despairing not hearing from Leo. My imagination was vivid with the dangers he faced in the wild jungle of an unknown world. I had to make an effort to block those thoughts, but it was easier said than done.

Leila would arrive a little later to attend the meeting with the Americans later that afternoon. I checked the time. It was past lunch-time already. There was no smell of food at home, so Rico and Zeno must be out. Harry was probably working in his office. I went to prepare myself a sandwich, giving double the amount of ham to Simba than I put in the sandwich. I washed it all down with a bottle of beer. I guiltily had a look at the Chronicles of Lil'London while eating. Every day I failed to advance my reading further than 5 pages: my progress was so painfully slow. On the positive side, it improved my understanding of old English and now I could read Shakespeare and understand it.

*

Just before 4pm, Sam arrived and informed us he would be next door should we need him during the meeting with the Americans. By next door, he meant the house facing our walled-in terraced houses. The British authorities had requisitioned every building surrounding us. Presumably it was for our security. We had taken the news of Her Majesty's Services surrounding us both with cynicism (we appreciated their care for our well-being) and pragmatism (if they had not done it and been open about it, we would have been even more suspicious). At exactly 4pm, six representatives of the American Embassy came through the checkpoints by the British security and ours. We greeted them at the main gate and led them to the office. As we walked through the old parking space, they discreetly looked around for the Fog. They immediately locked their eyes on the wooden wall hiding it, making a mental note of the location. While they were busy studying our ground, we were busy studying them. Their group comprised two women and four men. The older woman looked the stereotype of a high-level civil servant, fifty-something with a perfect shoulder length bob of dark blonde hair, a wrinkle-free silk shirt with a well-fitted suit and mid-heel court shoes. The other woman was younger, in her early to mid-thirties, and her appraisal of the situation seemed strategic rather than political. She made me think of a female Sam. She was also very fit and her way of walking betrayed military training. The same went for two of the men, who appeared also in their mid-thirties. Of the last two men, one had ginger blond hair and an engaging face, very tall and skinny. His suit was clearly made-to-measure and yet it gave the impression of being too big for him. The last man was chubby and bald, with a face that would have qualified as rough if not for his kind eyes, as if he had left behind a tough life for a more restful current one. He was in his fifties. My assessment of their backgrounds proved to be correct when they introduced themselves and their roles. The older man was the military Embassy attaché and the civil servant-looking woman a representative directly from the White House. She had travelled the previous day with the purpose of meeting us. The other three were unconvincing cultural and public relations attachés who did not speak a word during the whole meeting; instead, observing the room, windows, parking, us and any details that were worthy of being included in a thorough report about the Fog.

'Thank you for agreeing to see us,' said the White House representative with the perfect bob haircut.

'You are welcome.' I refrained from adding the meeting was unavoidable, opting to be charming instead of sarcastic, for as long as possible.

'We are sure that you have a very full diary, so we will try not to take too much of your time,' *Perfect Bob* said.

'Here is my card,' the ex-military man with kind eyes said. 'Should you need to contact the American Embassy for anything, you may contact me directly.'

'Thank you,' Harry, Zeno and I said as we took a card each. It felt a bit early to distribute cards, but what did I know about the American way?

'This is a beautiful dog you have here,' Kind Eyes said, caressing Simba. Simba let him do so, a good sign of his character, before coming to rest at my feet.

'Yes. She is a good companion. She's a malamute. I like big dogs.' I had gained confidence talking about Simba as if she were just large, even for her breed. I even managed to ignore the scrutiny of my wolf by the three so-called-attachés-more-likely-secret-agents.

'Yes. Very nice,' said Perfect Bob, in a tone that indicated she couldn't care less about my malamute. 'Miss Salelles, Mr Grande and Mr Baxton, we believe that the British have informed you we have a little bit of a 'situation' in our homeland with a Fog Gate and no Gatekeepers. By their intermediary, we suggested that maybe you would be able to help, which you regretfully declined. It was an error on our behalf not to make such a proposition directly and we would like to reiterate our invitation to come and help.'

Zeno looked at me and me at Harry to find out who would reply 'no' on behalf of us all, but Perfect Bob continued.

'Of course, your help would not go unrewarded. We offer you £1 million dollars each, per week, for your services, as well as transportation by private jet back and forth, staying in the best luxury hotels, and all that you may need to make your journey and visit the most comfortable and pleasant experience possible. Should you wish to establish a long-term relationship or remain with us, we would be delighted to offer you American citizenship and, of course, money. We will make sure the package is to your liking.'

Wow, I thought. It was an attractive deal. I shot a glance at Leila, who had stopped typing and was staring at Perfect Bob, trying to read her mind. She was appraising the risks for us to accept the proposal and move to the US, as well as calculating the all-round consequences.

'This is a very tempting proposal,' Harry replied. 'We appreciate the offer. However, would you care to be more explicit as to what you request in exchange for such generosity? Certainly your demands are more detailed than for just *our time* and *help*.'

'We would expect you to work with us by being at our disposal in testing the Fog, creating gates, liaising with locals of that other planet...' Perfect Bob replied.

'You already have one gate: why do you need more?' Zeno jumped into the conversation.

'To further explore this other planet,' Perfect Bob replied, with a smile.

'Those other gates, would they always be on American soil?' Zeno asked.

'Of course,' Perfect Bob replied.

'To be more specific, always located in one of the 50 American States?' I asked, remembering the American embassies are considered American soil.

'Miss Salelles, I understand your fear,' Kind Eyes replied, before Perfect Bob. 'Obviously, we are in the early stages of negotiation. The details of our partnership can be determined at a later date. Mostly, we wished to approach you to discuss the possibility of you coming to help us, if you are at liberty to do so.'

'We are glad to inform you that the British Government is not holding us captive in a golden London prison,' Harry said.

'It is our understanding your relations with them have not always been that clear,' Kind Eyes said.

'Is there any urgent issue we need to discuss on your Fog gate?' Harry asked, brushing away the reference and unspoken question about our relations with the British authorities.

'Well, we do indeed have some issues with the locals,' Perfect Bob replied. 'A few of our men have been relocated to the Other World after crossing the Fog and we lost contact with them. The communication we had was with a woman who used our military radio signal to confirm our men were safe and unharmed. We are trying to establish contact with her, but she refuses to talk. We are also looking for the original Gatekeepers who created this Fog, the Koplats. You wouldn't happen to have any information either on this woman or the Koplats, would you?'

Harry, Zeno and I had faces set in stone. She would learn nothing from us. Harry again took the lead in the conversation.

'Why would we know anything?' he asked.

'It is our understanding that the Gatekeepers are well connected,' Kind Eyes replied.

'I wonder where you get your *understanding* from?' I said.

'This is why we would like to hire your services in our homeland. We wish to have the real answers, not indirect ones,' Perfect Bob said.

'Come on… This is BS,' Zeno said. 'I am fed up with the politically correct talk. Let's be clear, here: we have done plenty of tests and the likes with the Brits and I have no wish to go through that again. The two countries are allies, so just sort something out between you and share the info you need, ok? Because I've had it with being a lab rat. In addition, there is no way we would open new Fog gates for you. Those things need maintenance, you know, and there are consequences in creating them. The only reason I would consider coming would be in view of your 'Relocated' problems. But this woman says they are safe, so no need. Your money, I don't care about.'

'Also, how do we know that once in the States you would honour our agreement?' I asked.

'For the same reasons the British are honouring theirs.'

'That's fair enough,' I thought. Though now that I felt secure, or secure-ish, in one place and trusted my interlocutors, I had no wish to budge. Like Zeno, money was not a motivator. However, it gave me an idea.

'Here is my email address,' I said, scribbling my secure email on a page of my notebook and ripping it for Kind Eyes. 'Send me the layout of your proposal. We will discuss it between us and get back to you.'

*

Sam was waiting outside for us when they left. As soon as they disappeared from earshot, he asked:

'So? They asked you to pay them a visit in the Great US of A, didn't they?'

'Of course,' I replied.

'And what did you say?' he continued.

'We said we didn't care about money,' Zeno replied. Sam smiled, but it wasn't the clear answer he wanted. He understood he would have none and dropped the subject.

Harry, Zeno, Rico and I – the four musketeers housemates - went for dinner at *The Jazzin*. Jazz, Big Tom and Nick were joining us. It had been a long time since we last gathered for a group meal. The Fishers and Molly were in Lil'London, being entertained by Barnaby Sparrow, the handsome forger and hunk. Apparently, Molly, like Jazz before her, had immediately started drooling when she saw him. However, Sparrow was already married and had several children. Sharing him with another wife was not ideal but Molly had such a crush on him she did not rule out the idea. As usual, we tried to have light conversation on our everyday lives and talk about random personal matters and anecdotes. It was difficult these days: we hardly had time for personal lives. The issues in both worlds were too much on our minds, so we soon put a movie on.

I decided to organise a visit to Ariel Ben-Chaim in the next few days. I had not seen the wise man for too long and would love to have a chat with him. He always gave good advice and more than anyone could help me understand the people of WII better. Now I was curious to hear what he would have to say about the rise of Clémence, and how his community viewed it. Indeed, the women of their town were not allowed to speak to non-Jews and had strict religious codes. Could they rebel, too?

Day 4 (Wednesday)

Over breakfast, we discussed the email received overnight from Perfect Bob. It did not give more information than the one provided during our meeting. As the offer concerned all the Gatekeepers, we passed on the message to the other Foggies. We wondered, mostly, what the Koplats would make of it. Leila joined us shortly afterwards, with concerns of her own.

'Aren't you worried it would create a discrepancy of incomes between Foggies?' Leila asked, after Harry's comment that the Koplats might take the offer.

'And so what? We can't lead an eccentric life, anyway. We are Fog-dependent,' Zeno said. 'Any one of us could have as much money as we wish:

we only have to ask a Government. Yet what more do we need that we don't already have? I think it's safe to say our future is secure, but first, we should work out what life we can have.'

'*Si*,' Rico commented. 'And as Gatekeepers, we all get a share of each other's earnings, even if a small percentage. Plus, we need each other, and if money goes to someone's head, we will remind them to get real.'

'Do you ask because you are scared of losing your connection with us, if we accept the American deal?' Harry asked Leila.

'A little... That and of the Americans coming after the Society,' Leila admitted, finishing her first cup of coffee and helping herself to another.

'It isn't in our interest, either, to have the Society endangered. You are protecting our freedom,' I told her.

'Someone could go to the US, quarterly, just to maintain the Fog and check on the Relocated. And on the Native Americans,' Harry suggested.

'Yes, I presume you're right,' Leila said, with a sigh. 'Elsie would welcome a bit of non-military company.'

'How is she doing?' Harry asked.

'She says she's fine. She is thrilled with her research and interactions with the Native Americans. She is compiling her discoveries and the whole experience in a daily report to me. We used to see each other, from time to time, in New York. She has a great energy, a positive spirit and she's a fighter. I still worry that the situation will take its toll on her soon. Right now, she is excited and flattered by the trust the Native Americans place in her, but what will happen when the novelty wears off? Will her spirits drop like a soufflé taken out of the oven too soon?'

Elsie had a routine already. Each day, she sat first thing in the morning with the Chief and Shaman of the tribe. Then she met with the relocated soldiers in one of the three tepees given by the Native Americans. The soldiers were uncooperative at first, angry at having their weapons and radio taken from them. They felt defenceless and arbitrarily cut from WI. Elsie patiently explained the radio would be returned when they had spent at least a month with the Native Americans. She wanted them to get to know their new community with total immersion. She also explained that it was possible for the door to close soon and they had to learn to adjust to a new life. Elsie also conceded to them that if she was trying to protect the Native Americans by removing the soldiers' weapons, she was also protecting them. This world was theirs now. They had to build a new life here. They wouldn't want to antagonise the locals from the start, would they? Elsie was adamant that as soon as they realised their old allegiances needed adjusting, they would be free to communicate and visit the Fog house. She warned them that even then, they would be strip-searched when coming back, for security reasons.

'As if we were terrorists,' sneered one of the soldiers.

'For this community, that's pretty much what you potentially are. A terrorist, a coloniser, an invader… A threat. This is not America. Anyway, there is no war and I would prefer not to have one lurking, so your weapons have no place here, especially if you intend to use them.'

The soldiers kept silent and nodded. On the matter of personal choice, there is rarely a right or wrong decision. Everything is relative; everything depends on the point of view. Theirs was still stuck in WI, but they were beginning to realise it might need to cross the Fog, too.

*

That Tuesday, none of us went back to our respective offices. We wanted to spend some time together, so worked from the dining room table. On my side, some administration work for Gatekeepers Associates with Sophia Koplat, and online classes access for WII with Leila, kept me occupied. My parents also got in touch to organise their arrival on Friday. Before we knew it, it was early afternoon and we were hungry.

'Ingis Chen has struck again,' Harry said, as Leila and I finished laying the table. Rico was in the kitchen tossing a mixed salad while Zeno filled burgers with meat, cheese and tomatoes.

'I'm afraid to ask,' I replied, with a frown.

'His latest is to request that the Gatekeepers 'fog' a hospital to extend the benefits of the Fog healing powers to a larger group of people on both sides, combining it with modern medicines. He claims the Government should have implemented this kind of project already and it is a shame it hadn't. He also claims that the public should be kept informed of all the research on the nature, benefits and risks of the Fog.'

'Has he dropped his more general claim that everyone must have right of access?' I asked, with suspicion.

Harry smiled and read on. 'Here it is. He considers it a key element of - wait for it – his *organisation*. Yes, you heard right: our Ingis has set up a non-profit organisation promoting the people's interest in view of the existence of the Fog and the parallel world.'

'Please, don't refer to him as 'our' Ingis…' I retorted.

Ingis Chen's latest antics did not surprise me. In truth, his public statements followed the same lines as before. It would only crescendo from now on. My fears were not about what he was currently demanding, even though it would make our lives difficult: I was wary of the power and influence he was gaining in the process. I did not trust him.

'He keeps saying we are a nice bunch who would love to help, and that it is up to the government to get cracking. He blames the Government for keeping things slow and for not making the best out of the Fog. Yeah right! As if it was so simple!' Rico commented, reading over Harry's shoulder.

'Well… there is nothing we can do about that,' I said as I sat down, grabbing one of the burgers.

'I am surprised you're not more upset,' Harry commented.

'My mind is still on the council's visit. Something is just not right in their attitude.'

They all waited for me to continue, pausing in their eating. Except Rico: nothing could stop Rico munching when he had food in his hands.

'Also, all these school children missing. We should help, not because we are taking sides but because children are involved. Plus, when Ushi Tsou abducted me, the town people helped. When I was targeted by this lunatic who wanted to kill me, they helped. Whenever we needed help, they helped.'

'Wait! For Maisie and Owen, the council almost caused a war with their fake letter?! How do we know they're not trying to use us again this time?' Zeno exclaimed.

'We have no proof the Council wrote that letter, and their children are involved.'

'Who else. But I see your point…' Harry said, thoughtful.

'But they are bastardi!' Rico retorted.

'Clémence is no English rose, mate. You forget that she is the prime suspect behind the lunatic's attempts to kill Yoko,' Zeno countered.

'We can just give out her location, thanks to the tracker, without giving the specifics,' I suggested.

'We could say it's her use of the radio that betrayed her,' Zeno says.

'The how is just details. We don't have to explain. The most important thing is: should we help them or not?' I snapped uncharacteristically. I had not realised, until then, how this issue had grown in my mind into a real ethical problem.

'Maybe we could ask for something in exchange?' Jazz suggested.

'Like what?' I asked her, suspiciously. We were still at the table, now on a conference call with Jazz. Her face took the whole of the widescreen television on the wall.

'We help them find the children in exchange for a decree abolishing the women's prison? Or their agreement on Open University for all?'

'You know that if we start stating conditions, when or if we need their support next, they will ask for something in return,' I said.

'They need us more than we need them,' she replied.

'Oh really? Because you don't need them? What would happen if they decide the Relocated are not welcome any more?'

'Nick would distribute grenades to us,' Jazz said without hesitation. What scared me was how serious she was. Was she turning into Ushi Tsou now?

'Right. Well… Let's see what we could do to turn this to your advantage, politically. Let's say that Nick is in charge of the tracking in WII and you are both Relocated. We could make this a negotiation between Woodfellas and the councils, not something to do with the Foggies, no? Like that, we protect our diplomatic neutrality – they know we watch your back anyway – and that gives you some powers of your own.'

'So you guys can wash your hands of it…' Jazz commented with a sneer.

'Oh please… Don't you start!' Harry remarked. 'You know we are doing the best we can and, as Yoko commented, we have your back. Who would give Nick the grenades, I wonder?'

'Fine. I will discuss with Maud and Molly for such negotiations. At least, are you interested in being kept in the loop?' Jazz was not happy.

'What is it with you today?!' I exploded. 'Why are you being so unpleasant?! We just suggested a way for you to win points towards your cause, as well as diminish Clémence's position. Can't you be a little grateful, and not so grumpy?!'

Jazz hesitated and looked a bit sheepish.

'Maybe it's that time of the month?' Zeno suggested. He turned to me. 'Looks like PMS to me.'

'It is not!' Jazz exclaimed. 'I…' She didn't get to finish her sentence as we heard Big Tom's voice in the background.

'You alright, Babe?' Jazz bit her lip and looked even more sheepish. OK, I thought, so here is the problem. Something to do with Big Tom.

'Right, we will talk about it later,' I said, in a calmer and conciliatory tone. 'I am coming in the afternoon to see Ariel Ben-Chaim.'

'Yes… Thank you.' Jazz was patently relieved.

I sorted a few more things and started to get ready for my trip to WII when Leila stopped me on the way out. She wanted to let me know that the memory stick Ingis Chen had provided had had a very complex virus on it, designed to mirror what was on my screen onto another device, and so they would be able to follow what we were up to. The Society had managed to separate the information content from the stick so that I could browse it safely.

'Have you read it?' I asked Leila.

'Just a quick look. It has an interesting insight on Native Americans. It will be useful to Elsie. That was possibly his target: getting access to the Nevada Portal.'

'He must have known the memory stick would be checked for viruses.'

'The mirror virus was activated not when you opened the document, but when you read its page 21 and moved on to page 22. A very clever trick.'

'So how did you work it out?'

'Our experts were interested in the read!'

'You mean we got lucky?'

'Yes. We all need luck from time to time.'

*

Just before heading to Ariel's, McRae messaged me suggesting dinner. He was already back from Morocco. I accepted. I didn't mention it to Jazz, as she would immediately say it was a date and tease me about it. She had decided to accompany me to Yerushaleim. My deductions had been correct: her grumpiness was due to tensions between Big Tom and her. She found him over-protective; he didn't like her political actions and the risks incurred with her being a 'feminist activist', as he put it.

We had intended to discuss with Ariel the status in Yerushaleim regarding Clémence's Women Liberation's uprising, and the reaction of its female population. We did not even allude to it once, as he had dismissed the subject immediately upon our arrival as non-relevant for the little town. Neither Jazz nor I wished to push the controversial subject any further. Instead, we enjoyed the warmth of his apothecary and welcoming home: a haven of peace and knowledge. Ariel taught us how to prepare traditional remedies and tried his hand at a couple of the recipes Elsie had sent from the WII natives. He was keen to reciprocate the favour and allowed me to take pictures of some pages from his family's traditional book of potions and remedies. Witnessing him at work proved to me, once more, that he was a man of science. The details with which he measured each ingredient and his expertise in assessing the right temperature to mix them was fascinating. Some ingredients I would never have thought to even try, like turnip water. He explained it was useful against coughs, for example. He read from his book:

'Take halfe a pack of Turnips, one quarter of a pound of Elliocompain Root, ten pippins. Pair them and slice them and put them into a Rose still and still them altogether. Tak the Water and boyl it to a surrup and drink of it for a Cough, in the boyling of the surrup you may put in a litle liquorish and sweet Fenel seeds.'

It was even worst to decipher than the *Chronicles of Lil'London*. Here, not only was the text in old English, it was manuscript. Elsie would have a hard time at it. She might also struggle to get the ingredients, as the Society was not able to pass them on to her.

*

As McRae's invitation for dinner intrigued me, I had accepted. Anyway, it was a much better alternative than staying at home, worrying over Leo's fate. The boys agreed to look after Simba for me and I got into the shower, speculating what the meeting could be about, aside from how to woo Leila or become better acquainted with the Society. I was also keen to hear the details of his mission in Morocco. Leila had told me in brief that the rescue had finally succeeded, helped by the fact that the extremists were unable to aggressively attack, unwilling to harm the Foggies. Their siege left them in a precarious situation once the mercenaries arrived and they were caught in a sandwich. It turned out they were newbie Muslim fanatics who had struck lucky in discovering the Fog. The young men, still teenagers, were hoping to get hold of the Fog and Foggies, then go back to the more established extremist groups to make an impression. They were now in the hands of the French Foreign Legion. I would rather not know what happened to them there. The Foggies on site would be moved to a new location in the mountains as soon as possible, with yet another increase in security.

*

McRae arrived by motorbike, to pick me up. I had foreseen this and put on a pair of skinny jeans and flat shoes, along with a silk shirt and a leather jacket. For the fun of it, I was wearing a long layered chestnut wig with bangs that covered half my face and Ray-Ban sunglasses. It felt good to look cool. McRae looked me up and down and smiled, giving me the thumbs up. Before climbing on the back of his bike, I checked with the Society's security that McRae had updated them on our destination and if someone was ready to follow us. They pointed to another biker waiting across the road and mentioned they had placed other drivers on the road. All good. I didn't know where we were going, but they did.

We passed the police blockade at the top of the road and turned left towards East London. McRae was generous in his use of the accelerator. I did not complain: give me speed and I am happy. After Angel, we turned left and in no time we entered Dalston, one of the hipster centres of London and a cool arty part of town. It has a rich mix of people and backgrounds and small delicious restaurants in abundance. Knowing what to expect, my stomach rumbled from pleasure and hunger. McRae opened the doors of a local Turkish diner and informed the waiter we had a reservation. The place was full of locals, which is always a good sign. We stood out from the crowd and all eyes were on us. That made me a bit nervous, not because I was the centre of attention, but to be recognised. The events in Kenya and Morocco were still fresh in my mind and I was not sure how people would react in my presence. However, McRae led me to our table and soon the diners turned back to their meal. Perusing the menu, everything looked delicious.

'Right,' I said folding the menu on the table. 'Lochy, it all looks wonderful and I already know I won't be able to make up my mind. Would you pick for me?'

'Sure. Any allergy?' McRae replied.

'No and I am happy to share, too.'

'Perfect, let's have a selection of dishes, then. I hope you're hungry: this place is the best!' McRae said, excitedly. He was obviously a food amateur, like me.

'Reassure me. We both agree this is not a date, right?' I told McRae, after he had placed the order and given me one of his wicked smiles. My question made him smile even more.

'It could be if you wanted it to be,' the Scot replied.

'What about your promise to Sam?' I asked him.

'If you take the lead, that wouldn't be my fault, would it?' The man was incorrigible. Who says Brits are shy? Or maybe the Scottish are to the British Isles what Italians are to Europe: irresistible and incorrigible flirts.

'Forget it. I am out of the dating scene. My heart is already taken by someone else,' I said, brushing away his comment. 'So, to what reason do I owe the pleasure of this dinner?'

'I wanted to get to know you a little better. In our line of work, we hardly get friendly with our colleagues - or targets - when on a mission. This situation is different. This could be a work relationship for life. So I wish to know more about you.'

McRae leaned back in his chair, in a relaxed attitude. He spoke with a calm and friendly tone, dropping the mask of the professional and that of the charmer.

'You are really involving yourself in this 'mission', aren't you? First, you managed to create a direct link with the Society, and now you work on setting up the ground for a more personal relationship with the Gatekeepers. Are you going to invite the other Foggies for dinner as well?'

My purpose in asking bluntly was not to be unfriendly; just to be clear from the start that I wouldn't and couldn't easily welcome people in my life any more. And yet, as soon as the words came out of my mouth, I regretted how cold they were. It was uncalled for. McRae had given us no reason to doubt his motivation. His achievements, to date, had proved he wanted to help us. My instincts were also telling me that he was reliable. Of course, all his actions could be interpreted as a plot to get in our good books when, in truth, he was a Trojan horse. I wasn't Rico though: I didn't read conspiracy into everything.

'I can see that even you don't recognise, yourself, how bitter that sounded…' McRae commented, while taking a piece of flat bread.

'No. I don't. I am sorry. It's just that striking up new friendships is not simple now.'

'I understand. It is also premature. As I said, I just want to get to know you better. It doesn't mean we'll be friends. You are not easy to read.'

'Maybe I prefer it that way?'

I was about to continue when my top was pulled slightly on the back. I turned and saw a toddler sitting in a high chair, just behind me. The mother smiled at me and moved the chair so that the child would not be able to grab my shirt again. I turned back to McRae.

'No one is an open book,' I continued. 'We all have our secret gardens. I don't know of anyone who shows the whole picture. We also show different sides to different people. Rare are those who even know or understand themselves fully, so that limits the chance for anyone else to do so.'

'True. I can tell you have a kind heart, though.'

That made me smile. At that moment, I felt a pull again from behind, but this time it was on the wig, which came off in a flash. I had taken off my glasses at the table, thinking I was safe as my back was to the main room. By reflex, I turned to look at the child and locked eyes with the mother. She started to apologise and then recognition sparked in her eyes. She put one hand to her mouth and pointed at me with the other, saying something in a language I did not know. Quickly, I grabbed the wig from the floor but it was too late. The whole room was now staring at me. Voices rose in a language that must have been Turkish. McRae stood up abruptly and was beside me in an instant, lifting me up from the chair by the arm. He had already grabbed our jackets with his free hand and we were walking towards the entrance as fast as possible. As he pushed the door open and slid outside, someone suddenly grabbed my shoulder and another person came in front of me, separating me from McRae and blocking my way out.

'You need to help me! I am sick. I am very sick. Please help! Please!' A woman in her forties, wearing a dark brown and gold outfit, told me.

A small part of me was moved by her pleas, but a bigger part was scared. 'I must get out!' was all I could think of. Before I had a chance to escape, several people had blocked the door, cutting me from the exit. McRae was outside, leaning against the door to push it open. A Society's bodyguard joined him. Someone from inside the restaurant shouted something – again, I assumed it was Turkish - and a table got pushed against the door. Then two more men carried another table on top of the first one and started adding chairs. I saw the Society bodyguard, already surrounded by two more men, call for backup. McRae was also talking on his mobile. I was rushed towards the back of the room, everyone talking to me at once. My internal panic button had been activated and I focused on keeping calm. 'What do they want from me?! I can't do anything for them here in the restaurant,' I thought. I was hyperventilating. The toddler started to cry.

'Leave me alone!' I screamed, pushing people away from me. In my confused state, I gathered there were two types of people in the room: one group focused on me and on getting my attention, asking questions and demanding help; the other, intent on keeping me inside, blocking my exit. I realised that I needed to regain control of myself. I stopped pushing, closed my eyes, steeled myself and shouted a firm 'STOP!' I repeated it several times, my eyes open from now on, looking directly into the eyes of my assailants. After a minute or so, the buzz calmed down and the room was quieter. I looked at the faces around me. Most appeared uncomfortable, maybe ashamed of their outbursts. A few were expectant, as if I held the solution to their problems and could change their lives, here and then.

'Ladies and gentlemen, may I ask you to give me some space and let me breathe?' I asked politely, doing my best to appear composed. The restaurant guests, about twenty people, moved back a little. Some among them exchanged glances.

'Thank you,' I said. 'Now, I understand that you may have queries. I would be happy to answer if I can, but you must understand that jumping on me like that and firing questions all at once is freaking me out! I am a normal person, you know.'

'You are the Gatekeeper!' an Asian in her thirties exclaimed, from the back.

'Yes, but …' I did not get a chance to finish. A young woman interrupted me to say that her husband was sick. She did not get a chance to finish as another person jumped in and said he needed to cross the Fog with his wife and children. Then, in a moment, they all started to speak again.

'STOP! SILENCE!' I shouted again, moving my arms up and down slowly in a calming gesture. It took a few seconds for everyone to stop talking. People, certainly McRae and the security from the Society, were banging at the door behind me.

'Please. You have to understand that I am not a miracle worker, nor can I solve all your problems. The situation is much more complicated than that.'

'All I want, all some of us want, is to cross the Fog,' a voice said.

'Is it true, can you really heal everyone?' another asked.

'What about that world? Is it really full of gold and diamonds? Can we get rich if we cross?'

'How do they treat us over there? Are we like… you know… Gods?'

'What? No. No to everything you just said!' I replied. 'We are certainly not gods and neither are we treated like that. As to diamonds and gold, it is, as I said, more complicated than that. Like here, you cannot just bend down and pick up diamonds as if they were mushrooms. This is preposterous. Also, no, everything cannot be healed, only viruses. Not everyone can cross to the WII, either.'

'But is it real? Is there a Fog with healing power and another earth?' someone asked.

'Yes.'

'And its population, are they aliens as well as humans?'

'I have only encountered humans.'

'Maybe they are aliens, not humans, and you are being fooled?'

Why is it that people tend to think of the worst, instead of the best, scenario? Do we always have to be suspicious of everything and everyone?

'We share the same ancestors,' I told the people before me. Now that a certain peace had settled, I could assess the situation. The door was still blocked and four men were holding the fort, simultaneously listening with attention to the exchange. Towards the kitchen, a frail man with determined features was observing the scene.

'Sir, is this your establishment? Are you condoning my being held captive in here?' I asked him. He looked to be the man in charge.

The man smiled. He disappeared into a side room and came out with a bottle of prosecco and two glasses. People parted as he came towards me and he handed me a glass.

'I approve of it. When I see an opportunity, I seize it,' he commented as he opened the bottle.

'An opportunity to do what?' I enquired.

'An opportunity to turn my restaurant into a Fog. If I keep you overnight, it will be. And soon I will be a rich man.'

'I think you have been misinformed. Portals are only created on specific days and that day is not today.'

'You might be saying this to get out. I'd rather wait and check for myself,' he replied.

'Hang on!' The mother of the toddler, holding him in her arms, jumped into the conversation. 'What if WE don't want to be locked inside?'

'Why wouldn't you want to be in the Fog and clear of all viruses?' the man in charge replied.

'I don't want to be transferred to this Other World!' she retorted.

'Chances are you won't. The odds are in your favour,' he snapped back.

'We don't want to gamble our life!' her companion said firmly, taking a step forwards in front of mother and child, in a protective gesture.

'Maybe we could just let the ones who want to leave go, and all the others stay,' another man intervened, talking about me and pointing at me as if I had no voice in the matter.

'Wait a minute. You do realise what you are doing is kidnapping, don't you?' I asked.

A teenager girl, maybe 14 or 15 years old, came running from the back of the restaurant and said something in the ear of the frail yet tough man, the owner of the place. He stood up and called for someone. A chef came out of the kitchen. After listening to the owner, the chef disappeared, running to the back.

'You don't speak Turkish, do you?' the mother with the toddler asked me.

'No, I don't.'

'Apparently there is a back door, and the child came to say there was some noise back there. The cook has gone to block it more,' she translated. 'I am telling you because I disapprove of the situation. I am sorry I was involved in creating it because my baby pulled your wig.'

'Don't worry. It is neither yours nor your child's fault. Certainly not,' I told her. She gave me a sorry smile. I turned back to the owner.

'Please be reasonable. You do understand that you will have the police, the secret services and who knows who on your back if you don't open these doors very soon. If you do it now, I will make sure nothing comes of it.'

'Miss, I don't think you understand. You are in a privileged situation; you don't know how difficult it is out there for normal people like us to make a living. We work hard day and night, and for what? We can hardly pay both mortgage and school fees. We hardly manage to scrabble enough money to all go and visit the family in Turkey once a year and close the restaurant. That is the only holiday we take and cannot even afford. Everywhere you turn, they talk of seizing opportunities, of taking chances, of going for it... This is not reality! In the real world, working your ass off every day doesn't leave you the time to browse for alternatives. And when you have a family to feed, how could you take the risk or the time to set up a new business and wait 3 years before it makes any profits. It could fail too! No... When I saw the commotion and understood who you were, I immediately knew that your presence here might be our blessing, the lucky break we've never had. You are our chance to finally come out of the long exhausting tunnel that is our life, and stop wondering if the clients will still come tomorrow. This is just for the night. Tomorrow you can go back to your life, but you would have improved mine for ever.'

'Tomorrow you will be arrested and put in prison. Tomorrow you will be known as the man who abducted a Gatekeeper for his personal benefit, and done it on the wrong day. Tomorrow, if you persist on holding me – us – captive, you will have ruined your life and anyone helping you will be suspected of complicity,' I told him as gently as I could. I felt sorry for the man. His actions were the consequences of his despair in life. Silence settled in the room as most of the dinners felt unsure how to react after my speech on the repercussions of keeping me against my will. None of them had planned to risk their future when they ventured out that evening!

'My mother is dying. You could cure her. If not today, you could create a healing Fog accessible to most that would save her,' an older teenage girl said, holding her mother's hand. The mother looked at her daughter with affection and put her arm around her shoulder, but she avoided looking at me.

'I understand. Though I can't help everyone.'

'Right now you are not helping anyone. Shouldn't it be why you have this gift, to help people? To help as many as you can?' the girl replied. This left me speechless and with a sense of guilt.

*

The banging against both door and windows had become worse for some time. At that moment, a loud shattering of glass indicated one window had caved in. Everyone inside ducked. Confusion followed and within seconds, a pair of arms grabbed me from behind, lifted me and put me on a shoulder. I tried to wiggle myself free, unsure if the back, bum and legs seen from above belonged to a rescuer or not.

'Yoko! Stop moving!' McRae's voice ordered. I stopped wiggling. Ten men from the Society soon joined McRae to escort me out in this very unladylike position. McRae sat me with authority on his motorbike and put a helmet on my head. A Society bodyguard arrived on a bike next to him and both started off at the same time, leaving a scene of chaos by the restaurant. The drive back home was not long, about 15 minutes. It still felt an eternity reliving the events of tonight in my head. Three things hit me hard: the first was how overwhelming a small crowd of people had become upon discovering who I was; the second was the hopes placed in me, or how I could appear as a cash cow; third, the more personally hurtful, was the girl's words. Was I misusing my gift? Was it a gift to use for the sake of others? Was I unworthy of it?

Day 5 (Thursday)

'Why does something always happen to you when I am not around?' Phil asked, with an annoyed look on his face. He had arrived for breakfast with Rico, Zeno, Harry and me, bringing a selection of pastries. 'And what were you doing with McRae anyway? Are you dating him now?'

I rolled my eyes. Can you not have dinner with a man these days without something sexual being read into it? Come to think of it, I had wondered that myself, at first…. McRae's reputation with the *lassies* was bound to lead to this type of question. So many women among the police, the Secret Services and even the Society had fallen for him, some of his male colleagues – maybe the jealous ones - were even calling him 'the disease'.

'No, it was a professional meeting.' Phil looked dubious at my reply. I persisted. 'Yes, the man is charming, but no, I haven't got the virus yet.'

'Yet?' Harry noted. I rolled my eyes once more.

'I won't!'

'Leo and she are back together,' Rico informed Phil, who looked at me with a nod of approbation. So much for having a private life.

'How is it going in Kenya?' Phil asked. As a key element of the Society's Foggies' protection team, he was aware of the Foggies' rescue mission.

'No news,' I replied with a pinch of the heart.

'Your parents are arriving tomorrow, aren't they?' Phil changed the subject. My face must have shown the Kenya topic was painful.

'Yes, they are.'

'I have assigned myself as security for their transport from the airport. They are staying here?'

'They don't want to. They are not sure how long they will stay, so they don't want to impose. Leila has organised a flat for them nearby.'

'You must be pleased to see them.'

'Very! I miss them. They have been under pressure lately, under the scrutiny of the French and the press.'

'It will be the same here if their link to you gets known,' Harry jumped into the conversation.

'Well, as usual in my life now, we will cross that bridge if or when necessary,' I replied. I refused to be stressed beforehand for what may or may not happen.

*

Leila arrived shortly after. She barely had time to sit before Sam and McRae joined us as well. Leila looked at them both and switched on her Ftab. She plugged it into the large screen and launched a recording of a BBC news report. The Turkish restaurant filled the screen. It was night time, shot soon after our departure.

'She wouldn't even listen to our plea,' an angry man said. 'All we wanted was for her to stay a couple of hours and enable us to get some of this Fog healing. We just want to be healthy!'

'I don't believe in it,' another person said. 'I wanted out but was blocked inside. That Gatekeeper woman seemed nice enough, but I agree she was unmoved by those begging for her help.'

'I don't understand.' The teenage girl came on the screen. She was shaking her head, confused and upset. 'If I could do what she does, I would travel all the time to open as many portals as possible. I would create doors open to anyone who wishes to cross. This is a gift. A gift from God. It doesn't matter which God. Or you can call it a gift from the Universe. It doesn't matter. It is a gift for humanity, a chance to save lives and help thousands of people. Why doesn't she do it? Why doesn't she help everyone? This is so magical, so wonderful. She should be out there. This is such a shame. No, I don't understand. She has been chosen. She has a mission. Doesn't she realise it?'

Ingis Chen then appeared in close-up on the screen. It was a sudden change and made us all lean back in our chairs.

'This young lady is right. We are living in extraordinary times. Yoko is a lovely person, she and the other Foggies wish nothing other than to help. If she had been able to Fog that venue last night, there is no doubt - no doubt! - she would have. Unfortunately, she told them the truth: she does not control her power. Only once every 7 days does she create the Fog. You must understand that Yoko was scared, too. The events in Kenya and Marrakech have shown how unpredictable the masses can be and how it may have dire consequences. Even though everyone in the restaurant was kind to her, she was locked inside against her wish, uncertain what the reactions would be when the Fog didn't occur. No, the blame of what happened yesterday does not fall on the Foggies' shoulders. It falls on the British government who seeks to control the Fog for their own benefit. It is with them that the Gatekeepers had to bargain for the 'healing lottery' for hospital patients to be able to prove their existence and the healing Fog. I say - let's help them, let's help the Gatekeepers! They should not have to fight. We must put pressure on any authority and institution to let the Gatekeepers accomplish their mission for humankind. The Fog is giving people another chance in life, a chance of better health and new horizons. For the lucky people who access that Other World, it is also a chance for a new beginning in an unspoilt land. Like a new America, it is a land of opportunities. We must stop the rigid structures of the State putting political and economic interest before the interest of the people. They are the ones stopping the opening of the gates.'

Ingis Chen paused for effect and looked straight at the camera. He was in a TV studio, a bland table in front of him and a blurred photographic landscape view of London behind him.

'The voice of the people from around the world must be heard. The Fog and the portals are here for us. All of us! We must claim our right to access them. I will make it my mission to support the Gatekeepers in theirs, and to make sure everyone - EVERYONE - benefits from the second chance in life the Fog offers.'

'So nice of him...' Rico grumbled. 'And the ones who don't want that chance, you will simply force it on them, won't you?'

Sam and McRae turned to Rico, a puzzled look on their faces. They did not know Ingis Chen like we did. They did not know his hidden agenda to relieve this planet of one billion people by sending them to WII, by coercion if required. They did not know he was not as selfless as he seemed.

'You may trust us on this,' I said to the two agents. 'Ingis Chen is dangerous.'

'He speaks well,' Sam commented.

'That is one of his most dangerous traits,' Harry said. 'He knows what will make people tick. He is promoting the ideology of freedom, life and hope. He tickles the dreams and aspirations that we all have of a better future. And to achieve this, all we have to do is rebel against the controlling States.'

'Wait!' Leila interrupted us. 'You need to hear the next one speaking. I am undecided who is worse - Ingis or her.'

'This is an abomination! Once again, humans act as if they were gods,' a petite and soft looking woman spoke, with eyes burning with intelligence and shining with invincible faith. She was in her forties, with a flawless skin radiating energy and shoulder-length white hair flowing in the wind. The interview was taking place outside, on the green lands of Wyoming.

'There is only one God. This Fog and these so-called portals are sacrilegious. They are our creation. Again and again, we play with nature and distort it for 'scientific' research. These people who have created the atomic bomb, the napalm, who create viruses, satellites and now this Fog! We have to stop playing God! We have to stop our egomaniac endeavour to be at the centre of the universe, to be bigger than ourselves. We have to go back to being humble creatures on earth and welcome what nature and God give us. We have to be grateful for our lives. We have lost ourselves in our thirst for grandeur. We are losing our soul, too. This latest thing, this Fog, this Other World: they are temptations from the devil. Do not believe the promises of the fake prophets for a land of wealth and health! Do not believe the glitter and the gold in their flowery words! Their mouth is foul; their words are toxic. In your search for more; in your constant lack of satisfaction with the present;

in your belief there is always better elsewhere, you do not live in the present, any more. In your discontent with your life, you listen in hope to this new chance of escape. Do not be fooled. There is no better than here. This is not your world. This is not natural. This is not the will of God. Be humble. Be...'

Leila cut short the video.

*

'Well, that's gloomy,' Zeno commented.

'So what are we in her eyes? Fallen angels doing the work of Satan?' I asked, pinching my nose.

'On the good side, that makes Ingis the devil's advocate,' Harry added.

After a beat to take in the pun, everyone smiled. It alleviated the tension a notch.

'I am sorry, Yoko,' McRae said, afterwards.

'Why? It's not your fault. You couldn't have known the toddler would pull off my wig and launch this mess,' I told him.

'I should not have put you in a dangerous situation,' he insisted.

'Oh drop it! You were only taking me out for a chat. It would have happened eventually, as I won't be homebound. So no more apologies.'

'The woman, who is she? Why did they interview her, of all people?' Sam asked.

'Lally O'Maleigh,' Leila answered. 'She is a Protestant reverend turned spiritual guru. Her aura has grown to such an extent, she is getting increasingly distant from her Church. She speaks her own mind and does not seek council from her peers any more. She has launched her own spiritual online channel and has been a guest on 'Oprah', who praised her on several occasions. O'Maleigh has also enchanted the crowd on 'Ellen' by her sense of humour. On the spiritual level, she does not appear extreme in her stance. However, she is uncompromising: everything is black or white with her.'

'So they interviewed Ingis Chen on a political and social ground, and Lally O'Maleigh on the spiritual. Both represented divergent opinions. Good. I still don't understand why they picked her, of all people, to describe us as Angels of Darkness.'

'You saw her. O'Maleigh has charisma. She is the perfect counter-balance to Chen. The press has done their job well.'

'Did you help them?' Rico asked, narrowing his eyes suspiciously.

'Give the media credit,' Leila told him. 'They know what they're doing, whether you like it or not.'

'So this Lally O'Maleigh, will she be a problem?' McRae asked.

'How would I know?' Leila replied and breathed out heavily. 'Hopefully not, but she has the potential to be a thorn in our side.'

'Great. One more on the list,' I whispered to myself.

*

'Leila, do you think I have received a gift? Do you think I am, or we Foggies are, on some kind of mission and making a mess of it?' I asked her when we went to the kitchen to refill the coffee pot. She had understood from my glance that I needed to talk to her in private and had come with me.

'My dear Yoko. We talked about this a long time ago. I do believe you have received a gift. You are the instrument of a force that is greatly superior to ours. I also believe that you are giving your best to do things right. This is not as easy as Ingis Chen presents it, or as the girl dreams. One thing they forgot but you don't: as a Gatekeeper, you are protecting not one side of the door but both. Also, you cannot help anyone if you are not looking after yourself first. This is true for life in general. Depressed, over-stressed, etc., you would not last long. Then this gift would be well and truly wasted.'

'Thank you, Leila.' I gave her a long hug.

'You are welcome, my friend,' she hugged me back.

As we walked back to the dining table, she added: 'Also, you need to know that some people think the Fog is a sign that the end of the world is coming and that the WII is the real Noah's Arch. The Relocated are the Chosen Ones whose purpose is to preserve the existence of humankind when Earth disappears.'

'You know, sometimes I despair with everyone's crazy ideas and interpretations of what is happening,' I shook my head. 'Can't they just see it as what it is: an inter-planetary door using a virus-cleaning fog?'

I felt the stare of those around the table and reflected on my own words.

'Uh-huh… Maybe I can understand how this might not satisfy

everyone out there.'

'I wonder how the people from Lil'London and Newtonsee explain the Fog? Are they religious?' McRae asked.

'From what I gathered, they don't question it. It just is.' Zeno told him.

*

That day, I filled my mind with one of my favourite projects: education. My aim was to instil respect and harmony between the two worlds by building strong foundations of knowledge and understanding of each community. I hoped that they would accept their differences and be able to live together. Instead of compromising – which always incurs the risk of dissatisfaction and problems in the long term – they would cooperate. My idea was to also provide education on what the Fog was and how it worked, as well as the background and traditions of Lil'London, Newtonsee and Yerushaleim. Their customs, especially around women, were not going to work in their favour, but hopefully the reforms instigated by Jazz and Maud would change things fast. The public needed proper information and no one could do it better than us. To prove that the Fog was not a scientific creation by some random laboratories, I needed the full results of the tests conducted by the Government. We should be privy to the information gathered, thanks to us anyway. The gist of it, already shared with us, was sufficient to give anyone a headache with all the incomprehensible terminology only meaningful to experts, so I would ask Sam for a 'translated' version. I winced at the thought of the governmental scientific team. They had failed to understand the mechanisms of the portal and had not been able to recreate it, or to determine who would turn out a Relocated. The one thing they predicted well, and it was just the beginning, was that the Fog had jolted the whole planet into new ways of thinking and acting, wrenching it away from past conceptions of time and space.

*

Aside from education, I dealt with personal matters: I wrote a letter to Leo. I had bottled up enough feelings in a few months to write a big book, so pouring a sample in a letter was easy. I needed this. Lally O'Maleigh was correct on one point: I was no God. I was a human being and also an idiot. For more than three months, I had denied myself the one thing that makes life complete: love.

Honestly, what a stubborn imbecile! Scarred by past hurts, scared by future pain, I had presently buried my emotions in the semi-conscious belief that it was self-protection. In fact, I was simply putting aside living on a personal level.

Carissimo Leo,

I miss you. I miss the time we could have had together in the past months, a time I let pass from fear of what might happen if we did not work together. I should have had more faith in you. You are so kind to me that you don't even blame me for the hurt I have caused you. I do not know the future and if something is written for us, yet 'everything will be fine in the end, and if not, then it is not the end'. I heard or read this somewhere, I don't remember where. But I want to believe today.

Leo, my heart aches. I fear for your safety; I fear not to see you anymore. I want to take you in my arms. I want to kiss your soft lips. I want you to carry me to my bed, or yours for that matter. I miss your touch, your caresses. And you are so far away and in danger. The idea that we could lose you is constantly in my mind. Why did it take this for me to realise how much I care, how much I need you in my life? I love you, Leo. I love you. You are the best thing the Fog brought to me, and I wasted it. I am such a fool! You are handsome, wonderful, loving and kind. Please come back, Leo. Please do not disappear in the jungle of the African WII. Please, come back and give me another chance.

Yours, very much yours,

Yoko.

I caught myself praying for Leo's safety out loud, a lump in my throat. In addition, I knew that if he was not coming back, I would not forgive myself for the time we could have had together and the hurt I had caused him.

Jazz shook me out of my heavy thoughts by calling me.

'We need you here. Can you come now?' The urgency in her voice made me stand straight away.

'On my way!'

'Is Zeno around?'

'I will find him. Anyone else?'

'We can do with as many heads as possible to mull this over!' she replied.

'Leila?' I added just as we were both going to hang up.

'As I said, the more the better.'

*

15 minutes later, Harry, Rico, Zeno and I were sitting on one side of *The Jazzins* largest table with Jazz, Big Tom and Nick, on the other side.

'There has been a cock-up,' Jazz looked both peevish and apprehensive.

'Go on,' I told her encouragingly, seeing her crankiness as a sign of stress.

'With Maud and Molly, we approached Lil'london and Newtonsee councils and offered our help to sort out Clémence's latest antics in exchange for the transformation of the women's punishing house into a simple prison without the imposed brothel aspect of it. These women might be guilty in the eyes of their laws, so we couldn't ask for their release. We also requested that *The Jazzin* and the Open University were open to all.'

'Hang on,' I interrupted her. 'Wasn't *The Jazzin* open to all already?'

'No, it wasn't. Didn't you notice that only men ever visited, aside from Molly and the wives of the council members?' Jazz asked.

'I didn't give any special thought to it…'

'Women were strongly advised not to come. The same for unmarried men; i.e., any young men under 18,' Big Tom told us.

'Anyway,' Jazz cut in. 'What matters is that we offered a deal for our help to track Clémence and recover the children. They didn't like it one bit but they complied. Next, the Council met with us here this morning, at dawn, as we used Maisie's earring locator to track Clémence.'

Jazz stopped and took a big in-breath.

'And?' Rico asked, with impatience.

'She fooled us,' Big Tom replied.

'When a group of men arrived at Clémence's camp, the sleeping bodies on the ground were, in reality, bundles of wood under blankets. Only one woman was there, and she wore the tracking earring herself! She was laughing out loud and mocking the army of men who had come to assault the Women Rebels.'

'Clémence knew about the earring?!' I exclaimed.

'Oh yes, she knew about the earring. She also knew about the planned

249

assault,' Jazz said in a dead tone.

'But that means…' I began.

'… That someone told her. Yes. And we know who that is,' Nick replied. 'Owen.'

'WHAT?' I yelped in surprise. 'Owen? It must be a mistake. Why would he do such thing?! Where is he?'

'No mistake here. He admitted it. His father is talking to him just now in their cabin. He is also the one who warned Clémence, by radio, of the use we intended to make of the tracker.'

'How did you work it out?' Zeno asked.

'I checked all the radio logs. The Fisher's was telling,' Nick told us. 'The look of bewilderment on James Fisher's face was enough to know it wasn't him. For the show, we blamed him, nonetheless, to force one or both children to tell us the truth. It could hardly be anyone else.'

'But why?' Rico asked. 'What did he have to gain from it?'

'Clémence won him to her cause,' Jazz replied, her jaw set.

'He is a man! How could she convince him that the 'reign of women folk' was overdue?' Rico shouted out. 'What did she do? Sleep with him or something? Has she bewitched him? Oh my God! She IS a witch, isn't she?'

Rico made the sign of cross. Big Tom looked at him in disbelief mixed with pity, and shook his head.

'No,' Big Tom said. 'She pointed out the fate that awaited Maisie if nothing changed in their society. Owen loves Maisie. He wants her safety first. He doesn't want her life broken by the rules of men here. Nor does he want her to have to marry out of duty and share her husband and marital duties with other women.'

'This is ridiculous!' I protested. 'He knows that you are fighting too, with Maud and Molly. And us. He knows we are onto it pacifically. What was he thinking?!'

'He doesn't believe in politics. He says that, in negotiations, something would have to give from our side too. Owen insists that if you look through our history, it took a change of mentalities during World War One for the suffragettes to see their request finally granted. Their political movement alone did not achieve it. Then on women's rights, things have improved slowly since. It only really started in the 60s and it took at least one generation to change the mentalities and practice. It is longer than the lifetime of the Fog - linked to yours - and so the risk of the men reclaiming their privileges afterwards is high.'

We all fell silent while thinking through the young man's arguments. That he had a point didn't mean he was right. The suffragette and feminist movements had been, and still were, for equal rights between men and women. Clémence's was for a complete shift in power, giving it all to women instead of men.

'Does he realise that Clémence intends to install a female dictatorship? Surely he can't approve of this?' I voiced my thoughts aloud.

'She was too astute to present it like that,' Jazz commented.

'I think I need to have a little conversation with him,' I said, to no one in particular.

'Don't bother. I have already,' Jazz said, in a firm tone. 'I opened his eyes to a few things Clémence has been involved in. I laid out for him, in detail, why WE decided not to back her up: the danger of revolution, her extreme position, her thirst for power. The anger she carries in her is a constant danger of future abuse, violence, hatred and intolerance. This cannot be what he wants, for his sister or for him.'

'Well said. How did he react?' I approved.

'I might have been a bit harsh. I was upset,' Jazz said, grimacing. She could be tough sometimes but she didn't like to be.

'And rightly so!' Rico interjected.

'It's worse than you think,' Nick pointed out. 'Clémence seized the opportunity to act, too.'

'What do you mean?' Harry asked, frowning like Zeno, Rico and me.

'Well, both towns had dedicated a large number of their strongest men to capture Clémence and her followers...' Nick began. He didn't have to finish his sentence before I put a hand to my mouth.

'Oh no! No, no, no, no, nooooooo!' I murmured.

'Cazzo!' Rico let out. His stomach rumbled. 'Scusi... It's the stress. It's past lunchtime. Mind if I gather a few things from the kitchen to bite?'

'Help yourself,' Jazz replied, as Big Tom murmured something about Italians and their priorities.

As the kitchen was an extension of the lounge with a counter for separation, we continued the conversation as Rico busied himself cooking.

'So what did she do?' I steeled myself for the bad news.

'She raided both Lil'London and Newtonsee. She freed the women from their so-called prisons, stole most the towns' food in the storage facilities, same with the armoury, and gathered clothes for her rebels. She didn't attack anyone or take from private houses; only the towns' storage. It is less damaging for her image even if the result will be the same,' Jazz explained. 'Her argument is that they have to survive, and as everyone is against them, their only option is to take. Her point of view is that, as inhabitants of the land, they are entitled to a chunk of the community's storage, anyway.'

'Needless to say, the councils are fuming. They are also blaming us for it,' Nick added. 'They accuse us of having sent them astray on purpose, that it was our plan to clear the way for Clémence all along. This is a big mess!'

'Dammit,' I murmured. So what are we supposed to do now, I wondered.

'This is not good,' Zeno growled.

'I am so sorry, Yoko! This is all a big mess!' Jazz was looking at me, her eyes filled with tears. I stood up and went to give her a hug.

'It isn't your fault, honey. You could not have known about Owen,' I whispered in her ears. 'Don't beat yourself up.'

'I blame myself!' Nick said. 'I should have been monitoring the communication. I have been slack. Owen should never have been able to be in contact with Clémence.'

'Oh stop it, all of you!' Harry burst out. 'This isn't helping. Owen is to blame and that is it. Yet again, he is young and easily influenced. Whatever! Now is not the time to point the finger, but think of solutions.'

Harry turned to me and pinched his lips. Then he spoke the words I dreaded to hear.

'Yoko, I am afraid it will be hard work for you on that one.' I braced myself as he continued. 'This is what I think we, and more specifically you, will have to do next. First, as an ambassador of WI and the Foggies, you will have to make a statement of how saddened we are for what both towns have gone through. Second, we need to make a mending gesture in replenishing their stocks. Third, and that will not be easy, you will have to reinforce your neutrality.'

'What about my movement? Or what we had negotiated? And our involvement in the failure of Clémence's capture and its consequences?' Jazz enquired.

'Do they know that it is Owen who spilled the beans?' Rico asked, munching an over-filled sandwich and putting a large plate on the table with a selection of food for us. We had not realised that we were all ravenous; within minutes, we were all eagerly eating.

'No, they don't know anything. They are blaming Molly, Maud and me for the fiasco of the raid. It's more convenient for them. That is a major blow for us! I am really, really upset!' Jazz angrily took another bite of her sandwich and munched it with ferocity. Big Tom put a hand on her shoulder and she looked at him gratefully and with affection. At least one thing was working out for her.

'I will try to talk to them,' I said, with more assurance than I felt. As was often the case, I felt out of my depth. I was determined to continue to do my best. Discreetly, I touched wood, caressing the under part of the table in front of me, more out of custom than superstition.

*

It was already mid-afternoon when I made my way to Lil'London. Nick had called the council to organise a meeting. I was dreading it. I made the journey with Zeno and Nick. Together we reviewed the various scenarios of what they might say, demand, reproach and object to. It seemed all my options were reactive, not pro-active. My best angle was to be flexible and adapt to the situation. Our strong advantage was the Fog, of course. Nick kept looking up as we journeyed. At some point I asked him why. He looked at me with a little smile and a glint in his eyes, but said nothing.

When we arrived in Lil'London, the town gave me the impression of mourning. The mood was gloom; the women and men stared at us with eyes full of questions, hope or anger. No one greeted us. Parents held their young children close to their bodies. Children were not playing in the street freely as usual, or rollerblading around. A cloud of sadness and fear had fallen heavily on the streets of Lil'London. A forbidding Augustus Hoare, reproachful Benjamin Snayth and anxious Edmund Poff were waiting for us on the threshold of the town hall as we parked our quad. Looking at the stern faces, I took a big breath, straightened myself and held my head high.

The good news was they had nothing against the Foggies. The bad news was that they had everything against Women's Equality, Jazz's political movement. Maud was now an outcast, Molly ignored, and Jazz looked upon as the head of a campaign to squash. The humiliation and loss they had endured was too raw for me to take a strong position in the defence of my friends. Instead, I reminded them that education, trade, access to the Fog and to *The Jazzin* for everyone were in the interests of the Relocated. It conformed to the neutrality of the Foggies as well: we did not want to take sides and eliminate anyone willing to get in touch with and learn about us. I emphasised how grateful we were for their continuous welcome and their support every time we needed it, especially me. It was the clue for Zeno to inform them we would supply them with the goods necessary to replace what had been stolen. That included the weapons. It was the point that bothered us the most: should we, shouldn't we? In the end, we decided to do it because we had some responsibility for their current vulnerability. We had to repair the damage Owen had caused to protect him and our relationship with the locals. Still, we did so on the condition that they made gestures towards the equal rights of anyone – including women – to get free access to what the Fog had to offer. They reluctantly agreed.

'Clémence: how did she know about our plans this morning?' August Hoare asked.

'I am afraid we underestimated her understanding of our technology,' I replied. Our answer was ready for the expected question. Stick to the truth and skip the details was the motto for today.

'What happened?' Benjamin Snayth pushed on.

'We thought she didn't know about our tracker. But she did. With this, she knew she could fool us regarding her whereabouts,' Nick replied for me.

'What about this morning? How did she know?'

'Have you considered that some of her followers might have stayed behind, disseminated within your communities?'

'So someone who heard about our plan must have passed the word,' Edmund Poff said and added, 'You might not be happy with Maud of late, but at least we know she is not on Clémence's side. So maybe instead of treating her like an enemy, you could see her as a potential ally.'

Snayth shot Edmund a dagger stare. It was rare to see Edmund stand up for himself in front of the council, even more so in our presence. His love for Maud was such, she might be the only the reason he would ever do so.

Before the meeting was over, Nick took out his radio and talked to Big Tom. About 20 minutes later, a couple of large drones appeared in the sky above Lil'London. Zeno and I turned inquiringly towards Nick. He grinned widely, asked for the main square to be cleared. He then gave the go-ahead to Big Tom, by radio, to release the loads. Within seconds, parcels dropped from the sky and hit the empty centre of the square. A crowd had formed on the side, fascinated and in awe. Nick went to the parcels and opened them, Zeno and I following. Soon, we distributed the presents of bread, ham, cheese and sugar. It would not replace what they had lost, not yet, but it would lighten the mood. We also informed them we had promised the council to replenish the town storehouse. Benjamin Snayth, needing to control information as usual, was not happy that we broke the news ourselves. Augustus Hoare let it pass, though. He had mellowed since Clémence's departure and her revolutionary activities. He was still stern and rigid in appearance, but less adamant in his convictions. He was not a bad man. Now, looking at the parcels and towards the sky, he asked Nick what new wonder this was. Nick explained about the drones. He then had to explain how, in the past 100 years, we had developed the technology and skills to fly. Nick explained the drones could be of use in the future for trade between the Fog and the towns of WII: for example, to use for the delivery of items for Ariel Ben-Chaim's apothecary, or for any medicines or urgent needs Lil'London and Newtonsee might have. Watching Augustus Hoare's positive reaction to the news, it confirmed it was not him we had as an enemy in town. Our main antagonists were Benjamin Snayth in town and Clémence outside town.

However, the whole day left a bitter taste. I was wearisome that night. We had just created the onset of a war, now that both sides were armed.

Day 6 (Friday)

Next to me, Simba refused to wake up as I stirred. It was too early, yet I did not manage to go back to sleep. I logged onto the Ftab in bed and checked my messages. Still no news from Leo. My letter to him had gone the previous night by courier, courtesy of the Society. I had chosen letter over email, something tangible for when he would surface back from his WII safari. Day 6 already… What took them so long? Were they safe? I wondered, too, if they would approve of our decision to compensate Lil'London and Newtonsee's loss in goods and weaponry. The other Foggies had. However, my sense of guilt proved I would make a terrible arms dealer.

*

In an attempt to turn my dark thoughts around, I checked my other messages. That wish failed: I just switched from one drama to another.

Sophia Koplat's email had the ominous title of 'The situation is unsustainable'. Its content was a long litany of her boredom on the shores of Alaska, grievances against her stepdaughter and frustrations with her family's isolation. I cringed whilst reading as, in addition to her issues with Michelle, she now had daily arguments with Rosario. It was hardly surprising that the two women had words: Rosario publicly eye-rolled most of Sophia's comments and Sophia did not take head-on criticism or disapprobation very well. The punch line of Sophia's message was that she wanted out by the beginning of the following week. The Koplats had already said they wished to move to London. It filled me with apprehension: I had enough problems without having Sophia putting her nose into them with an argumentative view on everything. Working with her on the administrative side of Gatekeepers Associates, it was clear that the only way to get her off anyone's back was to give her sole responsibility for one area. It was difficult to contain her to stay just in that one, but possible. It was a harsh opinion, but after a couple of months I had found a cruising pace with her. I had never exploded only because I was able NOT to see her every day and could remain professional with her when I did. If she were in London, there would be no chance of ignoring her: she would just turn up on our doorstep. So deep down, I hoped they would accept the American offer and return to Nevada.

Among the other emails was one from Adam. He wanted all Foggies on a call to discuss what we considered would be the best for them. I smiled when I read Rosario's email next. She ranted against Sophia's know-it-all and posher-than-posh attitude, always trying to get the last word on everything. She told me that for my sake and all the others' in London, she would recommend they move back to Nevada and work with the Americans. She believed the US would act like the UK, as both governments had similar aspirations and limitations, or thereabouts. She wrote that Sophia was not a bad person, just difficult to be around. Well, her wording might have been more colourful than this, but that was the gist of it.

More surprisingly, Christophe's email was pure positivism. After the emails from Alaska, it was a relief. He wrote that all was well between him, his wife and his baby. Louise was happy, too. She had lost one love and gained another: she adored Helo and dedicated most of her time to him. They were constantly together. For once, there was no jealousy between Isabelle and Louise at present.

*

Later, when I had made my way to the office and was working on the courses layout for the Inter-worlds education, Leila called:

'Hello Yoko, are you free to talk?' Her voice was tired and strained. It did not bode well.

'Yes. Tell me,' I replied

'We have a little issue with your parents.'

'What?! Are they all right?'

'They are, although detained by the French Government. They found a 'flaw' in your mother's ID papers and she won't be able to leave French territory anytime soon. Your father is refusing to leave without her.'

'This is nonsense!' There was nothing wrong in my mother's paperwork.

She had been naturalised French long ago and I said so to Leila.

'I know,' she replied. 'However, the French customs decided there was something amiss and they are blocked until we find a way to prove the contrary.'

'They are trying to get a hold of me. Damn governments!' I exploded. Nobody could treat my parents like that. This was something I would not forgive.

'They are wrong, but can you blame them? You are French but living in London, refusing to come back and to open a Fog in your own homeland. This might be their only way. As I said, wrong but expected.'

'I should have asked you to sneak them out discreetly.'

'This is what we tried to do even without you asking. We failed. We fooled the surveillance at your parents, not at the heliport. I suspect they had all the airports, heliports and harbours in your parents' vicinity under watch.'

I grumbled a few swear words.

'You know, there is an alternative,' Leila continued, taking no notice of my choice of words. 'The British Government has proposed to offer you and your family immediate British Citizenship due to extraordinary circumstances. It applies to any Foggy who wishes it.'

'With British citizenship, could my parents come right away?'

'They might. This is not a guarantee though.'

After thinking it through for a few seconds, I asked if my parents were back at home.

'The French government knows better than totally alienating you by putting them in prison! They are at home, under strict surveillance and with a request not to leave their town until your mother's situation is regularised.'

'Which I presume would be much faster if I were to visit and stay one Saturday night to give them a Fog gate. Bloody French!'

'You are French.'

'This is why I can insult them at will. I have the right to criticise my own.'

'Funny, that is exactly what Lochy said about the British.'

'Ah! Lochy. Come on, give me some good news. Be honest: you do like him, don't you?' The news about my parents had put me in a 'no messing around' frame of mind.

'That would be the worst match ever. No way,' she replied immediately.

'This is not what I asked. Do you like him?' I persisted.

'He is nice enough. He would make a good recruit for the Society if he didn't have this rogue side,' Leila replied.

'Do-you-like-him?' I repeated.

Leila sighed. I knew her a little by now. There were enough signs when she was in his presence to reveal that she was interested.

'Ok fine! I find him attractive and intriguing! Happy now? I still don't want anything to happen. I don't! The man is too big a flirt, there is no taking him seriously!' Leila insisted. 'Now can we move back to more serious subjects?'

'I would like to call my parents. This is really my priority now. Can the rest wait?'

'Fair enough. The rest can wait until after the call,' Leila replied.

We hung up and I dialled my parents. My father picked up. From the loud jazz music playing in the background, he was in his office. He informed me that my mother was in the kitchen, venting her nerves and frustration on a steak that she was hammering with fury. He expected to have steak tartare for lunch.

*

Dad related the morning's events for me. At dawn this morning, Dad and Mum adorned running gear and trainers and set out for a jog in the fields around the village. Their sentinel did not know their habits enough to be aware they never, ever, jog. I really couldn't fathom where they dug out those outfits and running shoes. Two men followed them. The Society had prepared a hiding spot on their route to lose their shadows, then several cars to transport them to a heliport a good 100kms from there. They toyed with the idea of taking off from a field, but they risked attracting attention with a non-authorised flight. The Society had not chosen a location close by on purpose: it was still not far enough. It was a mistake. My parents did not blame the Society for the failed escape; they were fuming against their own government for being under semi-official house arrest. It was outrageous. Like Leila, they could understand their reasons, even if it didn't justify their action. France was a democracy, the land of 'Liberté, Egalité, Fraternité'! Was nothing sacred anymore?!

It was rare to hear my father rant. I was seething, myself. I told him about the British citizenship offer and without hesitation, he gave me the green light to accept it.

'It might not be necessary in the end but at this point, it is good for us not to put all our eggs in the French basket.'

'I will inform the Brits and call the French right away. Maybe after I give them a piece of my mind they will think twice about pulling this ridiculous 'flaw' excuse on Mum's identity papers.'

'Let's hope so. I am French and still love my country! And I love our house. I don't want to leave it because the government is being an arse.'

'Maybe I should just come back home,' I said, feeling guilty putting my parents in such a difficult position.

'Don't be ridiculous! You have other priorities now. We can't start falling for blackmail. This is what it is, you know: emotional blackmail at national level.'

'It's disappointing. So disappointing.'

'I love you, my darling.'

'I love you, Daddy. Are you sure I can't talk to Maman?'

'I wouldn't recommend it yet. She really needs to unwind first.'

'Very well. Will you kiss her for me?'

'Of course, my love.'

*

I contacted Sam to ask if he could organise British citizenship for my parents and for me. He replied he would look into it straight away. Next, I called the French Embassy and asked to talk to the Ambassador and him only. I was in no mood to go through any intermediary.

'I am outraged. My mother, who has been a resident in France for close to 40 years and French for about 30 of them, is currently under review for being illegally settled in France. She has two grown-up French children. Her papers were renewed several times over the years and she never had her status as a French national called into question. Yes, she was born Japanese-Italian, but she has proved over several decades that she was proud of her adopted country. Now, suddenly, she decides to go on a trip to visit her daughter and she is treated like an illegal immigrant, sent back home under what is effectively house arrest, her papers taken from her. Her status is under review because a 'flaw' was found in her original application for citizenship... Whom are you kidding? Did you really, REALLY think it would go down well with me and my friends?' The Ambassador tried to interject. He stood no chance.

'I don't care whatever you may say: I really don't give a damn. Many governments would be happy to sort out new nationalities for them to help sort this mess. The British did not hesitate. I am French, I love being French: this is part of me, my culture, my blood and my traditions. French food is the best. French movies are awesome. French elegance has no par. Being French rocks. I don't want to give it up and neither do my parents. But if you force us, WE WILL. And then you can stuff it! You hear me? How dare you treat my mother like that! Sort it out! S-O-R-T I-T O-U-T!!!'

I angrily pressed the off button on my mobile several times. How I missed the old times when you could slam down the phone receiver on someone. It felt great to let my anger out loud. I cringed a little at how I had lashed out at the French Ambassador. He was not the one who made the decision to restrain my mother inland, so my outburst at him had been rather unfair. The guilty feeling did not last for too long though.

*

I called Leila back and updated her on my talk with my parents, the French Embassy and Sam. I was still very wound up and so, to change the subject, she told me the Society had made a discovery by accident regarding Ingis Chen. Apparently, the man had prepared for the worst-case scenario should the whole world go mad from an apocalyptic Fog-craze, everyone becoming dangerous predators fighting for survival. His back-up plan was a self-sufficient luxurious property on a small island in the Pacific, somewhere between New Zealand and Australia. Equipped with solar panels, water tank and filters, it also had a defence system against invasion by a possible hoard of starving people. Everything was already in place for agriculture. So if Ingis Chen's ideas failed and the world went to perdition, he could retire and hide on his island.

'How did you discover this? Chen would be extra careful to hide this type of secret den.'

'He is. However, one of the caretakers has young children. They use twitter, and they were very excited that their father's boss was on television and a friend of the Gatekeepers. The tweet has been deleted since, but not before it got our attention. It was a lucky break. One more piece of information on Chen we will store carefully.'

To further upgrade the mood of the day, Leila and I discussed my Open Education project. The Society would put at my disposal some of the information they had gathered on the Fog and the previous openings. For the time being, it would be limited to England, to avoid revealing the existence and location of the other Foggies and to keep it simple. Talking about the project was a pleasure. It was something constructive and positive in my life. Leila approved the idea and shared my excitement in spreading the history and knowledge from both sides of the Gate.

'Also, aside from the education, I would like to make the Fog more accessible to people. You see, what the teenager said in the restaurant, that I had a gift, a mission…' I began.

'Yoko, you can't let it affect you. You need to rise above the comments from the press and people. You do have a gift, and maybe a mission, but you need time to organise it. If you rush into anything because of pressure, it could be catastrophic.'

'I know, and yet there's so much going on in my life, sometimes I fear I could be losing sight of the bigger picture.'

'Trust me, I would remind you. That is what I am here for.' I could hear Leila's smile in her voice. Again, I felt lucky to have her in my life, as an advisor and as a friend.

*

The Foggies had much to discuss during our Board Meeting, our FBM. We went through the various governmental demands, public opinion and so-called rights, the omnipresence of Ingis Chen in the background and the novelty of Lally O'Maleigh's rise. Despite it all, there wasn't much more we could do towards the outside world than we were already doing: standing our ground and following the line of work we had assigned to ourselves. Gatekeepers Associates was a good structure to help us maintain a professional approach. For the observers, the Gatekeepers were strong and in control. On the inside, the Foggies were facing many dramas, ranging from mini to maxi.

What was directly affecting the Foggies was the location issue and moves. It was not as straightforward as one would hope for the Moroccan-based group to move to England with Isabelle and Chloé. Isabelle had finally relented and accepted flying for the journey. By then, the Society had two Relocated who could pilot planes. Due to the unknown ground for landing, they would have to use sea or float plane. They were already flying from London as far as they could into WII France – the one from Morocco doing the same in Spain - back and forth, to leave fuel tanks on the path planned by the de Rocque family. They could only go so far from the gates and Christophe had to create a new door, the following evening, in the Pyrenean mountains. By Sunday, good weather permitting (it should be fine in summer, but…), they would all be in England. They would stay in the Essex house. I was glad they were not staying in London with the WII potential Civil War looming. Isabelle was going to be introduced to Kim and Ed Epcott as a Relocated from Woodfellas moving away from the troubles with Clémence. Christophe and Louise would visit her daily as husband and cousin. Until further notice, Christophe and Louise would stay away from WII to hide the fact they were Foggies. The British Government was always on the watch; it would not be easy. Also, with the baby being so young, Christophe and Isabelle wanted to postpone test requests on Chloé. A solution was still pending for the long term, but that was on a later agenda.

The other move was for the Koplats. Despite Michelle's reluctance to leave Alaska, they were returning to Nevada on Sunday, after the switching night. Adam had asked me to liaise with the US Government to start preparing for their return: he wanted a deal similar to the one we had with the British Government, for which I planned to involve Sam to help in the negotiation. The British awareness of the Koplats' existence was one additional security for the family. The other person I intended to inform was Penny Thompson.

Adam's priority was Michelle's protection and future: he wanted her to have as normal a life as possible. Hearing this during the virtual Foggies Board Meeting (FBM), Michelle sneered that he was unrealistic and left the screen and the room. Adam had a difficult task being the father of a strong-headed teenager, as well as a Foggy.

Then there was the matter of Kenya. There was still no news from Mary, Jack, Leo and Mitch. Putu was back working in the hospital and helping the poor. She had lied through her teeth to her Embassy, saying she was only a friend and had been unaware of what was happening in Mary and Clare's household. The Embassy could do nothing but let her go, though the Society confirmed they continued to keep an eye on her. For security, the Society had increased their surveillance on her and provided two trained nurses to work in her team around the clock. Putu was delighted with this additional support to her hard work!

*

At night, trying to sleep, I sensed some events had been set in motion. It felt like something was stirring and would soon be awake and overtaking everything. Friendly beast or ravaging dragon?

Day 7 (Saturday)

'Even if we manage to protect the natives of WII from direct colonisation,' Harry said, as I bit into my toast generously spread with honey, 'by controlling the influx of people crossing and limiting relocation, we are still proceeding towards a colonisation in practice.'

'Per che?' Rico asked, after a sip of coffee.

'Because we are creating a situation of dependency,' Harry explained. 'Consider the British colonisation of India. It originated with trading posts and overseas possessions, swiftly gaining strength, power and domination through commerce. The advance in technology in the West played an additional role in establishing British supremacy and henceforth, control over what had become colonies.' Harry reached for a croissant with an apricot jam core.

'Well, it is different here, surely,' Zeno said.

'And why is that?' Harry asked, in a sarcastic tone.

'Because there was no stopping the British back then. Here, indigenous people, unhappy about the 'invasion' from their World, just have to block the door,' Zeno replied.

'They can't close the door,' Harry counter-argued.

'They can destroy it. They could kill everyone,' Rico interrupted. 'This has happened before!'

My look to Zeno clearly expressed my thought: 'Why - oh why - knowing Rico, would you give him anything that may feed his dark apocalyptic mind?!'

'Sorry... Sometimes I forget,' Zeno replied, with a fake smug look.

'Honestly guys! We should always - ALWAYS – be on our guard!' Rico proclaimed.

*

What triggered Harry's comment on colonisation was the sudden increase in offers for WI-WII business ventures, received by Gatekeepers Associates in the past few days. Requests from the wood industries, from gas and petrol companies, were also piling up in our online and desk inboxes. They quoted impossibly high figures if we would enable them to access and exploit the pristine resources of the Other World. We considered their proposals unacceptable in respect of WII. Plus, they were exactly what the Society had vowed to oppose: protecting the Other World against such abuse was their *raison d'être*. Nothing but green energy would pass. More to our taste, proposals from large or small agricultural projects, especially for organic products, flowed in. This had advantages for both worlds: in WII, it would provide an activity and a source of income for the Relocated, as well as expertise for this and future generations to better sustain themselves when the door closed. For our world, it had the benefit of putting the best pure and natural products on the market. We had a lot of work ahead to review them all. A myriad of eclectic ideas, suggestions and offers poured in from everywhere. The Society was of great help, as usual.

One of the filtered proposals triggered my attention: contrary to all the other publishing companies who only wanted my biography (I had no inclination towards this), one suggested publishing a history of WII. Such a book could spark interest for the Open University programme as an introduction to World II. We even had the core work done with the *Tales of Lil'London*, once the language was modernised. On this, we would need the Council of Lil'London's approval. It was their story and we shouldn't offend them with the disclosure of information they might want to keep restricted.

*

'There will be a peaceful demonstration tomorrow to demand access to the Fog for those in need,' Harry read from his tablet, interrupting my quick browsing through a proposal for a WII-inspired fashion design.

'A demonstration? I don't like that idea… Look what happened in Kenya!' Rico immediately reacted.

'Rico,' Harry rolled his eyes. 'This is not Kenya. This is London, Great Britain. People do not react the same. We are the nation that drinks tea, queues patiently and converses mostly about the weather.'

'Until there is a football match on and then you all turn into hooligans,' Rico replied.

'You are out of date in your stereotypes,' Harry commented, returning his attention to his tablet to read further. 'Hooliganism was just a temporary glitch of the 80s and it died in the 90s.'

'May I remind you of the London riots in the summer of 2011?' Zeno intervened. Harry shot him a glare and let out a sigh.

'Fine, so we have our moments, too,' Harry dismissed the reference with a flick of the hand. 'Still, neither hooligans nor rioters were a general movement of the masses; rather an epi-phenomenon of a disquieted and dissatisfied minority.'

'They still caused damage,' I said. 'In addition, a general movement of the masses often degenerates into minorities breaking off into violence. Then it is bedlam.'

'So either we leave today, or we have a helicopter ready to go in case of emergency tomorrow,' Harry said. 'The solution for us is simple.'

'Yes, that should be fine,' I nodded.

'They want you to express your opinion on the demonstration, Yoko!' Rico interjected, now also reading about the demonstration on his tablet.

'This will not happen,' I said, with a frown. 'I will not express my opinion, simply because I have no clue what to say. I do understand why they demonstrate. Hell! If I weren't a Foggy and a loved one or I was ill, I would be in the street demanding access! But in my position, I know it is impossible to give access to everyone, both for practical and moral reasons. So my heart feels for them, but my head is saying no.'

'I really don't envy you,' Rico commented. 'Nor you, or you,' he added, looking at Zeno and Harry. 'I like being an unknown Foggie.'

'You're not the only one, judging by the reaction of the others last night,' said Harry.

'Oh look! Guess who will be on the front row of the demonstrators?' Rico interrupted.

'Wild guess: Ingis Chen?' I replied.

'You're no fun. You could have hesitated a little for the game,' Rico pouted.

'Will we ever be rid of him?' Harry asked. We all knew it was a rhetorical question.

At least Ingis was praising the Foggies as nice individuals, not lambasting us as fraudsters and irresponsible cons, like Lally O'Maleigh did. She was even implying we were the limbs of the devil. In her words, we were Temptation personified, selling the promise of a new paradise, a fake one. We had never ever claimed such thing! When would people stop making assumptions and judgements without being properly informed? And where did the anger, the resentment, or fear, come from? I did my best not to take it personally and just brush away the attack, only to focus on the consequences her words might have. It was difficult. Since we turned Foggy, we had had to deal with people wanting to help us, use us, or control us. This was different. She aimed to destroy us in the eyes of the public, if not physically, and the latter possibility bothered me. She was now threatening that our actions had to be stopped by any means possible. I sensed danger in her voice as well as determination. Ill at ease, I left soon afterwards for the privacy of my home office, in the hope of crushing the worry by burying it under my workload.

*

First, I confirmed to my parents that their British Citizenship was being processed. The French did not need to be informed; they had been warned. Next, I called Sam. He and MacRae arrived within minutes. I needed them to organise a meeting with the Americans that afternoon, as an emergency. McRae and Sam were invited to join and, as an incentive, I told them the purpose of the meeting with the request they keep it confidential. We needed their support on this, so it would be a good thing they were prepared. Most of the world knew of the existence of a Fog in America; Penny Thompson had made sure of this. What no one knew was the Koplats' whereabouts, their connections to us and their individual roles as Foggies. Sam listened to my explanation of the Koplats' request for British Citizenship effective immediately, and the reason behind it. He immediately picked up his mobile and placed a call, launching the process. He smiled and winked in response to my question about how he could do that without any documents from them, answering that they only needed names, dates and places of birth to fill the paperwork on their behalf. Signatures were an unnecessary detail. Next, I told them how the Koplats, as British Citizens, were hoping the United Kingdom would ensure their decent treatment while in their residence abroad on American soil. McRae laughed.

'Blimey! You guys have guts!' he roared.

'The Brits benefit from our guts,' I replied, with a smile. 'If you appoint someone from your services to go to Nevada and protect the Koplats' interests over there, you will see, hear and learn everything that is going on,' I told them both.

'The Americans are not going to like this,' Sam said, with a wide grin.

'No, they are not,' McRae said.

'What if they say no?' Sam continued.

'The Koplats will not have any choice other than disappearing again, maybe in England.'

'I presume you know where they are now?' McRae asked.

'Maybe,' I replied, dismissively.

'I am impressed,' Sam said.

'Ditto,' McRae said, raising a bottle of beer as a 'cheers'.

*

Early afternoon, the fifty-something military attaché of the American Embassy, Kind Eyes, came for the meeting. Men and women, with Secret Service virtually tattooed on their foreheads, accompanied him. The White House representative, Perfect Bob, was not present. She was back in the US and we had not given the Americans enough notice for her to fly back in time for the meeting. Neither Harry, Zeno, nor I said much, aside from hellos and goodbyes. Sam led the meeting and stated the British demands and conditions on behalf of the Koplats, to emphasise the British role in defending their independence. Kind Eyes listened, took notes, asked a few questions, but did not comment or react. Sam had acted quickly and efficiently: temporary British papers were already prepared for the Koplats (and my parents). He also provided a detailed layout of their expectations surrounding their safe return, living conditions and working agreement between Adam, Sophia and Michelle with the American government. Their relations were to be limited to the authorities, not the press. The Koplats did not want to face the public, for whom I was to remain the official Gatekeepers speaker. Harry and Zeno and I would remain the only publicly acknowledged Gatekeepers.

*

When the Americans left, the French arrived. It was more difficult for me to keep silent then, as the French Embassy representative insisted on the paperwork requiring more time, the situation being misunderstood, etc. Harry could tell it was winding me up: he regularly put a hand on my knee to stop me intervening. In the end, Sam told the French that my parents were coming on Monday and that was it. Any attempt to stop them would result in a diplomatic incident and be leaked to the press. The French left, seriously upset.

*

'How are things in the Fisher family? With Owen?' I asked Jazz. It was switching night and we had our traditional dinner at *The Jazzin*. Big Tom and Nick would leave us after dinner when Jazz and I would watch a girlie movie.

'Not great. Father and son are constantly arguing. And Maisie is torn between her love for her brother and his treason,' Nick replied, before Jazz.

'And what of your Women's Equal Rights movement?'

'Molly is staying at Maud's tonight to work on it. They are reviewing our arguments and strategies towards the Councils of Lil'London and Newtonsee. The tension is terrible.' Jazz's face betrayed fear in addition to her seriousness. 'The men of both towns are receiving weapons and being trained on how to use them. Nick, thank God, had the brilliant idea to suggest the use of tranquiliser bullets before real ones. The men are angry, yet they still have no wish to kill the women. Their women. The mothers of their children. I don't know what they intend to do with them once the tranquiliser would have worn off, though. I mentioned that to Maud and Molly. This is when we could play a key role of reinsertion by integrating women into our structures. Men are frustratingly slow to understand the many, many advantages of working with us!'

'Have you explained this to Owen, too?' I asked.

'He is impossible to talk to at the moment. He just refuses to listen. It is infuriating,' Jazz said.

'The lad hurts, too,' Big Tom said.

'He is an idiot,' Nick stated, helping himself to roast vegetables. 'Because of him, both parties are now armed. I can't see how civil war can be avoided. Clémence is so inflexible.'

'He is young and suggestible,' I tried.

'Whatever,' Nick said, with a grunt.

'Any news from Clémence?' I tried. The Owen subject was a dead end for now.

'Nope. Nothing,' Nick said, with irritation.

The situation was uncontrollable and dangerous. It put us all in jeopardy. Nick had reinforced the video surveillance and booby-trapped the grounds around Woodfellas. He now spent most of his time in front of the monitors, or his tablet, checking what had triggered the motion sensors; i.e. squirrels and boars. He was growing to hate them.

What was Clémence going to do next, we all wondered?

WEEK IV

Day 1 (Sunday)

Waiting is one of the worse non-activities ever. I did not mind doing it as much before the Fog occurred. I could read at leisure, watch a movie, go for a walk, or just chill. These rare moments of free time were now a luxury. Even the stolen time of my long walks with Simba were not as relaxing anymore, because my brain was never at rest. There was too much to do, too much to oversee, too much to think about. So yes, waiting was the worst: all the worries, stress and potential issues to come assailed my thoughts and I was eager to get on with the tasks ahead. That Sunday was a day full of waiting. It was not a good day.

*

For a start, we waited for the arrival of Isabelle and Chloé who were flying blind across WII France. For the sake of the Epcotts and the officials in the Essex house, we couldn't make a big deal out of their arrival and we were not supposed to go and see them in the immediate future. Waking up late – and with difficulty - after a bad night's sleep, I was informed at 9.30am that Christophe had fogged a temporary cabin overnight, as planned, and that his wife and baby had already joined him. They were leaving shortly from the temporary fogged gate, which would then be burnt to leave no trace that the Fog was ever there. Christophe was coming separately, through our side of the fog, otherwise he would appear as Relocated and be stuck in WII. The small family arrived in the evening and we all breathed a sigh of relief. Isabelle and Chloé moved into a ready-made house, assembled in no time, close to the Fog house. Christophe and Louise were to spend the evening with them for dinner.

The silence and inaction from Clémence was even more worrying than her foray into towns. The longer we did not hear from her, the worse we expected her next coup to be. The tension mounted and was exhausting. The waiting continued for Leo and for news from the WII side of Kenya. 'What's taking them so long?' I kept wondering. If the situation were safe, surely it wouldn't take a week to find out where Mary was and what had happened to Clare?

Noises from the demonstration up the road were alarmingly high. Several helicopters, none from the Society, were flying above our heads and above the crowd. Was that what Clare and Mary had had to face, prior to being overtaken by the rioters? The stern look of my fellow Foggies and of Sam, McRae and Leila showed they shared my concern.

Leila spent the day with me and we occupied ourselves with Gatekeepers Associates' various projects. I could not go and wander into town without crossing the roadblocks and facing the demonstrators; I didn't want to stay at *The Jazzin* either, where Nick's grumpy mood was taking over the whole house. Because of the demonstration, and probably Leila's presence, McRae hovered around us the whole day. He displayed a certain shyness around her now: an unusual deference. She had resisted his classic seduction tactic, yet he could feel she was not immune to his charm. That was the one thing that made me smile during the day: their interactions. Something was growing between them and I couldn't wait for it to bloom. I was very fond of Leila, and I was learning to appreciate Lochy McRae.

Throughout the day, my name was often called on loud speakers, repeated afterwards by the crowd. The people, gathered up the road and filling the whole park in thousands, were asking for me, asking for a promise that I would open the gate to them. I could not make a promise I already knew would be a challenge to keep. More and more, I understood being a public figure would never bring me any joy. The pressure and frustrations were far exceeding the advantages. I could never be a politician! In the 'mixed junk' cupboard of the house, I found the sound blocking headsets used a few months back when the house was a building site. Leila and I were finally able to do some proper work.

*

Late afternoon, I was captivated by a project to pave the roads around Woodfellas with a customised heavy-duty solar panel system, when Jazz called. I was so engrossed in my reading that I missed her first, second and third call. Finally, Leila nudged me on the fourth.

'Yoko! Where are you? I have tried to call so many times!' Jazz said, stating the obvious.

'What is it? Are you all right?'

'Yes, but… You have to come now,' she continued, the urgency in her voice barely controlled.

'Coming now!'

'It's Ushi Tsou. She is back. With Eudes.'

'Oh my God! This is amazing! This …' I began.

'Julia is not with them,' Jazz interrupted.

I stopped in my move towards the front door. Conflicting feelings and thoughts assailed me in a blurry mess. Eudes only: not Julia. He was alive. Was she? My stomach knotted.

'I'm on my way,' I struggled to say, jogging down the stairs from the office, Simba on my heels and Leila behind her. I heard her phone ring and her talking to Nick. She was passing on the news to him.

When I rushed through the door of *The Jazzin*, the sight awaiting me in the lounge was shocking. Ushi Tsou, Ingis Chen's strikingly beautiful, hard, ruthless mercenary, was a shadow of her old self. She had lost a lot of weight, her complexion was grey and her whole body screamed exhaustion. In contrast, Eudes looked in perfect health; his hair long and shiny and his skin tanned. However, he looked lost and confused, holding on tightly to Ushi Tsou's leg for protection.

'Eudes, my darling, it's me, Yoko, your aunt,' I kneeled by him to speak at his level. I did not try to take him in my arms, not yet. He had not recognised me but looked at me with mistrust, tightening his grip on Ushi's leg.

'Eudes, tu te souviens de moi? Je suis la soeur de ta Maman. Ta tante?' I realised that introducing myself in French might stir a recollection. He frowned at the language familiar to him and looked at me anew.

'C'est moi, Yoko, tu te souviens?' I repeated my plea for him to try to remember his aunt.

Eudes slowly untied himself from Ushi's leg and made a step towards me. I opened my arms and gave him an encouraging smile. Eudes did not move: he just stood there with an inquisitive face. I took out my Ftab and quickly browsed for a photo of Eudes and me. After a while, I noticed the recollection in his eyes and he extended an arm to take the Ftab. I let him. He pointed at Julia in the background saying 'Maman'. Suddenly, he dropped the Ftab and ran into my arms. I breathed a huge sigh of relief and happiness. We stayed like this for a long time. At some point, I glanced up. Jazz was looking on us with tenderness, Big Tom seemed to have a tear in his eye and Leila was grinning. Ushi Tsou's focus was on Eudes. As usual, I could not read her and did not linger trying. It would have been like attempting to understand the feelings of a steel bar. I took Eudes' face in my hands and caressed his head.

'Thank you, Ushi, for bringing him back,' I told the mercenary, my eyes still on the little boy. When I turned them to Ushi, she nodded. I noticed something like concern fleetingly crossing her eyes. I could not be certain. She stepped forward and put a hand on Eudes' shoulder, bending to his level.

'Are you tired, Oudini?' she asked.

'Oudini?' I thought. 'She called him Oudini?'

Eudes immediately turned and hugged her. He then reached for her to take him into her arms, which she immediately did, with a smile. When talking and looking at him, she was a different person from the one we knew. Her attitude was mellow and gentle, her face showing care and affection. I realised it was love. She loved Eudes, and Eudes had adopted her as his.

'No, I don't want to sleep,' Eudes replied, nuzzling his head in her neck.

'Even if I tell you a story?' she asked him, softly. 'One with a magical cat who can speak to ghosts?'

Eudes' eyes glittered. He asked if the cat liked little boys and she said yes. He nodded excitedly. Ushi Tsou turned to Jazz in a manner to indicate she needed a room, and Jazz accompanied her upstairs. Eudes' basic English had improved greatly during his months with Ushi Tsou.

*

Returning alone, Jazz asked Leila and me to sit down. Big Tom went to put the kettle on. The front door opened and closed, and Nick came in. Once we were all seated, Jazz recalled Ushi and Eudes' arrival.

'We were outside in front of the house, reading and chatting,' she indicated Big Tom, 'when Nick came running towards us. He showed me an image on his tablet from a video surveillance camera, and asked if I could identify the toddler with the easily recognisable Ushi – despite the change in her. Nick and I jumped on a quad, Big Tom remaining behind to hold the fort, and we went to get Ushi and your nephew. When we arrived, Eudes was terrified. He would not let go of her. She would not let go of him, either. Not for one second.'

'Has she told you what happened?'

'Nothing. She has not spoken a word about her journey. I called you as soon as we were back home. All she asked was for some water for each of them and a biscuit for Eudes. Only one, she insisted.'

'She didn't want him to get sick by eating something his stomach was not used to any more,' Nick noted.

'So she didn't talk about Julia,' I insisted.

'No,' Jazz repeated.

I fell silent, numbed. I had known for months my sister and nephew's disappearance meant they might be dead; still the idea would neither settle nor be acceptable in my mind. Big Tom put a mug of tea in front of me. It was over-white and over-sweet. Again, exactly as the Brits drink it in difficult emotional times. It was perfect.

*

'We hit a storm,' Ushi began her story directly with the tough part. 'I looked for a place to land. There was none. I had to keep going. I hardly saw anything. Before I realised what was happening, there was a loud bang, a crash, and we hit the ground. Hard. Your sister was injured. If there had been a hospital around, maybe she would have made it.'

I couldn't breathe, as if there was no air in the room. Jazz spoke for me.

'Did she suffer?' she asked.

'No. There was morphine in the emergency kit of the helicopter. She was out of it most of the time. She didn't last long,' Ushi Tsou hesitated and added. 'I am sorry. I mean, I didn't know her, but I am sure she was a great sister and...'

'That depends,' I said, in a daze. Somehow, I couldn't lie: Julia had been a terrible sister for years. 'I loved her though. I did...'

Tears were flowing down my cheeks. My sister was dead. We would never make up our differences. We would never bond again. She had shown signs of trying just before they left to come and join me in London. Now it would never happen. Nick handed me a handkerchief to wipe my eyes and blow my nose.

'I buried her in the valley. We had little food, a map, a compass and other tools to survive in the wild. We had to move on,' Ushi added.

'It took you some time.'

'It was not an easy journey and the child is young. He cannot travel far without rest. Also, we tried to return to your parents first, but I couldn't find the place.' Ushi Tsou narrowed her eyes. 'I think I found the spot but there was no Fog any more.'

'We had to stop maintaining it after a few weeks. We have had a few problems of our own, on our side,' I replied, a feeling of guilt rising.

'After this, we had to make the whole journey back from the Mediterranean Sea to Woodfellas on foot. It was more difficult than I thought, especially crossing the Channel.'

'Did you build a boat?' Nick asked.

'A raft. My main concern was for Eudes. If he fell in the water, I could lose him.'

'You two seem to have bonded well. Thank you so much for looking after him. For not abandoning him,' I said, in a whisper.

'Of course I would not abandon him! He is such a good boy. He is wonderful!' Ushi said slightly cross, as if I had insulted her.

'Some people would have. Especially professionals aware he would slow them down. We would have been none the wiser,' Nick commented.

'No,' a stern Ushi snapped. She added with a defiant tone: 'I love the little guy. I will never let him go.'

She said this as a warning, not just as a statement. I knew in that moment Eudes would be safe in WII; she would make sure of it. It was as if she was claiming a right over him. It was best to dismiss this latter point for now and just be grateful. She had saved my nephew's life.

'Would you like something to eat? You must be ravenous. You are but skin and bones,' I told her.

'Yes. The choice was limited for food,' Ushi replied.

'Would you tell us about your journey?' Jazz asked. She was trying to be nice in acknowledgement of Ushi's care for Eudes.

'There isn't much to tell. It was a long trip in the wild.' Ushi had never been a big talker. A woman of few words ... Was she really telling stories to Eudes to help him sleep?

'What did you eat?' Jazz persisted.

'What I could find and what I could catch,' Ushi answered.

'He looks healthy. You gave him priority, didn't you?' Nick casually remarked. She acquiesced with a nod. She did not look healthy.

Big Tom went to the kitchen to prepare her something to eat. Nick brought her a beer.

'Why do you call him 'Oudini'?' I tried to continue the conversation before she closed up.

'He loves magic tricks. Also, Eudes - Oudini - it seemed obvious nickname,' she answered.

We all looked at her bemused. Did that mean she actually knew magic tricks?

Day 2 (Monday)

The headlines from the world press concerned the demonstration and us.

'It seems the Fog has at last attained some degree of credibility,' Harry said, over breakfast.

'Can't you speak like everyone and say *they believe the Fog is real*?' Rico asked. 'Something simple. You use these long sentences all the time.'

'You mean I have a wide range of vocabulary at my disposal and am proficient in using it? Thank you, I appreciate the compliment,' Harry replied.

Those two had been bickering since reading an article in The Times newspaper that morning. It traced and analysed the most discussed theories on the Fog's origins and purpose.

'How do you know the Fog is not a trick from aliens, messing with our minds?' Rico asked while pushing a mug of freshly made coffee Harry's way.

'Nonsense. Why would they do such thing?' Harry asked, adding sugar and milk to his cup. Rico winced, not from his comments but from his taste in coffee. He believed in the supremacy of espressos.

'How would I know? I am not an alien,' Rico replied.

'Are you sure? Are you absolutely certain you're not?' Harry asked, with a twinkle in the eye. Rico frowned and pondered. Harry had a knack for puzzling questions to unsettle Rico.

'What about the theory that the Other World is the Ark of Noah?' I asked them both. 'Then only the Relocated would survive the pending Apocalypse.'

'I don't believe in this,' Rico said. 'The door opened many times before and there was never an apocalypse afterwards. The world has never ended before.'

Harry shook his head at Rico's comments and smiled. So did I. Zeno was still bent down, reading and giggling.

'Oh! You are going to love that one, Rico!' Zeno interrupted. 'What about the theory that the Government and some big companies are behind it all, and that everyone in WII are just actors; that we have all been fooled into believing what is, in reality, a social experiment. A new kind of Big Brother show!'

We all looked at each other and laughed. We had experienced too much of the Fog to take an ounce of this idea seriously; even Rico.

'Yoko, your project to educate everyone about the Fog and both worlds is getting increasingly important. I won't be able to face all this balderdash for long,' Harry commented.

'It's almost as if they all get stoned for inspiration before writing their piece,' Rico added.

'Does that mean you're dropping the 'Alien' theory?' Zeno asked.

'Well...' Rico hesitated at first. 'Yeah, I think it is still a remote possibility, but let's put it aside. For now.'

'Thank God,' Harry whispered to himself.

'Plus, we have enough on our plate dealing with the pain-in-the-buttocks people here without adding some from space,' Zeno commented.

'That would be Ingis Chen and...?' Rico asked.

'Lally O'Maleigh,' Zeno said.

'Is she really a problem, that one? Her views are extreme, but I don't see how she can be a threat. On the contrary, she advises people not to cross or to idealise the Other World. It is rather helpful to us,' Harry commented.

'Any extreme belief is bad. She also gathers followers and that is dangerous. That's how fanatic beliefs and actions take shape,' Zeno explained. He spoke my mind.

'She is unpleasant, not dangerous,' Harry countered.

'Let's just play it safe and not underestimate her. Or anyone.' I replied. Religious extremism had always worried me, even more so when it was focused directly against us.

'Can I come with you to see Eudes later?' Rico asked.

'Of course. I have to warn you he might not remember you.'

'Not a problem. I liked the mini-man: it will be nice to see him anyway. When are you off?'

'I must go through a few things with Leila first. She should be here any time, so maybe in an hour.'

'Oh! Then I'll quickly train and get ready,' Rico said, already on his way upstairs.

That meant he would not be ready for a couple of hours, between training, showering and the long process of choosing what top would best go with the trendiest jeans. Let's not forget, too, the time taken to get each strand of his hair in its perfect spot.

'You can always join us there whenever you're ready?!' I shouted to him.

'I really won't be long!' he shouted back from his room. Zeno snorted, expressing his doubts. Even though our social life was non-existent over the past few weeks, could it be that once a metrosexual, always a metrosexual?

Rico was not perfect, but he had a gem for a heart.

*

My Ftab rang. I checked the caller ID and jumped in my chair. Leo! In my excitement, I dropped the tablet, picked it up quickly, and answered fearing I'd lost the call.

'Hello? Hello! Leo?'

'Yes, Yoko. It's me,' Leo replied, sounding both happy and exhausted.

'Oh my God, it is you! How are you? Where are you? Are you safe? Are you in Kenya? Where are you? Are you ok?' My thoughts were all over the place.

'I am fine, Yoko. Don't worry, I am fine. We are still in Kenya at the Society's villa, in the fogged tree house.'

'I am so relieved. So relieved! Is everybody well?' I asked, and added as an afterthought, 'When you say everybody, who is that?'

'Jack, Mitch, Mary and me. Putu as well. She helped us cross back,' Leo answered. His voice was heavy with tiredness and, yes, sadness.

'No Clare, then...' I muttered, more to myself than anyone. Harry and Zeno came by my side, listening to every word.

'No. Clare is gone,' Leo confirmed our fear. I shook my head to the others. Everybody lowered their eyes at the news.

'Poor Mary,' I thought.

'Mary is very shaken,' Leo said, reading my mind from miles away.

'So is she coming back with you guys? Kenya is not a place for her right now.'

'No, Yoko. She is not coming back.'

'What?' I began, but he didn't let me finish.

'She is distraught but determined. She wants nothing to do with her old world any more. Our world killed her mother.'

I didn't know how to react to this, unsure what he meant. Was he speaking literally or figuratively?

'What exactly happened?' I enquired.

One week ago, when Leo, Mitch and Jack arrived in Kenya, there was an intense discussion on whether or not Jack should join them in the search for Mary and Clare in WII, or if he should just stay safe in the Society's house. In the end, Jack's insistence won. Terrified as he was, he told them that if they got lost or, for any reason, could not make their way back to the fogged tree house, Jack would be their way out when the next Saturday came. What was most important, he had said, was to stay together and to be extra cautious. Jack looked petrified with fear, which made Mitch and Leo view him with new admiration. There is no bravery in facing adversity when there is no fear of it. Bravery is in overcoming fears, and moving forward despite and against them. Jack was being the bravest of us all. The three of them slept in the tree house on switching night. It was not just a little cabin perched high in the branches. The tree was very large with a hollowed trunk, big enough for a small 4x4 car to fit inside. Leo promised he would send me pictures to prove how a tree trunk could be large enough for such a vehicle. The idea worked. They left in the morning, driving the car packed with food, guns, ammunitions, map, water (a lot of water!), spare fuel and the boys' determination. Their first destination was towards the house Clare and Mary used to live in. It was not fogged anymore, but it was where their trail was bound to start. They had to beware of the Relocated people who would be close to the old Fog venue. As no one knew what had happened, the Relocated were a potential danger to be reckoned with in this rescue mission. The engine noise would give them away long before they reached their destination, so Leo and Mitch held their guns ready to shoot and Jack drove. He was a surprisingly good driver. He had learned to drive on his uncle's farm when he was under-aged. He couldn't go on the main roads then, so started in the fields. Driving rough was one of the rare 'manly' activities he had ever enjoyed. When close to the location where Mary and Clare's house should have been, the men studied the map. From Mary's previous messages, they vaguely knew the direction from the ex-fogged villa toward Mary's husband's Maasai village. This was the best chance they had to find her and, they hoped without much conviction, her mother.

They didn't meet anyone on that first day, or on the second day, mostly because they failed to find the village and had no idea where to look next. However, on the third day they heard shotguns being fired. They had to investigate. Knowing the people were armed, they left the car behind so they would not be shot at, hid their guns inside their jackets and made their way through the bush. They had to watch out for men and for wild animals. Soon, they came across a campfire where men and women sat, eating. Mitch went ahead on his own, leaving Zeno and Jack behind to watch his back. He was greeted at gunpoint. Mitch explained he was lost and had followed the sound of the gunshots. The settlers were suspicious and asked him a lot of questions about his crossing and where he had been so far. Mitch used his first experience in the Kenyan WII to describe his crossing and wandering in the jungle. He lied, saying that he was a reporter who had crossed during the riots, when he was intent on covering the whole event. He turned out to be a Relocated. Somehow, he became separated from the rest and had stumbled around since, very much concerned - day and night - about being eaten alive. So far he had been lucky, but when he heard the shots, he hastened to find the source. He longed for human contact and the safety in numbers! The group of men and women, 11 in total, softened towards him and offered him some of their food. Jack returned to the car to safeguard it and Leo stayed to watch the camp and check on Mitch. As silently as he could, he climbed a tree to its highest branch, staying in contact with Jack thanks to a military 2-way radio. He also used night-goggles to keep an eye on the camp and his friends.

Mitch spent most of the night listening to the Relocated's stories. They had split from a larger, more aggressive group who raided WII native villages and tried to gain control of the land as a form of survival. They especially targeted the locals who had helped the Gatekeepers to escape. They had tried to make a deal with Mary and Clare to gain control of the doors and have direct access back to our world at will, but the Foggies were having none of it. They had refused to agree to the Relocated's demand or be used by them. When the group turned more aggressive in their demands, they fled. Now, these Relocated were restless in their hunt for the two Gatekeepers. With the help of her husband and his family, Clare and Mary kept moving to safer places. Sadly, some of the Relocated had firearms and did not hesitate to use them in order to get Clare and Mary back. The Maasai had more traditional weapons and struggled to defend themselves when cornered. Mother and daughter disguised themselves as locals and, baring much more than they were accustomed to, were running from a camp to reach another village when Clare was hit. Mary buried her mother where she had died. She couldn't stop for long, though, and she and her bushman decided the best idea was to split from everyone. They did not want to endanger any more innocent tribesmen. They hoped that when the situation had settled down, or when Mary had turned so local she would be unrecognisable from her old self, the assailants would abandon their pursuit.

The undercover Foggies had come across a group who disapproved of the killing of the locals, even for the goal of capturing the Gatekeepers. As they had to live in this world from then onwards, they believed they should befriend the natives and learn how to survive here, instead of killing those who could help them adjust. They had left the main group in the middle of the night, only able to sneak one gun out with them. They were taking big risks in stealing it. Ammunition was rare and sparse. The others would not forgive them. They had taken all the precautions they could think of to not be followed and rarely used the gun, except in extremis, that afternoon when one of the children was attacked by a lioness and saved. When Mitch appeared, they feared the others had found them. The next day, they would have to move at dawn: if Mitch had found them, the others could as well. Mitch believed that they were not professional or dangerous. For one, they had not searched him. If they had, they would have found both the small gun nestled in his sock and the knife lodged in the back of his trousers.

Mitch considered they had made progress in the mission. He now knew what had happened to Clare and Mary. The boys still had to find the latter and, from what he had just learnt, that would prove tricky. Her husband would protect her at all costs and knew the area like the back of his hand. Mitch decided to dig for information a little further. He told them he had met Mary and Clare in the past, because of his work, and they were lovely ladies. He hoped to meet Mary again in this World. By then, Mitch believed that the only way they could get to Mary would either be by meeting her accidentally - and it was a very remote possibility - or by getting her to find them. For her to come, she would first need to know they were here, so he had to subtly pass the information to anyone and everyone. Talking to the Relocated was not the best option, though. After Clare's death, Mary must be wary of them all and unwilling to deal with them. The boys' best chance was with the local bushmen, which was equally challenging. Where were they? How to talk to them? How friendly would they be after the Relocated's attacks on their villages? Mitch could only see problems ahead. His hopes of finding Mary were plummeting as minutes passed and he reflected on the situation. However, his new and immediate concern was how to leave the settlers' camp and return to Leo and Jack. He couldn't just stand up and go. He had come, supposedly alone and in search of company. He had to find a way out, but how? Jack, Leo and he had been idiots, Mitch thought; they should have thought of this before. Well, he hoped the night would give him counsel and he would think of something in the morning. He looked towards where he knew Leo was in hiding and hoped he was safe.

Waking up at dawn, he informed the watchman of the hour that he was going to relieve himself and walked towards Leo's spot. He acted as though cautious of his surroundings, vigilant of wild animals. To attract Leo's attention, in case the latter was dozing, he sneezed loudly. Soon, he heard some rustling in the nearby bushes. Mitch braced himself and took out his knife for protection against a possible lion, when Leo spoke.

'How is it going? They seem friendly enough,' Leo said. 'Learned anything interesting?'

'Yes, I have,' Mitch answered. 'They are an okay bunch, but they might turn less friendly if I just stand up and say goodbye. No one likes to feel used or fooled. I need a way out.'

'A diversion?'

'That would do. Maybe I could disappear in the stampede if you create a bit of chaos,' Mitch suggested.

'Right,' Leo replied. He thought for a while on how he could possibly create a chaotic situation, but his mind was blank. 'Any ideas?'

'Nope,' Mitch replied, also thinking hard. They heard a branch cracking and Leo quickly hid back behind a tree

'Everything all right there?' a man from the camp asked, from a distance.

'All good!' Mitch replied. 'Just a bit stressed here,' Mitch played with his trouser zip to make the sound of closing his jeans and started moving towards the man without looking back. Leo climbed back up the tree and called Jack by radio, to update him.

Soon, everybody was gathered around the fire on which water was boiling for breakfast and tea. The ground suddenly shook, accompanied by a deafening bang. Soil and grass rose high in the sky, some of it falling back on the gathered individuals. A similar explosion occurred on the other side of the camp within seconds. The group was under attack, grenades being launched at them. They all stood up and ran for cover into the depth of the woods and bushes. A third grenade exploded towards the front of the camp and people fled in opposite directions. It was the chaos that Mitch had been hoping for. He ran with the others, yet slightly on the side. Within seconds, he split away and hid behind a tree. When a fourth grenade exploded, he faked panic, in case anyone had been watching him, and ran further away on the right, until he made another slight turn and circled back to where Leo had been. When he believed he had distanced himself from the group, he stopped running and walked carefully instead, to hear if anyone or anything was ready to pounce on him. Leo hissed at him from a branch and climbed down the tree. The two then walked at a fast pace to the truck's hiding place. Once back in the vehicle, they drove away until hunger made them stop the car and open some cans of food. They ate it cold, brainstorming on what should be their next move. It was already Wednesday: they had 3 days left before returning to the Fog Tree House or taking the risk of turning a temporary wood hut into a gate.

As they were talking, a Maasai knocked at the window. Jack screamed in shock, afterwards putting a hand on his heart, which was racing. Mitch and Leo had raised their guns simultaneously, aiming at the man. His head was shaved and his face bore many piercings with twigs, stones and elephant tusk. The lobes of his ears were stretched and ornate with what looked like bone-made jewellery. He was wearing fabric around his body and over his shoulders, and was looking at them intensely, a long spear in his right hand pointing towards the sky. From the folding of the fabric, he took out a rolled piece of animal skin, unfolded and studied it. He finally showed it to Mitch, Leo and Jack realised it was covered with drawings of the Foggies. The boys recognised themselves easily, along with Yoko, Zeno, Dante and all the others. Mary explained later that she had several drawn skins made like this: one to circulate within the Maasai communities of WII, the idea being for them to know the Foggies were friends, not foes. She knew we would come to her aid. She also knew this world was a dangerous place for us. Mary had advised the Maasai to organise a watch on the various groups of Relocated. Should they come too close to their villages or display belligerent behaviour, the watch could warn the villagers in time for them to flee. Last night, the Maasai man had recognised Mary's friends. Mary was the only one who could have drawn their portraits and given them to people she trusted. Mitch and Leo lowered their guns.

At nightfall, after an excruciatingly slow drive as the jeep followed the Maasai man on foot – he had refused to get into the vehicle – they reached a small 'enkang', or village. The Maasai tribes are semi-nomadic people, and their house-shelter reflects the impermanent nature of their dwelling. It was ideal for Mary and her beloved, who did not want to settle in one place for too long. When they arrived, Mary was ecstatic with joy at first. The emotions overwhelmed her: it didn't take long before she burst out crying. Over the past few weeks, her losses in life had been enormous. She was bickering with her mother constantly: nonetheless, they were very close and the void left by her passing was immense and painful.

Over the next two days, Mary, Mitch, Leo and Jack exchanged stories of what had happened since they had lost contact with each other. Mary's was by far the most heart wrenching. The only positive in her tragic days was the deepening of the love between her and her native Maasai husband. He had been the rock she relied on. She constantly repeated how blessed she was, in her misfortune, to have such a wonderful man. On the sixth day, they all departed to come back to the Gate tree house. Mary was adamant she did not intend to return to our world. There was nothing for her there, any more. Her mother was gone and she didn't like our society, nor its way of thinking. Her life was with her husband in WII now. What she wanted was to make sure we were able to return safely and to say goodbye to us all, especially Putu. The experience in the bush had given her a practical outlook though, and she requested a few key items from our world; a gun with ammunition to protect herself and her new family, should it be needed; some mobile solar energy panels; seeds and grains that could grow in the rich but dry soil of these parts; maps; and a few other objects that she believed would make her life slightly easier without affecting the ways of her adopted tribe too much. Hers was a drastic decision, to cut all links with her past, her origins, her world. Life in the African WII was hard. She believed she was following her path and it was what she really wanted. She knew that not visiting the Fog once every 49 days would create a withdrawal effect: she had decided to take the risk. She had faith in the natural medicine of the natives to help her get through it. The tribe had also told her that once she passed a certain point, the withdrawal effects would stop. This knowledge had been transferred orally from generation to generation. She believed it.

*

Listening to Leo and ignoring any other calls, I only took a break once to message Jazz to inform her of the boys' return to WI Kenya. During Leo's call, Leila had arrived and Rico had returned. They both sat down and listened to the update, catching it as Mary joined the call and took over from Leo, telling her side of the story. Her voice was shaky and emotional when she reached the point of her mother being shot. She was angry and feisty on the subject of the other Relocated, and soft when referring to how all the tribes had gathered behind her to face this new adversity. When she explained her decision to turn the page completely and settle for good in the Other World, some of us gasped; others frowned. I was sad that she found it necessary to abandon her links with us, despite the prospect of those debilitating withdrawal effects from the Fog. Was our world so terrible? We were willing to maintain a door for her, but she was uncompromising. She wanted to move on completely and let go of her past. It was her choice and, of course, we would respect it. She said she would contact each of us separately to say goodbye. This call was her goodbye to me in London. My throat tightened and my eyes welled. We had just found her again and she was one of us. Now she was leaving again, and for good.

When the call finished, there was a long moment when no one knew what to say and how to react to both her story and her wish to leave.

'What about Putu?' Harry asked, breaking the silence.

'I spoke with her,' Leila answered. 'As a Facilitor, she also needs to have access to the Fog one week in seven, minimum, to avoid the Fog withdrawal effect. As it now seems unreasonable to ask a Switcher to travel to Kenya to maintain a door there just for her, she agreed to consider a move to another Fog location.'

'She still isn't sure about moving from Kenya yet?' Rico asked. 'I mean, I know she is doing a good job there, but children are in need of support and care everywhere in the world. Even in London.'

'Very much in London!' Harry commented.

'Her passion and calling - as she puts it - is in Kenya. It is not easy for her to let it go,' Leila replied.

*

It was past lunchtime when I made it across the old parking lot to *The Jazzin* with Simba. Before stepping outside the house, Jazz had taken me aside to discuss the 'Ushi Tsou situation', as she put it.

'We need to sort out where we stand with her,' she said, point blank.

'What do you mean? And on what grounds exactly? There are so many,' I replied.

'On the more pressing one: we need to make sure she doesn't join Clémence, of course!' Jazz replied.

'What makes you think she would?'

'She's a mercenary. She is a hostile woman who will sell herself and her soul to the highest bidder. This is serious! She could train Clémence's bunch into real soldiers! Making them even more of a danger than they already are! We must prevent this.'

'Don't you think you are exaggerating a little?' It was a rhetorical question.

'No, I'm not. The threat of Clémence invading Woodfellas is real. We are in fear of this every day, as well as the constant need to negotiate and compromise with the councils. I have a permanent headache, you know.'

'Okay. Sorry. So what does she know of the situation? What have you told her?' I enquired.

'Nothing. I have told her nothing, but that doesn't mean she doesn't know. She could have met Clémence on her way here already. She could be a spy! A Trojan horse!'

I rolled my eyes. The last thing we needed was for Jazz to turn into a female Rico.

'Well, let's go talk to her and see how she reacts, shall we?' I said, putting down my empty mug and heading to the door.

'Where are they?' I asked her.

'Last I checked, they were just outside in the sun.'

'Good.'

Jazz, Simba and I walked to the door and crossed the Fog into WII.

*

Eudes and Ushi Tsou were playing in front of the house in the WII clearing. Maisie was attempting to befriend him but Eudes would not leave Ushi's side. When I walked towards him, he did recognise me and smiled, yet without moving towards me. Ushi was his anchor now. Simba's animal instinct told her that Eudes' confidence in other beings ran slim. She lowered herself to floor level and slowly crawled towards him, stopping regularly with gentle yelps. It intrigued the little boy. He observed her coming closer without fear. Only when she reached an arm's length distance from him did she stop, sensing the beginning of a hesitation from him. It was barely noticeable, yet she knew immediately how to react. She moaned softly, a barely audible sound. Eudes extended his arm and touched Simba between the ears. The wolf nodded slightly as a sign of appreciation and Eudes grew bolder, making a step towards her and caressing her with more confidence. In no time, he was by her side. She had turned to expose her tummy, her four legs up, and he was laughing, lying and holding her. Simba and Eudes had struck up a friendship. Ushi Tsou had observed the scene both with caution and pleasure. She enjoyed watching the boy's budding friendship with an animal, yet she kept a close eye on Simba, in case the wolf turned aggressive on the child.

'Oudini, it is time for your nap,' Ushi Tsou said to him after Simba and the child had played for some time. She spoke with softness, not in a commanding way but in a subtle and kind way.

'Do I have to? Can I sleep with Simba?' Eudes asked.

'Would you sleep or would you play? Ushi asked, with a smile.

Eudes hesitated. Simba nudged him with her snout and he giggled.

'I think that answers the question.' Ushi Tsou kneeled down and opened her arms towards Eudes. 'Come on, little one. Be a good boy.'

Eudes made a pout, looked at Simba, looked at Ushi, waved to the wolf and went to her. She lifted him on her shoulder and looked at both Jazz and me.

'I will be right back,' she said.

She returned within 10 minutes, carrying a mug of tea. She sat down, facing the clearing, and spoke rather coldly.

'So, what is it you want to talk to me about?'

'We need to update you on what has happened around here since you left,' I told her.

'I am listening,' she said.

'It has to do with Clémence,' I began. Ushi Tsou took a sip of her tea. She was still not looking at either of us. 'We know how you had dealings with her when you first crossed, and we know she was behind my assassination attempt.'

Ushi Tsou did not react. I continued.

'She has dropped her cover and left her husband. She is now heading a revolutionary movement for women to take the power in this World and overthrow the men. In short, she is after a role reversal: the women in control, the men the slaves.'

'The woman is nuts!' Jazz jumped in. 'She is armed! She is trying to indoctrinate the kids and has launched attacks on the communities. She has no limits! She is dangerous and endangering the whole society here! She is so extreme!'

Ushi Tsou smirked. She was not surprised to hear Jazz' description of Clémence.

'Maud Poff, Jazz and Molly – a newly Relocated, you might have met her already – have created a counter movement. A political one, not a revolutionary one. It is also in defence of women. Instead of a Revolution, they aim to rebalance the power between men and women. Instead of war, they wish to establish cooperation between genders, with mutual respect.'

Still silent, Ushi Tsou at least stopped staring into the distance and turned to look at me.

'And I presume you want to know in which camp I intend to be,' she stated.

'Exactly!' Jazz exclaimed. 'We can't have you here if you …'

'Jazz. Please. Let's hear what Ushi has to say before making threats. We just broke the news to her.'

Jazz turned grumpy and Ushi Tsou smirked some more. She took another sip of tea before speaking. It was the longest speech we ever heard her voice, to date.

'You have the correct information on Clémence. The woman hid her game well, but it was only a matter of time until she revealed her cards – or some of them. I had no doubt she would do so exactly at the right time and with a good hand. She is clever. Now, in the previous circumstances, I would probably have proposed my services to her, they would be invaluable for her cause …'

'No! You can't!' Jazz exclaimed.

'Jazz! Please!' I intervened.

'However,' Ushi Tsou continued, unperturbed, 'the situation has changed somewhat. I have no wish for her to create a society in which she will act as a dictator, controlling what people say and think, and reducing men to being women's doormats. Not that the idea is un-appealing…' She made an appreciative pout at the thought, before swiftly returning to her serious self. 'But that is not acceptable any more. Not with Eudes. Not FOR Eudes.'

At that point, leaning forward towards us, she continued in a determined tone.

'I have looked after Eudes for months and intend to continue doing so.' There was a challenge in her voice as she narrowed her eyes on me. 'You are his aunt and his only family. Yet, you don't live in this world. You can't look after him full-time. I can. The little one is a good boy. He has a good nature and... And I love him. I will not let anything or anyone stop him having the best that is possible in this world.'

I was stunned and it must have shown, as she commented, 'You think I have no heart, don't you? Maybe I just didn't have any reason to have one. Until Eudes. Yes, it surprised even me. It is what it is.'

'Hang on a second,' Jazz interrupted. 'What makes you think we will let you look after Eudes?! You don't come with the best recommendations, you know. Your antics are not exactly the ones of an appropriate nanny, even less of a surrogate mother!'

'What you think does not concern me,' Ushi Tsou replied with calm.

'Well it should, because I am much more suited to looking after Eudes than you are. I am Yoko's best friend. Yoko stays at mine every Saturday and so he would be with his aunt regularly. *The Jazzin* is a Fog house, so Eudes would remain in touch with both worlds and with his grandparents. Plus, we know what values would be transmitted to him, while yours...'

'Be careful of what you are going to say next...' Ushi Tsou hissed.

'Ladies, ladies...' I intervened. 'Please, let's not get into a fight,'

My brain was working at full speed, trying to think of all the options and their ramifications on this situation. There was much at stake, not only for Eudes but for the balance of powers in WII. I turned to Ushi Tsou.

'Ushi. I won't lie to you: the idea of you looking after my nephew does not fill me with joy. So far, you are not remotely a friend: you worked for Ingis Chen whom we distrust; you kidnapped both Simba and me and threatened us; you colluded with Clémence, who then tried to eliminate me. Yes, you agreed to fly to southern France to bring back my relatives, Julia and Eudes, but you had little choice in the matter: it was your only way to escape Lil'London's prison. Regarding your values, as Jazz pointed out, we are not sure what they are and if you have any. You were loyal to Chen until you got relocated, that we know. It is to your credit: you are at least capable of loyalty. However, you might have killed hundreds of people for money, and hopefully not for pleasure, too. So you must understand that leaving you in charge of one of the most valuable members of my family is not attractive to me.'

'Ha-Ha!' Jazz commented with a smug.

'However,' I continued, 'it is impossible to ignore that you have created a very special bond with Eudes. He seems to adore and respect you. You seem, indeed, to love him. I appreciate that. You brought him back when you could have easily left him behind and made your way back unburdened and faster. You saved his life and you took good care of him at your own expense. I am grateful, very grateful.'

'Yoko! You are not going to let her look after Eudes! You can't!' Jazz interrupted again.

'Jazz! Will you please let me speak?! You know me, you know I would only make a decision I truly believe is for the best.' I took a deep breath and turned to Ushi Tsou. 'So I am willing to try and give you a chance, under certain strict and non-negotiable conditions.'

Jazz looked at me horrified. Ushi Tsou was not revealing any of her thoughts as she listened attentively. I continued: 'I will let you look after Eudes if you agree that both of you will live here in Woodfellas. If I were to move and create a gate elsewhere in the future, you have to follow me there. You will look after him but I will always be his aunt and have the last words, and he will always have access to me and my parents, as we wish. We will decide if, what, and when regarding anything relative to him and his education. You will be like a nanny and we, the authorities. If we disagree with any of your ideas for him, you will have to cooperate and find a way to make it work to our principles. We want the best for him, and we want him happy. We love him! Aside from being his family, being close to us is also to his advantage: he will benefit from access and learning from both worlds. On that ground, I am willing to see how it works out. As I said, I am giving you a chance, but you do not have carte blanche. You will always, ALWAYS, have to answer to me. Am I being clear?'

'Yes, you are,' Ushi Tsou replied, stern.

'And...?' She had to verbally and clearly agree to respect my rules.

Ushi Tsou did not speak for some time. Her eyes were fixed on the table, her lips pursed. When she lifted her face, I realised that it wasn't because she was upset or thinking: she was holding back her tears.

'I was ready to fight for him,' she said, her voice strangled by the emotion. 'I was so scared you would take him away from me. I even hesitated coming back because I might lose him. In the end, I did, because I couldn't do that to the boy. For him, it was so important to have access to people, to society, to you.'

She swallowed a sob and breathed heavily, blocking her tears. Jazz took out a tissue and handed it to her. Ushi Tsou waved it away, frowning. She was trying hard to get back in control of her emotions.

'I accept your conditions. I will give him the best I have. I promise. I will.'

Ushi Tsou stood up abruptly and left, unwilling to further display the flow of emotion that had overwhelmed her.

'My God… I would never have thought…' Jazz whispered next to me.

'I am rather in shock, too,' I whispered back. I was moved and relieved at first, but soon I cringed. How were my parents going to take the news?

They were on their way to London. At last, the French administration had relented and allowed them to cross the borders. Mum and Dad had been overjoyed upon hearing the news of Eudes' return, the euphoria dying within seconds when they learned about Julia's death. The conflicted emotions left them numb, only eager to make their way to us as fast as possible. Their accommodation had been organised by the Society in partnership with McRae, who had gone in person to France to accompany them on the journey. Society's men also discreetly followed them.

Also on the move were the Koplats. The American Government had complied with all the demands and conditions presented by Sam and McRae on their behalf. Sam had gone to the States, along with a few other British representatives, to meet Adam, Sophia and Michelle at an agreed meeting point. From there, they were making their way to Nevada. The Society was, of course, in the background keeping an eye on things. Elsie, informed of the Koplat's return, was very excited at the prospect of renewed interactions with our worlds without fear of being controlled and invaded by the American authorities.

*

Late at night, in bed and exhausted, I switched off my light with a sad smile. I had just re-read another message from Leo sent early afternoon: 'Thank you for your letter, Yoko. It was the best welcome present I could ever have'. We had not had a chance to communicate again all day, as he was travelling back. Tomorrow he would be here. Would he give me another chance? Drained, my spirits were down and I worried more than I should about something I could not control.

It had been a difficult evening. When my parents had arrived, they intended to stay at *The Jazzin* for the first few nights to be with Eudes. Jazz was happy to comply and give them a room. Eudes had recognised my parents immediately and had run towards them with excitement. However, he had refused to stay away from Ushi Tsou for long. He also refused to sleep anywhere other than with her. My parents were distraught and upset, even if they did not say anything. When Ushi Tsou left to put Eudes to bed with a story, I explained to my parents my decision regarding Eudes and Ushi.

'You should have consulted us first,' my mother said, her voice betraying controlled anger.

'I agree with your mother. This is not the type of decision to be taken lightly and on the spur of the moment. The poor boy has lost his mother, his chance of a normal life in the world he was born into and his full access to us and to his father, too. Now you won't even take care of his education?!' My father barely articulated between clenched jaws.

'It is as if you can't be bothered,' my mother added.

'That is not true! I care! I care a lot!' I replied, with vehemence. 'How could you even conceive that I do not!?'

'Then why don't you look after him yourself!' my mother exploded.

'Because with the life I am leading right now, how reliable would I be for him?! I don't know when I might have to travel at the last minute to help a Foggy. I am juggling between two worlds when he is stuck in one only! I said I would oversee his education and be present. And I will. I will give him as much time and attention possible. But he needs somebody full time, someone who can look after him, care for him, fight for him. Ushi Tsou can. You can see it as clearly as I do: she adores him.'

'Why not Jazz? Jazz could, too! This Ushi, she ...' my mother began.

'Jazz has taken a stand in WII that puts her into a controversial position.

That could reflect back on Eudes. Also, Clémence is bound to hear about Eudes. As he is my nephew, she might be interested in getting her hands on him.'

My parents looked shocked.

'I didn't think of that…' my father whispered.

'Ushi Tsou is the best to protect him. She is a pro. No one will touch or harm him under her watch. In any case, she will only be his guardian on a trial basis for now. Be certain I will ask Nick, Jazz, Big Tom, everyone, to keep an eye on her and on Eudes!'

The discussion left me drained. Added to all the events and news of the day, I fell into a comatose-like sleep within minutes.

Day 3 (Tuesday)

I woke up with a start. It took me a few seconds to remember where I was. The light was unusually dim outside and Simba was not licking my face as she does in the morning. The shrilling sound filling the bedroom was not my alarm, but my Ftab's ringtone. I picked up the Ftab and answered 'hello' in a sleepy, cranky voice. It was 6.20am. Leila didn't bother saying hi and launched immediately into the object of her call. There was a new and major problem. Overnight, in more than 50 locations around the world, most of them being airports and buzzing hubs in large cities, breakouts of people suddenly taken ill had risen at an alarming rate. In only 8 hours, more than 2,500 men and women had been admitted to hospital as emergencies, suffering from fever, headache, rashes, dizziness, diarrhoea, to name only a few of the symptoms. Already, planes arriving from possibly contaminated airports were quarantined. So were the concerned airports and whole parts of town. Leila paused for a second before adding that it included Leicester Square and Piccadilly Circus in London, Heathrow and Los Angeles airports and Times Square in New York. London was one of the most hit by what was described, already, as a global epidemic outbreak.

'Is it a virus?' I asked, knowing what an affirmative answer entailed.

'It's too early to have the specifics on what causes the disease, but it is most likely a virus,' Leila replied. 'Yoko, if this is confirmed, I am afraid you will have a lot of pressure on your shoulders, you and all the Foggies.'

'I know,' I said. The thought of the whole planet in the grip of a pandemic virus and requesting access to the Fog was mentally too much to conceive at such an early hour of the day. Coffee was a must.

I put my slippers on and headed to the kitchen, with Simba on my heels. Minutes later, mug of coffee in hand, I switched on the English news. The health alert around the capital and airport was making the headlines, reminding us it was the third largest in the world in terms of passenger traffic. A map of the world illustrated the 50 original points where the epidemic had erupted simultaneously. Now, a web of lines and dots filled the map, showing how fast new cases of illness were reported. Growing mushrooms were taking over the screen.

'Oh my God...' I whispered to myself. I was horrified. No continent was unaffected. The anchor was in shock, too, at the extent and speed of the epidemic. She was finding it difficult to narrate the news without being emotional. She explained how the origins of the disease were not determined yet, aside from its sudden emergence the previous night around 10-11pm GMT. The similar timing around the world was an unlikely coincidence and suspicions of a planned released of the virus in targeted areas ran high. Multiple theories were presented, the main one being a terrorist attack.

'But why?' I thought. Only a fanatic could fully understand the reasoning and knots of another fanatic mind. I was glad not to be able to grasp such a twisted way of thinking. 'This is sickening. All these people affected. This is beyond terrible.'

For the first time of my life, the idea of breakfast was unappealing. The anchor stopped talking, listening to someone. When she spoke, there was anger and anxiety in her voice. Two babies and a 6-year-old child, among the first cases declared, had died. I felt sick in my stomach that anybody could purposely create such chaos and risk the health of so many, including babies and children. It was not just a mere virus now. It was a lethal one. I felt my eyes tingle. What was happening to this world?

Of course, the simultaneity of the outbreak could not be by chance. I didn't believe, either, that is was a coincidence that it would happen now, with the Fog and its healing power being public knowledge. London was the most affected by the virus; London was also viewed as the 'Gatekeepers headquarters'. The demonstration for open access to the Fog had taken place only two days ago and had failed in its aim. Could this fast-spreading pestilence have the same aim? Who would go to such extremes?! There was a niggling thought at the back of my mind, a recollection of my first encounters with Ingis Chen. He wanted the whole planet's population to cross the Fog. He wanted to save this planet, or so he claimed, by transferring a seventh of humans to that Other world, whether or not those concerned wished to cross. I had thought at the time, that even a tyrant would not be able to achieve this: it was an impossible task with 7 billion beings. However, a worldwide plague could achieve this end. It would force people into crossing the Fog for survival. And so Ingis Chen would reach his goal. Could he be behind this 'terrorist attack'? Did he have it in him to use such drastic means? I shook my head at the thought. Surely he would not stoop so low. I refocused on the news. An hour later, I was still watching reports from all over the world, drinking the remnants of a pot of lukewarm coffee.

*

My tablet beeped. A message from Leila shone yet another light on the pandemic infection.

'*Dear Yoko,*
A team of our scientists is studying any parallel between the Fog and the resurgence of viruses on earth. Some dates are, sadly, matching. As you know, the Fog occurs every 231 years. Although we do not have a list of all the locations for each Fog appearance, there was always a widespread pestilence or plague surrounding the time of the Fog, like in 1348 with the infamous Black Death in Europe. In 1551, England was suffering from what is often referred to as 'English sweating sickness'. The details of the disease and its causes still remain a mystery. It was a highly virulent disease, dramatic and sudden, that could be lethal within hours. The disease had been building up for some time, yet by the end of 1551 the sickness just vanished. In 1782, North America was dealing

with a lethal influenza plague. One can wonder if there is any cause-to-effect link between the Fogs and the plagues and if there is, which one comes first. I am afraid that like hen and egg, we will never know.

Just thought I would keep you in the loop of our studies.

X Leila'

As I closed her message, my eyes slid to the unread emails from Eudes' father, long overdue for attention. Leaning on the table, I took my head in my hands. It was barely 8am, I was already mentally exhausted and feeling guilty towards the whole world. The day ahead was going to be overwhelming considering the new Gatekeepers' duty towards the planet in the thrall of a virus. Yet the individual matters also needed to be looked at: I had to decide whether or not to inform Eudes' father of his child's current situation. He was the father; he had a right to know. I went to the kitchen, prepared a new pot of coffee and returned to the table.

My brother-in-law had sent vehement, threatening and worried emails. I wanted to be honest and tell him the truth. Nonetheless, I didn't want to write it down and leave a trace he could pass on to the government or the press. So I called him.

'Charles-Antoine. This is Yoko.'

'Yoko! At last! Do you know how long it has been?! This is outrageous! I …' He started.

'Charles-Antoine, I am sorry. You must understand my life has taken quite a turn and I have been caught in a whirlwind of events out of my control. It was also impossible for me to contact you earlier when the Fog was still hidden from public knowledge.'

'Where is my son?!' he exclaimed.

'I must ask you to listen to me first and refrain from asking your many questions. For you to understand, I must go back to the beginning.'

'I …' Charles-Antoine tried to speak, but I would not let him.

'This is not a happy story; I must warn you. So, here it comes. When the Fog first appeared months ago, I didn't know what was happening and how the Fog worked. I went to visit my parents the weekend after the Fog first appeared. Julia and Eudes were there, and when I created the Fog overnight, they were Relocated. Both of them. I was at a loss what to do, but they were safely looked after by my parents in the family house. Then I discovered that Julia and Eudes would never be able to come back to this world. I also learned that, thanks to the Fog, Julia was cured of the life-threatening sexually transmissible disease you passed on to her. Frankly, you were not particularly in anyone's good books for the way you left Julia for Ahmed - even if she was difficult to be around - but after hearing about the STD... Anyway, at this time we were trying to cope with the situation and Julia was very low. We were trying to protect our secret. Then ...'

'Why? Why did you try to hide your secret? I am the father! Do you realise what you have done?' An angry Charles-Antoine cut my monologue.

'You must see our circumstances are very unusual,' I replied, patient and calm. I would not let him wind me up.

'Ahmed is sick, too! I am a carrier. It hasn't declared itself with me and so I was unaware of it. But Ahmed! Ahmed is in very bad shape! He must cross the Fog. We must! We are coming to London. We will come to London this weekend and you WILL let us cross the Fog.'

I took a deep breath. Everything in its own time. I would deal with that request - well, order really – once I had finished my story. I continued where he had interrupted me.

'Then Julia and Eudes disappeared on their journey through WII back to me, here in London. There was a helicopter incident and ...'

'WHAT?' Charles-Antoine interrupted again. 'No! No, no, no! Where is Eudes? What happened to Eudes? Where is he? What did you do with my son?!'

'That is what I am trying to tell you, if you could stop interrupting! Ok, so Julia was depressed. She said she couldn't bear the emptiness of the Other World back in the South of France. Here, we have a community on the other side and she would be able to rebuild her life with other Relocated. So we organised for a helicopter to go through WII France. Unfortunately, they had to travel blind. There was bad weather on the way, the helicopter crashed. Julia died.'

'Oh… Julia… She…' Charles-Antoine whispered on the phone.

'Eudes survived.' I was determined to tell my story focusing on the facts, not lingering on the sore wounds. 'The pilot was able to make the journey back to us with him. It took the best part of 3 months. During that time, we had no news, no information, nothing. If we had told you this story before, when the Fog was unknown to the public, you would not have believed me.'

Charles-Antoine was silent on the other end of the line. This was a lot to register in one go. After a moment, he spoke.

'But Eudes is alive and he is with you. I am sorry for Julia. Really sorry. She could be a bitch but she was not a bad person deep down. I loved her, at the beginning… But Eudes, my son, is alive and with you. So when we come this weekend, I want to see him. And Ahmed will be healthy again. So will I, not carrying this disease any more and putting my loved ones at risk.'

This was a demand I could not refuse: I wanted Eudes to restore the link with his father. I had to remind Charles-Antoine of an important detail though.

'You know about the relocation to the Other World, right? It could happen to you. To Ahmed. Even to both, though it is unlikely. Of course, you might simply cross the Fog without being more affected than just perfect health. No one can predict.'

Once again, Charles-Antoine remained silent for a while before speaking.

'Ahmed and I talked about this. We thought that Julia and Eudes might be relocated. We agreed that if I were to reach you, I would request to cross despite the risks,' he paused, then asked, 'So, this weekend, will you give us access to the Fog?'

This time I was the one who took a minute to think, even if I already knew my answer was yes. When I told him so, he sighed with relief.

*

Hanging up, I put my head between my hands again, elbows on the table. The sound of steps coming downstairs - I recognised Zeno's – did not make me move. I greeted him without looking. He came and put a hand on my back, asking me if I was ok. Leila had left it to me to inform them and I had not had the courage to wake them up with the bad news. They would know soon enough upon waking. I switched the news back on, warning him that the world, and we Foggies, had a brand new big problem. Immediately, he frowned and sat down. I went to the kitchen and took a mug for him. He, too, would need a lot of coffee. Harry joined us, shortly after. Rico was blissfully sleeping, unaware of the panic among humankind. None of us made a move to wake him up, choosing instead to give him a few more hours of respite.

Out of habit, I headed back towards the kitchen to prepare breakfast, even though my stomach was still in knots. The doorbell rang as I was taking some eggs out of their box. From Simba's friendly reaction, I expected Leila, Sam or McRae. I opened the door to both Leila and McRae. Despite their seriousness, there was a shadow of a smile on their faces as they stopped their conversation to turn to me. McRae raised a hand to show me a bag of pastries and we went to the dining area.

'The Government is setting up a quarantine area in all the airports of the country and at St Pancras International. Eurostar trains from the continent are stopped,' Sam announced before he had even sat down.

'They are also working on emergency plans to close the borders,' Leila added.

Sam reacted sharply with 'How do you...?' He didn't finish his question. Instead he muttered to himself 'never mind' and went to the kitchen to fetch three more mugs and plates.

'Good that we managed to get your parents here before this mess. It's really getting out of control at the borders,' Leila said.

'What is this disease? Do we know?'

'We do now and it's not looking good. It's an evolved version of the Marburg virus, maybe the most dangerous virus known today,' Leila said.

'I have never heard of it,' Zeno said.

'The Marburg virus was first identified by scientists in 1967, when small outbreaks of haemorrhagic fever occurred in laboratories in Marburg and Frankfurt in Germany. The same happened in Belgrade in Serbia - then Yugoslavia. The scientists were exposed to infected green monkeys imported from Uganda, or to tissue from those monkeys. The identified Marburg virus had a 23% to 90% fatality rate. This virus spreads through close human-to-human contact. The symptoms are headache, fever and a rash on the trunk at first, then it progresses to multiple organ failure and massive internal bleeding. There is no cure,' Leila explained.

'Oh Lord…' Harry whispered.

'Wait! You said this is an evolved version. Is it worse?' I asked Leila.

'It is faster. Normally the incubation should be 5 to 10 days. Then the symptoms occur rather suddenly. However, in our case, the onset is immediate!'

'And how long before the symptoms become severe?' Harry asked.

'With the old Marburg virus, the first symptoms are similar to malaria or typhoid fever, with fever, chills, headaches and muscular pains. Only from the fifth day after the onset of symptoms may a number of other issues appear: rash, chest and abdominal pain, sore throat, nausea, vomiting and diarrhoea. It grows increasingly severe until the sick person suffers liver failure, massive haemorrhaging and multi-organ dysfunction.'

'So, how long does it take for the virus to cause death?' I asked.

'That depends on the person. Studies showed the average was 11.5 days for under twenties and increased to 25.5 days for over forties.'

'With this one, rash, nausea and vomiting appeared within 5 hours, not 5 days,' I recalled from the news. 'Young children and babies have already died. We just heard some elderly people have, too. The death toll is going up by the minute around the world, slowly but surely.'

'And how many people are affected right now? Do we know?' Harry asked.

'The figure might not represent the total number of people affected. In many countries, hospitals are not accessible easily …' Leila started.

'What is the official number?' Harry insisted.

'6,752 people are officially declared sick, showing signs to such an extent that it cannot be malaria or anything else. 7 individuals are already dead from it, either very young or old,' Leila said in a grim voice.

Ten hours. 6752 sick. 7 dead.

'The numbers are rising quickly,' Leila added. 'This is just the beginning.'

The pastries remained untouched on the plates. Zeno couldn't even swallow his coffee: he settled for water. Rico, running elephant-like down the stairs, broke the heavy silence. He entered the room with a beaming smile and greeted us with a loud cheery hello. One look around the table killed his joyous mood and wiped the smile off his face. Another look at the TV screen made him frown. He sat down and asked: 'OK guys. What have I missed this time?'. We filled him in on the outbreak of the virus overnight, the known details of the disease and the unknown threats of its evolution.

'We have to do something!' Rico exclaimed, when we had finished updating him.

'I agree,' Harry said, Zeno and I acquiescing as well.

'This is what we have come to talk to you about,' Sam said. He was hesitant and unwilling to talk. McRae looked upset. They were bearers of bad news.

'The Government does not want you to do anything. At least for now,' Sam continued.

'What! This is obviously a virus. So we can help all of these people. You know it would take less than a minute to cure them!' Rico roared. 'How could you?! How?!'

'Hey mate! Don't shoot the messenger! We don't even agree with this!' McRae snapped back.

Rico grumbled a couple of Italian swearwords in reply.

'How many people are affected in the British Isles?' I enquired of Leila.

'They were 703 before I stepped into this house. The figure is probably higher now. It's the highest toll in one single country,' she replied after checking her notes. It was more than 10% of the total worldwide figure in one place.

'Are they all in London?' Harry questioned.

'Most of them. 521 were. The others had time to finish their journeys before the symptoms caught on. They have also passed it on to more people along the way,' Leila answered.

'The recommendations of the Government are that anyone at risk of being contaminated, either by being in the original locations where the virus spread or in contact with someone who might have been there, must stay at home until further notice to avoid a potential transmission of the virus. Anyone who presents the symptoms of the virus must remain at home and call an emergency number created for this purpose. So must anyone who lives with them. A trained, kitted and protected team will go to their home and bring them to a special unit in a London hospital,' Sam explained.

'And why not make those special teams drive their ambulances through the Fog?' I asked, repeating Rico's question in another format.

'Because the Government does not want to involve the Gatekeepers and the Gates at this point,' Sam repeated, also with another wording.

'But why?' I pushed for a proper answer.

'Because of the logistics involved, because of the risk of unprepared relocation. Because once we start with the process of people crossing, it could not be stopped. Everyone with any other virus will demand a right of crossing. They already do. Because the Government is still uncertain about the long-term consequences of crossing the Fog, health-wise or other. Because of the risk with the local communities on the other side. The Government wants to strengthen its relations with them, especially in trade and science.'

'In brief, the British Government thinks it is too early for the public to be involved with the Fog,' McRae cut in.

'I understand, and agree, that it's frustrating,' Sam continued.

'You bet it is! People are dying out there!' Rico barked.

'Crossing the Fog has serious consequences in the short and long-term and in both worlds. Little is known about its long-term effect. The Government position is that it cannot just let people through blind.'

'They don't have to cross blind: we can inform them! Then it's their choice. Moreover, what if we wish to let them go through? It is our choice,' Harry said. 'If both parties accept the consequences and unknowns, the Government should not intervene.'

*

Harry's sentence triggered a switch in my approach of the Fog. With it came the seed of an idea. Its outline was barely defined, yet I felt myself beginning to smile despite the circumstances. A glance from Leila made me erase it immediately. I didn't want to attract Sam and McRae's suspicions. Both of them had learnt to spot when I was up to something, even it was just the shadow of an idea. I made a mental note to check more details and feasibility with Leila later. For the time being, with Sam and McRae, I would keep silent. It proved difficult when Sam mentioned that a Member of Parliament was affected by the epidemic. Also holding a Government office, he was applying pressure for access to the Fog. The Prime Minister had granted him his request as long as it remained in secrecy. The reasoning was that he was one of the men running the country and certain privileges were necessary to ensure the stability and the smooth running of the institutions. His wife and 17-year-old daughter were to cross with him. The three knew the risk of relocation and accepted it. They wanted to live. Rico exploded that it was nepotism, favouritism, elitism, unfair and an outrage. We all agreed that it was, including Sam and McRae. Rico noted politicians should also be models for the nation and practice what they preach. He argued we should all refuse to let this politician and his family cross the Fog. Sam rattled his throat and spoke up. He was uncomfortable when he commented they were already on their way to the Essex house. They wore eye-masks and headphones with music blasting, so they could not identify the location of this second house. If none of them were relocated, they would be sent back home within minutes. The Foggies were in front of a *fait accompli*. I narrowed my eyes on the agents. This we would not forget and would remind them, if or when necessary.

*

Finally, the agents left. All of us around the table felt deflated. Rico, in his frustration and anger at the situation, had binge-eaten half of the pastries. He stood up, annoyed, announcing he would exorcise his stress on a canvas. I asked him to sit down and listen to me first. For the following two hours, we talked about the plans that had formed in my head. Everyone listened at first, Leila taking notes when I asked her to check this or that. Soon, everyone voiced his or her opinion and ideas. What had been a small idea earlier turned into quite an elaborate plan. We were ready for action and shared a complicit smile. The next step was to discuss with the rest of the Foggies if they agreed to put the plan in motion. As was our rule when something could affect Gatekeepers Associates, the support had to be unanimous. It took us another hour to put down a project layout in an email to all the Foggies. During this time, the news coming from the monitor indicated slowly rising numbers of people affected by the New

Warburg pandemic. It was a strong incentive for us to get the plan into action as soon as possible.

*

In the afternoon, the fast-spreading New Warburg virus was too much on my mind for me to focus on the other project I had at heart: education on the Fog and the history of each world, for both worlds. The epidemic angered me. We had to do something! The words of the teenager, from the restaurants, rung again in my ears. If indeed the Fog was a gift to humanity, there was no better time to unwrap it than now, when it was the most needed. In an attempt to be more productive, I sat with Zeno while he worked on his common project with Leo: an online trading platform between WI and WII. Leo would be back in the evening – the thought filled me with relief, joy, anticipation and anxiety – and Zeno hoped that he would put his web designer skills to launch the platform as soon as possible. It was now even more needed. The trade would focus first on what WII was asking for most: sugar, salt, spices, peppers, tobacco, coffee, chocolate, tea, medicine, wine and spirits. There would be technology and more luxury items like porcelain, musk, pearls and metal such as tin, copper, iron or even silver and gold. Coming from the Other World, Zeno thought a few basics to start with would be attractive, due to their origins; like garments and woven cloths, textiles, carpets, jewellery and tools. He was also studying the mineral potential in WII England.

*

Late afternoon, my parents came to visit. It was a very emotional reunion. I hardly ever see my mother lose countenance, but that day, instead of my falling into her arms, she fell into mine. The mother-daughter roles were reversed. She told me how proud she was of me, how much she loved me, how worried she had been. She cried over what was happening to the world, the chaos in Kenya and the epidemic outbreak. She asked me if we could help, and I hesitated to tell her what we had in mind. 'We are trying, Mum, we are. It's not simple. We have a plan though. Slowly we are getting there.' She smiled and so did my father.

Mum and Dad wanted to see Eudes for a family dinner. It took me some time to convince them that Eudes was not ready to part with Ushi Tsou. He had just returned and needed time! She was now the core element of his life. My parents relinquished in the end. When we arrived at *The Jazzin*, my friend had prepared a table for us in the private room upstairs so that the comings and goings in the lounge would not bother us. To my parents' delight, again, Eudes immediately ran to them when he arrived. Nonetheless he did not stay long in their arms, sliding down soon after to grab Ushi Tsou's hand. My mother, back to herself and in full possession of her poise, did not flinch. My father did a little. Ushi Tsou was on guard at first, aware that my parents did not approve of her as a choice of guardian; she was aware, too, that she was the pilot of the helicopter that killed their older daughter when crashing. During the meal, Dad requested if she would kindly give a detailed account of what had happened. For once, I was glad Ushi Tsou was the least loquacious person I had ever met!

*

By 10pm, I was in bed and ready to switch off the light. The day had been emotionally and mentally draining for everyone, the whole planet included. My mind was a whirlwind of information, ideas and emotions that kept me awake in the dark. Leo's brief message in the middle of the night did not help. Due to the increased control at the borders and the need of discretion around his return (following his discreet exit), the Society had decided to make him come back first to Ireland and Northern Ireland, and then use a fishing boat to get him back to England. He had written from the boat still anchored in Northern Ireland, waiting for his departure. He would be with us in the morning. For once, I did not feel like a pathetic commitment-phobic miserable singleton. A deep longing for him had kicked my brain into braving my fear to be emotionally vulnerable to love someone.

'Finally!' I whispered. Simba came to lick my face.

Day 4 (Wednesday)

I woke up with a start, already feeling exhausted. Simba was nudging me with her snout. She was humming low, which meant an urgent need to go out and relieve herself. That was unusual: she could hold until the morning by now. A glance at the bedside table clock explained why she was slowly pushing me out of the bed. It was 9.47am, much later than my average waking time and a consequence of my struggle to fall asleep the previous night. I rushed to let Simba out. Then I checked who was, if anyone, in the living area. Leila was here and alone. Like we often did, she had plugged her tablet to the screen monitor and the news was on: a low hum barely loud enough to be comprehensible. Leila was multitasking, speaking on the phone with a headset while typing, her back to me. She was focused on her tasks and jumped when I greeted her good morning. She indicated the headset with a smile meaning that she was on a call, so I nodded and retraced my steps to the kitchen. When I returned with Simba as well as coffee, tea and toast, she had finished her call. She informed me where my housemates were: Zeno had gone to the Fog house to deal with some trading issues; Rico was there, too, with my parents playing with Eudes. He had announced he wanted to keep an eye on Ushi Tsou, even though Nick and Big Tom were already on the job. Leila suspected Rico was enjoying the sight of Ushi Tsou as well, even if he was adamant that he loathed her. Harry had gone to do some research for the Open University project. My interest in it had been contagious; the professor in him was excited at the idea of heading an Inter-Worlds Studies Department, even if only a virtual one.

*

Leila, usually full of energy, looked pale. Her shoulders were slouched and her cheeks hollow. She had lost weight quickly – too quickly - since the existence of the Fog was revealed. The huge pressure was getting too heavy for her to carry. She might have the Society behind her but she was still handling too much.

'Leila, how much did you sleep last night?' I pushed a cup of coffee in front of her.

'Maybe four hours,' she replied, taking the cup and bringing it to her lips. I winced.

'And when did you have a full, proper night? Something like 7 hours in a row?' I persisted.

'So long ago, I don't remember,' she replied with a tired voice.

'You can't go on like this,' I told her, with a sigh.

'I know. Lochy tells me that too,' she said. 'And yes, I know what you are going to say, about Lochy and me. I am still on my guard, although I am discovering another side to him. He has a good heart behind his Casanova *façade*. When he stops being a seducer, the man is both a gentleman and a good laugh. He does care about others.'

Having grown to appreciate the Scotsman, I agreed silently and returned the conversation to the matter of her health.

'You can't handle all the work as a liaison between the Society and us, the British Intelligence and us, or the Public and us ON YOUR OWN,' I told her.

'I don't. Really! There are other liaison officers in the States. I spend much of my time delegating to other teams within the Society.'

'You are still supervising everything,'

'Someone has to do it.'

'Yes but this someone still has to eat and sleep. Do you even take the time to go to the toilet?'

'The less I eat, the less I need to,' Leila replied with a smug smile.

'Very funny. Please, do me a favour: get a full time assistant or someone to help you. You look sick!' I was almost angry saying this to her. I valued her work with and for us, but I valued the person more. 'Promise you will try, otherwise our only resort to make you look after yourself will be to refuse to work with you.'

'Fine,' she said, annoyed. 'I will try to let go a bit more. I will. Happy now?'

'Thank you,' I smiled at her, and she saw that I only asked because I care. She stood up and took me in her arms in a big warm hug. We hold each other for some time, then we both sat back down without a word.

'Have you eaten this morning?' I had a suspicion she had not.

'No, I haven't,' she confirmed my doubts.

I pushed the plate of buttered toast covered with honey towards her and stood up, heading to the kitchen to prepare some more. When I returned, the plate was almost empty and she was licking her fingers. She already looked better.

I was engrossed in watching the news, cursing at the rising number of infected people, when Leila said to me that maybe I should have a shower and get ready.

'You're right. It's already mid-morning.'

'It's not that. Mitch and Jack have each taken a different route and will arrive later today, but Leo has travelled all night to be here as soon as possible. He will be here in less than an hour,' Leila grinned.

I stood up immediately. I expected Leo to arrive in the afternoon. He was supposed to sleep somewhere on the road. By the sound of it, he had skipped sleeping. I waved at Leila and went straight to my bathroom, Simba behind me.

*

An hour later, after five changes of clothes, my hair styled, light and discreet make-up applied to my tired eyes and a little gloss on my lips, I was ready. Pacing my room and wringing my hands, I wondered if he would call first or just ring the bell, if he would kiss me or not, if he would take me to my room, or ask that we 'sit and talk'. The doorbell rang and I ran to the door. There was no point in locking doors any more, but visitors still pressed the bell button to announce their visit. I steeled myself as I checked the peephole out of habit. My parents. I wrinkled my nose. Of course, I was happy to see them, just not at that exact time. I opened the door. They walked in, looking worn out. My mother suggested to me that water would be nice and headed for the living room. My father came with me to the kitchen and we prepared a jug of sparkling water with lemon and ice. Once seated, my mother asked me if I was expecting a special visitor. I batted my eyes in surprise, and she subtly raised her eyebrows. My father laughed. They both knew me too well not to have noted my make-up, however discreet it was. I attempted to dismiss their remarks, but it proved difficult when blushing and stuttering. The bell rang again and I stiffened. Muttering something unintelligible, even to myself, I went to the door and checked in the peephole. Leo. My heart started to beat faster and my mind went blank. I took a deep breath and opened the door. Leo looked at me and smiled. I looked at him and smiled. Simba looked at him and jumped. He could barely keep his balance as she continued to greet and jump on him with enthusiasm, yelping and even howling. It attracted attention.

Soon my father came to check on me and Phil, my assigned bodyguard from the Society, appeared by the front door. What I wanted to do was to take Leo's hand and go for a chat in a nearby coffee place. Such simple things were now a luxury for the Foggies and impossible for now. Therefore, I turned to my father and introduced Leo instead, then to my mother in the living room. They had heard of Leo only as a fellow Foggy. If they were suspicious of more, they did not show it. As Leo told them a little about himself, I observed him. The sun of Africa had tanned his already olive skin into a rich brown colour and his casual stubble had grown into a small beard. His eyes, which had turned a light version of hazelnut because of the Fog, were more striking than before. He was attractive, sensual and confident, as well as naturally charming to my parents. He was irresistible.

*

When Zeno and Rico returned, I gave up any chance of having any time alone with Leo. However, my parents took the cue from the glances Zeno shot them, along with the veiled questions on Leo's trip, that we could not talk freely in their presence. They announced they could not stay for lunch because they had made shopping plans in London. They had left all their belongings behind in France.

Harry joined us for lunch and it was 'friends reunited', like in the good old times. Leila did not join us. She had relented and went for a necessary rest. Leo entertained us with details of WII Kenya, the hard stories of harsh countryside and struggles of the Relocated mixing with tales of natural beauty, the fascinating nomad tribes and the Foggies' adventures. Afterwards, we updated him on what he had missed during the week, with the move of the other Foggies into old or new homes and the reappearance of Ushi Tsou and my nephew. He already knew about the highly contagious virus and its alarmingly fast spreading across the planet. Leo had had plenty of time to read and watch the news during his long journey back.

Soon, Leo's exhaustion started to show. Despite his best efforts, he could not keep his eyes open. He asked Rico if he could have a nap in his guestroom, which surprised and concerned me. What about my guest room? Or bedroom even? He noticed and said to me, with a tired smile as he left to go upstairs, that he would see me later, recharged in energy. He had no doubt he would need to be on top form to face me. I blushed at the innuendo and one of the boys giggled, probably Rico.

*

Leo did not wake up that day, and I did not see him until the following morning. The whole afternoon and evening, I was on edge, always keeping part of my attention on the sounds of the house not to miss him coming down the stairs. It was nerve-wracking. Sam and McRae came to question him, their security system having informed them of his return. Unofficially, they both knew Jack and he had gone to Kenya. They wanted to know more and had many questions. Officially, they knew nothing and had to find out details on their disappearance as well. They were disappointed to hear he was sleeping and we refused to disturb him. As Leo slept, their questions remained unanswered. So did mine.

Day 5 (Thursday)

Simba nudged me awake by softly patting my back. The light in the room indicated early morning and a sleepy glance at the alarm clock confirmed it. It was 6.45am. Slowly I realised there was a light knock at the door. It was more a scratching really. My head still asleep, I answered yes and the door cracked open to reveal Leo's cheeky face. He walked in, carrying two mugs with a plate full of croissants on top of one.

'I took the initiative to take out some pastries from the freezer for your breakfast. I know how dangerous you are in the morning and how carefully one must approach you until you have eaten. You are like a wild animal that needs to be tamed,' he said in a low voice, as he closed the door.

'And I presume you have gained experience with wild animals when in the jungle?' I replied, sitting in bed. My hair was a mess, my voice was croaky from sleep and, with my luck, there were probably pillow marks on my face. I was happy, despite the early hour of the day. Leo's presence in my room felt natural and a good sign. He was in boxer shorts and t-shirt, with strong tan marks mid-thigh and on his upper arm, making me want to laugh. He put the mugs and plate on the side table, gave me a kiss on the forehead, and sat on the bed at the level of my knee in a relaxed posture.

'I read your letter several times in the past two days. It moved me. Thank you. I couldn't have dreamt of a better welcome coming back to this world,' he said.

'I worried so much,' I told him. 'And I missed you so much.'

'I was always going to come back. I would not leave you, whether or not we were together. I will always protect you.'

I shook my head: 'It was not in your control if a lion attacked you or not, or if a bullet hit you.'

'Stop being a smart ass,' he retorted with a laugh.

'I am sorry,' I replied with a laugh as well, and then more seriously I repeated, 'I am sorry.'

'Don't,' he stroked my cheek. 'I understand you better than you think. Your decision did hurt. I disagreed, but I couldn't blame you. There is a logic in your wish to avoid a relationship in the current foggy circumstances… Pun intended.'

'Maybe. But maybe, or mostly, I am scared. I am protecting myself.'

'Yes, you are. I know that as well, and this is understandable, too. You have been hurt before.' He leaned and kissed me on the lips, a gentle, soft, tender kiss, before pulling back a little, his face still close to mine. A warm wave went through me and I felt heat rushing from my feet to my head. My core had reacted immediately to his touch and I wanted more. His stare turned to longing and slowly he cupped my face in his hands. He kissed me, this time with more intensity. The passion grew increasingly intense until Simba began to yelp and attempted to come between us. I broke the kiss.

'Maybe we should put her in the room next door?' I suggested in a husky voice. Leo grunted yes and stood up. Simba then went to the door and scratched it. I swore inwardly.

'She needs to go out,' I said, leaving the bed and heading out.

'Now?' Leo said with a hungry look at my legs. I was wearing an oversized T-shirt and a pair of shorts, and my bare legs were the only part of me he could see. There again, he had always liked my legs, especially caressing them.

'I'm afraid so,' I replied.

As I passed in front of him to leave the bed, he put a hand at the nape of my neck and squeezed lightly, then let his hand slide down my back, over my bottom and finishing on my thigh. It was so smooth and soft it made me shiver and long for him even more. It didn't take long when we reached the garden door and Simba had gone out, for him to take me in his arms and take the kiss back to where we had left it. His hands already under my t-shirt and mine about to lift off his top, we heard heavy footsteps coming down the stairs. I separated from Leo with reluctance and difficulty, as he would not let go that easily, then hastily readjusted my top and hair, just in time for Rico's entrance. I had never seen him up so early, and it didn't suit him. He looked the worse for wear.

'Rico? Are you ok?' I asked with concern.

'No. I have indigestion. Eudes and I finished a chocolate cake yesterday evening. I was sick all night. I haven't slept a wink.' His head turned from Leo to me. 'I heard Simba running down the stairs and thought you were alone, Yoko. Sorry guys.'

'What for?' I said, demure. Rico lifted an eyebrow to indicate he was not fooled. He picked up a glass and filled it with water.

'I don't even fancy coffee. Imagine. A morning without coffee... Tsss,' he commented on his own thoughts as he filled his glass.

'I will leave you to it, guys,' he was already moving to the door when he added as an after-thought. 'Yoko, have you mentioned the plan to Leo yet?' I had not. The previous day we had focused on sharing the updates from the past week first and had aimed to address this important project afterwards. However, as Leo's tiredness was slowly getting the better of him, we had postponed it to today. Now was not the time, either. Not only was it too early in the morning and the others were not here, I really had something else in mind. However, Leo's ears had pricked up.

'What project?' he asked with interest.

'It is best to tell you with the rest of the crew, if you don't mind. It's a bit complex,' I replied, avoiding his eyes. From experience of his protectiveness over me, he would not approve of the idea, let alone my role in it. My unease must have showed, because he narrowed his eyes and asked:

'What are you up to, Yoko?'

'It's not just me! And it's for a good cause!' I was on the defensive. I had no real reason to be,: the plan had been approved by all but the Foggies in Kenya who were not available then. Again, Leo picked up on my tone.

'Right, tell me.' He picked me up and sat me on the kitchen counter. 'I am listening.'

'Time for me to go,' Rico said, in an attempt to escape. Now I was not going to let him get away with it and I extended my leg to block his way out.

'Not so fast, you! You're the one who brought it up, you …' I begun.

'It's your idea,' Rico said.

'We all agreed on it,' I countered.

'Yes, but he is your boyfriend,' Rico replied.

'He isn't my …,' I stopped and shot a glance at Leo. His face was set in a serious and unhappy mood. 'Well, I don't know what we are but… That's not the point, anyway. I think we should wait until everyone is up. Mitch and Jack should arrive today as well, and they need to be informed, too.'

'I am sure you can tell me before. I promise not to ruin the surprise for them,' Leo said gravely.

'It's just… OK, if you want to know, I think you will like the concept and the cause. You might not like that I will expose myself to some very small risk. Really minor risk. Really. You might get a little protective, that's why I ….'

'That's because you don't know how to look after yourself. You are over-protective of your emotions, under-protective of your life.'

This made me flinch.

'Oopsy-daisy…' Rico whispered and tried to make himself very small. He asked me in a small voice: 'Have you had breakfast yet?'

'No' I replied, with contained anger. How could Leo say such a thing to me? Yes, there was some truth, but he was going too far. It was so patronising. Rico again tried to subtly leave the room.

'You stay right here,' I told my Italian housemate in such tone that he immediately froze on site. I got off from the kitchen counter.

'How dare you talk to me like that?' I turned to Leo, my voice low in anger. 'Granted, I bottle up my emotions. As you said yourself, I have my reasons for that. As to not being able to look after myself, you are being a macho ass! I am very capable of taking my life into my own hands, thank you very much. I can make my own decisions, take my own risks, and guess what - what is most important - I do take responsibility for the consequences of my actions! If I want to take risks because I believe in what I am trying to do, it's my choice and I can do what I want. I don't need either your approval or your protection. If I want some, I have Nick, I have Phil, I have Leila and the Society. I even have Sam and McRae.'

Leo was about to speak, but I was on a roll.

'One more thing: you don't even know what the plan is about. How can you be suspicious of me without having even heard what I want to do? Where is the trust, Leo?'

I went to the garden door. Simba was already behind it, no doubt alerted by my angry voice. She locked herself in my step as I walked out of the kitchen. Before leaving, I turned and said to Leo, in a business-like tone.

'I will see you both mid-morning for the Foggies' meeting. I am going back to bed.'

Walking off, I heard Rico say:

'She didn't have breakfast.'

'No. And – what a fool! - I woke her up, too.'

'Dude...'

*

I didn't come out of my room before 10am. I had not managed to get any more sleep but instead, ranted on my own on the machismo of men. Once the then-cold coffee was drunk and the croissants eaten, I felt a little better and admitted to myself that I might have overreacted - slightly - in response to a simple sentence. Just maybe. This was not the reunion with Leo I had dreamt of. I wondered if I had ruined everything, again. Was it always going to be a cause of disagreement, his determination to protect me with a hint of control when I was so fiercely independent? When the ringing of the doorbell informed me it was time for the Foggies' meeting, I made my way downstairs. We had already informed my parents, Sam and McRae that we needed to spend the morning dealing with business matters for Gatekeepers' Associates.

Leila, Mitch and Jack were here, and Leo had not left. I greeted Leila and hugged Mitch and Jack, delighted to see them. Both looked tanned and healthy. I wasn't sure how to act with Leo, so I just nodded at him with a small shy smile. He nodded back but there was no smile there. I felt a pinch of the heart. Mitch and Jack entertained us for a while with the tale of their return trip, the first one casually taking a flight to Aberdeen in Scotland and then an overnight train to London. As he was not a known Foggy, it was not necessary to hide his arrival and the Society had helped him go through the reinforced border controls. Jack had travelled by boat, like Leo, although separately, and had stayed overnight in Cornwall. He had caught an early train to London in the morning. Sam and McRae were certainly going to ask Leo and him many questions in the afternoon.

Leo, Mitch and Jack remained silent for some time after we exposed our new grand plan in response to the British Government's refusal to let the sick from the epidemic cross the Fog. Jack was the first to speak, and with an unusual confidence. He approved it by saying it was our duty to do something to help cope with the epidemic. Mitch agreed next. He noted that we were creating a Pandora's box, but the purpose and benefits of the project outweighed the problems in his opinion. Next, we waited for Leo to express his position. It was important that we all agreed among ourselves on this enterprise. Leo hesitated then, addressing everyone, he indicated he could not think of a better solution to send a clear message to the world that we wanted to help, even if we had to dismiss the authorities current positions on the Fog for it. Like Mitch, he feared there would be complicated consequences. He turned to me and added that many would not like it. As the Gatekeepers' representative and having a key role in the plan, fingers would point at me as mainly responsible. Leo didn't have to specify that this worried him. I knew he wished someone else would do the deed and take the blame. I could not let that happen. Everyone was doing their bit among us. Mitch, Jack and he had just been to Kenya and risked their lives to help Mary. Now it was my turn to act, and not just as an ambassador. No. I wanted to be a fighter. I was a woman of action AND words, not just the latter. As these thoughts crossed my mind, I also wished they would give me some courage as, of course, I was also scared of what might lie ahead. This would not be easy.

*

My parents were at *The Jazzin*, spending time with Eudes. Jazz enjoyed having them around. They were like family to her and she missed hers. Jazz had informed her relatives that she was a Relocated. Although they had not crossed the Fog, they had come to visit me to see it from afar. Jazz did not want them to take the risk of relocation, and neither did they. Coming to see me was a way to get closer to Jazz and get some personal news. They were not comfortable when they did. First, the security and control were making them feel they were going to see a prisoner. In a way, they were right. Second, their daughter had changed more than she had realised in the space of a few months. They were open minded, but her new political fight for Women Rights in the Other World, her romantic bond with a man who looked and spoke like an East End gangster, with a shaven head marked with tattoos and piercings: all of that was a lot to digest. Her stories of civil war and her learning to shoot did not help, either. From then on, they preferred to keep in touch via online video calls from their home. They had promised not to reveal she was Relocated or anything that she would tell them. So having my parents and Eudes visiting gave her both warm and longing feelings. When she messaged me around lunchtime, I was expecting to read stories about Eudes. Instead, she informed me the situation had become worse between Clémence and the locals.

*

The past few days had seen an aggravation of the conflict between the Revolutionary Women and the inhabitants of WII. Clémence had launched a series of attacks on the remote farms and small hamlets thanks to her stolen weapons, claiming these were necessary in times of war to feed and clothe the troops. She had taken to using the 2-way radio as well as proclamations placed on doors and houses to communicate her messages. For each house they stopped in, they approached the women with respect and asked them how their husbands had treated them. Depending on the reply, they would punish, or not, the husband by flagellation, before attempting to recruit the women. The homes in which the women protested and opposed the principles of the Women's Revolution saw 75% of their reserves emptied. In the others, only 25% was taken as a supporting tax for the Revolution. Clémence was proving well organised in her rebellion against the current social system in place. Nonetheless, two of the recent attacks had turned bad. The previous night, a man whose farm was under siege had shot one of the female aggressors and killed her. As a reaction, the other women had pillaged his home and set fire to the building. They had also taken the children of the household with them. Some of the women protested and were stripped naked and shaved bald. Others applauded and joined the rank of the revolutionaries. Clémence's group was getting more violent, as we had all feared. Consequently, an emergency meeting was planned that day between the members of the Lil'London and Newtonsee councils, along with the representatives of Yerushaleim and the other hamlets. The situation was so serious that they had also officially requested the presence of Maud, Jazz and Molly as a recognised political movement. It was the only silver lining: the councils had understood that, in time of war, they needed to put water into their wine and be open to cooperation! We could only hope compromises would emerge, and some of the women following Clémence would realise the violence she exhorted was extreme. Hopefully, they would choose the less belligerent option of Maud's and Jazz's party.

Jazz informed me she was leaving shortly for Lil'London to attend the meeting, accompanied by Big Tom and Nick. The two men insisted that, with the dangers of being on the road in WII, Maud, Molly and she needed as much security as possible. Ushi Tsou would remain in the house with Eudes and so would the Fishers. However, they asked if Zeno and Leo - and maybe also Rico and Harry - would go to Woodfellas and *The Jazzin* to keep an eye on things. The trust in Ushi Tsou was not yet deep-rooted. The boys immediately replied 'Present', Rico jumping on the opportunity to be in charge of the surveillance drone. He had been eager to 'play' with the drone for some time and Nick never let him, arguing it was not a toy. This time, he was granted his wish.

*

When Sam and McRae arrived later, Jack and I were discussing the Inter-Worlds Online University project. Trying to give him a new centre of interest to keep his spirits high, I suggested he could link his own studies and passion to the project: he could lead the Fashion and Fabrics department. He loved the idea so much he wanted to start working on it straight away! Jack also suggested that, with a large booster, the Internet signal would have a wider range in WII. We should check how far it could go and how many computers could connect to it. His trip to Kenya had done him good: he had gained confidence and inner-belief. It was a good thing that his morale was high: Sam and McRae wanted to speak to him alone, thinking, not without reason, that he was the weakest link of the lot. If they could get any information from any Foggy, they expected it would be from him. Jack's current frame of mind was strong and they did not get the answers they were seeking about his disappearance. He told them only that he had wanted a break and to get away for some time. Sam commented he was very tanned and Jack noted that it usually happened when you spend time in the sun. To McRae's direct question, had he gone to Kenya, Jack replied that it would not be his first choice for a break, considering the situation there. Mastering sarcasm: well done, Jack!

'Have you watched the news today?' Sam enquired. It surprised me to realise that I hadn't, despite all that was going on in the world. Nor had Jack.

'Well, maybe you shouldn't,' McRae suggested. 'You would not like what you hear.'

'Now we need to know! So either you tell us or I will just ignore your presence and switch on the news immediately,' I told them.

'For one, the Foggies are the subject of a heated dispute between Ingis Chen and Lally O'Maleigh,' Sam went on. 'Lally O'Maleigh is accusing you of being a fraud in claiming the Fog has a healing quality and is a door to another world. She adds that even if your outrageous assertions were founded, you would be guilty of using it as a means to gain power and control over the governments, states and people. Why else would you not speak up in these days of turmoil and crisis for the whole planet? Why else would you not offer your help and open the gate to save people? Not only this, she also maintains that even if, and she says it is a big 'if', the Fog were true and you were just overwhelmed by the current events, its existence goes against nature and God. She manages to make the Fog appear as the work of the devil to lead humanity into false salvation. She presents the Other World not like a chance of a new beginning, but a modern version of Hell. Listening to her, I was impressed that she manages to both question the existence of the Fog, and at the same time accept that if it does exist, it is evil.'

'Charming. I am feeling the love here,' I remarked. 'And what is Chen saying?'

'He is your strongest defender. He repeats that you and the other Foggies have great hearts and are dedicated to others. The only hindrance on your path to help save those suffering from the pandemic, or even everyone on earth, is the British authorities in collusion with most governments around the world. He reminds everyone that the Fog also exists in Kenya and the US, and that in these countries too, the men in power have blocked the access. You are but bound by the system in place that wants domination over both worlds. He claims you have been forced into silence by us.'

'Which is not true,' Sam interjected. 'You are free in movement and speech.'

'You are not stopping us from coming and going, this is true, but I wouldn't say I am feeling *free*. There again, it is also because I have to hide from the people in general,' I looked at McRae. The episode in the restaurant was still very fresh in my mind.

'How about you say a few words to stop this nonsense, and mention we are not holding you against your will?' Sam suggested.

'Is it your idea or a request from your boss?' I enquired.

'It comes directly from the Prime Minister,' McRae replied. 'In fact, he would love to have a chat with you. Off the record. The Prime Minister would like to take this opportunity to congratulate you on your newly acquired British Citizenship.'

I pulled a face. A few months ago, I would have struggled to contain my excitement at the prospect of a private conversation with the British Prime Minister. Today, it felt like a waste of time. He was either going to try and ingratiate himself with me, make some annoying requests, or demand my full cooperation as a citizen or mere human being. Still, it was an opportunity to make him understand we ought to help people in the current crisis. It was ridiculous to let people die in hospital when letting them cross the Fog could simply stop that. So I accepted the offer to talk to him. Sam pulled out his mobile and speed-dialled his team. He said a few words, waited a little, and then spoke in a more formal and tense tone.

'Good afternoon, Prime Minister. Agent Sam Riverson on the phone. I will pass you to Yoko Salelles now.' Sam handed me the mobile phone. I took it and stood up. I read somewhere that being up when talking on the phone makes you feel more in control and energetic, and that it transmits to your interlocutor.

'Good afternoon, Prime Minister. Yoko Salelles speaking.'

'Miss Salelles, it is a pleasure to speak with you,' the Prime Minister started. It was strange to hear his voice addressing me from the device, and not on the news. 'I have read the many reports about the Fog and about you, written by Intelligence. The most interesting was by Mr Riverson, whom I believe I just spoke to.'

'Indeed. Agent Riverson is the agent supervising the relations between the Fogg- the Gatekeepers and the British government. I expect his report is an excellent insight on the situation and us.'

'This is exactly what I thought. It is with regret I cannot experience the crossing of the Fog, for myself. In my position, the risk of relocation is unacceptable.'

'The United Kingdom would miss your leading of the country.' I was being politically correct. Someone else would replace him in no time. He was not that bad, but he was not an unforgettable Statesman.

'Thank you. I will not take too much of your time. You must be very busy.' Was the Prime minister telling *me* I was very busy?

'Please, take all the time you need. How can I be of help?'

'Ah! I appreciate you being direct. I trust you are aware of the current health threats caused by the emergence and escalating advance of the Modern Marburg virus?'

'Yes, I am.'

'I presume you are also aware that some of our British Citizens suggest a systematic crossing of the Fog as a medical solution to the problem?'

'Yes, I am. We Gatekeepers believe it could be a solution, as well.'

'You are? This is very generous of you. Impractical and unmanageable at present, but generous.'

'May I ask, why is that so impractical and unmanageable?'

'The structure is not in place – medical support, administrative support, control of symptoms and identity, security, to name a few. Some of the claimants could have an agenda to harm you or destroy the Fog. Also the long-term consequences of the Fog are not known, including concerning this virus. We need to do some tests on a limited number of people first with follow-ups over an extensive period of time. You might benefit from reading a couple of analyses I have received. I will have them sent to you. If you might treat them as highly confidential, I would appreciate it.'

During his talk, I bit my tongue several times to refrain from commenting. Yes, there was some truth in his words. No, he did not convince me. Structure, administration, blah-blah-blah! In an emergency situation, anything and anyone had a surprisingly fast capacity for reaction and adaptation. That included governments.

'Thank you. I will read them with interest,' I replied, keeping my thoughts to myself. The Foggies had enough enemies: I didn't need to antagonise the British Prime Minister, as well. He would be upset soon enough.

'Miss Salelles, some people claim that you are a prisoner in your own home and that it is our doing. Do you feel so? My understanding is that you are free to do whatever you wish and that you work with the Government on a partnership basis, am I correct?'

'Absolutely,' I replied, although this was not as smooth as he implied.

'I believe we would all benefit from your expressing this publicly in order to put an end to the nonsense and the growing wave of anger towards the government.'

'I see. However, I am afraid I have to decline.'

'May I ask why?'

'Certainly. Despite understanding your reasoning for not using the Fog - yet - to help those currently affected by the epidemic, I disapprove of this decision. If I were to speak in public in your support, I would have to mention you are the ones who block the access to the Gate, not us. I trust this is not what you want.'

'No, it is not. Wouldn't you be able to deny their claim without mentioning our divergence of views on the Fog crossing?'

'Prime Minister, considering the current affairs, Fog crossing can only be a key point of my speech. So no, I could not. Additionally, even if I were to make a statement to your credit, the sceptics would say you coerced me into it.'

'I appreciate your honesty. This said, in case you change your mind, I will have a speech prepared that would remain neutral and could be satisfactory for you, and have it sent along with the reports. They will be with you later today. I hope they might make you reconsider your position.'

'This is so thoughtful of you. Thank you.' This political correctness was exhausting. Nonetheless, it was so blatantly sarcastic on both sides, I almost enjoyed it.

I gave his mobile back to Sam. He let out a deep sigh and put the phone to his ear, then back in his pocket as no-one was on the line. He complained our stubborn lot would cost him his job one day. I put a hand on his shoulder and told him not to fear; we would hire him immediately to work for Gatekeepers Associates. Both McRae and he laughed. McRae discreetly peeked at Leila. I wasn't sure if it was a complicit look in reference to their bonding, or to his special links with Gatekeepers Associates and the Society. Sam begged us to at least read the speech: there could be something in it that would satisfy everyone and alleviate the tension. I promised him we were taking the situation seriously and would not dismiss any new information. By Sunday, our plans would have been launched and the speech would be obsolete, but I didn't tell him that. Better not.

*

Aside from my ambassador duties in the Other World and the online Inter-Worlds University, the integration of the relocated people – current and future - was always on my mind. Zeno was at the core of helping the residents of Woodfellas to relaunch their lives. By building a trading network between both worlds, he aimed to create new jobs and areas of expertise, and this was only the beginning. Lately, he thought that Ed Epcott, who loved hunting, could set up a venison supply business. Jazz and Molly had had serious conversations with him to discuss what roles could be offered to women, including the local inhabitants, in order to raise their profile as capable individuals. Jazz had modified her tone and was now more diplomatic in her approach to the Council. Molly was very excitable and direct by nature. She had to be silenced by her friends a few times, as she was antagonising even the men who supported her with her bluntness. Consequently, Maud and Jazz had to ask Molly to take care of the practical side of the fight for the women instead of the negotiations with the men. Molly was rather hurt at first, but thankfully, she had a good nature and followed their advice. She now worked with Zeno on creating opportunities for the women to prove their worth.

The presence of the Women's Party leaders at the emergency meeting between every town, village and hamlet was a crucial moment for our friends. They had won some credit before, even some cooperation, but this time they were officially recognised as key interlocutors in the affairs of WII. No Foggies had been invited to join. After our refusal to take sides and get involved (at least directly) in their affairs, they would not let us in now. Jazz was also acting as the representative of Woodfellas in the crisis meeting.

It was a dangerous time to be travelling in WII for someone holding such an important position as Jazz's. Clémence's revolution was getting violent and at any time she could cross the bridge towards a full blown and bloody war. She was unpredictable. When Jazz returned in the early hours of the evening, Rico immediately texted me and I made my way to *The Jazzin*. Leo was already there, monitoring the ground via Nick's surveillance system, and it was my cowardice towards him that stopped me waiting for her at her place. I was still building up the courage to talk to him after my outburst in the morning. I had tried to convince myself, for many reasons, that it was not a good time to talk; he needed to concentrate; he might not be alone. These were just excuses to delay the inevitable. When I arrived, Jazz's face was stern. She recounted the afternoon's events and emphasised the omnipresence of fear. Fear in the eyes of the people they passed in the countryside or in town; fear underlying the tension in the meeting room; fear in the said and unsaid words of the speakers. Never had the people of this part of WII lived in such dangerous times. They had had feuds, even bloody ones, murders and rivalries, but they had never known such a large group seceding from the system in place. Worse, this group were the women; those who carried in them the future generations of WII, the children who would ensure the survival of the human race there. At last, this afternoon, some of the council members had conceded that in addition to building up an army of men to defend themselves against the threats of Clémence's unruly rebels, they must work with Maud and Jazz to improve the position of women in their society. She pointed out that changes were now inevitable. With the men leaving to defend their families, their houses, their stocks and the towns, the women left behind would take over most of the tasks. They would prove their worth to men and to themselves, if any had doubts beforehand, and there was no going back after that. Jazz had done her research. This had happened for us after the First World War. It had been impossible afterwards to deny women the right to vote in England, for example. The suffragettes had not achieved this by their increasingly violent actions: the war did it. Also, by giving in and showing some understanding, the councils could prevent more women leaving to join Clémence's ranks. Jazz and Maud insisted that it was important that the concessions made in times of crisis did not appear temporary, and indeed were not, either. It was key that the Councils acted because they had heard, understood and agreed to the women's plea. Of course, the mentalities would not suddenly change, but giving women more respect and powers was the first step. Jazz suggested that each town, village and hamlet should add a woman as representative of half its population. Next, Jazz and Maud suggested that education should be accessible to boys and girls alike, under the same regime. This applied to adult education, as well. The members of the councils listened with their jaws set, except those from Chester who seemed to laugh inwardly, and Edmund who looked at his wife with pride. For all that, Jazz insisted that if the women wanted equal rights in education, work, representation and imprisonment, they should also give up specific women privileges. That had been a difficult point for Maud to accept at first. For example, men would soon be able to say to their wives that they might have to earn some money and work to contribute to family life. This was not particularly going to affect families living on farms where both genders were more often than not hard at work, but it might in town. In addition, with women claiming the right not to have to share their husbands or to be forced into marriage, some might end up single for life.

*

From that day on, Maud was a member of Lil'London Council, representing the women. Afterwards, Maud returned to her place with Edmund. This was a household Clémence was bound to hate, so they had men and dogs protecting their home now. Jazz had given Maud a shotgun and insisted she should begin daily practice from tomorrow.

*

Leo was giving me the cold shoulder. I had tried various strategies: the smile, the puppy eyes, the innocent questions about his day. His answers were laconic at best, monosyllabic at worst. He barely acknowledged my presence. My feeling of guilt was slowly giving place to annoyance. Yes, I might have overreacted (a little) in the morning, yet there were personal reasons behind it. He complained that I was over-protective of myself, yet so was he towards me! It would never work if he was going to stop me acting according to my beliefs and try to keep me in a soft secure cocoon. I was who I was, with my qualities, flaws, temper and all, and he was not going to change that. If he did not like my being an independent women or try to control me, it would never work! I was mulling those thoughts over as we all grabbed sandwiches for dinner. Any frustration vanished when Leo said he would go back to the Essex house that night and stay with Jack and Dante. He had already organised to meet Sam there, as the agent was still insisting on the need to discuss his sudden absence. It was time to cast aside my pride, the one of the seven deadly sins of which I was most guilty. So I asked if I could talk to him, in private, in my office upstairs.

'Leo, I overreacted this morning. Please accept my apologies,' I told him.

328

'Yes, you did,' he replied, his lips pressed thin together. I clenched my jaw tight to stop a defensive retort. Instead, I opted for silence. I had offered my apologies and he had not yet accepted them. The next move was still his. He took his time.

'Why do you do this, Yoko? It is almost as if you are self-sabotaging us.' His tone had mellowed.

'I don't...' I began.

'Look,' he interrupted me, 'I know the situation is not simple. I know you are a strong woman and you don't need to be looked after. I know you are scared to let somebody into your heart, scared of being hurt again. I know all of this. The way you face our situation, head held high - I admire that. Nonetheless, I WILL always want to look after you, because I love you and I care about your safety. I can't change you, but you can't change me.'

'Great. That's promising. We will get along just fine then, will we?'

'We could. I will try not to get upset when you bruise my manly pride and make me feel completely unnecessary. On your side, you can try not to blow a fuse when I attempt to be your dedicated super-hero.'

'When you put it like that...' I smiled. He had come closer. His hands were now on my waist, pulling me towards him.

'That said, you need to learn to ask for help, along with accepting offered help, and not just from me,' I pulled a face at his last words. This was something I had always struggled with.

'Yoko, sometimes when I am protective, it is only a wish to help. You are always keen to help without hesitation. Don't you understand others might wish to help, as well?'

He had a point, I knew he had a point. I had to work on this. I was even more convinced with Leo's lips on mine. Slowly, I felt myself melting into his arms. His lips parted and the kiss grew more intense and passionate. His hands slid under my top. Mine grabbed his trousers and I pulled him closer towards me. Simba, who always managed to open doors, sneaked between us making low throat noises, as if she wanted some attention too. Leo broke the kiss and whispered in my ear.

'Now that she is in this room, let's sprint from here to yours, block the door with a chair, and …?'

We made a run for it immediately.

Day 6 (Friday)

This was one of my least productive days in a long time. It started from the moment I woke up. I thought I would have to extract myself from Leo's arms to take Simba out for her morning routine. This was without counting on my housemates. I heard Zeno's steps walking towards the room next door, freeing Simba and going downstairs with her. I gratefully went back to sleep. I needed it after a night of hot passionate sex and tender cuddles, and only short moments of dozing in between. Knowing Simba was being looked after, I drifted back into dreamland, taking Leo with me. When we both woke up, and after some more playing with each other, I was horrified to note it was already past 1pm. I jumped out of bed and picked up my Ftab. Several messages, mainly from Sam, McRae, Leila and Jazz, were waiting for me. The four of them had stopped trying to contact me around 11am, after Rico informed them in a group email that neither Leo nor I 'were available at present, and until further notice', as we were 'busy catching up'. I cringed. It really wasn't necessary that Rico informed everyone of my intimate life. It was embarrassing enough that my housemates were privy to those details, but the British Intelligence? Leo pouted his disappointment as I wrapped myself into my dressing gown and headed for the bathroom to shower and dress. When I returned, he was reading the news on his Ftab with a frown. He left the bed and gave me a quick kiss on the lips, peeled the dressing gown off me to put it on, and left to have a shower. One hour later, we were having lunch with the others at the dining table.

*

My head was in the clouds. I could tell my face was glowing, beaming and blushing at the memories of the previous night. I chuckled at my naughty thoughts and did not dare look at Leo in case it would betray them. That day, I read the reports and speech proposal about the Fog sent by the Prime Minister's cabinet, with a constant smile. Even the scientific results (or lack of) and their assumptions felt light.

My spirits came crashing down when Leila came to visit early evening with the latest bad news: the United Kingdom had decided to close its borders. Trading flights, ships and trains would be limited to the strict minimum and handled with care by people wearing adequately protective outfits. The UK was determined to stop further contamination of the island. If isolating the country would not help those already sick, it should enable the spreading to be contained and that was good. On the other end, it could prove a problem with what we were about to do and, on a personal level, it put me in a difficult situation with my ex brother- in-law, due to visit this weekend. I raised the case with Sam.

'So how are you related, exactly?' he asked.

'He is my sister's ex-husband and father of Eudes, my nephew,' I answered.

'Is he a friend of yours?' Sam was taking notes, I presumed to complete the forms.

'Not really,' I then realised he did not know about Eudes and Ushi Tsou, their disappearance, their return and my sister's death.

'So why do you want him to come?' Sam asked. His eyes told me he had already understood there was more to it. He knew me well.

'It's a bit complicated. Do I really have to go into details?'

'You do. You are asking us to make an exception and reopen the borders for one single individual. That gives us the right to ask a few questions.'

'Two individuals,' I corrected.

'So father and son? That should make it easier: you want to see your nephew. This is a family reunion,' he jotted down with confidence.

'Well, no. Charles-Antoine is coming with his new partner, Ahmed.' My comment made Sam raise his eyebrows and smile.

'This is getting very interesting. You have quite a family. Now what about your sister? Where is she in all of this?'

'She is dead. She died in the Other World, a few months back. We learnt the news a couple of days ago.'

His face fell. He closed his notebook and put it on the table. I felt my throat tighten. I asked him to keep private what I was about to disclose. Then

I told him about the events that had led my sister to try to escape her remote relocation, taking her toddler son, Eudes, with her. I related the wait for them, and how I had lost hope. Then I explained that Ushi Tsou and Eudes had reappeared a few days ago, but Julia had died in the helicopter crash and that had caused their delay.

'You believe her, this Ushi Tsou?' Sam asked.

'All I know is that she loves my nephew and looked after him efficiently. I can't see what else could have happened to my sister. She had many flaws, but she loved her son: she would not have abandoned him.'

'What if Ushi Tsou killed her in order to be the only one looking after Eudes?' Sam persisted.

'It doesn't make sense: the only reason why she grew so close to him is because she had to look after him. If my sister had been around, this would not have been the case,' I replied. I had already thought and dismissed his argument days before.

'Fair point. I'll make sure we get a passage through for your late sister's ex-husband and his gay lover,' Sam gave in. 'I will level with you: we have been following his case for some time and I was aware of his link with you and claims regarding Eudes. He made it very public.'

'Yes… Of course you did.' Sometimes I really could miss the obvious.

'He might continue in this vein and make further claims. And he might increase his demands via public platforms. This is something we are cautious about. I am not saying we will not grant him exceptional entry; just that it is not a given and won't be unconditional. And yes, he is Eudes' father and should have a right to see him, but you see, Eudes is not really in England, is he? The rights are blurred there. Sorry, Yoko, I am just playing devil's advocate here.'

I nodded. Although I wanted to help reunite father and son, Charles-Antoine was not my priority, all things considered.

*

Loved up in Leo's arms that night, I told him about Charles-Antoine and how it illustrated my fears regarding anything private in my life; i.e. that things could go haywire at any time. It was not just my own love of independence, past hurts and insecurity over the future, it was that a part of me increasingly felt that my life was not my own. I was not a normal person any more, even if I would never give up the fight to remain true to myself and to my beliefs. Yet, could I really put myself as a priority when there were millions of lives on the line - sick people, Relocated, WII locals? I would never stop feeling, thinking, breathing. I couldn't just dismiss myself, but I was terrified the fragile balance would shift under the weight of my duties to the rest of the world.

Leo listened to me, patiently. When I started to sob, he tightened his arms around me and leaned his head against mine. My built-up anxiety surprised me. Coping daily by not asking myself too many questions - or trying to - had given me the illusion that I was adjusting somehow. Instead, I was slowly drowning.

'You are not drowning, my love,' Leo whispered to me, as you whisper to a child whose sorrow you wish to soothe. I focused on his last two words. Did he really just call me 'my love'? I immediately felt a little better.

'I can assure you, you are a better swimmer than you fear. You amaze me with your strength, your spirit, your determination. It takes a lot, and sometimes, like now, you just need to release the pressure. I know you: tomorrow, you will be back to your strong self, ready for your next action. You will continue to amaze me. This project of yours: you will antagonise the British Government and you know it. Still, you don't hesitate. I hate what you are going to do tomorrow because you are about to add danger and enemies to those you already have. I wish I could take it all away from you. However, I know there is no stopping you and really, I would not want to change you for anything in the world. I am proud of you. I love you.'

'Even when I am a being difficult?' I teased him.

'Even when you are a pain in the ass,' he smiled. 'Many would just simply do what is being asked of them without asking questions. It is difficult to say no, to challenge the system. You are not taking the easy road.'

'I could be wrong,' I said, and my mood darkened again.

'And that's why you seek advice and don't go ahead, kicking over like a crazy horse. We all appreciate that you do not solely trust your own opinion, but listen and respect those of others. You do not claim your own infallibility.'

Leo took my head in his hands and looked into my eyes. It was probably not a good sight: they were puffy and red from crying.

'For God's sake, woman!' he exhorted with a smile. 'Will you *please* give yourself some credit? You are navigating on unknown waters, with many parties trying to influence your direction according to their best interests. You are doing a brilliant job of staying sane. We all do! So let's focus on moving forward one step at a time, day after day. Okay?' He winked at me and I smiled back. He lowered his head and kissed me. Soon, we had a Simba problem all over again.

Day 7 (Saturday)

The first step of the project was to leave the house without being tailed by the British Secret Service, the British police and Chen's spies, or even by any other government, business and individual who would like to get their hands on a Foggy. Escaping the press was not a challenge to underestimate either, along with anyone who had taken to worship or hate us. Usually when venturing into town, Harry, Zeno and I left in an official car with blackened windows, changing vehicle regularly to lose any followers. Sam and McRae always helped us. Today, we had to lose them, too. I also needed to take Simba with me, and as I wouldn't normally if I were just running errands in town, it would raise suspicions. After discussion with Leila, we decided I would go *spiritual* on the authorities.

*

'I want to go on a retreat and meditate. I need to empty my mind, reconnect with my core. I need a day off. I am overwhelmed, tense and exhausted,' I said to Sam and McRae, when they visited at lunchtime.

'The Prime Minister is still waiting to hear your feedback on the speech drafted for your attention,' Sam needlessly reminded me. He was doing his job without drive. He already knew I did not intend to address the crowd and make this speech.

'Sam, you may want to reiterate to him that I do not want to make a speech, as mentioned when he called.' Sam let out a sigh: it was not a message he was looking forward to passing on to the Prime Minister.

'This is exactly why I want to take a day off,' I continued. 'So much is happening in the world, so much pressure from everywhere. I need to be by myself and breathe a little. After lunch, Phil and some other men - from our private security services - will escort me to the countryside. I wish to re-centre myself somewhere peaceful and quiet, away from anyone. I have reached the point when seeking the support of spiritual gurus to cope with the strains of my new life is an option I am seriously considering. I have even prepared a music meditation playlist for this afternoon.'

'We can provide you with excellent psychoanalysts,' Sam offered.

'I know. Every day one of your research team emails me suggestions for mental support, hypnotherapy, and goodness knows what. I want to find the balance within myself again, not reveal my deepest secrets to someone within your team.'

'We could have someone dedicated to help you, not for our research, but for you,' Sam insisted.

'Thank you. I'd rather try alternative ways first,' I pursued. 'Anyway, today I want to escape in nature and so I will disappear from the radar until tonight. I can assure you my protection will be excellent.'

'I don't like that,' McRae said. 'What's wrong with us keeping an eye on you while you do your Buddha thing.'

'My knowledge that your eyes are on me,' I replied.

'They are very appreciative,' he argued, cocky.

'You are incorrigible,' I replied. He did make me smile though. 'However, I really, really want to have a break the way I want it, not under the watch of Big Brother.'

'You will still have your security behind you. This is hardly normal.'

'They are private and my personal choice. I like you guys, but having the British Secret Service constantly on my back was not my choice.'

'Do you promise you will be back by nightfall? It is switching day...' Sam asked.

'I will be back in town by nightfall, I promise,' I meant it. I would be back in town. Somewhere in town.

McRae narrowed his eyes at me. Sam tapped his fingers on the table, thinking.

'So guys, are you going to let me off the hook for the rest of the day?' I asked them both.

'This is never going to work with my boss. This is what will happen. I will tell them your wish. They will say yes – you are supposedly free of movement – but they will have you followed and monitored nonetheless. They might, or might not, inform us they are doing so,' Sam admitted.

'Well, at least you are honest about it,' Leila commented.

'Then I will have to count on the ability of my people to lose your people and give me freedom,' I summarised. 'And because you know that is my purpose, you will not freak out and raise the alarm around the country to find me.'

'Yes.'

'Fine. So be it.'

'So we might still be watching your back in the end.'

'Oh no. You will not,' I grinned.

'You seem pretty confident,' McRae noted.

'Yes, I am!'

*

My backpack was ready and waiting with my bodyguard, Phil. In it were a little summer dress, two different wigs, two pairs of sunglasses, a pair of socks, a pair of trainers and a pair of ballerina pumps, a light foldable rucksack and a large foldable beach bag. Under my current shirt-dress, I wore running shorts and a tank top. When it was time, I grabbed a small handbag, took Simba with me and we got in the car with Phil. In there, I got rid of my shirt-dress and put on socks and trainers. I switched wig and shades, I stuffed the other sunglasses, wig, ballerina shoes and the beach bag into the foldable rucksack. Then I waited to reach the location where I would jump out of the car. There was a lot of traffic. Some roads were closed due to an annual London marathon. Phil slowed the car as we had reached the corner from which, in three or four strides, I could join the flow of the marathon participants. I checked my top and smiled: the number 737 was labelled over my chest. How fitting with the recurrence of those figures in the Fog history! I swiftly opened the door and ran out. It took just a few seconds to turn anonymous in the flow of thousands of runners. I tried to find a rhythm not to fall behind too fast. Barely 100 metres later, I made a quick left, got into the back of an old Rolls Royce with tinted windows and we departed. I changed again, pulling out the summer dress, with another wig, from the rucksack. The rest of the clothes went into the large beach bag except the last pair of sunglasses, now on my nose. Shortly after, we arrived at a large shopping centre. After a quick walk through the centre and a Starbucks coffee, I went down to the underground garage and got in the back of a mini-van, in which another change of clothes and wig was waiting for me. In the last vehicle, a mini this time, Simba was waiting for me. Her fur was now dyed the colour of a Pyrenean Mastiff: white, brown and cinnamon. At last, I drove on my own out of town. The Society monitored us both, me via the earring tracking device, Simba with an electronic implant. They also tracked and followed the car. I felt safe. The plan was for me to spend the rest of the day walking in the countryside, avoiding contact with anyone. Maybe I would truly attempt to meditate or reconnect with nature. Hug a tree or something. I had hours to pass. I wished Leo was with me, but it was easier for one to disappear than two.

As we walked along the edge of woods and fields in the beautiful English country, Simba ran behind squirrels and rabbits, or followed the scent of foxes and boars. She loved doing so in WII as well, but with the dangers of Clémence's rebels, she had not had such walks in the wild for some time. We were so lucky with the weather, I even took my shoes off and walked barefoot in a stream, playing with Simba and the water.

*

My alarm woke me up. Last I remembered, I laid down in the grass, looking at the sky and feeling good, Simba nestled against me. I had set up the alarm not to wake me up (I did not expect to fall asleep) but to warn me it was time to return to the car. I hurried back to the mini. It was not there any more. A Mercedes replaced it with a driver from the Society security. I got in the back seat, put my headset on and called Leila. Time to get an update on the situation and check everything was ready.

*

I arrived at my destination two hours later and waited another two hours in the car, eating a sandwich and a bar of dark chocolate. A food box left for me in the car also contained cheese and fruits, along with tea, coffee, orange juice and sparkling water. Leila had joined me a few minutes earlier, once she had launched the second phase of the plan. Outside, the shrieking sound of an alarm was unnerving, yet comforting. It confirmed the plan was on track. As expected, a large crowd of people was leaving the premises that I was about to enter. For thousands of people, some having travelled from far away, a fun night was ruined. It was all for a good cause I told myself, while admiring the building.

I had first seen it by day in the year 2000, when it was still called the Millenium Dome. It was so named because of its large dome-shaped structure and original purpose to host an exhibition celebrating the beginning of the third millennium. The building opened to the public from 1st January to 31st December 2000. In no time, the edifice became a London landmark and revived the Greenwich peninsula in East London with attractive new shows. Indeed, after failing to attract visitors and very public financial chaos, the large marquee-type construction turned into a successful entertainment complex with a state-of-the-art indoor arena, boasting a capacity seating of up to 20,000 for concerts. It was one of these big events we had just interrupted by raising the fire alarm. It was barely dark and the stars of the event had not even been on stage yet, as columns of upset people were evacuated under the watchful eyes of the fire brigades on site. Leila informed me it was far from being a full house that night. The Modern Marburg virus was keeping many people at bay from large events. The Society had tried to cancel the show altogether, or to build up a fake response team to the fake fire alarm, but it had proved impossible. So now, waiting in the car on a side street with the lights off, I was about to sneak into the building with the help of a few men the Society had put in place. They had access to the surveillance system and, when required, they would supervise Simba and me, remaining inside and unnoticed. A room for the night was prepared for me. In the morning, the O2 arena, as the complex was now known, would be transformed into the largest door to WII ever known. With 1km circumference of canopy, we Foggies aimed to clean millions of individuals from the viruses that plagued their lives.

*

Emptying the arena of its audience was relatively fast, but it took forever to get rid of the police, firemen, technicians, staff and all the others involved in the safety and security of the building. The Society was busy, discreetly intercepting communications and sending the right information for everyone to make a move and leave. By the time Simba and I were led inside and tucked into one of the star rooms, there were no more chocolate bars in the car.

As I settled for the night, I thought again of Harry's words:

'If those people want to cross the Fog, it is their choice. If we wish to let them go through, it is our choice. If both parties accept the consequences and unknowns, the Government should not intervene.'

At the time, his sentence reminded me there is such a thing as a private contract. If so, we needed a private venue. The O2 arena was the largest venue close by, that I could think of. However, we were imposing the Gate on the owners without knowing how they would react, and if they were kindred spirits ready to help. We were sorry to do that to them; it was just too sensitive a situation for us to consult the owners first. The Society and the Foggies hoped we could negotiate an acceptable solution for all. As for the British Government, if they could put us in front of a *fait accompli*, so could we!

*

Meanwhile, stating that Sam and McRae were upset would be a gross understatement. They were frantic to know my whereabouts, despite Leila informing them both that I was safe. They demanded reassurances that I would return soon and not switch an undisclosed location. Leila refused to answer any more questions. McRae and she argued. I sensed there was more in the argument than just the Fog. In the end, they decided to move Jack to the Essex house for security and McRae would stay with him. Sam would remain at ours and, for them, Jack was now the only Switcher located in England for certain, and they would not risk him staying in a place that was so high profile.

What they did not know was that Jack could not spend the night in the Essex house. Christophe was already there. He had to sleep in an already fogged building in order not to create another door, and he wanted to be by his wife and child. It was even more unfortunate timing that Jack had celebrated his return from Kenya, his renewed self-confidence and his fashion projects online by having a barbeque with Jazz and Big Tom during which he got very drunk. He was a sleepy drunk. When McRae insisted on taking him to Essex to stay with Dante and Leo, Jack didn't immediately get the implications of what the agent was saying and let him put him in the car. Only when he reached the house did he vaguely remember that he should not be there. He was not making much sense when fighting with McRae to not enter the Fog. Jack managed to run away, but drunk, he did not run very far. He fell in the arms of one of police officers who were discreetly guarding the entrance of the property. McRae tried to explain that he really ought to get in the house now, as it was Switching night. In the end, McRae had three men, who could cross the Fog unaffected, carry Jack inside. Within 5 minutes, they called him on the radio. Jack was anxiously trying to get out, so shaken he had sobered up, when he suddenly collapsed. When told they could hardly find his pulse, McRae ran inside: Jack had indeed fallen into a comatose sleep.

~

OPTIMUM

DEDICATION

*To You, dear Reader, for accompanying Yoko
on this Fog journey.
This book would not exist if not for my wish to share this
story with You.*

~

WEEK V

Day 1 (Sunday)

As soon as the sun rose, the news would spread that the colossal London landmark had disappeared under another type of dome, a dome of Fog. Hence, I had to leave the building before dawn.

It had been a surprisingly good night. The alarm, set for 15 minutes before sunrise, woke me up with a start. Like me, Simba disagreed with the abrupt and early end to her dreams. While I had a quick shower, and before we exited the premises, I suddenly had doubts: had it been possible to Fog such a large structure? I had simply assumed that whatever construction a Switcher would sleep in on any given Saturday would turn into a Fog door, whether igloo or palace. Now I wondered: and what would happen if I slept under a bridge or in the Eurotunnel?

*

Stepping out, the absence of lights from the city, along with the soft and subtle resistance of the Fog confirmed the building was now a gate to WII. When the veil lifted and the streetlights appeared in the distance, I hurried for fifty steps or so and turned to look at the building, or absence of it. It was still too dark to see much, but I could only vaguely discern the contour of the Fog-covered dome, blacker than the deep blue sky. We had done it! We had created a large, wide, Fog structure, which was already organised to let thousands of people in at any given time, even if for another purpose. Images from the news and the uncontrollable spread of the Marburg virus flashed behind my eyes, blending with those from blockbuster disaster movies, and I prayed the fogged dome could put an end to it. As the light grew, the sight became clearer and eerier. The size of dome was breathtaking before: now it was mesmerizing. It was a wide nothing, an act of disappearance. Someone tapped my shoulder and when I turned, Leila told me we ought to go. I nodded yet I could not move. I was captivated by the magnitude of the Fog coverage, increasingly apparent in the light. Leila put a hand on my back, and called my name softly. I took a deep breath, gave it one last look and we got to the car.

'We are going to the Essex House,' Leila said to me, as she handed me a large cup of coffee inside. I stared at it. Where had she found a coffee shop open at this time in the morning? It was still steaming, too.

'Ok, but why? I'd rather go home…' I said, sipping the cappuccino slowly and enjoying how the hot liquid felt on my tongue and in my throat.

'There has been a problem overnight,' Leila's tone left no doubt the problem was not a minor one. I stopped drinking and turned towards her, waiting for more.

'After your disappearance, British Intelligence decided it would be *intelligent* to move Jack to a more secure and remote location than the central London one. Not that the terraced-houses complex is insecure, but its location is known. So they picked him up from *The Jazzin* and moved him to the Essex house.'

'Ok… And what is the problem? Jack was there before. In fact, he lives there.' My head was not awake yet.

'Christophe de Rocque is also at the Essex house now,' Leila reminded me. Then I got it and gasped.

'Please tell me they did not put two Switchers under the same roof on Switching night?!' I already knew the answer, otherwise we would not be on our way there.

*

Leila recounted for me how the agents carried a drunk Jack inside against his wishes, and how he had collapsed. They tried to revive him in vain. The noise had woken Isabelle, Leo and Dante who were in the house. Not Christophe though, as he was in the same comatose state as Jack. As discreetly as they could, Leo and Dante carried Christophe outside in WII, where Isabelle joined him with Chloé. Dante stayed with him while Leo returned to Jack's side. He insisted repeatedly to McRae that Jack must be brought outside the Fog immediately. The medical emergency team was opposed to moving him, but McRae overrode them and ordered that they let Leo take Jack outside. As there was no Facilitator on site – McRae was not aware that Helo, currently in a Society's house close by, was a Facilitator - they put Jack in a wheeled foldable bed and Leo pushed him outside. To Leo's surprise, the duo did not emerge in the Other World, but ours. McRae arrived just behind him, his head bent over his mobile, ready to call Sam. Leo looked at him and narrowed his eyes. He knew McRae had reacted instinctively when he had heard Jack had collapsed and ran inside. He had only realised, as a second thought, that he was putting himself at risk of relocation, but when he had crossed again to check, he was in good old England, unaffected by the Fog. Leo turned to McRae.

'Mate, sorry to disappoint, but you are affected. You just led me out in our World as only a Facilitator could. You are the missing one, the unaccounted for. Welcome to the Foggies Club!'

As the car sped through the town, Leila's description of events was very succinct. The Government would be aware soon of the brand new and unmissable Fog Dome to handle, and she needed to get the Society's private security on the ground and liaise with her head office. As we headed towards the Essex house, she was checking the updates on the Society's first contact, the CEO and board members of the company running the O2 Arena. Speed was of the essence. Every detail had been planned, except their reactions. Leila now briefed me on the virtual Extraordinary Board Meeting currently taking place within the Society.

*

O2 is a leading mobile phone services company in the UK: I expected it to be the owner of the so-called O2 Arena. Absolutely not! The company owning the premises was a subsidiary of a wide international corporation, the world's largest owner of sports teams and sports events. They combined this with venues also used for live music and entertainment. The subsidiary was based in Los Angeles, the headquarters in Denver. Ultimately, the company belonged to one man and he wanted to speak to me. To Leila's silent question - did I accept - I acquiesced.

'Miss Salelles, good morning. Can you explain why you took it upon yourself to create this Fog on one of my most lucrative European venues?' The man had a deep voice and a strong American accent. He was direct and to the point, as only Americans can be.

'It's complicated,' I replied, aware it was high on the list of the most annoying answers ever. Nothing else had come to mind.

'You are giving me a case of conscience,' he continued. 'I am a businessman: I don't like having to mix conscience and business. It's usually counter-productive.'

'I have no doubt we will find a way to create a partnership you will be proud of.'

'I could just sue your ass,' he said in a non-aggressive tone. The American CEO did not sound that worried.

'You now own the largest virus-healing two-worlds-access gate on the planet, and you are talking to the person who can help you maintain this exclusivity for years to come. Your investment is worth billions more this morning than yesterday. If you want to sue me, go ahead. I have no financial means to compensate you and you will lose your chance to make a difference in this world. Just consider the number of people that you can save. It will be easy, too: people in, people out, in minutes. Yes, there will be administration involved and a need to control comings and goings, but most of the structure is already in place.'

'The venue costs millions to run and there is a mortgage...' Mr CEO started.

'As mentioned before, we will work it out. When there is a will, there is a way. Of course, we don't want you to be out of pocket. For example, there might be a symbolic fee for crossing, but we are hoping to keep it to a minimum.'

'We need to meet. I am scheduling a flight to London later today. I will meet with my local team first, then with you,' Mr CEO decreed.

I would have none of it. I didn't want to bend to his will from the start. We had to stop him from feeling he was in a position of power.

'A member of Gatekeepers Associates will be delighted to meet you tomorrow morning in our offices in Central London at 9am. Please be aware there is strict security to access our grounds and we will need a list of attendees from your side by the end of day, today. My wonderful assistant Leila will liaise with you for details. Also, it's highly probable that representatives of the British Government will be in attendance. I trust this will not be a problem for you,' I stated in a firm, confident tone. A battle of mind power was at play.

'Tomorrow, 9am. OK. I look forward to it.'

'In the meantime, be assured we will enforce maximum security around the Dome.'

'I will send some people, too.'

'Of course. Please ensure that your staff do not approach the Fog too closely, except if they are willing to be relocated to another world,' I reminded him.

'I will,' the CEO replied after a few seconds silence.

*

When we arrived at the Essex Fog house, a temporary medical tent was set outside the house, within the walls enclosing the property. It was early morning and activity in the street was non-existent. Leila and I entered the tent and the few heads inside turned towards us. The medical team was composed of Society experts - who knew that the issue was caused by the presence of two switchers, on switching night, under one roof - and the governmental experts, who had no clue. The origin of the problem did not matter though, when the real problem was that both sides were unable to wake Jack. McRae and Leo came towards us. Leo grabbed me by the waist and planted a kiss on my mouth that left me breathless. When I pulled out grinning, McRae exchanged a few words with Leila and indicated, with a look to both Leo and me, that he wanted to talk to us outside, away from the others.

McRae was mildly in shock at being a Facilitator. He had not revealed the news to anyone yet. I asked him if he agreed for me to disclose it to the other Foggies. After the fogging of the Dome, we had planned an extraordinary Board Meeting in the evening. He hesitated. McRae being a Facilitator should be a new line in the agenda of the meeting, but only if he was ready for it. While he was asking question after question on the implications of being a Facilitator, his mobile rang. It was Sam.

Within seconds, McRae roared a loud 'No!' and glared at Leila and me. As a wild guess, they knew about the Fog Dome. As McRae listened, we could see anger building up in his eyes, in the clench of his jaws and in the redness of his face. Leila, Leo and I steeled ourselves for the storm to come. We didn't have to wait long.

'How could you? How could you! Are you insane?!' He barked at me first, then turned to the others. 'All of you, are you insane? The O2 Arena? REALLY?'

His mobile beeped and he checked the screen. After looking at the screen wide-eyed, he held the device at us in an accusing manner. It displayed the Fog Dome in the light of a beautiful sunrise.

'I can't believe it! What have you done?' McRae took a deep breath in an attempt to control himself. I took his mobile and checked the pictures he had received from Sam. None of us had had a chance to see what the Dome looked like now, in daylight. I had to admit the sight of the covered edifice filled me with awe. It reminded me of an eerie alien space ship, or a gigantic dodgy whitish mushroom. It was undeniably daunting. When seen from above, via the aerial pictures from drones, it felt less overwhelming. The Dome only appeared to have disappeared under a white blotch, or a cloud. I gave back McRae's mobile.

'I think you need coffee,' Leo said to the Scotsman, putting a hand on his back.

'Yeah, a double espresso. And a Redbull. With whisky in it,' McRae replied in a low, irate tone.

'I'm on it. The whisky, in the espresso or in the Redbull?' Leo replied, ignoring McRae's tone and speaking politely like a well-trained waiter.

'What do you think? In both!' the Scot replied, true to his roots. 'Why did you do that? Do you realised the magnitude of what you have started?'

'The big picture, yes. The details we will have to adjust as we go along. We are kind of used to the practice by now,' I replied slowly to refrain from snapping back. I did not need to be defensive.

'What about you, Lochy? Don't you realise the magnitude of the Modern Marburg virus?' Leila jumped in. 'How long was the government going to wait? And how far would they let the virus spread before getting their act together and giving people's health the priority it deserves?' McRae didn't reply; just pursed his lips.

'Are you going to tell Sam about your new attribute?' Leo returned to the interrupted discussion on McRae being a Facilitator.

'Not yet,' McRae replied. 'I want to understand better where it places me first, with you Foggies, the Secret Services, the Society; how it will affect my life from now on.' He paused before adding, 'Also with you, Leila.'

Leila nodded. To refer to his relationship with her in a critical situation was a sign he was taking her seriously. It revealed that he had grown to really care for her. Despite the context, I smiled at the sight of the brief look of intimacy between them.

'You did not answer about revealing you are a Facilitator to the other Foggies?' I asked him. 'If yes, I can organise an introduction at the FBM later today.'

'How many are they?' he asked, instead of answering.

'You will know this if you answer by the affirmative and if they are willing to connect with you. Despite your links with British Intelligence, you have already been on missions for the Society and created a special link with them and us: it should play in your favour.'

McRae took a few seconds to think before accepting. He wanted to be introduced to the Foggies as the last Facilitator. Leila leaned over and whispered in my ear that Christophe was back in the house. He was awake and in full possession of his senses. He requested help to get back to this world and check on Jack. I suggested McRae. It could be the first introduction to a Foggy today. Leila quickly typed Christophe a message under the intrigued eye of McRae. He was still grumpy about the Dome. Christophe replied to send McRae to him inside.

'Lochy, would you go to the house now? Someone needs your help,' she told him.

Leo had just come back with coffee, Redbull and whisky, along with warm bacon and cheese croissants for everyone. McRae opened the can of Redbull, took a couple of sips from the can and then poured whisky into it, finishing the can in one go, afterwards. He then took the double espresso, poured one (or more…) shots of whisky in it, and drank bottoms up.

'I am on my way,' McRae said, as he started walking towards the house, taking a croissant on the way.

'Dante will also come out to see Jack,' Leo told us. I had forgotten all about Dante. 'He was keeping Ed and Kim away from Christophe and Isabelle and Baby Chloe. When Christophe said he wanted to come and see how Jack was doing, he decided he'd better tag along as he needed someone to help him cross as well.'

'How do you feel about Lochy joining your select little Fog-related club?' Leila asked Dante.

'This is going to be an interesting addition. So far, he's done good as a British Agent. He respected us. Not sure how he will juggle his current British allegiances with his *fogginess*, but we will see,' Dante answered.

'Ditto,' said Leo, coming next to me and putting an arm around my waist. He added mischievously: 'What about you, Leila, how do you feel about it?'

'I am loving it!' she replied with a wide grin. 'A maverick agent of the British Secret Service belongs to the Fog. This is a fascinating scenario. A good one, I think, as he already proved to have a penchant for our cause.'

'And on a personal level, where do you stand?' Leo went on.

'This is still to be determined, though I am feeling a bit better right now than I did an hour ago.' She repressed a smile, took out her Ftab, and acted busy until McRae, Christophe and Leo came out.

'Wow,' McRae exclaimed. 'So we have three Switchers in England now! And I finally met someone I helped in Morocco. I'm eager to discover what's coming next! But don't think I am not still upset about your Fog Dome…' McRae's mood had lifted at last, even if just a little. Another call from Sam somehow dampened it, as he walked away to speak with his colleague.

Leila turned to me. 'Right, Yoko, we have much to organise. Shall we get on with it?'

*

The Extraordinary FBM was at our usual video call time of 6pm. We needed everyone awake and with a clear mind in Nevada and Alaska. That left Leila and me the whole day to prepare notes to share on the latest events. We had also contacted the BBC newsroom for me to make a live declaration at noon, to be retransmitted to the rest of the world online. I wanted to make it brief and had been working on it during the week. It was still nerve wrenching. My wish was to avoid meeting the representatives of the British Government until after the live declaration, but it was utopian. Sam rejected every attempt to see him later in the afternoon and demanded to see us immediately at the Essex house. Leo prepared a tray with Redbull, espresso and whisky for Agent Sam Riverson, the combination having worked wonders with McRae. The latter snorted at the idea, saying that Sam was English, not Scottish, and he would probably settle for tea. I disagreed and suggested gin and tonic, but Leila countered me, saying that in summer, the Brits drink Pimms.

When Sam arrived, we all carried trays with our respective drink suggestions for him. He looked at them with distrust before bursting into laughter when we explained we just wanted to help him in the best way possible. The laughter gone, he still had to vent his anger seconds afterwards. None of us interrupted or reacted while he did so. He was still upset at our 'stupidity', 'inability to see the big picture', or 'dissident approach to everything'. Once he had finished, he put his boss – also McRae's - on a video call to us and she repeated pretty much the same thing. The one thing they both said though, and to which we ought to reply, was 'And now, what happens next?'

'We are going to make a statement to the press,' I told them.

'And what are you going to say?' Sam, McRae and their boss replied in perfect harmony.

'That it had been decided by the Gatekeepers and the authorities that the situation was critical. Something had to be done immediately to help contain the virus and save the lives of the contaminated,' I answered.

'Nicely played. And thank you for including us in taking the nice role. However, you have made a few people very angry. Don't be surprised if there is payback,' the boss said.

'Whatever we do, we seem to always upset half the population these days,' I said.

'These ones are powerful,' the boss said and added, 'Why the O2 Arena?'

'It was the best place when looking for a very large structure, already organised to filter people in and out, with a wide space inside and set in a location that can be manageable and controlled,' I explained.

'Did you have the owner's approval?' Sam enquired.

'We are hoping to get retroactive approbation for our charitable act towards helping infected people,' I replied.

'Good luck on that one,' the boss said. 'Not that it matters. They will not own the place for long. I expect that, for National Security, the venue will be taken over by the State in no time.'

'This is not what we want. We intend to negotiate the terms of the Fog Dome. we don't want you taking control over it,' I stated, sternly.

'It is not all about what the Gatekeepers want,' the boss replied.

'Let us disagree on this. First, I haven't spoken to the press yet. Second, what would you do with a nationalised building that turns back to normal in seven weeks? That is what will happen if we refuse to maintain the Fog because you are imposing your will on us.'

The boss, eyes closed, let out a deep sigh. 'You are an incredible asset to us yet a real thorn in our side. Sometimes I wish the Fog had picked a bunch of idiots who would just do as they are told.'

'Powerful, suggestible idiots are more dangerous, exactly because they are suggestible and could be as easily manipulated by other parties and not just you. Parties the like of Ingis Chen, for example,' Leila argued.

'Will you at least provide us with a copy of the speech before you talk to the press?' Sam asked.

'Or would you let us suggest one?' the boss added.

'The speech is not finalised yet. You are welcome to send suggestions,' I replied, noncommittal.

*

They did. They emailed them and sent hard copies directly from the Prime Minister's office. By fogging the Dome, we had forced him into action. It was impossible for him to refuse the public access to the Fog now for the people whose lives depended on it. When the Prime Minister called to check we had received his documents, he did not once express his dissatisfaction. We had expected threats, reprimands and anger: they were all absent. I was relieved, impressed, and made note of his attitude as one to adopt in similar situations. When something happens, just deal with it and don't dwell on it. His suggested speech had some good lines. Although I did not agree with it all, I used parts of the proposal when it matched our ideas and goals. I was determined to keep it short: under fifteen minutes.

*

At noon, Harry, Zeno and I were together on an empty square with the imposing Fog Dome behind us in the background. Leo and Dante had remained with Jack in the Essex house and Christophe stayed in WII with Isabelle and his baby daughter. The less they were seen around us, the better. We had not been able to secure Penny Thompson in time to proceed with the interview, even though we had an agreement with her to contact her first for breaking news. She was travelling to Nevada to see her daughter and ex-husband. This suited me fine. I could understand her anxiety on the whereabouts and safety of her daughter Michelle; nonetheless, the underlying anger and aggression in the way she handled situations and people was unnerving.

A team arrived from the BBC, with a famous presenter of worldwide renown. The Society covered the main security with a helicopter, ready in case we needed to escape. A crowd had gathered on the edge of the secure area. There were three zones: one set up by us, a larger one by the military and one last one, larger still, by the police. Other helicopters were flying low and surveying the ground. The same went on along the Thames, covered by boats.

When everything was ready, I closed my eyes and focused on taking deep breaths. I forced myself to smile in order to try and emanate positivity. Zeno came and gave me a little shoulder massage, whispering words of encouragement in my ear and reassuring me that every Foggy was by my side. Literally and physically, they were beside me in a show of support and strength as a group.

*

First, the presenter introduced me and summarised the appearance of the Fog Dome in London following the pressure on the British government to act. When my turn came to speak, my voice was shaky. As I spoke, it gathered momentum and confidence. I memorised most of my speech as best as I could and rarely glanced down at my notes. They were there to give me confidence if my memory failed. The gist of the speech put the emphasis on that we were all - Gatekeepers, governments, private companies (like the one owning the Dome) - learning as we went along and doing our best. The Fog was still neither the ultimate nor the perfect solution to any problem: it was to be used with caution. I reminded them that the Fog was not to cross on a whim. There was a 1 in 7 chances of relocation to that Other World, and that world was not ours to invade, impose upon, change, plunder, abuse and destroy because of its easily exploitable potential. We had to respect the communities already living in WII; there was much to learn from them. Of course, they could learn much from us as well, but the difference in culture and technology was such that they would require time and patience from us, and must be given a choice on what to learn and whether to do so or not. We had to accept that within this choice was their right to say no. I mentioned all of this to prepare them that not everyone would be given access to the Fog Dome:

'The priority must be given to cross the fog to those whose lives are threatened by a deadly virus like the current Marburg outbreak. Others would not be allowed through until a selection system is set up. The details of the selection process are being worked on, and we hope that people will be understanding and patient.

Until a few months ago, we Gatekeepers were mere human beings, carrying on our daily lives like any other average individual. In the same way, no state institution knew about or was prepared for the arrival of the Fog, along with its effects and consequences. We are all doing the best we can to deal with this extraordinary phenomenon and adjust our lives at the individual, national, international and inter-world level. There is no right or wrong way at this point: only a learning path. We have made and will make mistakes, though hopefully fewer and fewer. If this can be of reassurance, none of us Gatekeepers are seeking to increase our wealth or gain power at the expense of others, thanks to the Fog. Certainly, our standard of living has improved. We are well looked after while we work to organise the integration of the Relocated in WII and the management and maintenance of the Fog on this side of the Gate. However, we have refused many lucrative offers that were against our code of deontology, which aims *first and foremost to help communities in both worlds, respecting nature and humanity in the process.'*

*

As soon as I finished, Zeno and Harry came to join me and thanked the presenter and the public for their attention. We left the stage and headed to the Society's helicopter where Leila and Sam were waiting for us, to return to our house in Central London. Some movie stars and others in the public eye sometimes avoided reading celebrity magazines. I wondered back then if that was feasible, if I would be able to. I was now learning that it was not only feasible, it was necessary for one's mental sanity. Leila's team had turned into a filter to give us succinct reports from the media with only a summary of the various news and opinions about us, including the praise and constructive criticism that we could learn from. Harry, who was still reading the paper every morning with a cup of tea, was impressed by the accuracy and exhaustiveness of those reports. That was enough for me and much less depressing than having to go through the rants, gossip and accusations of the naysayers and negative people of this world. That afternoon, I made sure that I didn't go near a television and buried myself in work.

First, there were the preparations for the Extraordinary FBM. McRae was waiting impatiently to hear if the Foggies would allow him to join and virtually meet everyone in the evening. There was also the meeting with the CEO behind the O2 Arena to finalise for the next morning. Last but not least, I confirmed with Jazz and through her informed the decision-makers of WII, that we had created the Fog Dome. We had mentioned the project to them previously, in order to prepare them for the increase of Relocated as a consequence. All of them had been expecting, hoping even, for more people to arrive and so the news was generally welcomed. Sure, they had fears in front of the many unknown: numbers of newcomers, their adaptation and integration, or rejection and imposition. And yet they still approved the project, especially as we insisted we aimed to keep strict control of the flow of the people crossing.

*

McRae came to the house at 5pm. He was not the bearer of good news: Jack was still in a coma. The situation was worse than the last time two Switchers passed out when under the same roof on switching night. Indeed, the Fog tree house that Jack had created in Kenya had disappeared. This did not bode well: was Jack… dying? I could not bear to think of it.

We connected to the video conference for the Extraordinary FBM with gloomy spirits. The Foggies were now in just 4 locations: 2 in England (London and Essex) and 2 in the US (Alaska and Nevada). Before McRae joined us and once updated on the many details around the Fog Dome, Jack was the main topic of our conversation. We could speculate only, and it worried us more than any of the worldwide reactions to the Fog Dome. No one had any idea if Jack was ever going to wake up. Michelle suggested that if he did, maybe he wouldn't be a Switcher anymore; maybe this double-switching had annihilated the gift in one of them. It was a theory and it didn't matter if that was the case. The most important was that he woke up. Speculations…

McRae never once lost his relaxed confidence during the FBM. He remained in control, his interest and eagerness to discover who and where the other Foggies were only betrayed by the intensity of his gaze on each square of screen. Each group introduced each other, except us in London. In Essex, he had a small reaction of surprise to discover there was another crosser, Louise, and Facilitator, Helo, aside from Leo, Dante and Christophe. The six Foggies in the US had prepared questions for him on his link to the British Secret Service. We had him swear to secrecy the existence of the Foggies that British Intelligence did not already know about, otherwise he would be cut out of the Foggies.

'But I already knew of the existence of Foggies in Nevada,' he commented.

'True, but barely any information. We don't want you to reveal anything you learn about and from us. Now, Yoko, can you give him his file?' Adam said.

'Here it is,' I told McRae, pushing a thick folder in front of him. 'This is all you should keep in mind, regarding our rules of conduct, our codes, the workings of Gatekeepers Associates and how it came to be. We hope you will adhere to it and be an active part of the community. This is not compulsory, of course: in Kenya, Mary and Clare were Foggies but originally they did not wish to join the company. Events made them change their minds. Also summarised are our stories and connections. However, this folder is not going to leave this house, so we will ask you to study it only when visiting here. You are welcome to stay for the night.'

'Ok. What about the tablet you all carry around? Will I have one?' McRae asked.

'When you confirm being one of us first, a British agent second. We can't possibly give you one until we feel secure about your allegiances,' Zeno said, before I had a chance.

'Fair enough,' McRae replied, refilling his coffee cup.

Day 2 (Monday)

Leo stayed in Essex overnight, so Simba was back on the bed, taking over most of it. We woke up early and walked downstairs. A dishevelled McRae came into the kitchen as coffee was brewing. His eyes were puffy and the dark circles under them indicated a lack of sleep. His ginger-blond hair was a bird's nest, he was still wearing the same clothes as yesterday, now creased, and he looked devoid of energy. I asked him if he preferred tea or coffee and he opted for coffee. McRae told me he had been so absorbed in the details of each story that he could not put the files down. He had fallen asleep on the sofa while reading them. When Simba came back in, McRae's tired eyes lit up and he bent down to speak to her, saying that he always felt she was very special.

'Will you tell Sam about Simba?' McRae asked me.

'You know our main assumption on how she came to be both Crosser and Facilitator, which is that she was born on the first switching night in the midst of the Fog. Now imagine if this idea spread. What do you think any government, scientist, or anyone interested in developing better access to the Fog would do?'

'I know. Their probable reaction immediately crossed my mind,' McRae whispered to himself. 'They would try to induce births in the Fog on Saturday nights.'

'Exactly. As you worked for the Government, we couldn't tell you,' I added.

'I still do. Kind of. In partnership with the Society.'

'Now you are a Foggy. You will have to choose which comes first.'

'And I can't delay this decision, with my informing Sam, or not, that I am a Facilitator,' McRae said. He pinched his nose between two fingers and frowned.

'One thing I understand already,' McRae continued, 'is that your information is confidential. I will not talk. Not only do I appreciate your trust, I get that being bound to the Fog, I need you.'

'You should sleep on it. You clearly did not have a chance to last night.'

'Sleep will have to wait. Now, Yoko, aren't you having breakfast? I'd join you with pleasure.'

*

The CEO was not what I expected. Despite my best efforts to avoid having prejudices, I had envisioned a strong, bulky and jolly character in a grey suit with a cowboy hat and a cigar. Instead, he was a slim, young fifty-something, with vivid eyes and a stern face. He arrived with three people: his private secretary, who supervised the smooth daily running of his private and business affairs, the company Chief Operating Officer, and the in-house lawyer. The four men looked as determined to win the battle as Napoléon must have been before Waterloo. With Leila and the Society behind us, they did not stand a chance. Harry, Zeno and I greeted the men at the gates of the London Fog complex. Leila accompanied us as our private assistant. Sam and McRae were waiting for us in the office meeting room when we arrived. There was a moment of awkwardness when we all sat down. The circumstances were exceptional and rather bizarre. Harry broke the silence by thanking them for coming, and asked if they had had a chance to see the Fog Dome in reality. Unsurprisingly, they had. It had been a shock to them to see the large building completely covered.

During the whole meeting, only the CEO spoke. Within minutes, we reached the gist of the matter and things became heated.

'You owe us both explanations and compensation,' the CEO said and leaned forward on the table, his elbows firmly planted on it.

'National emergency. We requisitioned your premises for the sake of public health,' Sam replied, before Harry, Zeno or I had time to say anything.

I struggled to suppress my surprise. I looked at Sam and McRae and the latter winked at me. There were two ways of interpreting Sam's intervention: the first one was support for our action; the second was that they were taking credit for it. Either way worked for me as long as Gatekeepers Associates got the final word. What followed was a verbal tennis match between Sam, arguing for the nationalisation of the Arena, and the CEO, claiming both financial compensation and ownership rights to the Dome. The CEO asserted that the British Government had overstepped its legal rights in requisitioning their premises and allowing us to Fog the Arena. His argument relied on the large number of existing State-owned buildings, hospitals included, available to be fogged instead of theirs. He also alluded to the lack of prior consultation. Sam countered that the ultimate freehold of the land on which the Dome was built was owned by the Government through the Home and Communities Agency, and was not for sale. Because of this, the British Government was essentially still the landlord of the site. The CEO reminded Sam they had a decade left on the lease and he was ready to start a legal war.

The man was not at the head of one of the most successful companies in the world in his sector thanks to stupid stubbornness. His recriminations were only a stepping-stone to promote his proposal: running the Fog Dome like an enterprise, as efficiently and smoothly as his company did for all their activities. This time it was not surprise I suppressed, but a smile. This suggestion was what Gatekeepers Associates had hoped.

'The O2 Arena requires millions monthly to pay off the mortgage, maintenance, staff and more. Not even you could run it for free. I presume you could include it in your National Health system - your famous free NHS - and allocate funds towards it. It will enable you to save a lot of money on treatment against viruses, yet your NHS is running poor on funds... My suggestion: we run it like a clinic with free services for standard patients on the NHS, and paying services for private patients.'

'No,' I intervened. 'We do not want to promote inequality in health. The

NHS will only put forward those who desperately need to cross to survive, while others less in need would cross because they have the money for it.'

'It doesn't have to be expensive,' the CEO cut over me. 'It could even be just £10 per crossing. I had a very interesting conversation with a friend of yours yesterday, Mr Ingis Chen. He contacted me as an expert on the Fog and we went through some basic figures: the Arena has a seating capacity of 20,000, though we could easily have more standing. If we have just two scheduled crossings a day at £10 each per person, in addition to the health subvention of the British Government, this should be a successful venture for all.'

'No!' I was horrified. Not just by his involving Ingis Chen in the proposal, but also by what he was saying. With the ration of 7 to 1, the odds were that 6,000 people would be Relocated daily, out of 42,000 people crossing. That meant 42,000 people relocated per week. It was more than an invasion of the WII: it was a deluge of people. The locals would be overwhelmed, overruled, over-everything. Nothing and no one was ready to welcome or help so many people adjusting to a new life in WII. This was ethically unacceptable!

'I am sure you heard Yoko's address yesterday,' Harry spoke for me as I was left speechless by my own calculations. 'Only those affected by life-threatening or life degenerating viruses, and who accept taking the risk of relocation, will be allowed to cross. There will be a proper sorting process, and wealth will not be taken into consideration.'

'So let me repeat my original question: what's in it for me?' the CEO asked

'A new business venture and adventure,' I replied. 'The crossing will not be open to all, but we have projects for WII which will require a large venue. We will need places where Relocated and WII can train in and practice new skills. The Dome could be a large market platform between the two worlds. There are plenty of business opportunities, and a large interface like your venue will be key. If we use your whole place, you would have your cut. But you must work in partnership with the Government and with us.'

Leila glanced at me. This was the scheme we had in mind all along, a partnership between public sector, private sector, and Gatekeepers Associates, the three balancing each other. She took out the basic presentations the Society had prepared, laying out the ideas supporting this cooperation.

Everyone around the table bent over the document and read the main points, even us Foggies who already knew them. Once finished, the CEO raised his head and commented that some of it could work.

'You don't know them yet,' Sam said to him, in a blasé tone. 'Trust me, we have little choice. We are going to have to make it all work.'

We spent the whole morning and lunch around that table, negotiating and organising the foundations of a partnership between us. Any time there was a question on data, for a potential participation to the costs by a patient, an exception, or a statistic, Leila would have an answer within 2 to 3 minutes. The CEO was impressed. He believed that he could work well with us, solely on the strength of our organisation. He even suggested he would hire Leila on the spot if she wished. Beaming, she thanked him and brushed the offer away.

*

Once the CEO and his team had gone, Sam gathered his notes and commented that we had just increased his workload ten-fold.

'Na. You will just pass on the baby to the team of whatever Government department is concerned, maybe several, and they will do the work,' McRae corrected.

'I still have to be on top of things. Also, what is wrong with you? You kept mostly silent today and you look like crap. I have never seen you drink so much coffee. Even when hangovered. What's up?'

'Bad night's sleep,' McRae said with a scowl. He was not ready to talk yet. Sam had enough on his mind not to pursue, but the look he gave McRae clearly showed he was not fully satisfied with the answer. Sam did not linger and went back to his office. McRae remained behind.

'Are you going to check on Jack?' Zeno asked him. McRae looked a bit uncomfortable at the question.

'Not now,' he replied. 'I need some time to think. I need to be alone. I am going to disappear for a couple of days. You have my details: in case of an emergency, get in touch.'

He patted Simba's head with a crooked smile and started towards the door. Mid-way, he stopped, turned and swiftly walked to Leila. He grabbed her by the waist with one arm and pulled her towards him. He gently cupped the nape of her neck with his free hand and kissed her softly. It all happened so fast, none of us realised what he was up to at first, including Leila. McRae didn't give anyone time to recover before swiftly disappearing. Leila's wide bewildered eyes left no doubt that the kiss had not been expected and it was a big leap forward in her relationship with McRae.

'Leila, are you ok?' I asked her.

'Yes… Yes, I am fine,' she replied, a smile creeping up on her face before she caught herself, rattled her throat and frowned. 'Anyway, let's move on, shall we? We have work to do.'

'Ok. Anything we need to know about the public's reaction to the Fog Dome?'

'So far, everything is under control. People are just expectant on what use will be made of it,' Leila replied. 'The virus is still a major threat, even if the spreading is more controlled. The number of affected has increased again. If the Fog doesn't open its door soon, a lot more people will die.'

'The crossing must start tomorrow for the most urgent cases,' Zeno replied.

'I wonder how people will welcome the news that the crossing will still have set limits,' I wondered aloud.

*

At the Extraordinary FBM, we had come to the conclusion that we needed more flexibility in our approach to the Fog crossing. Our priority and focus was the crossing to save lives. On that ground, crossing would be based first on the imminent life threat by a virus – currently the Modern Marburg was the most obvious – then other viruses causing death in the long term. We were no gods and, as no one else on this earth was, it would always be difficult to be fair to everyone. The selection process outside immediate health needs still had to be by lottery.

For the time being, the only non-sick people allowed to go through the Fog would be those working within the Dome. Job offers were in preparation for anyone willing to take the risk of crossing the 'line', based on the skills and competences they would bring to the Relocated and WII locals; like surgeons, technicians, or energy experts. Their reasons for applying could be anything from curiosity, health, desire to change their life, or anything that was not malevolent or illegal. Every applicant would be fully informed of the odds and life-changing consequences of a relocation, including the need to build a new life from scratch with many opportunities but limited modern amenities and technologies. Also, and maybe the hardest, there was the severance, or sometimes loss, of their link to family and friends. Any of the applicants for the job would go through a strict screening of their characters, police records, and would need recommendations by peers and employers. They would have to build a rock-solid case to get the jobs. Gatekeepers Associates, with the Society's support, would review the files of the government's pre-selected 'skilled' applicants. If approved by us, the O2 Arena's company would organise the crossing and offices in their building.

For a third and last category, called 'New Life', the applicants were paying, partly to recoup the costs of administration for the Government yet mostly to compensate the O2 Arena company. The government suggested that we matched the cost of the only equivalent of starting a new life they could propose: new identity in the UK. To start with, there would be only 7 applicants per day, when the process was ready to be implemented. How it worked was that after a check of their credentials, through the application to the British Citizenship and payment of the usual fees of the process, the applicant would cross the Fog and be either relocated in WII, or offered a new British identity and name in the United Kingdom. The chance of a new start, either way. The attitude of the Government had surprised and impressed us on that one. It was a good offer!

*

After a long and hard day of work, Leo came and dragged me away from my desk to go on a date. I had mixed feelings about going out in town for a tête-à-tête dinner. Not because of Leo: no, for fear of being among people. I was apprehensive about being recognised, of people shouting at or pleading with me, of being pointed at, followed, facing aggression. I feared not being just like anyone in the crowd, anonymous. Leo was unknown to the public, so he didn't realise the trauma of my previous experience of a night out. I had not realised either, until now! Fears are the worst impediment in life. That is what stops you moving forward, and I was determined to give this new chance with Leo my best, so I bit my tongue and accepted with a show of enthusiasm, brushing away my apprehension like a nasty fly. I picked a cropped, strawberry blonde wig with a long fringe falling on my eyes. I drew my eyebrows a bit thicker than usual. Then, dressed in tight black jeans and a dove coloured chiffon halter neck top, I finished the look with a gold belt and gold earrings. Smart, casual and elegant. I did not know where he was taking me, so my attire had to suit a wide range of possibilities.

Leo had booked a table at the pub in Notting Hill where we had first met in person. It was more than 5 months ago now. It was a relaxed place that served surprisingly good Thai food. I appreciated his consideration in choosing that place. Leo was really such a caring person, and I was touched when he explained that there was no better way for him to feel we were back on the right path than to return to where it all started. Still, the situation was not as intimate as before: many of the restaurant's guests were Society bodyguards and British Intelligence. Also, Leo behaved much better than he had the first time and refrained from any torrid kissing in public. Nonetheless – and I insist on the nonetheless – we had a lovely night. As we sat back in the car taking us back to mine, he put his hand on mine, which was on my lap.

'This was extremely difficult,' he whispered in my ear, his lips brushing my neck: once, twice, thrice, slowly going down.

'I didn't realise I was such a bore,' I teased him.

'Oh Carissima… All I could think about all through dinner is how I longed to untie the bow of your halter neck and let the material fall, revealing your sculpted shoulders and… Even now…' He picked one of the ties and started pulling it with his teeth.

'I am afraid you are going to have to wait a bit longer,' I told him, unhurriedly lifting his head to mine and nibbling his bottom lip. 'I would prefer that only you see me naked, not the whole of British Intelligence.'

'You are right,' he said, pulling back his body but letting his hand slide between my thighs. 'I much prefer being the only one to see the very best of your body.'

He hesitated a little and added: 'Am I? The only one?'

'Of course you are!' I replied, surprised and a little hurt that he had to ask.

'In both worlds? I mean, Nick is always by your side in WII, and he is definitely interested and good looking. And you are not averse to his charms.'

'The answer is no, Nick has not seen me in my birthday suit,' I replied. My mood had switched to Ice Queen. I could understand that he had asked something that was on his mind, just why then was beyond me. Such a mood killer. I pushed his hand away from my leg.

'Yoko, please don't take it like that. I would not blame you if you had: we were on a break,' he murmured in my ear.

'We were not on a break. We were not at all,' I corrected him, glacial.

'Does it really matter? We are together now. Please forget that I asked: it was just out of curiosity. With a hint of jealousy. Let's brush it away. I have another surprise for you. We are not going back to yours. I have organised for Rico to look after Simba. You and I are going to spend the night together in the luxurious suite of a beautiful hotel in central London, with one of the biggest beds I have ever seen. I picked the room myself after visiting a few places. An overnight bag is waiting for you there – with a selection of wigs you can chose from in the morning. I even planned a selection of underwear for you.'

'You mean 'for you', as you will be the one admiring and playing with them,' I commented, back under his charm.

'No, Carissima. I am your slave tonight.'

I lifted an eyebrow and pouted, playfully. His mind was working in a nice way, and mine was on the fast fantasising track.

Day 3 (Tuesday)

Harry, Zeno, Leila and I had another meeting with Sam and the CEO in the morning. Each entity had worked separately on the management plans for the Fog Dome. We compared our projects, made amendments and negotiated on the details. All the participants were relatively happy with how things were developing despite each group having to make compromises. Afterwards, the boys and I wrote a report on the situation for Gatekeepers Associates to share with all the Foggies, including McRae. None of us had heard a word from him since his disappearing act. Even Leila was in the dark. In Leo's opinion, McRae was just in his man cave to assess the situation; he would return soon, and then it wouldn't take long before Leila and he were an item. I wasn't so sure about that: Leila was very much on her guard when it came to Lochy McRae. Leo laughed at my comment and told me perseverance was key: he was the living proof of it. As he leaned towards me and took me in his arms, his kiss proved his point.

*

Sam was also in the dark about McRae. He was sleep-deprived and grumpy. The Scot had left him only a frustrating laconic voicemail that he was taking a break, without giving any more details. For Sam, his friend was getting into the bad habit of doing what he wanted and when he wanted, even though he supposedly had a job! As we didn't have any information to share on McRae's whereabouts, Sam mumbled something unclear and left to return to his office.

*

The spirit of the Foggies that afternoon was gloomy, at best. In Essex, Jack had still not woken up. His coma was stable, yet he could remain in this state for months or years. Putu had decided to approach international non-profit organisations to suggest the creation of a worldwide programme supporting the children affected by life-threatening viruses. She wanted them to get access to the Fog and get a chance to live. She added that she could come and run the programme from the Fog Dome if necessary. I thought of Mary in the WII Kenya and how she had only the temporary fogged tree house as a link to this world, and how, if Putu left, she would definitely be cut from coming back. She did not want this link for now, but who knows if she wouldn't change her mind in the future. But then, how would we know?

*

Ingis Chen tried to contact me, as well. I decided to ignore his calls and messages. Dealing with him meant additional stress. It was hardly surprising, even though very annoying, that he had contacted the CEO directly and tried to sneak into Fog business as usual. I was wary of his methods and ultimate purpose. In addition, Chen gave another televised public appearance. He expressed his satisfaction that the authorities finally made the right decision and listened to the people's wish. However, he conveyed his disappointment about the limited use of the Fog Gate. Chen urged them, and the 'maybe too cautious' Gatekeepers, to consider that everyone should be able to cross the Fog at will, and that more Fog Gates should be opened around the globe.

'Hopefully, the Fog Dome is the beginning of a new way to approach health treatment and life in general,' he declared. 'Soon, everyone will have a new chance in life. We are truly living in exceptional times. This is very exciting.' Ingis Chen spoke with enthusiasm. He announced the creation of a new international non-profit NGO – non-governmental organisation - called *Fog Positive*, to promote the use of the Fog worldwide for health, cultural, ecological and economic purposes, as well as support after relocation for those concerned. He had already approached the United Nations, the European Union and every relevant international structure for funding and partnerships with his Fog Positive. His venture was welcome. Everyone had an interest in it, as the spread of the current virus had proved: what happened in any given country - economic, political, religious or social - had a ripple effect everywhere in the world, without exception. The boys and I were acutely aware there was no avoiding Ingis Chen. He had already gained international stature when it came to defending and promoting the Fog. He was a very convincing preacher, presenting himself as a disinterested party whose aim was to help mankind. His ruthless side was unknown to the public.

*

The other strong personality gaining international prominence, with an opposite opinion on the Fog to Chen's, was Lally O'Maleigh. She declared herself horrified by the creation of this *monstrous door to pandemonium*. In her words, this was only encouraging the weak and wrongly-advised minds to escape the lives they were destined for here on earth, instead of accepting what was God's wish. It was a dismissal of reality for the promises of a utopian world without stress, failures or a disturbing past. It was an illusion. Individuals had to stop running away from problems, circumstantial, physical or psychological, and start facing and dealing with them. God had created and moulded our lives for us to go through a specific journey. God had predestined each of our fates. Trying to skip it by crossing the Devil's door was an aberration. She claimed that indeed the Fog was the work of the Devil as a pure temptation to ignore the will and path of God.

Listening to her public allocution, Ingis Chen appeared to me a lovely character, even knowing his despotic tendency behind the scenes. Extremist ideologies had never been attractive to me. I did not mind religious beliefs and opinions opposite to mine, as long as they respected the right of others to differ and avoided proselytising. There was no denying that some people should learn to face their problems, but did she have to involve the Devil into this? When a journalist in the audience asked her about the fate of the people affected with the Modern Marburg and if it wasn't our obligation as human beings to save our *brothers and sisters*, her answer was that the Fog consequences on health and people were unknown, and what might be an apparent healing could, in reality, be a worse plague for the body, mind and spirit than we could anticipate. Lowering her voice in a warning tone, she reminded the listener that when something was too good to be true, it was either not true, or no good. The Fog was either or both, she concluded.

According to Leila, Lally O'Maleigh had a wide appeal among Christians around the globe. The lack of comprehension and scientific knowledge on the Fog was to blame, as well as voluntary and involuntary misinformation. We were trying to correct the latter as much as possible, but it was difficult to control people's imagination.

*

In the afternoon, out of the first group of sick people crossing the Fog, 8 were relocated; a lower ratio than the odds permitted. The 8 men and women had been willing to take the risk, but had raised new and knotty issues: should the members of their families willing to cross be allowed to do so? Of course they should, though we had to set up limits. For lack of a better solution, we decided that only the nucleus family of the concerned person would be given the right to cross, in the sense of partner and children. Not the parents, not the cousin, not the best friends etc. Rico promptly enquired about the polyamorous, the polygamous and the likes, the separated but not divorced, the reconstructed families and more, until Harry interrupted him to say that each case would have to be reviewed specifically and decisions made on an ad-hoc basis as humanly as possible.

'No, no, no!' Jazz exclaimed when I told her Rico's reaction at dinner. My parents, Eudes and Ushi Tsou had gathered at *The Jazzin* for a family dinner, along with Jazz and Big Tom. Leo was back at the Essex house to help Dante on one of their ecological building projects.

'Dismiss complex families! Just dismiss them! Remember we already have a case like that with Christophe, Louise and Isabelle. That's enough for me, thank you very much!'

'How is the baby doing?' my mother asked, subtly changing subject.

'Chloé is doing fine, and the parents seem to get along okay. It is a bit complicated to keep Christophe a secret from the officials at the Essex house, though. On paper, Helo is their adopted child and this is why they both visit Isabelle and the baby, daily. However, Christophe can't go to WII either, as it would reveal the truth.'

'What about Louise? How is she coping with Christophe and Isabelle being back together? Because that is it - they are together, right?' Jazz asked.

'So much drama in all these relationships. One should not get attached and dependent on others that way. It is pathetic,' Ushi Tsou commented, before adjusting Eudes' napkin and helping him cut his meat, with great care and affection. I refrained from pointing out her actions were contradicting her words, sharing instead a glance with my mother. There was worry in her eyes. She still wasn't convinced that Ushi Tsou could look after Eudes.

'I think Louise should go with Dante,' Jazz continued, unperturbed by Ushi Tsou's interruption. 'They have a good connection. I can see it happening. They might need just that little push, you know. It is so complicated with the Fog, so a little push would help.'

'I am afraid to ask… What kind of little push?' I enquired, suspiciously.

'Something romantic. Like he should invite her for a picnic under the stars, or something like that,' she suggested.

'That would imply that he is interested, and you don't know that,' I pointed out.

'True, so maybe you could throw a picnic with Leo and those two in the woods by the house in Essex, and then in the middle you have a headache and you leave them to it. Yes, this is what you should do,' Jazz was getting all excited by her idea.

'Jazz, please don't start matching everybody around you… Who will be next? Nick? You just want to spread relationships around.' I shook my head.

'It's not what I am doing at all. I am just helping two lovebirds who are slow to realise they are made for each other. That is all. And I have always been good at match-making.' That was news to me but I kept my surprise to myself.

'What about Charles-Antoine? Any news?' my mother asked. I would have been grateful for this new change of subject if it had been a better one.

'Yes. He is demanding that I organise a right of entry for Ahmed and him and wants to follow the *Fog Positive* programme,' I replied.

'Ingis Chen's NGO? Does a programme exist already?' my father asked.

'Yes, that one. No, there is no programme yet. I said so to Charles-Antoine. However, I have asked Sam to help them come across. He IS Eudes' father.'

'And Ahmed?' my mother asked in a cold tone, supressing anger. I wasn't sure if it was against Ahmed or Charles-Antoine.

'Him, too. He is seriously sick, Maman. And they are officially a couple. Charles-Antoine proposed last week. If Ahmed has to die, Charles-Antoine wants to make sure they spend the rest of their time together as husband and… Well, husband and husband.'

'I presume that, if you ask, it will not be refused,' my mother said.

'No, it will not.'

Ushi Tsou and my mother shared the same look of pursed lips and narrowed eyes when Charles-Antoine was mentioned. They reminded me of two women ready to enter into battle.

Day 4 (Wednesday)

We waited as long as possible before sending Jack to hospital because doing so felt like an acknowledgement that his situation was going to last. The previous night, we could not postpone it any longer and he was transferred to a military hospital in a special section, where family and Foggies could visit. The staff settled him in a timeless bland room where he could stay for an indefinite time. Today, tomorrow, next week or next year: if he still had not woken up, this room and Jack would not change. He was barely in his twenties; the Fog, the coma, it was all so unfair! I also wondered why it was Jack whom, first with me and now with Christophe, was most affected. Why? Jack was generally weaker in body and mind than Christophe: could it be the reason?

Calling Jack's parents had not been easy. They had finally accepted that their son was not crazy about the Fog in view of the whole world talking about it. They had organised a visit and landed early in the morning. Now it would not be the happy reunion they expected. In addition to the sorrow, we also feared an angry reaction. Jack's parents had so far abided by his wish to keep his link to the Fog secret: they had now announced they had contacted the US Government and requested to have their son brought home to the United States. Needless to say, the US Government had immediately set the wheels in motion and demanded from the British that they release Jack on the spot. Sam had reached a new level of stress, Leila had started biting her nails and we were at a loss as to what to do next. I went to meet the parents at the hospital after an early breakfast, notably to warn them of the danger of keeping Jack away from the Fog for too long. There was also the risk that Jack could create the Fog again when he woke up (I wanted to believe he would). His parents insisted, nonetheless, that they wanted him back home by their side. Under cover of Gatekeepers Associates, the Society had offered to set up his old bedroom as a hospital room with a nurse on call to help at any time, as well as security outside their home. The Government would no doubt apply pressure to look after Jack itself, and then Jack's parents would lose control over their son's fate. They were not used to such attention. They were leading a simple life and all they wanted was their son back. They were also intimidated by me, as if I were a celebrity. It played in my favour. They accepted our offer of assistance to both supervise Jack's return to the US and for the home settlement. It was a big relief for us, not for the US officials. Jack would be repatriated the next day, Thursday. His Ftab would be sent separately and kept on hold by a Society member there, ready for Jack when he woke up. Again, we refused to use the word 'if'.

*

'We have to learn to detach ourselves from the Fog we create, especially you as a creator,' Harry told me during dinner. 'The Fog Dome is not our own. And you Yoko, you should only act to maintain it for the public's benefit and double-check it is not misused; that's it. Don't start pushing to oversee it as if it were your responsibility to supervise everything. Or else it will ruin your life.'

'I created it, I feel responsible!' I exclaimed.

'And that's why Gatekeepers Associates and the Society are monitoring it, both for the WII and the Relocated. What I mean is that you must try and stop being too emotionally involved,' Leila continued where Harry had stopped.

'Now, I think if the United Nations decide to take over, we don't stand a chance,' Harry concluded.

The world was still in the grip of the Modern Marburg virus, so the leaders of our world had decided it was time to meet with the United Nations Organisation to discuss how they should ally to fight the spread of the disease. The United Kingdom had immediately come under pressure to give wider access to the Fog Dome. Now, in a confidential meeting, the British representative advocated that the Fog Dome was a joint venture with the CEO's company and Gatekeepers Associates, in an effort to create a balanced entity benefitting from the experiences from both the private and public sector. They did not have full control of the Fog Dome. They also put forward our arguments that the Fog should be limited to a strict need-to-cross basis, to control numbers.

This I learned later, when Sam made an impromptu appearance in my office, looking manic and begging me to join the video-conference to speak with the leaders of the most powerful countries in the world. It was just before lunch. I was at my desk, attempting to juggle between the work to be done for the online Inter-World University, the Fog Dome monitoring structure and other pending matters of Gatekeepers Associates. When Sam explained the reason for his sudden visit, I was awe-struck. Was he really suggesting that at such a last minute, unprepared, I was to defend our position to the key decision-makers on the planet? My immediate reaction was to say no; I was not ready. Sam looked down for a while, just standing there in front of me. Then he spoke.

'Yoko. You have to do this. This is part of your job now. I know you are scared, but you need get over it.'

'I am not ready! I… I would do more damage than good!'

'You will do fine. Be yourself, share your belief, speak with passion, keep it simple.'

He took out his laptop from a briefcase and set it up on the table, connecting it to a secure governmental network.

'Now? You are joking! You won't even let me have 5 minutes to gather my thoughts?' I told him.

'Yoko, you already have all the arguments in your head. They are waiting. And the quicker I am to connect you, the better chance I have to keep my job, and my boss's too.'

'What? Why?' I asked him, surprised.

'Let's just say the Government doesn't find us very efficient in convincing you to do what they want or, in other words, to impede you in doing whatever takes your fancy at any given time.'

*

I didn't have a chance to comment as the call connected. My hair was in a bundled mess on top of my head, I wore no make-up and had on a casual summer top with white trousers. I wasn't even sure whether I had any food between my teeth. I froze in front of the screen as a group of about 15 people stared back at me with a mixture of expectancy, curiosity and misgivings. Leila explained later they were the 15 Members of the UN Security Council, gathered in an "Arria-formula meeting". These were the Security Council members' informal and confidential meetings, allowing them to exchange their views openly between themselves, and enabling them to invite an external person to speak when it was believed to be beneficial for their decision-making. And how important were their executive powers! The Security Council was at the core of the maintenance of international peace and security, and under the UN Charter, all Member States were obligated to comply with Council decisions. In this case, there was no evident threat to peace or act of aggression, other than if the virus was the aggressor. The matter fell into another of their duties: *to develop friendly relations among nations; to cooperate in solving international problems and in promoting respect for human rights; and to be a centre for harmonising the actions of nations.*

Without knowing those details at the time, I was still highly intimidated and feeling out of my league. I clasped my hands together and muttered a weak 'Good morning' – it was afternoon. Harry, Zeno and Rico arrived hurriedly for moral support. Sam had kindly messaged them for me. As the British Member outlined the reasons for their meeting and briefly introduced the purpose of the Security Council for my benefit, Rico quickly prepared some coffee to give me a boost. As it contained whisky, it certainly gave me a jolt! I answered a few questions, my confidence slowly building. Zeno stood behind the laptop, drawing a smile with his fingers for me to give them one. I did and it helped. I began pleading my case.

'Ladies and Gentlemen,

As the British Representative has already kindly and accurately summarised the specificities of the Fog Dome and the existence of the Other World, I will not linger on the subject. As you know, the people crossing and being relocated can receive only limited help from this side of the door. Yes, our technology is developing fast and we will find ways to broaden the range of our help rapidly. Yet when the doors close, they will again be separated from us for another two centuries and will then have to fend for themselves. However, the locals can help, now and when the Fog disappears. We are lucky that in England, the local population of WII welcomed us gracefully: this was not the case in Mexico, as I am sure you know.'

'Miss Salelles, we understand and agree. We have no wish to alienate the inhabitants of this WII. We aim only to save as many lives as possible in this world by enabling a large number to cross,' one of the Members commented.

'This could lead to an invasion de facto, and the Other World is not ours to invade,' I insisted.

'We are not invading: we are giving people here another chance,' the same

Member of the Council politely corrected me.

I closed my eyes for a split second and smiled at what he had just said.

'Sir, of course I agree that we must save the people from this world. It would make sense to just let anyone and everyone cross if so they wish. And yet - yet it is wrong in many ways. You see, humankind has always had a tendency to look for an immediate solution, brushing away the long-term effects of their decisions. For example, how will you organise for the sick to travel without affecting more people around them? How will you help thousands and thousands of people once they have crossed? What will be their status with you as Relocated? Expats? Expats to where? Let's not forget also that another tendency of humankind is to think of themselves as the centre of the Universe. Sending people, in their thousands, to another world and helping them settle as comfortably as possible, using our technology, our knowledge, habits and customs is all very well, but some people already live there with their customs, their way of thinking, their traditions. Haven't we learnt anything from history? Doesn't it remind you of colonialism and imperialism? I said that the Other World is not ours to invade, because this is very close to what we would be doing; the same way we did with Australia, America, Africa...'

'This is not the same,' another Member interrupted. 'We are not doing it for economic or political purpose but for survival. The crossing to the Other World is the unfortunate consequence for one out of seven of the people whose lives will be saved.'

'We want to save as many people as possible: this is why we have created the Fog Dome,' I insisted. 'We just wish to ensure the crossing will be monitored appropriately, limited as a last option for those concerned, and taking into account the respect we owe to WII and its people. This planet might be similar to ours: this is still another planet the details of which we know nothing of. We strongly believe the crossing of the Fog should be a last resort; the last chance for anyone affected by a lethal virus. Traditional and modern medicine should continue to be our main defence against diseases and plagues affecting animals and human beings.'

I paused for effect, then continued just as another member of the council was about to speak. 'We fear that the Fog will be seen and used as a miraculous solution when it might just be a Band-Aid, covering deeper problems underneath. The limits we have put in place, enforcing a controlled crossing, are bound to evolve and adapt in practice. If there is one thing we have learned in the past 6 months, it is that we must remain flexible and open-minded when it comes to the Fog. We must think outside the box because, in our case, there is no box. Using what resourcefulness and ethos we have, we act for what we hope to be the best for everyone. We have made and will make mistakes, but we aim to limit them. This is why we are proceeding with caution on Fog crossing from this world and wish to respect the people of that world. Discovering the Fog and the world out there is a journey, and we are walking it one step at a time.'

'We should really name that other planet...' a Member commented, pensively.

'Should *WE*, or should we allow the locals this privilege?' I asked, unable to mask the sarcasm in my remark.

*

At dinner, I shivered at the memory of my virtual encounter with the UN Security Council. It confounded me that my life could have changed so much in such a short time: me, invited (or forced) to speak to a secret meeting of representatives of the almighty countries of the planet. However, it was so impersonal that it weighed less on my mind than the individual issues of the Foggies and their relatives. One of them was Charles-Antoine. The UK had granted him and his partner, Ahmed, a pass to come to London. They would arrive tomorrow and come to *The Jazzin* immediately, killing two birds with one shot: crossing the Fog for healing and seeing Eudes. My mother and father insisted they should be there and that Ahmed was not to meet Eudes. Ushi insisted she must be there, too, to comfort Eudes if needed. Jazz insisted she had to attend as well, to ensure the security of Charles-Antoine, in case Ushi tried to kill him for potentially claiming the child back if the father turned out Relocated. Big Tom was adamant he would not leave Jazz in an explosive situation. Nick jumped in and asserted he must be present for my protection and

Eudes'. Then Rico declared he would come because he didn't want to miss the show.

*

In Nevada, things were not rosy for the Koplats and Elsie either. With the Koplats' return to their own home, the US government had demanded to have access to their men in WII. After consulting the Indian Council, the American men were allowed to return to the house, wearing only a cloth covering their groin and bottom to ensure they would return unarmed. From what Elsie described by email, it was quite a sight. The American soldiers had complied somewhat unhappily, dreading meeting their former peers in such attire. Thanks to Elsie, they were getting used to the customs and life with the WII natives. They slowly understood that their survival in WII was linked to their respect and adaptability to the ways of this WII land, even if keeping their links with the army and the government would also be an asset for them in their new lives. The US government also asked to meet Elsie as a US Citizen. She refused, stating that she was now a member of the WII Indian tribe and had no order from them to receive. She would only comply as a porte-parole for the natives, with immunity as Foreign Ambassador and a promise they would not detain her in the house or impede her return back to her new homeland. The US Government reluctantly complied. When Elsie crossed the Koplats' threshold, Michelle threw herself into the woman's arms and cried out of happiness to see her. Immediately, Sophia had pursed her lips as a sign of her dislike for the Society's psychiatrist. The instant bond between her stepdaughter and Elsie had been a thorn in her side since the start, especially as Elsie was not siding with her opinion on the girl.

The Koplats found it difficult to adjust to having to deal with the authorities. For the time being, their return home had to be kept secret while they were getting organised. Adam was shocked on setting foot in their house: their home was not theirs anymore. Adam, putting Michelle's safety and future first, had decided that they ought to keep out of the public eye until they got settled. He also wanted to observe how things were evolving in London and learn from it. The US Government was delighted, not being ready (or keen) for a public Fog Dome-Gate yet. As pressure around the Modern Marburg was mounting, they were increasingly finding ways to prevent facing the public's demands. As for the Koplats, they wanted to act, like us in London and whatever the Government would decide. The Foggies were on a mission!

*

'At least everything, as usual, is going well for Tony, Rosario and Mitch in Alaska,' Harry commented at dinner. 'They are the only ones who have been able to live their lives with the Fog, avoiding chaos and drama. So far.'

'This gives us all hope,' Rico added.

'Hope for what?' Harry asked. 'It's too late for us, I am afraid. Not only that, but they don't have to deal with the Relocated and WII natives.'

'Damn,' I scowled, my mind brought back to the issue of Clémence's Revolution. She was more active than ever and continuing to raid local farms, recruiting women and children and terrorising those unwilling to join. We still had no news from Owen, much to the distress of his father and sister. I was also concerned for Jazz, now at the forefront of local politics in a context of civil war. She was in constant danger.

'You have to keep your head strong about that, too,' Harry said. He had sensed where my mind had wandered.

'Why not talk about something a bit more cheerful?' Rico intervened, with a telling naughty glint in his eyes. 'Any bawdy details to share on your reconciliation with Leo? Because really, you are the only one who is getting some, so you should at least be nice and entertain us.'

I shot him a mischievous look that told him more than words about my being 100% satisfied. That was all the detail he was going to get.

Dante, Leo and Zeno had been invited to Newtonsee for a business meeting regarding trading between the two worlds, including a discussion on how to improve the efficiency of their fishing boats. Dante was fast becoming a source of expertise on anything structural, despite not knowing anything about ships a few months back. For the purpose of research, the three men would sleep in town, waking up at dawn to go on a fishing trip. The idea of the three crossers sleeping in WII with limited protection, just as the tension and skirmishes with the Women's Revolution Movement were getting increasingly violent, kept me awake. Sharing my bed with Simba, I was watching TV shows online in my reduced portion of the bed in the middle of the night. This is when the explosion occurred.

Day 5 (Thursday)

The loud and sudden sound of the blast, in the peace of the night, made my heart skip a beat. The wall shook strongly and I sat in bed, frozen for a second, struggling to comprehend what was happening. Simba was immediately alert and growling. Another explosion roared on top of us and the whole house convulsed, paintings fell from the walls and my night table light died. Simba howled and I finally jumped out of bed. Simba joined me by the door, pushing me outside. Harry was shouting for help from the floor above. I ran to him. He was on the standing, trying to push open the door to Rico's quarters. The door was slightly ajar but the frame had suffered in the blast, blocking the door. Harry was too big to go through the opening. People were shouting downstairs and running footsteps indicated people coming up. It all happened in seconds. Harry and I looked at each other.

'Let me pass!' I urged Harry.

'Yoko, no! It's too dangerous!' he exclaimed. I had already squeezed myself inside, Simba following me, before he finished his sentence,.

My whole body shivered as I walked into the bedroom. The ceiling had completely collapsed and the bed had disappeared under its rubble. Rico! Another piece of the ceiling fell in a crash in the middle of the room, a few steps ahead. Simba was walking carefully in front of me when she suddenly stopped and turned, rushing and jumping on me. As she did, she pushed me back towards the door and I fell backwards. In a blur, I saw Rico's wardrobe collapse where I had stood, seconds before.

'Oh my God!' I whispered.

'Yoko! Yoko, are you all right!' Harry shouted, his voice full of fear.

'Yes! I am fine!' I exclaimed, turning to see him watching from the opening of the door. Sam had kneeled and was watching from below, too.

'Yoko, don't move! We are bringing wood beams to support the frame of this door and then we will axe our way through. Just don't move.'

Simba's attention had turned behind me. She made a throaty yelp and started towards Rico's studio. I turned and followed, a surge of hope filling me.

'Yoko! Stay where you are!' Harry shouted. I ignored him.

Simba was sniffing around the studio. Again, large pieces of the ceiling had fallen, but to a lesser extent than the bedroom. Colourful canvases stuck out between chunks of cement. Part of the external wall had collapsed, too, turning a corner of the room into a mess of bricks, wood and paints. I was looking around only for a sign of Rico. Simba rushed in and found him under several canvases, his face white, a mask of death. I hurried next to him and took his face in my hands. They turned white, too. Rico was covered in white paint. I quickly took his pulse and checked for signs of breathing. When I felt his heartbeat under my fingers, I slowly moved some of the canvas and saw that he did not seem harmed. I checked his head, cautiously passing my fingers through his hair. I felt a big bump with a gash. My hands came out red and white, from blood and paint. I looked around and saw a fragment of beam with blood on it not far from his head. It must have fallen on Rico and knocked him out.

'I found him!' I shouted to the others. 'He's been hit on the head. He's unconscious!'

'Don't move him!' a male voice I didn't know commanded. 'We'll be inside in a few minutes.'

I stayed by Rico, staring at his white face, oblivious to the sounds around me. I was vaguely aware of creaks coming from the unstable structure of the whole floor, or the sound of the work being done to support the door frame. Soon, two men with a stretcher entered the room and took Rico away. I went with them, Simba by my side. Outside, Phil was arguing with members of the government security that he would take us away to a secure location, not them. As he said so, a helicopter landed in the parking area.

'What is this? I haven't authorised any landing,' Sam scowled.

'I have,' Leila stepped in and grabbed my arm.

Members of the Society's security had stopped the medics carrying Rico, and Leila asked me if we agreed to all go to the emergency retreat, where there was also a care unit for Rico. The emergency procedure was set up so long ago, I had forgotten all about it.

'Jazz! I need to go check on Jazz and Eudes!' I burst out.

'They are fine, but their house has been hit as well... And... Big Tom is badly hurt.'

'Oh my God! No! I must go to Jazz.'

'There is nothing you can do for her right now. She insisted that you leave immediately.'

Harry was holding me back. I could not abandon Jazz and Eudes. An ambulance drove through the opened door of the Fog area. They couldn't take Big Tom to the hospital in this world, but they could bring medical attention to him in the house. While I looked, Leila had dialed Jazz and she handed me the phone.

'You must go!' Jazz said to me in an urgent tone.

'Jazz, are you ok? Is Eudes fine? I heard about Big Tom, how is he?' I pushed on.

'He... No, Yoko, we will talk about it later. You must go. Now! I couldn't bear it if something happened to you too. Go!' she hung up.

I was still very shaken and determined to go to her. My friend and nephew needed me. But so did Rico.

'Rico might need more than a basic care unit. He needs to go to hospital, and we can't let him go alone,' I told Leila.

'We can't abandon Rico,' Harry said, joining my side.

'Of course. You are right. I will go with him,' Leila said. 'Please be reasonable. This is a deliberate attack against you. We must proceed with the plan and get you to a safe location. I will bring him to safety as soon as possible, but you must go. You won't be able to help him by putting yourself in danger. Playing hero serves no purpose here.'

Harry and I looked at her, distraught at the decision to be made. Harry took me by the shoulders and turned me towards the helicopter.

'She is right. Come. It's what he would want. It is what you or I would expect from the unharmed if we were him. Come.'

Begrudgingly, I followed him and got inside the helicopter with Simba.

We flew over town to a landing spot, where we got into a discreet car to drive to a secret location. There, Leila called and explained what had happened.

*

There was a strong protection around Gatekeepers' block of houses in Central London. Radars, video camera surveillance, motion alarm; we had all kinds of electronics to ensure our safety. They were monitored 24/7 by the Society and by the Government, each for their own systems (although the Society was also checking the Government, to be sure). What nobody was doing was simply looking up at the sky. In the middle of a cloudy night, unnoticed by anyone, two hot air balloons went cruising in the dark sky. The hot air balloons kept to a certain height to avoid being spotted. When above the houses, one after the other, they launched rockets on the Fog houses and the one next to them. They had only one shot at it before the force of each would make them deviate considerably. The immediate security reaction was to shoot them down, killing the men inside. The government could not interrogate them. Some of the houses neighbouring ours, notably those opposite *The Jazzin* back garden, had suffered from the blast as well. They had been requisitioned by the army for their strategic positions and were mostly used by day. There had been no deaths among the few men and women in the neighbouring house that night, though three had been sent to hosptial with serious injuries. Out of everyone, Big Tom had suffered the most.

*

Harry, Louise, Helo and I settled in the living room of a little house somewhere near the river Thames in Richmond, on the south-west edge of London. It was dawn. The stress of the events, combined with tiredness, made us look like freshly unearthed zombies. Despite his protest, I picked up Helo and put him to bed. He fell asleep within seconds. Harry, Louise and I were the only other Foggies who had been home in London or in Essex and who were being evacuated here. Rico was in hospital; Leo, Dante and Zeno in Newtonsee in WII; Christophe had opted to go to safety in WII to stay with his wife and child in a house not far from the Essex house. Even though the Essex house did not have an immediate threat, it was on high alert, so he could not stay inside. When Christophe disappeared from the house without exiting to our world, British Intelligence understood he was a Foggy. Christophe was now on the authority's radar. For him, it didn't matter. He was in adoration of his baby girl and would do anything for her. The birth of his daughter had changed the man irremediably. Chloé came first. However, things were not always easy with Isabelle.

*

During the car journey, Jazz and I had talked on the phone. I felt terrible not to be with her when she was going through such a traumatic time. Big Tom and Jazz had been asleep in bed when the roof collapsed in the room next to theirs. Big Tom had taken her in his arms as she looked around sleepy and stunned, and dropped her on the landing of the stairs. He then went to investigate what had happened, urging Jazz to stay where she was. Unfortunately, the second explosion occurred on top of *The Jazzin* at that moment, shaking the house and causing more parts of the ceiling and roof to collapse on Big Tom. Jazz screamed when she heard the crash and rushed to the room to see Big Tom on the floor, with heavy slabs of cement over him. Blood was spreading everywhere around him. She had tried to move the heavy debris off his body but lacked the strength. She ran to get Nick, who was already coming through the front door. The medical team arrived at an impressive speed. It was a small team, but they managed to free him and bring him downstairs. Minutes afterwards, the ceiling of the main bedroom caved in. Jazz admitted she had to take it upon herself not to collapse and beg me to come. She did not want to have the two individuals closest to her in danger under a targeted house. Big Tom's state was still critical. I had to go and see her as soon as possible.

*

Drained, Louise, Harry and I were stunned by the latest event.

'What now?' Louise asked.

'I don't know,' Harry said, a cup of tea in hand. 'We should get some sleep.'

'I couldn't possibly sleep after this!' I said to him.

'I suggest we each go and lie down a little. That won't do us harm,' Harry persisted.

I slept like a log, hugging Simba.

*

Rico was awake. He had neither concussion nor trauma, and wanted coffee. His whole body ached from bruises and from the cut on his head, but he was told there would not be any long-term damage. As he lay in his private room in the hospital, we chatted via Ftab video call. He told us how he could not get to sleep the night before, awakened by the idea that if there was one alternative planet like earth, there could be more than one. What if a door opened to a planet where, in a role reversal, the population was technologically more advanced? What if, for *that* door, they were the ones who could come through in millions, and not us towards them? We would be the ones invaded then, wouldn't we?

'Were you thinking about this before or after you were hit on the head?' Harry asked him.

'Ha-ha. Very funny,' Rico said, before brushing away the comment. 'Yoko, maybe this is something you should say to the public. Just to make them think a little that if the roles were reversed, they would not like a rush of newcomers from another planet coming through.'

It was not a bad idea and I made a mental note of it.

Rico had not yet seen the damage but there was no doubt his loss of art was great. Many of his canvases, on which he had worked so hard over the years, had been shredded. He forgot all about it when he heard about Big Tom. On the ground floor of *The Jazzin*, his condition was critical. He was unconscious and his body was slowly shutting down.

Leila joined the video and tried to change the subject. Focusing on our security, she told us preparations to clean the rubble and render the houses safe again had already begun. She recommended that we did not move to the Essex house, as it would be difficult to keep it out of the public spotlight for long if we were all there. An alternative was to move to a secure location close to the Fog Dome. The government was already working on ways to accommodate the affluence of newly Relocated in the long term. They also had to handle how to organise visits from their close ones. Prices for buying or renting in the area were rocketing. In WII, the Fog Dome was much further away from Lil'London, yet still well located between that town,

Newtonsee and Yerushaleim. With the Fog Dome offering the possibility for the immediate relatives to come and visit, most of the new WII inhabitants would want to stay nearby. The Relocated of Woodfellas might wish to move to the vicinity of the Fog Dome, as well, including Jazz. Business-wise, it made sense: she would have a growing number of customers over there. Not that it mattered at the time. Everything was on hold for her, as Big Tom had not regained consciousness. Worse, the team battling to save his life had little hope of victory. He needed to be in hospital and could not be.

'What would happen to the two Fog houses in the terraced houses?' Rico asked.

'They would return to normal in 7 weeks or so,' Leila replied.

'It will be quite impersonal, no? Living so close to this big hub of activity, of crossing, businesses, emotional dramas etc. Like having home and office in the middle of a train station,' Rico thought out loud.

'When you put it like that… Especially when we only need to be there one Saturday in seven,' I said, pensively. A new thought was burgeoning.

'Well, Gatekeepers and the Society will need offices by the Fog Dome for supervision,' Leila commented. 'I could look into getting a building or structure to accommodate you, as well. It makes sense. Then we will try to recoup the cost – for you and the Society – by renovating your houses and selling them later. If you wish, of course.'

'I don't know…' Rico continued. 'Isn't the Fog Dome an even bigger target for attack? It's also difficult to miss.'

We heard a door open and shut, some footsteps, two hands carrying take-away cups of coffee for Rico and Leila, before seeing the smug smile of McRae on screen.

'Hello,' he said cheerily. 'Missed me?'

'Hey! McRae. Welcome back,' Harry greeted the Scot.

'Good morning, Lochy. Nice to have you back,' I said, with genuine pleasure to see him. He winked at me.

'Hello, Mr McRae,' Louise told him, more formally. She had seen him only once, virtually, on Sunday's online Board Meeting.

'Hello. Louise, isn't it? Nice to see you online again. You can call me Lochy.

That's the name lassies tend to prefer,' he said with his charmed turned on maximum. Leila rolled her eyes and took a sip of coffee. McRae gave her a tender kiss on the temple. They looked good together.

*

McRae had called Leila early in the morning to check if she was in London and to invite her on a date. She had informed him of the attacks and he had rushed to the hospital. Sam's reception had been colder when the latter arrived, informed of his colleague's presence by the team on site. McRae's disappearance without notice was unprofessional, then to contact Gatekeepers Associates first, as Sam saw it, was also unacceptable. The agent sensed McRae's loyalty was shifting and he was right. McRae explained that he felt responsible for Jack's fate and needed some time alone. Sam didn't accept this explanation easily and he and McRae had a major bust-up. It was a very public argument: Harry and I witnessed it in person at the hospital, late morning. Jack and Rico were in the same hospital, and we had insisted we come to visit. As Sam and McRae launched into a shouting match, Leila, Harry and I were spectators. It was soon obvious that Sam's resentment was not all professional. He was worried for his friend and felt personally betrayed. When McRae realised this, he stopped shouting and went to his friend to give him a big hug. That silenced Sam but did not appease him. He just stared and scowled at McRae, then turned on his heels and left.

*

McRae then told us that he had gone to Scotland to recharge and review his situation. He had re-read his notes on Facilitators. He already knew the pros and cons of being a Facilitator prior to learning he had become one. The question was, could he continue to work for the Secret Service? Should he not be independent from the Society as well?

'Joining Gatekeepers Associates is enough,' Rico suggested. 'You don't have to join the Society: we already work together.'

'Technically, we even work for you,' Leila remarked.

'I disagree. We are working willingly together, with common interests,' I told her. 'You told us long ago that should our interests diverge or should you disagree with us, you would stop supporting us.'

'True,' she admitted.

'Thomas Lochlan Alastair McRae, Associate Facilitator for Gatekeepers Associates: that will look good on your business cards,' Rico joked.

'You have business cards?' McRae asked, bemused.

'No, we don't,' I laughed. 'And for us you will be Lochy McRae, Fellow Foggy Facilitator.'

'So I could be with Gatekeepers Associates, and do some consultant work for the British Government and Secret Services,' McRae continued.

'Yes, you could. Although there is no doubt you will lose access to their resources,' I told him.

'But you will gain ours. The Society's are not too bad, either,' Leila said.

'That I noticed!' McRae exclaimed. 'Right. It confirmed my conclusions. I might be a bit of a maverick but I'd rather not be a double agent. And the first person I will break the news to is Sam.'

*

McRae went to find Sam to reveal the truth. We heard afterwards that Sam was shocked, finding it hard to accept his friend's new situation or why it had happened to him. So far, all the Foggies on a given location had some kind of strong prior connection, either through family or friendship. McRae did not. Maybe we would find one later, or maybe this would just be added to the list of the mysterious ways of the Fog. The two men left to meet with their boss, but only after McRae had secured a date with Leila in the evening.

Meanwhile, Leo, Dante and Zeno had got back home to the London house and were told there was no Facilitator on site to help them back to WI. They arrived as the house was in crisis. The medics' fight to save Big Tom was in vain: Jazz's boyfriend was dying. In a last desperate effort, Zeno and Nick had left right away to get Ariel Ben-Chaim, in the hope that the wise man and apothecary might be able to save him with some alternative healthcare. This was not to be. Big Tom died within 15 minutes of their departure. Nothing and no one could prevent me going to *The Jazzin* now. Jazz was suffering! She was like a sister to me, and me to her. It wasn't open to discussion: I had to be by her side. To protect Simba's secret, it was decided that McRae would join me there to help as Facilitator. The meeting with his boss was cut short.

*

Big Tom's lifeless body was lying on a medical bed in the living room, covered with a white sheet. Jazz had her arms wrapped around his torso, crying. Ariel Ben-Chaim was there with Leo, Dante, Zeno and Nick. Ushi was with Eudes and the Fishers outside in Woodfellas, staying away to respect Jazz's privacy. The same went for the medics and everyone else from the Society or the Secret Services. Ariel came to talk to me before I approached Jazz. He told me he had prepared a special concoction to calm her nerves and help her sleep. I walked to Jazz and wrapped myself around her in the same way she was embracing Big Tom. She wailed and cried his name. Jazz turned and fell into my arms. Her body shook from weeping. We stayed in this position for a long time, until I felt her strength had drained to the point she was going to collapse. I slowly moved her towards the sofa, almost holding her in my arms. She was still weeping uncontrollably, my poor friend. I gave Ariel a glance for him to bring me his preparation. He left it in a mug on the side table.

'Jazz, my dear Jazz, I am so sorry. So, so, so sorry,' I said.

'Why Yoko? Why? He was so kind. Such a big softie teddy bear on the inside,' Jazz said amid tears. 'A real marshmallow core!… I loved him, Yoko. I really did. I lost everything else but had found love, and this was taken from me, too. I wish it was me who had gone, not him. Not him…'

'Please don't say that. It was an accident…'

She interrupted me before I finished my sentence.

'It wasn't an accident! They killed him! Those bastards, whoever they are, they killed him! You will find who did this, won't you?' She grabbed my shoulders. 'Promise me you will find those motherfuckers and make them pay! Promise me!'

'Of course we will,' I replied, my mood vacillating between sorrow for my friend and rage against who had done this to her, against who had killed Big Tom. Underneath his rough exterior and despite his mobster connections, he was a good man. I couldn't believe what had happened.

'Here, drink this,' I pushed the mug towards her gently, feeling foolish. Drinking was certainly the last thing she could care about right now.

'Thanks.'

She took a sip and winced.

'It's a kind of soothing herbal tea prepared by Ariel,' I told her.

'Do me a favour: add whisky to this. Or cognac. Whatever can make this drinkable and knock me out as well!' She glanced at Big Tom's body and added in a whisper. 'Oh my God. I can't believe it. I just… My Tommy bear…'

Her throat blocked. I took the mug from her hands and put one hand on her thorax, telling her to inhale and exhale slowly. Her eyes were a pool of grief and panic as she struggled to take a breath. Zeno rushed to our side with a small paper bag for her to breathe into. It helped. We took her outside for a short walk, Harry following with the mug in which he had added whisky. We led her to Nick's small cabin where she was to stay the night: the house was just not safe enough. Alone with Jazz, I helped her undress and get into bed. She finished Ariel's special herbal tea. As I lay next to her, she nestled against me and continued sobbing. She asked me for a sleeping pill. I was not keen on those and neither was she, but these were extraordinary circumstances.

'I will ask Zeno to get one. He's outside. I will be back in one second.'

'No! Don't leave me! Don't leave me. Please,' she begged. I knocked at the window until Zeno came rushing in. I whispered Jazz's request to him and he disappeared, only to reappear a few minutes later with a box of pills. I gave one to Jazz. Twenty minutes later, she was sleeping like a baby.

I wished I could take one as well, but I still had pressing matters. Like dealing with Charles-Antoine who kept calling me. He was alarmed that no one would let Ahmed and him through the Fog. They had arrived at the appointed time hours ago, but they were unable to meet anyone and were concerned by my silence, as well as angry to be cast aside as non-important. However, along with my parents, they were shown the destruction of the houses next door: the four of them then understood how grave the situation was. Part of me felt it was wrong to make the two men cross in this moment of mourning: the other part just wanted to get rid of this chore. Charles-Antoine insisted they would only be a few minutes and would come back the next day to spend more time with Eudes. In the end, he wore me out. Tired of arguing, I gave up and acquiesced to his request. Ahmed looked very poorly, and I had to admit his appearance also made me bend to the couple's plea.

*

My parents, Charles-Antoine, Ahmed and I had arrived together and Ushi was waiting for me with my nephew. Big Tom's body was in the fogged storage house used for the inter-world trading, in one of the cold rooms. Jazz and his mother would decide later how to proceed with the funeral. Eudes recognised his father immediately and was at first ecstatic with joy to see him. Shortly after though, he returned to hold Ushi's hand, now the cornerstone of his life. Within minutes, Ahmed looked visibly healthier and Charles-Antoine was beaming to see his son. Whatever we thought of his attitude towards Julia, he loved the child. The difficulty started when the couple crossed back, as Ahmed came out in the forest clearing. Somehow, even though the chances of it happening were almost 15%, they did not think it could happen to them.

People never think it can happen to them.

This created a brand new set of problems, as Charles-Antoine immediately suggested he should move next to the Fog so that he could come and visit Eudes and his husband-to-be every day. Then he implied that Ahmed should be looking after Eudes. Ushi had immediately tightened her grip on Eudes' hand and instinctively, the toddler asked her to pick him up. Charles-Antoine flinched and said he would take his son. Ushi retorted that the child had asked her, not him. The father came forward, upset, arguing that Eudes was his son and he was the one who would choose who picked him up and who would look after him. Ushi argued that he could go to hell, Eudes had picked her as his new carer, and anyone in their way would meet their maker earlier than they hoped. Charles-Antoine was taken aback at the strength of the threat, even more so when announced calmly and coldly in a tone that sent shivers down my spine. It was not an empty threat. Ahmed scowled during the whole exchange. The rising animosity and tension in the room was palpable, and the mechanic was obviously uncomfortable with his role in it.

Ahmed was a tall and good looking young French man of North African origin, with hair cut short and aquiline features. He was fit and lean, without the camp attitude some gay men might have, like Jack. He was about to say something when my father intervened between Ushi and Charles-Antoine, who remained dangerously too close to Ushi. I would not have bet on him to win in close combat against the well-trained mercenary. Maybe Dad knew this, too. Ushi took this opportunity to say she had had enough and swiftly went through the door with Eudes, leaving for WII where Charles-Antoine could not go. He tried, forgetting for a minute the strange situation he was in. He came rushing back, asking Ahmed to go and get his son back. Ahmed hesitated and bitterly remarked that maybe it was not the time just then, and that it would be nice of Charles-Antoine to think about his partner, too. Indeed, Ahmed was glad to be healthy again, but he had lost his normal life in the process and just then, his partner did not seem to care. Even if he understood how Eudes could monopolise his father's thoughts, Ahmed's bitterness was now switching to indignation. He declared he had no wish to antagonise from the start the people he was going to live with from now on, including Ushi Tsou. He was also upset that Charles-Antoine made plans for what he wanted, but did not consult him first. What about their wedding? What about their life together? Could they really be a couple two worlds apart when they could only meet in one house, and not even theirs? Also Ahmed protested that he might not want to look after Eudes alone! The last comment left Charles-Antoine speechless. Ahmed added that it was one thing to help care for Eudes at home with Charles-Antoine by his side, it was something else to be in charge of a child he had never met before in a foreign land, with a life to build from scratch. Ahmed insisted that he did not say he would not, just that he was fed up with Charles-Antoine not taking his feelings into consideration. Ahmed loved Charles-Antoine and knew it was reciprocated. He was very grateful his husband-to-be had managed to make him cross the Fog and thus saved his life. Yet, Ahmed was put in a brand new situation. He still had to appraise all the ramifications of his relocation. It was one thing to read articles in the press, interviewing the newly Relocated, to watch the TV reports of their families and more; it was another to live it. Charles-Antoine was tongue-tied when his partner went through his long monologue. By the end of it, both had tears in their eyes and Ahmed went to hug my ex-brother-in-law and kissed him.

Afterwards, Ahmed left to be introduced to the Woodfellas inhabitants. It would take some time for both of them for the new situation to sink in.

Charles-Antoine did not stay in the house either, as the damage and risks caused by the explosion needed to be assessed. The couple planned to meet later that day and Nick would serve as liaison officer for now.

*

While this new drama was unrolling, the Members of Lil'London Council had arrived, along with Maud and Barbara. They had come as soon as they had heard from their watchmen about the bombing and Big Tom's death, and had waited patiently outside. Barbara Snayth was just doing her duty as far as I could tell, while Maud experienced real sadness. She knew everyone at Woodfellas and had grown close to Jazz in their partnership to fight for the better fate of women in their community. Maud was sorry not to see Jazz, who was sound asleep. She had brought some homemade pie, apologising that she had done it at the last minute and it might not be her best. She longed to try and bring some comfort to Jazz in her distress. Augustus Hoare was also distraught at Big Tom's death. Nick, Big Tom and he had built an unlikely friendship over the past months, based on their love of boxing. They often went for drinks afterwards. It made me notice I had not seen much of Nick since the morning. All my attention had been on Jazz, forgetting that Nick had lost the one real friend he had in this world: a Relocated, like him.

Edmund Poff and Augustus Hoare came to visit regularly due to the personal bond they had created with some Woodfellas people, so they were not as surprised as the Snayths by our little hamlet's development and recent increase in population. We now had a long row of large wooden houses, with signal boosters for the Internet and mobile phones through the Fog, as well as quads by the side of each. The clearing saw goats, cows, horses, ducks, dogs and cats roaming around, except in a protected area dedicated to vegetable gardens. Unable to have a meeting inside the Fog house, we sat around a large table outside *The Jazzin*. Hearing the visitors express their condolences brought me close to tears. It felt strange to be the receiver of sympathies for the loss of Big Tom, as so far I had focused on giving solace to Jazz. The compassion hit me hard. I liked Big Tom and would miss him too. Clenching my jaw to keep composure and hold back the tears, I swallowed with difficulty the ball of pain and anger rising in my throat. They were curious about the attack and I explained the chain of events to them: how Rico had been injured and how Big Tom had first ensured Jazz was safe before going to investigate and being harmed.

'So you mean Jazz and Big Tom were living in sin in the Fog house?' Barbara Snayth asked with a scowl. Augustus Hoare and Edmund Poff fidgeted in their seats, uncomfortable. They were both aware of the relationship that had bloomed between Jazz and Big Tom. They had closed their eyes to it; Edmund because of his character, Augustus because he had put a lot of water in his wine since Clémence had left the marital home.

'Are you certain that now is the time and place to make such comment, Barbara?' Maud snapped. The animosity between the two women had increased with Maud's new role as Member of the Council. Barbara could not bear that Maud was now more important than she was in town, politically if not socially. It got worse when Edmund had asked her, as a matter of priority, to support Maud for the sake of fighting Clémence. At Maud's comment, Barbara's whole face closed up and her eyes became venomous slits. If thoughts had the power to kill, Maud would have joined Big Tom in the cold room that instant.

*

Naturally, the conversation evolved towards the Women's Revolution. Clémence and her followers were less violent of late, but rumour had it that they were more insidious: instead of asking women who adhered to their cause to join the rank of the fighters, they set them as spies within their social circles and their homes. Word spread that some of the kidnapped children had, in truth, been sent by their mothers to Clémence to rid them of the male dominance dogma. Suspicions even reached the women protesting against Clémence, as it could only be a cover to gain trust and access information. Whether Clémence had acted consciously or not, it was divide and conquer.

'What about the Women's Party?' I asked Maud.

'I think we are gaining ground,' Maud replied, in a heavy tone. 'A lot of women are backing us up and following our recommendations to widen and empower the roles of women in the community. What pleases me are the reactions of men, as well: not only do some support their wives more often than we expected, they also pass on the message to their sons. They are still a minority, but it is a good start. However, the veil of suspicion concerning women does not help us. Any expression of interest for the women's causes is tainted with the fear that anyone could be a follower of Clémence. Of course Clémence is playing on this and fuels the rumours of spies and partisans within the town on purpose.'

'This woman is a snake,' Benjamin hissed.

'Yes! She is poisonous! The only way to deal with her is decapitation!' Barbara burst out.

Augustus winced but said nothing. None of us did, even if everyone, apart from Edmund, bore expressions betraying discomfort or disapproval at the idea.

'Even you are not immune to her filth. What about the young fellow that left his family to join her rank?' Benjamin enquired about Owen Fisher.

'I am afraid we haven't heard from him,' I replied.

'She probably seduced him and soiled his mind. Maybe his body too,' Edmund commented, shaking his head.

From the corner of my eye, I saw Augustus Hoare bit his tongue. He never opened up about his feelings regarding Clémence and her betrayal. He was handling the whole situation with dignity. Maud told me that he had gained a different type of respect in town for his attitude.

'How about your women?' Benjamin asked Ariel Ben-Chaim, who had remained silent for most of the discussion. 'How come you are hardly affected by Clémence's Revolution and no woman has absconded from your community?

'One woman has,' Ariel corrected.

'Oh. I am sorry for your loss,' Benjamin replied, sardonic.

'The women of our Jewish community are not belittled. They are our equals; we each have a role determined for us by our faith. The reason for them not addressing strangers is for self-protection from sins, not because the men do not trust them.'

'So what about the one who left?' Maud asked.

'She lost her faith. She came to us and asked if she could go. We told her no faith was compulsory; it was a personal choice. If she wished to leave, she was free to do so. Should she want to come back and return to our Jewish ways, she would be welcome.'

'How do you know she went to the Women's Revolution?' Maud continued.

'She told us. She said she had observed what was happening in the other communities here and it offended her. The appeal to fight, by Clémence's side, was stronger than her faith. I am sorry about that. I hope she will see the light soon and return to us. That day, we will celebrate.'

The members of Lil'London's Council listened to Ariel Ben-Chaim with grim expressions, Maud included. At first, I thought it was the subject of the Women's Revolution that caused their sour faces, until I saw Maud fiddle with the cross she wore on a necklace around her neck. Then it hit me: by referring to the Jewish faith holding their communities together and being a source of respect between people, he had undervalued the faith of the people of Lil'London and any of the other communities in WII England. Even the Poffs, usually the most open-minded of the lot, looked wounded. Ariel clearly did not intend to undermine their faith in any way, but the effect was there. The last thing we needed was another division between the towns. It just would give Clémence more grounds to conquer.

'Things will change with the opening of the new Fog Dome further east,' I changed the subject. 'It will bring a new wave of Relocated with independent women and men used to equality between genders. They will help prove that a change is possible with the right frame of mind and does not require a violent revolution.'

'I hope so. I very much hope so,' she replied.

'Exactly how many people are we expecting? We went to see the site: it is enormous,' Augustus commented.

'Lil'London would easily fit in it, wouldn't it?' Edmund added. 'Benjamin mentioned that he already saw about 30 houses built in the vicinity and Mr Bopani indicated he was planning for a hundred of your wooden houses to be 'assembled' by the middle of next week. What a strange yet efficient way to build a house! He also mentioned this was just the beginning. It seems a alarmingly large number in such a short time,'

We had already had a conversation about the Fog Dome and how it would increase the rate of newcomers. No one could provide them an exact number, only probabilities. Even so, they had been shocked by our estimates and were doubtful of our calculations.

'We intend to control the crossing as much as possible so that relocation is contained. Already, we have avoided the possibility of thousands going through the door daily.' Apart from Maud and Edmund, who knew about the events in Kenya, the other attendees looked at me in awe. They had no idea how easily it could have happened and I summarised the events since last Sunday. When I finished, Augustus Hoare thanked me.

'Do we have your promise you will do everything in your power for the numbers to be controlled? I know we did hope for more Relocated, but we did not expect such sudden and large arrivals. It is unheard of. Never before in our history did we have to face so many Relocated.'

'I presume we ought to be grateful,' Benjamin Snayth said, gratitude not apparent in his tone. 'You have prevented a mass invasion of our land. For now. Instead, I presume we will have a slightly slower influx. What about the land they will occupy?'

'Please don't tell me that it was your land and you want to apply a tax on it. You would soon have another Revolution on your hands,' I snapped. It was *not* the best day to get on my nerves.

Benjamin Snayth clamped his mouth shut and Barbara Snayth turned her murderous stare towards me. Next Christmas I would offer her sunglasses.

Day 6 (Friday)

Hot coffee was ready in a thermos. An aspirin and a large glass of water were waiting on the side table. Bread was in the toaster. Butter and a selection of jam, honey, peanut butter and marmite were on the set table. I was working on my Ftab on Nick's small sofa while Jazz was sleeping in the adjacent room. Whenever she opened her eyes, I would be here for her.

Jazz had woken up in the middle of the night, surprised to see me asleep next to her. Until she remembered why. When she burst into tears, Simba echoed her wailing. Leila had brought the wolf for me. The three of us had shared the bed and Simba was definitely the one who slept the best. Jazz then took another sleeping pill, using a bottle of whisky to help her swallow. One gulp directly from the bottle was not sufficient, and I looked gob-smacked as she drank a third in one go. Jazz was not usually a drinker of spirits; it showed in the morning.

The choice proved difficult for her to make when she came out of the room, zombie-like: what to take first, aspirin or coffee? She went for the aspirin first. At my offer of food, she wrinkled her nose. She had not eaten anything since the evening prior to the attack - 36 hours ago - so I was not going to let her starve herself, whether she was hungry or not. I prepared a plate with scrambled eggs and toast, and sat her down telling her to eat it all. She began to argue with me, so I softly took her in my arms, and told her that I loved her and was just looking after her. That made her cry again, but she agreed to eat a little something. She nibbled at the toast and had two or three mouthfuls of the eggs. Mildly satisfied, I broached a difficult subject with hesitation.

'Jazz, honey, I am afraid we have some burdensome matters to talk about.'

'I can't deal with anything right now,' she grunted.

'He needs a funeral,' I told her anyway, with a wince.

Her jaw tightened and she put all her strength into holding her tears.

'His mother also needs to be involved. I can do it if you wish. Then you two need to sort something out for the funeral.'

'I will do it,' she said between clenched teeth.

'I am so sorry, Jazz,' I murmured.

She did not speak any more for some time. Her expression slowly switched from struggle to keep the tears away to determination and steel. Jazz put her left hand on mine and smiled, a tense, sad, hard smile. Then, with her right hand, she picked up the toast and ate it all.

'I will need more coffee. And I will finish the food. I must have all my strength today,' she said. Jazz had always been a tough cookie with a melting core. Now her toughness was an armour she would use to deal with the days, weeks and months to come.

'Big Tom, where is he?' she asked.

'In the cold room of the fogged storage house.'

'Have you... Have you tried to move the body out of the Fog? Is it coming out in WII or in London?'

If the body had come out of the Fog in London, his mother could hold the ceremony for Big Tom in East London with his relatives and friends there. Jazz would not be able to attend his requiem. In contrast, if his lifeless body were bound to WII, as it was when he was alive, his burial would be here, close to her.

'We did. He will have to be buried here in this world.'

She let out a sigh of relief, at the same time frowning at the thought of his mother now alone and cut off from her son's tomb.

'I will suggest that he is cremated. His heart belonged to both of us. If she agrees, we could both have him.'

It was a strange thought, the mother and the girlfriend sharing the ashes. I thought of Big Tom and wondered if he would have liked this. Probably yes. He would go with whatever made them happy.

'Now, can you tell me something – anything - that would take my mind off this for just a minute? I can really do with some uplifting thoughts to re-centre myself before I call his mother.'

*

The latest positive story was one I had heard about Leila and McRae. While waiting for Jazz to wake up, Leila and I chatted about her date the previous night. McRae was certainly a man full of surprises. Instead of taking her to a nice restaurant for the classic evening of food, chat and seduction, he led her instead to a private art gallery with a special exhibition of.... A ball pool for adults. The whole loft of the gallery was filled with colourful balls. In preparation, he had recommended that she wore comfortable trousers and no heels. The request triggered enough curiosity in Leila for her not to cancel the evening despite being buried under work. McRae's instinct had been correct; she did have a big kid side. The minute she entered the room, she started jumping, crawling, throwing and laughing. She had climbed on his shoulders and dived. She had attacked him from under the sea of balls, plunging back below and disappearing from view before he could retaliate. McRae had managed to make her relax and forget her duties for an hour. Relaxed and happy, she and McRae had dined and danced in a low-key Scottish restaurant with a live jazz band. Not once did he try to seduce her, or act as a playboy. He acted like an old-fashioned gentleman, giving her the attention and respect a woman could expect in the old times of chivalry, and she loved every minute of it. She found him irresistible and could not fight the attraction. When they separated, he kissed her softly on the lips, cupping her face in his hands, stopping before the kiss grew strong and passionate.

'You are the real deal, Leila. I don't want to mess this up,' he murmured in her ear. Next, McRae took her hand, kissed it and left. Leila, standing outside the door of her building, was confused and elated. It was the best date she had had in a long time, if not ever. She knew she was falling for him.

*

I was about to relate the story to Jazz when I stopped myself. How could I tell her about a romantic evening between two lovebirds when she had just lost her boyfriend?! As an alternative, I recalled for her the encounter between Charles-Antoine, Ahmed, Ushi Tsou and Eudes. It was not as cheery a subject but it would have to do. I had barely finished my story when Ahmed knocked vigorously at the door. Out-of-breath and looking frantic, he apologised for interrupting but claimed he urgently needed to talk to me. Ushi Tsou had just threatened to slit his throat if he ever tried to take Eudes away from her. Ahmed was not scared: he was upset. He insisted he had done nothing wrong. He had not even tried to meet with her. He was just walking around the edge of the clearing, trying to make sense of what was happening to him, when she emerged from nowhere, stood in front of him like a tigress, made her machete shine in the sunlight and quietly suggested he did not want her to demonstrate her skills with it.

'Yep, this is Tsou Bitch all right,' Jazz commented.

'Who is this woman? She is nuts! How can you let her look after Eudes? Are you insane too?' Ahmed shouted.

'She is a trained mercenary, a modern Amazon,' Jazz replied.

'Well, you can't deny she is equipped to protect him in an unknown world where a band of rebellious women are intent on enslaving men,' I pointed out, using a slightly distorted but not totally untrue view of what was happening in WII.

'What do you mean? What rebellious women?' Ahmed had immediately calmed down and was now scowling. The situation in WII was so evident to me I had forgotten it was not known for everyone else. I summarised it for him. His face was losing its colour by the minute.

'I wouldn't worry, if I were you,' Jazz tried to reassure him. 'They might not consider you as a man.'

She then turned to me. 'Yoko, I will make the call to his mother now. You should go: you have a lot to do. Go.' She gave me a big hug while I protested, then closed the door on me. I stood, confused for a few seconds, before turning to Ahmed and telling him I would speak with Ushi.

*

'I have a deal for you,' Ahmed said to Ushi Tsou before I had a chance to talk. She was standing by the door of her little house, her face menacing. Her eyes squinted on Ahmed in such a way I thought she might be evaluating what was the most efficient way to make him disappear. She didn't react to his sentence, nor did she slam the door in our face either, so he continued.

'I grew up with 6 brothers and sisters,' Ahmed began, with forced confidence. His attempt at aplomb was impressive. 'My mother and father worked very hard but they had little money and, as the oldest, I helped a lot around the house and looked after my siblings. I know how to take care of children and how to take care of a house. Moreover, I am a mechanic. I will be of use here. What I lack are the skills to defend Eudes or myself in this world. I know how to live in the rough suburbs, not in the wild. Yoko told me about you, what you did, and I think we could find a way to make it work.'

'Clever,' Ushi Tsou retorted. She then fell silent, her eyes not leaving his, deep in thought.

'And I am gay. I am not interested in having sex with you.'

'What if I am? You are not bad looking,' she replied giving him the once over.

'No,' Ahmed said firmly.

'I like your attitude,' she replied, with the faintest of smiles. 'I'll think about it.' With that, she slammed the door in our faces.

*

Charles-Antoine listened with increasing alarm when Ahmed shared his idea and actions with him. He did not approve at all of his initiative, even though Ahmed told him he had all to gain in this, especially as he could keep an eye on Eudes. I thought it was a good idea. Ahmed was growing fast in my esteem. He was smart, self-assured and fearless in dealing with Ushi Tsou. Like Ushi Tsou, I liked his attitude.

*

Back on good old planet earth, the world was in turmoil. The Modern Marburg illness continued to progress, especially in the highly populated areas that were also the poorest. The health benefits of the Fog were now backed by medical reports. And so the Fog appeared the only way to save life and control the disease. Stories about relocation to WII did not deter most of the people affected by the virus. The will to live (or the instinct of self-preservation) was stronger than the fear of the unknown and the absence of family and friends. The Security Council of the United Nations had declared that the whole world was in a state of emergency, and that the priority was to stop the spread of the disease and find a cure at all cost. To the United Kingdom, it recommended the creation of special exemptions to its closed borders and the creation of international health corridors giving access to the Fog. This caused a logistics problem for the UK government, as well as an ethical one for us. We were battling to set up and control the crossing for both worlds. The thought of an international influx terrified me. Gatekeepers Associates expressed official concerns and reiterated the need to keep control of the numbers of people crossing. Moreover, we were concerned about the fairness of the process and costs of travelling to England for Fog healing. The lottery system applied in the United Kingdom, for both emergency cases and long-term life-threatening viruses, was a temporary solution. How could we organise this worldwide? Also, who would pay for the travel and accommodation, and settlement of the Relocated from abroad? The Security Council's recommendations had the best purpose in mind: they appeared impossible to put into practice, at least in the short term.

*

On a video call between Foggies, later that day, Rosario raised the issue of all the Foggies disclosing their existence. From the tone of her voice, it was clear she was not keen on the idea. Mitch, Tony and Rosario enjoyed their peaceful and relatively normal life in Alaska, while still providing support to the rest of us, either as a safe house or for secret missions. They were our back-up plan and happy to remain so. Christophe was also against publicly revealing himself as a Switcher. His focus was on his baby daughter. He had observed the pressure of the media and authorities on Zeno, Harry and me. He was aware that the British now knew he was a Foggy, and it was enough that the whole family would be under scrutiny, and at risk, in WII as well. The 'hidden' Foggies agreed they could achieve more without being constantly under watch and free to roam around. So our decision to conceal the existence of all the Foggies was confirmed until further notice. The British government knew more than the public, and we trusted they would keep their knowledge a secret. It gave them the upper hand over other States.

Soon, Putu would join us in the UK too, but not as a Foggy. It had been a difficult decision for her to leave Africa, and she did not hide that she longed for the day when we would be able to create another public door on the African continent. She was part of the medical team that would work within the Fog Dome. Her goal was to supervise the department for visiting children at the Fog door in Africa or from Africa, and help at their habilitation in WII. Thanks to a little push by the Society, she already had accommodation organised close to the Fog for the weekend, and would start her new work on Monday.

Jack had left in the morning for the US. He was not an 'active' Foggy any more. On Saturday nights, he would still sleep in a separate area to avoid a potential Fog gate. Leila was going to monitor his progress, if any.

As for the official Foggies and Rico, adjacent luxury suites were waiting for us in a requisitioned hotel overlooking the river, a stone's throw from the Fog Dome. Moving out of the terraced houses was difficult. Living there had enabled me to retain the illusion of some normality in my life. We were living like a family. Our furniture and art was a mix of our own tastes and gave the home a warmth, an eccentricity and an edge that we could not have achieved individually. It enabled us to ignore the buzz around us and I would miss our coffees in the back garden together.

*

Before joining Jazz for dinner, I made sure to shake all these black clouds from my mind. I brushed away fears, worries and regrets to ensure I could be present for her. She needed a friend and she deserved my full attention.

At dinner, Jazz told me about her arrangement for Big Tom's farewell. Exceptionally, Edmund Poff would hold his usual Sunday mass at Lil'London's church in the evening, so he could give a private ceremony at *The Jazzin* in the morning. Leila had promised the building would be safe and secure by then. Afterwards, Edmund had organised the body's cremation. It was not common practice in WII; quite to the contrary. As they inherited the traditions of England in the late 18th - early 19th century, the Christians of the Other World's communities thought cremation was a heathens' and pagans' practice. Only from the late 19th century did the mentality change, notably because the Victorians had a problem of space to bury bodies in the growing cities. As to the Jews of Yerushaleim, they strictly applied the Jewish Law that forbids cremation. However, Edmund played on Jazz's Asian background and Big Tom being her betrothed – a little lie that hurt no one – to have the decision accepted by the funeral director. From his history studies, he was aware that the Hindus in the British Empire practised the burning of loved ones' dead bodies. Jazz did not care why or what was said if Big Tom's mother's wish and her own was implemented. They would then split the ashes between two worlds, between the two women he loved and loved him back. Suddenly Jazz stopped mid-sentence and threw the cup of tea she had in her hand against the wall where it shattered. She banged the table with her fist and implored with rage:

'Do we know yet who killed my Tom?'

'Not yet Jazz. Not yet. Leila is doing what she can. It shook her too, you know. It shook us all. We are all in this together. We are a team,' I told her, gripping her arm tight.

'More than that, Nutella. We are a family.'

'Yes, we are,' I replied, a heavy weight on my chest. I thought of how Big Tom had entered our lives and how concerned I was about him at first. He had turned out to be the best person Jazz could have hoped for.

*

As recalling the events of the day got too much for Jazz and she seemed on the verge of a nervous breakdown, I attempted to distract her with anecdotes from both worlds. I mentioned to her that one of the new activities that Zeno and Leo were working hard on was the creation of new business, WII-style. To facilitate the integration of the Relocated within the local communities and enable a feeling of mutual contribution and benefit, new businesses and activities should not be in competition with what already existed in the Other World. This was in accordance with the agreement between the WII towns, and between them and the Foggies. Some of the obvious examples were retail shops with products from our planet, or shops like a bicycle and repair centre. Inside the Fog Dome, they planned a cinema, restaurants and markets, as well as some shops run by the locals. Molly was hoping there could be a primary school, too. Even if she supported the Virtual University project, she pointed out that children should have new schooling encompassing programmes from both worlds. From the start, Lil'London then Newtonsee, and even Yerushaleim had demonstrated a keen interest to learn from us on specific subjects, mainly in technological advances and history. However, it was always with a certain reserve and apprehension. Educating the new generations was essential!

On our side, the planet was developing a global and fervent fascination for anything about WII. Fashion and furniture were jumping back in time and getting inspiration from the early 19th century. Restaurants were opening with new menus based on vintage recipes. TV shows, newspapers and book editors were hungry for the stories of the Foggies, Relocated and WII. We kept receiving requests for copies of the Chronicles of Lil'London. News of the Inter-worlds University programmes excited the minds and the list of applicants for attending the courses was already building up.

'Big Tom wanted me to go beyond my actions for the women here,' Jazz interrupted me. I did not know when she had stopped listening.

'Did he? What did he want you to do?' I enquired.

'Well, you see, there will be a lot of people around the Fog Dome. Very soon, it won't be a village that we'll have, but a town. And you are an Ambassador and you already have your hands full.'

'Okay... So what did he suggest?' I scowled, unsure where she was going with this.

'Big Tom said that if we had a town, we should have a structure for it, with our own council, our religious buildings, our own prison etc. He said I should be a mayor. I was not sure. For me, gaining equal rights for the women here would already be achievement enough. Apart from that, I had my lounge and my man, and I could create a life for myself. But now... Now I think that he was right, I should do it. He said something else, and the more I think about it, the more convinced I am.'

'What did he say?' I asked her softly. Big Tom was not a talker and he rarely got into this type of conversation with me. I regretted it even more now.

'He said that when it came to equal society, the best way to change the mentalities was by example. Already, Maud is a member of the Council of Lil'London, Molly is a great Secretary for the Women's Party. By being the mayor of the Relocated new town, I could not only promote our cause, I would make it global.'

'Jazz, this sounds great,' I told her cautiously. I liked the idea, yet I worried for my friend. This would give her a purpose as well as a sense of belonging in her new life. However, It could be to the detriment of her personal life. She would throw herself in the political battle with all her strength and would let nothing stand in her way.

'What about the lounge? Are you going to give this up?'

'Yes and no. It will be my source of income. I will invest in various projects to avoid having all my eggs in the same basket. I will get some land around the Dome and create a farm, and keep parts as a forest, too. As I want something in the Dome as well, maybe the lounge could move there. I haven't worked out all the details, but I want to have a certain security. I might not always be elected, plus I don't think the elected should get an income from their position. It has rotted most political systems! This is just an idea to be tweaked and trimmed. Mind you, this is not a dream! It will happen, a new town based on a fair and equal society. This is what I am going for, and I won't let go until we've got it.'

*

That night, I slept with Jazz again. In the loneliness of the room, she needed the presence of her friend. Despite another sleeping pill, she still tossed and turned for some time before falling asleep. It took me even more time than her to quieten my mind. I thought of the attack on the Fog and Foggies and the consequences on the people around me, and how to make sure that being a Foggy was not about to slowly kill us due to the dangers and pressure. I thought of our global duties to the world. I thought of McRae and for what reasons he could have been 'chosen' as a Facilitator. I thought of many things and I decided we needed a back-up plan to remain sane. I spent the rest of the night trying to think of one. Something slowly emerged, but would it be possible?

Day 7 (Saturday)

Some people are either swift to react to new circumstances or they have a talent to foresee what is to come. Ingis Chen was one of them. He always seemed to have a trump card up in his sleeve. Today, he unveiled the details of his new company, dedicated to promote and support access to the Fog. It offered services linked to the crossing, including travel planning, specialised legal advice for forms and applications and the like. His company also proposed grants and consulting for starting a new life in case of relocation. It was the first of its kind. His reputation for Fog knowledge and expertise gave it immediate success. Millions of people registered on the first day, the company's app was downloaded to mobiles around the world, and the short documentary he had prepared on the Fog - how to welcome it, not fear it - had gone viral within its first few hours online. Despite my misgivings on his core ethics, I had to admire the man. One of the branches of this company was even dedicated to help businesses apply to the call for tenders for trading with WII. Indeed, Leo and Zeno had announced the launch of an online

410

market platform for Fog-related businesses.

If Ingis Chen's was the first private structure of its kind, the British Government had not wasted time either to prepare the ground for the current and future Relocated. The main difficulty was administrative and financial: WII was foreign soil, the Relocated did not have to pay taxes there, yet they needed help to settle and had paid taxes up until now. What was their status? Should they be associated with refugees? Should they be given an early pension as a form of support?

*

Jazz came out of the bedroom with eyes puffy from the tears and the strain. Her first words were that she did not want to talk about *it*. Not once. She wanted to keep busy all day with research on the minimum administrative, political and economic structures a new town required. I intended to stay by her side all day. Anything else would have to wait. So I let the other Foggies deal with their private affairs and Leila monitored the negotiations between the British Government, the CEO and the UN. Zeno, Dante and Leo helped on site for the settlement around the Fog Dome. Ingis Chen shone in the media. Lally O'Maleigh verbally attacked the Fog and the Gatekeepers. My parents, Ushi Tsou and Charles-Antoine could be grown-ups without me and find a way to make things work. Harry and Rico supervised plans to move our belongings to our new homes near the Fog Dome. I just kept Jazz company.

Leo asked to join us for lunch. I had not seen him for a couple of days and missed him terribly. However, Leo's presence could be a reminder of what Jazz did not have any more and I said as much to Leo. I should have known Jazz better. As we walked in the forest with Simba, for a break late morning – we had worked on her projects non-stop until then - she approached the subject of love and the Fog.

'How are things going with Leo?' she asked.

'He is wonderful. He is so patient, you know. He manages to climb each of my inner walls, one after the other. I have built so many over the years to protect myself against emotional vulnerability.'

'He is taming you.'

'I'm not that bad!' I scowled at her. She laughed.

'Don't you remember? You are the one who read me an extract from this short story once, about a boy and a fox.'

She was referring to *The Little Prince*, by Antoine de Saint-Exupery. This wonderful book teaches a lot to adults, too, under pretence of being a children's book. It relates interplanetary adventures and encounters the so-called Little Prince has on the planets he visits. On one of the planets, he meets a fox whose wisdom summarised some easily forgotten truths about human relationships. The fox explains to the Little Prince that to be friends with him, he needs to be patient, to take the time to know him, to create a bond, to *tame* him. It is the time, as well as the quality of this time spent creating the bond, that makes the other one important and unique. Moreover, creating such a bond is not to be taken lightly, as the fox adds. "*You become responsible, forever, for what you have tamed.*" My favourite quote from the whole book was also from the fox: "*One sees clearly only with the heart. What is essential is invisible to the eyes.*" To see with the heart, and be seen by it, one needs to take the time to open these hearts.

'You are right. Leo is taming me,' I said to Jazz, with a smile.

'Poor guy, it took him long enough. I was even beginning to wonder if you had become frigid.'

'What? Jeez, thanks!'

'Well, you didn't even go for Nick! One of the hottest guys I've ever set eyes on. He had his eyes set on you, and you resisted. I was getting worried the Fog had made you lose your sex drive.'

'Absolutely not! I still have a very good libido, thank you very much. I am just good at controlling my animal impulses,'

'Yeah. If you want my honest opinion, it was getting frustrating just watching as an outsider how you kept controlling yourself.'

'I really don't understand this fascination you all have for my sex life...'

'We just all care for your sanity... Anyway, where is Leo? You've been here for two days and I haven't seen him around.'

'He is in Essex.'

'Why don't you invite him for lunch or dinner? He will be here tomorrow morning for Big Tom, so he might as well arrive tonight.'

'Are you sure? I don't want his presence to…'

'I am sure. It helps me to see you happy,' she said smiling. I loved this woman. 'What about Nick? I have to tell you, Nick took your going back with Leo more personally than he let show. And now Big Tom…'

'There was nothing serious in….'

'Take it from me, who took it from Big Tom. When you chose Leo, he compensated on the ring and with renewed assiduity on his job. In addition, you were less around and he felt less useful. Nick has been much grimmer than you are aware.'

'Maybe Nick for lunch and Leo for dinner?' I suggested. Jazz raised an eyebrow.

'Are you burning the candle at both ends now?' she asked, with a smirk. I rolled my eyes.

'I like Nick but I love Leo. Nick is a good guy: there's no reason we can't be friends.'

Jazz said nothing and just shook her head.

'Sometimes, Yoko, you really underestimate the effect you have on men. Or their feelings. They are as sensitive as women, you know. They just don't express it or deal with it the same way.'

'Will you stop it? You make it sound as if I am terribly naïve.'

'Sometimes you are. You are brilliant when not personally emotionally involved, terrible when you are.'

I cringed and finished the conversation, then called Leo to invite him for dinner. He instantly accepted.

Nick did not speak much at lunch. I tried to entertain both Jazz and him with anecdotes from London. It was difficult to find uplifting stories in the gloom of the virus and the pressure surrounding the Fog. And Big Tom … In the end, Nick grabbed us both by the waist and dragged us to his little house, settled us on his sofa on each side of him, and put old movies on the large screen he had installed for his nights at home. He told us later that we both fell asleep against him, and that it made his day. He could still be there for us, as well as protect us. As he spoke, both Jazz and I noted that his eyes were red from crying.

*

Before dinner, we had a Foggies Board Meeting. Every Foggy wanted to give personally - even if by way of the Ftab screens - their condolences to Jazz. We insisted Nick joined as well and he was touched to be included. The FBM also helped change the mood as Adam gave further details of his plans for tonight. I had hinted to Jazz that the US was going to be shaken up in the morning. Nick and Jazz, the only ones not privy to the details of the operation until then, were stunned when they heard. During dinner afterwards, it offered a welcome distraction from conversation about the funeral, the next morning.

How could it not? Overnight, Alcatraz would be turned into a door to the Other World!

As you might expect, the choice of venue had been subject to much deliberation within our group. There had been controversy that it was not the easiest to access for maintenance purposes. Also, for the Relocated in the long term, having a Fog Gate on an island would make trading and exchanges more complex. However, it was what Adam aimed for: it was a good way to protect the door from excessive use and abuse. The Dome had not been the first choice for the others either, but they had granted me my wish and accepted my arguments. This time, we gave in to Adam's.

'Gosh!' Nick exclaimed. 'The Rock fogged. Of all the movies set there before, none ever imagined that one.'

'That's probably Ingis Chen's next venture: a movie trilogy set on Alcatraz. A Fog adventure with a love story of teenagers from the 18th and 21st centuries. He will probably throw some witches in the middle for the sake of it,' Leo sneered.

'I wouldn't joke about it, if I were you. He will probably add a character after you ...' I teased him. He did not find it funny.

WEEK VI

Day 1 (Sunday)

It took us by surprise. Jazz and Big Tom's mother wished for a small and private ceremony with the Foggies and Relocated who knew him. They hoped the members of Lil'London boxing Club and the few WII *The Jazzin* customers who had bonded with him would join as well. They joined. They all joined. We had underestimated the importance of rites in the relatively small and old-fashioned population of the Other World's England. We also underestimated how attractive the first funeral of a Relocated would be: it was attended by the illustrious Yoko, the controversial if not infamous Jazz and the charming resourceful Italians Zeno, Leo and Dante. For the ceremony, we were a small group inside the warehouse. It was when we left the house for the forest clearing that we got the shock of our lives. Big Tom's mother, the Facilitators, Leila and Sam Riverson, who were attending the ceremony via online video, also gasped at the sight. The whole clearing was full of people from Lil'London and Newtonsee. They had brought tables and picnic baskets with them and the place was buzzing with activities, though the assembly immediately fell silent when we emerged from the Fog. Nick rushed towards me. He had discreetly left during the service without us being aware of it. When the alarm monitors on his mobile had gone frantic with everyone starting to arrive, he had checked the video feed and understood what was happening. He decided not to disturb the funeral and went to switch off the alarm. He was agitated and anxious: with such a crowd, security was difficult to enforce. He feared for our safety and urged us not to mix with visitors but remain on the side. It was impossible. They had come to pay their respects to the dead man and present their condolences to Jazz for her loss: we couldn't just dismiss them. Jazz was touched by the true kindness she read on many faces. In addition, Maud said that as a public figure, a politician, even a role model for some of the women in attendance, Jazz could not discomfit them. She should not use this as an opportunity to advance her cause, but she was not going to be rude.

I asked Maud why she had not warned us that so many people would come. She replied she could not be certain it would happen and did not want to concern us. Augustus had organised additional security. Armed local men were talking with Nick and placing themselves under his supervision in key positions at the corners of the forest's clearing and among the crowd.

*

By early evening, everyone was merry, Jazz included, Nick excluded. Food and wine were consumed aplenty. People played and sang sad songs. The crowd was emotional and phased. This was when the commotion started.

In my tipsy state, I heard a scream and felt a weight on me. Before realising what happened, I was on the floor with a body on top of me. Nick's. People started running and screaming around me, I heard my name. Leo was calling me. I was about to answer when Nick moved off me and grabbed my hand, pulling me up. He inspected me and looked satisfied.

'You're not hurt, are you?' he asked.

'No, I am fine.'

Now Leo and Jazz were calling me.

'She is with me!' Nick replied to them at the same time I shouted 'Leo! Leo, are you ok? Jazz? You are ok? And you Zeno, Dante?'

'Come, we need to bring you to safety!' Nick hushed me as he pulled my arms and we ran towards the hangar on the edge of the forest, where the quad bikes were.

'Wait! What about the others? We need to make sure they are fine,' I said trying to stop him in his run.

'You are my priority!' He stopped, turned and with one strong lift put me on his shoulders. He started to run again but his attempt was interrupted by Simba. She jumped in front of him and bared her teeth dangerously, growling.

'Hey! Easy girl! I am helping her!' Nick said to the wolf.

'Put me down! Put me down right now! Nick!' I shouted at Nick.

Nick let me down to the ground, not letting Simba from his sight.

When I got down to pat her, she calmed down.

'Nick, we must check on the others! And… What on earth happened?'

Nick had already taken my hand and was about to pull me into a run when he saw my face. I was staring at the chaos in the clearing. My eyes had grown wide and I swore. People were running in all directions. There was a lot of dust in the air. The closest to the centre of the clearing, the more bodies were lying on the ground, wounded if not worst. Nick held me back from running towards them. I scanned the space to find my friends, oblivious to anything else.

'Yoko, the Fog!' Nick shouted.

I promptly refocused my attention onto the Fog. Only then did I realise I had been looking at the scene in front of me without seeing the obvious. There was no Fog. Where the two fogged houses had been, *The Jazzin* and the storage house, there was now only a thick cloud of dust. A rumble of stones was scattered where the buildings had once been. Then came the sounds. Whether the explosion had deafened me or I was in a bubble prior, a chaotic mix of screams, shouts, cries and calls now assailed me. I noticed Ushi on the ground, Eudes in her arms. She saw me looking and gave me the thumbs up. Then in the dust, I distinguished Leo and Zeno running behind Jazz. She was shouting my name. I started running towards her but Nick pulls me back again.

'No! Yoko, they blew the houses! It's dangerous, you can't go there. We don't know who…' Nick attempted to reason with me. In a sudden movement, with my free hand I grabbed his arm that was holding me back and pulled myself free.

'Let me go! I don't fucking care! I need to check they are fine! Let me go!' I shouted at him, then ran towards my friends screaming: 'I am here! Leo! Leo! Jazz! Zeno! Over here!'

Next thing I knew, Nick had tackled me to the ground again, belatedly yelling 'down!' I looked back at him in anger, and to my astonishment, he had pulled out a gun and started shooting in the direction of one of the

Woodfellas' wooden houses. Squinting, I saw figures and rifles. Next came the sound of shots and the whizz of bullets above our heads. Nick was still shooting and one of the figures fell to the ground. The detonations continued. I yelled in the direction of the remaining people in the clearing, telling them to get down.

'We need to go for cover! When I tell you, run for the closest trees, get to the ground and hide. I'll follow,' Nick shouted above the noise.

'What about the others?' I began.

'Yoko! Shut up and do what I say. You cannot help them if you are dead! Where is your gun?'

'In my bag. Back there,' I pointed to the centre of the clearing.

Nick bent his knee and took a knife from under his trousers.

'Take this, just in case.'

I had no idea how to use a knife, but I took it eagerly.

'Go! Go now! And stay low!' Nick barked.

I ran as fast as possible, bent in half, scrutinising the forest ahead for any sign of danger. Simba had preceded me and was watchful, ready to pounce on anything or anyone coming to harm me. When I reached the woods, a bullet whizzed pass me and hit a tree close to Simba, much too close for comfort. I let myself collapse on the ground and grabbed her, forcing her to the ground too.

'Down Simba! Down!' I ordered her. She immediately obeyed and continued her vigilance. Lying on the floor, I turned my attention back to the clearing. The shots had stopped and I could not see any of the attackers. Nor could I see my friends. There was no movement anywhere. No movement, and no sound. If I screamed Leo's name, or Jazz's, or anyone's, I risked revealing my position. Or theirs if they replied. I felt helpless, useless and terrified. The anguish was nauseating and the silence unbearable. When Nick stood up and ran towards me, I was both terrified he would get shot and longed for his company. Never had a few seconds felt so much like hours, and never had a run looked so much like a slow motion movie. In the silence of that moment, his steps seemed to echo like the tread of an elephant herd.

'Yoko, put the knife down. You are clutching it so tight you are cutting the blood flow to your hands,' he said to me as he lay down by my side and started to inspect our surroundings. I tried to open my hands but could not, as if my body were frozen.

'I can't… I can't do it…' I was panicking and hyperventilating. He put his two hands on top of mine and slowly massaged my wrists. I instantly felt my whole body relax.

'Better?'

'Much better. Thank you.'

Nick did not let my hands go. The moment turned strangely eerie for a minute, until I broke it by retrieving my hands and lowering my gaze. The forest was still and silent aside from the wind shaking the branches. No bird singing, no animals making the wood crack under their steps. As I whispered to Nick that we must check on the others, Leo called my name. I glanced at the clearing. The dust was slowly settling and I could see people hiding within the rubble.

'Leo! Are you ok? Jazz? Zeno? Is everyone safe?' I shouted, standing up to see, only for Nick to pull me back down where it was safer.

'We are fine, but some are wounded and need to be looked after. Are you ok? I am coming!' Leo shouted back.

'Stay where you are!' Nick stopped him. 'We haven't asserted that the situation is safe yet!'

'No! I am coming! Just watch my back!' Leo bawled.

Next, Leo stood up and broke into a run, zigzagging towards us. More exactly, towards where he estimated that we were, which was not our exact position. Or maybe all this zigzagging threw him off route. Simba, observing the scene like us, howled. I could have sworn she was trying to guide him. Leo redirected his course and when he reached us, Nick could not stop me standing up and throwing myself into Leo's arms. His face was dusty, his shirt torn, and he was holding a gun in his hand. There was blood on his shirt.

'Oh my God! Are you hurt?' I screamed.

'Just scratches. Come here,' Leo pulled me against him and kissed me. In that instant, all my fears lifted and I felt some of my strength return.

'Hey! You two love birds, get the fuck down!' Nick said, bringing us back to reality. On the ground, Nick was every bit the professional, surveying and assessing the dangerous situation. Yet it seemed to me that his focus away from Leo and me was not entirely due to professionalism.

'How come you have a gun?' I whispered to Leo.

'How come you don't?' he murmured back.

'My bag dropped in the chaos back in the clearing,' I told him. 'I hope it hasn't fallen into the wrong hands!'

Leo pulled out his radio from his belt. Nick instinctively put his hand where his own device should have been. It must have fallen during the chaos.

'Dante, all good here!' Leo said, into the device. 'Yoko's bag is somewhere around. Can you find it? It has Ftab, gun and probably other stuff that shouldn't fall into the wrong hands.'

'Only a woman would worry about her handbag at a time like this,' Dante replied. I grabbed Leo's hand holding the radio and spoke to Dante.

'Are you sure you are all fine? Jazz, is she with you?' I asked.

'We are all fine!' I heard Jazz say in the background. Zeno said something in Italian that I couldn't make out.

'What about Maud and Edmund and Molly, and…?' I continued.

'I think our attackers were just shooting to cover their escape,' Nick said.

'They shot at me!' I exclaimed. Then I thought they could have targeted Simba. 'Or maybe not,' I finished, caressing my wolf. Nick understood my last comment.

'Without Simba, you would have been alone. Easy to abduct,' Nick thought aloud.

'It wouldn't be that easy! I would defend myself, you know!' I scowled at him. He raised an eyebrow and smirked. My saying that I had self-defence skills was apparently an over-statement. I was in no position to argue.

'Anyway, does that mean they are gone now?' I asked Nick.

No one could answer this for sure. Nick announced it was time to unblock the situation and spoke with Augustus by way of radio. One after the other, the sheriff sent his deputies to the edge of the woods at equal distance to ensure our safety.

*

Nobody had died; for this we were all grateful. Maybe it was a stroke of luck; maybe the attackers intended only to scare us. We all joined efforts to tend to the seriously wounded, including one of our rare helicopter pilots. They were plenty, although I thanked whoever might be out there – God, the Universe, the almighty aliens, everyone – for sparing every one of my friends, who bore cuts and bruises only. Unfortunately, our supply of medicines was limited, as the storage house where most of it had been was gone. In addition, one of the people badly hurt was the Lil'London doctor-surgeon. I asked if Ariel Ben-Chaim was anywhere around and was told he had not come. Nobody from Yerushaleim had. They had sent ahead some food, but the women could not have been in attendance, and with the current threat from Clémence's group, the men had stayed to protect them. Soon, teams were organised for the care, transportation and safety of everyone's return to their towns.

*

It was late and dark already. I had had no contact with London since the morning, and knew they would be worried. I suggested we head to the Essex house or the Fog Dome, whichever would be the fastest and safest to reach. Nick pulled a face as I said so.

'Neither,' he replied.

'What do you mean, 'neither'? I can't leave my parents, or Harry and Rico, or Leila, in the dark! Or the other Foggies and even Sam! We must tell them we are ok; we must tell them what happened. They must be worried sick.'

Leo and Nick exchanged a look.

'Ariel Ben-Chaim sent a messenger this afternoon. Christophe, Isabelle and Chloé, along with the Epcotts and other military Relocated based at the Essex Fog House, appeared at his. Christophe is badly wounded. The Fog house was destroyed there, just as here.'

'What?!' Zeno and I exclaimed in unison.

'They tried to go to the Fog Dome, but Owen told them not to.'

'Owen? But Owen is with Clémence,' I protested.

'No. Not any more, he isn't.'

Leo and Nick then related the events as the messenger, one of Ariel Ben-

Chaim's sons, had told them.

At a similar time as here and also using the element of surprise, a group of Clémence's rebels blew up the house in Essex. Like here, they had a target: they wanted to take Christophe and Chloé, probably in the same way they were after Simba and me. I was surprised when they told me this, but Leo said he had checked, and the bullet in the tree was a tranquiliser. Owen was ashamed to admit that he was the one who had revealed - he insisted it was by accident - that Simba was special to me. Through informants, Clémence also learned of Christophe's presence in Essex as a new Foggy, and that Chloé was his daughter. She interrogated Owen using her sharp mind and her seductive assets, and his answers unconscioulsy passed on key information. Casually talking with Clémence, answering her subtle questioning, he had also revealed how someone can be neutralised yet not killed through tranquilisers, some of which she had stolen. It was enough for her to plot Chloé's abduction; a baby girl she could educate with revolutionary ideas. When Owen realised today what Clémence was doing, his eyes opened to what was really happening. He could not let her enact her plans. He came to the rescue of Christophe's family in their escape, leaving the rebel ranks. However, in the debacle as he led the group from the Essex house through the weakest link of the siege, a stray bullet hit Christophe in the back, in the middle of the right scapula. Owen urged them not to flee towards the Fog dome. It was the reaction Clémence expected from all Foggies and Relocated: she had set groups of her followers in strategic locations around the Fog Dome, de facto circling it and ready to intercept anybody trying to communicate with London. The Fog Dome was too big to destroy, so she aimed to control access to and from it. Her message to London and our World was that in this world, it was going to be her way, or no way.

It left the escapees from the Essex Fog house no choice but to go to Yerushaleim. Christophe was fighting for his life, carried away by Relocated English soldiers on the journey. He needed urgent treatment as soon as possible, as much as they all required a secure place for the night. Ariel's medical knowledge and Yerushaleim seemed the safest bet.

'We must go there too! And the sooner the better!' Leo announced.

422

'And we must bring as much ammunition and weapons with us as possible,' Nick added.

Clémence's women had not destroyed the motorhomes and quads. Maybe simply because they didn't know how to drive them. However, we only had what fuel remained in the vehicles' tanks, and that was not much. We gathered what could be salvaged into two motorhomes' tanks and packed them with any technology we could find that was still working. With arms and ammunitions, we were luckier. Nick had made sure they were not easily accessible: he had set up a small building dedicated to our armament with thick walls, strong doors and heavy locks. Our aggressors had tried to get in, as the marks on the doors and locks clearly showed. A pity the fuel did not have such a building too. Once the motorhomes were ready, we split the groups in two: Jazz, Ushi, Eudes, Leo, Simba and I got into one, Zeno, Dante and the Fishers into another. It was a slow procession towards Yerushaleim and a dangerous one in the dark of the night. One of the motorhomes in front, one at the back, and the Relocated of Woodfellas walked in-between. Nick was the only one to drive on a quad, alone. He was making journeys back and forth between motorhomes to ensure security. We also had a small group of armed men on horses that the two Councils of Lil'London and Newtonsee had left behind, to help reinforce the security for our journey.

On the road, the tension was palpable. As Leo drove, the women kept guns leaning on the window frame, pointed towards the dark countryside. When we arrived, exhausted and scared, we saw that the inhabitants of the small Jewish community had raised wooden walls around their towns and were keeping watch. They were expecting us and greeted us with joy, relief and food.

As Ariel Ben-Chaim led Jazz and me to one of their spare rooms for the night, Jazz was tightly holding the urn that should have contained Big Tom's ashes. She burst into tears. Edmund would try to have the ashes brought to her soon. However, she knew it was not a priority any more, and she would have to be patient.

Day 2 (Monday)

Early in the morning, Ushi and Nick did the tour of Yerushaleim to assess the weak and strong points of the village's outline in case of an attack, and to work out the best defence strategy. On a professional level, they worked well together. Their presence was reassuring. There was little doubt Clémence would soon know that all the Foggies currently in WII had found refuge with the Jewish community. When she did, she would try to get to us. Why did she want this now? What had changed? I was hoping Owen would be able to provide some answers.

*

As Isabelle was in a state of shock, Jazz and I were looking after Eudes and Chloé. It kept Jazz occupied and she really needed this. Ariel was doing his best to help Christophe, but the injury was severe. Nick had tried to reassure us the night before, saying that chances of survival from gunshots were much higher than is generally believed; that is, if one is not shot in the head or directly in the heart. Ushi added that the human body is surprisingly resilient and about 80 per cent of shots to the body do not turn out to be fatal. They were less positive in the morning, listening to Ariel's description of the damage caused by the bullet. After encountering the bone, instead of it absorbing most of the force and limiting the harm, the bullet created splinters that turned into projectiles, travelling through the body. The bullet also continued inside and lodged itself into the lungs, causing yet further tissue damage. Furthermore, Christophe had suffered significant blood loss. He had the same A- blood type as Dante, and the latter immediately stepped forward to give blood. It was a complicated blood transfusion to organise, as such a procedure was unheard of in Yerushaleim.

Nick and Ushi had more knowledge of gunshots than Ariel, and they provided him with as much information as possible on the immediate risks to life. According to them, most deaths by gunshot are from blood loss or wound infection rather than from the damage to internal structures caused by the bullet. The removal of the bullet is not always necessary, although they hesitated in this situation. It could prevent the risk of embolism in one of the lungs. In any case, Ariel was adamant he had to do it and proceeded with the surgery at dawn. I knew Nick and Ushi Tsou were trying to minimise the trauma Christophe's body was dealing with, for our sakes. It was obvious that a vital organ, the lung, was seriously affected. I also remembered my research of a few months back, when Nick had been stabbed just under the lungs, and Christophe's symptoms were distressingly matching those of a collapsed lung, also called a 'sucking chest wound'. Christophe's breathing was fast and shallow. He looked pale with a cool, clammy skin. Instead of his lungs expanding properly with the breathing, the chest looked flatter than it should have been, with a barely audible hiss from the wound as the air came in and out of the lungs. This I did not hear myself: Ariel had covered the wound to prevent the air using this entrance/exit instead of the mouth and nose, but when he explained it, a chill settled in the room. Poor Christophe was in pain and anxious: it was terrible to watch, and it felt as though we could do so little. I wanted to give him shots of morphine from our emergency kit to relieve the pain, but Ushi stopped me, warning me that morphine is not for people with breathing problems. She added with a sorry look that only if he was dying should we go down that line, to make his last moments bearable.

*

We used the morphine around midday. When the drug kicked in, Christophe lost the pain and gained lucidity. Even though everything around him had turned psychedelic, he asked to see his wife and his daughter one last time. He might have a few hours left, but he wanted them to see him when he could still think and speak. He wanted them to see him smile, even though Chloé would be too young to remember. Christophe's last hours were full of dignity and love. His ego had too often hidden these qualities of his, and I regretted I did not have a chance to get to know this side of him better.

When his family left, he called me in and grabbed my hands. He had two special requests for me. Because of them, I would review all our current options and take a step back.

'Yoko, I would like you to be Godmother to Chloé,' he asked me in a breathy voice, panting between each word.

'Christophe, I am honoured. I...', I began.

'Isabelle and I had already discussed this. We agreed. Please. We cannot imagine anyone better suited for the role, or a better role model. I have never told you this, but I do appreciate all that you are trying to do. Please!' Every word he uttered was an effort for him. I was touched. I accepted with gratitude.

'Now, and it is as important, if not more,' Christophe continued. 'I would like you to promise you will look after Isabelle and Chloé.'

'Christophe, I will. Of course I will,' I replied eagerly and meant it.

'You need to bring them somewhere safe. You need to bring my wife and daughter somewhere where they will not be torn between the politics of either worlds, somewhere they will be free, somewhere where they will not have fears or abuse. Especially Chloé. Chloé, she is special. When Owen told me of Clémence's interest in my baby girl, I understood she would never be safe. Because, you see, Clémence is right. Chloé, she is like Simba. She can cross between worlds.'

'What!' I blurted.

'Isabelle and I worked it out in Morocco. We decided to try one night, just the baby and me. I crawled with Chloé in my arms, so that if the Fog split us, she would not fall from high. I was able to crawl a long way until I realised we had gone far into the Fog and she was accompanying me in the space between two worlds where there is only Fog. That's when I started to believe she might be like your wolf. So the next day, I hid her in a bag she could breathe in, and I went out with Louise when the baby was sleeping. Both Chloé and I came out with Louise in Morocco. I told Louise I had forgotten something and quickly returned home, where Isabelle was waiting for me. Together, we went to the Other World, Chloé still in the bag. It confirmed it. My baby girl can travel to both worlds and even into the Fog with me. She is too young for us to try anything else, and I don't know if she is exactly like Simba, but she is very special. Not a Relocated, a Facilitator or a Crosser. Just special. And in danger. She will always face the risk of abduction, brainwashing and being used. We didn't tell anyone, to protect her. Now... Now Isabelle can't cope with this alone. She can't. We need you. Chloé needs you. Please.'

'Christophe, I will look after her. I promise,' I told him, putting a hand on his shoulder in a gesture of reassurance. I was still trying to grasp all the implications of what he had just shared and what it meant for Chloé's future.

'She is not safe here, Yoko. You must bring her somewhere she will be safe,' Christophe added.

'Alaska?' I asked, a little confused.

'No. Isabelle cannot go to Alaska. This is too far away for her to travel in WII,' he was weakening. His voice was feeble. It was now only a whisper, and I had to bend over and place my ear close to his mouth to comprehend his next words. 'Somewhere else. Safe. Remote. Somewhere where the demands and strains from both worlds won't be able to reach her.'

'I… I will do my best. I promise,' I hurried to say. He was drifting away, I hoped it was only towards sleep.

*

Christophe was resting. His eyes had closed with a last breath of relief after hearing my promise. He was resting forever. While I was with him, Ariel and Leo had been in the room by the door, set back to give us some privacy. Now I was staring at Christophe's body, stunned, incapable of accepting I was looking at a corpse. Ariel came to check Christophe's pulse and confirmed he was dead. Leo put his arms around my shoulders. I felt tears running silently down my cheeks and I closed my eyes, too. My thoughts went back to a couple of days before, to Big Tom's death, to Jack in a coma. My mind went back to Julia, to Helo's family, to all the deaths around the Fog and me. Why had it come to this? Leo's grip got tighter. He was pulling me towards the door. I felt in a daze, everything blurred around me. I entered the living room. Isabelle took one look at me and understood. She let out a shrieking wail and broke into tears. Feeling the distress of her mother, Chloé began to cry. Eudes, with the natural instinct of the children, immediately came to me and hugged my leg. Jazz went to Isabelle to try to comfort her. Zeno, who had disappeared seconds after my entrance, returned with a steaming cup of tea that he handed to Isabelle. She took it gratefully, and even before taking a sip, holding the cup in her hand seemed to calm her down a little. Ariel's wife then arrived holding a tray with a large samovar and many cups with tea for everyone.

Ushi and Nick returned promptly, alerted by a messenger sent by Ariel. Nick immediately went to the room to check Christophe was indeed dead. Ushi was at loss as to what to do. She did not know Christophe, and in general, she was not prone to any display of emotions. Her love for Eudes was the first indication to us that she had any.

'Did he say anything? Before he… before he left?' Isabelle managed to say after a few sips of tea.

'His last words were for Chloé and you. It's all he talked about,' I answered softly.

'He wanted you to be Chloé's Godmother. We wanted…' she said as if to herself, lost in thought.

'Christophe asked me. I would be delighted. He also asked me to look after her, after you both. I promised I would,'

I kneeled next to Isabelle.

'It will not be like in Morocco, Isabelle. You are not alone here in WII. We will all look after you and Chloé,' I added and Isabelle nodded.

Jazz came to sit next to her. She was crying. I knew that her tears were as much for her loss as for Isabelle's, and maybe Isabelle realised it too when she took Jazz's hand. They looked at each other for an instant and fell into each other's arms, crying. Isabelle wanted to go and see Christophe to say one last goodbye. I proposed to go with her and so did Jazz. She refused; she needed to go alone. When she was gone, silence fell heavily in the room.

Ariel's wife had discreetly put food on the dining table and he suggested we should eat something. We might need all our strength in the days to come. Then, to avoid letting sorrow and gloom overtake us, we tried to numb our minds for the rest of the day by busying ourselves to secure Yerushaleim. Isabelle had gone to bed with a sleeping pill, following Jazz' suggestion of her own experience to deal with the first shock. During that time, Jazz discussed with Ariel what type of funeral and burial could be organised for Christophe. She would not make the decision, it was Isabelle's, but she wished to make it easier for the new widow by preparing the options available. While Ushi Tsou was arranging reinforcements for the security of the village with Dante's help, I was working along with Nick and Leo on how to get in touch with Leila through the Fog Dome. Based on Owen's story, we would not be able to reach the Dome unimpeded. Thanks to a solar-powered drone, we could check this information by sending images of the ground around the Fog Drone from the air. The drone would help us locate the camps from the Women's Revolution Movement and would serve as an intermediary radio to communicate with Leila. The apparatus needed a few hours in the sun to recharge its batteries. The wait was excruciatingly agonising. I longed to connect with parents, friends and Leila in London, and most importantly, we needed help.

*

However, this wait was also an opportunity to think. I had some difficult choices to make. I had made a promise to Christophe, and now had to respect it. Protecting Chloé and Isabelle was not the problem; his request to bring them somewhere safe and remote was. I wondered where that would be, or how to make sure it remained 'safe and remote'? An idea was forming. Not a plan yet, but an idea. Based on a recent memory. My need to communicate with London grew even more urgent.

Zeno, Leo, Nick and I crammed into one of the motorhomes and stared at the screen displaying the drone's images from its flight. To avoid Clémence spotting the strange bird and shooting at it, we had to make it fly slightly too high to have a detailed image of the ground. However, we detected a couple of the rebels' camps around the Fog Dome. It confirmed Owen's story. Next, we connected my Ftab to the drone's transmitter and dialled Leila.

'Yoko! Is that you, Yoko?' Leila answered with anxiety, after half a ring.

'Yes! Leila, it's me. I am with Zeno, Leo and Nick. We…'

'Where are you? What happened?' she interrupted me before I finished my sentence. 'Yoko, both the Fog houses in London and in Essex, they are blown and gone. And the Fog house in the mountain in Morocco, it is not fogged anymore… So we fear that… Christophe…'

'Christophe passed away this morning.'

'Oh no!' she said in a whisper. 'Nooooo…'

I related the events of the previous day to her: the explosion, the brief attack and what happened to Christophe, Isabelle and Chloé. I explained Clémence's interest in Simba and me. For the time being, I decided not to mention anything about Chloé. Leila listened quietly to the last updates on our situation in Yerushaleim. On her side, she told us that she had immediately asked Louise to go to the Fog Dome, but when she got there, the few new

Relocated informed her that a band of feisty women warned them not to venture out of the Fog Dome. They were circled.

*

Our helicopter was on the roof of *The Jazzin* when the house blew up. Pieces of the house and the helicopter had travelled to both worlds in the explosion. Otherwise, Ushi Tsou could have flown us to the Fog Dome and we would have had a chance to leave this world. Ushi Tsou and Nick were thinking an alternative could be that one of them broke through the lines of the rebels into the Fog Dome, get another helicopter and fly back to us; the other helicopter pilot among us was too injured for such a mission. They believed it was feasible; they had the training for it. However, Ushi Tsou hesitated about leaving Eudes and we did not want to take the risk of losing Nick. Additionally, I didn't want to flee to London and leave my friends and family here. They needed us.

*

With that line of thought, I broached a very specific subject with McRae, requesting that he and Leila must keep the rest of the conversation private. In both worlds, the Foggies' situation was unstable and could become intolerable. Something had to be done. The promise I made to Christophe had been the trigger to step forward and say enough was enough.

'Lochy,' I said to McRae. 'When we went to Scotland, it often felt like we were in the middle of nowhere. Do you know the land well?'

'I do.' I could hear in his voice that he was surprised at my reference to the Scottish trip. It had no link with the current situation.

'How remote is it? Could a small community live there in peace, with no questions asked?' I asked.

'You want to move to Scotland?' McRae asked, in return.

'Not just me, all the Relocated. My idea is that any one of them and of us who wish to have a proper new start, should be able to do so. One free of civil war and dangers linked to the politics of this world. Maybe this is another Utopia, but... In my promise to look after Isabelle and Chloé and take them somewhere safe, I knew it involved creating a new Fog Gate. They can't be far from the Fog. Yet, no Fog gate will be safe if there is anyone close by on either side of the door,' I explained.

'This is a bit extreme, isn't it?' Leila commented, quietly.

'I just wish to create a little haven of peace, like they have in Alaska. Without drama, death, politics...' I replied, vehemently.

'That's because nobody knows they are Foggies. The minute you move to Scotland and it becomes known, people will go there. The problems will just follow you,' McRae counter-argued.

'Not if my presence is not known!' I replied.

*

The idea was still vague, with many grey areas. Globally, the concept was that in a remote part of Scotland, maybe even a small island, the Foggies could establish a secret Fog location. Ideally it would be a large mansion (in my dreamy head, I imagined a romantic Highland castle) that we could use as a base to monitor the Gatekeepers and Relocated operations. Only a small separate house nearby (again, dreamy head imagined an old caretaker's cottage) would be fogged. Luxurious private properties with helicopter landing fields were not unusual in Scotland. One just assumed they belonged to some politician or financial big shot who enjoyed having a retreat with some privacy. As the public only knew Zeno, Harry and me, only us three would have to be cautious and discreet, locally. The other Foggies could travel as they wished. In WII, the Relocated would have a chance to settle down and create their town as they pleased, without the strain of Clémence's radical views and dangerous ways, or the backward mentalities of Lil'London and Newtonsee. Eudes and Chloé would grow up safe there. Isabelle and Jazz could rebuild their lives on new ground, leaving the bad memories behind.

Leila raised the subject of the newly Relocated through the Fog Dome, present and future: what about them? Would they also be invited to travel to Scotland and join the Fog community there? My thought was yes. It would have been unacceptable and ill-advised not to. The community in Scotland would benefit from the input of newcomers and an increase in numbers. Once the gate closed and they did not have access to our planet any more, it would give them a chance to survive and prosper. However, to protect the secrecy of the Scottish Fog, the newly Relocated would be told about a northern community, but not that there was a Fog gate there as well. As such, they would not expect to keep any links with their estranged past. Even those in the know would not have access to the Gate: only Foggies. The Relocated travelling north would be the ones ready for a real change and a new life.

Nick put an end to our conversation when the drone was on its way back. It could fly for only so long and it was partly cloudy. It was frustrating to end the conversation so abruptly. There was much more I wanted to know about the situation in London and the rest of the world.

*

In the evening, we gathered in Yerushaleim's small synagogue. Together, all those who had fled from Clémence's threat and the Jewish council of wise men, Ariel at their head, reviewed the situation. The town defences were very weak. We had arrived with limited weapons and the town had practically none. If Clémence decided to launch an attack on us with all her might, we would not last for long. It was unfortunate that the other pilot from the Society, who would be able to help now that they knew our location, had been injured during the attack that killed Big Tom. Ushi announced to the people present that she had decided there was no other way: she had to force her way into the Dome that night, pack as much as she could in a helicopter and come back here. Nick wanted to accompany her as a back-up but she refused. It would leave us without any military expert on site. As she stood up to go and say goodbye to Eudes, she looked at me with an intensity that was worth a thousand words. Should anything happen to her, she was counting on me to look after the child. I refrained from blurting out that he was my nephew and that I was ultimately the one looking after him anyway. It was not the moment to antagonise her. So I nodded. Later that night or more exactly early that morning, she slid out of town like a shadow. I had little doubt of her skills, but I feared the worst nonetheless. We had not been very lucky lately.

*

In a closer committee of Foggies and Relocated, we put Owen on the spot to further explain why Clémence was so intent on coming after us. Hesitantly at first, he shared his experience and how Clémence fascinated him; He admitted she had used him cleverly, kissing him though never sleeping with him. She was tantalising him, keeping him captive to his emotions and attraction for her.

Clémence had a double motivation to make a foray into Yerushaleim. First, her interest in Simba, Chloé and me. If she could have a Switcher along with two-way crossers, it would establish her own links to our world. I asked Owen why she had this sudden interest in having direct access when, in the past, she had tried to eliminate me. Owen then told me that with the apparition of the Fog Dome and the large number of Relocated expected to come through, she realised she soon risked losing control of the Women's Revolution. Clémence understood that she needed either to get rid of the Switcher, or control her. She opted for the second, believing it was more to her advantage, notably because of the access to weapons and advanced technology it entailed. However, if she did not manage to capture me and use me, then she would kill me.

'Slowly, I saw her become more ruthless, more determined. Originally, she was trying to avoid killing people, but soon she saw it as a means to an end,' Owen said, with a voice shaky with tears. He felt ashamed that she had fooled him.

'When I thought of Maisie and of the dangers Clémence put her through in attacking Woodfellas, I couldn't go along with the woman's plans. My love for Maisie was stronger than the fire Clémence had instigated in my heart. My mind cleared, and I knew I must come to you.'

I nodded. I was still angry with the young man for his betrayal. Yes, he was young; he was seduced, used, stupidly in love. It did not excuse his choices, though it made them less unforgivable.

'You mentioned there is a second reason why you believe she will want to attack Yerushaleim?' I continued.

'Yerushaleim… She has a distrust of the town with something that felt almost like a personal affront. You see, she is furious at the women of this town for dismissing her ideas and appeals. In addition, it is well known that this community has a better pregnancy and birth rate than others. It has been the case ever since they arrived. Often the councils or desperate barren women came and begged for their 'secret'. Always, they were told there was no secret, but Clémence, like anyone from Newtonsee and Lil'London, disbelieved them. I tried to tell her what I gathered from Ariel: that the 'secret' is medical. The Jews have a better understanding of the woman's cycle. Ariel's medical knowledge and that of his ancestors is evidently at the core of this practice. Clémence refuted my hypothesis, arguing that in this case, the doctors from our world would know it too, as they were more advanced. Yet she had enquired and learned that fertility in the United Kingdom is below 2 children per couple on average. In her mind, it proved that only Yerushaleim had the key to fertility, and she is determined to get it. Clémence could not comprehend that, in our modern times, people do not want a string of children to look after for various reasons.'

*

Struggling to sleep, Jazz sharing the bed next to me, I thought of the inhabitants of Yerushaleim. Would they never be free from the stigma their religion and specificities brought them? Not even crossing to another planet, to another world had managed to give them a clean slate. And as I stared at the ceiling in the dark, I wondered if they shouldn't come with us up north, too.

Day 3 (Tuesday)

Ushi left early in the morning. It was barely light. She proceeded very carefully in the knowledge that the women rebels were certainly watching the comings and goings of the Jewish town. So, instead of exiting and heading directly towards the Fog Dome, Ushi Tsou slowly and carefully circled the small town, keeping an eye out for signs of Clémence's group. She saw them easily. The rebels' watchers were beginners, yet Ushi felt they were learning fast: they had picked good positions, were holding their rifles properly, and were focused. When she was further away in the local woods, she called Nick on the 2-way radio and told him her observations and their locations. Nick made careful notes of it all. Ushi Tsou remained in contact regularly, as long as the radio had signal coverage.

Ushi's progression was slow. She was cautious. As WII's few basic roads must have been under surveillance, she stayed clear of them. However, Clémence and her women were also tracked and avoiding them, so she could encounter them anywhere. She was at a disadvantage of not knowing the ground and being short of time, having to avoid making too long a detour. Within an hour of careful walking and in the dim light of dawn, she spotted a large group of rebel women on the move. They were heading at a relatively fast speed in the opposite direction, towards Yerushaleim. Ushi, who still had radio connection with Nick – albeit feeble - hurriedly informed him. As she looked on, she hesitated taking on the group. If Clémence was amongst them, Ushi could behead the movement and put an end to the Civil War. She toyed with the idea for some time, but decided against taking the risk that something might go wrong; They were heavily armed and she was on another mission. Still, Clémence had lost the element of surprise.

*

In the meantime, Nick came to shake me out of my half-sleeping, half-awake state, to inform me we would have unwelcome visitors soon.

'Damn! What should we do?' I blurted, immediately on my feet and trying to raise Jazz. She was groggy from sleep and struggling to open her eyes, the normal effect of taking sleeping pills to give her aching heart some peace.

'We can't take the risk of you falling into Clémence's hands. We must get you out and hide you,' Nick said, firmly.

'No. I will not leave. I want to stand up to her, not flee,' I retorted, with a firm tone.

'Don't make me make you, because I will. And take Simba with you, as well as Eudes, Isabelle and Chloé,' Nick ordered.

'Who made you decide what is best?' I retorted.

'Yoko, stop being a stubborn ass and go,' Jazz joined the conversation with a sleepy voice. 'I've already lost one of the people that matters the most to me. I do not want to lose another.'

'Guys, she doesn't want to kill me yet,' I replied.

'She didn't want to kill Christophe, either,' Nick hit back. 'Yet it happened. Don't underestimate the random casualties of war.'

'I will not go,' I put on my determined face, crossed my arms and stamped my feet. Just like a child having a tantrum.

'That, we will see,' Nick said, crossing his arms and looking at me with a smirk. 'I need to warn the others, but I'll be back shortly. Get ready.'

As he left, Jazz and I got out of the long, thick and old-fashioned nightgowns worn by Yerushaleim women and dressed in comfortable jeans, hiking boots, summer tops and warm jackets. It was cold at this early time of the morning. Jazz did not say a word at first, but I felt her tension and her being upset with me. I knew she would soon be on my back, like Nick, urging me to leave. I understood their reasons, but I did not want to run away while Yerushaleim was under attack from afar. I could not leave my friends behind, nor did I want special treatment. I was fed up with special treatment. It did not make me feel privileged but useless, a coward. I was going to stand my ground with the rest of Yerushaleim, and that was it! Unfairly upset at Jazz for the probable nagging she was about to do but had not yet done, I told her I was going downstairs to help prepare tea and food for everyone. We were going to need it. Soon enough, Leo and Zeno arrived with Nick, and Jazz came down. They told me Isabelle would bring Eudes and Chloé, shortly. I went to the kitchen to help bring the plates of food. On my return, there was awkwardness in the room. Jazz avoided my eyes. Zeno and Leo both told me they agreed with Nick that I should leave Yerushaleim. I answered a definite no and poured tea for everyone, acting as if the discussion was closed. I ignored the look Zeno and Leo gave each other, and the sigh coming from Nick, sat down and slowly sipped my tea, determined to face their renewed attempts to convince me. I was tired and my head felt heavy. Then everything started to look blurry. I grabbed the table as the room swirled around me. In an instant, I understood they had drugged me. Drugged by my own friends! All went black.

*

I woke up, 6 hours later, in a dark and humid space that looked like a cavern. A few candle lanterns lit the room. Isabelle was breast-feeding Chloé at the foot of the makeshift mattress where I was lying. Jazz was reading a story to Eudes and trying to keep him quiet. I turned a heavy head and spotted Zeno at the entrance, keeping guard with a shotgun. I later learnt that Leo and Nick were outside, acting as lookouts close by. When I sat up, my head throbbed as if I was suffering from a hangover, Jazz and Isabelle shared a look. Jazz handed the children's book to Isabelle who took over the story telling. My dear friend brought me a jug and a full glass of water as I tried to clear my head. The sooner I got my wits together, the sooner I would be able to give them all a piece of my mind. I took the glass with a grunt, drank it all in one go and she replenished it. When I finished the second glass, I was ready for a fight and immediately began with Jazz. Stoically, she let me rant and wind myself up. The throbbing in my head grew in unison with my frustration at her lack of reaction. No one spoke in the room; everyone just ignored my explosion. I went on about how unacceptable their action had been, how I had the right to do what I wanted, how they had been sneaky and back-handed. I finally shouted that they had broken my trust. This was the only moment Zeno showed a sign of acknowledgement of my loud ranting, as he waved a hand down to indicate I should lower my voice. That was it: that was the last straw and I swore out loud: 'Fuck you! Fuck you all!'

I was still a bit shaky on my legs, but my anger was giving me wings. I started to walk towards the entrance and Zeno barred my way.

'Where do you think you are going?' Zeno asked me, softly but firmly.

'I am returning to Yerushaleim,' I answered with my chin up and a tone of defiance.

'Don't be ridiculous,' Zeno replied.

'Yoko, come back here. Come and sit down. We have news you will want to hear,' Jazz called from inside.

'Dammit!' I said to myself. Now I was torn between my scorned ego and free will, and my curiosity. A brief thought made me realise that I had no idea where I was and how to get to Yerushaleim. Therefore, I went back inside, sulking, and put myself down on the mattress. Jazz placed some ham and cheese and a piece of bread on a plate before giving it to me. It made me realise I was starving.

'We are all sorry we had to go to the extent of knocking you out with an animal tranquiliser...' Jazz began.

'You drugged me with an animal tranquiliser!' I exclaimed.

'More specifically the one that Clémence had aimed at Simba and missed,' Zeno offered. Jazz shot him a look indicating it would not be a good idea to give further details on the subject.

'Anyway,' Jazz continued, 'We all agreed that whatever happened, you should not fall into the hands of the rebels. Too much was at stake. We also agreed that you would be a pain about it and refuse to back down. None of us could be bothered arguing and wasting valuable time. The decision to take drastic measures to get you out to safety was unanimous. The blame falls on all of us, as a group.'

'That doesn't make it more acceptable!' I blurted.

'Well, what is done is done. Just accept it and move on. You are usually good at that! We have enough problems already for you to make a fuss. Honestly woman, if you were not always so stubborn and if your main sin was not pride, we would not have had to do this.'

I was about to retort something spiteful but she stopped me in my tracks, raising a hand and her voice.

'Yoko, I *really* have a lot to tell you. Just listen.'

*

Jazz was right: it was already lunchtime and a lot had happened.

To be able to get all the Foggies out of Yerushaleim, Nick and Zeno had had to create a clean and safe way out. This is when the Italians' compulsory military services came in handy. Nick's experience in organising such operations became crucial. Ushi Tsou had had it easy: sneaking out in the dark was standard for a professional. It was more difficult to get a large and mostly untrained bunch through 'enemy lines'. The fact that I was knocked out added to the difficulty, as well. Additionally, Nick did not want to leave the motorhomes behind, with drones, technology and ammunition. We also had a serious conundrum: what would happen to Yerushaleim once we had left? When asked if the other two larger towns would offer some support, Ariel gave a small, kind smile. Lil'London and Newtonsee were willing to send a few groups of their 'soldiers' but argued they did not have many to spare, as they had to ensure the safety of their own people first. In brief, their help would be very limited. There had never been much love lost towards the Jewish community in WII, and they were not going to start spreading the love now.

The Foggies and Relocated had an emergency meeting. Nick, Leo and

Zeno, who were aware of my wish to create a Fog Gate in the Highlands, took the discretionary decision to share the information with the rest of the Relocated and Foggies, and review the various options it entailed. They regretted having drugged me before the meeting, not after. At least they had some form of regret, I thought.

The prospect of going on a long journey through uncharted land in this world was daunting. Nevertheless, it was better than the local dangers and threats. The group then made another discretionary decision: to invite Ariel and the population of Yerushaleim to join our journey. From the start, they had never judged us: on the contrary, they had displayed respect, warmth and generosity, despite our differences. Whenever a life was in danger, Ariel never hesitated to assist. They knew the risks in letting us come and find refuge with them. They never asked for anything in return for their help. We could not just abandon them to their fate, fending for themselves with few weapons and little expectation to withstand a siege for long, even though they argued that the Foggies must go, for their own protection. From Owen, we knew Clémence was intent on getting to Yerushaleim, whether or not we had found refuge in the town. They had been here for us; we wanted to be here for them. Even though asleep when it was discussed, everyone knew I would agree with this statement.

First, Ariel met with the wise men leading the town. Then, the heads of each family discussed the wise men's recommendations. To our surprise, the conclusion was that the whole town would come with us on our journey north.

'Our people have a nomadic tradition,' Ariel announced to the gathered Foggies and Relocated. 'More often than not, it was not by choice. On this land, we were lucky to settle for centuries. Now it looks like we need to end this sedentary life and get back on the road, like so many of our ancestors had to before us. We will join and help you on the journey.'

Instead of a dozen of us, we would be travelling as a couple of thousand, including babies, children and elderlies. It would be slow, noticeable and easy for the Women Rebels to track. On the other hand, the numbers could be an advantage, as it would be more difficult for Clémence to overcome us. Or so I hoped.

The only two people who showed hesitation in joining the journey were Jazz and, to a lesser extent, Molly. Jazz stated that she had found her place here. She had found a purpose in fighting alongside Maud for a better society. She believed in her work, she believed in pursuing it with the newly relocated at the Fog Dome, and she believed she could make a difference. She also knew that I would have to come back regularly, and that we would still see a lot of each other. So, in this cave, Jazz announced to me that she would not be coming with us and our paths would part in a few hours. I never saw this coming. I understood, but something collapsed in me.

*

Back on the events of the morning, the Italians and Nick neutralised the small rebel camps promptly before the larger group, spotted by Ushi, arrived. We had the element of surprise. Every one of the women was immobilised and tied up to a tree with a gag. In the meantime, the town was getting ready for a swift exit. The essentials - tools, fabric, food, religious artefacts and other family transportable valuables - were packed on horses and wagons. People packed heavy bags to carry on their shoulders, too. The journey was too long for the motorhomes to have sufficient fuel: ripped of their furniture and mechanics, they were light enough for horses to pull. One was filled with some local treasures, like religious items and Ariel's precious jars with ointments and healing herbs. There was very little time. A first group of the community and the Foggies left for the secret caves the Jews had built for their own protection, in case they needed to flee and hide. Again, the Jews were putting us first before their own safety. We had barely arrived in our underground hidden spot, I was told, when the rebels appeared and soon circled Yerushaleim. Most people were still in town. Weapons were drawn and shots were fired. The men from the caves – Nick and Foggies aside, but including Owen – were placed in strategic positions to shoot at the rebels as well, from outside town. Although brave, they were not numerous enough. We did not have an accurate number on the women rebels, but we estimated them to be at least a couple of hundred and they were well armed. The total population of Yerushaleim far exceeded this, but weapons were scarce. We needed Ushi Tsou to get back and fast.

Ushi had left signal-relays on her way to the Fog Dome. It did not work with the radios, just served as a signal boost to communicate with us via Ftab once she had arrived. When she called, everyone had hopes it was to confirm her immediate return. She could make it back in less than 20 minutes by helicopter. However, the news was not good. She had been shot while making her way inside the Fog Dome. Though the injury was not lethal, it had gone through her shoulder and incapacitated her. She was unable to use her arm, or to fly. This was a real blow to our morale and defence. Aside from the sparsity of our weapons, we also had only one professional, Nick, to supervise the safe retreat of the whole community.

The Italians argued that Nick should not put himself in danger and supervise only from the back, remaining in a safe position. They wanted him to stay with the women to protect us. Nick counter-argued that their training was basic and out of date, even more so in comparison with his. He was our best chance as a commander for the battle. However good his arguments, he stood no chance against three determined Italians. They finally reminded him that his mission was to protect me, first and foremost.

'I am her boyfriend, not a professional bodyguard,' Leo had said. 'And because I am her boyfriend and want the best for her, I will swallow my pride and acknowledge that you can protect her best. Well, let's limit this to the rebels. I will take care of the close-body protection though.'

'Well said!' Zeno patted Leo on the back. 'And this is why I will be the one in the front line. You stay with Yoko.'

And thus followed another argument between the Italians on who would get in the line of fire, all of them volunteering. It only got sorted when Dante picked up the short straw. Literally, they drew straws. He waved it around with a beaming smile.

'If I see that Clémence, she is dead! Oh yeah!' he whispered to himself afterwards, the smile gone.

That is what war does to you; the architect had turned into a fighter ready for the kill.

Nick's suggested strategy was to attack the women rebels as soon as possible, ideally before they had a chance to take their position of siege, circling the town. His idea: make an impression by an offensive with a bang. Using grenades. Relatively speaking, we had plenty of them: a whole box full. They were distributed to all the Relocated, even Owen and Maisie, with a quick training on how to use them. No one was happy with the idea of throwing them at the women, not even Nick. Even if we had already suffered losses because of the Women Rebels, we were not comfortable with the idea of killing anyone (except for Clémence, for some). It was war and war always brought deaths. However, we would first try to scare them and not hit the rebels directly.

'I have killed many people in my life already,' Nick said, grumpily. 'And too many were innocent casualties of war. They haunt you, those deaths. I don't want you to have their ghosts during your sleep, like I do.'

Dante and Zeno, armed with a rocket-launcher and grenades, went ahead and released their weapons on the advancing band of women, trying to deter them first by avoiding direct shots into the group. However, there came a time when they had no choice other than to launch a rocket in the middle of them, as the rebels became aware that we were unwilling to kill. We hoped one of the early casualties would be Clémence and that, without their leader, the women rebels would scatter away. We did not even know for certain if, indeed, Clémence was there, if she was hurt or killed, but the women did retreat. A small group of our fighters pursued them as far away as possible to give room to the villagers to escape. Lookouts were also set up for our security.

*

All of this had happened during my sound sleep and I was listening avidly, grateful that we were all safe. The story was too captivating for me to remain upset much longer. Isabelle joined the conversation after she put a sleeping Chloé into a makeshift cradle.

'We are going to bury Christophe here in Yerushaleim. The Jews have agreed to make an exception for him on the edge of their cemetery, despite him being a catholic. Like that, when Chloé will want to see where her father is, she will be able to locate him.' She began to cry quietly. 'I don't want any of you to come. I know you would and I am grateful, but I wish, no, I *need* to have those last minutes alone with him. Ariel has organised for some people from Yerushaleim to do the burial and leave. I will be very quick, then I will leave with you all.'

*

The rest of the afternoon, on our own and as a group, we prepared for the long trip ahead. Regularly, the lookouts continued to make cautionary tours to check the women rebels were not making a comeback. We were aware that Clémence had probably left spies behind to keep an eye on Yerushaleim. She was a calculating and determined woman; if alive, she would not give up on her goals and ideas. She could be patient too in her determination, as she had proved acting as the ingénue young wife of Augustus Hoare for years, waiting for her time to come.

An hour before it was time to leave, Jazz came to say goodbye. A couple of men from the village were to accompany her so that she was not going to travel across the land unassisted. They would then make their way back towards us, informed of our short-term destination with a basic map. They would also act as watchers for our rear. If the situation were unsafe, they would catch up with us by horse and warn us.

Separating from Jazz broke my heart.

'Are you sure? Are you absolutely sure? This doesn't have to be your fight. Maud is doing a good job alone, and…' I didn't want her to go. Not only was I worried for her safety, I also selfishly wished to keep my friend by my side.

'I don't have the choice: I don't do walking! No way can I join this long walk of yours!' She joked. I smiled but my heart was not in it. Jazz continued. 'I know I don't have to: I want to. This is something I believe in and there isn't much left in my life now other than my beliefs. I will not let it go. And you will visit often. I know this. Moreover, you will need me to liaise with the Relocated and the towns. Wait and see: soon you will be happy to have your trustworthy friend keeping you up-to-date and helping you with the locals. I know you will be incapable of staying away. If you think the reverse, you are delusional.'

'Hey!' I protested, but Jazz silenced me with a laugh.

'Nutty, sometimes your friends know you better than yourself on how to handle you. Why do you think we all acted in unison this morning!'

'About that...' I started.

'Oh no. We will not see each other again for some time. No bickering!'

I smiled. She was going to get away with it, wasn't she? We hugged each other. I felt a big lump in my throat and my eyes burned, ready to cry.

'My dear friend, my heart-adopted sister, I love you.' My voice was shaky as I held Jazz tight.

'Oh Nutty! I love you so, so much! Promise me you will not take stupid risks. Promise me!

'As if anyone would let me,' I laughed.

Leo came and stood by me as I waved Jazz goodbye. I forced myself not to shed any tears. It was only goodbye. Everything would be just fine. Soon, Leo tore me away from watching the empty space ahead. We had to make a start on our journey, as well. We planned to walk until sunset, seven hours away.

*

Halfway through our first stretch of walk, everyone was silent, concentrating on the way ahead, on their sore feet and their aching backs. Despite my own pain, I felt elated. I had begun to understand this journey was not just necessary through the circumstances; it was beneficial for my sanity. It carried an unexpected spiritual feel, as if I was going to find myself again. I had not realised, until then, how close I was to getting lost within myself.

Day 4 (Wednesday)

My feet hurt. My legs hurt. My back hurt. My neck was sore. To make it worse, the coffee at breakfast was absolutely disgusting. Even the Italians decided to do without one. As Zeno said, it was a dreary thought to face a whole day of walking without a good dose of caffeine. It was a psychological need as well as physical. I opted for tea instead. Even after years in Great Britain, I had still failed to gain quintessential Britishness: I had not packed any tea bags. I suspiciously sipped one of the brews specially prepared by Ariel, but it was a good surprise: I liked the sweetness of Ariel's drink with its touch of spice.

It was hot goat's milk with honey and cinnamon, a special treat for those who had not had such spices for generations. With this, breakfast consisted of ham, cheese, bread. Nick practically force-fed me half a dozen boiled eggs as well. Apparently, it was the best source of protein and energy for the day ahead. I was ravenous but that didn't help the eggs go down. Neither did the tea.

*

To keep my spirits up, I focused on the thought that Ushi Tsou would be able to reach us by helicopter within a few days. Before we all got to sleep the night before, we talked to her. It might be our last chance; the signal was very poor. She had been adamant her injury was not going to stop her flying for long. Leila, my parents and others from London had recorded news and messages. During the night and thanks to the low bar of signal that we had, they were downloaded onto our Ftabs. Leila had had the foresight to think of this way to inform us with audio files we could listen to during the walk. There were the general files for everyone, and individual ones, like one from my parents to me.

During our brief chat, Ushi Tsou proved disinterested in what was happening in London.

'My priority is to get on with the mission here, not gather information on the mess,' she replied, dismissively.

'The mess? What mess?' Zeno enquired, eagerly.

'Politicians, ecology, pandemic, whatever. Same old, same old. I can't be bothered with them any more,' she snapped.

'And Ingis Chen? I am surprised your old boss has not tried to get in touch,' I asked her. His name had not been around for some time. From past experiences, it was not a good sign.

'Of course he did. He left messages for me to contact him as soon as I could,' she told us.

'What did he want?' I asked her.

'I don't know. I didn't call him. Not my priority.' Her firm tone and her demeanour indicated that she didn't want to discuss the matter any further. Instead, she asked after Eudes and how he was coping with the event. She gave us tips on how to help him, what were his physical limits and other tricks she had learned in the months looking after him. Ahmed and I were the ones she saw as her replacement. Temporary replacement. When talking about Eudes and how to handle him, her whole voice slowly switched from stern and cold to soft and loving. It was fascinating to hear. It didn't last, the second she stopped instructing us about Eudes, she returned to being as hard as nails.

When she would be ready to fly again, Ushi Tsou's role was tri-fold. She was to watch our backs from the air so that Clémence did not catch up with us; liaise with the Fog Dome; prepare fuel stops ahead for the journey up north. On the fuel issue, she would have to fly and leave fuel tanks at strategic points where refuelling would be required, later. The idea was that she needed to stock as much as possible on each stop to enable her, ultimately, to cover the whole journey. It meant we would be left without our backup for long periods of time while she was on her round trips, north or south. Not a reassuring thought, yet still better than now; not having her at all. It was a big project for someone who was still unable to even fly. I never expected to look forward to seeing her that much.

*

Leila's idea of recording information for us was brilliant. Listening to her calm voice on the Ftab helped to pass the time and to feel connected with my loved ones, despite the news from London not being uplifting. Sadly, the Ftab battery would not last forever and it was a temporary treat.

First, the Modern Marburg virus still did not have a cure. The pandemic had considerably slowed in the northern hemisphere and in Australia and New Zealand, but the situation was still out of control in the rest of the world. Europe, North America and the Australasia faced a wave of immigrants never witnessed before. They knocked at the wealthier countries' doors in their thousands of thousands. More exactly, the immigrants attempted to knock down their doors, as those countries had closed their borders.

The worst was at the borders between Mexico and the United States. It was under strict military control with orders to shoot-on-sight. The pressure at the borders was even stronger than usual as, for three full days now, the US had had its own Fog in the public eye. As planned, Adam had stayed overnight in Alcatraz on Saturday, escaping before dawn by helicopter, courtesy of the Society. Now the government had to deal with the same demands, protests and dilemmas the British government faced, from inside and outside. The UN had immediately applied their recommendations previously addressed to the British only. It should not come as a surprise that the USA dragged its feet in applying the recommendations they had promoted so strongly a few days prior. At the time, the Government had presented them as exigencies more than suggestions…

Adam and Sophia Koplat were giving selected interviews to explain their decisions and their side of the story,

especially as one of the consequences of Fog Alcatraz was an increase in followers for Lally O'Maleigh. The latest issues raised by the new Fog on American soil fed her argument that the Fog was the work of the devil; that it brought out the worst in people. She even used the Koplats' Jewish origins to emphasise that the Fog was unchristian! For all his faults, I was beginning to feel that Ingis Chen was a light piece of cake by comparison. He was manipulative with dangerous dictatorial tendencies but he was no religious fanatic. In many ways, he was even helpful to anyone interested in the Fog. Leila confirmed that his Fog advisory and legal support consulting firm was thriving. He was also the main UN specialist and consultant on the Fog now.

'Good for him,' I thought, with a twinge of cynicism. 'With a bit of luck, this will satisfy his thirst for recognition and power and he won't push his ridiculous project to save mankind by force-crossing 7 billion people through the Fog. If he sticks with this current attitude, he could even be bearable to have around as a business partner.'

*

Next, my parents' voices came up, speaking to me alternately or together as if in front of me. It really filled me with happiness to hear them. They began with light chit-chat about their time in London, visiting the town's hidden gems, like the Wallace Collection museum, the Greenwich area or even beautiful cemeteries. Slowly, they broached more serious subjects, the like of Charles-Antoine having a fit, cut from his son and his partner. He demanded that Ahmed and Eudes be led to the Fog Dome immediately, refusing to understand that the situation was unsafe. Ahmed had been given the option to return with Jazz to Lil'London, yet he had chosen to accompany us instead. He would rather be somewhere he could choose his new life without new prejudices, and Charles-Antoine could go there to see them. He asked if we could pass on a message to Charles-Antoine, informing him they had to travel to a secure and secret location. Charles-Antoine had work opportunities in London: Scotland was less of an option for him. Would Charles-Antoine adjust? If he did, he would have to agree to our terms, as his coming back and forth would otherwise risk revealing our whereabouts… I had a lot of time to think on the road and my mind wandered on all the possibilities.

On a more positive note, my parents wished to join us in Scotland. They had nothing and no one more important than Eudes and me: they wished to be by our sides.

'At whatever age, you will always be our little girl. And now, as much as ever before, we want to be there for you. We will follow you and support you wherever you go. As Eudes will be there as well, it is an obvious choice. Also, he can do with having his family around,' my mother said.

They planned to go to the Highlands with McRae the following day, Thursday. The preparations for our arrival were complex and already in full swing. First, they planned to gather food, large tents and warm clothes. The technology would come later. We had to proceed carefully, to not attract attention, especially from the British Government. We might inform them later, or not. McRae had carefully selected the best location for us. At first I considered an island the best option. He talked me out of it: depending on weather and sea conditions, the islanders would be cut from the mainland for indefinite periods of time. Also, our comings and goings would be more notable and conspicuous.

On another subject still, Putu's arrival in London and her energy had surprised everyone. This young woman, who appeared so pale and fragile, had imposed herself with aplomb. She was softly-spoken and didn't make waves; we already knew this. We also knew her mind was made of rock and she was determined to help those in need. What we had never had a chance to witness was how she could silence a room of officials by stating, in a quiet firm voice, what she was going to do, how she was going to do it and what she expected them to provide for her task. As I listened, I could visualise the scene and felt so proud of her. I had grown attached to and protective of each Foggy, even if they sometimes annoyed me (Ah… Sophia). In the end, we all completed each other. Often I wondered if the Fog, or whatever was behind the Fog, had picked us on purpose or at random. I liked to think there was some kind of mastermind behind it all. As the thought crossed my mind, the Foggies who had died came back into my thoughts. The family in Indonesia who, apart from Helo, disappeared before we even got a chance to know them. Clare and Christophe. And Jack, who was in a state between life and death. He was so endearing and, well - unlucky. So if we were all to complete each other and we were all part of a big plan, could we proceed without them?

*

As we studied the map of our journey at lunchtime and compared it with our current rhythm, I was filled with doubt. We had just under 590 miles to walk, or about 940kms, which, at our average speed and walking 8 hours per day, would take about 3.5 weeks. *What was I thinking?!* I said to myself, not for the first time. Choosing a remote corner of the Scottish Highlands sounded like a great idea when it was just for us Foggies and a few Relocated. I had not realised how long and difficult it would be to walk. Now, we were about two thousand people … Me and my grand ideas! Sometimes I really felt I was making things worse, instead of helping anyone. Ariel did not flinch when he heard the result of our calculations. He only nodded and smiled.

'Will there be any others there?' he asked.

'Not as far as we know,' Zeno replied. 'We were there a few weeks back and we didn't encounter any sign of human life in WII. On the other hand, it's a hunter's paradise. The wild life was blooming.'

'This is good. Tell me more about the land that is to be our new home, please.' Ariel replied. It was time to leave again, so we continued talking while we walked.

*

The Italians and I talked about Scotland, a land that we had discovered only recently. It had bewitched me with its rough beauty. The others had felt as strongly as me. We described the lakes - or lochs, the windy hills, the pure water and depth of the blue sky. We tried to share the sense we had to be an integral part of nature, to belong. Then naturally, the conversation turned to our true homelands as another beloved memory. I described the Mediterranean coast of my childhood, the small hills with the tortuous olive trees, or picking the ripe apples directly from the trees around my parent's village. I spoke of running in vineyards and lavender fields at weekends with my sister, when we were still young and got along. I explained how we could hear the cicadas by day and the crickets at sunset, and how there is only a limited time when you might, just might, hear them both together. I struggled to find the words to convey the blissful feeling when lying on the sand under the warm sun of May, listening to the sound of crashing waves, watching the clouds and birds in the sky, with hardly anyone else on the long beaches.

When I couldn't speak any more, my throat dry but with a beaming smile at the wonderful memories, Dante and Leo took over. They spoke with passion and wide hand gestures about Rome and its surroundings. One of Leo's favourites was to randomly drive his motorbike, late at night, when the streets were quieter and without tourists. He knew the places to go to have the freshest *cornetto* directly out of the oven at dawn, and where else they served the best espresso. Dante also spoke of his *Roma*, giving us an oral tour of the monuments, not by location but in chronological order, so that we benefitted from a class in history as well as one in architecture.

'Si, si, si,' said Zeno. 'Ma, I still think my hometown is the best.'

'Does it have a fascinating history, too?' Ariel asked.

'No,' Zeno replied.

'Unique monuments?' Dante took over.

'No,' Zeno answered.

'Beautiful beaches?' Leo offered.

'No.'

Dante and Leo gave Zeno a dubious look.

'It's the people. We are just the best,' Zeno finally said, with a grin. He then proceeded to tell us fun local stories, including what mischief he got up to growing up. We all laughed.

Unbeknownst to us, we had started a trend that continued for the following days. Each of us would talk for at least a couple of hours about some experiences, locations, history or travels that touched us. We would open up on what we loved only; never did we refer to anything we disliked. Anything negative was spontaneously brushed away. The walk was still long and extenuating, yet the sharing and learning from each other made it warm. The bond between us grew stronger and even deeper than it was.

*

That night, I could barely keep my eyes open when it came to typing notes in my diary. Leo, next to me on the makeshift bed, gently took the Ftab from my hands and closed it.

'You should really save its battery and recharge yours. You will need both,' he whispered and softly kissed me behind the ear. We were too exhausted to have more than a cuddle and we soon fell asleep under a beautiful sky and thousands of stars. I slept better than ever before, cosy in Leo's arms, despite the pain of my whole body.

Day 5 (Thursday)

I dreamed of blister plasters and broccoli. The food we had was quite good, though based essentially on bread and meat. I longed for fruit and vegetables. However, my mind was mostly focused on the blisters covering the soles and sides of my feet. Strangely, the problem affected the Foggies more than the Yerushaleim people. So much for our top of the range hiking boots.

Our group was falling into a good rhythm, adjusting quickly. Several times during the day, looking back at our lot, I thought of the numerous stories of exodus through the history of mankind. It must have looked like this, entire families with babies, young children, parents and elderlies, travelling side by side. No one had been left behind. The older people were the only ones on horses or sitting amid the belongings on the wagons. Jews were the most well known community to have suffered imposed or necessary exodus. Even though, there were many others with such experiences. I thought of the lines of refugees fleeing African countries at war; of the Indians and Pakistanis at the creation of Pakistan in 1947, to name a couple only. And now here. I shivered: was it another consequence of the Fog gate creation? Had we brought it with us? It reminded me of a line from Agent Smith in the movie 'The Matrix': '*Human beings are a disease, a cancer of this planet*'. Sadly, the Fog was not able to cure humans from spreading that virus in the wiring of their brain.

These were gloomy thoughts and were far from representative of my mood. On the contrary, I felt spiritually and surprisingly rejuvenated by the thought of the days ahead. I slowly became oblivious to my aching body – it hurt so much everywhere, I could not distinguish a specific pain any more. My mind seemed clearer and I began to appreciate the beauty of the wild nature surrounding me, as well as the support each and everyone gave each other. I was learning to listen again to my surroundings without a thousand other thoughts crossing my mind at the same time. Simply, I was rediscovering living in the here and now. I caught myself closing my eyes and breathing deeply, or focusing on the song of one single bird in a distant forest. Adding the other sounds around me, one by one, the ensemble created a strange new music that made me smile. There is no other way to define it: I was learning to meditate.

One of my pleasures was also to observe Simba blooming in the nature. It was a long journey for her and she was still young for it. In the morning, she was full of energy and would run after the small animals we encountered, or growl at those that could be dangerous. As I observed the landscape, she would run across it and stop, alert, taking in any new scenery. Afterwards, she would run back to me, confident she could protect me.

Moreover, the journey was bringing me even closer to Leo. What we lacked in intimacy, we gained in spending time together, creating our own bubble of privacy. In the long moments of silence, sensing his presence filled me with a tenderness towards him that was often overwhelming. All his actions were full of attention and affection towards me. He put me first in everything he did. His love was so real, so present, I wondered how it could not be touched. Sometimes, when I had doubt or when the exhaustion brought my mood down, I would fall into his arms and lean my head on his shoulder, feeling his arms around me. Within a few minutes, I would be appeased, re-energised even, as if his love and care had quietened all my physical and mental aches.

*

Eudes also brought a smile to my face. He was a good child and he coped with the circumstances well. I thought of Ushi Tsou. He was her only focus, and the reason that made me believe we could count on her. She was working hard for us as it meant securing his future. She clearly loved and missed him as he missed her. Aside from her and me, he had also accepted Leo and Ahmed carrying him to bed. Things were looking good for him: he would be well looked after. I was ready to end this day on this good note. That was not to be.

*

The sky was already dark when we heard the ominous sound of horses galloping towards our camp. We were not expecting anyone to return from hunting, so it was foreboding. They had to be the lookouts left behind, coming to warn us of danger. Should the messenger be the bearer of good news, he would have waited until the morning. It was a dangerous trip by night in the unknown land. A heavy silence fell on our already quiet group and we quickly lit some torches.

'I came as fast as I could,' the horseman said, on reaching us. 'It's Clémence. She is following you with a large group. They appear on the offensive.'

'Hell!' I burst out. The inner peace gained during the day drained in one go, like bath water once the plug is pulled.

'They are not far, either,' his face was frightened.

'Where are they?' asked Zeno.

'About 10 miles south,' the horseman replied. 'It was too dark to determine, for certain, how many they are.'

'So how do you know they are after us?' I asked.

He glanced at Nick, who glanced at Ariel, who looked south at the forest.

'When we were preparing for the journey,' Nick said, 'we knew chances were Clémence would organise some of her women to keep track on our movements. She is a very determined woman; she wouldn't just let us go that easily. So we asked Ariel if even more brave members of his communities would be willing to work as watchers at the rear, miles away from the end of our moving column, to keep an eye on any followers. There are twenty watching our back, not just four as you believed – the four who accompanied Jazz back. We gave them several tracking signals and I check on them at the end of each day.'

'Thank God you are a pro and thought ahead!' I said to Nick.

'Has Eudes got a tracking device? And Chloé? And Isabelle?' Owen asked. Nobody had heard him arrive.

'Eudes has one. Chloé and Isabelle don't,' Nick replied.

'Do you have spares? They really ought to have one each,' Owen insisted. 'Clémence really wants to get her hands on the two children. Especially Chloé. What about Simba?'

'Simba is tagged and can be tracked. Why is Clémence interested in Chloé?' Nick looked inquisitively at Owen. Seeing the young man uncertain and avoiding my eyes, Nick turned his attention to me and repeated: 'Why is Clémence especially interested in Chloé?'

'She is the daughter of a Switcher and born between two worlds. She believes Chloé might have 'special powers',' I answered, reluctantly.

'Like Simba?' Nick persisted.

'Yes, like Simba,' I replied.

'I see… Does she?' Nick asked the obvious question. I didn't want to get into this subject.

'Nick, Chloé is not even two months old! I don't want to even think about it! The only thing I care about is making sure she is safe. So, do you have a spare tracking device for her?'

'No, I am afraid I don't.' Nick's look was apologetic.

'Please take mine!' Owen offered immediately. 'Dad gave it back to me on Sunday. She needs it more than I do. I still feel terribly guilty over my behaviour. So much of what happened is my fault!'

'Clémence used you. One way or another, she would have done it. You were young and foolish. She has no excuse,' I said to Owen, kindly.

'Also, you provided us with valuable information. Thanks to you, we knew of her interest for Yerushaleim, Yoko and Simba, and… Chloé,' Nick added.

'And Eudes,' Zeno added. 'I am going to talk to Ahmed and give him speed-training to use a shotgun. Right now.'

'Not now.' Nick stopped him. 'We don't want the shotgun to be heard.'

'Then I will teach him how to use a bow,' Ariel said.

'A bow?' Leo and Dante said, in unison.

'Yes, it is what we teach the young when they start hunting. Maybe Owen and Maisie could come and join as well. And you all if you wish.'

That brought a few seconds silence around the group. I quite fancied learning to use as many weapons as possible.

'Yes, I will come,' I replied.

'Clémence is taking it to another level,' Leo said. 'I believe this is also turning personal. Imagine, we are robbing her of the opportunity to get what she believes to be the Jews' 'fertility secret' from Yerushaleim. And she probably wants to brainwash all the Jewish children. I am not even referring of her old rivalry and envy towards you, Yoko.'

'Yes, I fear you are right,' Zeno commented.

'Ok... So... What do we do now?' I asked, turning to our professional, Nick.

*

According to the watcher and the uncertain estimate from the information provided, Clémence's group could be between a hundred and a hundred and fifty women. They were far less numerous than us but well equipped. However, as a smaller group, they were faster. They did not have young and older people making them lose speed. A third of them were on horses, including Clémence – the watcher had heard two rebels speaking of her presence among them. Nick believed that they intended to use the horses to encircle us and use their weapons as a threat, while the other two-thirds would force their way in. They could be upon us by tomorrow and either attack at sunset when we would be tired from a day of walking, or at dawn when we were asleep.

Nick suggested that we should split into four groups that would detach themselves during the day. One group would walk ahead and two were to walk slightly back, further east and west from the main larger group in the centre. The new separate groups would have the strongest men, the more adept to defend our flanks. The strongest and fittest women would remain in the larger group in the centre, to defend it. The idea was that Clémence would attack a column of women as determined as she was, ready to defend their families and community. Hopefully, the presence of children and the elderly would also soften the attackers' hearts, if that were still possible. Then the three other groups could intervene from the outside and take Clémence in a sandwich. Each group would be given flares to raise the alarm if they were under attack, too. We could not stop the rebels' progress and we could not prevent their attack, but we could use our numbers to our advantage and counter-attack. So at dawn, we would split.

'Yoko, you must not be in the main group. Take a horse and go ahead with Nick as fast as you can. In fact, you should go, just the two of you, away from any danger.' Leo said.

'You are not going to force me again to do something against my own will, are you? Or try to drug me?' I protested. 'I told you before and I will tell you again. All of you. I believe Ushi will make it to us by Saturday. She will bring more weapons and ammunition and then take me to our destination in Scotland by helicopter, where I will spend the night and create a new Fog. But until then, I will stick by your side and be part of the fight. I will not leave now. I will also be here for my nephew and for Chloé. I made a promise to look after them and I will keep it. No, I am not fleeing with Nick.'

I looked around at everyone, challenging them to go against me.

'I have received basic training from the Society and the British Intelligence,' I continued. 'And even though basic, it is invaluable here. So, I am an asset in the fight to come. And to conclude, I do *not* want to spend my time running away from danger and anyone intent on getting at me. I want to confront them!'

Again, I checked that everyone understood my position before I spoke again.

'You might argue that I am a Switcher, that my role is too important for me to take risks, that you can't afford to lose me. Blah-blah-blah. Let me remind you that through history, Kings and Queens, Princes and Lords, and other leaders were participating in the fight, even when deemed irreplaceable. They did it because they had self-respect and values, because it was part of who they were, because they led by example. If I go, I will lose this self-respect. Whatever you might say, in my mind I would be abandoning you. I can't do that. So, for all these reasons and more, I want to stay. I NEED to stay.'

The attendees of our emergency meeting looked at each other, attempting to read each other's thoughts on the matter. As for me, I looked at Simba. I tried to mentally ask her to keep a watch on my friends so that none of them would approach me with a needle overnight, to pacify me and lead me away against my will.

Day 6 (Friday)

The threat of an imminent attack by Clémence and her followers, added to the risk that my fellow Foggies and friends might try to send me away during my sleep, kept me awake for a long time. I doubted I could sleep a wink that night, but I underestimated my body's exhaustion. When I did sleep, it was so deep that it took a good hour for me to fully wake up in the morning.

We didn't linger over breakfast, which was very brief. People barely spoke. Everyone was focused on getting ready and on the road as soon as possible, wanting to put more distance between the women rebels and us. It was futile: Clémence would catch up with us, nonetheless, but the later the better, to give Ushi a chance to join us. More space between them and us also meant more time to organise our defence and counter-attack. The positive mood that had settled over the past couple of days was gone. Instead, the silence was ponderous, the mood dark.

*

I wanted to travel with the core group, but I could not win on everything. I had to concede to travelling with Leo and Nick in the smaller group ahead. Isabelle, Chloé and Eudes were also with us. Zeno and Dante were each in one of the groups that flanked the core group. Because of the general tension, Simba was very much on edge and not leaving my side, even squeezing between Leo and me as we walked. Leo was also over-protective of me, even if he tried not to let it be too apparent to avoid irritating me. To my surprise, I found his care endearing, unlike my reactions in the past when I would rebuff him for such an attitude. Maybe Leo had cut through the thick armour of my pride at last.

Thanks to the 2-way radios, we were in constant contact with each other. This comment was a small relief among all my worries for the villagers and the people I loved. Tomorrow was Saturday, 'Switching Day', and Clémence probably intended to catch us before I created a Gate and could escape through it. My grievances against the woman were accumulating from her attempts to kill me, her extreme and dangerous revolutionary ideas, her violent methods and, now, her interest in Chloé, Eudes and Simba. They were innocent creatures I would never let them fall into her hands!

I experienced feelings I had never thought existed in me. I felt the visceral fear of the hunted, of the prey about to be caught. At the same time, a rage slowly rose that made me want to grab my shotgun when I thought of Clémence. To protect the children, the thought of coldly killing her crossed my mind. And … I was not appalled by it.

*

The day's walk was made harder by the travellers' fear and silence. At midday, I had to take my shoes off, due to burst blisters on the sides of my feet. Leo made some kind of flip-flop with old soles and pieces of soft fabric. Soon, several pairs were created for others like me. I knew this would cause a new pain on the heel and the arch of the feet, but there was no other choice. I couldn't feel my legs any more, and my feet were on fire, so how much worse could a little more pain be?

'Tonight, you will get a foot bath and an especially long foot massage. My treat!' Leo said to me, after he helped secure the handmade shoes with an additional leather rope around the ankle.

'You must need one too. I'll take care of that,' I told him, softly.

'I am fitter than you are and my feet rougher. I don't need it as much as you do,' he said, shaking his head.

'Well, I'll give you a sample, and we will see if you want me to stop,' I said, teasing.

'If I ask you to stop, it will be more by decency than by choice. We do not have much privacy... A foot massage is a very sensual gift,' he replied, giving me a kiss.

'Could it also be a reason why you wish to offer me one?' I whispered, kissing him back.

We tried to continue walking into the night that evening, to move forward as much as we could. It was not possible to do this for long without lights, and the presence of lights would have informed Clémence's patrol of our positions. The possibility of such patrols was already a worry, as we wanted to keep some element of surprise at us being split into groups. Our spies on the road had not seen signs of any such lookouts, but it didn't mean they didn't exist.

As we settled for the night, Leo attached a horse close to our sleeping area.

'If at any moment we are in danger, you take Eudes and Chloé, you get on the horse, and you go far away from here. You just go!'

I hesitated. Again, I didn't want to leave everyone behind, yet I agreed for the children.

Day 7 (Saturday)

All through the night, I wondered if I would pull the trigger. Should one of the women-rebels be in front of me, a gun in her hand, could I aim and shoot? I believed I would if anyone pointed a gun at someone I cared about, or at me. It was a defensive action, to save their life or mine. But my taking the offensive and initiating the first shot, I was not so sure about. I had never even gone hunting. I had never taken the life of an animal, let alone one of a human being. Even for bugs, it was limited to moths and mosquitoes. Some others had also expressed their reluctance at killing any of the rebels. Only Nick and the Italians, having retrieved their military training mindset, argued that it was out of our hands now: should we kill someone during the battle, it was because of war.

'I don't think I could just point and shoot, though,' Zeno tempered. 'Except Clémence. Her, I wouldn't have any problem. She is the reason for the war. I don't want to kill anyone, but if we kill her, we could save everyone else on both sides.'

'You are right.' Nick replied. 'I also wish to limit the death toll. Many of them are like Owen, seduced by Clémence's bullshit and fooled into thinking there is no alternative. A massacre is uncalled for.'

'I really want to be the one spotting Clémence,' Leo said. 'I have a personal vendetta against her, for Yoko.'

Each time the subject was raised, they all claimed they were the one with the best reason to eliminate Clémence in person. In truth, it was less personal than they said: they all wanted to avoid the dangers of a long siege and the loss of lives, along with protecting her key targets, me included. Nick was the most composed, but his stern face hid a strong and a deep personal grievance. He was the most dangerous to her, I felt.

*

I fell asleep late. My body was exhausted, yet my mind too active and anxious to find rest. So when I was woken up with a start by the shout of men raising the alarm, it took what felt like an eternity to remember where I was. Leo jumped on his feet and immediately started gathering our packs on the horses. We had slept fully dressed, ready to fight or run if necessary. Everybody seemed in control, tidying the camp in a rush but quietly. Even Simba did not make a sound. She circled around me, keeping a protective watch. The horses were nervous, feeding on the atmosphere of the group. They had become used to having Simba around during the walk, but it was different that morning. They could sense how edgy she was, ready to jump on any threat, and so they were restless. We could not keep them calm enough to mount them. Leo decided to take Simba away just long enough for us to get on the horses.

'It might be dangerous to have her around, even after,' he commented. 'She makes the horses too nervous. I don't want them to kick out when we are on them.'

'What are you suggesting? We can't leave her behind! She is coming with me, no matter what. You know Clémence wants to get her hands on her, too!' I explained.

'Then let's do it one step at a time. First, we get her out of the way and calm the horses, then we get on them, then we see if they can handle Simba.'

Next, Leo tried to grab Simba. She would have none of it. For the first time ever, she bared her teeth at him, in a manner indicating he should not even think of separating her from me. It was clear from her demeanour that she might attack him if he persisted. Simba was intent on protecting me and no one would stop her doing this, not even Leo. As we pondered how to proceed next, Nick ran towards us.

'A group of women rebels is coming!' He was holding the radio in his hands, listening to the latest update on their progress.

'Are they far?' I asked.

'They are on horses. We have 10 minutes; 15 minutes max,' Nick replied.

'Do they know about us being ahead, or are they following their own strategy to go ahead of the main group?' Leo enquired, still trying to quieten the horses.

'How would I know?' Nick snapped.

Leo was about to retort when I put a hand on his back in an appeasing gesture. We were all highly-strung. Now was not the time to bicker. The situation was critical.

'So, what do we do now?' I said, instead.

Nick looked around. The whole group, about 150 hundred people, was ready.

'We hide in an ambush,' Nick finally answered. 'I was told there are 50 to 60 on horses. We can take them. They have the advantage of mobility, so trapping them is better than risking a frontal assault. And I am not good enough on a horse to shoot well from the saddle. With an ambush, whether they know we are here or not, we can still surprise them.'

'What about Yoko?' Leo immediately asked. 'Time to send her away for her protection. We discussed this: I will stay and hide. You go with her with a small group to protect her, along with the children and Isabelle.'

'Hey! Don't speak as if I were not here with you,' I interrupted him.

'Leo, I must stay here to organise the ambush.' Nick replied. 'You go with Yoko. With the children. Take a few men with you. We need to go and fast!

'Wait!' I began but didn't have a chance to continue. Leo was still holding the horses. Nick grabbed me by the waist and put me, by force, on the back of mine. The animal was agitated and Leo struggled to keep him quiet. Simba was on edge and circling the horse. Nick tried to come close to her and to everyone's surprise, Simba jumped on him with such strength, he fell back. Simba perched herself on top of him and growled, then left and came back towards me. My horse was getting out of control. Fearing a fall, I jumped off. Simba immediately came to my side and stood her ground in a menacing manner.

'For fuck's sake! We don't have time for this!' Nick yelled.

'OK, that settles it. I am staying and will fight with you. Leo, you take Isabelle and the children and go with the men Nick referred to. Hide them somewhere not too far from here. Nick, do you have a radio for him?'

Nick handed a radio to Leo, in silence. Isabelle and the children arrived on their horses with ten men. Leo gave me a quick kiss. He refused to say goodbye *'for such a short time'*. I moved away with Simba for the horses to calm down. Leo got on a horse, then Eudes was placed on the saddle in front of him. Isabelle was on the horse behind, with Chloé tied up in a blanket around her mother. After one last look between us all and a little wave from my nephew, they turned their horses and broke into a gallop. I didn't stand there to watch them go; there was no time to waste.

Nick had already defined the layout for our ambush of the rebels and where everyone should be. As quickly as possible, we went ahead with his plan. The previous evening, we had settled under cover of trees not far from a stream, on the edges of a clearing. Nick had woken up early to check the ground at the first sign of daylight. If we would not walk in the open in full daylight, too visible from afar, he expected that the women behind us would have the same strategy. He also believed they must have seen our tracks. How could it not be? A hundred people leave traces that no one could ignore. So certainly, they would stop where we had settled to gather any information. This is when we were to act.

*

Nick and I were together in position. He was eyeing Simba with anger. She had ruined his plans, and in his view, she was putting me in danger instead of protecting me. On my part, I was not upset with her: she was acting from instinct with my best interest at heart.

We were slightly in retreat but still with a good view of the clearing where the old camp was. Nick had some men positioned behind us to watch our backs and to build a protective shield around me. We laid low on the ground, covering ourselves as much as we could with leaves and branches. The horses were hidden in the bushes a bit further away, in a spot Nick had shown me so that I could make a run for it, if needed.

The dew seemed to slowly infiltrate every layer of fabric I was wearing. The damp chilled my bones. Or maybe it was fear.

'How do we know they will come that way?' I whispered to Nick as we lay on the grass next to each other.

'We don't know for certain. It just makes sense. They are following our tracks, so they will come that way. It might just be a scouting group… We will know soon enough.'

The silence between us settled for barely a few seconds, I had more questions for him.

'Nick, you woke Leo and me because we needed to get a move on the main group. Are they under attack? Do you have more information? What happened to the other Foggies? I also worry for the people of Yerushaleim!'

'Yes, they are. There is nothing we can do to help them for now. Ariel just informed me that they were holding on. They have a strong spirit. He also knows we are getting ready to face a group of rebels. For now, we each need to focus on sorting our own group.'

'But…'

'Yoko, we will get in touch with them again as soon as we can. Now, I need to focus.'

He hesitated a few seconds, then bent towards his leg and undid the strap holding a sheath with a knife to his leg. He tied it around mine.

'If your assailant is on top of you, don't plant the knife straight or it would go through you as well. Plant it upward. And aim to kill.'

I nodded, but prayed I would never have to pull that knife out of this sheath.

*

We had tied ropes between trees all around the camp, covering them with leaves and twigs on the ground to hide them. Some of our men were waiting for Nick's signal to pull on them when necessary. It was an old tactic but still a good one. It might happen soon. The sounds of the forest, mainly birds singing and branches cracking, turned to an ominous silence just prior to the muffled sound of hoofs hitting the ground reached us. They were nearly there. As the sound became closer and clearer, I caught myself thinking how beautiful a sound it was, the galloping of horses in nature.

A large group of women on horses suddenly filled the space we had just left. When the first horses stopped, those behind slowly did the same. Their nostrils fumed from their run. Three of the women in front got on the ground and checked the signs of our overnight stay.

'They are fresh!' a woman shouted. 'They can't be far ahead.'

'Here! Those are large paws. That must be the wolf's,' another shouted, pointing to the ground.

By now, all the horses had stopped. Another voice rose.

'If Simba was there, so was Yoko.' I recognised Clémence's voice. 'I was right: they are trying to deceive us with separate groups. Let's go!'

Their horses started towards us, following the tracks we had deliberately left. At this moment, Nick raised his arm and sliced it down through the air. The men from Yerushaleim promptly pulled the ropes, using trees as levy. They tied them as quickly as possible to opposite trees and grabbed their weapons. Only the first horses were not able to stop in time, but all the animals became agitated. Everyone was shouting and there was confusion within the riders. Our men raised their guns and Nick shouted for the rebels to throw down their weapons. Clémence bawled from the centre of the rebels' group.

'No! Women, charge north!' she commanded.

'Men! Fire!' Nick ordered.

The men had hesitated for a split second than shot cautiously, lacking determination. The riders were already on the move, having urged the horses on to launch a foray ahead. They headed to the left of Nick and me. They had also started to shoot, at random.

'Fire! Fire! We must stop them exiting! Tighten the ropes!' Nick shouted.

'Jump the ropes!' I heard a woman yell.

It was chaos. Some of the first horses jumped, some refused. The blocked riders, half-panicked, half-angry, began to fire at anything on the ground opposite. They made their horses gallop back to the centre or in any direction not already blocked by other horses. Some women were falling to the ground, hit by gunshots.

My eyes were wide open, disbelieving the carnage occurring in front of me, I was in shock. The scene of women dead on the ground, of horses bleeding and of men collapsing, was like a bad dream. For a moment, I struggled to believe it was real, that I was not watching a 3D movie. Every sound was dulled, every image seemed in slow motion.

Nick shook me out of my reverie. I had not pulled the trigger once.

'Yoko, go now!'

'What?'

'You need to go. Clémence and too many of them have managed to get over the ropes. They will circle and shoot at us from the other side!'

I looked back at the women on the inside of the rope circle. A lot of them were sheltering behind fallen horses to shoot back at the men. Simba, I only just realised, had climbed on top of me and was lying low, watching out for possible threats against me.

'What about you?' I asked him, anxiously.

'I'll cover your exit and join you after. When I tell you, run - keep low. Go to the horses.'

'OK.'

'And Yoko, use your gun.'

'Right.'

'Ready?'

'Yes.'

I pushed Simba on the side and got on my feet, bending my body to stay low, as close as possible to the ground. Nick checked around and gave the command to run. I broke into a jog, Simba sprinting next to me. I focused on a man ahead, one of the watchmen defending our back. I ran as fast as I could but it was difficult. The floor of the forest was uneven with branches and dead trees. Several times, I felt myself slipping, catching back my footing without knowing how. When I reached the man after running like a lunatic, I felt a surge of relief quickly followed by horror as a bullet hit him in the jaw in front of my eye. I threw myself on the floor and he fell next to me. Simba grabbed my jacket, pulling me to move forward. I looked back and saw Nick not far behind me, leaning against a tree and aiming in the direction where the bullet had come from. I jumped back on my feet and looked ahead. I had to keep moving, I had to reach the horses. I heard a noise on my right and raised my gun.

Strangely, I was not scared, I was angry. Very angry. A man came out from behind a tree. He was from Yerushaleim, another watchman whom Nick had given the mission to protect me. I lowered my gun and we both started running. Another man joined us on the run within seconds, and both of them kept an eye out on either side of us for danger. Simba ran in front of me. My senses seemed suddenly more acute. I could hear the breathing of the men next to me. I could also hear horses getting closer and closer and shots aimed at us. Again, the world slowed down around me. When I reached the hidden horses, three men were waiting for us. They held the animals tight, much agitated by the pandemonium, so that I could quickly jump on the back of one. Four of them and Nick got in the saddle as well, the others staying to cover our way out. Immediately, we pushed the horses into a gallop. The men surrounded me with their horses. I was effectively placed into a protective circle. Simba ran on the side. She was slowly losing speed. Looking back, at least a dozen rebels were pursuing us, fiercely pushing their steeds. I worried for Simba. She was too young to keep up with the horses for long.

'We need to get out of the forest!' Nick shouted, as not for the first time we had to slow down and break up the group to pass through trees. It was leaving me exposed each time and at risk of being shot at.

*

My horse suddenly trembled. He was still moving forward but something was amiss. Before understanding what was happening, I felt myself slipping from the horse and falling to the ground. Nick was immediately beside me. Seeing me going down, he had tried to grab my jacket and pull me on his horse, yet between my weight and his horse on full speed, his heroic endeavour failed. He had fallen.

My horse was unable to stand up. The men accompanying us, noting our absence, slowed down further ahead, already at a distance. The horse had stopped shaking. When I looked into his eyes, he was staring right at me, through me. I couldn't bear it. I looked back at the women who were almost upon us and jumped into action, taking cover behind the horse's dead body. Nick joined me as the women begun to shoot. Simba, also by my side, howled. I put my hand on her nuzzle and whispered to her to keep silent. She seemed to understand and stopped.

'Yoko! Shoot at them!' Nick shouted at me.

'I am,' I shouted back through the noise, turning my gun toward the riders and trying my best to avoid their horses. I wished to hit them in the shoulders instead of killing them, but it was a ridiculous hope. Not only was I an average shot (at best) during relaxed practice, my current targets were moving! The shooting stopped on both sides. For me, it was because I had run out of ammunition. A group of Jewish men arrived to our rescue and immediately attacked the women rebels. The confrontation between the two groups happened just in front of Nick and me.

'Stay down!' Nick shouted unnecessarily. I didn't intend to go for a stroll just then.

'I'm out of ammunition,' I told him.

'Take my gun!' He said, trading his for mine and putting new bullets in my old gun from his pockets.

'What shall we do now?'

'First, we kill Clémence. Then we run.'

I turned my head and scrutinised the group of women. At the back, protected by her followers, rode Clémence. She was giving orders to the women. Most of them had shotguns with knives attached to the ends. They had no qualms about planting them into the bodies of the men's horses to force them down, or into the men directly if they could. The women seemed enraged and bloodthirsty. In contrast, the men were obviously reluctant to kill. They would only do so to protect themselves, or me.

Nick was one who did not hesitate to shoot to kill. Women fell like flies under his aim, yet his deadly shots were limited as both sides mixed in front of us. Then he shouted: 'Fuck! I am out!'

'Take my gun,' I pushed it towards him.

'No, you must keep it. You must be able to defend yourself. I'll go and get one of the weapons on the ground.'

'You're not going over there!' I urged him.

'You stay here. Shoot any woman coming your way. I'll be back in no time,' he replied standing up. He ran fast and found cover behind another horse corpse. I positioned myself ready to shoot, trying to locate Clémence. I had to spare my bullets, but when I had a clean shot, I did fire. Two women fell, dead. It left me cold. As if I were emotionless. From the corner of my eyes, I saw Nick going for a spot where both men and women had fallen, leaving their weapons lying around. Then I saw Clémence raising her gun and taking a shot. I was not fast enough to react. Nick collapsed. I screamed; she laughed of victory. It felt that she had been waiting all along for an opportunity to get to one of us, that she spared her shots especially for us. Next, it would be me.

Anger took hold of me again. More than anger: rage. At the same time, a strange peace filled me. A determination to kill. This woman would die. I would take care of it myself. It was not just to save my life: she had to pay for the hurt and death she had inflicted on those I loved. As I looked at her hiding place, I felt like an animal watching her prey, calculating the best approach to hunt, catch, and kill. These thoughts crossed my mind in the space of a nanosecond, but they were as clear as spring water and the change in me was instantaneous. Nick was immobile. I held my breath, unwilling to believe he was dead. Then he turned his head slightly. He was close enough for me to see him looking at me, but too far to read what he was mouthing. Was he praying or trying to pass on a message, an instruction? He winked. A huge relief filled me: he was fine. Yet my rage against Clémence had not abated. She had found refuge in the middle of her group again, and I only got a glimpse of her twice. Each time, her attention was on Nick and me. Nick could not move, he had fallen in clear sight and any movement would reveal that he was alive. Then he would immediately be shot. He still had no weapon to defend himself.

My brain was working in overdrive. I needed to find a way to steer the danger away from Nick. If I appeared to flee, Clémence would come after me without doubt, along with some of the women surrounding her. I did a quick calculation: the probability was one to five, at best: at worst, one to ten. I checked my gun: it had four bullets left. Maybe making a move was not such a good idea, after all. However, Nick would then be able to get a gun, find a horse, and follow us, increasing our chances to get her. It was a risky bet. I looked around. Many horses were now rider-free and loose in the forest, confused. One was not too far from me. I took it as a sign. I decided to make myself the bait, but truly, I felt the hunter. Then I noticed the silence. Shouts, screams, neighs were still loud, and yet no sound of gunshots resonated in the forest. Had everyone run out of ammunition? Underestimating my adversary would be a mistake: she was too clever not to have kept more than a couple of bullets for Nick and me, or to have instructed her right-hand women to do the same. I had to hope that they only had a few spares. It was time to act. I turned to my wolf.

'Simba, you see this horse over there?' I whispered to her, making a discreet gesture towards the horse. 'I am going to go for it. I will call you after. Until then, stay. You understand? Stay!'

Even though Simba was well trained, she could play deaf to my request in the current circumstances. I had already noted that morning, that her determination to protect me trumped my orders. By talking calmly, I hoped she would understand it was important and would obey. I gave one last look at Nick. He had slowly moved his upper body to a partial protection of a tree trunk, lying on the ground. He still didn't have a weapon.

As I looked at him, a group of women riders suddenly made a move out of the battle scene in my direction. This spurned me into action. I jumped out and ran to the horse close by. The animal had a moment of surprise, and I managed to grab its reins just as he began to canter away. I didn't have the time to panic; I had to get on that horse! By instinct, I adjusted my running to his rhythm and swiftly jumped on his back. I hadn't tried this trick since my teenage years. Back then my teacher had taught me to jump on the back of a galloping horse, but it was indoors, on a slow gallop, and without a saddle. This time, the saddle was on the way and I landed so low on its back that I almost slid back to the ground. It was good luck that the horse did not kick out. I scrambled to get on the saddle. Simba was already in a run beside the horse. The sight of her must have given wings to my steed, because the animal went at the speed of light. Six horses were on my heels, Clémence in the vanguard.

'OK,' I thought. 'And now?'

I needed to turn hunter; stop and hide, wait for them to pass by me, then take them by surprise. That meant I had to get out of their sight first. The horse was heading towards the open space, so my priority was to change its course. I veered him back towards the forest and scanned ahead for a denser area or a good hiding place. There was nothing. My horse was slowly putting some distance between the women rebels and us. Simba was struggling to follow. She was a good sprinter for a short while only. She would not last long. When I checked again on her, she had disappeared. Further back, the women riders were still on my tail. They were too far away now for me to determine who was who. I had to keep going until I found a spot to hide and hope Simba was out of their way and safer than I was.

Finally, I reached a denser part of the forest. It was about time, as my horse was losing speed. The incentive of a wolf scaring him into motion had more weight than my heels. The ground was awkward and rocky. Not far away on the side, I spotted large rocks covered with moss. I pulled the reins and swerved. Once there, I quickly jumped off the horse and roughly attached him out of sight. I might still need him for an emergency exit. Afterwards, I took a sniper position on top of a rock, camouflaging myself as best as I could. I took big breaths to steel myself. Already, I could hear the horses arriving.

*

They were six. I had four bullets. This was not looking good. Reviewing my other options, I remembered the knife Nick had attached on my leg. Good. With one hand, I checked my pockets. Feeling the items instead of looking, I recognised my small Swiss pocket knife and a lip moisturiser. Instinctively I pinched my lips together to feel if they were dry. They were.

'Maybe it can wait until later...' I said to myself.

As the women entered my target zone, I aimed for Clémence at their head.

I had a clean shot. They were so close I could not miss her, so I fired.

I missed. Well, not totally - the rider on the right of Clémence screamed and fell to the ground. I had just killed someone and my first thought was 'Damn. One bullet less!'. No remorse whatsoever. This was how war and fighting for my life, along with the thirst of revenge, can transform someone. Guilt and shame would come later.

The effect of surprise was now lost. As I aimed again at Clémence, the rebels moved behind trees for shelter, pointing their guns in the direction of my hiding rock. It was large and multi-layered, and I could tell that they could not see me. One of the women fired her weapon twice, but Clémence shouted at her not to shoot. The rebel shooter shook her shotgun and threw it to the ground in anger. One gun less against me. I glanced at the dead woman's shotgun, on the ground, wondering how many bullets were in this one. It was out of reach on either side, except by coming into the open. If one of them tried, should I use one of my few bullets to stop her? I had only three left now.

Clémence must have thought alike, because next she indicated to one of her rebels to go and grab the dead woman's shotgun. I aimed at the rebel and shot. I hit her between the shoulder and the breast. She collapsed and lay there, dead. I had taken a gamble. I had lost one more bullet but hoped Clémence would believe it meant I still had enough bullets for them all.

Two bullets left.

A branch cracked behind me. I turned my head with a feeling of panic and saw Simba creeping towards me. Instinctively, she moved close to the ground. She came to a stop next to me, her eyes fixed right ahead on the rebels' location. I returned my attention to the danger. Clémence had not sent anyone else to retrieve the shotgun. I had to try and get my hands on it, the sooner the better. At some point, they would make a move to circle me. Maybe they were already trying. I had to be two steps ahead. Very slowly, to avoid being seen, I moved backwards, then slid away my shotgun from its position. Putting it across my back, I told Simba to stay. I moved as fast and silently as possible to the horse and quietly got on it. When I whispered her name, Simba appeared. Her presence and me ramming my heels in the horse's flanks, made him jump into a sprint. My shotgun slung on my back, my body leaning as low as possible on the side of the horse opposite the rebels, I directed the horse towards the body of the woman I had killed, ready to extend my arms and grab the shotgun. It was a desperate effort, and indeed, I was desperate. I needed this gun, and I needed to be fast. I knew they could shoot the horse at any time.

At long last in this chase, I had a lucky break. It didn't look like one at first. When the horse reached the dead body, he tripped. This made him slow down, change his course, and a bullet aimed at him missed. The tripping also brought the horse lower, thus placing the shotgun in my reach. I would have struggled otherwise. The sound of the shot made the horse react. He immediately jolted ahead and sprinted. Unbelievably, I had gotten away with my daring action. I had another shotgun, hopefully with bullets, and I was on the move. Not that I knew where I was going or what to do next. Simba was back running next to me, the women not far behind us. There was an impression of déjà-vu that was unnerving.

*

Now what? With difficulty, I opened my new rifle and noted there were two bullets inside. Things were looking up with four bullets against four women. A shape of a horse and rider seemed to appear out of nowhere, far away on my left. He or she was still too far away to determine if the rider was friend or foe. In doubt, I veered to my right to avoid the encounter. The newcomer, whoever that was, began shooting at the women rebels. They replied with a couple of shots. A wave of joy ran through me; joy at not being alone in the middle of nowhere; joy at having someone watching my back. As I turned to look at my rescuer and check if I was holding my distance between the women, I saw him or her falling from his horse and hitting the ground. Someone - I did not even know who - had been hit trying to help me. Again. I prayed it was not Leo, or Dante, or Zeno. It could be Nick, too. The women rebels had suffered losses, too. Only three were behind me, slowly catching up. My rage against Clémence was such that I hoped that she was still alive among my pursuers, so that I could kill her myself. A voice in my head warned me: 'Be careful, don't let anger blind you. Don't underestimate her. Be careful. Keep your mind clear.'

With my four bullets against the three of them, I had a proper chance of survival. All I needed was to hit my targets. I even had one miss allowed. This made me wince. I would never manage to shoot from a galloping horse. My riding skills were fine, my shooting skills much less. I had to stop to barely stand a chance. I scanned around me. Simba had disappeared again. I worried less this time. She was safe, recuperating somewhere. She would find me again. Further away, there were bushes and dead tree trunks on the ground. It was as good as any, as a sniper spot. As I reached it, I made the horse turn sharply and jumped off. While he continued galloping, I hid in the bushes hoping the women had not seen my tactic. They were coming fast, so there was little time to get ready and in position. I knelt on the ground, trying to repeat my past months' practices with Nick. Taking a deep breath, focusing on keeping the panic away as the women were closing in on me, I aimed through the branches at the one heading the group – Clémence - and pulled the trigger.

'For God's sake!' I swore in a low voice. It was a miss.

The women stopped and immediately went for cover behind large trees. I barely had the time to aim again and shoot at one of the rebels before she reached them. This time, I did not fail. The woman collapsed from her horse. The animal fled, the woman lay immobile on the ground. With a knot in the stomach, I wished that she were dead. Not just wounded: dead! Otherwise, she could still harm me. I quickly brushed away the thought that it was wrong. I did not have the time to dwell on the negative aspects of my current frame of mind. I stared at the body of the woman on the ground. She was crawling with difficulty towards her rifle. I had two bullets left. I couldn't waste one more on her. She was in agony as she clutched her weapon and aimed it at the bushes, at me. I quickly aimed at her and was about to shoot her when she was knocked away by an animal. The woman fired her gun but the bullet whistled through the air above me. No one had seen Simba coming. In one swift movement, the wolf snapped her powerful jaw shut on the woman's throat. Seconds later Simba was gone, disappeared. The body of the woman lay, inert. I reviewed the situation. It was not one against two, but two against two. Simba might not have a shotgun, but she had a killer instinct and the teeth for it. She was also a thorn in the rebels' side: she might attack them any time and from anywhere.

*

'Yoko!' Clémence shouted. 'Yoko! It doesn't have to end like this.'

'For you or for me?' I thought but did not say. I did not want to reveal my exact location in the bushes by responding. To be safe, I decided to move next time she spoke, in case she already knew from the gunshot.

'We are going to win, Yoko. You know we will. We are the future! There is only one way to start afresh: clean the slate. I can quote so many of your books on this. We need to drastically break with the old. We need to break the men.'

I pinched my lips to contain my longing to argue. They had to remain shut tight. Instead, I slid inch by inch backward and to a new shooting position.

'As to the newcomers and Fog Gate,' Clémence continued. 'At first, I hoped your modern ways would be in our favour, but your easy life has rendered you mellow. You would not change things. Yes, your women have more rights; they still don't have the role they deserve. We ought to be in charge! WE are at the source of life, the source of everything.'

It really was difficult to keep my mouth shut. I tried to stop listening and focused on settling anew in the bushes. I might have an angle to see them and shoot. The longer she kept talking, the more I moved at snail pace. I was also trying to keep an eye on her hiding spot, which was difficult. Finally, I reached a position where I had an angle on a woman. It was Clémence. I placed my rifle against my shoulder, in the hollow at the junction of arm and torso, and levelled my eyes with the rear and front sights on the gun. Next, I took a couple of deep breaths, steadying my body and mind. I could not miss this shot. Clémence was still talking. She had dismounted and attached the horse to the tree. She was looking around constantly, no doubt checking if Simba was creeping in on them. She looked anxious; it surprised me, as it had not come across from her poised voice. My mind was blocking her words now. 'You talk too much,' I whispered as I concentrated on my target. I kept breathing, focusing not on the human being in front of me but on the enemy. I pulled the trigger.

The shot hit her in the hip. I fired again. As I did, Clémence looked in my direction and our eyes locked. There was fear and rage and longing and hope in hers. They had so much humanity that, when the bullet hit her in the chest, my arm extended towards her and I shouted 'No!' Clémence fell backwards to the ground. She lay immobile. She was no more. I stared at her body and felt empty. There was no relief or joy, no sadness, nothing. I just stared, my mind blank.

The sound of a shotgun quickly followed by a sharp, excruciating pain in my left arm shook me back to reality. Clémence was dead, but one woman was still after me. Stupidly, Clémence's death had symbolised the end of all dangers in my mind, but clearly that woman-rebel disagreed. My rifle was useless, empty of bullets, while she had hers and Clémence's. I felt faint. Looking down at the source of the excruciating pain, blood was running down my arm from the wound, at the top of the humerus. I took off my scarf and wrapped it tightly around the arm, pulling one end with my teeth. Aside from the pain, the fear and the helplessness, for a (very) brief moment, I felt like Rambo.

'Right, Yoko. Focus!' I said to myself, inwardly. My horse was gone, my rifle only of use as a cricket bat in close combat, my head was swirling and I was about to pass out. On the other hand, she did not know any of this. To prevent myself from fainting, I pressed my right hand against the wound. The acute pain immediately woke me up. It was a temporary fix. I was not sure how long I would last.

*

A piercing sound woke me up. I tried to move my head. It was difficult; it felt so heavy. Even opening my eyes hurt. I was lying face-down on the ground. Through the base of the bushes, I saw the woman rebel lying on the ground still, with Simba on top of her. She was struggling to get Simba off, using the rifle held across her chest to push the wolf away. I forced myself onto all fours, closing my eyes as the world turned around me. As I pushed on my arms, I stifled a scream of pain, but again the sting cleared and sharpened my mind. I had to act fast. As quickly as possible, I got on my feet. I retrieved Nick's knife from my leg, then ran towards them. It required all my strength. The woman saw me arrive and made a last effort and pushed Simba away from her. Kneeling, she aimed her rifle at me. Simba closed her jaw on her shoulder. The woman shrieked and kicked back her shotgun into Simba's stomach. My wolf was projected backward with a yelp of pain. The woman aimed again as I threw myself on top of her, pushing aside the rifle with one arm and planting Nick's knife into her chest. As I fell on her exhausted, surprise was still showing in her wide-opened eyes. Was she dead? I was not sure. There was still a rasping sound in her throat. I did not have the force to retrieve the blade from her body. Weakness hit me hard. Her eyes narrowed, she could see my failing strength. When she pushed me, I squealed and fell to the side. As my vision blurred and my head drifted into blackout, I saw Simba jumping on the woman's back.

*

An acute migraine brought me back to my senses. The sound of the blood pumping inside my head was too loud. My whole body was numb. I was lying on my back but the ground was shaky. Opening my eyes was too much of a struggle and I gave up. Slowly gaining some focus, I understood the noise that disturbed me was not my blood pumping. It was a familiar sound, one I could not place. The pain in my arm took over that from the migraine.

'Simba...' I tried to mumble. It sounded more like a gurgle.

'She is awake!' a muffled voice said. A hand took mine, feeling my pulse. The voice said something again that I did not hear. A wet towel wiped my cheek several times. After a moment, it became clear it was not a wet towel; it was Simba licking me. The joy mixed with relief helped me open my eyes. Two sets of eyes observed me: one animal, one human. They were both smiling in their own way.

'Welcome back, babe!' Nick said, with a smile. Simba told me the same with another lick. I gave them both the best smile I could master in the circumstances.

We were in the air at full speed. Ushi Tsou informed us the helicopter was already above what would be Scotland in WI. We had already stopped once to refuel from the spare barrels she had dropped there on a preparatory trip. Sunset was falling faster as we travelled north. Nick gave me a painkiller and explained how they had found me.

Ushi Tsou had been true to her word and as soon as she could deal with the pain and could fly, she requested it. She said to me that her wound in the shoulder was less severe than mine - she was being strangely kind to me (Nick's later theory was that her respect for me had increased now that I had killed people with my own hands. Charming). Ushi demanded a Eurocopter able to transport fuel barrels, which could then fly to our Scottish destination with one stop only. The Eurocopter was also a lethal machine, and she made it even more dangerous by filling it with weapons. Following our roadmap, she soon picked up the tracking signals from the Foggies and arrived that morning on the main battle site, between our larger group and the rebels. Immediately, she dropped weapons in our camp. She then launched a few missiles into the ranks of the rebels and dropped a couple of grenades where she deemed it necessary. Her show of power did a perfect job of morale destruction within the rebels. Afterwards, Ushi went further north in search of Eudes. She had no difficulty in finding his signal, and soon she met Nick and heard about my escape. When Ushi arrived, the men had the upper hand on the rebels. They were many, too many, dead and wounded, especially among the rebels. After having neutralised their attackers, the men were attempting to save the lives that could be saved. Nick claimed his wound was only a scratch, but he did look in pain. When Ushi was certain that Eudes was safe with Leo, who also looked after Isabelle and Chloé, she took Nick along to come and find me. The tracker was my lifesaver, as it had enabled them to find me. Ushi dropped Nick as close to me as the landscape allowed, then landed a bit further away, in an open space. Nick was fully equipped, as if ready to take on the White House. He saw Simba before he saw me. I was inert on the floor, covered in blood. The only reason he didn't panic was that the wolf was not howling. Otherwise, he knew I would be dead.

Isabelle, Eudes and Chloé had joined us for the long flight, but not Leo. We had to limit the number of people in the aircraft or the helicopter would not make it to our destination. Before leaving, Ariel had checked my wound and bandaged me. He assured everyone I would be fine but needed rest.

Drowsy and in pain, I was drifting in and out of consciousness as Nick recalled the story, before I passed out again, into deep sleep.

WEEK VII

Day 1 (Sunday)

Leila and McRae had filled the fridge, freezer and pantry with most of my favourite food in the hope of my arrival overnight. So now McRae put a selection of pastries on the table for breakfast.

'Nick has briefed us on what happened in the Other World,' McRae said. 'Hell! It's a proper civil war, isn't it?'

'Yes. Based on an ideology and, as usual, a thirst for power,' I replied, sipping a cup of tea.

*

I had woken up an hour before, in a large, old fashioned bed. I did not remember how I had come to be in this bed. The mattress had seen better days, the ceiling was showing marks of water stain and paint strips, yet most importantly the duvet was warm, thick and smelling fresh. The room felt homely. From the window, I could see the Highlands under a bright blue sky. I was alone. Putting one foot on the floor, my head got a little fuzzy and I steadied myself, leaning against the bed. I checked my arm. I did not feel much pain, probably thanks to some of the pills on the night table next to a bottle of Scottish still water. The room had two doors; a large one I assumed to lead to the rest of the house and a small one I hoped to open to the bathroom. I longed for a bath or a shower.

As the water slowly ran into the bath-tub, there was a knock at the bedroom door. Leila had come to enquire how I felt. Satisfied by my answer and look, she recounted for me what had happened the previous day. I was sleeping deeply when the helicopter landed at our destination, so Nick carried me on his shoulder to my bed, concerned for the whole journey that he might cause pain. He should not have worried: Ushi had injected me with enough morphine to dull any pain. We slept in three cabins. One for Nick and me – he refused to leave me alone; one for Isabelle and Chloé and one for Ushi and Eudes. As Simba refused to stay out of the cabin, Nick soon had to give up his place and sleep outside. Or, more exactly, keep watch. In the morning, the Fog covered my cabin. Nick took out his mobile and called Leila. She answered immediately, relieved to hear his voice. It meant we had succeeded. It was still quite dark and the Fog was not yet apparent. Leila, McRae and a couple of men from the Society immediately made their way through the woods from the mansion. The fogged cabin was at the back of the property. McRae went in and brought me back into my world, Simba on his heels. Once in my room, Leila changed my clothes and put a nightdress on me. A nurse from the Society cleaned and treated my wound as best as possible. She agreed with Ariel that there was no long-lasting damage. Leila had taken my hand in hers and did not let go for a long time. There was real relief and tears of joy in her eyes. She had feared never to see me again. For days, she had dreaded the disappearance of the Fog Dome meaning I was dead.

In the kitchen, the sweet smell coming from the oven, mixed with that of freshly made coffee, gave the room an atmosphere so welcoming and peaceful, one could almost forget the dramatic events occurring in both worlds. McRae and Leila updated me.

*

Lally O'Maleigh was furious. She confronted the US government about the turning of Alcatraz into a gate to the Other World, claiming they were behind it. Repeatedly, she presented Fog, Foggies and governments working together against the interests of humanity. O'Maleigh was clever; she did not deny humankind could benefit from the Gate or that it could help eradicate the disease currently plaguing the planet. Her case was that humanity was at the core of humans; that the true value of people was in their spirit. Using the Fog to save people was, in her opinion, an illusion created by the devil, or, to quote her own words, *'whatever people wish to call the negative forces of dark spirits'*. If saving us at all costs meant losing our humanity, then she would fight against it until her last breath. O'Maleigh was adamant that the

Gate offered a fake solution to the problems our planet was facing, that faith only could rescue us. When asked how she could justify the deaths of tens of thousands when it could be avoided, Lally O'Maleigh answered that the spirit of the dead would be pure and it would find its place in a better world by the side of God, the side of the Light. The Fog was the devil's way of leading us along the wrong path.

I rolled my eyes. This was such nonsense.

'You will be surprised,' McRae said, sitting at the table with a fresh pot of tea. 'The number of her followers is increasing rapidly, and not just in the US.'

'People are feeling lost,' Leila added. 'She plays on their fears. They are seeking answers, reference points, reassurance. We don't offer any on the origins and reasons for the Fog or the WII. We can't explain the sudden apparition and lightning spread of the plague, either. Whether we like it or not, right or wrong, she does have an answer for those who need one.'

'People are idiots,' McRae commented. Leila put a hand on his arm in a calming gesture. He turned to look at her. In the look they exchanged, it was clear that their relationship had evolved during the week. The emotion was stronger than the previous flirting and signs of affection. At her touch, McRae immediately allayed. His composure and facial expression betrayed how smitten he was. Her eyes also told a story of intimacy, care and deep feelings towards him. It was but a brief gesture, yet it brought a smile to my face. Those two looked good together.

'It's the same old story,' Leila said in a soothing voice. 'The unknown terrifies most, except when it is based on faith.'

'Then why don't we give them faith?' I asked. 'Could we just say that the Gate is a door created by God to give humans another chance, another start?'

'Could you do this when you don't believe it? You would be lying. Would you be able to? And keep up with the lie?' Leila asked. She was eyeing me with concern, in a way she had never done before.

'No... No, I couldn't,' I replied. 'You are right. I couldn't. I would feel like a fraud.'

'She is a fanatic, not a fraud. She now believes what she is saying.' Leila continued, relieved and happy with my answer. 'It is much, much, much more dangerous.'

*

Ingis Chen was also pro-active on the international scene. He was now advising not just the United Nations Organisation but the President of the United States. His legal support and advisory company had branches working for governments, institutions and corporations around the globe. High net worth individuals sought him out, either as a client or a friend. He was *en vogue.* Chen cleverly pushed aside any attempt from the press to turn him into the latest fashionable celebrity, instead carefully playing with his image as a heart-motivated, caring, brilliant mind who understood early on the opportunities lying in the Fog. He presented the Fog and his support for it as the path to spiritually and physically help every human on this planet. He was the opposite to O'Maleigh. Ingis Chen portrayed himself as practical and business-like with a light spiritual touch – not a guru. This appealed to the men in power. It was positive and inoffensive. On the surface, at least.

'There has been a shift of conscience in the past fifty to sixty years,' Leila read a quote from him. 'We have become more open to the notion that we are all connected, that we all share a universal human experience. My personal belief is that the Fog occurred because we were ready to welcome the extraordinary. The Gates have enlarged the boundary of our physical world as well as opened our mind to a higher spiritual level.'

'On the Modern Marburg virus, he even counter-argued O'Maleigh's, using her own line of thought,' McRae interrupted Leila. 'He suggested that her point of view on the devil was too narrowed on the Fog, when maybe the virus is the devil's attempt to stop mankind on their spiritual path. Maybe the virus is making them question their faith, whereas God sent the Fog for salvation. Chen claims that he doesn't have the answers, but neither has O'Maleigh, except, of course, if God speaks to her directly.'

'Wow,' I pulled a face. 'O'Maleigh must have loved this.'

'She was enraged!' Leila confirmed. 'War is practically declared between those two.'

*

The Society had mixed feelings about Chen's Fog ventures. At present, his activities and official position on the Fog were beneficial to their actions and goals. Still, there was no love lost between him and them (and the same between him and the Foggies). We had not forgotten how he had first come into our lives and his backhanded actions. We were wary that, for him, the means justified the end. It was difficult to believe that he had turned into an amazingly kind-hearted man who devoted his life to others - even though he applied high fees for his advice. Consequently, the Society was strictly monitoring him and his movements. However, the Koplats were more forgiving of his old ways. They were slowly building closer relations with him. After switching Alcatraz into a Fog Gate, they relied on Ingis Chen to defend their image with the media and to intercede with the US Government. The Society was still their secret ally, but they wanted an official representation. The family decided there could be no better agent than Ingis Chen. He had the international stature and charisma required. In accordance with our code of practice, they contacted all the Foggies currently available; the number was considerably reduced in the UK. Everyone had reservations, even the Koplats, themselves, but no one could argue against Chen being the best candidate as public relations for the American Foggies. It was just a professional arrangement. One with strict limits.

'Chen is beaming,' McRae said, his jaw set tight. 'I don't trust that bastard. Something is off about him.'

'I said to the Koplats that they should distance themselves from him,' Leila said. 'We have a lead and are investigating.'

'What is it?' I asked her.

'I will know more soon. We want to be certain. I will let you know as soon as possible,' she replied, avoiding a direct answer. 'It would be good if you would reappear on the public scene. There have been a lot of questions on your whereabouts. The more present the Koplats and you are with the media, the better. That would limit Chen's role. It is not good that he is associated too closely with you in the public's mind.'

'Did you mention this to the Koplats? I am surprised Sophia relinquished being more present in the press,' I ventured slowly. I didn't want to criticise a fellow Foggy too strongly, but Sophia was quite susceptible to flattery and being the centre of attention.

'Sophia was certainly not averse to the celebrity status. However, Adam refused to make any public appearance to protect Michelle from overwhelming attention. He insists on remaining as private as possible. Hence, as you know, the decision to use Ingis Chen. Now that you have returned, all the Foggies and we are hoping that you will be able to take over, the Koplats included.' Leila concluded, with a grimace expressing apologetic hope.

'What reason did you give them for my absence?' I enquired.

'You were on a touring visit of the WII communities, in the equivalent of England there. As usual, we stayed as close as possible to the truth. Not that it made much difference. As your assistant, I received all kinds of requests for further details from the press, corporations, countries, and the UNO.'

'I have already called Sam to let him know you are back and safe. He was really worried. He knew, more than anyone, something was off,' said McRae.

'What did he say to his boss? As a matter of fact, what did *you* say to your boss?' I asked him.

'He says to British Intelligence that they should consider themselves lucky we keep him informed at all. I tell them that I have gained a foot inside the close Foggies' *clan,* now that I am dating their irreplaceable personal assistant, and I need to tread carefully.' He winked at me and kissed Leila gently on the lips.

I smiled.

'OK, so what do you need me to do, and when?' I said, with a sigh.

*

Late afternoon, Leila recorded a video during which I explained why I had been absent. I spoke calmly, sitting on a standard chair against a bare wall, light classical music playing in the background to blank out any sound from wild nature that might betray my location. We had spent hours writing and rehearsing what I would say about my disappearance. We wanted to stick to the facts, yet be thorough, as I recounted my personal history with Clémence.

First, I spoke – not for the first time – of the striking differences between the ways of life in WII and ours, in addition to the discrepancies in technologies, recent history and scientific knowledge. Then I revealed the two attempts against my life, months ago and recently. In detail, I described the rise of the women rebels and their claim to the right of role reversal in favour of their gender. It was difficult not to make personal comments, and thus subjective ones. I could not help but express that the WII Amazon-like fighters aimed for a women totalitarian regime, possibly even more unfair, strict and inflexible as the one they fought. We had to remain brief to avoid losing the audience with too many details, and so I moved swiftly to the civil war between genders and the attacks against Foggies and Relocated. My voice trembled when I mentioned the death of two friends from WI; Big Tom and Christophe (that he was a Switcher remained a secret). Then I explained how we ended up cut off from the gate and had to flee. We were hunted down, engaged in battle, and lost too many people on both sides. After gaining the upper hand, we found a safer place and I could reconnect with my peers and with my world.

'I share this story,' I emphasised, 'to demonstrate that WII is neither an idyllic world where rebuilding one's life is easy and risk-free, nor the den of the devil, as some people try to make you believe. It is just another planet where humans are being humans, with their qualities, flaws, doubts, beliefs, fears and aspirations. There, life is more difficult in terms of communication, technology, transportation, but it is also more natural, organic and pollution-free. It is simply another way of life that will suit some, less others, but for those who decide to cross the gate, *it will not be a holiday*.'

My conclusion was that, being back, I would regain my role as the Foggies' speaker, including on the newly opened Gate in Alcatraz.

*

In the video, there was no mention of Ingis Chen or Lally O'Maleigh. Every Foggy available was consulted prior to disclosing the video. It won unanimous consent for release to the press. My peers and friends were delighted that I was back and safe. Rosario, always direct and honest, declared: 'Gosh! You do look like shit. It's obvious you went through hell. You should have gone for a professional make-up session before shooting the video.'

'I disagree,' Michelle commented. 'It makes her story more believable than if she had looked fresh and pampered. It is pretty obvious she went through a real ordeal.'

Adam was also relieved to have me back and dealing with the press. He expressed that he was happy with the work done by Ingis Chen so far, but he much preferred that it all stayed within the 'family', so to speak. Sophia defended Chen, saying that he had been excellent, and that maybe we should review our opinion of him, and that we might have judged him too harshly. She shut up, though, when Leila reminded her he had killed one of the Society's agents, kidnapped Jack, attempted to kidnap Louise, and more often than not acted on his own agenda and without consulting the Foggies on matters directly linked to them. Leila's tone was stern and did not invite contradiction. It was rare to hear her speak to us in such an uncompromising tone. Michelle turned towards me with a personal question on the recent events in WII.

'How do you feel to have killed someone? Not just a woman you didn't know, but Clémence; a person you had lunched and dined with?'

'Michelle!' Adam burst out. 'Michelle, this is a very inappropriate question. Sorry, Yoko! Please dismiss it.'

And I did dismiss it. The question had been pushed to the back of my mind since opening my eyes. It was a sore nagging thought I refused to face, the thought that I was a killer. A point blank killer. When the thought came, the event replayed in slow motion in my head. Me, carefully aiming my shotgun at Clémence and pulling the trigger, going for the kill. And there was not just Clémence. The look of surprise, pain and fear of that other woman when my knife went through her chest. No, I was not ready to face the memory, to acknowledge how cold and determined I was then. Those actions had been necessary to save my life, but my wish to kill had such strength! Such violence … So, I pushed the thought away like dust under the carpet, trying to cover it with the many other issues ahead. I hoped the blend of painkiller and sleeping pill would knock me out that night, so that Clémence's eyes would not creep up at bedtime to haunt my sleep.

*

The Society released the recorded video to the mainstream news broadcasters around the world and on social media online. It made the headlines of the BBC evening news, but instead of watching myself on the screen, I went back to the Fog cabin in WII to meet up with Ushi and Nick, and to check on Eudes, Isabelle and Chloé. Despite being exhausted from her injury and the long journey, Ushi was beaming. She was reunited with Eudes who had never been happier. He had even started calling her 'Mum'. She loved it; however, in an effort to avoid confusion and criticism from his blood family, she corrected him. She repeated to him her name was 'Ushi'. He immediately adjusted to the best of his understanding. As a young child, and from then on, Ushi Tsou had become 'Mumushi' to him. Children really do have a gift. She loved the name and adored Eudes. Even to us, she presented a calm, serene, blissful face.

*

The councils of both Lil'London and Newtonsee had been informed of our misadventure and Clémence's death. Nick had contacted Jazz on her Ftab to update and reassure her, and she had passed on the information. The councils were ecstatic to be rid of Clémence, and the women rebels' stamina was already showing signs of fatigue. However, the council members were rather bitter at the lack of consultation prior to our departure and our special alliance with the people of Yerushaleim. It irritated them even more to be informed via Jazz and Maud instead of us contacting them directly. Zeno and I would normally be their direct point of contact on Fog matters. They recognised the two women and the need for their strong political presence but they remained reluctant to embrace them as peers. My first intention was to write them a letter explaining the journey had been unforeseen but then I stopped myself. It was better to meet them in person, to explain the circumstances of our decision and the urgency of the situation. To explain, not to justify! The difference between the two words would be put across very clearly. They had taken our actions slightly personally and as a rebuff to their mild advances, yet we had done nothing wrong. In fact, their reproaches were even inappropriate. They knew we had taken refuge in Yerushaleim because we had no choice, and they offered very little help at the time. After a few deep breaths and some inner ranting, I focused on my duty as ambassador and liaison agent between both worlds. I had to remain diplomatic.

*

The following day I would be on the move again, back to London, then WII, to meet with representatives from the press, the Government, Lil'London and Newtonsee, and whomever it was my chore to meet. This included dealing with my ex-brother-in-law, Charles-Antoine, to discuss his son and his boyfriend's future location or his part in it, if he wished.

Part of me dreamed of staying longer here in the Highlands, to recover from my wounds, physical and mental. On the other hand, I feared dealing with the memories of what happened in the woods if I stayed inactive. Because of this, I was glad to go. I hoped my parents and Jazz would find the right words to help me deal with the chill I felt at the thought, at the flashback, of Clémence's eyes when the bullet hit her.

'I *had* to do it…' I repeated to myself. 'It was war. It was either her – them - or me.' I shook my head and pushed the images as far away as possible to bury them in the depths of my brain. For the painkiller and sleeping pill to act faster, I poured myself a glass of wine.

Day 2 (Monday)

Leila left ahead of me to avoid attracting attention to our group. She was unknown to the public, but too many officials knew her and her role, so she also had to disguise herself. Instead of taking the train from Edinburgh to London, she was travelling from Glasgow under a false identity. For McRae and me, it had been an early start by car to reach Edinburgh. McRae had turned bright ginger to be more anonymous, adding a large and, frankly, horrid ginger beard to his disguise. He was not a man for beard. Four bodyguards from the Society surrounded my seat. I played the role of businesswoman in a suit, with dark hair tied in a bun and my face hidden by a thick fringe and glasses with a large rim. A set of fake teeth finished the look to render me unrecognisable. Whenever I glanced at the window, the reflection made me start in surprise. If it could even fool me, the disguise must be good. The hours stretched endlessly. I missed Leo terribly. It was a consolation that when next in the Highlands, Leo would be there. Whatever the hardship of the journey, the blisters, or the tendonitis, he would be there.

To control my thoughts, I concentrated on the news. Even though it was abundant, I was bored within an hour after having learnt the gist of it. The carriage was half-empty, which was unusual; it was a popular commute between the Scottish and English capitals. For the most part the Modern Marburg had considerably reduced the will of people to travel. I would have thought about it twice, too, if the Fog did not protect me from most diseases. Leila had kindly given me a couple of books, but I couldn't concentrate on either. It was raining outside. Absent-mindedly, I caressed Simba who was sitting at my feet, her head on my lap. In the morning, she had gone for a thorough trimming, followed by a black and fire colouring of her fur. She had not enjoyed it at all, but she looked nothing like her old self. She was still a huge dog in appearance, though now of indeterminate breed: a large mongrel beast. Her fur felt strange under my fingers. My poor baby. She was staring at me with her beautiful eyes and I gave her another treat. Maybe she did not mind the trimming that much and was using my weakness for nibbles.

*

The list of tasks was long and kept growing. I mentally reviewed what was waiting for me upon my arrival. The train was due to arrive at London Kings Cross station in the late afternoon. From there, I would head to see Sam. To prepare for the meeting with the British Secret Service, I needed to raise a couple of matters with McRae. I could not go and talk to him in the train, so I logged into the *instant messaging* system of my Ftab.

'Hi Lochy! Free to chat?' I wrote.

'Go ahead,' he replied.

'As we are meeting Sam later, could you tell me what he knows and what he doesn't know?'

'My dear lass, you are wondering if you can trust me not to reveal to him any Foggies' secret. Don't worry, I am a Foggy now. I am adjusting my allegiances to what I have become. Like Nick. And like him, I will remain true to my beliefs. Contrary to him, I'll keep the fun in it.'

'Nick is fun!' I wrote, defending the man who had put his life on the line for me so many times since we first met. He could be fun; things had just been tough for him lately.

'Aren't you a protective one? Anything I should be aware of? Anyway, I meant no offence. I like the guy. Only he is English, not Scottish, so he can't help himself if he is a bit dry.'

'Whatever. Moving on. My point is: does Sam know you are a Facilitator?'

'No, and it is best he doesn't, yet.'

'Are you sure he doesn't suspect anything?'

'When I announced that I was dating Leila, it appeased his fears about my suspicious behaviour. For our Department, it gives me a step further into the Foggies' world. They probably wished it would have been you, but hey, Leila caught me first.'

'I'm heartbroken.'

'It's better not to tell them I am a Facilitator. Already, they have reservations regarding my impartiality because my interest in Leila is real. And to add to the problems, they are putting pressure on me to influence Leila. They have strongly suggested she should work for them. Now, Leila has an idea to get them off her back.'

'Which is?'

'To tell them *she* is a Facilitator. Her, instead of me. She believes it could make my job easier too.'

'She didn't mention this to me...' I said with a frown.

'It is just an idea for now; one I do not condone. She has enough on her plate,' McRae continued.

'I agree!'

'She can't go ahead unless you support it. Yoko, please nip this in the bud. She is exhausted. She needs to take care of herself.'

'I will talk to her.' His reaction pleased me. He cared about her enough to put her first. 'How do you feel about betraying your old chums?'

'I don't betray them. Being a Foggy is a fact, not a job. My job is to liaise between you and the British Intelligence and this I will continue. Telling them I am a Facilitator would just complicate things more than anything else. I don't need any more complications in my life.'

'You know there might be cases when they ask you to provide information on us, or give you info you should not be privy to.'

'Then I will act as I have always done, according to what my conscience is dictating to me. There is a reason why they consider me a maverick. However, if the information is one only the Facilitator should know, not the agent, then I will not pass it on as an agent. I will not betray you guys. I will also do my best to be a good agent. Now, I have a question for you.'

'Yes?'

'This Chloé: she is the daughter of Christophe and Isabelle, born in Morocco, isn't she?'

'Yes.'

'Born in the Fog, I assume? Is she... special?'

I made a promise to Christophe to keep Chloé safe, and one to Isabelle not to reveal the Simba-like quality of Chloé for as long as I could. Therefore, I played a little with the truth.

'She is just a lovely baby girl who has gone through too much already in her short life, not least losing her father. In this she is special, and I wish she wasn't. My goal now is to give her the happiest childhood possible, with as much love as we can all give her.'

McRae did not push the point, but I knew I had not answered this question. The doubt remained in his mind.

*

Isabelle was right, it was best for Chloé that no one knew of her 'special' talent for the time being. First Simba, then Chloé, both born in the Fog, and both sharing two of the Foggies' idiosyncrasies: being able to go across between worlds and to facilitate other Foggies to go with them, as well. If their abilities were discovered, how long before the authorities set up schemes for pregnant women to give birth in the Fog? Or worse, how long before people demanded it? What would happen to all these babies when they grow up? Would they just be pawns in the hands of the men in power? And what about when the Fog disappeared? What would they become? Would they suffer Fog withdrawal syndromes, as well? I already worried for the other Foggies when it happened, especially the younger ones. The only remaining active Switchers were Adam, Rosario and me. Of the original seven, one had disappeared almost immediately in Indonesia, then Clare and Christophe were killed, and Jack was in a coma.

I must have pulled a face or grunted, because Simba nudged my hand. It broke the dispiriting chain of thoughts. Returning to my Ftab, I decided to prepare for the next meeting with the Councils. Maud and Jazz were already working on what we hoped could be a positive ending to the gender's civil war. The goal was to prevent the women rebels reorganising themselves to continue their actions, despite losing their guru. They had suffered heavy losses during their offensives against the Yerushaleim people and us. The appeal of their movement was decreasing in their ranks: the deaths, the difficult life in the wild, the absence of loved ones and family: all brought doubts to the minds of many fighters. Nevertheless, the Women's Revolution was not dead. Plenty of angry women were still out there, determined to change the rules of leadership and society, as well as avenge Clémence. Jazz and Maud were determined to further promote their action of peaceful political activism as the best alternative to violence. Even if my friends won, I wondered if a few women rebels would remain in the future; outlaws, roaming around the country and robbing travellers and remote farms. The next editorial in Jazz and Maud's gazette, a weekly paper launched the previous Monday, was on the theme of 'Reconstruction, not Retribution'. They aimed to make it a motto to promote a positive end of the hostilities. The gazette was distributed in shops and read in public by a growing number of supporters. In addition, Jazz and Maud were working on a new and more general name, for their party. The names currently making the top five were Equality For All (EFA), Equal Rights (ER), People United (PU), Together and, simply, Equality. Jazz had convinced Maud that it would be much easier for men to support equality between both genders, not just focusing on women. By renaming the party to defend any group whose status and rights were unclear, their party would gain audience and credit. It was necessary. The friction between men and women was the predominant problem in WII, yet it was not the only serious social issue.

The fragile equilibrium established with the councils, regarding the

Relocated, was on the verge of collapse. The social unease was spreading, due to the sudden and large influx of people from WI. The councils still expected that the newcomers, aside from the novelties they were bringing, would be the ones making most of the adjustments to live among them. When Maud and Jazz introduced the idea of facilitating divorces, it had caused uproar in the Lil'London council boardroom. However, it was one of the best ways to acknowledge something had changed. Divorce was quasi non-existent in WII and seriously frowned upon, even from a man's initiative. Maud and Jazz argued that some of the women who had left to fight alongside Clémence might rethink their tempestuous ways, if given a chance to be in control of their lives. Plus, the abandoned husbands might wish to divorce them, too. 'I could sympathise with this,' August Hoare had commented. Not only was a change in mentalities necessary, it also involved a reshaping of the justice systems to ensure the fairness of the divorces, including legal texts, premises and lawyers, and the neutrality of the Court of Justice. As all the key official roles for both towns were held by three or four people, redistribution was in order. Maud and Jazz had not introduced these facts to the councils yet. They had already swallowed enough bitter pills that day. The two women did not want the counsellors to choke on them and spit them out.

*

When the train arrived at London Kings Cross station late afternoon, McRae and I made our way directly to see Sam at my new flat. This flat had been assigned to me in one of the Fog-dedicated buildings near the Fog Dome. Only a few people knew its exact location and security was high. It was modern, newly refurbished and decorated by experts. I found it cold, without soul or personality and hated it. It was like staying in a beautiful luxury hotel suite, except that I was supposed to call it my home.

It was a relief to take off my disguise. Speaking with fake teeth was awkward and the fake fringe kept falling behind the glasses, so I could hardly see.

Afterwards, I met with Putu and a representative of the UN Fog–dedicated agency, newly created in my absence. Putu briefed me on the health and security measures set in place and how the Fog Dome was now fully operative. The remaining problems were still its restricted access and the rehabilitation of the Relocated. There were no solutions in sight for them. At least, one of the positive consequences of my video released the previous day, was that people seemed more understanding of the Fog's complexity. However, this understanding did not mean they accepted the imposed limits on crossing the Gates. The pressure to open the Gate wider was still strong.

*

Despite my wish, it had not been possible to see Jazz at the Fog Dome. The WII roads were still unsafe for her to visit at will. She had to plan ahead of time and travel with protection. Today, Jazz was staying with Maud to be able to attend important meetings in Lil'London. Putu would pass her a message and hopefully, she would come the next day.

*

I had been adamant that dinner would be private with just my parents and me. Though first, I had one last duty to perform: the dreaded meeting with Charles-Antoine. His body language expressed anger and frustration when he arrived at the flat.

'Good evening, Yoko,' my ex-brother-in-law said, putting a briefcase on a chair in the entrance with a brief look around. 'Nice place you have here. Quite in contrast to your video released yesterday.'

'Good evening, Charles-Antoine,' I replied, ignoring his bitter comment.

'Where are Eudes and Ahmed? When am I going to see them?'

'Eudes is in a safe location, far from the civil war in WII. Ahmed is on his way there. I don't know when you will be able to see them. As soon as possible I hope. It will also depend on you.'

'What do you mean, it will depend on me? I want to see them: that's simple!'

'As I said, they will stay in a secure and remote location, not easy to access from here. If you want to see them daily, you should move there. Even if you want to see them weekly, we will expect you to move there. Because of your links to me and because you are under surveillance, your journeys to that secret location would eventually be noticed. We can't have you jeopardising the tranquillity of everyone there. So to see them regularly, you will need to change your life completely. No more living in Paris or London. No more city life or lavish lawyer's income.'

Charles-Antoine's eyes focused on an invisible point on the perfect and brand new wooden floor.

'It's the eternal choice between family and career, isn't it?' he said.

'Yes. I am afraid it is.'

'I must think about it. If both of them were in this world, my choosing to move with them would mean we would really be together. I would not hesitate. But in the present case... Even if I go there, we would only meet in the fogged venue, wouldn't we? It would still be limited. Maybe... Maybe I could try a long distance relationship first and see how it works?' He was speaking to himself more than to me. I let him continue his self-addressed monologue without interruption.

'Maybe I could travel there every couple of months and stay for a week or two, and in-between, we could have daily online chat? Would that work?' The last question might or might not have been directed to me. In doubt, I answered.

'Well, it doesn't depend on me. The three of you are the ones who will have to make any arrangement work,' I said, treading carefully in this dangerous zone.

'You mean 'the four of us', I presume?' he commented, bitterness back in his tone. 'You are forgetting that Ushi Tsou woman who managed to bomb into our family picture.'

'I can assure you she is going to extreme lengths for Eudes' care. We could not have found a person more dedicated to him.'

Charles-Antoine listened carefully to my narration of Ushi's misadventures during the previous week. What seemed to please him most was how Ushi had come to realise Ahmed was not a threat to her: to the contrary. The last time she saw him, she was even showing signs that she appreciated the young man. It was not just Charles-Antoine who felt relieved: I was glad to tick the relationship between Ushi and Ahmed off the list of tricky problems to handle.

*

My parents were wonderful. They could see I was exhausted and in pain from the bullet wound. I did not tell them that I was also dreading my agenda the following day, with a line-up of officials, press and Ingis Chen. The latter had messaged me to request a meeting and I found a slot for him in the afternoon. So they took it upon themselves to entertain me with funny anecdotes from the past. They told me how long-lost family members were suddenly resurfacing, now that I was 'famous'; at best to request access to the Fog, at worst to claim a crumb of my celebrity status. Mum and Dad succeeded in making me laugh.

Unfortunately, when my Ftab beeped the arrival of several messages and rang simultaneously, the stress rose again. I picked up the call. Leila immediately announced the bad news: the Koplats' ranch-like house in Nevada had just blown up. The Fog Gate was destroyed, reduced to dust. The powerful blast had taken the lives of many among the Americans present - military, FBI, scientists and others - who were working in and around the Fog. Thankfully, the Koplats were not in the house. They were safe in San Francisco, helping the first Relocated to settle around the Alcatraz-Fog. Any communications with the WII Nevada were cut-off. We did not know if Elsie, the Native Americans and the Relocated had suffered any losses as well. We could only hope their camps had been distant enough to be unaffected by the explosion. I wondered if the attack had come from WI or from WII this time. In London, we had had attacks against the Fog Gate from both worlds, but we were not aware of any Clémence-like threat in WII Nevada. So, it must be from this world, I thought. Who this time? The same people who attacked us in London?

Day 3 (Tuesday)

The painkillers helped soothe the pain in my shoulder; they did not dull my worries. How could someone's principal focus be to explode the Fog Gates? More than one person and in different planets. A deep feeling of unfairness lowered my spirits. We were good people, normal people: we just happened to wake up one day with a strange gift. I knew the attacks were not against us as individuals. It was against the Fog, the Gates, the Other World and we were just in the middle of it. Well, ok - we were the direct cause of it.

Our most prominent and loudest opponent just then was Lally O'Maleigh. It was almost too obvious for her to be the culprit. Most often, the loudest were not the ones who acted. Plenty of other religious or ideological groups condemning the Other World as heretical could be behind the Nevada explosion. They could have fanatics crazy enough. What about pharmaceutical companies: the Fog healing powers threatened their businesses, didn't they? The list went on… It could be anyone for the most ridiculous reason or fears.

Sophia was badly shaken by the destruction of her house. It affected Adam too, though differently; more because of what would have happened had they been home. Michelle was in tears. For once in agreement, they had decided to return to Alaska and keep a low profile for a while. Adam planned to return to Nevada in a week or two to switch a cabin where their house once stood, for Elsie and the Relocated to recover their connection with our world.

At breakfast with Harry and me, Rico was adamant the US Government must be involved, somehow. As he was struggling to find which conspiracy theory to apply to this case, he started to browse various websites and forums dedicated to such hypotheses. Rico was soon lost to us, totally focused on his Ftab. He only emerged when Leila messaged that she was on her way with more news. We expected the Society had found the perpetrators of the attack. They had found something else.

*

Hate and rage: that's what I felt when she told us. Hate and rage! *That bastard*, I fumed. Ingis Chen was the most malevolent person ever. How could anyone be so twisted, have so little care for the life of others. Horrible… He was horrible!

Leila had hinted at some news about him the previous day, yet it was so extreme, she didn't want to reveal anything until it was confirmed. Overnight, the Society researchers had tied up the threads: Ingis Chen was behind the release of the Modern Marburg virus. He had used secret laboratories to give the original Marburg a deadlier speed, selected key locations and used – sacrificed – carrier people to release this modern plague into the world. He had succeeded.

'What a fucking asshole!' Harry exclaimed. Hearing him swear was a rarity, let alone seeing him lose his nerve.

'I'm going to kill that guy! Let me! Please let me! Just give me a gun!' Rico shouted to no one specifically.

I was about to reply I might kill him first, when the image of Clémence's shocked eyes when my bullet hit her popped up in my mind. I clamped my mouth shut.

'We can't let him get away with it,' Harry continued. 'Leila, we must nail that sycophant!'

Harry had regained a control of himself, as his vocabulary indicated.

'I couldn't agree more,' she replied, her jaw set and her eyes venomous. 'This is the plan.'

*

The Society had tracked down the laboratories where Ingis Chen had developed the virus. The silver lining to their discovery was that a man-made virus, even partially man-made, did increase the chances of a cure. In all probability, Chen's laboratories would have the molecular structure of the virus and developed a cure already. Chen would want to protect himself against the Modern Marburg, like anyone else. The Society's plan was to raid the laboratories and get their hands on the original virus, the codes of its modern version, and the antidotes. Only after that would they inform the authorities of Ingis Chen's role in the worldwide pandemic. That way, they could give the formula to every nation on the planet – something they were not certain any Government would do as fast - and reveal Ingis Chen as a fraud and danger to humanity. The assault had already started.

'Let it be that the antidote really exists,' Harry said.

'It's likely,' Leila commented. 'And if it doesn't, we should be able to create one relatively quickly, once we have their Modern Marburg's formula.'

As Leila received live feed of the laboratories' break-in, we all fell into silence.

*

Once the laboratories were secure, physician experts took over the place and found not only the formula for the antidotes but samples as well. The mood turned victorious. The Society immediately sent copies to research centres, hospitals and governments around the world. Simultaneously, the Society anonymously leaked the information on Chen to anyone with influence on the planet, from politicians to secret services and Interpol. They also released it to the press and the most followed blogs, Twitter and Facebook accounts. Within minutes, the news had gone viral. Within hours, an international arrest warrant was launched against Chen. People called for him to be charged for crimes against humanity.

When the Society prepared the attack on his laboratories, they also pinpointed Chen's exact location, to catch him when the time came. However, Ingis Chen would never stay anywhere without having secured an escape plan, and his diary often changed. So, when he decided to travel to London earlier than planned, the raid on his laboratories had not started. The Society could not stop him without indicating they were up to something. They had to watch him get in his plane and leave. He must have heard about the laboratories raid when he was in the air. His flight suddenly went off route and disappeared from radars. The Society was now monitoring the place where he was most likely to find refuge: his own island. Mid-afternoon, their suspicions were confirmed: his plane had landed there. They swiftly leaked his whereabouts to secret services around the world. Afterwards, the Society decided they had done their duty. Now was the time to wait and watch.

'Why? Why did he do that?' Rico was in shock.

'The man is crazy, this is why!' McRae exploded. He had joined us by lunchtime. 'He is a lunatic!'

'Because he never lost sight of his goal,' Leila answered. She contained herself better than the others, but her cold voice revealed a real and deep anger.

'First he revealed the existence of the Fog to the world and created an interest,' I continued on Leila's line of thought. 'Then he released a virus that would force the people to consider the Fog as their only hope of survival; he forced their need to cross the Gate at whatever cost. He even kindly advised everyone how to deal with the Fog issues.'

'You might have been the only person he was honest with when you first met him,' Leila added. 'Chen said it clearly then. He wanted every single individual on earth to cross the Fog. He wanted to 'save the planet' by reducing its population, and make a fortune in the process.'

'Yes, I remember all too well. The means justified the end… Just as he told us. But why he told us, I am not sure,' I replied.

'Because if he had convinced you, his goal might already be achieved,' Leila concluded.

I knew of Chen's ultimate goal, and yet I had not followed the idea that he was at the origin of the pandemic. He was just too obvious a suspect, it could not be him. Wrongly, I had dismissed the obvious. And not just me.

*

In the meantime, the Fog Dome's health team was already proposing to the applicants affected by the Modern Marburg virus, that they would get the antidote instead within a few days. Due to the delay, the most serious cases were still going through, but the other cases were put on hold. Putu was proving very efficient in encompassing the roles of doctor and administrator of the health department. She did not have to; she could have just practiced her art. When asked, she replied that the blinkers, structural inefficiencies and lack of understanding had frustrated her in Kenya. This time she would try and influence the system positively. She had also launched the creation of a department to train Relocated as nurses and midwives. It was all very well that anyone could benefit from the state-of-the-art technology for medical assistance and surgery within the Fog Dome, but there were a few basics that needed teaching for outside emergencies.

Putu was one of the Foggies I knew the least. She had never been much of a talker during the Foggies' conference calls. Her interest was mainly in helping others medically, not in the Fog, the WII or the Foggies. I always sensed that, as a Facilitator, she was only doing her duty. She had a calling and was true to it. Meeting her that afternoon in the Fog Dome, I warmed to the woman. She was mature beyond her age, sensible and grounded. Determined, too. Putu struck me as one of those people who would only commit to something after much thought and consideration, though once they did, nothing would stop them. She slowed down for ten minutes to talk to me before continuing her tour through the hospital section of the Dome. I trotted by her side to continue our conversation. She talked about medicine, treatment, diseases and care in a simple way that made it comprehensible. Before, I considered it a foreign language. Putu would join us for a short while when the council representatives arrived to discuss health improvement opportunities. One of the projects was a class for all the Other World's local doctors, apothecaries, midwives and other healing practitioners to update them on modern medicine's basics. I already knew the offer of help by some of the local practitioners would not be as welcome as she hoped.

*

There was nothing exciting about the meeting with the towns' councils; nonetheless, I was waiting eagerly for their arrival. Among them were Maud and, most importantly, Jazz. She had never spent so much time alone in WII, away from the Foggies and most of the Relocated she knew. To ensure a safe passage to the Fog Dome, the councils travelled in a large group, surrounding themselves with armed men. The soldiers, who just a few weeks ago were farmers, retailers, or smiths of various guilds, had adjusted to their new roles to various degrees. Some did not look cut out for battle. Really not.

At first, it was not possible to spend personal time with Jazz. We agreed to meet when the councils were touring the increasingly large Relocated settlement.

Benjamin Snayth was curt and irritable. From various comments, I gathered that the councils had lost their immunity to criticism. Many of the adherents to the Equality Party – Jazz and Maud's choice of name for their party - had joined because they felt the councils were too risk-averse towards the necessary changes to the welfare and development of their society. Despite my misgivings towards Snayth, I sympathised with him. Their situation was a complex one. Aside from the opposition of women rebels, they also had to deal with the conflicting demands among their communities for more access to the knowledge, technology and trades with our world or, on the contrary, to stop the influx of new arrivals and sever the links that could further damage (some said destroy) the balance and foundations of their society. Therefore, when Benjamin Snayth berated me for leaving them and leading the people of Yerushaleim away, I kept silent. When he continued with the accusation that I belittled their authority by not seeking their help, my mouth remained shut (even though…). It was more difficult not to pipe a word when Snayth begun to criticise our handling of the Fog and the arrival of so many Relocated. John Chester, the mayor of Newtonsee and Churchill look-a-like, let Snayth vent his frustration and rant until he was looking ready to explode, before he intervened.

'Miss Salelles, we are aware, of course, that your ordeal was not a pleasant one and that you encountered many losses. In the name of Newtonsee, we sincerely regret that you had to go through these terrible events. I can assure you that our World is civilised. The sufferings you have endured were caused by the chaos and shock of cultures and mentalities. We thought we were ready to welcome everyone and anyone coming through, as well as any changes you may bring. We were not.'

'If I may add something,' Augustus Hoare interrupted. 'In my opinion, we are lucky. In view of your advances in weaponry and sciences, you could have taken over and imposed your ways upon us more easily than we could imagine. Instead, you wish to share your knowledge and help us grow. I appreciate your respect towards us even if… Even if sometimes it is clear that you do not approve.'

Snayth scowled at Augustus for his intervention. John Chester harboured a side smile that told me he approved of Hoare's words, or that Snayth was upset by it. Maybe both. Edmund Poff turned cheerful.

'Well said, Augustus,' Edmund said.

'Transitions are always messy,' Jazz commented. She looked tired and pale. She had lost too much weight and gained years in only a few days. Nonetheless, there was the fire of passion in her eyes. This reminded me of Clémence's eyes. In that moment, I was glad my friend had a lot of common sense and was well grounded. Otherwise, she might have turned into another Clémence, stopping at nothing for what she believed was right.

Slowly, the Councils were introducing the amendments put forward by the Equality Party to the local systems. Maud, Jazz and I believed they were the foundation stone for the people of WII and the Relocated to live side by side. They would enable the first group to adjust to the views we had brought along with the Fog, and to the second to live in harmony with the locals. Online classes aimed to broaden education in both worlds and enable each to learn about the other; trading was to be encouraged and spread; new regulations were drafted for all men and women to rebalance rights. It would take time; many old-fashioned people from all backgrounds were dragging their feet in WII. We hoped the young generation would consolidate the integration of old and new.

*

After the meeting, I first had tea with Maud and Jazz, then spent an hour with Jazz only. It was so nice to be together, to share the details of what had happened in our lives during the week. On her side, she had buried herself in chores and actions to keep her mind busy. If she stopped for too long, she would cry. An hour in her company went too fast and I longed for more. I suggested we could both spend the night at the Fog Dome to keep chatting. Rare were the people I could open up to and talk about my deeper feelings. It was even difficult with my mother and father these days. The child wanted to protect the parents. As their representative with the other town councils and de facto mayor, Jazz also had a pied-à-terre in the Relocated settlement, by the Fog Dome. The place was empty, but she was glad to invite me to stay. We would use yoga mats as mattress and blankets were easy to find.

'It's a good thing that I stay here, anyway. I ought to be here, in my constituency. Well... I haven't been elected yet, and that is also something to work on. Ed Epcott is helping me. He is our sheriff for now. It makes sense; he used to be a police officer. Anyway, time for me to show my face here. I have delayed it long enough.

'You were working with Maud. You had your reasons,' I told her. She looked at me, raising an eyebrow with an air saying '*Give me a break. I know that you know that I know I was delaying being alone in a new place and facing Big Tom's death.*'

It didn't take long before she asked me how I felt about Clémence's death. I took my time to answer this question. The knot of my emotions was difficult to entangle, and even more challenging to put into words. Guilt to have taken a life, resentment towards Clémence to have forced me into this situation, anger at myself to have let it go so far. Frustration, sadness, shame... Even fear that it would change me somehow; that it could turn me into a cold, inhumane person, over time. These confused thoughts swirled in my mind, still I did not doubt it had been my only option. The pressure on my chest grew stronger and when the tears began to flow, Jazz took me in her arms.

'Yoko. I am sorry. I wished it had been me pulling the trigger. I would not have seen her eyes. I would have seen Big Tom lying on the ground, dead.'

'You think I have avenged him? Maybe,' I said, between sobs, 'but it ought to make the unease go and it doesn't. It doesn't… Her and all the others I shot… All those deaths! All of them! All because I have opened those Gates!'

Jazz remained silent, hugging and patting me on the back. She was sobbing, as well. After a while, when I felt there was not a drop of water left in us to cry, I stood straighter and held her by the shoulders.

'I am sorry, Jazz. I am being selfish. What you went through, your loss, is much bigger.'

'We have both lost. It is not comparable,' she whispered.

'Ah… The good old truth… Everything is relative, a matter of perspective,' I replied.

'And now you are getting all French and philosophical on me,' she joked with a smile. 'At least reassure me on something. With Leo, you have someone good who loves you. Don't mess it up, okay? Seize every minute of it. It can go so quickly.'

'He is still on the long walk to the Highlands' Fog. It will take weeks,' I winced at the idea. My body yearned for him; my skin itched for his touch. I missed Leo, his voice and his laugh. Jazz looked at me with a sad smile and nodded.

'Good. About time you feel and think straight on that one,' she said.

Day 4 (Wednesday)

Ingis Chen had declared his island a free State overnight. By doing so, Chen was gaining immunity on the soil of his own State. Leila explained how he could do this, as I met her over breakfast in the Fog. The existence of a State is independent of recognition by other States, who are not free to intervene in its affairs. However, international laws have a clear definition of what defines a State, derived from the Montevideo Convention of 1933 (or Convention on Rights and Duties of States). A State must have a permanent population, a defined territory, a government (however basic it might be) and the capacity to enter relations with other States. Chen had covered all these points. He had now reached the stage of the *Declaration of Independence*. In normal circumstances, the creation of a new State would raise a few eyebrows, produce a little stir in the press, cause some grunts at the United Nations should the State accept their invitation to join (they would have to squeeze an additional seat), along with sceptical speculations on how long the country would last.

Still, those were not normal circumstances.

Any countries may be subject to an invasion, though de facto an armed invasion is a declaration of war. That Wednesday, the UN was voting to support the creation of a coalition to launch an assault against Chen Island and force him to stand down. Ultimately, the UN wanted to place him in front of the International Court of Justice in The Hague to stand trial for crimes against humanity. Not one person around the world rose to his defence, at least not publicly. The press praised the swift reaction of the UN, although many believed Special Forces should have been sent in a secret mission the instant his location became known.

'Every country wanted to,' Leila told me. 'China, Russia, the US, the UK, Israel, France... All of them. That was the problem. 20 or more Special Forces could not launch an uncoordinated mission onto the Island to get Ingis Chen. They would have killed each other. Too many were not speaking the same language on site.'

'I see... Does Chen still have people defending him behind the scenes?' I asked.

'He does. Either he pays them extremely well, or they share his ideals. Or both,' she answered.

'Well, money will run out.'

'Don't underestimate him, Yoko. He knows how to surround himself with the best. He must have protected his back.'

'Have you looked into it?'

'Of course we have, and we are struggling. He has several fake IDs, multitudes of accounts disseminated off-shore, most of which we cannot trace,' Leila's tone was upset and vehement. Obviously, she was frustrated in her wish to nail him.

'In many good movies,' I interrupted her, 'not least *The Untouchables*, the way to get the bad guy is through his accountant. Do you know who created the wiring web for the funds and who holds the keys to the accounts?'

'We are looking for him, too.'

'Would he be on the island?'

'Who knows?' she sighed.

'Well… Never mind the money. The UN coalition will catch him and condemn what he has done for eternity. Money won't help him there.'

'I hope so,' Leila said, her eyes narrowed and her jaw set.

*

The UN was not just busy dealing with Ingis Chen, they were also arguing on our fate: the fate of the Foggies. Even though the antidote lightened the threat of the Modern Marburg virus, the Fog still held 'miraculous' healing powers and opened the doors to extraordinary opportunities every country wanted a share of. They demanded to know the names and roles of everyone linked to the Fog, as well as the exact location of each Gate and our links with governments. Their aim was that their newly created UN Fog department would coordinate our actions. It felt like an additional layer of supervision. I mourned the days when no government, no institution and no member of the public was aware of our existence. To think I considered my life was complicated then; I had no idea. We could and would never satisfy everyone.

The Foggies in Alaska had no wish to reveal their existence and location. The Koplats seconded their decision, grateful to have a safe and discreet haven where they could hide when necessary, like now - recovering from the shock of the attack to their family home. I did not intend to reveal the creation of the little Fog cabin in Scotland, either. Interestingly, the United Nations' request – not a demand, not yet – was on the assumption that working with them would be beneficial to the Foggies in that they would help harmonising the work between us internationally. They underestimated the structure of Gatekeepers Associates or the support we received from the Society. How long did we have before Ingis Chen disclosed the existence of the latter, when arrested? Certainly, he would do this as revenge for their revelation of his links to the virus and whereabouts.

*

'Where is Simba?' Leila asked. We were working together in our office inside the Fog Dome. Jazz was out, checking the development of the Relocated settlement's future Town Hall.

'I left her with my parents yesterday. Too many witnesses have seen her by my side in both worlds. She was not a happy wolf, separating from me.'

'Wise decision. Scientists here are beginning to suggest tests should be made on various situations linked to the Fog, including birth and long periods within or outside the Fog. They wish to start studies on the Fog withdrawal effect and its symptoms. One of you will be asked, soon, if you 'wouldn't mind experimenting a little withdrawal' so they can understand it.'

'They'd better not ask Rico. That would not go down very well…'

'I think it would be better Simba doesn't come close to the Fog Dome. Ever. As for Chloé…' Leila let the sentence finish in mid-air, then switched to me. 'I would not be surprised if they also suggest you should get pregnant.'

'They'd better not! And as for Chloé, she will stay in Scotland for as long as possible,' I replied in my most determined tone. Leila immediately understood there was no room for negotiations there, not that she wanted any.

*

The morning flew by, getting updated with the current affairs and dealing with the mountains of paperwork and messages accumulated in my absence. I was grateful to the team working with Leila. They helped skim through the hate letters, death threats and marriage proposals. I could not keep track of the many reports and meeting proposals from the UN Fog Department, the British Government and other institutions.

Early afternoon, I returned to my soulless flat. I needed a break, wanted to see my parents and walk Simba. I also worried for Leo and missed him, the comfort of his arms and the warmth of his love. Leila had plans of her own for

506

a late lunch. She would join me afterwards to start planning my next public address, the meetings we could not escape and the ones we were to impose, among other chores at hand. Sitting at my desk at home, I looked around at my cold surroundings. I switched on my computer with determination.

'I have to do it. Now. It's just too depressing!' I said aloud to myself. I must have sounded upset, as Simba put her head on my thigh, looking up at me.

'Don't worry, sweetie,' I said to her, patting her head. 'It's all good. You will see. You'll like what I am up to. It will be better for you, too.'

For the next two hours, I browsed the world of online shops, spending an indecent amount of time and money on eBay. Colourful curtains, trendy cushions, boho chic sofa, classic movie posters, fake humongous silk flower arrangement, funky lamps… This flat was the subject of a total transformation; it was going to be a real home: welcoming, hearty and mine. The address for delivery was to the care of Sam at the Fog Dome, and to keep him in the loop I emailed him confirmation of all the orders. After my retail therapy, I went for art therapy and got a wide selection of canvases, paints and brushes. During this outrageous afternoon of shopping spree, loud background music played my best blues-busters tunes. When Leila rang the doorbell, my mood was much better.

*

My parents joined Leila and me for a casual dinner at the kitchen table. I made smoked salmon and spinach lasagne, a comfort food for a relaxed evening. They explained their decision to move to Scotland. Charles-Antoine's hesitation left them with little doubt that his contact with his partner and son would be long distance. In contrast, Mum and Dad wanted to be with Eudes. Sometimes, they could even travel to London or abroad. For them, the most important aspect was that Eudes felt his family had not abandoned him. I would be there often, as well, but I would have unavoidable commitments taking me away. They had not. I would miss them when in London. I liked having them around: their presence was calming. Being alone was not the problem. It never bothered me. The novelty was that, when alone these days, I was feeling lonely. I missed my parents, Jazz, Leo and old housemates. The Fog had brought us even closer, yet now it also kept us apart.

During dessert, the doorbell rang again. I was not expecting anyone and so prepared myself for bad news. When I opened the door, Leo was smiling in front of me. After a split second of surprise, I threw myself in his arms, dismissing the pain in my shoulder. His lips met mine and we kissed. Simba jumped on him, delighted to see him and breaking us apart.

'I am so happy you're here!' I said, looking at him in wonder before frowning at the sight. His small, untamed beard barely hid a badly-healed slit on his left cheek. He also had bruises on his forehead and jaw, and a split lip. Leo was scruffy and marked by battle. I passed a hand on his face.

'My poor darling. We need to have you looked at.'

'It's cosmetic damage. I am fine.' He looked at my arm sling. 'What about you? What did the doctors say?'

I looked down at my arm. I had awakened the pain but tried not to show it.

'Nothing to worry about,' I replied. 'How did you arrive here?'

'Never underestimate the power of women's solidarity. Jazz talked to Leila who convinced McRae to approach Ushi. He talked her into flying back and collecting me, then she dropped me at the Fog Dome.'

'Such a long trip… Why?' I asked. I snuggled against him. 'Not that I'm unhappy to have you back.'

'Because you were brooding and down. Apparently, they believe you were missing me,' Leo smiled his wonderful and cheeky smile. His eyes sparkled as he looked right at me. I felt blissful.

'I love you,' I told him.

'And I love you,' he said back.

*

The shout of 'Nooooo! I can't believe it!' coming from the kitchen broke the romance of the moment. We ran to see what had made Leila sound so upset. When Leo and I arrived, she was pacing the kitchen floor. My parents were looking at her, worried. I had never seen her like this: Leila was listening intently to someone on her mobile, grinding her teeth in contained rage. She was scarily pale. My heart stopped beating. I didn't know what to expect, but I feared the worst: who had died?

Ingis Chen.

Not dead, but free. He had escaped.

Within a minute of the UN vote supporting the arrest of Chen for trial on the grounds of crimes against humanity, an attack was launched against his island. Everything had been ready. Agreements and coalitions were formed, plans of action set, coordination determined. For the first time in human history, each secret service was working together to get the '*bastard*'. Unbelievably, he still managed to slip out. When the coalition of Special Forces raided his island, broke into his mansion and hunted every inch of his domain, Ingis Chen could not be found anywhere. He was gone. It was hardly surprising that he did not want to stay and wait at home: however, protected his fortress was, he did not stand a chance against the rest of the world united. What no one could fathom was how he had disappeared from the island without being spotted by any of planes, submarines and ships surrounding it, or the satellites focused on it. For Leila, there could be only one explanation: he was not on Chen Island to begin with. He must have fooled them from the start.

'That could be a problem,' Leila said, between clenched teeth.

'A big problem. This man is dangerous and on the loose!' I exclaimed.

'Yes. But I was referring to another problem,' Leila pointed out. We all waited for her to continue. 'We leaked the information on his whereabouts, anonymously. The world out there will assume we misinformed them on purpose, so he could disappear. Speculations as to the source will spread fast. Who will be in the crossfire?'

'I see what you mean. International relations can consequently worsen; countries might turn against each other...' I reflected aloud.

'Exactly,' Leila said.

'And before long, Foggies are bound to be accused as well,' my father added, a line of worry appearing on his forehead.

'It's not past Chen to have predicted that if the mission was not successful, everyone would turn against each other,' Leo fumed. 'I hate him, but I have to concede he has the brilliance of mind for it. The motherf... Sorry. The bastard is just applying the 'divide and conquer' strategy.'

I sat down at the table and put my head in my hands. Why did it always have to get worse and worse and worse? I had always refused to feel the victim of my destiny, a victim in life, but sometimes, when everything and everyone seemed to want to pick a bone against you, one had to wonder. Leo came next to me and put an arm around my shoulder.

'What are we going to do?' I asked no one in particular.

'We need to pre-empt the attacks and attack first,' my mother said. 'Nobody is going to touch my baby if I can stop it!'

I looked up at my mother and burst into laughter. She was on a warpath for her daughter.

'Right. Let's start brainstorming. How are we going to proceed?' my mother said, with a brief smile. She had turned into a general in charge of an impossible mission.

My Ftab rung. It was Sam.

Day 5 (Thursday)

On the BBC morning news, the anchor announced that the British Government was investigating the chain of events that triggered the assault on Chen Island, in the belief that Chen was holed-up there. The BBC reported that, following the Foggies' recent misgivings on Ingis Chen, British Intelligence had dug deeper into his activities. Upon discovering the truth, they had tried to arrest Chen but he had made a first escape. The British Government was aware future action would require international support: they were adamant Chen should face the International Court of Justice. Therefore, they refrained from sending the SAS on an undisclosed mission, choosing instead to release the information to the world.

In short, the British were taking the blame for the cock-up of letting Ingis Chen leave their country. That had been a bitter pill to swallow for Sam when my mother first presented him with her idea.

*

When I answered Sam's call the previous night, my mother had leant forward and pressed the speaker key on the Ftab screen. Taking the lead in the conversation, she immediately summarised for Sam, stunned into silence by my mother's commanding voice, that it was essential to preserve the Foggies' image.

'These days, everything is being turned into conspiracy theories,' she started, 'so there is little chance that Ingis Chen's disappearing act will not. The hunt for a culprit will be relentless and heads will roll. You *must* make sure my daughter will not be one of them. First and foremost, because she is my daughter. Second, because you know she and the Foggies are good people who are doing their best. Third, because you must protect the Fog, the Foggies and all that is linked to them by defending their image. The purpose of the Fog is unclear, but it is not evil. Maybe there is no purpose at all and just an offer of an alternative. It does not matter. Two people are likely to attack the Foggies online: Ingis Chen, whose destroyed 'Empire' makes him even more dangerous in his anger, and Lally O'Maleigh, who would use anything against the Fog.'

My mother stopped for one deep breath before continuing.

'Anyway, do you know what happened? How did he pass through the cracks? Why were there cracks in the first place?'

'We don't know,' Sam managed to answer, just before my mother asked another question. 'We have reviewed all the 'anonymous' data circulating between worldwide authorities. In addition to your secret little helpers, several agencies were constantly monitoring him. They backed up the leaked information regarding his movements.'

'Could the flight have stopped unnoticed on its way to Chen Island?' Leo asked.

'Possible,' Leila answered.

'Or could he have jumped on parachute or something?' I enquired.

'Possible,' Sam answered.

'What about if it needed to stop to refuel?' I continued. 'He could have left then!'

'We caught the pilot. We are interrogating him now,' Sam commented.

'Why wasn't he arrested then?' Leo lost his temper and turned to Leila. 'You knew what he had done. How could you not have sent a team or something?!

It's not as if you haven't employed mercenaries before! Even if you were not 100% sure, it was worth the risk!'

Sam listened to the exchange, obviously curious and hoping to learn more about Leila and the Society.

'Leo, I told you. We tried,' Leila replied with calm, refusing to fall into an argument.

'Do you have any idea where he could be now?' Sam asked Leila.

'No, I don't. I would need to check with our 'secret little helpers' as you put it,' Leila replied. Leo winced as he realised he might have blown Leila's cover. 'But I know they are reviewing all the information the Foggies have on him and hope to find even the minutest clue, a shred of a thread that could help. Then they will share it with us.'

'In the meantime,' my mother's voice rose above all the others, 'because the source of the information was anonymous, it will be considered suspicious. And because in the public eye Ingis Chen was close to the Foggies, so will they.'

My mother then said that the best option was for the British Secret Service to take the blame. The idea was that the British authorities had released the information to the world anonymously, because it was contrary to Secret Services' policy to openly divulge their data.

'Everyone will think we were feeling guilty; that we have let Ingis Chen go,' moaned Sam.

'Look on the bright side,' Leila smiled sweetly, even though Sam was not in the room to see it. 'You get the credit for discovering Chen's true nature. You should be able to regain a few brownie points with the International community of spies for this, no?'

*

The British Government reluctantly agreed with my mother's suggestions. Heads started rolling, including Sam's. He came after breakfast to say goodbye. Harry, Rico, Leo and I were sitting at the table when he messaged us that he was outside, and would it be a convenient time to visit. He had never been so formal, so we knew something was wrong.

When he told us he had been given the sack, we all fell silent. Rico then dialled Leila and asked her to join us, if she could. She arrived within fifteen minutes. Rico made fresh coffee for everyone, even those who did not want any. He stood at the end of the table and, leaning forward, announced that Sam losing his job was unacceptable because Sam was trustworthy, efficient, a '*good bloke who didn't deserve that crap*', and he knew how to keep a secret. After his little speech, Rico slammed his knuckle on the table – from the way he held it afterwards, it hurt - and turned to each of us, one after the other.

'Now, guys, if we refuse to work with anybody other than Sam, they will have to keep him, right?' he said around.

'I am still here,' Sam pointed out.

'Yeah, yeah. Don't worry. We'll sort you out.'

We all looked at Sam. I smiled, put down my cup on the table, and said 'I'm on board.'

'Me too,' Harry followed.

'And me,' Leo added.

'And me, not that I have a say in the matter, but I'll help build a case,' Leila concluded.

'That is… Do you want to continue working with us?' I asked him.

Sam looked around, his smiles and soft eyes showing how moved he was by our support. It was an important decision to make; he would go against the grain of important people within British Intelligence. To our relief, he accepted. Then I asked if he would come with me to walk Simba.

*

During the walk, I further explained our spontaneous backing. There was an unspoken understanding that Gatekeepers Associates would only hold in the long term if surrounded by reliable partners, by people or entities we trusted. We needed to be strong on the inside as well as on the outside. First, we had just been our household: Harry, Zeno, Rico and me. Then more Foggies appeared and we found a way to work together. It was in our mutual interest. We lived in our little bubble for a while, even though we knew that our secret was at risk of coming out in the open, any day. We hoped we would be able to cope and manage when that happened. If it had not been for the likes of Leila, Sam and McRae in this world, or in WII for Maud, Ariel Ben-Chaim and the Councils – however begrudgingly for the latter - we would not have made it.

We were part of a whole. Short of hiding in the most remote and secret cave in Siberia, interaction with others was necessary. Therefore, we might as well choose those we wished to interact with.

'As my father repeated to me, growing up,' I quoted, "a clever person can rise to the top; For him to remain there, he will need to surround himself with even more clever and competent people in their fields."

'A bright man, your father,' Sam commented with a smile.

'That's why he married my mother. He still says she is the cleverest woman he has ever met. And the cherry on the cake is that they are still madly in love with each other.'

'They are part of a lucky few.'

'Yes, they are.' I replied. 'Though more often than not, we are the ones who don't allow our own luck to bloom. We are often so blind, set in our ways, with one fear or another – or fear of one another - that we miss the signs.'

'Nah. I just haven't met the person that rocks my boat. Not that I'm complaining: you guys do that enough.'

'Do I detect a slight compliment?'

'I never wanted a boring life. The Fog is clearly making sure my wish comes true. It's frustrating though. You keep a lot under wraps.' With this he bent down and patted Simba, then looked up at me, knowingly.

'Don't take me wrong, I don't blame you,' he continued. 'I understand why you keep some of the things quiet. Like this one. I reviewed all the tapes with Simba, all the records, and noted when some of you let slip she was in WII. So I know. She can double-cross.'

We continued walking on a protected path along the Thames in silence. The path was limited to a short section, but safe. The fact that he knew did not scare me, which was further confirmation of my trust in him.

'Since when did you know?'

'A few weeks.'

'Have you told anyone?'

'No. And I won't. As I told you, some things are better left under wraps. Some scientists out there would not resist playing God in their laboratories. Scientifically, this is fascinating, but in human terms? We are talking about life, about babies, and people… Anyway, if news about Simba's abilities spread, it would take barely hours for pregnant women to be brought to the Fog and births to be induced.'

'Once upon a time, you said to me that the Fog was too big an event to consider at the individual level. What happened to this idea?'

'I still believe it. The Fog is too big a discovery to keep from the world just because you wish to protect yourself as individuals. However, it is now clear that some aspects of the Fog should remain hidden to protect humanity against itself. Humans do not always show humanity, far from it. Even if there are signs that more individuals act united in displays of humanity and spirituality, we are not there yet.'

'I didn't know you had this spiritual side,' I looked at him, a little surprised.

'Oh, come on. Don't we all?'

*

I was never able to fathom how Rico could drink so much coffee and not be a nervous wreck. He was always hyperactive, that is true; however, it was abnormal to drink up to 3 litres of coffee by midday and still function normally. That Thursday, he was bursting with anger by early afternoon, gesticulating vehemently in front of the news broadcast on television. As expected, Lally O'Maleigh had swiftly pointed a finger at the Foggies and accused us of consorting with Ingis Chen in releasing the Modern Marburg. She denounced us for using the virus to pretend to be the saviours of humanity. She emphasised that she had warned the world we were agents of the Dark Forces. What was new was that she now presented herself as an alternative, as an agent of the Light. This triggered Leila off. I had never seen Leila lose her temper like this before. Soon we learned why she was so enraged. When we did, the Foggies were fuming against both Lally O'Maleigh and Leila.

*

Leila came clean. She revealed that Lally O'Maleigh was an old acquaintance of hers from when they sat on the benches of the Society's University, learning their skills to prepare for the coming Fog. They each had an assignment: Leila as a liaison agent with direct interaction with the Foggies, Lally as a balancing act. Should it be necessary, Lally was to defend the case against the Fog and its crossing to help control an excessive afflux of people to WII. Until full disclosure of the Fog to the public, she would remain a dormant agent, waiting for the Society's green light to spring into action. There were many such dormant agents to target political, ecological, social and other consequences of the Fog. Lally O'Maleigh's role was to balance the spiritual side. The Society had compartmentalised each section and actors: information was limited to what was essential for their activity. Even though Leila was at the top level of the structure and knew the bigger picture, she did not know every detail and name of the schemes supporting their global action and purpose. It was crucial to protect identities: the Society had implanted key contacts and experts at the core of large companies, institutions, governments and laboratories. The Society had worked for decades laying out the various scenarios following the revelation of the Fog's possibilities and the existence of a parallel Universe. Thanks to technology, they used – ahem… stole - ill-earned funds hidden in offshore accounts to finance their researches and goals. Through their presence in leading IT companies, they could break into most devices. The Society's secret tentacles spread in all directions. They were a spider's web of good intentions, frighteningly wide and well connected. However, they still relied on people and sometimes people take a different turn than expected. Lally O'Maleigh was one of them.

Lally O'Maleigh had always been a little intense, Leila told us. She had a talent for speeches and hesitated at first between politics or law for her dormant role. When hearing about the religious approach, she chose that. She liked the idea that, aside from the Fog, she would help people find their way spiritually. Indeed, Lally was a Christian. The idea that God governed the Universe intrigued her, and she liked to consider the Fog as an Act of God to prepare men for a new age of many interconnected worlds. It was one of the possibilities the people within the Society believed, but Lally often argued it was the only one that made sense to her. Leila and Lally were never close friends. Over the years, they grew more distant. Looking back, Leila saw how Lally was increasingly isolating herself. It should have rung alarm bells, yet they failed to notice and follow up on this, thinking it suited her role. Now, Leila explained, the Society realised something had switched inside the agent.

The character she played caught up with her and she started to believe her own words. Like in a role-play game, she identified herself with her character. Therefore, when Lally raised her voice against the Fog as the work of the devil, the Society was unprepared. She went to the media on her own mission. The Society then understood she was a problem. They tried to stop her by blocking her access to the public, but she had already built her own network through her followers and her own contact with the press. Lally was clever and well trained. She knew the ropes.

*

I was irate. How could Leila have kept such important information from us? How could she not have told us that Lally O'Maleigh belonged to the Society, even if she was their black sheep?

'What would it have changed?' Leila argued. 'In a strange way, she does the job we assigned her, though she surpasses it all by presenting herself as a new Messiah of sorts. We are trying to contain her.'

'It changes a lot! Lally being an ex-Society member makes her more dangerous to us. She knows a lot more than it appears. We should have known!' I was indignant. 'She is against us. An adversary. As such, any information about her is useful. To retain such information was unacceptable!' Leo came and put his hand on my back to calm me down. His body language indicated he was upset, but more in control. His gesture appeased me a little and I continued, slightly more composed.

'Leila, could she be a danger to you?' I asked.

'Yes. She is more a danger to us than for you. Chen vaguely knows about our existence; she knows everything, or almost everything! She can pinpoint our main locations, like the university or the address in New York. She knows the faces and names of some key agents and alumni. She knows how we work, and how we have infiltrated networks worldwide. She can create a scandal any day; one that could destroy our cover. And us.'

'So why doesn't she?' Leo asked.

'We're not sure...' Leila replied.

'Of course she can't,' Rico interjected. 'She would have to reveal how she knows this. Which also means revealing she started as a fraud, that she knew about the Fog all along and didn't warn anyone. That would feed our blogs!'

'What blogs?' Leo asked.

'The ones on every conspiracy out there!' Rico exclaimed.

I had to close my eyes and take a deep breath. Rico needed to learn to choose his time better.

'Anyway,' I continued, 'obviously something needs to be done. She is going off-rail!'

'Wait!' Rico yelled, startling us all. 'Did she know the Foggies' locations?'

'What do you mean?' Leila asked with a frown.

'Our houses in London and Nevada were blown out, remember?'

'No. No, she isn't behind the attacks,' Leila's reply was adamant.

'Why not?' Rico challenged her.

'It's just... I can't conceive... I have known her since we were teenagers. We dreamed about the Fog, about what it would be like. As I said, we were never that close, but still, I cannot imagine.'

'You said it yourself. She kind of *switched*,' Rico persisted.

'Rico, it is one thing to have an extremist view. It is another to have extremists' actions,' Harry, as usual, was acting as a moderator.

'Well, Leila, what did you come up with in your investigations?' Rico would not let it go. Neither would I.

'Yes, any more clues on the London and Nevada bombings?' I enquired.

'No. No one has so far. Not the Americans, the British, or us. We can't move past the direct perpetrators. They claim they acted alone. It is highly unlikely,' Leila replied.

'What about torture? Don't they speak under torture?' Rico asked, exasperated.

'Rico, I can't believe you sometimes,' Harry commented. 'You are not condoning torture, are you?'

'Not in general, though as with everything, sometimes there can be exceptions,' Rico replied, helping himself to more coffee.

'We are not giving up,' Leila ignored Rico's comment and put the torture subject aside. 'Our problem is that we can't go on sites and interrogate the witnesses like officials. It is frustrating.'

'Instead, you just break into their IT system and get all the data. Not too bad, though,' Leo commented.

'Yes,' Leila smiled. 'But nothing can replace gut feeling and sixth sense. And before you ask, no - still nothing on Chen's whereabouts, either.'

*

Seeing Jazz in the afternoon was a relief, even if the circumstances were not for pleasure. She had organised a whole day of discussions and events with the newly Relocated to address the way ahead. There were workshops on how to keep contact with family and friends on Earth, on how to use their experience or acquire new ones to relaunch their lives, or how to deal with the psychological trauma of the Relocation. She had organised it like a fair, with a section in the Fog Dome and with therapists to help with mental and medical questions. Molly supervised the online university stand, one of the busiest along with the information on maximising energy and adapting to modern technologies. Both Lil'London and Newtonsee had sent representatives for their main trades to explain their work and daily life. Even Barbara Snayth had her own stand to introduce the values and ways in WII and emphasised that everyone should respect them, including the newcomers. Her audience watched with curiosity mixed with shock. Benjamin Snayth roamed around, acting important but without much to do. As for me, Jazz had planned that I would go on stage late afternoon. Tea, coffee, scones and cucumber sandwiches would be served afterwards on the brand new main square. It was just a way of introducing myself and answering a few questions: there was no long speech planned. In the meantime, smiling and walking around, I shook hands and accepted requests of selfies with people I didn't know. I clearly held the status of mini-celebrity. Most were friendly, if not a little awkward around me. A few were aloof, one even hostile, refusing to shake my hand and turning their back on me. I wondered why: crossing the Fog had been their choice, anyway. It reminded me of *The Matrix* and the character Cypher in this movie. He took a red pill to awake to the real world. However, he hated that reality, his life there, and wished to return to being oblivious to the truth. Cypher was ready to do anything to go back in time. He blamed the one who freed him for not warning him enough that the new reality was hard.

*

Answering some of the questions about the Fog, I tried to explain the limit of our knowledge of it.

'I am just the one who creates the Fog weekly, that's it,' I told them. 'I can't even control it and I don't know how it works. Aside from this, I am just like anybody else, like you. It isn't even a talent or a skill. A gift, yes. I can't take any credit for it.'

I wasn't being falsely humble. I meant it.

'This 'gift' has put me in a situation of being able to go back and forth between two worlds and having a certain importance in both. My simple wish is to use this position to act as an ambassador to promote positive relations between the people there (I pointed to the Fog) and here (opening my arms in a wide gesture, I indicated all our surroundings). I will do my very best, but will not achieve anything without other Gatekeepers (I had almost said Foggies, before realising this was not the known word for us). Some cannot be here today, but Leo, who is accompanying me, is a Crosser. You will see him often, working hard for all of us.'

Pushing Leo centre stage, I let him explain his role, working alongside Zeno and Dante. Many women in the crowd eyed him with interest. He was a good-looking man, a Crosser, and with a job for life. A smile crept up, tinted with a tiny feeling of threat or jealousy. Leo was a good catch for any women here. One should never take a relationship for granted. Instinctively, without realising it, I took a small step closer to him. Looking at the audience, its size struck me: more than a hundred people were standing there. It was only the beginning: the number accrued every day.

'Before long,' I thought, 'they will be thousands.' The idea terrified me. My fears were coming true.

*

Back in my flat, a few parcels waited for me on the threshold. Whoever left them there did not consider theft as an option in the building. They were right. Leo and I swiftly brought them inside and I ripped them open with the eagerness of a child dealing with Christmas presents. In one was a selection of multi-coloured cushions, in the other were three posters of paintings by Dali, an artist I had a passion for.

Leo and I were exhausted, but he insisted he wanted a 'date' night at home with dinner and movie. He had planned a special Italian meal based on family recipes and I was not to step in the kitchen or allowed to set the table. Instead, he gently pushed me into the living room and made me sit on the sofa.

'Read this. Harry gave it to me this morning, you should find this interesting.' Leo put a news magazine in my hands, opened to a page entitled 'Quantum Fog'. I wrinkled my nose. I could not see how another article on the Fog by people who had never experienced it, yet thought they could theorise it, could be a good read before dinner.

I was wrong; it was fascinating.

It was not the first time I had heard of the quantum theory. It was also not the first time that someone espoused the theory and its variations as an explanation to the Fog. So far, the terms were still unclear to me and I remained unconvinced. This article was a revelation.

The quantum theory analyses nature and the behaviour of matter (quantum physics) and energy (quantum mechanics), more specifically at the atomic and subatomic level. This aside, what interested me at this point was not the mathematic formula and the study of the atom, but the implications of the study's findings. The quantum theory asserts that a particle is whatever it is measured to be: it could be either a wave or a particle under the scrutiny of the scientist, whether he is looking for a wave or looking for a particle. Indeed, without explanation, it appeared that a particle 'travelled as a wave but arrived as a particle'. Hence, until measured, that particle-wave does not have specific properties. It might not even exist. Based on this theory, objective reality did not exist. Going further, *nothing is real until it has been observed*. The article then referred to the Schrödinger's cat experiment and it helped me clarify this aspect of the theory - a bit blurry in my head, I will concede this - with a practical example.

Erwin Schrödinger was an Austrian quantum physicist who applied the quantum theories to the following test: he placed a living cat into a steel chamber, along with a device containing a vial of hydrocyanic acid and a minuscule quantity of the same acid directly on the chamber floor. The hydrocyanic acid is a radioactive substance and, if the smallest particle of it decayed during the test period, a relay mechanism would trip a hammer, which in turn would break the vial. The cat would not survive this. From the outside, the observer could not know whether an atom of the substance had decayed, whether the vial had been broken and, the cat killed. Without this observation, according to quantum law, the cat was both dead and alive. This superposition of states, or quantum indeterminacy (also called *observer's paradox*), only stopped with the opening of the box and the cat became one or the other (dead or alive). The outcome did not exist unless the measurement was made.

From there, in 1957, another quantum physicist, Hugh Everett, developed the idea of multiple worlds, or multiple universes. The 'Many-Worlds Interpretation' (MWI) of quantum theory stated that all possible alternate histories and futures are real, each representing an actual "world". There was, thus, a possibly infinite number of worlds, in which everything that could have happened in our past, but did not, had occurred in the past of some other world. Each universe branches into a bunch of new universes every time a quantum measurement is made. All possibilities are therefore realised. According to this theory, these multiple worlds were similar, yet different, to ours. They were equally real and processing through time, with their own specificities.

Applying this theory to the WII seemed obvious. Here we had a parallel world, a new Universe, similar yet different. Could it be that in that universe, something happened millions of years ago, and apes never rose and evolved into men? If so, what could that event be? The principal question remained on the Fog: if it created a link between two universes, what part of the quantum theory could apply there?

*

The article was mind-blowing. Science met science fiction. It raised so many possibilities and questions. Despite the lack of answers, it was riveting. When Leo came to tell me that dinner was ready, he laughed at my bewildered look.

'Fascinating, isn't it?'

'Yes! Scary, too… How did you come up with this article?'

'Leila gave it to me. She has tried to get me to read books on quantum theories for some time. I never gave it a second thought.'

'Same with me. I just put them on top of the big pile of must-reads. Well, in truth, more at the bottom of the pile than on top. Gosh! How many other universes could be out there?!' The question was general, but Leo had an answer.

'I would say at least one more than WII, the one which is only Fog. The one only Switchers or Simba can access, the one you could get lost in...'

'It could be either another world, or a hallway leading to a multitude of worlds I just walk by, not knowing how to see or open the doors.' I shivered. 'That makes my back crawl. I am in awe, terrified by the idea.'

'Please no! Don't forget however fitting it is, quantum theory and the multiple universes remain one interpretation, one theory. Don't get too stressed about it and taste my pasta: it will help.'

*

That evening, we watched *The Matrix*. Despite knowing it almost by heart, I never failed to get engrossed in the story. So did Leo. After the quantum theory article, it was even more appropriate for the evening. No reality was objective. Though I was still bemused by the Multi-Worlds Interpretations, it was not what had made me choose that movie for the night. Something in my thoughts from that afternoon was bothering me. I had a hunch, but could not pinpoint it. The idea lingered through the night as I dreamt of futuristic worlds.

Day 6 (Friday)

It was barely dawn. It had been a terrible night of bad sleep. Our argument with Leila the previous night had left a sour taste in my mouth. I was still upset with her for withholding such a large piece of information and wondered what else of importance the Society kept from us. Just after 8am, when it was a decent time to call, I picked up the Ftab and dialled her number. My tone was a bit abrupt as I cut to the chase, asking her who else knew that Lally O'Maleigh was part of the Society.

'Lally and I met at university, in the Society's student group. Anybody else present at the time may recognise her, even though she has changed a lot. Lally interacted with others, too, at least at the start of her mission, when their respective roles required it. Why?'

'I had a thought last night,' I replied. 'Call it a hunch, but it would explain things. You see, the attack on the houses in London: anyone could pinpoint the exact address. However, the way it was done, the perpetrator had specific information on our security and weaknesses. I am thinking of a leak.'

'Not necessarily. The Koplats have lived there for a long time, and when Alcatraz was fogged and the Koplat's truth became public, someone in their hometown must have talked. Penny Thompson might have disclosed some information, too.'

'It doesn't make sense. Why attack an empty house in Nevada? Going to such an extent just to destroy a Fog doesn't make sense. One would want to destroy the Foggies. Like in London.'

'They probably didn't know...' Leila retorted.

'It was done by a professional. I have read your report. If they wanted to make a statement, they would have gone for Alcatraz. If they wanted to attack the Foggies, they would have waited to get confirmation on their location. It is almost as if they wanted it to be empty. Why? What are we missing?'

'Let's not dismiss Chen. He is probably involved somewhere, somehow...' Leila snapped. She knew where I was heading.

'Leila, the Society wouldn't be the first organisation to have leaks...' I told her in a soft tone. She was always so protective about the Society. It was her family.

'Fine!' she replied, upset but compliant. 'I will request a thorough review of all archives on Lally and private communications from and to her with any Society's agents – active or dormant. I'll get back to you. Happy now?'

Leo came and took me back to bed, murmuring in my ear that in the future, he would forbid the use of the Ftab until after breakfast, which would come after coffee, which would come after morning sex. During his whispers, he put his arm around me and began to caress the most sensitive and sensual parts of my body. I slowly mellowed into his arms and forgot what preoccupied me. He leaned forward and put the Ftab on silent, setting it aside.

'Leila is going to call me back,' I protested weakly.

'It will take some time,' Leo replied, taking hold of my lips.

'Is that a wish?' I whispered, my mouth against his.

'Stop talking,' he said, pushing me against the mattress.

*

Three hours later, I was feeling in a much happier mood when Leila called. I quickly threw a light jacket on my shoulders and took the call on my way for a walk with Simba. I had just had enough coffee to face the day ahead, or so I thought.

'Hello again, Leila,' I began. 'First, please accept my apologies. I was a bit aggressive with you on the phone. It's only that I have had this nagging idea since yesterday...' I didn't get to finish my sentence.

'Lally and Elsie. They had an affair.' Leila's voice was beaten.

'What?!' I gasped. 'Are you sure? When?'

'We don't know all the details yet. Hell, we didn't know anything until we started to check intra communication records from way back. It uncovered that ten years ago, they were often in contact with each other. They were not saying or writing much, but they were scheduling to meet. So I tracked down their family, friends and colleagues at the time. Though Lally was always very discreet and kept to herself, Elsie was more open about her private life. Yet at the time, she remained vague, which was out of character. Some of her old acquaintances thought she might be seeing a married man, but the closest one had guessed she was having a relationship with a woman.'

'*Wow!*' was all I managed to say.

'So from there, we had to determine if they were still in touch, or worse, still together.'

'And?' I asked Leila, when she remained silent.

'We found no direct link, but they could have used disposable mobiles.'

'When Elsie turned out Relocated, any mobile call from the Fog in Nevada would have been picked up by you, no? You were constantly monitoring signals,' I commented.

'Yes, but we might have overseen one lead... There were calls to Michelle's

Ftab from two or three mobile numbers that are not registered. We eventually traced them back to Lally's Church headquarters.'

'Michelle? Oh! Of course! Lally and Elsie used Michelle's mobile.'

'Michelle is sleeping right now, but we will ask her in a couple of hours if she knows anything about these calls,' Leila said, with a heavy voice.

Both of us stopped talking, lost in thought on each side of the line.

'Where are you? Shall we meet and discuss this?'

'It's impossible now,' Leila replied. 'I am in a jet heading towards Lally. I am going to confront her.'

'Leila, no! You can't! The woman is dangerous! She is not the same person you met so long ago. You can't go there alone, you can't!'

'Who says I am going there alone? To protect my back, I tipped the American Government that Lally had a secret past. I released to them part of our files on her - the one relevant to her basic military, psychological and infiltration training. Of course, we have switched reference from the Society to mercenary activities.'

'Wait! She has such training?' I asked bemused, wondering why the Society had deemed it necessary for her to be so prepared.

'Yes. So do I. This reinforces your theory that she could have planned and supervised the attack on the Fog House. I just can't fathom that she could do that. But I must envisage the possibility and so, in a couple of hours, the FBI will raid her centre of operations at dawn there. They might or might not find anything. However, when they extract Lally, we will intercept her. Then and only then will I confront her. I am not stupid, Yoko. I am not going to enter her nest of fanatics and just ring the doorbell.'

'You are still playing a dangerous game: how can you be certain you will be able to get your hands on Lally? What will happen if there is nothing incriminating against her? Will it not just reinforce her position against the Fog, the authorities and you?'

'I know we are taking a risk, but she has to be stopped. She is going too far in her claims and turning herself into a so-called prophet.'

'Promise me you will be careful.'

'I promise. I still have so much I want to do for you and the Fog. I will not jeopardise my mission because of her.'

'I have an even more good use of you as a friend,' I told her. I meant it.

'I am sorry we didn't tell you about Lally. We should have, but... Oh! Before I forget, check your emails, I have a surprise for you. A good one!'

'What is it?' I asked suspiciously despite her 'good' warning.

'Ingis Chen. We didn't find him, but his second in command has started to talk.'

*

Ingis Chen knew that his movements and communications were under constant scrutiny. He also knew the moment the authorities – any authorities – would close in on him, he must go on the run somewhere and hide. His island was an obvious place to go to, except that it was obvious. Only after the extent of his problem had been clarified and depending on the gravity of the situation, might he go to the Chen State. In the meantime, no one should know his whereabouts. So Ingis Chen had played his cards right: he had disappeared at the airport. He was never on that flight. The man driving the rolling stairs to his private jet did not belong to the airport staff, but to Chen's. Ingis Chen swapped clothes and rode with him and drove the mobile stairs back into the air shed. From there, he had a vehicle waiting with a few essentials. He had several fake passports, cash in various currencies and vehicles in various safe locations around town, ready for him. Chen simply vanished.

Thanks to his accountant, the international community had frozen all his accounts. I did not ask how the information had been extracted from him, I was just satisfied that Chen did not have access to his millions. He was public enemy number 1; his picture posted in every airport, station, harbour, newspaper and police station. Billions of people, all around the globe, hated him and would happily denounce him to the police - if they could refrain from lynching him themselves. Of course, a small group of people might still agree with him in private. After all, he was not the only one to argue that our planet was not made to support 7 billion humans, and that our attempts to delay or stop death in all its forms was against nature. A virus, some argued, was the natural way to eliminate an excess of people on Earth.

In the past, even renowned scientists had defended these theories. However, no one rose publicly to defend Chen now. They would have faced immediate vituperation if not rage. Could Chen have found refuge with someone who secretly supported his beliefs and methods? Ingis Chen's sister was adamant she knew nothing of his activities and openly criticised him. Nonetheless, she was under scrutiny day and night and her offshore accounts were also blocked. Many of Chen's hidden accounts were in her name and, up until the disclosure to the public of his involvement with the virus, brother and sister had enjoyed an excellent relationship. She was the only person Chen was known to have been close to and her protests of innocence were simply dismissed.

It was good news that Chen had no financial resources – at least, none direct - and his wings cut off. It was good news, though unsatisfying. I would not be happy until the man was under arrest.

*

I spent the afternoon with my parents and Leo. To my relief, Leo was very relaxed around them, and they with him. After the break up months ago, my parents had never either criticised or praised him. They chose not to meddle in my private life or question my choices. Still, I noted from their attitude that afternoon that they liked him and were glad we were back together. It was important to me. They were leaving the next day, Saturday, on a 24- hour journey with long detours to lose any followers. When I reluctantly asked what they wanted to do with the family house in the South of France, they said we ought to sell it. They never planned to go back without Eudes and me, and it was unlikely Eudes could ever go there again. It was another one of my roots torn away from me. I had to let go: it was difficult but I had to move on and leave the past to the past. I had to travel forward without this luggage from the past, travelling light if I wanted to continue without a hernia.

*

It was already late when Leila contacted the Foggies with updates from the US via a video-conference call. She did not waste any time and immediately launched into a description of the day's events, cutting short any interruption and asking us to raise our queries afterwards.

'When the Americans broke into her headquarters, they arrested Lally O'Maleigh and her followers. The believers were gathered in a sports hall nearby, under a tight watch, while Lally was brought to a high security prison for interrogation. As you know, we had aimed to intercept her on the way. We couldn't. At the last minute, the Americans changed their plans, deciding to transport Lally by helicopter for speed and security. The Americans did not find anything in her headquarters linking Lally to the attack against the Fog and the Foggies. No documentation, no trace of explosive, no records on their computer. Everything is clean, excessively clean. Lally knows what she is doing; she did not leave any traces. However – thank goodness! - not every one of her followers are as diligent as she is. The woman has created a cult: there is no other word for it! A few of them kept notes or diaries, and three or four fanatics wrote down her words and calls to arms in their prayer books. One even made discreet videos of her sermons. Lally has created a sect of religious extremists who aimed to destroy the Fog and the Foggies as *'creations of the Devil and the cause of Mankind's downfall'.* Their writings reveal them as extremists, based on a singular interpretation of the religions around the Book. It has attracted Christians, Jews and Muslims, alike. She could almost have called her cult 'Fanatics United'... How they got along on a daily basis, I have no idea.'

Leila then told us that she went to the American high security building and presented herself as our representative. She explained and argued with the officials that the purpose of her presence was to goad Lally to make her crack and reveal her true nature. At this point, Leila had nothing to lose anymore. Lally could reveal everything she knew about the Society at any time. The organisation was already destroying secret files, transferring computer databases to a new location and warning key people from the University and headquarters to disappear until further notice. The University would go on, but its use by the Society was limited from now.

When Leila sat in front of her, Lally looked at her with contempt. They were both silent for some time before Leila spoke.

'Hello, Lally. It's been a long time.' The FBI agents in the room frowned at this comment. They did not expect the two women to be acquainted.

'What happened, Lally?' Leila continued, calmly. 'What caused you to turn into such a zealot? Why go so far with the attacks on the Fog? Why Nevada?'

As Lally remained silent, simply staring at her old acquaintance with a sarcastic smirk, Leila persisted. 'Nevada is not that far from Alcatraz. It would have made a bigger impact. Come on: if you don't tell us, we will go and ask Elsie. The Foggies plan to recreate a Fog there tomorrow.'

The side of Lally's mouth turned slightly down. It was subtle, but it turned her grin into a mean sneer.

'Poor Elsie,' Lally said, casually. 'She is bright, but she lets her feelings control her head.' She added more thoughtfully, 'I did love her, though in the magnitude of the situation it didn't matter. And in the end, she was getting in my way.'

'That's why you destroyed the house in Nevada? You were trying to eliminate her?'

'Me? I do not destroy anything, I only preach the word of God,' Lally said, with a sickening sweet smile.

'According to records kept by your disciples – written and videos – your words and your God are very violent,' Leila replied, with an equally sickening sweet smile.

'The imbeciles!' Lally said between clenched teeth, her anger obvious.

'Your time is over. It is the end of your dangerous activities. With the information found, you don't stand a chance. You are a fraud, Lally,' Leila continued.

'One you created,' Lally retorted with a sneer. 'They don't know, do they?' Lally nodded towards the FBI agent who, indeed, had no clue what was happening but who knew better than to intervene and cut the flow of unexpected information.

'Do you think I would be here if they didn't?' Leila bluffed. 'Do you think they would have raided your so-called Church, otherwise? They were bound to find out at some point, so we chose to have it done on our terms, not on yours. Now, we can talk about it gently together and get the answers we seek, or we can leave it to professionals to get them out of you.'

'I presume asking for my lawyer is not an option?'

'Not when it comes to international terrorism, as you very well know. I don't envy the many, many, MANY years you have ahead of you.'

'What do you want, Leila?' Lally spit her words at Leila.

'I came here to let you know that you have no room for bargaining. You are done,' Leila replied in a deep, calm voice. One too calm and composed. 'But also, I came here because of two promises that I intend to keep. One made recently to a friend, and one we made to each other as students when we all swore-in together, a long time ago.'

Leila and Lally stared at each other. In the silence, many words were said through their eyes. They were understood by both sides.

'I am not a fraud, Leila. I believe in what I am fighting for and against. The Society is blind. They are blinded by their positive approach. They want to see only the good in what is happening with the Fog, but in doing so they are naïve. In every class I took, every report I read, every single document the Society put in front of me, there was always this belief that something amazing was about to happen. And always, I felt an element was missing. Later I began to question: What if it was not amazing? What if it was not all a gift? What if it was not such a great opportunity? And then, when I took on my dormant agent's role, I began to see the other side, a darker side. You thought you were giving information for my cover that was erroneous, but what you dismissed was the key, the truth. You only cast it aside because it displeased you.'

'You are wrong, Lally,' Leila interrupted. 'We did not *dismiss* it. We know it is one interpretation of the event. We did not dismiss it because we thought it untrue. We dismissed it because we chose, CHOSE, not to go down the negative path. There is no right or wrong answer, we do not know what is behind the Fog, the same way we do not know what other secrets the Universe holds. We do not have the answers, but we have the choice. We can choose to believe in the positive, even though we protect our backs by preparing for the bad. We can choose to have faith and trust in the opportunities and take our chances. We can choose to lead our life looking for what can be good, instead of denouncing what could be bad.'

'You are so naïve,' Lally repeated.

'And you are so sad,' Leila responded.

Again, a silence ensued. The FBI agents in the room were observing the scene, wondering what information they would learn next.

'What about Elsie?' Leila asked, returning to one of her original questions.

'Elsie? Elsie... We ran into each other in the corridors of the New York headquarters, so long ago now. It was an instant love crush. The minute we met, we knew we were made for each other. It was awkward at first: we were unsure if our relationship would be accepted by the Society, with regard to our opposite roles. Neither of us wished a reassignment, so we decided to keep our affair under wraps. It was difficult to see each other so little and having to avoid leaving any traces of our relationship. With time, it grew easier for me. When I found my path, I knew my duty against the Fog had to come first. It was more difficult for Elsie, of course. I know she suffered; there was nothing I could do about it. One morning, I woke up and I knew I was not in love with her any more. I still loved her, but the passion was gone. Her lack of understanding of the truth behind the Fog created a distance between us. I hid that from her knowing the time would come when she would be able to help me, even without her awareness of it. Whatever information the Society was not providing me, they might provide to her. I was right. In the past months, she told me - the love of her life - when the Fog was discovered, when the authority got involved, when the Foggies, especially in Nevada, had second thoughts or moods. I urged her that Michelle should speak to her mother, hoping Penny Thompson's journalist instinct would trigger her to go public. It worked in a way: the mother went to that scum-of-the-earth, Chen. Finally, what I had been praying for happened. The Fog was disclosed to the public and I could fulfil my mission. At last!'

'You killed innocent people,' Leila snapped.

'No one touching the Fog is innocent!' Lally retorted angrily, before leaning back and continuing her story. 'Elsie began to have doubts. She investigated and discovered the Society had not given me the instructions to go active. We had an argument. More exactly, she was screaming, while I could not care less. That is, until she threatened to reveal the truth about me. She said she had kept copies of the rare messages and photos of us together.

She would denounce me to the world as a fake. She threatened to turn to the Society and do everything in her power to destroy me and my new mission by ruining my image. In our age of multimedia, image is everything. I could not let it happen. It presented another opportunity to destroy a Fog house. Unfortunately, the Koplats were not at home.'

'You didn't know that?' Leila was surprised.

'Elsie had been my source of information. Your secrets are well protected, as you know. This time, she had stopped talking.'

'The Switchers can easily create a new door...' Leila continued.

'I took my chances. If the Koplats had been in the house, the number of Switchers would have dropped to two, and the others would be reluctant to come to Nevada under the American authorities. In any case, I acted for the better good of this planet and its people.'

*

Leila had heard enough. She stood up to leave and started for the door, accompanied by two FBI agents. At the last minute, before stepping out, she turned and walked to Lally. When in front of her, Leila bent slightly and reached a hand behind the prisoner's neck. She pulled Lally's head towards hers. When the two heads almost touched each other, Leila murmured 'I gave my word, whether I like it or not'. She then straightened up and left without another word or a look back.

The two FBI agents accompanied her to a room next door, where more agents were waiting for her. It was her turn to face an interrogation, or so they intended. Thanks to her work for Gatekeepers Associates, Leila was protected by international immunity and she was fast to remind them. They had to release her. Without wasting another minute, she boarded a private plane and left towards the closest bordering country, Canada, from which she also promptly fled. She had to create a distance between herself and America as fast as possible.

'You don't trust them either, then,' Rico said, nodding his approval.

'I don't think this is it, Rico...' I said. Leila's eyes were red. She was holding her tears.

'Leila, what did you promise?' I asked softly. I had my suspicions.

'I promised you and Jazz whomever killed Big Tom would pay. And when we joined the Society, after we were sworn in, all the students in my year made each other the promise we would never let one of us be questioned or tortured if we could stop it by any means possible.' She paused. 'I killed Lally. Before getting into that interrogation room, I slipped on a poison ring. When I grabbed her neck with my hand, I punctured her with the small needle on the inside of the ring. Within one hour, Lally was incapacitated. Within two hours, she was dead. I killed her.'

Leila shut her eyes tight, trying to control her tears. She had never killed before, let alone an old acquaintance. I knew how she felt.

*

The Americans would be furious with her. The authorities had been made a fool and Leila had stopped them getting valuable information. They would come for her. For her safety, until further notice - maybe forever - Leila would have to hide. This was not her main preoccupation, though: she asked us all if we still trusted her to work alongside the Foggies and if we could accept what she had done.

It was an important decision, one on which all the Foggies had to agree. Harry asked her to disconnect from the call while we deliberated on the issue. It would be a temporary decision, as too many of us were missing. Zeno and Dante were still on the long walk to Scotland in WII. As for McRae, he had not participated in the conference call. Leila had told him privately just before the call, and kept him out of it. So whatever we decided would be pending Zeno, Dante and McRae's points of view. As for Helo, we agreed he was still too young to take part. We were twelve to review the situation - Harry, Rico, Leo, Louise, Putu and me in London; Rosario, Tony, Mitch, Adam, Sophia and Michelle in Alaska.

Leila's action had shocked me. She had premeditated her action. This was murder. She was not in mortal danger, but intent on keeping her promises. Could protecting the Society be considered self-defence? Was the protection of the Society worth taking someone's life? This thought left me uncomfortable. However, I was less bothered that she had killed a fanatic who attacked us verbally and physically at every chance she had! She had dropped explosives on my home, on *The Jazzin*. She had killed Big Bob and could have killed me, Leo, the Koplats and many others. What about Elsie?! She had seriously injured many others working for the governments in the UK and in the US. The promise to avenge the death of our friends did not mean killing the perpetrator in cold blood; still, I could not deny a part of me was glad Lally was no more. The other Foggies shared the same split feelings.

'You know what, guys?' Rico exclaimed, as everyone was mulling over Leila's case in silence. 'I know one thing: if it had been me who had made the promise, I would have done it. I would have been Leila. I would have nailed that bitch! Hell, she was a danger for all of us! I don't trust the Americans to keep her in check. Even in prison she could continue to preach and lead her followers into bombarding us with their shit.'

'Putting aside your colourful, explicit and renowned distrust for the American government...' Harry started.

'Any governments!' Rico corrected.

'Right. Putting aside your colourful, explicit and renowned distrust for any governments,' Harry amended, 'that is a good question to ask: what would any of us have done in her shoes?'

'I don't know what I would have done,' Sophia replied. 'It is difficult to conceive... But part of me... Part of me hopes I would have been strong enough to do the same, despite the moral condemning that goes with it.'

'I can understand, too. I do not approve. I cannot... But I understand,' Rosario added. 'In truth, if Mitch or Tony had died because of Lally, I would be singing Leila's praises right now.'

'She used Elsie! Even the ones she said she loved, she didn't even respect!' Michelle burst out.

'We are not meant to be judges. We are not supposed to find Leila guilty or not, to condemn or not her actions. What we need to determine is whether we still trust her and if we will still be able to work with her, or not,' Adam said.

'I am willing to. As you rightly said, Rosario, I do not approve of her actions but I understand them.' I said, in Leila's defence. 'But it shows one thing for certain: we can trust her to be loyal. She has faith and fights for a cause I adhere to. It might be immoral, but knowing that she means it when she says she is watching my back, I find that comforting.'

'She didn't tell us about Lally O'Maleigh being from the Society, though…' Tony pointed out.

'Darling, she was being a good assistant,' Rosario told her husband.

'In what way?' he asked, surprised at her words.

'One of my previous bosses told me that an efficient assistant will always aim to smooth the problems first, instead of just putting them in front of the boss for him to find a solution. We have enough to bug our minds!'

'Let's be realistic here,' Tony persisted. 'I am willing to agree with you, if you also agree she was scared that, by telling us, we might move away from the Society.'

'Fine. I will concede that she was protecting them, too,' Rosario gave in a little.

'By the way, the Society might not accept what she had done. It might be against her code of deontology…' Harry commented.

*

A ping indicated that McRae had requested to join the video conference call. We accepted his request and a new window appeared on the screen. McRae looked drained and anxious. Before anyone asked, he told us that what Leila had done did not change anything about his opinion or feelings towards her. On the contrary, he appreciated how much bravery she had had to summon up the courage to carry out a promise that cost her dearly, psychologically and emotionally. She knew that she risked losing everything and everyone who mattered in her life. McRae announced that his vote was in favour of keeping Leila by our side.

We decided to vote anonymously and to use sound for it. Each of us cut the microphone and the image of the video call, except McRae. He switched off his phone, so that calls would reach his voicemail. We all called him with our numbers hidden, and made either two knocks in favour of Leila, or five knocks against her. McRae stayed on the screen with his mobile set on the table in front of him, not touching it, so that we could check the phone was not meddled with. When the twelve voters reappeared on the screen and reactivated their microphones, everyone had voted. The thirteenth was McRae, and we knew what his vote was. We needed to have unanimity for this vote of confidence. Only one 'no' and we would stop our relationship with Leila.

There were none. We all wanted Leila in.

Day 7 (Saturday)

McRae rang the bell at 8am and woke us up. Leo and I had fallen asleep late in the night, still rediscovering each other and giving special attention to reviewing each detail of our anatomies. Therefore, Leo was rather grumpy when he went to open the door in boxer shorts. I quickly put on his shirt and my panties, and went to check why the unexpected visit on an early Saturday morning. McRae was standing in the entrance to the flat, carrying a heavy-looking travel bag on his shoulder.

'Are you moving in?' Leo asked, with non-hidden sarcasm.

'Hell no!' McRae laughed. 'I wouldn't sleep a wink in a room next to yours.'

I smiled and nodded at the bag.

'It's for you,' McRae replied, to my unspoken question.

We went to the kitchen and McRae put his burden on the table, where he unzipped it. He took out various bottles of champagne, orange and mango juices. Then came the food: pains au chocolat, croissants, macaroons, fresh papaya, grapes and kiwi. Finally, he took out a box containing eggs, bacon, black pudding, sausages, haggis, mushrooms and tomatoes. Leo and I looked at the drinks and food piling on the table, our surprise increasing. Then opening each cabinet door, McRae took out glasses, plates and pots and began to prepare a full breakfast.

'What are you doing?' I asked him.

'Preparing breakfast, of course,' he replied, without a look at us, adding water to a large pot. 'Rico will be here shortly. He is in charge of coffee. I thought you might prefer his to mine. Harry is coming, too. I didn't want to wake up Louise and Putu; I don't know them that well.'

'So considerate of you...' Leo said, still caustic.

McRae continued unperturbed. 'Haggis takes from 45 minutes to 1 hour to cook, so I'll start with that. Leo, why don't you open one of the bottles?'

'Lochy…' I stopped Leo grabbing a bottle and waited for McRae to explain himself. He put a pot on the hob for the haggis and turned to us.

'What you did for Leila, I will never forget it,' he said to me, solemnly.

'It was not just me: all the Foggies agreed, Leo included!' I protested with a laugh.

'And I am grateful to all, but especially you. You are the closest one to her, and the one who could have felt the strongest that she had let you down. You did not. You were her advocate.'

Leo smiled, took a bottle, and made the cork pop. We set up the table, each with a glass in hand.

*

Rico arrived shortly after, looking frumpy and grumpy. The time was 'outrageously' early for him. He arrived with his own coffee maker, an old and battered brewing pot that he put directly on the stove.

'I only forgive you because that's a nice thing to do,' he told McRae, in a voice husky from sleep.

'You could have stayed in bed and continued sleeping,' Leo told Rico.

'Impossible. I suffer from FOMO,' Rico retorted.

'What's that?' Leo asked, a little suspicious. He was getting to know Rico.

'FOMO – Fear Of Missing Out. Especially when it comes to family events. Where's Harry?'

As if on cue, Harry knocked at the door. Both Rico and Harry had keys, but preferred to announce their visit instead of letting themselves in. I went to let Harry in.

'We are missing Zeno. I wish he could join us,' Rico said, as he poured coffee into his coffee maker and put it on the stove.

'And Dante,' Leo remarked.

'No offence mate, but it's not the same,' Rico replied. 'We all used to live together as a family. Breakfast with one of us missing is just wrong.'

'And I grew up with Dante. He is like a brother to me,' Leo snapped back.

'Hear, hear! This is a happy breakfast. Have a drink, you will feel better,'

Harry said, as he put the kettle on for tea. He took a sip of champagne in the meantime.

'You don't know?' McRae looked around at us, in surprise. I did not like surprises any more: they were hardly ever good these days. 'Zeno and Dante are on their way to London. Leila got in touch with Ushi Tsou last night.'

*

Leila was aware that her situation was still pending until Zeno and Dante had expressed their opinions. Overwhelmed by guilt, she had asked Ushi Tsou to help. She recorded a video for them, explaining her actions and the current situation. She also added some news reports for them to be updated on what was happening in this world. Ushi Tsou travelled at dawn to find the Italians on their walk to Scotland. Again, she found them easily thanks to the tracker. After watching Leila's video and hearing the news, they had a meeting with Nick, the Relocated and Ariel Ben-Chaim. The conclusion was favourable for their return to London via the Scottish Fog. They would join the travellers again in a few days.

'Where are they now?' Rico asked, with trepidation.

'They have just arrived at the Scottish Fog house. Using various kinds of transport, they should be with us this afternoon. We should keep some champagne for them,' McRae said.

'I take it they backed up Leila, as well?' I grinned. It was obvious; otherwise McRae would not have been here and would not have looked forward to seeing them.

'Aye. They are good guys!' McRae replied, brandishing the piece of black pudding he was about to put in a pan.

*

The Foggies indeed had some important decisions to make and we needed Zeno and Leo. We were under unbearable international pressure and it was crucial that we dealt with it immediately. National and international organisations increasingly demanded that we opened new gates around the globe for more opportunities of 'Fog healing'. The United Nations had already taken over the company, set up by Ingis Chen, under its special Fog Department. Other non-profit organisations, or even some less charitable companies, were appearing like mushrooms after the rain, proposing legal, financial and travel support to access the Fog. They even offered a full paperwork and integration programme for Relocated, as well as grants and financing options to rebuild their lives. Considering that quarantine and closed borders were still in place in many countries, including the United Kingdom and the US, those companies' claims were preposterous. That was not for us to deal with but the pressure linked to them was. We could never satisfy everyone. Moreover, even though one of our fiercest opponents, Lally O'Maleigh was gone, others would rise.

We had to make a proposal that would be acceptable for the international community and realistic for us. If we took too much weight onto our shoulders, we would simply collapse.

*

Over breakfast, McRae explained that Leila planned to hide in Scotland until further notice. He would stay with her most of the time. McRae would remain active for the British Secret Service only to accompany me on my travels abroad, while Sam would remain in London as the Fog Dome liaison officer with the Foggies. Aside from these missions, McRae would officially enjoy living on his ancestors' land. Anyone knowing him was aware of his passion for his homeland, so his decision would not surprise his colleagues and friends. Rico pointed out that it was a serious commitment towards Leila, a surprisingly fast one considering how much of a player he was merely weeks ago. McRae replied that he knew the minute he saw her that she was the only one he wanted from now on. That they were now to settle in Scotland together just proved that he was right.

'You know, the good thing about me being in Scotland, as well as regularly on a mission with you,' McRae said, as I was eating some of his overfilling breakfast, 'is that we can become friends, both officially and in reality, and that gives you a reason to come and visit me in Scotland. I can formally invite you over for your 'holidays'. It's the best cover for your visit to your family and your friends there.' It was a good idea and I felt a bit lighter for the future.

McRae didn't realise how much his words meant to me. My travelling to Scotland had worried me: I was wondering how often I would be able to return without jeopardising the secret of the Scottish Fog's existence, let alone location. To have the excuse to go there to visit friends was very helpful. It was not perfect, of course, and I would still have to sneak out of London and head there taking the long route most of the time, but his idea was still a relief. However, working with Rosario and Adam, we realised it might not have to be that way. It might be the reverse!

*

Indeed, Rosario, Adam and I spent the rest of the morning on a video call together. We were the only active Switchers left, Jack still being in a coma. His state was deteriorating and the doctor warned his family and us that they had no expectation he would survive for more than a few weeks. The news saddened us all. For the three Switchers, it also confirmed the pressure was on us to create and maintain the Fog. We had six active crossers with Zeno, Leo, Dante, Mitch, Sophia and Louise. On the Facilitators count, we were seven with Harry, Rico, McRae, Putu, Tony, Michelle and Helo. We all had important roles to play, though the Switchers were the most in demand and the most limited in numbers and abilities. We could only create a door per week, and it lasted only seven weeks. Therefore, the three of us had to work out how we could manage to satisfy most and still keep our sanity. Then we would discuss with the others in the afternoon if they agreed, too.

*

As soon as Zeno and Dante crossed back into this world, they drove to Glasgow to take a train from there to London. They had not changed, showered, or trimmed their beards, and proudly took selfies on the train that they sent to us. They looked like Russians having just stepped out from Siberia after a winter of hibernation. They clearly did not need any means of disguise to travel incognito. Only when they arrived in London did they go to a pub and shave, cleaning their faces and hair as well they could in the wash basin. They also changed and disposed of their clothes in front of a charity shop (which must get them dry-cleaned!).

*

All the UK Foggies sat around my dining table, the Ftab connected to the large wall screen. The Foggies' Board Meeting had started.

Here was the plan: Gatekeepers Associates was going to create and maintain twelve Fog gates around the world. Aside from the Society, everyone believed there were only two Gatekeepers able to create the Fog: Adam and me. At the rate of one a week, with a need of maintenance every seven weeks, Adam and I would offer to 'work' six Saturdays in a row and get the seventh off, before revisiting each Fog to keep them open. In reality, Rosario, Adam and I would share the task of maintaining four Gates each, at random, to avoid creating a pattern and our movements being traceable. It would also limit the dangers of being held hostage by a country, or kidnapped, or killed.

As a cover for their travel to Fog Gates, Tony would use his insurance background and Rosario her current travel agency to set up a fake business of travel insurance specialising in Fog Gate destinations. The couple would often travel around visiting the Gates for business. It would be more difficult for Adam and me to remain incognito when we travelled. Both he and I would need to be disguised most of the time when travelling, anyway, except on official travels or between our headquarters in San Francisco and London.

We added a little twist to our proposal: only nine of the twelve Gates would be permanent, three would be fogged at random in locations picked from a list of hundreds established by the United Nations. Those would only exist for seven weeks.

And last, we would create the gates, then it was up to the United Nations to manage them.

The three Switchers would have to run a tight ship to make sure Rosario was not spotted. To best confuse the authorities, we would have to travel anonymously. It suited us all: the Koplats had decided to live in Alaska, and I in Scotland. We had finally chosen to be where life was simple and live in the present, surrounded by nature and people who greeted us daily, as family and friends. I had wondered how the Koplats would deal with the change in their lives, but after the turmoil of the past week, they found themselves breathing anew when they returned to Alaska.

'And we are still in the US,' Sophia said briefly in the morning, eating Oreo biscuits. 'It is a bit simple here, but we can make a good life for ourselves. We can enjoy the day. Here I do not have to look over my shoulder for a machine gun, or the paparazzi, to steal my life away from me.'

When she was gone, Adam told me that Michelle and Sophia were even starting to accept each other's company. They would never like each other, but they could get along.

Of course, we knew no proposal would ever be ideal in this world or the other. There would always be risks that we open doors in locations where the local WII people would not welcome us. There would always be more demands and more detractors. The world out there, whichever it was, would always judge us harshly. That is what people do. We just had to do what we believed was right. We were decent people, with decent values, and we found strength in them. We had faith in doing the best we could for all. That is also why we decided to continue working with Leila and the Society, even though they had disappointed us with Lally O'Maleigh. We were doing our best but we made and would make more mistakes. It was the same for them.

*

'Wow! We are going to be like superheroes,' Rico laughed, as ever either wonderfully positive or incredibly suspicious. 'Acting in secret in the background; jumping out of our bat cave to save humanity!'

'So who's the bad guy?' Harry asked.

'What do you mean?' Rico did not like being interrupted in his elation. He was ecstatic that Gatekeepers Associates had finally stood their ground and found a balance, a way to move forward.

'Where there are super-heroes, there are super-villains,' Zeno spoke for Harry, as he understood his point.

'Gone. Pfffft! No more! They have lost,' Rico declared, with a wide gesture of his arms.

'Chen is still around, somewhere…' I said, as much to the friends around the table as to myself.

'No, he is not,' Zeno replied. 'He is history. His face is despised all around the world. He is penniless. All his friends and relatives are under scrutiny.

There is an international arrest warrant accepted by every single State on the planet. His only chance of survival is to make himself very small in a remote location without Internet and media, and to live a life as simple and unremarkable as possible.'

'A new villain can always rise...' Harry added.

'Harry, don't ruin the moment. Just help yourself to more tiramisu. Life is always a little lighter with a full stomach. Especially with tiramisu.' Rico brushed away further negative comments by passing the dessert around.

*

In bed, a little later, my head resting on Leo's chest, I joked with him that he would have to get used to haggis, tattie scones and black pudding now that we were to move to Scotland. He winced and replied that he planned to bring Italian food to the Highlands.

Playing with my hair, Leo spoke softly.

'What would you say if I were to ask you to marry me?'

Leo was being cheeky, testing the water instead of really popping the question. He wasn't going to get away with it.

'Well, if you were to ask me, I would answer you,' I told him with a smile, my head still against his torso. Leo remained silent for a minute or so. His hand was caressing my back.

'Then, let me ask you properly: would you spend the rest of your life with me as my wife?'

My smile grew wider.

~

Acknowledgements

First and foremost, I would like to express my gratitude to my family – Minouche, Maman, Antoine and Helena - for their continued assistance and trust. They have been wonderful in their patience, standing by me while I wrote Horizons (and Gatekeepers!).

The support of many friends has been invaluable to the completion of this passionate project. I am especially thankful to Alaa (the patient mentor), Alexandra (the fervent advocate), Angelica (the energy booster), Arun (the visualiser), Emma (the enthusiast), Katya (the brainstormer), Laurent & Marine (the champions) and Patricia (the ever-supporter) for kindly and steadily encouraging me in moving forward.

I also wish to thank Cem and Joy for being who they are. Their kindness, respect and trust make the office hours so pleasant that, when at last I turn to writing, it is always with a composed mind. Such serenity is priceless in life and for creativity.

To you all, thank you.

About the author

Virginie Bonfils-Bedos was born and raised in Southern France and moved to London for her studies. After reading political science and European legislation, she earned master's degrees in European public policy and management of European affairs, and went on to begin a career in strategic communication, office and project management, company secretary and more. In her own words, she is an *Optimiseur*.

A lifelong writer with a passion for words, Virginie Bonfils-Bedos has always kept notebooks filled with fictional or real stories she shared with her family and friends. Along with her love of writing, she began dedicating more time to her creativity over the years, with activities such as acting, mixed media art, and photography.

Walking through London one foggy morning, an unusual idea caught her imagination. It paved the way for her surprising and captivating series, The Fog Chronicles. She is also a screenwriter, collaborating with movie directors on feature film projects and TV series.

Discover More

...about The Fog Chronicles and Virginie Bonfils-Bedos at:

Virginiebb.com

...and on social media at:

www.facebook.com/virginiebonfilsbedos/

www.twitter.com/virginiebb

www.instagram.com/virginiebb_

~

www.ingramcontent.com/pod-product-compliance
Lightning Source LLC
Chambersburg PA
CBHW022233020726
47496CB00004B/876